THE PRINCESS CASAMASSIMA

THE

PRINCESS CASAMASSIMA

A Novel

BY

HENRY JAMES

THOMAS Y. CROWELL COMPANY

ESTABLISHED 1834/NEW YORK

Apollo Edition 1976
Introduction copyright © 1976
by Thomas Y. Crowell Company, Inc. All rights reserved.
Published simultaneously in Canada.
Manufactured in the United States of America

L.C. Card 75-27312
ISBN 0-8152-0395-0

INTRODUCTION

The tradition in which THE PRINCESS CASAMASSIMA enlists itself is that of the great "panoramic and processional" novels of
the nineteenth century. No critic has failed to remark upon its
sweep and inclusiveness, and James himself offers an important
clue in describing the book's genesis in his walks through
London—in "the assault directly made by the great city" (James,
The Art of the Novel, ed. Blackmur, N.Y., 1962, pp. 59, 90).
What lies at the heart of his inspiration is not so much a character or a personal dilemma as the life of the city itself, the life
of the city as representative of the whole of society and the
human possibilities it offers. Readers of James's more familiar
novels may at first be surprised by a shift in focus. It is not the
act of perception that is problematic—as so often in the later
works—but the world that is perceived. Motives are clear and
distinct, but the contradictions of the world in which these
motives must be acted upon make a final resolution impossible.
The misery on which this society is based and the grace and
beauty of its accomplishments, the justice of the revolutionary
cause and the meanness of its probable motives, the fatuity of
the great and their humanity—all these are seen unblinkingly
and held in balance with no "reconcilement of disparities" (p.
471). Hyacinth is the center of the novel's awareness because
he confronts these contradictions most intensely—"Whatever he
saw, he saw ... so many other things besides" (p. 434)—and
indeed enacts them in his own life, caught as he is in "the perpetual laceration of the rebound" between the two currents of
his inheritance, "the blood of his passionate, plebeian mother
and that of his long-descended, supercivilized sire" (p. 471).
But if we think about THE PRINCESS CASAMASSIMA in the

context of the ancestry it seems to claim for itself, what is odd, and perhaps most "modern" about James's treatment of these themes, is the unsubstantiality of that very society whose institutions and ethics the novel exists to call into question. This makes James's work very different from its predecessors. In *Pride and Prejudice,* for example, when Elizabeth visits Darcy's estate, she comes to realize the nature of the life that might be hers as part of the aristocracy; Hyacinth's visit to Medley serves as a similar initiation, an awakening to new possibilities. But unlike Darcy, the Princess is only renting her great house for a season. What Hyacinth encounters there is not so much the embodiment of social functions as it is a gossamer museum-like glamour (the still more enlarging corridors of the Louvre dazzle in much the same way) or else a pastoral charm that suggests a transcendence of the merely social—a liberating moment of vision all the more luminous for being so inevitably transient. Elizabeth observes at Pemberly the manifestation of her lover as "a brother, a landlord, a master," and the landscape is appraised in terms that ultimately are social—civility, fitness, the union of artifice and nature. For Hyacinth, Medley is a vast treasure-house, an "enchanted palace" (p. 303), where the "dust of centuries" seems "peopled with recognitions" (pp. 278-79), and where he longs to lose himself, on rambles through the countryside, in "the mystery and sweetness of blue distances" (p. 318). When he tries to define all that has separated him from the revolutionary cause, his imagination summons up a "vast, vague, dazzling presence, an irradiation of light from objects undefined" (p. 434).

It is for this reason that the ethical language which comes naturally to Austen, or to George Eliot, a language having to do with decorum and responsibility, with the laws or possibilities governing the relationships between classes, is not very elaborately employed in working out Hyacinth's divided loyalties. The particular intuition it is his tragic destiny to bear is of the elusiveness of the charm that glitters above the darkness and wreckage of ordinary lives, a glitter as poignantly short-lived as the ministrations of the Princess Casamassima herself. This element of romantic charm, quite literally of a magical glamour, is not. I think, a mere vehicle for James but the very substance of what he has to say about Hyacinth's quest and about the world in which he pursues it. When the Princess "turns on" her charm (xiv; p. 572), Hyacinth feels "good enough for anything"

(p. 367), just as in culture's supreme moments, "rescued and redeemed" as it were from an "immeasurable misery"(p. 434), experience attains a spaciousness and intensity that does not, perhaps, justify the bitterness and exploitation, but does nevertheless make the "world . . . less impracticable and life more tolerable" (p. 380). (In a revision of this passage, James underlines the sense of holiday or release implicit in Hyacinth's perception: the world seems "less of a 'bloody sell' and life more of a lark.") But then the doors close; the face is averted, or words continue while the mind is elsewhere; and finally it is the emptiness of London's streets, after all the bustle and turmoil, that most impresses us, a blankness with "nothing to look at" under empty skies and far-off stars (p. 555). In this reading, the Princess herself, with her seductive call and ineluctable withdrawal, enacts for Hyacinth the very nature of the society to which he is so implacably bound by desire and hatred: all those promises and capacities he can see—as if through a glass window, she tells him (pp. 316-17)—but can possess only fitfully in his own existence.

Perhaps the best way to formulate what we have been considering is to say that James is not concerned so much with society as with civilization. And that he conceives of civilization not as a complex of institutions (his "sociological" impotence has been lamented) but as something achieved, the elusive radiance of a certain style—what Hyacinth calls "the idea of beautiful arrangement" (p. 364). The questions by which James is most deeply engaged have to do with the ways in which civilization, conceived in these terms, may be possessed in one's personal life, or allowed to transform it; and with the costs of such transfigurations. "The reward of romantic curiosity," he writes of Hyacinth, "would be the question of what the total assault, that of the world of his work-a-day life and the world of his divination and his envy together, would have made of him, and what in especial he would have made of them" (*Art of the Novel*, p. 61). In this connection we may notice that in THE PRINCESS CASAMASSIMA the "people"—with the significant exception of Paul Muniment, a chemical engineer and genuinely a "new man"—are all on the margins of the arts: musicians, bookbinders, costumers. And the grievance registered most feelingly against English society is an "anguish of exasperated taste" (p. 408), for which a soiled shirt front or a vulgar intonation speaks more tellingly of dilapidations of the spirit than the rather abstract miseries sometimes evoked. This blighting of style, a pervasive "resigned seediness" (p. 340), is for James, much more than any actual suffering, the measure of his culture's failure and guilt, a failure to provide, except sporadically and for "the happier few" (p. 380), the fulfillment of those human capacities it has been its particular glory to envision.

As we have seen, James discusses the book as the fruit of his walks through London, so that the social scene of the novel comes to life for him—and for us—first of all as a series of impressions to be received, of appearances to be deciphered; a "public show," he calls it, to be watched until it ripens into understanding. James himself reminds us that "little Hyacinth" watches this show "from outside" very much as his creator had (*Art of the Novel,* pp. 60-61). And perhaps we may add that just the crucial difference between the two ("for one's self, all conveniently, there had been doors that opened") is embodied by the Princess, who (like James in this, also) remains no actual part of the world whose glamour she seems to embody: "I have not the manners of this country," she admits, "not of any class" (p. 165). Certainly it is significant that nowhere in the book do we see in actual *operation* either of the "two nations" whose dependencies it intends to traverse—neither the homely pulse of Dickens' poor (though James's prose seems sometimes rather oddly to lay claim to the tradition of Dickens) nor the bourgeois imbroglios of Austen or Eliot or even Trollope. All the major characters and most of the minor ones, in fact, are outcasts, observers of the social scene rather than participants in it. This is obvious for the Princess or for Hyacinth, the little gentlemen incognito in apron and cap. The transplanted revolutionaries, a critic has observed, are "not so much shaped by a foreign culture as they are cultureless" (J. A. Ward, *The Search for Form,* Chapel Hill, 1967, pp. 118-19). Rose Muniment has reminded more than one reader of Dickens' Jenny Wren, the doll's dressmaker, equally crippled and equally shrill; but Rose observes the great world from a sinecure that comes to Dickens' heroines—if not in death—only in the apocalyptic endings by which the world of his novels is restored to a simpler and safer estate.

Even for characters less evidently detached from their surroundings, the society on which their attention is fixed is not so much a set of functions or duties imposed upon them as an aching awareness of what they lack: a system not of duties but of deficiencies, of negations. One is tempted to apply the linguist's assertion that "in language there are only differences" : which would explain why the notion of "equality" comes to seem so devastating (to Hyacinth as well as to Rose), and why characters both high and low so continuously need to identify each other as "specimens" (p. 196) of a different life in order to place their own existences. Both Vetch and Pinnie, for example, are defined by the gentility they have forgotten or never quite attained. Vetch's deterioration is a failure to fill out the lineaments of a style the Princess, at least, is keen-sighted enough to recognize. The little seamstress is from the opening paragraphs of the novel intensely conscious of heights and distances, though her social sense is sufficiently askew to find in the sheer physical bulk of the prison matron—and this is surely the beginning of what leads Hyacinth so scarifyingly to his mother—an intimidating "elevation." Much of the book's rueful comedy is based not on the familiar mode of violated roles but on just this interplay of incongruous perspectives. All the formidable energy of the Princess's will is spent on her determination to see Hyacinth as one of "the people," while he casts Millicent Henning in a similar role. She, in turn, is genteely upset by the grime of his labor—"it had been a source of endless comfort to her . . . that she herself never worked with her 'ands" (p. 530)—and clings to her dress shop as the badge of her respectability. The tangle is summed up in this exchange, where (in James's revision) Pinnie's *h* drops neatly into the gap between the characters' understandings :

> *"And pray doesn't she think you good enough*
> *—for one of the beautiful 'Ennings?"*
>
> *"You don't understand, my poor Pinnie," he*
> *wearily pleaded. "I sometimes think there*
> *isn't a single thing in life that you under-*
> *stand. One of these days she'll marry an*
> *alderman."*
>
> *"An alderman—that creature? (x; p. 115)*

Of all the novel's characters, Rose Muniment speaks most clearly for this aspect of James's sense of society, and she makes for society the same claim Nietzsche did (and at about the same time) : what it crucially provides is the "pathos of distance" by which one can measure one's aspiration or one's failures *(Be-*

yond Good and Evil (p. 257). "I don't want to see the aristocracy lowered an inch," she says, "I like so much to look at it up there" (p. 107). And Pinnie, in much the same spirit, would gladly offer the services of her needle to poor frazzled Lady Aurora in a probably futile attempt to "keep up her rank for her" (p. 232). Other characters in the novel may be more skeptical of the available "grandees" than Rose or Pinnie, but they are equally preoccupied with the distances of their society, and in particular with a feeling for "height" and with puzzlements over the true nature and likely effects of such elevation. "It is better not to be lifted up high, like our friend," says Madame Grandoni. "It doesn't give happiness." "Not to one's self, possibly," Hyacinth replies, "but to others !" (p. 281).

James recognized and defended the vagueness of his conspiratorial world by saying that what he wanted was not a sense of "sharp particulars, but . . . loose appearances, vague motions and sounds and symptoms, just perceptible presences and general looming possibilities" (*Art of the Novel,* p. 76). Perhaps the impulse that most comprehensively informs the book's vision is Christina's passionate need to get in touch, through a sort of clairvoyance, with what "*is* real, *is* solid" in a world that seems very much to militate against this need. "The holy of holies," Hyacinth says, is "beyond anything I can say" :

> *Nothing of it appears above the surface; but there is an immense underworld, peopled with a thousand forms of revolutionary passion and devotion. . . . And on top of it all, society lives! People go and come and buy and sell, and drink and dance, and make money and make love, and seem to know nothing and suspect nothing and think of nothing (p. 308).*

Christina's flight from banality is a flight from a world drained of its solidity, an aimless and witless "charade"; Lady Aurora, too, finds that her position is "the deadness of the grave" and wants only "to live" (p. 188). In the degree to which they are aware of their true situation, James's Londoners feel not so much trapped in their social station, as anxiously adrift and in search of some solid ground. Like Lou Witt in D. H. Lawrence's *St. Mawr*—James's sense of society anticipates much of Lawrence's diagnosis—the Princess has "had her own way so

long that ... she didn't know where she was," and like Lou she
sometimes longs for a purging "barbarism" that would restore
her to "seriousness" (pp. 229, 290). The very distance of "the
people" guarantees, or seems to hold out the promise of, a flight
from self into some purer air (p. 440). And it is this same
promise, although in quite different ways, that Hyacinth or Rose
Muniment see in the splendidly or dangerously elevated existence
of the rich: a reminder of distances within the soul itself, a spur
(as Nietzsche said) to continuous "self surmounting," or at
least the source of a vicarious intensity of experience. In any
case, each world seems to be preoccupied with the other chiefly
as an image of the reality it finds lacking in its own existence.
And I suppose the envy Hyacinth comes to think is the basis
of revolution is only a cruder or despairing form of this same
passion; certainly the conspirators too are preoccupied with
"the real thing," with discovering an "irresistible reality" in
the midst of an "eternal dirty intellectual fog" (p. 255).

In such a world, sustaining environments are not given, but
must be fabricated out of the general muddle. Rose Muniment
constructs a world around her pink nightgown and wonders if
she can hope for a gilt mirror as well—"when you were stretched
on your back like that," Hyacinth muses, "you had the right to
reach out your hands ... and seize what you could get" (pp.
179, 426). In Sholto's apartment, Hyacinth wonders a trifle
naively over the "thousands of things" it takes to "make an accomplished man" (p. 196). Christina's drawing room throws
the Captain quite into the shade, and what most dazzles is not
mere splendor but the almost frightening vistas of sensibility
suggested by its "refinements of choice" (p. 212). Even the
Prince is forced grudgingly to recognize, for all his wife's
wanderings (moral as well as physical), her remarkable powers
of collection and arrangement: "no one had such a feeling as
she for the *mise-en-scène* of life" (p. 200).

Christina is above all concerned with choosing, and therefore
with creating, not merely the style of a room but the style of a
life. "I try to occupy my life, my mind, to create interests, in
the odious position in which I find myself," she says; and then
of her husband, "What interests could he create?" (p. 227). If
the Prince is a comic character it is because, so anxious over his
name and tradition, he believes that society *exists;* while Christina's charm is the "high, free, reckless" spirit in which she "plays
with life" (p. 405), fabricating her own position and creating

her own "society." "Please remember this," she says to
Hyacinth, "you cease to be insignificant from the moment I
have anything to do with you" (p. 298). His first meeting with
her, during a performance of *The Pearl of Paraguay,* is paradig-
matic. James exploits all the atmosphere of melodrama—the
first glimpse of an extended arm, the gargoyle attendant, the
mysterious summons—to suggest that there is about the world
into which Hyacinth is being initiated, the world of money and
power and culture, an element of the "fictive" and phantasma-
goric (p. 149). And that this is perhaps what redeems it. The
"new term" by which Hyacinth finds himself prepared to understand what is offered by Paris and Venice is just Christina's
theatricality; it is the actresses of Paris who bring before him
most vividly the way in which his mind has been "renewed,"
and when he "confronts" their manner and movement, they
seem only to be poorly imitating the Princess (p. 366).

"I've sold everything to give to the poor" (xxxii; p. 401). For
all the Biblical solemnity of her announcement, what Christina
calls "the last sacrifice" is not really to embrace poverty; "not
even a good imitation of it," Madame Grandoni observes sourly,
and even Hyacinth must admit that the Princess's economies are
sometimes rather expensive (p. 510). The real sacrifice, perhaps more mortifying to the spirit, is to relinquish "style and
elevation," to dispense with all the "beautiful things" of a cultivated existence, to immerse herself in the ugliness and vulgarity of the world she wishes to redeem (p. 403). And yet,
just because this relinquishment is itself an act of choice, Christina retains in her new role all her dazzling virtuosity. This
"most finished entertainment" (p. 411) verges, to be sure, on
the ridiculous. Christina Light leading the "homely" life on
Madeira Crescent is surely one of the funnier versions of
pastoral—which is what Paul Muniment must mean rudely to
suggest when he compliments her on the "loveliness" of her new
home (p. 445). But this is, I think, just a part of the gallantry
of her gesture—the sheer riskiness of its high spirits—and why
Christina finally strikes us, for all the destruction she unwittingly
leaves in her wake, as touching and vulnerable. The question
of her "sincerity," unanswerable as it is, seems in the end not
to matter. Even if we must grant, as Hyacinth does, that "her
behavior ... was more addressed to relieving herself than to
relieving others" (p. 469), the crucial point is the one Madame
Grandoni has already made in *Roderick Hudson,* the novel in

which Christina first appears: "I think she's an actress, but she believes in her part while she's playing it" (Chap. X).

James is of course aware of the costs of such performances, which is why so much of the novel is in the comic vein I have been describing. More portentously, Madame Grandoni is made to voice the claims of "station" (p. 330) and the certainties of work over against the vagrancies of what we have seen James calling a "romantic curiosity." Doing anything well, she says, is better than paying "extraordinary visits:" "Do not give up *yourself*," she warns (p. 211). If the wholly factitious Sholto stands as a frightening parody of the Princess, frightening because he lacks her saving conviction (pp. 332-33), Millicent Henning ("a loud-breathing feminine fact," James calls her in his revision) is the embodied presence of the human and "spontaneous" life—which is to say, the "conventional" (pp. 521-22). Nothing is more characteristic of James than this unexpected identification, but for all the comedy he extracts from his paradox, he is generous in recognizing Millicent's claims. Numbed and exhausted by the Princess's apparent betrayal, Hyacinth sinks gratefully into the embrace of Millicent's "vague primitive comfort" (p. 588). The park through which they stroll on a memorable Sunday ("there's nothing so pretty as nature," she observes (p. 523), affords a "small cheap pastoral" (xli, p. 529) quite unlike Medley with its shimmering distances. But perhaps their relationship is the more enduring because it is based—so Hyacinth muses—not on intense fidelities but on their fallibilities and shared weaknesses (p. 522). And as for the Princess, what freedom, after all, does she win for herself, isolated as she remains from the inner sanctum of the conspirators and still entangled in the bonds of money and position?

Nevertheless, in any contest between "the beauty of the original and the beauty of the conventional" (p. 521), there is little doubt where Hyacinth's final allegiance must lie. Surely we cannot suppose that only Millicent's flirtation with Sholto drives Hyacinth from her arms, bruising to his sensibilities as the last scene at the shop must be. As much as the Princess, he is driven by a passion for "fine moments" (p. 311). Open to all the sometimes undecodable "communications of life" (x; p. 117), he must achieve for himself, invent really (as Vetch claims to have "invented" him [p. 453]), an identity that will put him in touch with what is always but dimly adumbrated in the life around him, "the genuine article" (p. 270). Ironically, it is this need he shares with the Princess that carries them apart. What is "interesting" to her has for him the banality of mere fact, while the tedious charade on which she turns her back reveals to him the perspectives of romance. However torn Hyacinth may be, "society" and revolution have this much in common, that both come upon him as summons, calls toward a more intense life in which the mundane self, "the bad air of the personal" (xlv; p. 577), may be left behind. All he loses when he sees Millicent's betrayal is "the one, the last, sore personal need" (xlvii; p. 589) that in his last hours—embarrassed, half ashamed, and as it were retrospectively—he has allowed himself to acknowledge.

That the last summons should be to his own death is of course the measure of the insolubility of the contradictions he faces. But it is also consonant with the quality of Hyacinth's perception throughout the novel. The cultivated world becomes humanly real to him only when he sees it under that final sentence of which he finds himself the executor (p. 315); and in Paris and Venice the brilliance and dazzle play off against the darkness that seems to be stealing upon the old life and the old assumptions. His own life too, "the sweetness of not dying" (p. 377), seems vivid to Hyacinth only when the sentence hanging over him makes him aware of how conditional his existence is—when death itself offers a holiday, a "lark," from the half-felt routines of convention, and allows him to improvise those "fine moments" of which he had been dreaming. It is the death Hyacinth carries with him that frees him from banality, and allows him to meet the Princess on something like her own level. This is the meaning, I take it, of the striking ellipsis between Book Two and Book Three. Hyacinth rides off into the gloom and drizzle with the conspirators and then seems without transition to awaken at Medley, a world abruptly "everywhere...like a picture" (p. 275); we first learn of the sinister Hoffendahl from the Princess herself, "her hands full of primroses" (p. 304).

Hyacinth's suicide is not a blind defeat, but neither perhaps is it an intensely conscious moral act—at least in the traditional sense. It is interesting to speak of him assuming, through his deed, the guilt of both worlds, the cruelty of the rich and the envy and meanness of the poor; but this is probably to go beyond what is offered us of his actual consciousness. Hyacinth quite simply—James makes it explicit in his revisions—wants to be "splendid" (xxiv; p. 315). This is the motive the Poupins cannot grasp when they see that ideology no longer sustains him, and this is why he *is* sustained in the end by the Princess, even though he feels she has deserted him. The language of James's revision makes especially clear where his sympathies lie in their last confrontation:

> "... *there is no one in the world and has never been any one in the world, like you.*"
>
> "*Oh, thank you!*" *said the Princess impatiently. And she turned from him as with a beat of great white wings that raised her straight out of the bad air of the personal. It took her up too high, it put an end to their talk; expressing an indifference to what it might interest him to think of her today, and even a contempt for it, which brought tears to his eyes. His tears, however, were concealed by the fact that he bent his head low over the hand he had taken to kiss; after which he left the room without looking at her.* (xlv; p. 577)

At once absurd and genuinely grand, the radiance of the Princess's style, even while denying Hyacinth the human warmth he craves—such warmth is after all merely for sale in Millicent's shop—sustains him "caryatid like" in the expensive gesture he is about to complete. While he is aware of the gulf between them, he is overwhelmed by the sheer conviction she lends the idea of "an unregarded sacrifice" (p. 577)—"one who could shine like silver and ring like crystal" (xlv)—and his own tears are concealed in the gallantry of his leavetaking. As Hyacinth has felt before, the Princess has the capacity to "raise him higher and higher and absolutely highest ... to make him feel that he was good enough for anything" (xxix; p. 367). For Hyacinth, as for many of James's heroes, a moral code seems important not so much for its specific content as for its nature as a code, as the basis for a style—a "standard of fitness in place of exploded proprieties" (p. 315). "I didn't promise to believe," Hyacinth says, "I promised to obey" (p. 552). Mr. Vetch is perhaps not wide of the mark when he compares Hyacinth's silent commitment to that of a duelist (p. 460).

And we must suppose that the "careful" Schinkel betrays a want of imagination in seeing no more than the sad waste of a pistol and of a life (p. 596).

Early in the novel there is an episode that is revealing of James's instinctive sympathies and scale of values. Hyacinth, impressed by Paul Muniment and egged on by Rosy—"Oh, do say something of that kind; we should enjoy it so much! (p. 96) —has been seeing "how far" he can go in the direction of revolutionary ferocity, and Paul has ended on a rather threatening note:

> *"Enjoy your privileges while they last; it may not be for long."*
>
> Lady Aurora listened to him with her eyes on his face; and as they rested there Hyacinth scarcely knew what to make of her expression. ... She got up quickly when Muniment had ceased speaking; the movement suggested that she had taken offense, and he would have liked to show her that he thought she had been rather roughly used. ... Then he saw that he was mistaken and that, if she had flushed considerably, it was only with the excitement of pleasure, the enjoyment of such original talk and of seeing her friends at last as free and familiar as she wished them to be. "You are the most delightful people—I wish every one could know you!" she broke out.

(pp. 99-100)

To a certain kind of committed revolutionary this would have a satirical ring, or at least a deflating one. But I think James would agree that the finally pertinent achievement, the only important kind of "elevation," is the quality of lived experience, its freedom and originality. If Paul Muniment is a sinister figure, it is because in his pursuit of power he refuses to charm (although he will use this very refusal to manipulate others); because he is a "system" and not (like the Princess or Hyacinth or Lady Aurora) "an embodied passion" (p. 469): "tremendously reasonable" but humanly unengaged, like the touch of a hand "at once very firm and very soft, but strangely cold" (pp. 430-31). When all allowances have been made for self-delusion and fatuity, what is real for James is not ideology and not statistics, but the human gesture and the "fund of life" it embodies (p. 405). And such gestures, even gestures of abnegation or of rage and denial, are the hard-won triumph of what is meant by "civilization."

Terry Comito

A NOTE ON THE TEXT

The present edition is a reprint of James' original 1886 version of THE PRINCESS CASAMASSIMA. His later revisions are sometimes interesting for the light they throw on his intentions. In the Introduction, when reference is made to the language of the revised version, a chapter number is cited along with the page of the corresponding passage in this edition. Readers interested in comparing in detail the two versions of *The Princess Casamassima* should consult the New York Edition of the novel, first published in 1907-1909.

A NOTE ON FURTHER READING

The classic essay on *The Princess Casamassima* is by Lionel Trilling, and it is included in *The Liberal Imagination* (N.Y., 1950). There is an interesting discussion of the novel in F. W. Dupee, *Henry James* (N.Y., 1951). The Princess herself makes her first appearance as Christina Light in *Roderick Hudson,* which is brilliantly discussed in Richard Poirier, *The Comic Sense of Henry James* (N.Y., 1960).

BOOK FIRST

THE PRINCESS CASAMASSIMA

I

'OH yes, I daresay I can find the child, if you would like
to see him,' Miss Pynsent said; she had a fluttering wish to
assent to every suggestion made by her visitor, whom she
regarded as a high and rather terrible personage. To look
for the little boy she came out of her small parlour, which
she had been ashamed to exhibit in so untidy a state, with
paper 'patterns' lying about on the furniture and snippings
of stuff scattered over the carpet—she came out of this somewhat stuffy sanctuary, dedicated at once to social intercourse
and to the ingenious art to which her life had been devoted,
and, opening the house door, turned her eyes up and down
the little street. It would presently be tea-time, and she
knew that at that solemn hour Hyacinth narrowed the circle
of his wanderings. She was anxious and impatient, and in
a fever of excitement and complacency, not wanting to keep
Mrs. Bowerbank waiting, though she sat there, heavily and
consideringly, as if she meant to stay; and wondering not
a little whether the object of her quest would have a dirty
face. Mrs. Bowerbank had intimated so definitely that she
thought it remarkable on Miss Pynsent's part to have taken
care of him gratuitously for so many years, that the humble
dressmaker, whose imagination took flights about every one
but herself, and who had never been conscious of an
exemplary benevolence, suddenly aspired to appear, throughout, as devoted to the child as she had struck her solemn,
substantial guest as being, and felt how much she should
like him to come in fresh and frank, and looking as pretty
as he sometimes did. Miss Pynsent, who blinked con-

fusedly as she surveyed the outer prospect, was very much
flushed, partly with the agitation of what Mrs. Bowerbank
had told her, and partly because, when she offered that
lady a drop of something refreshing, at the end of so long
an expedition, she had said she couldn't think of touching
anything unless Miss Pynsent would keep her company.
The cheffonier (as Amanda was always careful to call it),
beside the fireplace, yielded up a small bottle which had
formerly contained eau-de-cologne and which now exhibited
half a pint of a rich gold-coloured liquid.   Miss Pynsent
was very delicate; she lived on tea and watercress, and she
kept the little bottle in the cheffonier only for great emer-
gencies.   She didn't like hot brandy and water, with a
lump or two of sugar, but she partook of half a tumbler
on the present occasion, which was of a highly exceptional
kind.   At this time of day the boy was often planted in
front of the little sweet-shop on the other side of the street,
an establishment where periodical literature, as well as
tough toffy and hard lollipops, was dispensed, and where
song-books and pictorial sheets were attractively exhibited
in the small-paned, dirty window.   He used to stand there
for half an hour at a time, spelling out the first page of
the romances in the *Family Herald* and the *London Journal*,
and admiring the obligatory illustration in which the noble
characters (they were always of the highest birth) were presented to the carnal eye.   When he had a penny he spent
only a fraction of it on stale sugar-candy; with the
remaining halfpenny he always bought a ballad, with a
vivid woodcut at the top.   Now, however, he was not at
his post of contemplation; nor was he visible anywhere to
Miss Pynsent's impatient glance.

   'Millicent Henning, tell me quickly, have you seen my
child?'   These words were addressed by Miss Pynsent to
a little girl who sat on the doorstep of the adjacent house,
nursing a dingy doll, and who had an extraordinary luxuri-
ance of dark brown hair, surmounted by a torn straw hat.
Miss Pynsent pronounced her name Enning.

   The child looked up from her dandling and patting, and
after a stare of which the blankness was somewhat exaggerated, replied: 'Law no, Miss Pynsent, I never see him.'

'Aren't you always messing about with him, you naughty little girl?' the dressmaker returned, with sharpness. 'Isn't he round the corner, playing marbles, or—or some jumping game?' Miss Pynsent went on, trying to be suggestive.

'I assure *you*, he never plays nothing,' said Millicent Henning, with a mature manner which she bore out by adding, 'And I don't know why I should be called naughty, neither.'

'Well, if you want to be called good, please go and find him and tell him there's a lady here come on purpose to see him, this very instant.' Miss Pynsent waited a moment, to see if her injunction would be obeyed, but she got no satisfaction beyond another gaze of deliberation, which made her feel that the child's perversity was as great as the beauty, somewhat soiled and dimmed, of her insolent little face. She turned back into the house, with an exclamation of despair, and as soon as she had disappeared Millicent Henning sprang erect and began to race down the street in the direction of another, which crossed it. I take no unfair advantage of the innocence of childhood in saying that the motive of this young lady's flight was not a desire to be agreeable to Miss Pynsent, but an extreme curiosity on the subject of the visitor who wanted to see Hyacinth Robinson. She wished to participate, if only in imagination, in the interview that might take place, and she was moved also by a quick revival of friendly feeling for the boy, from whom she had parted only half an hour before with considerable asperity. She was not a very clinging little creature, and there was no one in her own domestic circle to whom she was much attached; but she liked to kiss Hyacinth when he didn't push her away and tell her she was tiresome. It was in this action and epithet he had indulged half an hour ago; but she had reflected rapidly (while she stared at Miss Pynsent) that this was the worst he had ever done. Millicent Henning was only eight years of age, but she knew there was worse in the world than that.

Mrs. Bowerbank, in a leisurely, roundabout way, wandered off to her sister, Mrs. Chipperfield, whom she had come into that part of the world to see, and the whole history of the dropsical tendencies of whose husband, an undertaker with a business that had been a blessing because you could always count on it, she unfolded to Miss Pynsent between the sips of a second glass. She was a high-shouldered, towering woman, and suggested squareness as well as a pervasion of the upper air, so that Amanda reflected that she must be very difficult to fit, and had a sinking at the idea of the number of pins she would take. Her sister had nine children and she herself had seven, the eldest of whom she left in charge of the others when she went to her service. She was on duty at the prison only during the day; she had to be there at seven in the morning, but she got her evenings at home, quite regular and comfortable. Miss Pynsent thought it wonderful she could talk of comfort in such a life as that, but could easily imagine she should be glad to get away at night, for at that time the place must be much more terrible.

'And aren't you frightened of them—ever?' she inquired, looking up at her visitor with her little heated face.

Mrs. Bowerbank was very slow, and considered her so long before replying, that she felt herself to be, in an alarming degree, in the eye of the law; for who could be more closely connected with the administration of justice than a female turnkey, especially so big and majestic a one? 'I expect they are more frightened of me,' she replied at last; and it was an idea into which Miss Pynsent could easily enter.

'And at night I suppose they rave, quite awful,' the little dressmaker suggested, feeling vaguely that prisons and madhouses came very much to the same.

'Well, if they do, we hush 'em up,' Mrs. Bowerbank remarked, rather portentously; while Miss Pynsent fidgeted to the door again, without results, to see if the child had become visible. She observed to her guest that she couldn't call it anything but contrary that he should not turn up, when he knew so well, most days in the week, when his tea was ready. To which Mrs. Bowerbank rejoined, fixing her companion again with the steady orb of justice, 'And do he have his tea, that way, by himself, like a little gentleman?'

'Well, I try to give it to him tidy-like, at a suitable

hour,' said Miss Pynsent, guiltily. 'And there might be some who would say that, for the matter of that, he *is* a little gentleman,' she added, with an effort at mitigation which, as she immediately became conscious, only involved her more deeply.

'There are people silly enough to say anything. If it's your parents that settle your station, the child hasn't much to be thankful for,' Mrs. Bowerbank went on, in the manner of a woman accustomed to looking facts in the face.

Miss Pynsent was very timid, but she adored the aristocracy, and there were elements in the boy's life which she was not prepared to sacrifice even to a person who represented such a possibility of grating bolts and clanking chains. 'I suppose we oughtn't to forget that his father was very high,' she suggested, appealingly, with her hands clasped tightly in her lap.

'His father? Who knows who *he* was? He doesn't set up for having a father, does he?'

'But, surely, wasn't it proved that Lord Frederick——?'

'My dear woman, nothing was proved except that she stabbed his lordship in the back with a very long knife, that he died of the blow, and that she got the full sentence. What does such a piece as that know about fathers? The less said about the poor child's ancestors the better!'

This view of the case caused Miss Pynsent fairly to gasp, for it pushed over with a touch a certain tall imaginative structure which she had been piling up for years. Even as she heard it crash around her she couldn't forbear the attempt to save at least some of the material. 'Really—really,' she panted, 'she never had to do with any one but the nobility!'

Mrs. Bowerbank surveyed her hostess with an expressionless eye. 'My dear young lady, what does a respectable little body like you, that sits all day with her needle and scissors, know about the doings of a wicked low foreigner that carries a knife? I was there when she came in, and I know to what she had sunk. Her conversation was choice, I assure you.'

'Oh, it's very dreadful, and of course I know nothing in particular,' Miss Pynsent quavered. 'But she wasn't low

when I worked at the same place with her, and she often
told me she would do nothing for any one that wasn't at
the very top.'

'She might have talked to you of something that would
have done you both more good,' Mrs. Bowerbank remarked,
while the dressmaker felt rebuked in the past as well as in
the present. 'At the very top, poor thing! Well, she's at
the very bottom now. If she wasn't low when she worked,
it's a pity she didn't stick to her work ; and as for pride of
birth, that's an article I recommend your young friend to
leave to others. You had better believe what I say, because
I'm a woman of the world.'

Indeed she was, as Miss Pynsent felt, to whom all this
was very terrible, letting in the cold light of the penal
system on a dear, dim little theory. She had cared for the
child because maternity was in her nature, and this was the
only manner in which fortune had put it in her path to
become a mother. She had as few belongings as the baby,
and it had seemed to her that he would add to her importance in the little world of Lomax Place (if she kept it a
secret how she came by him), quite in the proportion in
which she should contribute to his maintenance. Her
weakness and loneliness went out to his, and in the course
of time this united desolation was peopled by the dressmaker's romantic mind with a hundred consoling evocations.
The boy proved neither a dunce nor a reprobate ; but what
endeared him to her most was her conviction that he
belonged, ' by the left hand,' as she had read in a novel, to
an ancient and exalted race, the list of whose representatives
and the record of whose alliances she had once (when she
took home some work and was made to wait, alone, in a
lady's boudoir) had the opportunity of reading in a fat red
book, eagerly and tremblingly consulted. She bent her
head before Mrs. Bowerbank's overwhelming logic, but she
felt in her heart that she shouldn't give the child up for all
that, that she believed in him still, and that she recognised,
as distinctly as she revered, the quality of her betters. To
believe in Hyacinth, for Miss Pynsent, was to believe that
he *was* the son of the extremely immoral Lord Frederick.
She had, from his earliest age, made him feel that there

was a grandeur in his past, and as Mrs. Bowerbank would be sure not to approve of such aberrations Miss Pynsent prayed she might not question her on that part of the business.   It was not that, when it was necessary, the little dressmaker had any scruple about using the arts of prevarication ; she was a kind and innocent creature, but she told fibs as freely as she invented trimmings.   She had, however, not yet been questioned by an emissary of the law, and her heart beat faster when Mrs. Bowerbank said to her, in deep tones, with an effect of abruptness, ' And pray, Miss Pynsent, does the child know it ? '

' Know about Lord Frederick ? ' Miss Pynsent palpitated.

' Bother Lord Frederick !   Know about his mother.'

' Oh, I can't say that.   I have never told him.'

' But has any one else told him ? '

To this inquiry Miss Pynsent's answer was more prompt and more proud ; it was with an agreeable sense of having conducted herself with extraordinary wisdom and propriety that she replied, ' How could any one know ?   I have never breathed it to a creature ! '

Mrs. Bowerbank gave utterance to no commendation ; she only put down her empty glass and wiped her large mouth with much thoroughness and deliberation.   Then she said, as if it were as cheerful an idea as, in the premises, she was capable of expressing, ' Ah, well, there'll be plenty, later on, to give him all information ! '

' I pray God he may live and die without knowing it ! ' Miss Pynsent cried, with eagerness.

Her companion gazed at her with a kind of professional patience.   ' You don't keep your ideas together.   How can he go to her, then, if he's never to know ? '

' Oh, did you mean she would tell him ? ' Miss Pynsent responded, plaintively.

' Tell him !   He won't need to be told, once she gets hold of him and gives him—what she told me.'

' What she told you ? ' Miss Pynsent repeated, openeyed.

' The kiss her lips have been famished for, for years.'

' Ah, poor desolate woman ! ' the little dressmaker murmured, with her pity gushing up again. 'Of course he'll see she's fond of him,' she pursued, simply. Then she added, with an inspiration more brilliant, 'We might tell him she's his aunt !'

'You may tell him she's his grandmother, if you like. But it's all in the family.'

'Yes, on that side,' said Miss Pynsent, musingly and irrepressibly. 'And will she speak French?' she inquired. 'In that case he won't understand.'

'Oh, a child will understand its own mother, whatever she speaks,' Mrs. Bowerbank returned, declining to administer a superficial comfort. But she subjoined, opening the door for escape from a prospect which bristled with dangers, 'Of course, it's just according to your own conscience. You needn't bring the child at all, unless you like. There's many a one that wouldn't. There's no compulsion.'

'And would nothing be done to me, if I didn't?' poor Miss Pynsent asked, unable to rid herself of the impression that it was somehow the arm of the law that was stretched out to touch her.

'The only thing that could happen to you would be that *he* might throw it up against you later,' the lady from the prison observed, with a gloomy impartiality.

'Yes, indeed, if he were to know that I had kept him back.'

'Oh, he'd be sure to know, one of these days. We see a great deal of that—the way things come out,' said Mrs. Bowerbank, whose view of life seemed to abound in cheerless contingencies. 'You must remember that it is her dying wish, and that you may have it on your conscience.'

'That's a thing I *never* could abide !' the little dressmaker exclaimed, with great emphasis and a visible shiver; after which she picked up various scattered remnants of muslin and cut paper and began to roll them together with a desperate and mechanical haste. 'It's quite awful, to know what to do—if you are very sure she *is* dying.'

'Do you mean she's shamming? we have plenty of that —but we know how to treat 'em.'

'Lord, I suppose so,' murmured Miss Pynsent; while

her visitor went on to say that the unfortunate person on whose behalf she had undertaken this solemn pilgrimage might live a week and might live a fortnight, but if she lived a month, would violate (as Mrs. Bowerbank might express herself) every established law of nature, being reduced to skin and bone, with nothing left of her but the main desire to see her child.

'If you're afraid of her talking, it isn't much she'd be able to say. And we shouldn't allow you more than about eight minutes,' Mrs. Bowerbank pursued, in a tone that seemed to refer itself to an iron discipline.

'I'm sure I shouldn't want more; that would be enough to last me many a year,' said Miss Pynsent, accommodatingly. And then she added, with another illumination, 'Don't you think he might throw it up against me that I *did* take him? People might tell him about her in later years; but if he hadn't seen her he wouldn't be obliged to believe them.'

Mrs. Bowerbank considered this a moment, as if it were rather a super-subtle argument, and then answered, quite in the spirit of her official pessimism, 'There is one thing you may be sure of: whatever you decide to do, as soon as ever he grows up he will make you wish you had done the opposite.' Mrs. Bowerbank called it oppo*site*.

'Oh, dear, then, I'm glad it will be a long time.'

'It will be ever so long, if once he gets it into his head ! At any rate, you must do as you think best. Only, if you come, you mustn't come when it's all over.'

'It's too impossible to decide.'

'It is, indeed,' said Mrs. Bowerbank, with superior consistency. And she seemed more placidly grim than ever when she remarked, gathering up her loosened shawl, that she was much obliged to Miss Pynsent for her civility, and had been quite freshened up : her visit had so completely deprived her hostess of that sort of calm. Miss Pynsent gave the fullest expression to her perplexity in the supreme exclamation :

'If you could only wait and see the child, I'm sure it would help you to judge !'

'My dear woman, I don't want to judge—it's none of

our business !' Mrs. Bowerbank exclaimed ; and she had no
sooner uttered the words than the door of the room creaked
open and a small boy stood there gazing at her. Her
eyes rested on him a moment, and then, most unexpectedly,
she gave an inconsequent cry. 'Is that the child? Oh,
Lord o' mercy, don't take *him !'*

'Now *ain't* he shrinking and sensitive?' demanded Miss
Pynsent, who had pounced upon him, and, holding him an
instant at arm's length, appealed eagerly to her visitor.
' Ain't he delicate and high-bred, and wouldn't he be thrown
into a state?' Delicate as he might be the little dressmaker shook him smartly for his naughtiness in being out
of the way when he was wanted, and brought him to the
big, square-faced, deep-voiced lady who took up, as it were,
all that side of the room. But Mrs. Bowerbank laid no
hand upon him ; she only dropped her gaze from a
tremendous height, and her forbearance seemed a tribute
to that fragility of constitution on which Miss Pynsent
desired to insist, just as her continued gravity was an
implication that this scrupulous woman might well not
know what to do.

'Speak to the lady nicely, and tell her you are very
sorry to have kept her waiting.'

The child hesitated a moment, while he reciprocated
Mrs. Bowerbank's inspection, and then he said, with a
strange, cool, conscious indifference (Miss Pynsent instantly recognised it as his aristocratic manner), 'I don't
think she can have been in a very great hurry.'

There was irony in the words, for it is a remarkable fact
that even at the age of ten Hyacinth Robinson was
ironical ; but the subject of his allusion, who was not
nimble withal, appeared not to interpret it ; so that she
rejoined only by remarking, over his head, to Miss Pynsent,
' It's the very face of her over again !'

' Of *her?* But what do you say to Lord Frederick?'

' I *have* seen lords that wasn't so dainty !'

Miss Pynsent had seen very few lords, but she entered,
with a passionate thrill, into this generalisation ; controlling
herself, however, for she remembered the child was
tremendously sharp, sufficiently to declare, in an edifying

tone, that he would look more like what he ought to if his face were a little cleaner.

'It was probably Millicent Henning dirtied my face when she kissed me,' the boy announced, with slow gravity, looking all the while at Mrs. Bowerbank. He exhibited not a symptom of shyness.

'Millicent Henning is a very bad little girl; she'll come to no good,' said Miss Pynsent, with familiar decision, and also, considering that the young lady in question had been her effective messenger, with marked ingratitude.

Against this qualification the child instantly protested. 'Why is she bad? I don't think she is bad; I like her very much.' It came over him that he had too hastily shifted to her shoulders the responsibility of his unseemly appearance, and he wished to make up to her for that betrayal. He dimly felt that nothing but that particular accusation could have pushed him to it, for he hated people who were not fresh, who had smutches and streaks. Millicent Henning generally had two or three, which she borrowed from her doll, into whom she was always rubbing her nose and whose dinginess was contagious. It was quite inevitable she should have left her mark under his own nose when she claimed her reward for coming to tell him about the lady who wanted him.

Miss Pynsent held the boy against her knee, trying to present him so that Mrs. Bowerbank should agree with her about his having the air of race. He was exceedingly diminutive, even for his years, and though his appearance was not positively sickly it seemed written in his attenuated little person that he would never be either tall or strong. His dark blue eyes were separated by a wide interval, which increased the fairness and sweetness of his face, and his abundant curly hair, which grew thick and long, had the golden brownness predestined to elicit exclamations of delight from ladies when they take the inventory of a child. His features were smooth and pretty; his head was set upon a slim little neck; his expression, grave and clear, showed a quick perception as well as a great credulity; and he was altogether, in his innocent smallness, a refined and interesting figure.

'Yes, he's one that would be sure to remember,' said Mrs. Bowerbank, mentally contrasting him with the undeveloped members of her own brood, who had never been retentive of anything but the halfpence which they occasionally contrived to filch from her. Her eyes descended to the details of his toilet : the careful mending of his short breeches and his long, coloured stockings, which she was in a position to appreciate, as well as the knot of bright ribbon which the dressmaker had passed into his collar, slightly crumpled by Miss Henning's embrace. Of course Miss Pynsent had only one to look after, but her visitor was obliged to recognise that she had the highest standard in respect to buttons. 'And you *do* turn him out so it's a pleasure,' she went on, noting the ingenious patches in the child's shoes, which, to her mind, were repaired for all the world like those of a little nobleman.

'I'm sure you're very civil,' said Miss Pynsent, in a state of severe exaltation. 'There's never a needle but mine has come near him. That's exactly what I think : the impression would go so deep.'

'Do you want to see me only to look at me ?' Hyacinth inquired, with a candour which, though unstudied, had again much of the force of satire.

'I'm sure it's very kind of the lady to notice you at all !' cried his protectress, giving him an ineffectual jerk. 'You're no bigger than a flea ; there are many that wouldn't spy you out.'

'You'll find he's big enough, I expect, when he begins to go,' Mrs. Bowerbank remarked, tranquilly ; and she added that now she saw how he was turned out she couldn't but feel that the other side was to be considered. In her effort to be discreet, on account of his being present (and so precociously attentive), she became slightly enigmatical ; but Miss Pynsent gathered her meaning, which was that it was very true the child would take everything in and keep it : but at the same time it was precisely his being so attractive that made it a kind of sin not to gratify the poor woman, who, if she knew what he looked like to-day, wouldn't forgive his adoptive mamma for not producing him. 'Certainly, in her place, I should go off easier if I had seen them curls,'

Mrs. Bowerbank declared, with a flight of maternal imagination which brought her to her feet, while Miss Pynsent felt that she was leaving her dreadfully ploughed up, and without any really fertilising seed having been sown. The little dressmaker packed the child upstairs to tidy himself for his tea, and while she accompanied her visitor to the door told her that if she would have a little more patience with her she would think a day or two longer what was best and write to her when she should have decided. Mrs. Bowerbank continued to move in a realm superior to poor Miss Pynsent's vacillations and timidities, and her impartiality gave her hostess a high idea of her respectability; but the way was a little smoothed when, after Amanda had moaned once more, on the threshold, helplessly and irrelevantly, 'Ain't it a pity she's so bad?' the ponderous lady from the prison rejoined, in those tones which seemed meant to resound through corridors of stone, 'I assure you there's a many that's much worse!'

II

Miss Pynsent, when she found herself alone, felt that she
was really quite upside down; for the event that had just
occurred had never entered into her calculations : the very
nature of the case had seemed to preclude it. All she knew,
and all she wished to know, was that in one of the dreadful
institutions constructed for such purposes her quondam
comrade was serving out the sentence that had been sub-
stituted for the other (the unspeakable horror) almost when
the halter was already round her neck. As there was no
question of *that* concession being stretched any further, poor
Florentine seemed only a little more dead than other people,
having no decent tombstone to mark the place where she
lay. Miss Pynsent had therefore never thought of her
dying again ; she had no idea to what prison she had been
committed on being removed from Newgate (she wished to
keep her mind a blank about the matter, in the interest of
the child), and it could not occur to her that out of such
silence and darkness a second voice would reach her,
especially a voice that she should really have to listen to.
Miss Pynsent would have said, before Mrs. Bowerbank's
visit, that she had no account to render to any one ; that
she had taken up the child (who might have starved in the
gutter) out of charity, and had brought him up, poor and
precarious as her own subsistence had been, without a
penny's help from another source ; that the mother had
forfeited every right and title ; and that this had been
understood between them—if anything, in so dreadful an
hour, could have been said to be understood—when she
went to see her at Newgate (that terrible episode, nine
years before, overshadowed all Miss Pynsent's other
memories) : went to see her because Florentine had sent

for her (a name, face and address coming up out of the still recent but sharply separated past of their working-girl years), as the one friend to whom she could appeal with some chance of a pitying answer. The effect of violent emotion, with Miss Pynsent, was not to make her sit with idle hands or fidget about to no purpose; under its influence, on the contrary, she threw herself into little jobs, as a fugitive takes to by-paths, and clipped and cut, and stitched and basted, as if she were running a race with hysterics. And while her hands, her scissors, her needle flew, an infinite succession of fantastic possibilities trotted through her confused little head; she had a furious imagination, and the act of reflection, in her mind, was always a panorama of figures and scenes. She had had her picture of the future, painted in rather rosy hues, hung up before her now for a good many years; but it seemed to her that Mrs. Bowerbank's heavy hand had suddenly punched a hole in the canvas. It must be added, however, that if Amanda's thoughts were apt to be bewildering visions they sometimes led her to make up her mind, and on this particular September evening she arrived at a momentous decision. What she made up her mind to was to take advice, and in pursuance of this view she rushed downstairs, and, jerking Hyacinth away from his simple but unfinished repast, packed him across the street to tell Mr. Vetch (if he had not yet started for the theatre) that she begged he would come in to see her when he came home that night, as she had something very particular she wished to say to him. It didn't matter if he should be very late, he could come in at any hour—he would see her light in the window—and he would do her a real mercy. Miss Pynsent knew it would be of no use for her to go to bed; she felt as if she should never close her eyes again. Mr. Vetch was her most distinguished friend; she had an immense appreciation of his cleverness and knowledge of the world, as well as of the purity of his taste in matters of conduct and opinion; and she had already consulted him about Hyacinth's education. The boy needed no urging to go on such an errand, for he, too, had his ideas about the little fiddler, the second violin in the orchestra of the Bloomsbury

Theatre. Mr. Vetch had once obtained for the pair an order for two seats at a pantomime, and for Hyacinth the impression of that ecstatic evening had consecrated him, placed him for ever in the golden glow of the footlights. There were things in life of which, even at the age of ten, it was a conviction of the boy's that it would be his fate never to see enough, and one of them was the wonder-world illuminated by those playhouse lamps. But there would be chances, perhaps, if one didn't lose sight of Mr. Vetch; he might open the door again; he was a privileged, magical mortal, who went to the play every night.

He came in to see Miss Pynsent about midnight; as soon as she heard the lame tinkle of the bell she went to the door to let him in. He was an original, in the fullest sense of the word: a lonely, disappointed, embittered, cynical little man, whose musical organisation had been sterile, who had the nerves, the sensibilities, of a gentleman, and whose fate had condemned him, for the last ten years, to play a fiddle at a second-rate theatre for a few shillings a week. He had ideas of his own about everything, and they were not always very improving. For Amanda Pynsent he represented art, literature (the literature of the play-bill), and philosophy, and she always felt about him as if he belonged to a higher social sphere, though his earnings were hardly greater than her own and he lived in a single back-room, in a house where she had never seen a window washed. He had, for her, the glamour of reduced gentility and fallen fortunes; she was conscious that he spoke a different language (though she couldn't have said in what the difference consisted) from the other members of her humble, almost suburban circle; and the shape of his hands was distinctly aristocratic. (Miss Pynsent, as I have intimated, was immensely preoccupied with that element in life.) Mr. Vetch displeased her only by one of the facets of his character—his blasphemous republican, radical views, and the contemptuous manner in which he expressed himself about the nobility. On that ground he worried her extremely, though he never seemed to her so clever as when he horrified her most. These dreadful theories (expressed so brilliantly that, really, they

might have been dangerous if Miss Pynsent had not known
her own place so well) constituted no presumption against
his refined origin ; they were explained, rather, to a certain
extent, by a just resentment at finding himself excluded
from his proper place.   Mr. Vetch was short, fat and bald,
though he was not much older than Miss Pynsent, who was
not much older than some people who called themselves
forty-five ; he always went to the theatre in evening-dress,
with a flower in his button-hole, and wore a glass in one
eye.   He looked placid and genial, and as if he would
fidget at the most about the 'get up' of his linen ; you
would have thought him finical but superficial, and never
have suspected that he was a revolutionist, or even a critic
of life.   Sometimes, when he could get away from the
theatre early enough, he went with a pianist, a friend of his,
to play dance-music at small parties ; and after such expeditions he was particularly cynical and startling ; he indulged
in diatribes against the British middle-class, its Philistinism,
its snobbery.   He seldom had much conversation with
Miss Pynsent without telling her that she had the intellectual outlook of a caterpillar ; but this was his privilege
after a friendship now of seven years' standing, which had
begun (the year after he came to live in Lomax Place) with
her going over to nurse him, on learning from the milk-
woman that he was alone at Number 17—laid up with an
attack of gastritis.   He always compared her to an insect
or a bird, and she didn't mind, because she knew he liked
her, and she herself liked all winged creatures.   How
indeed could she complain, after hearing him call the
Queen a superannuated form and the Archbishop of
Canterbury a grotesque superstition ?

He laid his violin-case on the table, which was covered
with a confusion of fashion-plates and pincushions, and
glanced toward the fire, where a kettle was gently hissing.
Miss Pynsent, who had put it on half an hour before, read
his glance, and reflected with complacency that Mrs. Bowerbank had not absolutely drained the little bottle in the
cheffonier.   She placed it on the table again, this time
with a single glass, and told her visitor that, as a great
exception, he might light his pipe.   In fact, she always

made the exception, and he always replied to the gracious
speech by inquiring whether she supposed the greengrocers'
wives, the butchers' daughters, for whom she worked, had
fine enough noses to smell, in the garments she sent home,
the fumes of his tobacco. He knew her 'connection' was confined to small shopkeepers, but she didn't wish others to know
it, and would have liked them to believe it was important that
the poor little stuffs she made up (into very queer fashions,
I am afraid) should not surprise the feminine nostril.   But it
had always been impossible to impose on Mr. Vetch ; he
guessed the truth, the untrimmed truth, about everything
in a moment.   She was sure he would do so now, in regard
to this solemn question which had come up about Hyacinth ;
he would see that though she was agreeably flurried at
finding herself whirled in the last eddies of a case that had
been so celebrated in its day, her secret wish was to shirk
her duty (if it *was* a duty) ; to keep the child from ever
knowing his mother's unmentionable history, the shame
that attached to his origin, the opportunity she had had
of letting him see the wretched woman before she died
She knew Mr. Vetch would read her troubled thoughts,
but she hoped he would say they were natural and just :
she reflected that as he took an interest in Hyacinth he
wouldn't desire him to be subjected to a mortification that
might rankle for ever and perhaps even crush him to the
earth.   She related Mrs. Bowerbank's visit, while he sat
upon the sofa in the very place where that majestic woman
had reposed, and puffed his smoke-wreaths into the dusky
little room.   He knew the story of the child's birth, had
known it years before, so she had no startling revelation
to make.   He was not in the least agitated at learning that
Florentine was dying in prison and had managed to get a
message conveyed to Amanda ; he thought this so much
in the usual course that he said to Miss Pynsent, ' Did you
expect her to live on there for ever, working out her terrible
sentence, just to spare you the annoyance of a dilemma, or
any reminder of her miserable existence, which you have
preferred to forget ? '   That was just the sort of question
Mr. Vetch was sure to ask, and he inquired, further, of his
dismayed hostess, whether she were sure her friend's message

(he called the unhappy creature her friend) had come to her
in the regular way.   The warders, surely, had no authority
to introduce visitors to their captives ; and was it a question
of her going off to the prison on the sole authority of Mrs.
Bowerbank ?   The little dressmaker explained that this lady
had merely come to sound her, Florentine had begged so
hard.   She had been in Mrs. Bowerbank's ward before her
removal to the infirmary, where she now lay ebbing away,
and she had communicated her desire to the Catholic
chaplain, who had undertaken that some satisfaction—of
inquiry, at least—should be given her.   He had thought
it best to ascertain first whether the person in charge of the
child would be willing to bring him, such a course being
perfectly optional, and he had some talk with Mrs. Bowerbank on the subject, in which it was agreed between them
that if she would approach Miss Pynsent and explain to
her the situation, leaving her to do what she thought best,
he would answer for it that the consent of the governor of
the prison should be given to the interview.   Miss Pynsent
had lived for fourteen years in Lomax Place, and Florentine
had never forgotten that this was her address at the time
she came to her at Newgate (before her dreadful sentence
had been commuted), and promised, in an outgush of pity
for one whom she had known in the days of her honesty
and brightness, that she would save the child, rescue it from
the workhouse and the streets, keep it from the fate that
had swallowed up the mother.   Mrs. Bowerbank had a
half-holiday, and a sister living also in the north of London,
to whom she had been for some time intending a visit ; so
that after her domestic duty had been performed it had been
possible for her to drop in on Miss Pynsent in a natural,
casual way and put the case before her.   It would be just
as she might be disposed to view it.   She was to think it
over a day or two, but not long, because the woman was
so ill, and then write to Mrs. Bowerbank, at the prison.   If
she should consent, Mrs. Bowerbank would tell the chaplain,
and the chaplain would obtain the order from the governor
and send it to Lomax Place ; after which Amanda would
immediately set out with her unconscious victim.   But
should she—*must* she—consent ?   That was the terrible,

the heart-shaking question, with which Miss Pynsent's
unaided wisdom had been unable to grapple.

'After all, he isn't hers any more—he's mine, mine only,
and mine always. I should like to know if all I have done
for him doesn't make him so !' It was in this manner that
Amanda Pynsent delivered herself, while she plied her
needle, faster than ever, in a piece of stuff that was pinned
to her knee.

Mr. Vetch watched her awhile, blowing silently at his
pipe, with his head thrown back on the high, stiff, old-
fashioned sofa, and his little legs crossed under him like a
Turk's. 'It's true you have done a good deal for him.
You are a good little woman, my dear Pinnie, after all.'
He said 'after all,' because that was a part of his tone.
In reality he had never had a moment's doubt that she was
the best little woman in the north of London.

'I have done what I could, and I don't want no fuss
made about it. Only it does make a difference when you
come to look at it—about taking him off to see another
woman. And *such* another woman—and in such a place !
I think it's hardly right to take an innocent child.'

'I don't know about that; there are people that would
tell you it would do him good. If he didn't like the place
as a child, he would take more care to keep out of it
later.'

'Lord, Mr. Vetch, how can you think ? And him such
a perfect little gentleman !' Miss Pynsent cried.

'Is it you that have made him one ?' the fiddler asked.
'It doesn't run in the family, you'd say.'

'Family ? what do you know about that ?' she replied,
quickly, catching at her dearest, her only hobby.

'Yes, indeed, what does any one know ? what did she
know herself ?' And then Miss Pynsent's visitor added,
irrelevantly, 'Why should you have taken him on your back ?
Why did you want to be so good ? No one else thinks it
necessary.'

'I didn't want to be good. That is, I do want to, of
course, in a general way : but that wasn't the reason then.
But I had nothing of my own—I had nothing in the world
but my thimble.'

'That would have seemed to most people a reason for not adopting a prostitute's bastard.'

'Well, I went to see him at the place where he was (just where she had left him, with the woman of the house), and I saw what kind of a shop *that* was, and felt it was a shame an innocent child should grow up in such a place.' Miss Pynsent defended herself as earnestly as if her inconsistency had been of a criminal cast. 'And he wouldn't have grown up, neither. *They* wouldn't have troubled themselves long with a helpless baby. *They'd* have played some trick on him, if it was only to send him to the workhouse. Besides, I always was fond of tiny creatures, and I have been fond of this one,' she went on, speaking as if with a consciousness, on her own part, of almost heroic proportions. 'He was in my way the first two or three years, and it was a good deal of a pull to look after the business and him together. But now he's like the business—he seems to go of himself.'

'Oh, if he flourishes as the business flourishes, you can just enjoy your peace of mind,' said the fiddler, still with his manner of making a small dry joke of everything.

'That's all very well, but it doesn't close my eyes to that poor woman lying there and moaning just for the touch of his little 'and before she passes away. Mrs. Bowerbank says she believes I will bring him.'

'Who believes? Mrs. Bowerbank?'

'I wonder if there's anything in life holy enough for you to take it seriously,' Miss Pynsent rejoined, snapping off a thread, with temper. 'The day you stop laughing I should like to be there.'

'So long as you are there, I shall never stop. What is it you want me to advise you? to take the child, or to leave the mother to groan herself out?'

'I want you to tell me whether he'll curse me when he grows older.'

'That depends upon what you do. However, he will probably do it in either case.'

'You don't believe that, because you like him,' said Amanda, with acuteness.

'Precisely; and he'll curse me too. He'll curse every one. He won't be happy.'

'I don't know how you think I bring him up,' the little dressmaker remarked, with dignity.

'You don't bring him up; he brings you up.'

'That's what you have always said; but you don't know. If you mean that he does as he likes, then he ought to be happy. It ain't kind of you to say he won't be,' Miss Pynsent added, reproachfully.

'I would say anything you like, if what I say would help the matter. He's a thin-skinned, morbid, mooning little beggar, with a good deal of imagination and not much perseverance, who will expect a good deal more of life than he will find in it. That's why he won't be happy.'

Miss Pynsent listened to this description of her *protégé* with an appearance of criticising it mentally; but in reality she didn't know what 'morbid' meant, and didn't like to ask. 'He's the cleverest person I know, except yourself,' she said in a moment; for Mr. Vetch's words had been in the key of what she thought most remarkable in him. What that was she would have been unable to say.

'Thank you very much for putting me first,' the fiddler rejoined, after a series of puffs. 'The youngster is interesting, one sees that he has a mind, and in that respect he is —I won't say unique, but peculiar. I shall watch him with curiosity, to see what he grows into. But I shall always be glad that I am a selfish brute of a bachelor, that I never invested in that class of goods.'

'Well, you *are* comforting. You would spoil him more than I do,' said Amanda.

'Possibly, but it would be in a different way. I wouldn't tell him every three minutes that his father was a duke.'

'A duke I never mentioned!' the little dressmaker cried, with eagerness. 'I never specified any rank, nor said a word about any one in particular. I never so much as insinuated the name of his lordship. But I may have said that if the truth was to be found out, he might be proved to be connected—in the way of cousinship, or something of the kind—with the highest in the land. I should have thought myself wanting if I hadn't given him a glimpse of that. But there is one thing I have always added—that the truth never *is* found out.'

'You are still more comforting than I !' Mr. Vetch exclaimed. He continued to watch her, with his charitable, round-faced smile, and then he said, 'You won't do what I say ; so what is the use of my telling you ?'

'I assure you I will, if you say you believe it's the only right.'

'Do I often say anything so asinine ? Right—right ? what have you to do with that ? If you want the only right, you are very particular.'

'Please, then, what am I to go by ?' the dressmaker asked, bewildered.

'You are to go by this, by what will take the youngster down.'

'Take him down, my poor little pet ?'

'Your poor little pet thinks himself the flower of creation. I don't say there is any harm in that : a fine, blooming, odoriferous conceit is a natural appendage of youth and cleverness. I don't say there is any great harm in it, but if you want a guide as to how you are to treat the boy, that's as good a guide as any other.'

'You want me to arrange the interview, then ?'

'I don't want you to do anything but give me another sip of brandy. I just say this : that I think it's a great gain, early in life, to know the worst ; then we don't live in a fool's paradise. I did that till I was nearly forty ; then I woke up and found I was in Lomax Place.' Whenever Mr. Vetch said anything that could be construed as a reference to a former position which had had elements of distinction, Miss Pynsent observed a respectful, a tasteful, silence, and that is why she did not challenge him now, though she wanted very much to say that Hyacinth was no more 'presumptious' (that was the term she should have used) than he had reason to be, with his genteel figure and his wonderful intelligence ; and that as for thinking himself a 'flower' of any kind, he knew but too well that he lived in a small black-faced house, miles away from the West End, rented by a poor little woman who took lodgers, and who, as they were of such a class that they were not always to be depended upon to settle her weekly account, had a strain to make two ends meet, in spite of the sign between her windows—

MISS AMANDA PYNSENT.

Modes et Robes.

DRESSMAKING IN ALL ITS BRANCHES. COURT-DRESSES, MANTLES AND FASHIONABLE BONNETS.

Singularly enough, her companion, before she had permitted herself to interpose, took up her own thought (in one of its parts), and remarked that perhaps she would say of the child that he was, so far as his actual circumstances were concerned, low enough down in the world, without one's wanting him to be any lower. 'But by the time he's twenty, he'll persuade himself that Lomax Place was a bad dream, that your lodgers and your dressmaking were as imaginary as they are vulgar, and that when an old friend came to see you late at night it was not your amiable practice to make him a glass of brandy and water. He'll teach himself to forget all this : he'll have a way.'

'Do you mean he'll forget *me*, he'll deny me ?' cried Miss Pynsent, stopping the movement of her needle, short off, for the first time.

'As the person designated in that attractive blazonry on the outside of your house, decidedly he will; and me, equally, as a bald-headed, pot-bellied fiddler, who regarded you as the most graceful and refined of his acquaintance. I don't mean he'll disown you and pretend he never knew you : I don't think he will ever be such an odious little cad as that ; he probably won't be a sneak, and he strikes me as having some love, and possibly even some gratitude, in him. But he will, in his imagination (and that will always persuade him), subject you to some extraordinary metamorphosis ; he will dress you up.'

'He'll dress me up !' Amanda ejaculated, quite ceasing to follow the train of Mr. Vetch's demonstration. 'Do you mean that he'll have the property—that his relations will take him up ?'

'My dear, delightful, idiotic Pinnie, I am speaking in a figurative manner. I don't pretend to say what his precise position will be when we are relegated ; but I affirm that

relegation will be our fate.   Therefore don't stuff him with
any more illusions than are necessary to keep him alive ; he
will be sure to pick up enough on the way.   On the contrary, give him a good stiff dose of the truth at the start.'

'Dear me, dear me, of course you see much further into
it than I could ever do,' Pinnie murmured, as she threaded
a needle.

Mr. Vetch paused a minute, but apparently not out of
deference to this amiable interruption.   He went on suddenly,
with a ring of feeling in his voice.   'Let him know, because
it will be useful to him later, the state of the account
between society and himself; he can then conduct himself
accordingly.   If he is the illegitimate child of a French
good-for-naught who murdered one of her numerous lovers,
don't shuffle out of sight so important a fact.   I regard that
as a most valuable origin.'

'Lord, Mr. Vetch, how you talk !' cried Miss Pynsent,
staring.   'I don't know what one would think, to hear
you.'

'Surely, my dear lady, and for this reason : that those
are the people with whom society has to count.   It hasn't
with you and me.'   Miss Pynsent gave a sigh which might
have meant either that she was well aware of that, or that
Mr. Vetch had a terrible way of enlarging a subject, especially
when it was already too big for her ; and her philosophic
visitor went on : 'Poor little devil, let him see her, let him
see her.'

'And if later, when he's twenty, he says to me that if I
hadn't meddled in it he need never have known, he need
never have had that shame, pray what am I to say to him
then ?   That's what I can't get out of my head.'

'You can say to him that a young man who is sorry for
having gone to his mother when, in her last hours, she lay
groaning for him on a pallet in a penitentiary, deserves more
than the sharpest pang he can possibly feel.'   And the little
fiddler, getting up, went over to the fireplace and shook out
the ashes of his pipe.

'Well, I am sure it's natural he should feel badly,' said
Miss Pynsent, folding up her work with the same desperate
quickness that had animated her throughout the evening.

'I haven't the least objection to his feeling badly ; that's not the worst thing in the world! If a few more people felt badly, in this sodden, stolid, stupid race of ours, the world would wake up to an idea or two, and we should see the beginning of the dance. It's the dull acceptance, the absence of reflection, the impenetrable density.' Here Mr. Vetch stopped short; his hostess stood before him with eyes of entreaty, with clasped hands.

'Now, Anastasius Vetch, don't go off into them dreadful wild theories !' she cried, always ungrammatical when she was strongly moved. 'You always fly away over the house-tops. I thought you liked him better—the dear little unfortunate.'

Anastasius Vetch had pocketed his pipe ; he put on his hat with the freedom of old acquaintance and of Lomax Place, and took up his small coffin-like fiddle-case. 'My good Pinnie, I don't think you understand a word I say. It's no use talking—do as you like !'

'Well, I must say I don't think it was worth your coming in at midnight only to tell me that. I don't like anything —I hate the whole dreadful business ! '

He bent over, in his short plumpness, to kiss her hand, as he had seen people do on the stage. 'My dear friend, we have different ideas, and I never shall succeed in driving mine into your head. It's because I *am* fond of him, poor little devil; but you will never understand that. I want him to know everything, and especially the worst — the worst, as I have said. If I were in his position, I shouldn't thank you for trying to make a fool of me ! '

'A fool of you ? as if I thought of anything but his 'appi-ness !' Amanda Pynsent exclaimed. She stood looking at him, but following her own reflections; she had given up the attempt to enter into his whims. She remembered, what she had noticed before, in other occurrences, that his reasons were always more extraordinary than his behaviour itself; if you only considered his life you wouldn't have thought him so fanciful. 'Very likely I think too much of that,' she added. 'She wants him and cries for him ; that's what keeps coming back to me.' She took up her lamp to light Mr. Vetch to the door (for the dim luminary in the passage had long since been extinguished), and before he left the house he turned, suddenly, stopping short, and said, his composed face taking a strange expression from the quizzical glimmer of his little round eyes—

'What does it matter after all, and why do you worry? What difference can it make what happens—on either side —to such low people?'

III

MRS. BOWERBANK had let her know she would meet her,
almost at the threshold of the dreadful place; and this
thought had sustained Miss Pynsent in her long and devious
journey, performed partly on foot, partly in a succession of
omnibuses. She had had ideas about a cab, but she decided to reserve the cab for the return, as then, very likely,
she should be so shaken with emotion, so overpoweringly
affected, that it would be a comfort to escape from observation. She had no confidence that if once she passed the
door of the prison she should ever be restored to liberty
and her customers; it seemed to her an adventure as
dangerous as it was dismal, and she was immensely touched
by the clear-faced eagerness of the child at her side, who
strained forward as brightly as he had done on another
occasion, still celebrated in Miss Pynsent's industrious
annals, a certain sultry Saturday in August, when she had
taken him to the Tower. It had been a terrible question
with her, when once she made up her mind, what she
should tell him about the nature of their errand. She determined to tell him as little as possible, to say only that she
was going to see a poor woman who was in prison on
account of a crime she had committed years before, and
who had sent for her, and caused her to be told at the same
time that if there was any child she could see—as children
(if they were good) were bright and cheering—it would
make her very happy that such a little visitor should come
as well. It was very difficult, with Hyacinth, to make
reservations or mysteries; he wanted to know everything
about everything, and he projected the light of a hundred
questions upon Miss Pynsent's incarcerated friend. She
had to admit that she had been her friend (for where else

was the obligation to go to see her?); but she spoke of the
acquaintance as if it were of the slightest (it had survived
in the memory of the prisoner only because every one else
—the world was so very hard!—had turned away from her),
and she congratulated herself on a happy inspiration when
she represented the crime for which such a penalty had
been exacted as the theft of a gold watch, in a moment of
irresistible temptation.   The woman had had a wicked
husband, who maltreated and deserted her, and she was
very poor, almost starving, dreadfully pressed.   Hyacinth
listened to her history with absorbed attention, and then he
said :

'And hadn't she any children—hadn't she a little boy?'

This inquiry seemed to Miss Pynsent a portent of future
embarrassments, but she met it as bravely as she could, and
replied that she believed the wretched victim of the law
had had (once upon a time) a very small baby, but she was
afraid she had completely lost sight of it.   He must know
they didn't allow babies in prisons.   To this Hyacinth
rejoined that of course they would allow him, because he
was—really—big.   Miss Pynsent fortified herself with the
memory of her other pilgrimage, to Newgate, upwards of ten
years before ; she had escaped from that ordeal, and had
even had the comfort of knowing that in its fruits the interview had been beneficent.   The responsibility, however,
was much greater now, and, after all, it was not on her own
account she was in a nervous tremor, but on that of the
urchin over whom the shadow of the house of shame might
cast itself.

They made the last part of their approach on foot, having got themselves deposited as near as possible to the
river and keeping beside it (according to advice elicited by
Miss Pynsent, on the way, in a dozen confidential interviews with policemen, conductors of omnibuses, and small
shopkeepers), till they came to a big, dark building with
towers, which they would know as soon as they looked at
it.   They knew it, in fact, soon enough, when they saw it
lift its dusky mass from the bank of the Thames, lying
there and sprawling over the whole neighbourhood, with
brown, bare, windowless walls, ugly, truncated pinnacles,

and a character unspeakably sad and stern. It looked very
sinister and wicked, to Miss Pynsent's eyes, and she wondered why a prison should have such an evil face if it was
erected in the interest of justice and order—an expression
of the righteous forces of society. This particular penitentiary struck her as about as bad and wrong as those who
were in it; it threw a blight over the whole place and made
the river look foul and poisonous, and the opposite bank,
with its protrusion of long-necked chimneys, unsightly gaso-
meters and deposits of rubbish, wear the aspect of a region
at whose expense the jail had been populated. She looked
up at the dull, closed gates, tightening her grasp of Hyacinth's small hand ; and if it was hard to believe anything
so blind and deaf and closely fastened would relax itself to
let her in, there was a dreadful premonitory sinking of the
heart attached to the idea of its taking the same trouble to
let her out. As she hung back, murmuring vague ejaculations, at the very goal of her journey, an incident occurred
which fanned all her scruples and reluctances into life again.
The child suddenly jerked his hand out of her own, and
placing it behind him, in the clutch of the other, said to
her respectfully but resolutely, while he planted himself at
a considerable distance—

' I don't like this place.'

' Neither do I like it, my darling,' cried the dressmaker,
pitifully.   ' Oh, if you knew how little ! '

' Then we will go away.   I won't go in.'

She would have embraced this proposition with alacrity
if it had not become very vivid to her while she stood there,
in the midst of her shrinking, that behind those sullen walls
the mother who bore him was even then counting the
minutes.   She was alive, in that huge, dark tomb, and it
seemed to Miss Pynsent that they had already entered into
relation with her.   They were near her, and she knew it ;
in a few minutes she would taste the cup of the only mercy
(except the reprieve from hanging!) she had known since
her fall.   A few, a very few minutes would do it, and it
seemed to Miss Pynsent that if she should fail of her charity
now the watches of the night, in Lomax Place, would be
haunted with remorse—perhaps even with something worse.

There was something inside that waited and listened, something that would burst, with an awful sound, a shriek, or a curse, if she were to lead the boy away. She looked into his pale face for a moment, perfectly conscious that it would be vain for her to take the tone of command; besides, that would have seemed to her shocking. She had another inspiration, and she said to him in a manner in which she had had occasion to speak before—

'The reason why we have come is only to be kind. If we are kind we shan't mind its being disagreeable.'

'Why should we be kind, if she's a bad woman?' Hyacinth inquired. 'She must be very low; I don't want to know her.'

'Hush, hush,' groaned poor Amanda, edging toward him with clasped hands. 'She is not bad now; it has all been washed away—it has been expiated.'

'What's expiated?' asked the child, while she almost kneeled down in the dust, catching him to her bosom.

'It's when you have suffered terribly—suffered so much that it has made you good again.'

'Has *she* suffered very much?'

'For years and years. And now she is dying. It proves she is very good now, that she should want to see us.'

'Do you mean because *we* are good?' Hyacinth went on, probing the matter in a way that made his companion quiver, and gazing away from her, very seriously, across the river, at the dreary waste of Battersea.

'We shall be good if we are pitiful, if we make an effort,' said the dressmaker, seeming to look up at him rather than down.

'But if she is dying? I don't want to see any one die.'

Miss Pynsent was bewildered, but she rejoined, desperately, 'If we go to her, perhaps she won't. Maybe we shall save her.'

He transferred his remarkable little eyes—eyes which always appeared to her to belong to a person older than herself, to her face; and then he inquired, 'Why should I save her, if I don't like her?'

'If she likes you, that will be enough.'

At this Miss Pynsent began to see that he was moved.
'Will she like me very much?'

'More, much more than any one.'

'More than you, now?'

'Oh,' said Amanda quickly, 'I mean more than she
likes any one.'

Hyacinth had slipped his hands into the pockets of his
scanty knickerbockers, and, with his legs slightly apart, he
looked from his companion back to the immense dreary
jail. A great deal, to Miss Pynsent's sense, depended on
that moment. 'Oh, well,' he said, at last, 'I'll just step
in.'

'Deary, deary!' the dressmaker murmured to herself,
as they crossed the bare semicircle which separated the
gateway from the unfrequented street. She exerted herself to pull the bell, which seemed to her terribly big and
stiff, and while she waited, again, for the consequences of
this effort, the boy broke out, abruptly:

'How can she like me so much if she doesn't know
me?'

Miss Pynsent wished the gate would open before an
answer to this question should become imperative, but the
people within were a long time arriving, and their delay
gave Hyacinth an opportunity to repeat it. So the dressmaker rejoined, seizing the first pretext that came into her
head, 'It's because the little baby she had, of old, was
also named Hyacinth.'

'That's a queer reason,' the boy murmured, staring
across again at the Battersea shore.

A moment afterwards they found themselves in a vast
interior dimness, with a grinding of keys and bolts going
on behind them. Hereupon Miss Pynsent gave herself up
to an overruling providence, and she remembered, later,
no circumstance of what happened to her until the great
person of Mrs. Bowerbank loomed before her in the
narrowness of a strange, dark corridor. She only had a
confused impression of being surrounded with high black
walls, whose inner face was more dreadful than the other,
the one that overlooked the river; of passing through gray,

stony courts, in some of which dreadful figures, scarcely
female, in hideous brown, misfitting uniforms and perfect
frights of hoods, were marching round in a circle; of
squeezing up steep, unlighted staircases at the heels of a
woman who had taken possession of her at the first stage,
and who made incomprehensible remarks to other women,
of lumpish aspect, as she saw them erect themselves,
suddenly and spectrally, with dowdy untied bonnets, in
uncanny corners and recesses of the draughty labyrinth.
If the place had seemed cruel to the poor little dressmaker
outside, it may be believed that it did not strike her as an
abode of mercy while she pursued her tortuous way into
the circular shafts of cells, where she had an opportunity of
looking at captives through grated peepholes and of edging
past others who had temporarily been turned into the
corridors—silent women, with fixed eyes, who flattened
themselves against the stone walls at the brush of the
visitor's dress and whom Miss Pynsent was afraid to glance
at. She never had felt so immured, so made sure of;
there were walls within walls and galleries on top of
galleries; even the daylight lost its colour, and you couldn't
imagine what o'clock it was. Mrs. Bowerbank appeared to
have failed her, and that made her feel worse; a panic
seized her, as she went, in regard to the child. On him,
too, the horror of the place would have fallen, and she had
a sickening prevision that he would have convulsions after
they got home. It was a most improper place to have
brought him, no matter who had sent for him and no
matter who was dying. The stillness would terrify him,
she was sure—the penitential dumbness of the clustered or
isolated women. She clasped his hand more tightly, and
she felt him keep close to her, without speaking a word.
At last, in an open doorway, darkened by her ample person,
Mrs. Bowerbank revealed herself, and Miss Pynsent thought
it (afterwards) a sign of her place and power that she should
not condescend to apologise for not having appeared till
that moment, or to explain why she had not met the bewildered pilgrims near the principal entrance, according to
her promise. Miss Pynsent could not embrace the state
of mind of people who didn't apologise, though she vaguely

envied and admired it, she herself spending much of her
time in making excuses for obnoxious acts she had not
committed.   Mrs. Bowerbank, however, was not arrogant,
she was only massive and muscular; and after she had
taken her timorous friends in tow the dressmaker was able
to comfort herself with the reflection that even so master-
ful a woman couldn't inflict anything gratuitously disagreeable on a person who had made her visit in Lomax Place
pass off so pleasantly.

It was on the outskirts of the infirmary that she had
been hovering, and it was into certain dismal chambers
dedicated to sick criminals, that she presently ushered her
companions.   These chambers were naked and grated,
like all the rest of the place, and caused Miss Pynsent to
say to herself that it must be a blessing to be ill in such a
hole, because you couldn't possibly pick up again, and
then your case was simple.   Such simplification, however,
had for the moment been offered to very few of Florentine's
fellow-sufferers, for only three of the small, stiff beds were
occupied—occupied by white-faced women in tight, sordid
caps, on whom, in the stale, ugly room, the sallow light itself seemed to rest without pity.   Mrs. Bowerbank discreetly paid no attention whatever to Hyacinth; she only
said to Miss Pynsent, with her hoarse distinctness, 'You'll
find her very low; she wouldn't have waited another day.'
And she guided them, through a still further door, to the
smallest room of all, where there were but three beds,
placed in a row.   Miss Pynsent's frightened eyes rather
faltered than inquired, but she became aware that a woman
was lying on the middle bed, and that her face was turned
toward the door.   Mrs. Bowerbank led the way straight up
to her, and, giving a business-like pat to her pillow, looked
invitation and encouragement to the visitors, who clung
together not far within the threshold.   Their conductress
reminded them that very few minutes were allowed them,
and that they had better not dawdle them away; whereupon, as the boy still hung back, the little dressmaker
advanced alone, looking at the sick woman with what
courage she could muster.   It seemed to her that she was
approaching a perfect stranger, so completely had nine

years of prison transformed Florentine. She felt, immediately, that it was a mercy she hadn't told Hyacinth she
was pretty (as she used to be), for there was no beauty left
in the hollow, bloodless mask that presented itself without
a movement. She *had* told him that the poor woman was
good, but she didn't look so, nor, evidently, was he struck
with it as he stared back at her across the interval he
declined to traverse, kept (at the same time) from retreating by her strange, fixed eyes, the only portion of all
her wasted person in which there was still any appearance
of life. She looked unnatural to Amanda Pynsent, and
terribly old ; a speechless, motionless creature, dazed and
stupid, whereas Florentine Vivier, in the obliterated past,
had been her idea of personal, as distinguished from social,
brilliancy. Above all she seemed disfigured and ugly,
cruelly misrepresented by her coarse cap and short, rough
hair. Amanda, as she stood beside her, thought with a
sort of scared elation that Hyacinth would never guess that
a person in whom there was so little trace of smartness—
or of cleverness of any kind—was his mother. At the
very most it might occur to him, as Mrs. Bowerbank had
suggested, that she was his grandmother. Mrs. Bowerbank
seated herself on the further bed, with folded hands, like a
monumental timekeeper, and remarked, in the manner of
one speaking from a sense of duty, that the poor thing
wouldn't get much good of the child unless he showed
more confidence. This observation was evidently lost
upon the boy ; he was too intensely absorbed in watching
the prisoner. A chair had been placed at the head of her
bed, and Miss Pynsent sat down without her appearing to
notice it. In a moment, however, she lifted her hand a
little, pushing it out from under the coverlet, and the
dressmaker laid her own hand softly upon it. This gesture
elicited no response, but after a little, still gazing at the
boy, Florentine murmured, in words no one present was
in a position to understand—

' *Dieu de Dieu, qu'il est beau !* '

' She won't speak nothing but French since she has
been so bad—you can't get a natural word out of her,'
Mrs. Bowerbank said.

'It used to be so pretty when she spoke English—and
so very amusing,' Miss Pynsent ventured to announce,
with a feeble attempt to brighten up the scene. 'I suppose she has forgotten it all.'

'She may well have forgotten it—she never gave her
tongue much exercise. There was little enough trouble to
keep *her* from chattering,' Mrs. Bowerbank rejoined, giving
a twitch to the prisoner's counterpane. Miss Pynsent settled
it a little on the other side and considered, in the same
train, that this separation of language was indeed a mercy;
for how could it ever come into her small companion's head
that he was the offspring of a person who couldn't so
much as say good morning to him? She felt, at the same
time, that the scene might have been somewhat less painful
if they had been able to communicate with the object of
their compassion. As it was, they had too much the air of
having been brought together simply to look at each other,
and there was a grewsome awkwardness in that, considering
the delicacy of Florentine's position. Not, indeed, that
she looked much at her old comrade; it was as if she were
conscious of Miss Pynsent's being there, and would have
been glad to thank her for it—glad even to examine her for
her own sake, and see what change, for her, too, the horrible
years had brought, but felt, more than this, that she had
but the thinnest pulse of energy left and that not a moment
that could still be of use to her was too much to take in
her child. She took him in with all the glazed entreaty of
her eyes, quite giving up his poor little protectress, who
evidently would have to take her gratitude for granted.
Hyacinth, on his side, after some moments of embarrassing silence—there was nothing audible but Mrs. Bowerbank's breathing—had satisfied himself, and he turned
about to look for a place of patience while Miss Pynsent
should finish her business, which as yet made so little show.
He appeared to wish not to leave the room altogether,
as that would be a confession of a vanquished spirit, but to
take some attitude that should express his complete disapproval of the unpleasant situation. He was not in sympathy, and he could not have made it more clear than by
the way he presently went and placed himself on a low

stool, in a corner, near the door by which they had entered.

'*Est-il possible, mon Dieu, qu'il soit gentil comme ça ?*' his mother moaned, just above her breath.

'We are very glad you should have cared—that they look after you so well,' said Miss Pynsent, confusedly, at random ; feeling, first, that Hyacinth's coldness was perhaps excessive and his scepticism too .marked, and then that allusions to the way the poor woman was looked after were not exactly happy.   They didn't matter, however, for she evidently heard nothing, giving no sign of interest even when Mrs. Bowerbank, in a tone between a desire to make the interview more lively and an idea of showing that she knew how to treat the young, referred herself to the little boy.

'Is there nothing the little gentleman would like to say, now, to the unfortunate ?   Hasn't he any pleasant remark to make to her about his coming so far to see her when she's so sunk ?   It isn't often that children are shown over the place (as the little man has been), and there's many that would think they were lucky if they could see what he has seen.'

'*Mon pauvre joujou, mon pauvre chéri,*' the prisoner went on, in her tender, tragic whisper.

'He only wants to be very good ; he always sits that way at home,' said Miss Pynsent, alarmed at Mrs. Bowerbank's address and hoping there wouldn't be a scene.

'He might have stayed at home then—with this wretched person moaning after him,' Mrs. Bowerbank remarked, with some sternness.   She plainly felt that the occasion threatened to be wanting in brilliancy, and wished to intimate that though she was to be trusted for discipline, she thought they were all getting off too easily.

'I came because Pinnie brought me,' Hyacinth declared, from his low perch.   'I thought at first it would be pleasant. But it ain't pleasant—I don't like prisons.'   And he placed his little feet on the cross-piece of the stool, as if to touch the institution at as few points as possible.

The woman in bed continued her strange, almost whining plaint.   '*Il ne veut pas s'approcher, il a honte de moi.*'

'There's a many that begin like that!' laughed Mrs. Bowerbank, who was irritated by the boy's contempt for one of her Majesty's finest establishments.

Hyacinth's little white face exhibited no confusion; he only turned it to the prisoner again, and Miss Pynsent felt that some extraordinary dumb exchange of meanings was taking place between them. 'She used to be so elegant; she *was* a fine woman,' she observed, gently and helplessly.

'*Il a honte de moi—il a honte, Dieu le pardonne!*' Florentine Vivier went on, never moving her eyes.

'She's asking for something, in her language. I used to know a few words,' said Miss Pynsent, stroking down the bed, very nervously.

'Who is that woman? what does she want?' Hyacinth asked, his small, clear voice ringing over the dreary room.

'She wants you to come near her, she wants to kiss you, sir,' said Mrs. Bowerbank, as if it were more than he deserved.

'I won't kiss her; Pinnie says she stole a watch!' the child answered with resolution.

'Oh, you dreadful—how could you ever?' cried Pinnie, blushing all over and starting out of her chair.

It was partly Amanda's agitation, perhaps, which, by the jolt it administered, gave an impulse to the sick woman, and partly the penetrating and expressive tone in which Hyacinth announced his repugnance : at any rate, Florentine, in the most unexpected and violent manner, jerked herself up from her pillow, and, with dilated eyes and waving hands, shrieked out, '*Ah, quelle infamie!* I never stole a watch, I never stole anything—anything! *Ah, par exemple!*' Then she fell back, sobbing with the passion that had given her a moment's strength.

'I'm sure you needn't put more on her than she has by rights,' said Mrs. Bowerbank, with dignity, to the dressmaker, laying a large red hand upon the patient, to keep her in her place.

'Mercy, more? I thought it so much less!' cried Miss Pynsent, convulsed with confusion and jerking herself, in a wild tremor, from the mother to the child, as if she wished to fling herself upon one for contrition and upon the other for revenge.

'*Il a honte de moi—il a honte de moi!*' Florentine repeated, in the misery of her sobs. '*Dieu de bonté, quelle horreur!*'

Miss Pynsent dropped on her knees beside the bed and, trying to possess herself of Florentine's hand again, protested with a passion almost equal to that of the prisoner (she felt that her nerves had been screwed up to the snapping-point, and now they were all in shreds) that she hadn't meant what she had told the child, that he hadn't understood, that Florentine herself hadn't understood, that she had only said she had been accused and meant that no one had ever believed it. The Frenchwoman paid no attention to her whatever, and Amanda buried her face and her embarrassment in the side of the hard little prison-bed, while, above the sound of their common lamentation, she heard the judicial tones of Mrs. Bowerbank.

'The child is delicate, you might well say! I'm disappointed in the effect—I was in hopes you'd hearten her up. The doctor'll be down on *me*, of course; so we'll just pass out again.'

'I'm very sorry I made you cry. And you must excuse Pinnie—I asked her so many questions.'

These words came from close beside the prostrate dressmaker, who, lifting herself quickly, found the little boy had advanced to her elbow and was taking a nearer view of the mysterious captive. They produced upon the latter an effect even more powerful than his unfortunate speech of a moment before; for she found strength to raise herself, partly, in her bed again, and to hold out her arms to him, with the same thrilling sobs. She was talking still, but she had become quite inarticulate, and Miss Pynsent had but a glimpse of her white, ravaged face, with the hollows of its eyes and the rude crop of her hair. Amanda caught the child with an eagerness almost as great as Florentine's, and drawing him to the head of the bed, pushed him into his mother's arms. 'Kiss her—kiss her, and we'll go home!' she whispered desperately, while they closed about him, and the poor dishonoured head pressed itself against his

young cheek. It was a terrible, irresistible embrace, to which
Hyacinth submitted with instant patience. Mrs. Bowerbank
had tried at first to keep her *protégée* from rising, evidently
wishing to abbreviate the scene; then, as the child was
enfolded, she accepted the situation and gave judicious
support from behind, with an eye to clearing the room as
soon as this effort should have spent itself. She propped
up her patient with a vigorous arm; Miss Pynsent rose
from her knees and turned away, and there was a minute's
stillness, during which the boy accommodated himself as he
might to his strange ordeal. What thoughts were begotten
at that moment in his wondering little mind Miss Pynsent
was destined to learn at another time. Before she had
faced round to the bed again she was swept out of the room
by Mrs. Bowerbank, who had lowered the prisoner, exhausted, with closed eyes, to her pillow, and given Hyacinth
a business-like little push, which sent him on in advance.
Miss Pynsent went home in a cab—she was so shaken;
though she reflected, very nervously, on getting into it, on
the opportunities it would give Hyacinth for the exercise of
inquisitorial rights. To her surprise, however, he completely neglected them; he sat in silence, looking out of
the window, till they re-entered Lomax Place.

'WELL, you'll have to guess my name before I'll tell you,' the girl said, with a free laugh, pushing her way into the narrow hall and leaning against the tattered wall-paper, which, representing blocks of marble with beveled edges, in streaks and speckles of black and gray, had not been renewed for years and came back to her out of the past. As Miss Pynsent closed the door, seeing her visitor was so resolute, the light filtered in from the street, through the narrow, dusty glass above it, and then the very smell and sense of the place returned to Millicent; a kind of musty dimness, with the vision of a small, steep staircase at the end, covered with a strip of oilcloth which she recognised, and made a little less dark by a window in the bend (you could see it from the hall), from which you could almost bump your head against the house behind. Nothing was changed except Miss Pynsent, and of course the girl herself. She had noticed, outside, that the sign between the windows had not even been touched up; there was still the same preposterous announcement of 'fashionable bonnets'—as if the poor little dressmaker had the slightest acquaintance with that style of head-dress, of which Miss Henning's own knowledge was now so complete. She could see Miss Pynsent was looking at her hat, which was a wonderful composition of flowers and ribbons; her eyes had travelled up and down Millicent's whole person, but they rested in fascination on this ornament. The girl had forgotten how small the dressmaker was; she barely came up to her shoulder. She had lost her hair, and wore a cap, which Millicent noticed in return, wondering if that were a speci-men of what she thought the fashion. Miss Pynsent stared up at her as if she had been six feet high; but she

was used to that sort of surprised admiration, being perfectly
conscious that she was a magnificent young woman.

'Won't you take me into your shop?' she asked. 'I
don't want to order anything; I only want to inquire
after your 'ealth; and isn't this rather an awkward place
to talk?' She made her way further in, without waiting
for permission, seeing that her startled hostess had not yet
guessed.

'The show-room is on the right hand,' said Miss
Pynsent, with her professional manner, which was intended,
evidently, to mark a difference. She spoke as if on the
other side, where the horizon was bounded by the partition
of the next house, there were labyrinths of apartments.
Passing in after her guest she found the young lady already
spread out upon the sofa, the everlasting sofa, in the right-
hand corner as you faced the window, covered with a light,
shrunken shroud of a strange yellow stuff, the tinge of
which revealed years of washing, and surmounted by a
coloured print of Rebekah at the Well, balancing, in the
opposite quarter, with a portrait of the Empress of the
French, taken from an illustrated newspaper and framed
and glazed in the manner of 1853. Millicent looked about
her, asking herself what Miss Pynsent had to show and
acting perfectly the part of the most brilliant figure the
place had ever contained. The old implements were there
on the table: the pincushions and needle-books; the pink
measuring-tape with which, as children, she and Hyacinth
used to take each other's height; and the same collection
of fashion-plates (she could see in a minute), crumpled,
sallow and fly-blown. The little dressmaker bristled, as
she used to do, with needles and pins (they were stuck all
over the front of her dress), but there were no rustling
fabrics tossed in heaps about the room—nothing but the
skirt of a shabby dress (it might have been her own), which
she was evidently repairing and had flung upon the table
when she came to the door. Miss Henning speedily arrived
at the conclusion that her hostess's business had not increased, and felt a kind of good-humoured, luxurious scorn
of a person who knew so little what was to be got out of
London. It was Millicent's belief that she herself was

already perfectly acquainted with the resources of the metropolis.

'Now tell me, how is Hyacinth ?   I should like so much to see him,' she remarked, extending a pair of large protrusive feet and supporting herself on the sofa by her hands.

'Hyacinth ?' Miss Pynsent repeated, with majestic blankness, as if she had never heard of such a person. She felt that the girl was cruelly, scathingly, well dressed ; she couldn't imagine who she was, nor with what design she could have presented herself.

'Perhaps you call him Mr. Robinson, to-day—you always wanted him to hold himself so high.   But to his face, at any rate, I'll call him as I used to : you see if I don't !'

'Bless my soul, you must be the little 'Enning !' Miss Pynsent exclaimed, planted before her and going now into every detail.

'Well, I'm glad you have made up your mind.   I thought you'd know me directly.   I had a call to make in this part, and it came into my 'ead to look you up.   I don't like to lose sight of old friends.'

'I never knew you—you've improved so,' Miss Pynsent rejoined, with a candour justified by her age and her consciousness of respectability.

'Well, *you* haven't changed ; you were always calling me something horrid.'

'I dare say it doesn't matter to you now, does it ?' said the dressmaker, seating herself, but quite unable to take up her work, absorbed as she was in the examination of her visitor.

'Oh, I'm all right now,' Miss Henning replied, with the air of one who had nothing to fear from human judgments.

'You were a pretty child—I never said the contrary to that ; but I had no idea you'd turn out like this.   You're too tall for a woman,' Miss Pynsent added, much divided between an old prejudice and a new appreciation.

'Well, I enjoy beautiful 'ealth,' said the young lady ; 'every one thinks I'm twenty.'   She spoke with a certain artless pride in her bigness and her bloom, and as if, to show her development, she would have taken off her jacket or

let you feel her upper arm. She was very handsome, with
a shining, bold, good-natured eye, a fine, free, facial oval,
an abundance of brown hair, and a smile which showed
the whiteness of her teeth. Her head was set upon a fair,
strong neck, and her tall young figure was rich in feminine
curves. Her gloves, covering her wrists insufficiently,
showed the redness of those parts, in the interstices of the
numerous silver bracelets that encircled them, and Miss
Pynsent made the observation that her hands were not
more delicate than her feet. She- was not graceful, and
even the little dressmaker, whose preference for distinguished
forms never deserted her, indulged in the mental reflection
that she was common, for all her magnificence; but there
was something about her indescribably fresh, successful
and satisfying. She was, to her blunt, expanded finger-
tips, a daughter of London, of the crowded streets and
hustling traffic of the great city; she had drawn her health
and strength from its dingy courts and foggy thoroughfares,
and peopled its parks and squares and crescents with her
ambitions; it had entered into her blood and her bone, the
sound of her voice and the carriage of her head; she
understood it by instinct and loved it with passion; she
represented its immense vulgarities and curiosities, its
brutality and its knowingness, its good-nature and its impudence, and might have figured, in an allegorical procession, as a kind of glorified townswoman, a nymph of
the wilderness of Middlesex, a flower of the accumulated
parishes, the genius of urban civilisation, the muse of
cockneyism. The restrictions under which Miss Pynsent
regarded her would have cost the dressmaker some fewer
scruples if she had guessed the impression she made upon
Millicent, and how the whole place seemed to that prosperous young lady to smell of poverty and failure. Her
childish image of Miss Pynsent had represented her as
delicate and dainty, with round loops of hair fastened on
her temples by combs, and associations of brilliancy arising
from the constant manipulation of precious stuffs—tissues
at least which Millicent regarded with envy. But the
little woman before her was bald and white and pinched ;
she looked shrunken and sickly and insufficiently nourished ;

her small eyes were sharp and suspicious, and her hideous cap did not disguise her meagreness.   Miss Henning thanked her stars, as she had often done before, that she had not been obliged to get *her* living by drudging over needlework year after year in that undiscoverable street, in a dismal little room where nothing had been changed for ages ; the absence of change had such an exasperating effect upon her vigorous young nature.   She reflected with complacency upon her good fortune in being attached to a more exciting, a more dramatic, department of the dress-making business, and noticed that though it was already November there was no fire in the neatly-kept grate beneath the chimney-piece, on which a design, partly architectural, partly botanical, executed in the hair of Miss Pynsent's parents, was flanked by a pair of vases, under glass, containing muslin flowers.

If she thought Miss Pynsent's eyes suspicious it must be confessed that this lady felt very much upon her guard in the presence of so unexpected and undesired a reminder of one of the least honourable episodes in the annals of Lomax Place.   Miss Pynsent esteemed people in proportion to their success in constituting a family circle—in cases, that is, when the materials were under their hand.   This success, among the various members of the house of Henning, had been of the scantiest, and the domestic broils in the establishment adjacent to her own, whose vicissitudes she was able to follow, as she sat at her window at work, by simply inclining an ear to the thin partition behind her—these scenes, amid which the crash of crockery and the imprecations of the wounded were frequently audible, had long been the scandal of a humble but harmonious neighbourhood.   Mr. Henning was supposed to occupy a place of confidence in a brush-factory, while his wife, at home, occupied herself with the washing and mending of a considerable brood, mainly of sons.   But economy and sobriety, and indeed a virtue more important still, had never presided at their councils.   The freedom and frequency of Mrs. Henning's relations with a stove-polisher in the Euston Road were at least not a secret to a person who lived next door and looked up from her work so often that it was a

wonder it was always finished so quickly.   The little Hennings, unwashed and unchidden, spent most of their time
either in pushing each other into the gutter or in running
to the public-house at the corner for a pennyworth of gin,
and the borrowing propensities of their elders were a theme
for exclamation.   There was no object of personal or
domestic use which Mrs. Henning had not at one time or
another endeavoured to elicit from the dressmaker ; beginning with a mattress, on an occasion when she was about to
take to her bed for a considerable period, and ending with
a flannel petticoat and a pewter teapot.   Lomax Place had,
eventually, from its over-peeping windows and doorways,
been present at the seizure, by a long-suffering landlord, of
the chattels of this interesting family and at the ejectment
of the whole insolvent group, who departed in a straggling,
jeering, unabashed, cynical manner, carrying with them but
little of the sympathy of the street.   Millicent, whose
childish intimacy with Hyacinth Robinson Miss Pynsent
had always viewed with vague anxiety—she thought the
girl a ' nasty little thing,' and was afraid she would teach
the innocent orphan low ways—Millicent, with her luxu-
riant tresses, her precocious beauty, her staring, mocking
manner on the doorstep, was at this time twelve years of
age.   She vanished with her vanishing companions ; Lomax
Place saw them turn the corner, and returned to its occupations with a conviction that they would make shipwreck on
the outer reefs.   But neither spar nor splinter floated back
to their former haunts, and they were engulfed altogether in
the fathomless deeps of the town.   Miss Pynsent drew a
long breath ; it was her conviction that none of them would
come to any good, and Millicent least of all.

When, therefore, this young lady reappeared, with all the
signs of accomplished survival, she could not fail to ask
herself whether, under a specious seeming, the phenomenon
did not simply represent the triumph of vice.   She was
alarmed, but she would have given her silver thimble to
know the girl's history, and between her alarm and her
curiosity she passed an uncomfortable half-hour.   She felt
that the familiar, mysterious creature was playing with her ;
revenging herself for former animadversions, for having been

snubbed and miscalled by a peering little spinster who now could make no figure beside her.   If it was not the triumph of vice it was at least the triumph of impertinence, as well as of youth, health, and a greater acquaintance with the art of dress than Miss Pynsent could boast, for all her ridiculous signboards.   She perceived, or she believed she perceived, that Millicent wanted to scare her, to make her think she had come after Hyacinth ; that she wished to inveigle, to corrupt him.   I should be sorry to impute to Miss Henning any motive more complicated than the desire to amuse herself, of a Saturday afternoon, by a ramble which her vigorous legs had no occasion to deprecate ; but it must be confessed that when it occurred to her that Miss Pynsent regarded her as a ravening wolf and her early playmate as an unspotted lamb, she laughed out, in her hostess's anxious face, irrelevantly and good humouredly, without deigning to explain.   But what, indeed, had she come for, if she had not come after Hyacinth ?   It was not for the love of the dressmaker's pretty ways.   She remembered the boy and some of their tender passages, and in the wantonness of her full-blown freedom—her attachment, also, to any tolerable pretext for wandering through the streets of London and gazing into shop-windows—she had said to herself that she would dedicate an afternoon to the pleasures of memory, would revisit the scenes of her childhood.   She considered that her childhood had ended with the departure of her family from Lomax Place.   If the tenants of that obscure locality never learned what their banished fellows went through, Millicent retained a deep impression of those horrible intermediate years.   The family, as a family, had gone down-hill, to the very bottom ; and in her humbler moments Millicent sometimes wondered what lucky star had checked her own descent, and indeed enabled her to mount the slope again.   In her humbler moments, I say, for as a general thing she was provided with an explanation of any good fortune that might befall her.   What was more natural than that a girl should do well when she was at once so handsome and so clever ?   Millicent thought with compassion of the young persons whom a niggardly fate had endowed with only one of these advantages.   She was good-natured, but she had no idea of gratifying Miss Pynsent's curiosity; it seemed to her quite a sufficient kindness to stimulate it.

She told the dressmaker that she had a high position at a great haberdasher's in the neighbourhood of Buckingham Palace; she was in the department for jackets and mantles; she put on all these articles to show them off to the customers, and on her person they appeared to such advantage that nothing she took up ever failed to go off. Miss Pynsent could imagine, from this, how highly her services were prized. She had had a splendid offer from another establishment, in Oxford Street, and she was just thinking whether she should accept it. 'We have to be beautifully dressed, but I don't care, because I like to look nice,' she remarked to her hostess, who at the end of half an hour, very grave, behind the clumsy glasses which she had been obliged to wear of late years, seemed still not to know what to make of her. On the subject of her family, of her history during the interval that was to be accounted for, the girl was large and vague, and Miss Pynsent saw that the domestic circle had not even a shadow of sanctity for her. She stood on her own feet, and she stood very firm. Her staying so long, her remaining over the half hour, proved to the dressmaker that she had come for Hyacinth; for poor Amanda gave her as little information as was decent, told her nothing that would encourage or attract. She simply mentioned that Mr. Robinson (she was careful to speak of him in that manner) had given his attention to bookbinding, and had served an apprenticeship at an establishment where they turned out the best work of that kind that was to be found in London.

'A bookbindery? Laws!' said Miss Henning. 'Do you mean they get them up for the shops? Well, I always thought he would have something to do with books.' Then she added, 'But I didn't think he would ever follow a trade.'

'A trade?' cried Miss Pynsent. 'You should hear Mr. Robinson speak of it. He considers it one of the fine arts.'

Millicent smiled, as if she knew how people often con-

sidered things, and remarked that very likely it was tidy,
comfortable work, but she couldn't believe there was much
to be seen in it. 'Perhaps you will say there is more than
there is here,' she went on, finding at last an effect of irritation, of reprehension, an implication of aggressive respectability, in the image of the patient dressmaker, sitting for
so many years in her close, brown little den, with the foggy
familiarities of Lomax Place on the other side of the pane.
Millicent liked to think that she herself was strong, and she
was not strong enough for that.

This allusion to her shrunken industry seemed to Miss
Pynsent very cruel ; but she reflected that it was natural
one should be insulted if one talked to a vulgar girl. She
judged this young lady in the manner of a person who was
not vulgar herself, and if there was a difference between
them she was right in feeling it to be in her favour. Miss
Pynsent's 'cut,' as I have intimated, was not truly fashionable, and in the application of gimp and the distribution of
ornament she was not to be trusted ; but, morally, she had
the best taste in the world. 'I haven't so much work as
I used to have, if that's what you mean. My eyes are not
so good, and my health has failed with advancing years.'

I know not to what extent Millicent was touched by the
dignity of this admission, but she replied, without embarrassment, that what Miss Pynsent wanted was a smart young
assistant, some nice girl with a pretty taste, who would
brighten up the business and give her new ideas. 'I can
see you have got the same old ones, always : I can tell
that by the way you have stuck the braid on that dress ;'
and she directed a poke of her neat little umbrella to the
drapery in the dressmaker's lap. She continued to patronise
and exasperate her, and to offer her consolation and encouragement with the heaviest hand that had ever been
applied to Miss Pynsent's sensitive surface. Poor Amanda
ended by gazing at her as if she were a public performer of
some kind, a ballad-singer or a conjurer, and went so far as
to ask herself whether the hussy could be (in her own mind)
the 'nice girl' who was to regild the tarnished sign. Miss
Pynsent had had assistants, in the past—she had even,
once, for a few months, had a 'forewoman ;' and some of

these damsels had been precious specimens, whose mis-
demeanours lived vividly in her memory. Never, all the
same, in her worst hour of delusion, had she trusted her
interests to such an extravagant baggage as this. She was
quickly reassured as to Millicent's own views, perceiving
more and more that she was a tremendous highflyer, who
required a much larger field of action than the musty bower
she now honoured, heaven only knew why, with her presence.
Miss Pynsent held her tongue, as she always did, when the
sorrow of her life had been touched, the thought of the slow,
inexorable decline on which she had entered that day,
nearly ten years before, when her hesitations and scruples
resolved themselves into a hideous mistake. The deep
conviction of error, on that unspeakably important occasion,
had ached and throbbed within her ever since like an
incurable disease. She had sown in her boy's mind the
seeds of shame and rancour; she had made him conscious
of his stigma, of his exquisitely vulnerable spot, and condemned him to know that for him the sun would never
shine as it shone for most others. By the time he was
sixteen years old she had learned—or believed she had
learned—the judgment he passed upon her, and at that
period she had lived through a series of horrible months, an
ordeal in which every element of her old prosperity perished.
She cried her eyes out, on coming to a sense of her
aberration, blinded and weakened herself with weeping, so
that for a moment it seemed as if she should never be
able to touch a needle again. She lost all interest in her
work, and that artistic imagination which had always been
her pride deserted her, together with the reputation of
keeping the tidiest lodgings in Lomax Place. A couple of
commercial gentlemen and a Welsh plumber, of religious
tendencies, who for several years had made her establishment their home, withdrew their patronage on the ground
that the airing of her beds was not what it used to be, and
disseminated cruelly this injurious legend. She ceased to
notice or to care how sleeves were worn, and on the
question of flounces and gores her mind was a blank. She
fell into a grievous debility, and then into a long, low,
languid fever, during which Hyacinth tended her with a

devotion which only made the wrong she had done him seem more bitter, and in which, so soon as she was able to hold up her head a little, Mr. Vetch came and sat with her through the dull hours of convalescence. She re-established to a certain extent, after a while, her connection, so far as the letting of her rooms was concerned (from the other department of her activity the tide had ebbed apparently for ever) ; but nothing was the same again, and she knew it was the beginning of the end. So it had gone on, and she watched the end approach ; she felt it was very near indeed when a child she had seen playing in the gutters came to flaunt it over her in silk and lace. She gave a low, inaudible sigh of relief when at last Millicent got up and stood before her, smoothing the glossy cylinder of her umbrella.

'Mind you give my love to Hyacinth,' the girl said, with an assurance which showed all her insensibility to tacit protests. 'I don't care if you do guess that if I have stopped so long it was in the hope he would be dropping in to his tea. You can tell him I sat an hour, on purpose, if you like ; there's no shame in my wanting to see my little friend. He may know I call him that !' Millicent continued, with her show-room laugh, as Miss Pynsent judged it to be ; conferring these permissions, successively, as if they were great indulgences. 'Do give him my love, and tell him I hope he'll come and see me. I see you won't tell him anything. I don't know what you're afraid of ; but I'll leave my card for him, all the same.' She drew forth a little bright-coloured pocket-book, and it was with amazement that Miss Pynsent saw her extract from it a morsel of engraved pasteboard—so monstrous did it seem that one of the squalid little Hennings should have lived to display this emblem of social consideration. Millicent enjoyed the effect she produced as she laid the card on the table, and gave another ringing peel of merriment at the sight of her hostess's half-hungry, half-astonished look. 'What *do* you think I want to do with him ? I could swallow him at a single bite !' she cried.

Poor Amanda gave no second glance at the document on the table, though she had perceived it contained, in the corner, her visitor's address, which Millicent had amused herself, ingeniously, with not mentioning : she only got up, laying down her work with a trembling hand, so that she should be able to see Miss Henning well out of the house. 'You needn't think I shall put myself out to keep him in the dark. I shall certainly tell him you have been here, and exactly how you strike me.'

'Of course you'll say something nasty—like you used to when I was a child. You let me 'ave it then, you know !'

'Ah, well,' said Miss Pynsent, nettled at being reminded of an acerbity which the girl's present development caused to appear ridiculously ineffectual, 'you are very different now, when I think what you've come from.'

'What I've come from ?' Millicent threw back her head, and opened her eyes very wide, while all her feathers and ribbons nodded. 'Did you want me to stick fast in this low place for the rest of my days ? You have had to stay in it yourself, so you might speak civilly of it.' She coloured, and raised her voice, and looked magnificent in her scorn. 'And pray what have you come from yourself, and what has *he* come from—the mysterious "Mr. Robinson," that used to be such a puzzle to the whole Place ? I thought perhaps I might clear it up, but you haven't told me that yet !'

Miss Pynsent turned straight away, covering her ears with her hands. 'I have nothing to tell you ! Leave my room—leave my house !' she cried, with a trembling voice.

V

It was in this way that the dressmaker failed either to see or to hear the opening of the door of the room, which obeyed a slow, apparently cautious impulse given it from the hall, and revealed the figure of a young man standing there with a short pipe in his teeth. There was something in his face which immediately told Millicent Henning that he had heard, outside, her last resounding tones. He entered as if, young as he was, he knew that when women were squabbling men were not called upon to be headlong, and evidently wondered who ·the dressmaker's brilliant adversary might be. She recognised on the instant her old playmate, and without reflection, confusion or diplomacy, in the fulness of her vulgarity and sociability, she exclaimed, in no lower pitch, 'Gracious, Hyacinth Robinson, is *that* your form?'

Miss Pynsent turned round, in a flash, but kept silent; then, very white and trembling, took up her work again and seated herself in her window.

Hyacinth Robinson stood staring; then he blushed all over. He knew who she was, but he didn't say so; he only asked, in a voice which struck the girl as quite different from the old one—the one in which he used to tell her she was beastly tiresome—'Is it of me you were speaking just now?'

'When I asked where you had come from? That was because we 'eard you in the 'all,' said Millicent, smiling. 'I suppose you have come from your work.'

'You used to live in the Place—you always wanted to kiss me,' the young man remarked, with an effort not to show all the surprise and agitation that he felt. 'Didn't she live in the Place, Pinnie?'

Pinnie, for all answer, fixed a pair of strange, pleading eyes upon him, and Millicent broke out, with her recurrent laugh, in which the dressmaker had been right in discovering the note of affectation, 'Do you want to know what you look like? You look for all the world like a little Frenchman! Don't he look like a little Frenchman, Miss Pynsent?' she went on, as if she were on the best possible terms with the mistress of the establishment.

Hyacinth exchanged a look with that afflicted woman; he saw something in her face which he knew very well by this time, and the sight of which always gave him an odd, perverse, unholy satisfaction. It seemed to say that she prostrated herself, that she did penance in the dust, that she was his to trample upon, to spit upon. He did neither of these things, but she was constantly offering herself, and her permanent humility, her perpetual abjection, was a sort of counter-irritant to the soreness lodged in his own heart for ever, which had often made him cry with rage at night, in his little room under the roof. Pinnie meant that, to-day, as a matter of course, and she could only especially mean it in the presence of Miss Henning's remark about his looking like a Frenchman. He knew he looked like a Frenchman, he had often been told so before, and a large part of the time he felt like one—like one of those he had read about in Michelet and Carlyle. He had picked up the French tongue with the most extraordinary facility, with the aid of one of his mates, a refugee from Paris, in the work-room, and of a second-hand dog's-eared dictionary, bought for a shilling in the Brompton Road, in one of his interminable, restless, melancholy, moody, yet all-observant strolls through London. He spoke it (as he believed) as if by instinct, caught the accent, the gesture, the movement of eyebrow and shoulder; so that if it should become necessary in certain contingencies that he should pass for a foreigner he had an idea that he might do so triumphantly, once he could borrow a blouse. He had never seen a blouse in his life, but he knew exactly the form and colour of such a garment, and how it was worn. What these contingencies might be which should compel him to assume the disguise of a person of a social station lower still than his own, Hyacinth would not for the world have mentioned to you; but as they were very present to the mind of our imaginative, ingenious youth we shall catch a glimpse of them in the course of a further acquaintance with him. At the present moment, when there was no question of masquerading, it made him blush again that such a note should be struck by a loud, laughing, handsome girl, who came back out of his past. There was more in Pinnie's weak eyes, now, than her usual profession; there was a dumb intimation, almost as pathetic as the other, that if he cared to let her off easily he would not detain their terrible visitor very long. He had no wish to do that; he kept the door open, on purpose; he didn't enjoy talking to girls under Pinnie's eyes, and he could see that this one had every disposition to talk. So without responding to her observation about his appearance he said, not knowing exactly what to say, 'Have you come back to live in the Place?'

'Heaven forbid I should ever do that!' cried Miss Henning, with genuine emotion. 'I have to live near the establishment in which I'm employed.'

'And what establishment is that, now?' the young man asked, gaining confidence and perceiving, in detail, how handsome she was. He hadn't roamed about London for nothing, and he knew that when a girl was as handsome as that, a jocular tone of address, a pleasing freedom, was *de rigueur;* so he added, 'Is it the Bull and Gate, or the Elephant and Castle?'

'A public house! Well, you haven't got the politeness of a Frenchman, at all events!' Her good-nature had come back to her perfectly, and her resentment of his imputation of her looking like a bar-maid—a blowzy beauty who handled pewter—was tempered by her more and more curious consideration of Hyacinth's form. He was exceedingly 'rum,' but this quality took her fancy, and since he remembered so well that she had been fond of kissing him, in their early days she would have liked to say to him that she stood prepared to repeat this graceful attention. But she reminded herself, in time, that her line should be, religiously, the ladylike, and she was content to exclaim.

simply, ' I don't care what a man looks like so long as he's
clever.   That's the form *I* like ! '

Miss Pynsent had promised herself the satisfaction of
taking no further notice of her brilliant invader ; but the
temptation was great to expose her to Hyacinth, as a mitigation of her brilliancy, by remarking sarcastically, according
to opportunity, ' Miss 'Enning wouldn't live in Lomax
Place for the world.   She thinks it too abominably low.'

' So it is ; it's a beastly hole,' said the young man.

The poor dressmaker's little dart fell to the ground, and
Millicent exclaimed, jovially, ' Right you are ! ' while she
directed to the object of her childhood's admiration a smile
that put him more and more at his ease.

' Don't you suppose I'm clever ? ' he asked, planted
before her with his little legs slightly apart, while, with
his hands behind him, he made the open door waver to
and fro.

' You ?   Oh, I don't care whether you are or not ! ' said
Millicent Henning ; and Hyacinth was at any rate quick-
witted enough to see what she meant by that.   If she
meant he was so good-looking that he might pass on this
score alone her judgment was conceivable, though many
women would strongly have dissented from it.   He was as
small as he had threatened—he had never got his growth
—and she could easily see that he was not what she, at
least, would call strong.   His bones were small, his chest
was narrow, his complexion pale, his whole figure almost
childishly slight ; and Millicent perceived afterward that he
had a very delicate hand—the hand, as she said to herself,
of a gentleman.   What she liked was his face, and something jaunty and entertaining, almost theatrical in his whole
little person.   Miss Henning was not acquainted with any
member of the dramatic profession, but she supposed,
vaguely, that that was the way an actor would look in
private life.   Hyacinth's features were perfect ; his eyes,
large and much divided, had as their usual expression a
kind of witty candour, and a small, soft, fair moustache
disposed itself upon his upper lip in a way that made him
look as if he were smiling even when his heart was heavy.
The waves of his dense, fine hair clustered round a fore-

head which was high enough to suggest remarkable things, and Miss Henning had observed that when he first appeared he wore his little soft circular hat in a way that left these frontal locks very visible.   He was dressed in an old brown velveteen jacket, and wore exactly the bright-coloured necktie which Miss Pynsent's quick fingers used of old to shape out of hoarded remnants of silk and muslin.   He was shabby and work-stained, but the observant eye would have noted an idea in his dress (his appearance was plainly not a matter of indifference to himself), and a painter (not of the heroic) would have liked to make a sketch of him.   There was something exotic about him, and yet, with his sharp young face, destitute of bloom, but not of sweetness, and a certain conscious cockneyism which pervaded him, he was as strikingly as Millicent, in her own degree, a product of the London streets and the London air.   He looked both ingenuous and slightly wasted, amused, amusing, and indefinably sad. Women had always found him touching; yet he made them—so they had repeatedly assured him—die of laughing.

'I think you had better shut the door,' said Miss Pynsent, meaning that he had better shut their departing visitor out.

'Did you come here on purpose to see us?' Hyacinth asked, not heeding this injunction, of which he divined the spirit, and wishing the girl would take her leave, so that he might go out again with her.   He should like talking with her much better away from Pinnie, who evidently was ready to stick a bodkin into her, for reasons he perfectly understood.   He had seen plenty of them before, Pinnie's reasons, even where girls were concerned who were not nearly so good-looking as this one.   She was always in a fearful 'funk' about some woman getting hold of him, and persuading him to make a marriage beneath his station. His station!—poor Hyacinth had often asked himself, and Miss Pynsent, what it could possibly be.   He had thought of it bitterly enough, and wondered how in the world he could marry 'beneath' it.   He would never marry at all —to that his mind was absolutely made up; he would never hand on to another the burden which had made his own young spirit so intolerably sore, the inheritance which had darkened the whole threshold of his manhood. All the more reason why he should have his compensation; why, if the soft society of women was to be enjoyed on other terms, he should cultivate it with a bold, free mind.

'I thought I would just give a look at the old shop; I had an engagement not far off,' Millicent said. 'But I wouldn't have believed any one who had told me I should find you just where I left you.'

'We needed you to look after us!' Miss Pynsent exclaimed, irrepressibly.

'Oh, you're such a swell yourself!' Hyacinth observed, without heeding the dressmaker.

'None of your impudence! I'm as good a girl as there is in London!' And to corroborate this, Miss Henning went on: 'If you were to offer to see me a part of the way home, I should tell you I don't knock about that way with gentlemen.'

'I'll go with you as far as you like,' Hyacinth replied, simply, as if he knew how to treat that sort of speech.

'Well, it's only because I knew you as a baby!' And they went out together, Hyacinth careful not to look at poor Pinnie at all (he felt her glaring whitely and tearfully at him out of her dim corner—it had by this time grown too dusky to work without a lamp), and his companion giving her an outrageously friendly nod of farewell over her shoulder.

It was a long walk from Lomax Place to the quarter of the town in which (to be near the haberdasher's in the Buckingham Palace Road) Miss Henning occupied a modest back-room; but the influences of the hour were such as to make the excursion very agreeable to our young man, who liked the streets at all times, but especially at nightfall, in the autumn, of a Saturday, when, in the vulgar districts, the smaller shops and open-air industries were doubly active, and big, clumsy torches flared and smoked over hand-carts and costermongers' barrows, drawn up in the gutters. Hyacinth had roamed through the great city since he was an urchin, but his imagination had never

ceased to be stirred by the preparations for Sunday that
went on in the evening among the toilers and spinners, his
brothers and sisters, and he lost himself in all the quickened
crowding and pushing and staring at lighted windows and
chaffering at the stalls of fishmongers and hucksters.   He
liked the people who looked as if they had got their week's
wage and were prepared to lay it out discreetly; and even
those whose use of it would plainly be extravagant and
intemperate; and, best of all, those who evidently hadn't
received it at all and who wandered about, disinterestedly,
vaguely, with their hands in empty pockets, watching others
make their bargains and fill their satchels, or staring at the
striated sides of bacon, at the golden cubes and triangles of
cheese, at the graceful festoons of sausage, in the most
brilliant of the windows.   He liked the reflection of the
lamps on the wet pavements, the feeling and smell of the
carboniferous London damp; the way the winter fog
blurred and suffused the whole place, made it seem bigger
and more crowded, produced halos and dim radiations,
trickles and evaporations, on the plates of glass.   He
moved in the midst of these impressions this evening, but
he enjoyed them in silence, with an attention taken up
mainly by his companion, and pleased to be already so
intimate with a young lady whom people turned round to
look at.   She herself affected to speak of the rush and
crush of the week's end with disgust: she said she liked
the streets, but she liked the respectable ones; she couldn't
abide the smell of fish, and the whole place seemed full of
it, so that she hoped they would soon get into the Edgware
Road, towards which they tended and which was a proper
street for a lady.   To Hyacinth she appeared to have no
connection with the long-haired little girl who, in Lomax
Place, years before, was always hugging a smutty doll and
courting his society; she was like a stranger, a new
acquaintance, and he observed her curiously, wondering
by what transitions she had reached her present pitch.

  She enlightened him but little on this point, though she
talked a great deal on a variety of subjects, and mentioned
to him her habits, her aspirations, her likes and dislikes.
The latter were very numerous.   She was tremendously

particular, difficult to please, he could see that; and she
assured him that she never put up with anything a moment
after it had ceased to be agreeable to her.   Especially was
she particular about gentlemen's society, and she made it
plain that a young fellow who wanted to have anything to
say to her must be in receipt of wages amounting at the
least to fifty shillings a week.   Hyacinth told her that she
didn't earn that, as yet; and she remarked again that she
made an exception for him, because she knew all about
him (or if not all, at least a great deal), and he could see
that her good-nature was equal to her beauty.   She made
such an exception that when, after they were moving down
the Edgware Road (which had still the brightness of late
closing, but with more nobleness), he proposed that she
should enter a coffee-house with him and 'take something'
(he could hardly tell himself, afterwards, what brought him
to this point), she acceded without a demur—without a
demur even on the ground of his slender earnings.   Slender
as they were, Hyacinth had them in his pocket (they had
been destined in some degree for Pinnie), and he felt equal
to the occasion.   Millicent partook profusely of tea and
bread and butter, with a relish of raspberry jam, and
thought the place most comfortable, though he himself,
after finding himself ensconced, was visited by doubts as
to its respectability, suggested, among other things, by
photographs, on the walls, of young ladies in tights.
Hyacinth himself was hungry, he had not yet had his tea,
but he was too excited, too preoccupied, to eat; the situation made him restless and gave him palpitations; it
seemed to be the beginning of something new.   He had
never yet 'stood' even a glass of beer to a girl of Millicent's stamp—a girl who rustled and glittered and smelt of
musk—and if she should turn out as jolly a specimen of
the sex as she seemed it might make a great difference in
his leisure hours, in his evenings, which were often very
dull.   That it would also make a difference in his savings
(he was under a pledge to Pinnie and to Mr. Vetch to put
by something every week) it didn't concern him, for the
moment, to reflect; and indeed, though he thought it
odious and insufferable to be poor, the ways and means

of becoming rich had hitherto not greatly occupied him.
He knew what Millicent's age must be, but felt, nevertheless, as if she were older, much older, than himself—she
appeared to know so much about London and about life ;
and this made it still more of a sensation to be entertaining
her like a young swell.   He thought of it, too, in connection with the question of the respectability of the establishment ; if this element was deficient she would perceive it
as soon as he, and very likely it would be a part of the
general initiation she had given him an impression of that
she shouldn't mind it so long as the tea was strong and
the bread and butter thick.   She described to him what
had passed between Miss Pynsent and herself (she didn't
call her Pinnie, and he was glad, for he wouldn't have
liked it) before he came in, and let him know that she
should never dare to come to the place again, as his mother
would tear her eyes out.   Then she checked herself.   'Of
course she ain't your mother !   How stupid I am !   I keep
forgetting.'

Hyacinth had long since convinced himself that he had
acquired a manner with which he could meet allusions of
this kind : he had had, first and last, so many opportunities
to practise it.   Therefore he looked at his companion very
steadily while he said, ' My mother died many years ago ;
she was a great invalid.   But Pinnie has been awfully good
to me.'

' My mother's dead too,' Miss Henning remarked.
' She died very suddenly.   I daresay you remember her in
the Place.'   Then, while Hyacinth disengaged from the
past the wavering figure of Mrs. Henning, of whom he
mainly remembered that she used to strike him as dirty,
the girl added, smiling, but with more sentiment, ' But I
have had no Pinnie.'

' You look as if you could take care of yourself.'

' Well, I'm very confiding,' said Millicent Henning.
Then she asked what had become of Mr. Vetch.   ' We
used to say that if Miss Pynsent was your mamma, he was
your papa.   In our family we used to call him Miss Pynsent's young man.'

' He's her young man still,' Hyacinth said.   ' He's our

best friend—or supposed to be.   He got me the place I'm
in now.   He lives by his fiddle, as he used to do.'

Millicent looked a little at her companion, after which
she remarked, 'I should have thought he would have got
you a place at his theatre.'

'At his theatre?   That would have been no use.   I
don't play any instrument.'

'I don't mean in the orchestra, you gaby!   You would
look very nice in a fancy costume.'   She had her elbows
on the table, and her shoulders lifted, in an attitude of
extreme familiarity.   He was on the point of replying that
he didn't care for fancy costumes, he wished to go through
life in his own character; but he checked himself, with the
reflection that this was exactly what, apparently, he was
destined not to do.   His own character?   He was to
cover that up as carefully as possible; he was to go through
life in a mask, in a borrowed mantle; he was to be, every
day and every hour, an actor.   Suddenly, with the utmost
irrelevance, Miss Henning inquired, 'Is Miss Pynsent some
relation?   What gave her any right over you?'

Hyacinth had an answer ready for this question; he
had determined to say, as he had several times said before,
'Miss Pynsent is an old friend of my family.   My mother
was very fond of her, and she was very fond of my mother.'
He repeated the formula now, looking at Millicent with
the same inscrutable calmness (as he fancied), though what
he would have liked to say to her would have been that his
mother was none of her business.   But she was too handsome
to talk that way to, and she presented her large fair face to
him, across the table, with an air of solicitation to be cosy
and comfortable.   There were things in his heart and a
torment and a hidden passion in his life which he should
be glad enough to lay open to some woman.   He believed
that perhaps this would be the cure ultimately; that in
return for something he might drop, syllable by syllable,
into a listening feminine ear, certain other words would
be spoken to him which would make his pain for ever less
sharp.   But what woman could he trust, what ear would be
safe?   The answer was not in this loud, fresh laughing
creature, whose sympathy couldn't have the fineness he

was looking for, since her curiosity was vulgar. Hyacinth
objected to the vulgar as much as Miss Pynsent herself;
in this respect she had long since discovered that he was
after her own heart. He had not taken up the subject of
Mrs. Henning's death; he felt himself incapable of inquiring about that lady, and had no desire for knowledge of
Millicent's relationships. Moreover he always suffered, to
sickness, when people began to hover about the question
of his origin, the reasons why Pinnie had had the care of
him from a baby. Mrs. Henning had been untidy, but at
least her daughter could speak of her. ' Mr. Vetch has
changed his lodgings : he moved out of No. 17, three
years ago,' he said, to vary the topic. ' He couldn't stand
the other people in the house ; there was a man who played
the accordeon.'

Millicent, however, was but moderately interested in this
anecdote, and she wanted to know why people should like
Mr. Vetch's fiddle any better. Then she added, ' And I
think that while he was about it he might have put you
into something better than a bookbinder's.'

' He wasn't obliged to put me into anything. It's a
very good place.'

' All the same, it isn't where I should have looked to
find you,' Millicent declared, not so much in the tone of
wishing to pay him a compliment as of resentment at having
miscalculated.

' Where should you have looked to find me ? In the
House of Commons ? It's a pity you couldn't have told
me in advance what you would have liked me to be.'

She looked at him, over her cup, while she drank, in
several sips. ' Do you know what they used to say in the
Place ? That your father was a lord.'

' Very likely. That's the kind of rot they talk in that
precious hole,' the young man said, without blenching.

' Well, perhaps he was,' Millicent ventured.

' He may have been a prince, for all the good it has
done me.'

'Fancy your talking as if you didn't know!' said
Millicent.

' Finish your tea—don't mind how I talk.'

'Well, you *'ave* got a temper!' the girl exclaimed, archly. 'I should have thought you'd be a clerk at a banker's.'

'Do they select them for their tempers?'

'You know what I mean. You used to be too clever to follow a trade.'

'Well, I'm not clever enough to live on air.'

'You might be, really, for all the tea you drink! Why didn't you go in for some high profession?'

'How was I to go in? Who the devil was to help me?' Hyacinth inquired, with a certain vibration.

'Haven't you got any relations?' said Millicent, after a moment.

'What are you doing? Are you trying to make me swagger?'

When he spoke sharply she only laughed, not in the least ruffled, and by the way she looked at him seemed to like it. 'Well, I'm sorry you're only a journeyman,' she went on, pushing away her cup.

'So am I,' Hyacinth rejoined; but he called for the bill as if he had been an employer of labour. Then, while it was being brought, he remarked to his companion that he didn't believe she had an idea of what his work was and how charming it could be. 'Yes, I get up books for the shops,' he said, when she had retorted that she perfectly understood. 'But the art of the binder is an exquisite art.'

'So Miss Pynsent told me. She said you had some samples at home. I should like to see them.'

'You wouldn't know how good they are,' said Hyacinth, smiling.

He expected that she would exclaim, in answer, that he was an impudent wretch, and for a moment she seemed to be on the point of doing so. But the words changed on her lips, and she replied, almost tenderly, 'That's just the way you used to speak to me, years ago in the Plice.'

'I don't care about that. I hate all that time.'

'Oh, so do I, if you come to that,' said Millicent, as if she could rise to any breadth of view. And then she returned to her idea that he had not done himself justice.

'You used always to be reading: I never thought you would work with your 'ands.'

This seemed to irritate him, and, having paid the bill and given threepence, ostentatiously, to the young woman with a languid manner and hair of an unnatural yellow, who had waited on them, he said, 'You may depend upon it I shan't do it an hour longer than I can help.'

'What will you do then?'

'Oh, you'll see, some day.' In the street, after they had begun to walk again, he went on, 'You speak as if I could have my pick. What was an obscure little beggar to do, buried in a squalid corner of London, under a million of idiots? I had no help, no influence, no acquaintance of any kind with professional people, and no means of getting at them. I had to do something; I couldn't go on living on Pinnie. Thank God, I help her now, a little. I took what I could get.' He spoke as if he had been touched by the imputation of having derogated.

Millicent seemed to imply that he defended himself successfully when she said, 'You express yourself like a gentleman'—a speech to which he made no response. But he began to talk again afterwards, and, the evening having definitely set in, his companion took his arm for the rest of the way home. By the time he reached her door he had confided to her that, in secret, he wrote: he had a dream of literary distinction. This appeared to impress her, and she branched off to remark, with an irrelevance that characterised her, that she didn't care anything about a man's family if she liked the man himself; she thought families were played out. Hyacinth wished she would leave his alone; and while they lingered in front of her house, before she went in, he said—

'I have no doubt you're a jolly girl, and I am very happy to have seen you again. But you have awfully little tact.'

'*I* have little tact? You should see me work off an old jacket!'

He was silent a moment, standing before her with his hands in his pockets. 'It's a good job you're so handsome.'

Millicent didn't blush at this compliment, and probably didn't understand all it conveyed, but she looked into his eyes a while, with a smile that showed her teeth, and then said, more inconsequently than ever, 'Come now, who are you?'

'Who am I? I'm a wretched little bookbinder.'

'I didn't think I ever could fancy any one in that line!' Miss Henning exclaimed. Then she let him know that she couldn't ask him in, as she made it a point not to receive gentlemen, but she didn't mind if she took another walk with him and she didn't care if she met him somewhere—if it were handy. As she lived so far from Lomax Place she didn't care if she met him half-way. So, in the dusky by-street in Pimlico, before separating, they took a casual tryst; the most interesting, the young man felt, that had yet been—he could scarcely call it granted him.

ONE day, shortly after this, at the bindery, his friend
Poupin was absent, and sent no explanation, as was
customary in case of illness or domestic accident. There
were two or three men employed in the place whose non-
appearance, usually following close upon pay-day, was better
unexplained, and was an implication of moral feebleness;
but as a general thing Mr. Crookenden's establishment was
a haunt of punctuality and sobriety. Least of all had
Eustache Poupin been in the habit of asking for a margin.
Hyacinth knew how little indulgence he had ever craved,
and this was part of his admiration for the extraordinary
Frenchman, an ardent stoic, a cold conspirator and an
exquisite artist, who was by far the most interesting person
in the ranks of his acquaintance and whose conversation,
in the workshop, helped him sometimes to forget the smell
of leather and glue. His conversation! Hyacinth had
had plenty of that, and had endeared himself to the passionate refugee—Poupin had come to England after the Commune of 1871, to escape the reprisals of the government of
M. Thiers, and had remained there in spite of amnesties
and rehabilitations—by the solemnity and candour of his
attention. He was a Republican of the old-fashioned sort,
of the note of 1848, humanitary and idealistic, infinitely
addicted to fraternity and equality, and inexhaustibly surprised and exasperated at finding so little enthusiasm for
them in the land of his exile. Poupin had a high claim
upon Hyacinth's esteem and gratitude, for he had been his
godfather, his protector at the bindery. When Anastasius
Vetch found something for Miss Pynsent's *protégé* to do, it
was through the Frenchman, with whom he had accidentally
formed an acquaintance, that he found it.

When the boy was about fifteen years of age Mr. Vetch
made him a present of the essays of Lord Bacon, and the
purchase of this volume had important consequences for
Hyacinth. Anastasius Vetch was a poor man, and the
luxury of giving was for the most part denied him; but
when once in a way he tasted it he liked the sensation to
be pure. No man knew better the difference between the
common and the rare, or was more capable of appreciating
a book which opened well—of which the margin was not
hideously chopped and of which the lettering on the back
was sharp. It was only such a book that he could bring
himself to offer even to a poor little devil whom a fifth-rate
dressmaker (he knew Pinnie was fifth-rate) had rescued
from the workhouse. So when it became a question of
fitting the great Elizabethan with a new coat—a coat of
full morocco, discreetly, delicately gilt—he went with his
little cloth-bound volume, a Pickering, straight to Mr.
Crookenden, whom every one that knew anything about the
matter knew to be a prince of binders, though they also
knew that his work, limited in quantity, was mainly done
for a particular bookseller and only through the latter's
agency. Anastasius Vetch had no idea of paying the bookseller's commission, and though he could be lavish (for him)
when he made a present, he was capable of taking an
immense deal of trouble to save sixpence. He made his
way into Mr. Crookenden's workshop, which was situated
in a small superannuated square in Soho, and where the
proposal of so slender a job was received at first with coldness. Mr. Vetch, however, insisted, and explained with
irresistible frankness the motive of his errand : the desire to
obtain the best possible binding for the least possible
money. He made his conception of the best possible
binding so vivid, so exemplary, that the master of the shop
at last confessed to that disinterested sympathy which,
under favouring circumstances, establishes itself between
the artist and the connoisseur. Mr. Vetch's little book was
put in hand as a particular service to an eccentric gentleman whose visit had been a smile-stirring interlude (for the
circle of listening workmen) in a merely mechanical day;
and when he went back, three weeks later, to see whether

it were done, he had the pleasure of finding that his in-
junctions, punctually complied with, had even been bettered.
The work had been accomplished with a perfection of skill
which made him ask whom he was to thank for it (he had
been told that one man should do the whole of it), and in
this manner he made the acquaintance of the most brilliant
craftsman in the establishment, the incorruptible, the
imaginative, the unerring Eustache Poupin.

In response to an appreciation which he felt not to be
banal M. Poupin remarked that he had at home a small
collection of experiments in morocco, Russia, parchment,
of fanciful specimens with which, for the love of the art, he
had amused his leisure hours and which he should be
happy to show his interlocutor if the latter would do him
the honour to call upon him at his lodgings in Lisson
Grove. Mr. Vetch made a note of the address and, for
the love of the art, went one Sunday afternoon to see the
binder's esoteric studies. On this occasion he made the
acquaintance of Madame Poupin, a small, fat lady with a
bristling moustache, the white cap of an *ouvrière*, a knowledge of her husband's craft that was equal to his own, and
not a syllable of English save the words, ' What you think,
what you think ? ' which she introduced with startling frequency. He also discovered that his new acquaintance had
been a political proscript and that he regarded the iniqui-
tous fabric of Church and State with an eye scarcely more
reverent than the fiddler's own. M. Poupin was a socialist,
which Anastasius Vetch was not, and a constructive democrat (instead of being a mere scoffer at effete things), and a
theorist and an optimist and a visionary ; he believed that
the day was to come when all the nations of the earth
would abolish their frontiers and armies and custom-houses,
and embrace on both cheeks, and cover the globe with
boulevards, radiating from Paris, where the human family
would sit, in groups, at little tables, according to affinities,
drinking coffee (not tea, *par exemple!*) and listening to the
music of the spheres. Mr. Vetch neither prefigured nor
desired this organised felicity ; he was fond of his cup of
tea, and only wanted to see the British constitution a good
deal simplified ; he thought it a much overrated system,

but his heresies rubbed shoulders, sociably, with those of
the little bookbinder, and his friend in Lisson Grove became
for him the type of the intelligent foreigner whose conversation completes our culture.   Poupin's humanitary zeal
was as unlimited as his English vocabulary was the reverse,
and the new friends agreed with each other enough, and
not too much, to discuss, which was much better than an
unspeakable harmony.   On several other Sunday afternoons
the fiddler went back to Lisson Grove, and having, at his
theatre, as a veteran, a faithful servant, an occasional privilege, he was able to carry thither, one day in the autumn,
an order for two seats in the second balcony.   Madame
Poupin and her husband passed a lugubrious evening at
the English comedy, where they didn't understand a word
that was spoken, and consoled themselves by gazing at
their friend in the orchestra.   But this adventure did not
arrest the development of a friendship into which, eventually, Amanda Pynsent was drawn.   Madame Poupin,
among the cold insularies, lacked female society, and Mr.
Vetch proposed to his amiable friend in Lomax Place to
call upon her.   The little dressmaker, who in the course of
her life had known no Frenchwoman but the unhappy
Florentine (so favourable a specimen till she began to go
wrong), adopted his suggestion, in the hope that she should
get a few ideas from a lady whose appearance would doubtless exemplify (as Florentine's originally had done) the fine
taste of her nation ; but she found the bookbinder and his
wife a bewildering mixture of the brilliant and the relaxed,
and was haunted, long afterwards, by the memory of the
lady's calico jacket, her uncorseted form and her carpet
slippers.

The acquaintance, none the less, was sealed three months
later by a supper, one Sunday night, in Lisson Grove, to
which Mr. Vetch brought his fiddle, at which Amanda presented to her hosts her adoptive son, and which also
revealed to her that Madame Poupin could dress a Michael-
mas goose, if she couldn't dress a fat Frenchwoman.   This
lady confided to the fiddler that she thought Miss Pynsent
exceedingly *comme il faut—dans le genre anglais;* and
neither Amanda nor Hyacinth had ever passed an evening

of such splendour.   It took its place, in the boy's recollection, beside the visit, years before, to Mr. Vetch's theatre.
He drank in the conversation which passed between that
gentleman and M. Poupin. M. Poupin showed him his
bindings, the most precious trophies of his skill, and it
seemed to Hyacinth that on the spot he was initiated into
a fascinating mystery.   He handled the books for half an
hour ; Anastasius Vetch watched him, without giving any
particular sign.   When, therefore, presently, Miss Pynsent
consulted her friend for the twentieth time on the subject
of Hyacinth's ' career '—she spoke as if she were hesitating
between the diplomatic service, the army and the church
—the fiddler replied with promptitude, ' Make him, if you
can, what the Frenchman is.'   At the mention of a handicraft poor Pinnie always looked very solemn, yet when Mr.
Vetch asked her if she were prepared to send the boy to
one of the universities, or to pay the premium required for
his being articled to a solicitor, or to make favour, on his
behalf, with a bank-director or a mighty merchant, or, yet
again, to provide him with a comfortable home while he
should woo the muse and await the laurels of literature—
when, I say, he put the case before her with this cynical,
ironical lucidity, she only sighed and said that all the money
she had ever saved was ninety pounds, which, as he knew
perfectly well, it would cost her his acquaintance for evermore to take out of the bank.   The fiddler had, in fact,
declared to her in a manner not to be mistaken that if she
should divest herself, on the boy's account, of this sole
nest-egg of her old age, he would wash his hands of her and
her affairs.   Her standard of success for Hyacinth was
vague, save on one point, as regards which she was pas-
sionately, fiercely firm ; she was perfectly determined he
should never go into a small shop.   She would rather see
him a bricklayer or a costermonger than dedicated to a
retail business, tying up candles at a grocer's, or giving
change for a shilling across a counter.   She would rather,
she declared on one occasion, see him articled to a shoemaker or a tailor.

A stationer in a neighbouring street had affixed to his
window a written notice that he was in want of a smart

errand-boy, and Pinnie, on hearing of it, had presented
Hyacinth to his consideration. The stationer was a dreadful bullying man, with a patch over his eye, who seemed
to think the boy would be richly remunerated with three
shillings a week ; a contemptible measure, as it seemed to
the dressmaker, of his rare abilities and acquirements.
His schooling had been desultory, precarious, and had
had a certain continuity mainly in his early years, while
he was under the care of an old lady who combined
with the functions of pew-opener at a neighbouring church
the manipulation, in the Place itself, where she resided
with her sister, a monthly nurse, of such pupils as could
be spared (in their families) from the more urgent exercise of holding the baby and fetching the beer. Later,
for a twelvemonth, Pinnie had paid five shillings a week
for him at an 'Academy' in a genteel part of Islington,
where there was an 'instructor in the foreign languages,' a
platform for oratory, and a high social standard, but where
Hyacinth suffered from the fact that almost all his mates
were the sons of dealers in edible articles—pastry-cooks,
grocers and fishmongers—and in this capacity subjected
him to pangs and ignominious contrasts by bringing to
school, for their exclusive consumption, or for exchange
and barter, various buns, oranges, spices, and marine
animals, which the boy, with his hands in his empty pockets
and the sense of a savourless home in his heart, was obliged
to see devoured without his participation. Miss Pynsent
would not have pretended that he was highly educated, in
the technical sense of the word, but she believed that at
fifteen he had read almost every book in the world. The
limits of his reading were, in fact, only the limits of his
opportunity. Mr. Vetch, who talked with him more and
more as he grew older, knew this, and lent him every
volume he possessed or could pick up for the purpose.
Reading was his happiness, and the absence of any direct
contact with a library his principal source of discontent ;
that is, of that part of his discontent which he could speak
out.   Mr. Vetch knew that he was really clever, and therefore thought it a woful pity that he could not have furtherance in some liberal walk ; but he would have thought it a

greater pity still that so bright a lad should be condemned to measure tape or cut slices of cheese. He himself had no influence which he could bring into play, no connection with the great world of capital or the market of labour. That is, he touched these mighty institutions at but one very small point—a point which, such as it was, he kept well in mind.

When Pinnie replied to the stationer round the corner, after he had mentioned the 'terms' on which he was prepared to receive applications from errand-boys, that, thank heaven, she hadn't sunk so low as that—so low as to sell her darling into slavery for three shillings a week—he felt that she only gave more florid expression to his own sentiment. Of course, if Hyacinth did not begin by carrying parcels he could not hope to be promoted, through the more refined nimbleness of tying them up, to a position as accountant or bookkeeper; but both the fiddler and his friend—Miss Pynsent, indeed, only in the last resort—resigned themselves to the forfeiture of this prospect. Mr. Vetch saw clearly that a charming handicraft was a finer thing than a vulgar 'business,' and one day, after his acquaintance with Eustache Poupin had gone a considerable length, he inquired of the Frenchman whether there would be a chance of the lad's obtaining a footing, under his own wing, in Mr. Crookenden's workshop. There could be no better place for him to acquire a knowledge of the most delightful of the mechanical arts; and to be received into such an establishment, and at the instance of such an artist, would be a real start in life. M. Poupin meditated, and that evening confided his meditations to the companion who reduplicated all his thoughts and understood him better even than he understood himself. The pair had no children, and had felt the defect; moreover, they had heard from Mr. Vetch the dolorous tale of the boy's entrance into life. He was one of the disinherited, one of the expropriated, one of the exceptionally interesting; and moreover he was one of themselves, a child, as it were, of France, an offshoot of the sacred race. It is not the most authenticated point in this veracious history, but there is strong reason to believe that tears were shed that night, in Lisson Grove, over poor

little Hyacinth Robinson. In a day or two M. Poupin
replied to the fiddler that he had now been several years in
Mr. Crookenden's employ; that during that time he had
done work for him that he would have had *bien du mal* to
get done by another, and had never asked for an indulgence,
an allowance, a remission, an augmentation. It was time,
if only for the dignity of the thing, he should ask for something, and he would make their little friend the subject of
his demand. '*La société lui doit bien cela*,' he remarked
afterwards, when, Mr. Crookenden proving drily hospitable
and the arrangement being formally complete, Mr. Vetch
thanked him, in his kindly, casual, bashful English way.
He was paternal when Hyacinth began to occupy a place in
the malodorous chambers in Soho; he took him in hand,
made him a disciple, the recipient of a precious tradition,
discovered in him a susceptibility to philosophic as well as
technic truth. He taught him French and socialism,
encouraged him to spend his evenings in Lisson Grove,
invited him to regard Madame Poupin as a second, or rather
as a third, mother, and in short made a very considerable
mark on the boy's mind. He elicited the latent Gallicism
of his nature, and by the time he was twenty Hyacinth,
who had completely assimilated his influence, regarded him
with a mixture of veneration and amusement. M. Poupin
was the person who consoled him most when he was
miserable; and he was very often miserable.

His staying away from his work was so rare that, in the
afternoon, before he went home, Hyacinth walked to Lisson
Grove to see what ailed him. He found his friend in bed,
with a plaster on his chest, and Madame Poupin making
tisane over the fire. The Frenchman took his indisposition
solemnly but resignedly, like a man who believed that all
illness was owing to the imperfect organisation of society,
and lay covered up to his chin, with a red cotton handkerchief bound round his head. Near his bed sat a visitor,
a young man unknown to Hyacinth. Hyacinth, naturally,
had never been to Paris, but he always supposed that the
intérieur of his friends in Lisson Grove gave rather a vivid
idea of that city. The two small rooms which constituted
their establishment contained a great many mirrors, as well

as little portraits (old-fashioned prints) of revolutionary heroes. The chimney-piece, in the bedroom, was muffled in some red drapery, which appeared to Hyacinth extraordinarily magnificent; the principal ornament of the salon was a group of small and highly-decorated cups, on a tray, accompanied by gilt bottles and glasses, the latter still more diminutive—the whole intended for black coffee and liqueurs. There was no carpet on the floor, but rugs and mats, of various shapes and sizes, disposed themselves at the feet of the chairs and sofas; and in the sitting-room, where there was a wonderful gilt clock, of the Empire, sur-mounted with a 'subject' representing Virtue receiving a crown of laurel from the hands of Faith, Madame Poupin, with the aid of a tiny stove, a handful of charcoal, and two or three saucepans, carried on a triumphant *cuisine.* In the windows were curtains of white muslin, much fluted and frilled, and tied with pink ribbon.

VII

'I am suffering extremely, but we must all suffer, so long as the social question is so abominably, so iniquitously neglected,' Poupin remarked, speaking French and rolling toward Hyacinth his salient, excited-looking eyes, which always had the same proclaiming, challenging expression, whatever his occupation or his topic. Hyacinth had seated himself near his friend's pillow, opposite the strange young man, who had been accommodated with a chair at the foot of the bed.

'Ah, yes; with their filthy politics the situation of the *pauvre monde* is the last thing they ever think of!' his wife exclaimed, from the fire. 'There are times when I ask myself how long it will go on.'

'It will go on till the measure of their imbecility, their infamy, is full. It will go on till the day of justice, till the reintegration of the despoiled and disinherited, is ushered in with an irresistible force.'

'Oh, we always see things go on; we never see them change,' said Madame Poupin, making a very cheerful clatter with a big spoon in a saucepan.

'We may not see it, but *they'll* see it,' her husband rejoined. 'But what do I say, my children? I do see it,' he pursued. 'It's before my eyes, in its luminous reality, especially as I lie here—the revendication, the rehabilitation, the rectification.'

Hyacinth ceased to pay attention, not because he had a differing opinion about what M. Poupin called the *avènement* of the disinherited, but, on the contrary, precisely on account of his familiarity with that prospect. It was the constant theme of his French friends, whom he had long since perceived to be in a state of chronic spiritual inflammation. For them the social question was always in order, the political question always abhorrent, the disinherited always present. He wondered at their zeal, their continuity, their vivacity, their incorruptibility; at the abundant supply of conviction and prophecy which they always had on hand. He believed that at bottom he was sorer than they, yet he had deviations and lapses, moments when the social question bored him and he forgot not only his own wrongs, which would have been pardonable, but those of the people at large, of his brothers and sisters in misery. They, however, were perpetually in the breach, and perpetually consistent with themselves and, what is more, with each other. Hyacinth had heard that the institution of marriage in France was rather lightly considered, but he was struck with the closeness and intimacy of the union in Lisson Grove, the passionate identity of interest: especially on the day when M. Poupin informed him, in a moment of extreme but not indiscreet expansion, that the lady was his wife only in a spiritual, transcendental sense. There were hypocritical concessions and debasing superstitions of which this exalted pair wholly disapproved. Hyacinth knew their vocabulary by heart, and could have said everything, in the same words, that on any given occasion M. Poupin was likely to say. He knew that 'they,' in their phraseology, was a comprehensive allusion to every one in the world but the people—though who, exactly, in their length and breadth, the people were was less definitely established. He himself was of this sacred body, for which the future was to have such compensations; and so, of course, were the Frenchman and his consort, and so was Pinnie, and so were most of the inhabitants of Lomax Place and the workmen in old Crookenden's shop. But was old Crookenden himself, who wore an apron rather dirtier than the rest of them and was a master-hand at 'forwarding,' but who, on the other side, was the occupant of a villa almost detached, at Putney, with a wife known to have secret aspirations toward a page in buttons? Above all, was Mr. Vetch, who earned a weekly wage, and not a large one, with his fiddle, but who had mysterious affinities of another sort, reminiscences of a phase in which he smoked cigars, had a hat-box and used cabs—besides visiting Boulogne? Anastasius Vetch had interfered in his life, atrociously, in a terrible crisis; but Hyacinth, who strove to cultivate justice in his own conduct, believed he had acted conscientiously and tried to esteem him, the more so as the fiddler evidently felt that he had something to make up to him and had treated him with marked benevolence for years. He believed, in short, that Mr. Vetch took a sincere interest in him, and if he should meddle again would meddle in a different way: he used to see him sometimes looking at him with the kindest eyes. It would make a difference, therefore, whether he were of the people or not, inasmuch as in the day of the great revenge it would only be the people who should be saved. It was for the people the world was made: whoever was not of them was against them; and all others were cumberers, usurpers, exploiters, *accapareurs*, as M. Poupin used to say. Hyacinth had once put the question directly to Mr. Vetch, who looked at him a while through the fumes of his eternal pipe and then said, 'Do you think I'm an aristocrat?'

'I didn't know but you were a *bourgeois*,' the young man answered.

'No, I'm neither. I'm a Bohemian.'

'With your evening dress, every night?'

'My dear boy,' said the fiddler, 'those are the most confirmed.'

Hyacinth was only half satisfied with this, for it was by no means definite to him that Bohemians were also to be saved; if he could be sure, perhaps he would become one himself. Yet he never suspected Mr. Vetch of being a 'spy,' though Eustache Poupin had told him that there were a great many who looked a good deal like that: not, of course, with any purpose of incriminating the fiddler, whom he had trusted from the first and continued to trust. The middle-class spy became a very familiar type to Hyacinth, and though he had never caught one of the infamous brotherhood in the act, there were plenty of persons to whom, on the very face of the matter, he had no hesitation in attributing the character. There was nothing of the Bohemian, at any rate, about the Poupins, whom Hyacinth had now known long enough not to be surprised at the way they combined the socialistic passion, a red-hot impatience for the general rectification, with an extraordinary decency of life and a worship of proper work. The Frenchman spoke, habitually, as if the great swindle practised upon the people were too impudent to be endured a moment longer, and yet he found patience for the most exquisite 'tooling,' and took a book in hand with the deliberation of one who should believe that everything was immutably constituted. Hyacinth knew what he thought of priests and theologies, but he had the religion of conscientious craftsmanship, and he reduced the boy, on his side, to a kind of prostration before his delicate, wonder-working fingers. 'What will you have? *J'ai la main parisienne,*' M. Poupin would reply modestly, when Hyacinth's admiration broke out; and he was good enough, after he had seen a few specimens of what our hero could do, to inform him that *he* had the same happy conformation. 'There is no reason why you shouldn't be a good workman, *il n'y a que ça ;*' and his own life was practically governed by this conviction. He delighted in the use of his hands and his tools and the exercise of his taste, which was faultless, and Hyacinth could easily imagine how it must torment him to spend a day on his back. He ended by perceiving, however, that consolation was, on this occasion, in some degree conveyed by the presence of the young man who sat at the foot of the bed, and with whom M. Poupin exhibited such signs of acquaintance as to make our hero wonder why he had not seen him before, nor even heard of him.

'What do you mean by an irresistible force?' the young man inquired, leaning back in his chair, with raised arms and his interlocked hands behind him, supporting his head. M. Poupin had spoken French, which he always preferred to do, the insular tongue being an immense tribulation to him ; but his visitor spoke English, and Hyacinth immediately perceived that there was nothing French about *him*— M. Poupin could never tell him he had *la main parisienne.*

'I mean a force that will make the bourgeois go down into their cellars and hide, pale with fear, behind their barrels of wine and their heaps of gold !' cried M. Poupin, rolling terrible eyes.

'And in this country, I hope in their coal-bins. *Là-là*, we shall find them even there,' his wife remarked.

''89 was an irresistible force,' said M. Poupin. 'I believe you would have thought so if you had been there.'

'And so was the entrance of the Versaillais, which sent you over here, ten years ago,' the young man rejoined. He saw that Hyacinth was watching him, and he met his eyes, smiling a little, in a way that added to our hero's interest.

'*Pardon, pardon,* I resist !' cried Eustache Poupin, glaring, in his improvised nightcap, out of his sheets ; and Madame repeated that they resisted—she believed well that they resisted ! The young man burst out laughing ; whereupon his host declared, with a dignity which even his recumbent position did not abate, that it was really frivolous of him to ask such questions as that, knowing as he did— what he did know.

'Yes, I know—I know,' said the young man, good-naturedly, lowering his arms and thrusting his hands into his pockets, while he stretched his long legs a little. 'But everything is yet to be tried.'

'Oh, the trial will be on a great scale—*soyez tranquille !* It will be one of those experiments that constitute a proof.'

Hyacinth wondered what they were talking about, and perceived that it must be something important, for the stranger was not a man who would take an interest in anything else. Hyacinth was immensely struck with him—he could see that he was remarkable—and felt slightly aggrieved that he should be a stranger : that is, that he should be, apparently, a familiar of Lisson Grove and yet that M. Poupin should not have thought his young friend from Lomax Place worthy, up to this time, to be made acquainted with him. I know not to what degree the visitor in the other chair discovered these reflections in Hyacinth's face, but after a moment, looking across at him, he said in a friendly yet just slightly diffident way, a way our hero liked, 'And do you know, too ?'

'Do I know what?' asked Hyacinth, wondering.

'Oh, if you did, you would!' the young man exclaimed, laughing again. Such a rejoinder, from any one else, would have irritated our sensitive hero, but it only made Hyacinth more curious about his interlocutor, whose laugh was loud and extraordinarily gay.

'*Mon ami*, you ought to present *ces messieurs*,' Madame Poupin remarked.

'*Ah ça*, is that the way you trifle with state secrets?' her husband cried out, without heeding her. Then he went on, in a different tone: 'M. Hyacinthe is a gifted child, *un enfant très-doué*, in whom I take a tender interest —a child who has an account to settle. Oh, a thumping big one! Isn't it so, *mon petit?*'

This was very well meant, but it made Hyacinth blush, and, without knowing exactly what to say, he murmured shyly, 'Oh, I only want them to let me alone!'

'He is very young,' said Eustache Poupin.

'He is the person we have seen in this country whom we like the best,' his wife added.

'Perhaps you are French,' suggested the strange young man.

The trio seemed to Hyacinth to be waiting for his answer to this; it was as if a listening stillness had fallen upon them. He found it a difficult moment, partly because there was something exciting and embarrassing in the attention of the other visitor, and partly because he had never yet had to decide that important question. He didn't really know whether he were French or English, or which of the two he should prefer to be. His mother's blood, her suffering in an alien land, the unspeakable, irremediable misery that consumed her, in a place, among a people, she must have execrated—all this made him French; yet he was conscious at the same time of qualities that did not mix with it. He had evolved, long ago, a legend about his mother, built it up slowly, adding piece to piece, in passionate musings and broodings, when his cheeks burned and his eyes filled; but there were times when it wavered and faded, when it ceased to console him and he ceased to trust it. He had had a father too, and his father had

suffered as well, and had fallen under a blow, and had paid
with his life; and him also he felt in his mind and his
body, when the effort to think it out did not simply end in
darkness and confusion, challenging still even while they
baffled, and inevitable freezing horror. At any rate, he
seemed rooted in the place where his wretched parents had
expiated, and he knew nothing about any other. Moreover, when old Poupin said, 'M. Hyacinthe,' as he had
often done before, he didn't altogether enjoy it; he thought
it made his name, which he liked well enough in English,
sound like the name of a hair-dresser. Our young friend
was under a cloud and a stigma, but he was not yet prepared to admit that he was ridiculous. 'Oh, I daresay I
ain't anything,' he replied in a moment.

'*En v'là des bêtises !*' cried Madame Poupin. 'Do you
mean to say you are not as good as any one in the world?
I should like to see !'

'We all have an account to settle, don't you know?'
said the strange young man.

He evidently meant this to be encouraging to Hyacinth,
whose quick desire to avert M. Poupin's allusions had not
been lost upon him; but our hero could see that he himself would be sure to be one of the first to be paid. He
would make society bankrupt, but he would be paid. He
was tall and fair and good-natured looking, but you couldn't
tell—or at least Hyacinth couldn't—whether he were
handsome or ugly, with his large head and square forehead, his thick, straight hair, his heavy mouth and
rather vulgar nose, his admirably clear, bright eye,
light-coloured and set very deep; for though there
was a want of fineness in some of its parts, his face
had a marked expression of intelligence and resolution,
and denoted a kind of joyous moral health. He was
dressed like a workman in his Sunday toggery, having
evidently put on his best to call in Lisson Grove, where he
was to meet a lady, and wearing in particular a necktie
which was both cheap and pretentious, and of which
Hyacinth, who noticed everything of that kind, observed
the crude, false blue. He had very big shoes—the shoes,
almost, of a country labourer—and spoke with a pro-

VII THE PRINCESS CASAMASSIMA 85

vincial accent, which Hyacinth believed to be that of
Lancashire. This didn't suggest cleverness, but it didn't
prevent Hyacinth from perceiving that he was the reverse
of stupid, that he probably, indeed, had a tremendous
head. Our little hero had a great desire to know superior
people, and he interested himself on the spot in this strong,
humorous fellow, who had the complexion of a ploughboy
and the glance of a commander-in-chief and who might
have been (Hyacinth thought) a distinguished young *savant*
in the disguise of an artisan. The disguise would have
been very complete, for he had several brown stains on his
fingers. Hyacinth's curiosity, on this occasion, was both
excited and gratified; for after two or three allusions, which
he didn't understand, had been made to a certain place
where Poupin and the stranger had met and expected to
meet again, Madame Poupin exclaimed that it was a shame
not to take in M. Hyacinthe, who, she would answer for it,
had in him the making of one of the pure.

' All in good time, in good time, *ma bonne*,' the invalid
replied. ' M. Hyacinthe knows that I count upon him,
whether or no I make him an *interne* to-day or wait a
while longer.'

'What do you mean by an interne?' Hyacinth asked.

'Mon Dieu, what shall I say!' and Eustache Poupin
stared at him solemnly, from his pillow. 'You are very
sympathetic, but I am afraid you are too young.'

'One is never too young to contribute one's *obole*,' said
Madame Poupin.

'Can you keep a secret?' asked the other visitor, smilingly.

'Is it a plot—a conspiracy?' Hyacinth broke out.

' He asks that as if he were asking if it's a plum-pudding,'
said M. Poupin. ' It isn't good to eat, and we don't do it
for our amusement. It's terribly serious, my child.'

' It's a kind of society, to which he and I and a good
many others belong. There is no harm in telling him that,'
the young man went on.

' I advise you not to tell it to Mademoiselle; she is quite
in the old ideas,' Madame Poupin suggested to Hvacinth,
tasting her *tisane*.

Hyacinth sat baffled and wondering, looking from his

fellow-labourer in Soho to his new acquaintance opposite.
'If you have some plan, something to which one can give
one's self, I think you might have told me,' he remarked, in
a moment, to Poupin.

The latter merely gazed at him a while; then he said to
the strange young man, 'He is a little jealous of you. But
there is no harm in that; it's of his age. You must know
him, you must like him. We will tell you his history some
other day; it will make you feel that he belongs to us in
fact. It is an accident that he hasn't met you here before.'

'How could *ces messieurs* have met, when M. Paul never
comes? He doesn't spoil us!' Madame Poupin cried.

'Well, you see I have my little sister at home to take
care of, when I ain't at the shop,' M. Paul explained.
'This afternoon it was just a chance; there was a lady we
know came in to sit with her.'

'A lady—a real lady?'

'Oh yes, every inch,' said M. Paul, laughing.

'Do you like them to thrust themselves into your apartment like that, because you have the *désagrément* of being
poor? .It seems to be the custom in this country, but it
wouldn't suit me at all,' Madame Poupin continued. 'I
should like to see one of *ces dames*—the real ones—coming
in to sit with me!'

'Oh, you are not a cripple; you have got the use of your
legs!'

'Yes, and of my arms!' cried the Frenchwoman.

'This lady looks after several others in our court, and she
reads to my sister.'

'Oh, well, you are patient, you English.'

'We shall never do anything without that,' said M. Paul,
with undisturbed good-humour.

'You are perfectly right; you can't say that too often.
It will be a tremendous job, and only the strong will prevail,' his host murmured, a little wearily, turning his eyes to
Madame Poupin, who approached slowly, holding the *tisane*
in a rather full bowl, and tasting it again and yet again as
she came.

Hyacinth had been watching his fellow-visitor with
deepening interest; a fact of which M. Paul apparently

became aware, for he said, presently, giving a little nod in
the direction of the bed, ' He says we ought to know each
other. I'm sure I have nothing against it. I like to know
folk, when they're worth it ! '

Hyacinth was too pleased with this even to take it up ;
it seemed to him, for a moment, that he couldn't touch it
gracefully enough. But he said, with sufficient eagerness,
' Will you tell me all about your plot ? '

' Oh, it's no plot. I don't think I care much for plots.'
And with his mild, steady, light-blue English eye, M. Paul
certainly had not much the appearance of a conspirator.

' Isn't it a new era ? ' asked Hyacinth, rather disappointed.

' Well, I don't know ; it's just a little movement.'

' *Ah bien, voilà du propre ;* between us we have thrown
him into a fever ! ' cried Madame Poupin, who had put
down her bowl on a table near her husband's bed and was
bending over him, with her hand on his forehead. Eustache
was flushed, he had closed his eyes, and it was evident there
had been more than enough conversation. Madame Poupin
announced as much, with the addition that if the young
men wished to make acquaintance they must do it outside ;
the invalid must be perfectly quiet. They accordingly
withdrew, with apologies and promises to return for further
news on the morrow, and two minutes afterward Hyacinth
found himself standing face to face with his new friend on
the pavement in front of M. Poupin's residence, under a
street-lamp which struggled ineffectually with the brown
winter dusk.

' Is that your name—M. Paul ? ' he asked, looking up at
him.

' Oh, bless you, no ; that's only her Frenchified way of
putting it. My name *is* Paul, though—Paul Muniment.'

' And what's your trade ? ' Hyacinth demanded, with a
jump into familiarity ; for his companion seemed to have
told him a great deal more than was usually conveyed in
that item of information.

Paul Muniment looked down at him from above broad
shoulders. ' I work at a wholesale chemist's, at Lambeth.'

' And where do you live ?

'I live over the water, too ; in the far south of London.'

'And are you going home now ? '

'Oh yes, I am going to toddle.'

'And may I toddle with you ? '

Mr. Muniment considered him further ; then he gave a laugh. 'I'll carry you, if you like.'

'Thank you ; I expect I can walk as far as you,' said Hyacinth.

'Well, I admire your spirit, and I daresay I shall like your company.'

There was something in his face, taken in connection with the idea that he was concerned in a little movement, which made Hyacinth feel the desire to go with him till he dropped ; and in a moment they started away together and took the direction Muniment had mentioned. They discoursed as they went, and exchanged a great many opinions and anecdotes ; but they reached the south-westerly court in which the young chemist lived with his infirm sister before he had told Hyacinth anything definite about his little movement, or Hyacinth, on his side, had related to him the circumstances connected with his being, according to M. Poupin, one of the disinherited. Hyacinth didn't wish to press him ; he would not for the world have appeared to him indiscreet ; and, moreover, though he had taken so great a fancy to Muniment, he was not quite prepared, as yet, to be pressed. Therefore it did not become very clear to him how his companion had made Poupin's acquaintance and how long he had enjoyed it. Paul Muniment nevertheless was to a certain extent communicative about himself, and forewarned Hyacinth that he lived in a very poor little corner. He had his sister to keep—she could do nothing for herself ; and he paid a low rent because she had to have doctors, and doses, and all sorts of little comforts. He spent a shilling a week for her on flowers. It was better, too, when you got upstairs, and from the back windows you could see the dome of St. Paul's. Audley Court, with its pretty name, which reminded Hyacinth of Tennyson, proved to be a still dingier nook than Lomax Place ; and it had the further drawback that you had to pass through a narrow alley, a passage between high, black walls,

to enter it.   At the door of one of the houses the young
men paused, lingering a little, and then Muniment said, 'I
say, why shouldn't you come up?   I like you well enough
for that, and you can see my sister; her name is Rosy.'
He spoke as if this would be a great privilege, and added,
humorously, that Rosy enjoyed a call from a gentleman,
of all things.   Hyacinth needed no urging, and he groped
his way, at his companion's heels, up a dark staircase, which
appeared to him—for they stopped only when they could
go no further—the longest and steepest he had ever
ascended.   At the top Paul Muniment pushed open a door,
but exclaimed, 'Hullo, have you gone to roost?' on perceiving that the room on the threshold of which they stood
was unlighted.

'Oh, dear, no; we are sitting in the dark,' a small,
bright voice instantly replied.   'Lady Aurora is so kind;
she's here still.'

The voice came out of a corner so pervaded by gloom
that the speaker was indistinguishable.   'Dear me, that's
beautiful!' Paul Muniment rejoined.   'You'll have a party,
then, for I have brought some one else.   We are poor, you
know, but I daresay we can manage a candle.'

At this, in the dim firelight, Hyacinth saw a tall figure
erect itself—a figure angular and slim, crowned with a large,
vague hat, surmounted, apparently, with a flowing veil.   This
unknown person gave a singular laugh, and said, 'Oh, I
brought some candles; we could have had a light if we had
wished it.'   Both the tone and the purport of the words
announced to Hyacinth that they proceeded from the lips
of Lady Aurora.

VIII

PAUL MUNIMENT took a match out of his pocket and lighted it on the sole of his shoe; after which he applied it to a tallow candle which stood in a tin receptacle on the low mantel-shelf. This enabled Hyacinth to perceive a narrow bed in a corner, and a small figure stretched upon it—a figure revealed to him mainly by the bright fixedness of a pair of large eyes, of which the whites were sharply contrasted with the dark pupil, and which gazed at him across a counterpane of gaudy patchwork. The brown room seemed crowded with heterogeneous objects, and had, moreover, for Hyacinth, thanks to a multitude of small prints, both plain and coloured, fastened all over the walls, a highly-decorated appearance. The little person in the corner had the air of having gone to bed in a picture-gallery, and as soon as Hyacinth became aware of this his impression deepened that Paul Muniment and his sister were very remarkable people. Lady Aurora hovered before him with a kind of drooping erectness, laughing a good deal, vaguely and shyly, as if there were something rather awkward in her being found still on the premises. 'Rosy, girl, I've brought you a visitor,' Paul Muniment said. 'This young man has walked all the way from Lisson Grove to make your acquaintance.' Rosy continued to look at Hyacinth from over her counterpane, and he felt slightly embarrassed, for he had never yet been presented to a young lady in her position. 'You mustn't mind her being in bed—she's always in bed,' her brother went on. 'She's in bed just the same as a little trout is in the water.'

'Dear me, if I didn't receive company because I was in bed, there wouldn't be much use, would there, Lady Aurora?'

Rosy made this inquiry in a light, gay tone, darting

her brilliant eyes at her companion, who replied instantly,
with still greater hilarity, and in a voice which struck
Hyacinth as strange and affected, 'Oh, dear, no, it seems
quite the natural place!' Then she added, 'And it's such
a pretty bed, such a comfortable bed!'

'Indeed it is, when your ladyship makes it up,' said
Rosy; while Hyacinth wondered at this strange phenomenon of a peer's daughter (for he knew she must be that)
performing the functions of a housemaid.

'I say, now, you haven't been doing that again to-day?'
Muniment asked, punching the mattress of the invalid with
a vigorous hand.

'Pray, who would, if I didn't?' Lady Aurora inquired.
'It only takes a minute, if one knows how.' Her manner
was jocosely apologetic, and she seemed to plead guilty to
having been absurd; in the dim light Hyacinth thought
he saw her blush, as if she were much embarrassed. In
spite of her blushing, her appearance and manner suggested
to him a personage in a comedy. She sounded the letter
r peculiarly.

'I can do it, beautifully. I often do it, when Mrs.
Major doesn't come up,' Paul Muniment said, continuing
to thump his sister's couch in an appreciative but somewhat subversive manner.

'Oh, I have no doubt whatever!' Lady Aurora exclaimed, quickly. 'Mrs. Major must have so very much
to do.'

'Not in the making-up of beds, I'm afraid; there are
only two or three, down there, for so many,' Paul Muniment remarked loudly, and with a kind of incongruous
cheerfulness.

'Yes, I have thought a great deal about that. But
there wouldn't be room for more, you know,' said Lady
Aurora, this time in a very serious tone.

'There's not much room for a family of that sort anywhere—thirteen people of all ages and sizes,' the young
man rejoined. 'The world's pretty big, but there doesn't
seem room.'

'We are also thirteen at home,' said Lady Aurora,
laughing again. 'We are also rather crowded.'

'Surely you don't mean at Inglefield?' Rosy inquired eagerly, in her dusky nook.

'I don't know about Inglefield. I am so much in town.' Hyacinth could see that Inglefield was a subject she wished to turn off, and to do so she added, 'We too are of all ages and sizes.'

'Well, it's fortunate you are not all *your* size!' Paul Muniment exclaimed, with a freedom at which Hyacinth was rather shocked, and which led him to suspect that, though his new friend was a very fine fellow, a delicate tact was not his main characteristic. Later he explained this by the fact that he was rural and provincial, and had not had, like himself, the benefit of metropolitan culture ; and later still he asked himself what, after all, such a character as that had to do with tact or with compliments, and why its work in the world was not most properly performed by the simple exercise of a rude, manly strength.

At this familiar allusion to her stature Lady Aurora turned hither and thither, a little confusedly ; Hyacinth saw her high, lean figure sway to and fro in the dim little room. Her commotion carried her to the door, and with ejaculations of which it was difficult to guess the meaning she was about to depart, when Rosy detained her, having evidently much more social art than Paul. 'Don't you see it's only because her ladyship is standing up that she's so, you gawk? We are not thirteen, at any rate, and we have got all the furniture we want, so that there's a chair for every one. Do be seated again, Lady Aurora, and help me to entertain this gentleman. I don't know your name, sir ; perhaps my brother will mention it when he has collected his wits. I am very glad to see you, though I don't see you very well. Why shouldn't we light one of her ladyship's candles? It's very different to that common thing.'

Hyacinth thought Miss Muniment very charming : he had begun to make her out better by this time, and he watched her little wan, pointed face, framed, on the pillow, by thick black hair. She was a diminutive dark person, pale and wasted with a lifelong infirmity ; Hyacinth thought her manner denoted high cleverness—he judged it impos-

sible to tell her age. Lady Aurora said she ought to have
gone, long since; but she seated herself, nevertheless, on
the chair that Paul pushed towards her.

'Here's a go!' this young man exclaimed. 'You told
me your name, but I've clean forgotten it.' Then, when
Paul had announced it again, he said to his sister, 'That
won't tell you much; there are bushels of Robinsons in the
north. But you'll like him; he's a very smart little fellow;
I met him at the Poupins.' 'Puppin' would represent
the sound by which he designated the French bookbinder,
and that was the name by which Hyacinth always heard him
called at Mr. Crookenden's. Hyacinth knew how much
nearer to the right thing he himself came.

'Your name, like mine, represents a flower,' said the
little woman in the bed. 'Mine is Rose Muniment, and
her ladyship's is Aurora Langrish. That means the morning, or the dawn; it's the most beautiful of all, don't you
think so?' Rose Muniment addressed this inquiry to
Hyacinth, while Lady Aurora gazed at her shyly and
mutely, as if she admired her manner, her self-possession
and flow of conversation. Her brother lighted one of the
visitor's candles, and the girl went on, without waiting for
Hyacinth's response: 'Isn't it right that she should be
called the dawn, when she brings light where she goes?
The Puppins are the charming foreigners I have told you
about,' she explained to her friend.

'Oh, it's so pleasant knowing a few foreigners!' Lady
Aurora exclaimed, with a spasm of expression. 'They are
often so very fresh.'

'Mr. Robinson's a sort of foreigner, and he's very fresh,'
said Paul Muniment. 'He meets Mr. Puppin quite on
his own ground. If I had his command of the lingo it
would give me a lift.'

'I'm sure I should be very happy to help you with your
French. I feel the advantage of knowing it,' Hyacinth remarked, finely, and became conscious that his declaration
drew the attention of Lady Aurora towards him; so that he
wondered what he could go on to say, to keep at that level.
This was the first time he had encountered, socially, a
member of that aristocracy to which he had now for a good

while known it was Miss Pynsent's theory that he belonged; and the occasion was interesting, in spite of the lady's appearing to have so few of the qualities of her caste. She was about thirty years of age; her nose was large and, in spite of the sudden retreat of her chin, her face was long and lean. She had the manner of extreme near-sightedness; her front teeth projected from her upper gums, which she revealed when she smiled, and her fair hair, in tangled, silky skeins (Rose Muniment thought it too lovely), drooped over her pink cheeks. Her clothes looked as if she had worn them a good deal in the rain, and the note of a certain disrepair in her apparel was given by a hole in one of her black gloves, through which a white finger gleamed. She was plain and diffident, and she might have been poor; but in the fine grain and sloping, shrinking slimness of her whole person, the delicacy of her curious features, and a kind of cultivated quality in her sweet, vague, civil expression, there was a suggestion of race, of long transmission, of an organism highly evolved. She was not a common woman; she was one of the caprices of an aristocracy. Hyacinth did not define her in this manner to himself, but he received from her the impression that, though she was a simple creature (which he learned later she was not), aristocracies were complicated things. Lady Aurora remarked that there were many delightful books in French, and Hyacinth rejoined that it was a torment to know that (as he did, very well), when you didn't see your way to getting hold of them. This led Lady Aurora to say, after a moment's hesitation, that she had a good lot of her own and that if he liked she should be most happy to lend them to him. Hyacinth thanked her—thanked her even too much, and felt both the kindness and the brilliant promise of the offer (he knew the exasperation of having volumes in his hands, for external treatment, which he couldn't take home at night, having tried that system, surreptitiously, during his first weeks at Mr. Crookenden's and come very near losing his place in consequence), while he wondered how it could be put into practice—whether she would expect him to call at her house and wait in the hall till the books were sent out to him. Rose Muniment exclaimed that that was

her ladyship all over—always wanting to make up to people
for being less fortunate than herself: she would take the
shoes off her feet for any one that might take a fancy to
them. At this the visitor declared that she would stop
coming to see her, if the girl caught her up, that way, for
everything; and Rosy, without heeding this remonstrance,
explained to Hyacinth that she thought it the least she
could do to give what she had. She was so ashamed of
being rich that she wondered the lower classes didn't
break into Inglefield and take possession of all the
treasures in the Italian room. She was a tremendous
socialist; she was worse than any one—she was worse,
even, than Paul.

'I wonder if she is worse than me,' Hyacinth said,
at a venture, not understanding the allusions to Inglefield and the Italian room, which Miss Muniment made
as if she knew all about these places. After Hyacinth
knew more of the world he remembered this tone of
Muniment's sister (he was to have plenty of observation
of it on other occasions) as that of a person who was
in the habit of visiting the nobility at their country-seats;
she talked about Inglefield as if she had stayed there.

'Hullo, I didn't know you were so advanced!' exclaimed Paul Muniment, who had been sitting silent,
sidewise, in a chair that was too narrow for him, with his
big arm hugging the back. 'Have we been entertaining
an angel unawares?'

Hyacinth seemed to see that he was laughing at him,
but he knew the way to face that sort of thing was to
exaggerate his meaning. 'You didn't know I was advanced? Why, I thought that was the principal thing
about me. I think I go about as far as it is possible
to go.'

'I thought the principal thing about you was that you
knew French,' Paul Muniment said, with an air of derision
which showed Hyacinth that he wouldn't put that ridicule
upon him unless he liked him, at the same time that it
revealed to him that he himself had just been posturing
a little.

'Well, I don't know it for nothing. I'll say some-

thing very neat and sharp to you, if you don't look out
—just the sort of thing they say so much in French.'

'Oh, do say something of that kind; we should enjoy
it so much!' cried Rosy, in perfect good faith, clasping
her hands in expectation.

The appeal was embarrassing, but Hyacinth was
saved from the consequences of it by a remark from
Lady Aurora, who quavered out the words after two or
three false starts, appearing to address him, now that
she spoke to him directly, with a sort of overdone consideration. 'I should like so very much to know—it
would be so interesting—if you don't mind—how far
exactly you do go.' She threw back her head very far,
and thrust her shoulders forward, and if her chin had
been more adapted to such a purpose would have appeared
to point it at him.

This challenge was hardly less alarming than the other,
for Hyacinth was far from having ascertained the extent
of his advance. He replied, however, with an earnestness
with which he tried to make up as far as possible for his
vagueness : 'Well, I'm very strong indeed. I think I see
my way to conclusions, from which even Monsieur and
Madame Poupin would shrink. Poupin, at any rate; I'm
not so sure about his wife.'

'I should like so much to know Madame,' Lady
Aurora murmured, as if politeness demanded that she
should content herself with this answer.

'Oh, Puppin isn't strong,' said Muniment; 'you can
easily look over his head! He has a sweet assortment of
phrases—they are really pretty things to hear, some of
them; but he hasn't had a new idea these thirty years.
It's the old stock that has been withering in the window.
All the same, he warms one up; he has got a spark of the
sacred fire. The principal conclusion that Mr. Robinson
sees his way to,' he added to Lady Aurora, 'is that your
father ought to have his head chopped off and carried on
a pike.'

'Ah, yes, the French Revolution.'

'Lord, I don't know anything about your father, my
lady!' Hyacinth interposed.

'Didn't you ever hear of the Earl of Inglefield?' cried
Rose Muniment.

'He is one of the best,' said Lady Aurora, as if she
were pleading for him.

'Very likely, but he is a landlord, and he has an hereditary seat and a park of five thousand acres all to himself,
while we are bundled together into this sort of kennel.'
Hyacinth admired the young man's consistency until he
saw that he was chaffing; after which he still admired the
way he mixed up merriment with the tremendous opinions
our hero was sure he entertained. In his own imagination
Hyacinth associated bitterness with the revolutionary passion; but the young chemist, at the same time that he was
planning far ahead, seemed capable of turning revolutionists
themselves into ridicule, even for the entertainment of the
revolutionised.

'Well, I have told you often enough that I don't go
with you at all,' said Rose Muniment, whose recumbency
appeared not in the least to interfere with her sense of
responsibility. 'You'll make a tremendous mistake if you
try to turn everything round. There ought to be differences, and high and low, and there always will be, true as
ever I lie here. I think it's against everything, pulling
down them that's above.'

'Everything points to great changes in this country, but
if once our Rosy's against them, how can you be sure?
That's the only thing that makes me doubt,' her brother
went on, looking at her with a placidity which showed the
habit of indulgence.

'Well, I may be ill, but I ain't buried, and if I'm content with my position—such a position as it is—surely
other folk might be with theirs. Her ladyship may think
I'm as good as her, if she takes that notion; but she'll
have a deal to do to make *me* believe it.'

'I think you are much better than I, and I know very
few people so good as you,' Lady Aurora remarked, blushing, not for her opinions, but for her timidity. It was easy
to see that, though she was original, she would have liked
to be even more original than she was. She was conscious,
however, that such a declaration might appear rather gross

to persons who didn't see exactly how she meant it; so she added, as quickly as her hesitating manner permitted, to cover it up, 'You know there's one thing you ought to remember, *àpropos* of revolutions and changes and all that sort of thing; I just mention it because we were talking of some of the dreadful things that were done in France. If there were to be a great disturbance in this country—and of course one hopes there won't—it would be my impression that the people would behave in a different way altogether.'

'What people do you mean?' Hyacinth allowed himself to inquire.

'Oh, the upper class, the people that have got all the things.'

'We don't call them the people,' observed Hyacinth, reflecting the next instant that his remark was a little primitive.

'I suppose you call them the wretches, the villains!' Rose Muniment suggested, laughing merrily.

'All the things, but not all the brains,' her brother said.

'No, indeed, aren't they stupid?' exclaimed her ladyship. 'All the same, I don't think they would go abroad.'

'Go abroad?'

'I mean like the French nobles, who emigrated so much. They would stay at home and resist; they would make more of a fight. I think they would fight very hard.'

'I'm delighted to hear it, and I'm sure they would win!' cried Rosy.

'They wouldn't collapse, don't you know,' Lady Aurora continued. 'They would struggle till they were beaten.'

'And you think they would be beaten in the end?' Hyacinth asked.

'Oh dear, yes,' she replied, with a familiar brevity at which he was greatly surprised. 'But of course one hopes it won't happen.'

'I infer from what you say that they talk it over a good deal among themselves, to settle the line they will take,' said Paul Muniment.

But Rosy intruded before Lady Aurora could answer. 'I think it's wicked to talk it over, and I'm sure we haven't any business to talk it over here! When her ladyship says that the aristocracy will make a fine stand, I like to hear her say it, and I think she speaks in a manner that becomes her own position. But there is something else in her tone which, if I may be allowed to say so, I think a great mistake. If her ladyship expects, in case of the lower classes coming up in that odious manner, to be let off easily, for the sake of the concessions she may have made in advance, I would just advise her to save herself the disappointment and the trouble. They won't be a bit the wiser, and they won't either know or care. If they are going to trample over their betters, it isn't on account of her having seemed to give up everything to us here that they will let *her* off. They will trample on her just the same as on the others, and they'll say that she has got to pay for her title and her grand relations and her fine appearance. Therefore I advise her not to waste her good nature in trying to let herself down. When you're up so high as that you've got to stay there; and if Providence has made you a lady, the best thing you can do is to hold up your head. I can promise your ladyship *I* would!'

The close logic of this speech and the quaint self-possession with which the little bedridden speaker delivered it struck Hyacinth as amazing, and confirmed his idea that the brother and sister were a most extraordinary pair. It had a terrible effect upon poor Lady Aurora, by whom so stern a lesson from so humble a quarter had evidently not been expected, and who sought refuge from her confusion in a series of bewildered laughs, while Paul Muniment, with his humorous density, which was deliberate, and clever too, not seeing, or at any rate not heeding, that she had been sufficiently snubbed by his sister, inflicted a fresh humiliation by saying, 'Rosy's right, my lady. It's no use trying to buy yourself off. You can't do enough; your sacrifices don't count. You spoil your fun now, and you don't get it made up to you later. To all you people nothing will ever be made up. Enjoy your privileges while they last; it may not be for long.'

Lady Aurora listened to him with her eyes on his face; and as they rested there Hyacinth scarcely knew what to make of her expression. Afterwards he thought he could attach a meaning to it. She got up quickly when Muniment had ceased speaking; the movement suggested that she had taken offence, and he would have liked to show her that he thought she had been rather roughly used. But she gave him no chance, not glancing at him for a moment. Then he saw that he was mistaken and that, if she had flushed considerably, it was only with the excitement of pleasure, the enjoyment of such original talk and of seeing her friends at last as free and familiar as she wished them to be. 'You are the most delightful people—I wish every one could know you!' she broke out. 'But I must really be going.' She went to the bed, and bent over Rosy and kissed her.

'Paul will see you as far as you like on your way home,' this young woman remarked.

Lady Aurora protested against this, but Paul, without protesting in return, only took up his hat and looked at her, smiling, as if he knew his duty; upon which her ladyship said, 'Well, you may see me downstairs; I forgot it was so dark.'

'You must take her ladyship's own candle, and you must call a cab,' Rosy directed.

'Oh, I don't go in cabs. I walk.'

'Well, you may go on the top of a 'bus, if you like; you can't help being superb,' Miss Muniment declared, watching her sympathetically.

'Superb? Oh, mercy!' cried the poor devoted, grotesque lady, leaving the room with Paul, who asked Hyacinth to wait for him a little. She neglected to bid goodnight to our young man, and he asked himself what was to be hoped from that sort of people, when even the best of them—those that wished to be agreeable to the *demos*—reverted inevitably to the supercilious. She had said no more about lending him her books.

'SHE lives in Belgrave Square; she has ever so many
brothers and sisters; one of her sisters is married to Lord
Warmington,' Rose Muniment instantly began, not apparently in the least discomposed at being left alone with a
strange young man in a room which was now half dark
again, thanks to her brother's having carried off the second
and more brilliant candle. She was so interested, for the
time, in telling Hyacinth the history of Lady Aurora, that
she appeared not to remember how little she knew about
himself. Her ladyship had dedicated her life and her
pocket-money to the poor and sick; she cared nothing for
parties, and races, and dances, and picnics, and life in
great houses, the usual amusements of the aristocracy; she
was like one of the saints of old come to life again out of
a legend. She had made their acquaintance, Paul's and
hers, about a year before, through a friend of theirs, such
a fine, brave, young woman, who was in St. Thomas's
Hospital for a surgical operation. She had been laid up
there for weeks, during which Lady Aurora, always looking
out for those who couldn't help themselves, used to come
and talk to her and read to her, till the end of her time in
the ward, when the poor girl, parting with her kind friend,
told her how she knew of another unfortunate creature (for
whom there was no place there, because she was incurable),
who would be mighty thankful for any little attention of
that sort. She had given Lady Aurora the address in
Audley Court, and the very next day her ladyship had
knocked at their door. It wasn't because she was poor—
though in all conscience they were pinched enough—but
because she had so little satisfaction in her limbs. Lady
Aurora came very often, for several months, without meeting

Paul, because he was always at his work; but one day he
came home early, on purpose to find her, to thank her for
her goodness, and also to see (Miss Muniment rather shyly
intimated) whether she were really so good as his extravagant little sister made her out. Rosy had a triumph
after that : Paul had to admit that her ladyship was beyond
anything that any one in his waking senses would believe.
She seemed to want to give up everything to those who
were below her, and never to expect any thanks at all.
And she wasn't always preaching and showing you your
duty ; she wanted to talk to you sociable-like, as if you
were just her own sister. And *her* own sisters were the
highest in the land, and you might see her name in the
newspapers the day they were presented to the Queen.
Lady Aurora had been presented too, with feathers in her
head and a long tail to her gown ; but she had turned her
back upon it all with a kind of terror—a sort of shivering,
sinking feeling, which she had often described to Miss
Muniment. The day she had first seen Paul was the day
they became so intimate (the three of them together), if she
might apply such a word as that to such a peculiar connection. The little woman, the little girl, as she lay there
(Hyacinth scarcely knew how to characterise her), told our
young man a very great secret, in which he found himself
too much interested to think of criticising so headlong a
burst of confidence. The secret was that, of all the people
she had ever seen in the world, her ladyship thought Rosy's
Paul the very cleverest. And she had seen the greatest,
the most famous, the brightest of every kind, for they all
came to stay at Inglefield, thirty and forty of them at once.
She had talked with them all and heard them say their
best (and you could fancy how they would try to give it
out at such a place as that, where there was nearly a mile
of conservatories and a hundred wax candles were lighted
at a time), and at the end of it all she had made the
remark to herself—and she had made it to Rosy too—that
there was none of them had such a head on his shoulders
as the young man in Audley Court. Rosy wouldn't spread
such a rumour as that in the court itself, but she wanted
every friend of her brother's (and she could see Hyacinth

was that, by the way he listened) to know what was thought
of him by them that had an experience of talent. She
didn't wish to give it out that her ladyship had lowered
herself in any manner to a person that earned his bread in
a dirty shop (clever as he *might* be), but it was easy to see
she minded what he said as if he had been a bishop—or
more, indeed, for she didn't think much of bishops, any
more than Paul himself, and that was an idea she had got
from him. Oh, she took it none so ill if he came back
from his work before she had gone ; and to-night Hyacinth
could see for himself how she had lingered. This evening,
she was sure, her ladyship would let him walk home with
her half the way. This announcement gave Hyacinth the
prospect of a considerable session with his communicative
hostess ; but he was very glad to wait, for he was vaguely,
strangely excited by her talk, fascinated by the little queer-
smelling, high-perched interior, encumbered with relics,
treasured and polished, of a poor north-country home,
bedecked with penny ornaments and related in so unexpected a manner to Belgrave Square and the great landed
estates. He spent half an hour with Paul Muniment's
small, odd, crippled, chattering, clever, trenchant sister,
who gave him an impression of education and native wit
(she expressed herself far better than Pinnie, or than
Millicent Henning), and who startled, puzzled, and at the
same time rather distressed, him by the manner in which
she referred herself to the most abject class—the class that
prostrated itself, that was in a fever and flutter in the presence of its betters. That was Pinnie's attitude, of course ;
but Hyacinth had long ago perceived that his adoptive
mother had generations of plebeian patience in her blood,
and that though she had a tender soul she had not a
great one. He was more entertained than afflicted, however, by Miss Muniment's tone, and he was thrilled by the
frequency and familiarity of her allusions to a kind of life
he had often wondered about ; this was the first time he
had heard it described with that degree of authority. By
the nature of his mind he was perpetually, almost morbidly,
conscious that the circle in which he lived was an infinitesi-
mally small, shallow eddy in the roaring vortex of London,

and his imagination plunged again and again into the waves that whirled past it and round it, in the hope of being carried to some brighter, happier vision—the vision of societies in which, in splendid rooms, with smiles and soft voices, distinguished men, with women who were both proud and gentle, talked about art, literature and history. When Rosy had delivered herself to her complete satisfaction on the subject of Lady Aurora, she became more quiet, asking, as yet, however, no questions about Hyacinth, whom she seemed to take very much for granted. He presently remarked that she must let him come very soon again, and he added, to explain this wish, 'You know you seem to me very curious people.'

Miss Muniment did not in the least repudiate the imputation. 'Oh yes, I daresay we seem very curious. I think we are generally thought so; especially me, being so miserable and yet so lively.' And she laughed till her bed creaked again.

'Perhaps it's lucky you are ill; perhaps if you had your health you would be all over the place,' Hyacinth suggested. And he went on, candidly, 'I can't make it out, your being so up in everything.'

'I don't see why you need make it out! But you would, perhaps, if you had known my father and mother.'

'Were they such a rare lot?'

'I think you would say so if you had ever been in the mines. Yes, in the mines, where the filthy coal is dug out. That's where my father came from—he was working in the pit when he was a child of ten. He never had a day's schooling in his life; but he climbed up out of his black hole into daylight and air, and he invented a machine, and he married my mother, who came out of Durham, and (by her people) out of the pits and misery too. My father had no great figure, but *she* was magnificent—the finest woman in the country, and the bravest, and the best. She's in her grave now, and I couldn't go to look at it even if it were in the nearest churchyard. My father was as black as the coal he worked in: I know I'm just his pattern, barring that *he* did have his legs, when the liquor hadn't got into them. But between him and my mother, for grand,

high intelligence there wasn't much to choose.   But what's
the use of brains if you haven't got a backbone?   My
poor father had even less of that than I, for with me it's
only the body that can't stand up, and with him it was the
spirit.   He discovered a kind of wheel, and he sold it, at
Bradford, for fifteen pounds : I mean the whole right of it,
and every hope and pride of his family.   He was always
straying, and my mother was always bringing him back.
She had plenty to do, with me a puny, ailing brat from the
moment I opened my eyes.   Well, one night he strayed so
far that he never came back ; or only came back a loose,
bloody bundle of clothes.   He had fallen into a gravel-pit ;
he didn't know where he was going.   That's the reason my
brother will never touch so much as you could wet your
finger with, and that I only have a drop once a week or
so, in the way of a strengthener.   I take what her ladyship
brings me, but I take no more.   If she could have come
to us before my mother went, that would have been a
saving !   I was only nine when my father died, and I'm
three years older than Paul.   My mother did for us with
all her might, and she kept us decent—if such a useless
little mess as me can be said to be decent.   At any rate,
she kept me alive, and that's a proof she was handy.   She
went to the wash-tub, and she might have been a queen, as
she stood there with her bare arms in the foul linen and
her long hair braided on her head.   She was terrible handsome, but he would have been a bold man that would
have taken upon himself to tell her so.   And it was from
her we got our education—she was determined we should
rise above the common.   You might have thought, in her
position, that she couldn't go into such things ; but she
was a rare one for keeping you at your book.   She could
hold to her idea when my poor father couldn't ; and her
idea, for us, was that Paul should get learning and should
look after me.   You can see for yourself that that's what has
come about.   How he got it is more than I can say, as we
never had a penny to pay for it ; and of course my mother's
cleverness wouldn't have been of much use if he hadn't
been clever himself.   Well, it was all in the family.   Paul
was a boy that would learn more from a yellow placard

pasted on a wall, or a time-table at a railway station, than many a young fellow from a year at college. That was his only college, poor lad—picking up what he could. Mother was taken when she was still needed, nearly five years ago. There was an epidemic of typhoid, and of course it must pass me over, the goose of a thing—only that I'd have made a poor feast—and just lay that gallant creature on her back. Well, she never again made it ache over her soapsuds, straight and broad as it was. Not having seen her, you wouldn't believe,' said Rose Muniment, in conclusion; 'but I just wanted you to understand that our parents had intellect, at least, to give us.'

Hyacinth listened to this recital with the deepest interest, and without being in the least moved to allow for filial exaggeration; inasmuch as his impression of the brother and sister was such as it would have taken a much more marvellous tale to account for. The very way Rose Muniment sounded the word 'intellect' made him feel this; she pronounced it as if she were distributing prizes for a high degree of it. No doubt the tipsy inventor and the regal laundress had been fine specimens, but that didn't diminish the merit of their highly original offspring. The girl's insistence upon her mother's virtues (even now that her age had become more definite to him he thought of her as a girl) touched in his heart a chord that was always ready to throb—the chord of melancholy, bitter, aimless wonder as to the difference it would have made in *his* spirit if there had been some pure, honourable figure like that to shed her influence over it.

'Are you very fond of your brother?' he inquired, after a little.

The eyes of his hostess glittered at him for a moment. 'If you ever quarrel with him, you'll see whose side I'll take.'

'Ah, before that I shall make you like *me*.'

'That's very possible, and you'll see how I'll fling you over!'

'Why, then, do you object so to his views—his ideas about the way the people will come up?'

'Because I think he'll get over them.'

'Never—never!' cried Hyacinth. 'I have only known him an hour or two, but I deny that, with all my strength.'

'Is that the way you are going to make me like you—contradicting me so?' Miss Muniment inquired, with familiar archness.

'What's the use, when you tell me I shall be sacrificed? One might as well perish for a lamb as for a sheep.'

'I don't believe you're a lamb at all. Certainly you are not, if you want all the great people pulled down, and the most dreadful scenes enacted.'

'Don't you believe in human equality? Don't you want anything done for the groaning, toiling millions—those who have been cheated and crushed and bamboozled from the beginning of time?'

Hyacinth asked this question with considerable heat, but the effect of it was to send his companion off into a new fit of laughter. 'You say that just like a man that my brother described to me three days ago; a little man at some club, whose hair stood up—Paul imitated the way he glowered and screamed. I don't mean that you scream, you know; but you use almost the same words that he did.' Hyacinth scarcely knew what to make of this allusion, or of the picture offered to him of Paul Muniment casting ridicule upon those who spoke in the name of the down-trodden. But Rosy went on, before he had time to do more than reflect that there would evidently be a great deal more to learn about her brother: 'I haven't the least objection to seeing the people improved, but I don't want to see the aristocracy lowered an inch. I like so much to look at it up there.'

'You ought to know my aunt Pinnie—she's just such another benighted idolater!' Hyacinth exclaimed.

'Oh, you are making me like you very fast! And pray, who is your aunt Pinnie?'

'She's a dressmaker, and a charming little woman. I should like her to come and see you.'

'I'm afraid I'm not in her line—I never had on a dress in my life. But, as a charming woman, I should be delighted to see her.'

'I will bring her some day,' said Hyacinth. And then

he added, rather incongruously, for he was irritated by the
girl's optimism, thinking it a shame that her sharpness
should be enlisted on the wrong side, 'Don't you want, for
yourself, a better place to live in?'

She jerked herself up, and for a moment he thought she
would jump out of her bed at him. 'A better place than
this? Pray, how could there be a better place? Every
one thinks it's lovely; you should see our view by daylight
—you should see everything I've got. Perhaps you are
used to something very fine, but Lady Aurora says that in
all Belgrave Square there isn't such a cosy little room. If you
think I'm not perfectly content, you are very much mistaken!'

Such a sentiment as that could only exasperate Hyacinth,
and his exasperation made him indifferent to the fact that
he had appeared to cast discredit on Miss Muniment's
apartment. Pinnie herself, submissive as she was, had
spared him that sort of displeasure; she groaned over the
dinginess of Lomax Place sufficiently to remind him that
she had not been absolutely stultified by misery. 'Don't
you sometimes make your brother very angry?' he asked,
smiling, of Rose Muniment.

'Angry? I don't know what you take us for! I never
saw him lose his temper in his life.'

'He must be a rum customer! Doesn't he really care
for—for what we were talking about?'

For a moment Rosy was silent; then she replied, 'What
my brother really cares for—well, one of these days, when
you know, you'll tell me.'

Hyacinth stared. 'But isn't he tremendously deep
in——' He hesitated.

'Deep in what?'

'Well, in what's going on, beneath the surface. Doesn't
he belong to things?'

'I'm sure I don't know what he belongs to—you may
ask him!' cried Rosy, laughing gaily again, as the opening
door readmitted the subject of their conversation. 'You
must have crossed the water with her ladyship,' she went
on. 'I wonder who enjoyed their walk most.'

'She's a handy old girl, and she has a goodish stride,'
said the young man.

'I think she's in love with you, simply, Mr. Muniment.'

'Really, my dear, for an admirer of the aristocracy you allow yourself a license,' Paul murmured, smiling at Hyacinth.

Hyacinth got up, feeling that really he had paid a long visit; his curiosity was far from satisfied, but there was a limit to the time one should spend in a young lady's sleeping apartment. 'Perhaps she is; why not?' he remarked.

'Perhaps she is, then; she's daft enough for anything.'

'There have been fine folks before who have patted the people on the back and pretended to enter into their life,' Hyacinth said. 'Is she only playing with that idea, or is she in earnest?'

'In earnest—in terrible earnest, my dear fellow. I think she must be rather crowded out at home.'

'Crowded out of Inglefield? Why, there's room for three hundred!' Rosy broke in.

'Well, if that's the kind of mob that's in possession, no wonder she prefers Camberwell. We must be kind to the poor lady,' Paul added, in a tone which Hyacinth noticed. He attributed a remarkable meaning to it; it seemed to say that people such as he were now so sure of their game that they could afford to be magnanimous; or else it expressed a prevision of the doom which hung over her ladyship's head. Muniment asked if Hyacinth and Rosy had made friends, and the girl replied that Mr. Robinson had made himself very agreeable. 'Then you must tell me all about him after he goes, for you know I don't know him much myself,' said her brother.

'Oh yes, I'll tell you everything; you know how I like describing.'

Hyacinth was laughing to himself at the young lady's account of his efforts to please her, the fact being that he had only listened to her own eager discourse, without opening his mouth; but Paul, whether or no he guessed the truth, said to him very pertinently, 'It's very wonderful: she can describe things she has never seen. And they are just like the reality.'

'There's nothing I've never seen,' Rosy rejoined. 'That's

the advantage of my lying here in such a manner. I see everything in the world.'

'You don't seem to see your brother's meetings—his secret societies and clubs. You put that aside when I asked you.'

'Oh, you mustn't ask her that sort of thing,' said Paul, lowering at Hyacinth with a fierce frown—an expression which he perceived in a moment to be humorously assumed.

'What am I to do, then, since you won't tell me anything definite yourself?'

'It will be definite enough when you get hanged for it!' Rosy exclaimed, mockingly.

'Why do you want to poke your head into black holes?' Muniment asked, laying his hand on Hyacinth's shoulder, and shaking it gently.

'Don't you belong to the party of action?' said Hyacinth, solemnly.

'Look at the way he has picked up all the silly bits of catchwords!' Paul cried, laughing, to his sister. 'You must have got that precious phrase out of the newspapers, out of some drivelling leader. Is that the party you want to belong to?' he went on, with his clear eyes ranging over his diminutive friend.

'If you'll show me the thing itself I shall have no more occasion to mind the newspapers,' Hyacinth pleaded. It was his view of himself, and it was not an unfair one, that his was a character that would never beg for a favour; but now he felt that in any relation he might have with Paul Muniment such a law would be suspended. This man he could entreat, pray to, go on his knees to, without a sense of humiliation.

'What thing do you mean, infatuated, deluded youth?' Paul went on, refusing to be serious.

'Well, you know you do go to places you had far better keep out of, and that often when I lie here and listen to steps on the stairs I'm sure they are coming in to make a search for your papers,' Miss Muniment lucidly interposed.

'The day they find my papers, my dear, will be the day you'll get up and dance.'

'What did you ask me to come home with you for?'
Hyacinth demanded, twirling his hat.   It was an effort for
him, for a moment, to keep the tears out of his eyes; he
found himself forced to put such a different construction on
his new friend's hospitality.   He had had a happy impression that Muniment perceived in him a possible associate,
of a high type, in a subterranean crusade against the ex-
isting order of things, and now it came over him that the
real use he had been put to was to beguile an hour for a
pert invalid.   That was all very well, and he would sit by
Miss Rosy's bedside, were it a part of his service, every
day in the week; only in such a case it should be his
reward to enjoy the confidence of her brother.   This
young man, at the present juncture, justified the high
estimate that Lady Aurora Langrish had formed of his
intelligence: whatever his natural reply to Hyacinth's
question would have been, he invented, at the moment, a
better one, and said, at random, smiling, and not knowing
exactly what his visitor had meant,

'What did I ask you to come with me for?   To see if
you would be afraid.'

What there was to be afraid of was to Hyacinth a
quantity equally vague; but he rejoined, quickly enough,
'I think you have only to try me to see.'

'I'm sure if you introduce him to some of your low,
wicked friends, he'll be quite satisfied after he has looked
round a bit,' Miss Muniment remarked, irrepressibly.

'Those are just the kind of people I want to know,'
said Hyacinth, ingenuously.

His ingenuousness appeared to touch Paul Muniment.
'Well, I see you're a good 'un.   Just meet me some
night.'

'Where, where?' asked Hyacinth, eagerly.

'Oh, I'll tell you where when we get away from *her*,'
said his friend, laughing, but leading him out of the room
again.

X

SEVERAL months after Hyacinth had made the acquaintance of Paul Muniment, Millicent Henning remarked to
him that it was high time he should take her to some
place of amusement. He proposed the Canterbury Music
Hall; whereupon she tossed her head and affirmed that
when a young lady had done for a young man what she
had done for him, the least he could do was to take her to
some theatre in the Strand. Hyacinth would have been a
good deal at a loss to say exactly what she had done for
him, but it was familiar to him by this time that she regarded him as under great obligations. From the day she
came to look him up in Lomax Place she had taken a
position, largely, in his life, and he had seen poor Pinnie's
wan countenance grow several degrees more blank.
Amanda Pynsent's forebodings had been answered to the
letter; that bold-faced apparition had become a permanent
influence. She never spoke to him about Millicent but
once, several weeks after her interview with the girl; and
this was not in a tone of rebuke, for she had divested herself for ever of any maternal prerogative. Tearful, tremulous, deferential inquiry was now her only weapon, and
nothing could be more humble and circumspect than the
manner in which she made use of it. He was never at
home of an evening, at present, and he had mysterious
ways of spending his Sundays, with which church-going
had nothing to do. The time had been when, often,
after tea, he sat near the lamp with the dressmaker, and,
while her fingers flew, read out to her the works of Dickens
and of Scott; happy hours when he appeared to have
forgotten the wrong she had done him and she almost
forgot it herself. But now he gulped down his tea so fast

that he hardly took off his hat while he sat there, and
Pinnie, with her quick eye for all matters of costume,
noticed that he wore it still more gracefully askew than
usual, with a little victorious, exalted air. He hummed
to himself; he fingered his moustache; he looked out
of the window when there was nothing to look at; he
seemed pre-occupied, absorbed in intellectual excursions,
half anxious and half delighted. During the whole winter
Miss Pynsent explained everything by three words murmured beneath her breath: 'That forward jade!' On
the single occasion, however, on which she sought relief
from her agitation in an appeal to Hyacinth, she did not
trust herself to designate the girl by any epithet or title.

'There is only one thing I want to know,' she said to
him, in a manner which might have seemed casual if in
her silence, knowing her as well as he did, he had not
already perceived the implication of her thought. 'Does
she expect you to marry her, dearest?'

'Does who expect me?   I should like to see the
woman who does!'

'Of course you know who I mean.   The one that came
after you—and picked you right up—from the other end
of London.'   And at the remembrance of that insufferable
scene poor Pinnie flamed up for a moment.   'Isn't there
plenty of young fellows down in that low part where she
lives, without her ravaging over here?   Why can't she
stick to her own beat, I should like to know?'   Hyacinth
had flushed at this inquiry, and she saw something in his
face which made her change her tone.   'Just promise me
this, my precious child: that if you get into any sort of
mess with that piece you'll immediately confide it to your
poor old Pinnie.'

'My poor old Pinnie sometimes makes me quite sick,'
Hyacinth remarked, for answer.   'What sort of a mess do
you suppose I'll get into?'

'Well, suppose she does come it over you that you
promised to marry her?'

'You don't know what you're talking about.   She
doesn't want to marry any one to-day.'

'Then what does she want to do?'

'Do you imagine I would tell a lady's secrets?' the young man inquired.

'Dear me, if she was a lady, I shouldn't be afraid!' said Pinnie.

'Every woman's a lady when she has placed herself under one's protection,' Hyacinth rejoined, with his little manner of a man of the world.

'Under your protection? Laws!' cried Pinnie, staring. 'And pray, who's to protect *you*?'

As soon as she had said this she repented, because it seemed just the sort of exclamation that would have made Hyacinth bite her head off. One of the things she loved him for, however, was that he gave you touching surprises in this line, had sudden inconsistencies of temper that were all for your advantage. He was by no means always mild when he ought to have been, but he was sometimes so when there was no obligation. At such moments Pinnie wanted to kiss him, and she had often tried to make Mr. Vetch understand what a fascinating trait of character this was on the part of their young friend. It was rather difficult to describe, and Mr. Vetch never would admit that he understood, or that he had observed anything that seemed to correspond to the dressmaker's somewhat confused psychological sketch. It was a comfort to her in these days, and almost the only one she had, that she was sure Anastasius Vetch understood a good deal more than he felt bound to acknowledge. He was always up to his old game of being a great deal cleverer than cleverness itself required; and it consoled her present weak, pinched feeling to know that, although he still talked of the boy as if it would be a pity to take him too seriously, that wasn't the way he thought of him. He also took him seriously, and he had even a certain sense of duty in regard to him. Miss Pynsent went so far as to say to herself that the fiddler probably had savings, and that no one had ever known of any one else belonging to him. She wouldn't have mentioned it to Hyacinth for the world, for fear of leading up to a disappointment; but she had visions of a foolscap sheet, folded away in some queer little bachelor's box (she couldn't fancy what men kept in such places), on which Hyacinth's name would have been written down, in very big letters, before a solicitor.

'Oh, I'm unprotected, in the nature of things,' he replied, smiling at his too scrupulous companion. Then he added, 'At any rate, it isn't from that girl any danger will come to me.'

'I can't think why you like her,' Pinnie remarked, as if she had spent on the subject treasures of impartiality.

'It's jolly to hear one woman on the subject of another,' Hyacinth said. 'You're kind and good, and yet you're ready——' He gave a philosophic sigh.

'Well, what am I ready to do? I'm not ready to see you gobbled up before my eyes!'

'You needn't be afraid; she won't drag me to the altar.'

'And pray, doesn't she think you good enough—for one of the beautiful Hennings?'

'You don't understand, my poor Pinnie,' said Hyacinth, wearily. 'I sometimes think there isn't a single thing in life that you understand. One of these days she'll marry an alderman.'

'An alderman—that creature?'

'An alderman, or a banker, or a bishop, or some one of that kind. She doesn't want to end her career to-day; she wants to begin it.'

'Well, I wish she would take you later!' the dressmaker exclaimed.

Hyacinth said nothing for a moment; then he broke out: 'What are you afraid of? Look here, we had better clear this up, once for all. Are you afraid of my marrying a girl out of a shop?'

'Oh, you wouldn't, would you?' cried Pinnie, with a kind of conciliatory eagerness. 'That's the way I like to hear you talk!'

'Do you think I would marry any one who would marry me?' Hyacinth went on. 'The kind of girl who would look at me is the kind of girl I wouldn't look at.' He struck Pinnie as having thought it all out; which did not surprise her, as she had been familiar, from his youth, with his way of following things up. But she was always delighted when he made a remark which showed he was conscious of being of fine clay—flashed out an allusion to his not being what he seemed. He was not what he seemed, but even with Pinnie's valuable assistance he had not succeeded in representing to himself, very definitely, what he was. She had placed at his disposal, for this purpose, a passionate idealism which, employed in some case where it could have consequences, might have been termed profligate, and which never cost her a scruple or a compunction.

' I'm sure a princess might look at you and be none the worse !' she declared, in her delight at this assurance, more positive than any she had yet received, that he was safe from the worst danger. This the dressmaker considered to be the chance of his marrying some person like herself. Still it came over her that his taste might be lowered, and before the subject was dropped, on this occasion, she said to him that of course he must be quite aware of all that was wanting to such a girl as Millicent Henning—she pronounced her name at last.

' Oh, I don't bother about what's wanting to her; I'm content with what she has.'

'Content, dearest—how do you mean ?' the little dressmaker quavered. ' Content to make an intimate friend of her ?'

' It is impossible I should discuss these matters with you,' Hyacinth replied, grandly.

' Of course I see that. But I should think she would bore you sometimes,' Miss Pynsent murmured, cunningly.

' She does, I assure you, to extinction !'

' Then why do you spend every evening with her ?'

' Where should you like me to spend my evenings ? At some beastly public-house—or at the Italian opera ?' His association with Miss Henning was not so close as that, but nevertheless he wouldn't take the trouble to prove to poor Pinnie that he enjoyed her society only two or three times a week; that on other evenings he simply strolled about the streets (this boyish habit clung to him), and that he had even occasionally the resource of going to the Poupins', or of gossiping and smoking a pipe at some open house-door, when the night was not cold, with a fellow-mechanic. Later in the winter, after he had made Paul Muniment's acquaintance, the aspect of his life changed considerably, though Millicent continued to be exceedingly mixed up with it. He hated the taste of liquor and still more the taste of the places where it was sold; besides which the types of misery and vice that one was liable to see collected in them frightened and harrowed him, made him ask himself questions that pierced the deeper because they were met by no answer. It was both a blessing and a drawback to him that the delicate, charming character of the work he did at Mr. Crookenden's, under Eustace Poupin's influence, was a kind of education of the taste, trained him in the finest discriminations, in the perception of beauty and the hatred of ugliness. This made the brutal, garish, stodgy decoration of public-houses, with their deluge of gaslight, their glittering brass and pewter, their lumpish woodwork and false colours, detestable to him; he was still very young when the ' gin-palace' ceased to convey to him an idea of the palatial.

For this unfortunate but remarkably organised youth, every displeasure or gratification of the visual sense coloured his whole mind, and though he lived in Pentonville and worked in Soho, though he was poor and obscure and cramped and full of unattainable desires, it may be said of him that what was most important in life for him was simply his impressions. They came from everything he touched, they kept him thrilling and throbbing during a considerable part of his waking consciousness, and they constituted, as yet, the principal events and stages of his career. Fortunately, they were sometimes very delightful. Everything in the field of observation suggested this or that; everything struck him, penetrated, stirred; he had, in a word, more impressions than he knew what to do with— felt sometimes as if they would consume or asphyxiate him. He liked to talk about them, but it was only a few, here and there, that he could discuss with Millicent Henning. He let Miss Pynsent imagine that his hours of leisure were almost exclusively dedicated to this young lady, because, as he said to himself, if he were to account to her

for every evening in the week it would make no difference—she would stick to her suspicion; and he referred
this perversity to the general weight of misconception under
which (at this crude period of his growth) he held it was his
lot to languish.   It didn't matter to one whether one were
a little more or a little less misunderstood.   He might
have remembered that it mattered to Pinnie, who, after her
first relief at hearing him express himself so properly on the
subject of a matrimonial connection with Miss Henning,
allowed her faded, kind, weak face, little by little, to
lengthen out to its old solemnity.   This came as the days
went on, for it wasn't much comfort that he didn't want to
marry the young woman in Pimlico, when he allowed himself to be held as tight as if he did.   For the present,
indeed, she simply said, ' Oh, well, if you see her as she is,
I don't care what you do '—a sentiment implying a certain
moral recklessness on the part of the good little dressmaker.   She was irreproachable herself, but she had lived
for more than fifty years in a world of wickedness; like an
immense number of London women of her class and kind,
she had acquired a certain innocent cynicism, and she
judged it quite a minor evil that Millicent should be left
lamenting, if only Hyacinth might get out of the scrape.
Between a forsaken maiden and a premature, lowering
marriage for her beloved little boy, she very well knew
which she preferred.   It should be added that her impression of Millicent's power to take care of herself was such as
to make it absurd to pity her in advance.   Pinnie thought
Hyacinth the cleverest young man in the world, but her
state of mind implied somehow that the young lady in
Pimlico was cleverer.   Her ability, at any rate, was of a
kind that precluded the idea of suffering, whereas Hyacinth's
was rather associated with it.

    By the time he had enjoyed for three months the ac-
quaintance of the brother and sister in Audley Court the
whole complexion of his life seemed changed; it was pervaded by an interest, an excitement, which overshadowed,
though it by no means supplanted, the brilliant figure of
Miss Henning.   It was pitched in a higher key, altogether,
and appeared to command a view of horizons equally fresh

and vast.   Millicent, therefore, shared her dominion, without knowing exactly what it was that drew her old play-
fellow off, and without indeed demanding of him an account
which, on her own side, she was not prepared to give.
Hyacinth was, in the language of the circle in which she
moved, her fancy, and she was content to occupy, as regards
himself, the same graceful and somewhat irresponsible position.   She had an idea that she was a very beneficent
friend : fond of him and careful of him as an elder sister
might be ; warning him as no one else could do against the
dangers of the town ; putting that stiff common sense, of
which she was convinced that she possessed an extraordinary supply, at the service of his incurable verdancy ; and
looking after him, generally, as no one, poor child, had ever
done.   Millicent made light of the little dressmaker, in this
view of Hyacinth's past (she thought Pinnie no better than
a starved cat), and enjoyed herself immensely in the character of guide and philosopher, while she pushed the young
man with a robust elbow or said to him, ' Well, you *are* a
sharp one, you are ! '   Her theory of herself, as we know,
was that she was the sweetest girl in the world, as well as
the cleverest and handsomest, and there could be no better
proof of her kindness of heart than her disinterested affection for a snippet of a bookbinder.   Her sociability was
certainly great, and so were her vanity, her grossness, her
presumption, her appetite for beer, for buns, for entertainment of every kind.   She represented, for Hyacinth, during
this period, the eternal feminine, and his taste, considering
that he was fastidious, will be wondered at ; it will be
judged that she did not represent it very favourably.

It may easily be believed that he scrutinised his infatua-
tion even while he gave himself up to it, and that he often
wondered he should care for a girl in whom he found so
much to object to.   She was vulgar, clumsy and grotesquely
ignorant ; her conceit was proportionate, and she had not a
grain of tact or of quick perception.   And yet there was
something so fine about her, to his imagination, and she
carried with such an air the advantages she did possess,
that her figure constantly mingled itself even with those
bright visions that hovered before him after Paul Muniment

had opened a mysterious window. She was bold, and free, and generous, and if she was coarse she was neither false nor cruel. She laughed with the laugh of the people, and if you hit her hard enough she would cry with its tears. When Hyacinth was not letting his imagination wander among the haunts of the aristocracy, and fancying himself stretched in the shadow of an ancestral beech, reading the last number of the *Revue des Deux Mondes*, he was occupied with contemplations of a very different kind; he was absorbed in the struggles and sufferings of the millions whose life flowed in the same current as his, and who, though they constantly excited his disgust, and made him shrink and turn away, had the power to chain his sympathy, to make it glow to a kind of ecstasy, to convince him, for the time at least, that real success in the world would be to do something with them and for them. All this, strange to say, was never so vivid to him as when he was in Millicent's company; which is a proof of his fantastic, erratic way of seeing things. She had no such ideas about herself; they were almost the only ideas she didn't have. She had no theories about redeeming or uplifting the people; she simply loathed them, because they were so dirty, with the outspoken violence of one who had known poverty, and the strange bedfellows it makes, in a very different degree from Hyacinth, brought up, comparatively, with Pinnie to put sugar in his tea and keep him supplied with neckties, like a little swell.

Millicent, to hear her talk, only wanted to keep her skirts clear and marry some respectable tea-merchant. But for our hero she was magnificently plebeian, in the sense that implied a kind of loud recklessness of danger and the qualities that shine forth in a row. She summed up the sociable, humorous, ignorant chatter of the masses, their capacity for offensive and defensive passion, their instinctive perception of their strength on the day they should really exercise it; and as much as any of this, their ideal of something smug and prosperous, where washed hands, and plates in rows on dressers, and stuffed birds under glass, and family photographs, would symbolise success. She was none the less plucky for being at bottom a shameless Philistine, ambitious of a front-garden with rockwork ; and she presented the plebeian character in none the less plastic a form.   Having the history of the French Revolution at his fingers' ends, Hyacinth could easily see her (if there should ever be barricades in the streets of London), with a red cap of liberty on her head and her white throat bared so that she should be able to shout the louder the Marseillaise of that hour, whatever it might be. If the festival of the Goddess of Reason should ever be enacted in the British metropolis (and Hyacinth could consider such possibilities without a smile, so much was it a part of the little religion he had to remember, always, that there was no knowing what might happen)—if this solemnity, I say, should be revived in Hyde Park, who was better designated than Miss Henning to figure in a grand statuesque manner, as the heroine of the occasion ?   It was plain that she had laid her inconsequent admirer under a peculiar spell, since he could associate her with such scenes as that while she consumed beer and buns at his expense.   If she had a weakness, it was for prawns ; and she had, all winter, a plan for his taking her down to Gravesend, where this luxury was cheap and abundant, when the fine long days should arrive.   She was never so frank and facetious as when she dwelt on the details of a project of this kind ; and then Hyacinth was reminded afresh that it was an immense good fortune for her that she was handsome.   If she had been ugly he couldn't have listened to her ; but her beauty glorified even her accent, interfused her cockney genius with prismatic hues, gave her a large and constant impunity.

SHE desired at last to raise their common experience to a loftier level, to enjoy what she called a high-class treat. Their conversation was condemned, for the most part, to go forward in the streets, the wintry, dusky, foggy streets, which looked bigger and more numerous in their perpetual obscurity, and in which everything was covered with damp, gritty smut, an odour extremely agreeable to Miss Henning. Happily she shared Hyacinth's relish of vague perambulation, and was still more addicted than he to looking into the windows of shops, before which, in long, contemplative halts, she picked out freely the articles she shouldn't mind calling her own. Hyacinth always pronounced the objects of her selection hideous, and made no scruple to tell her that she had the worst taste of any girl in the place. Nothing that he could say to her affronted her so much, as her pretensions in the way of a cultivated judgment were boundless. Had not, indeed, her natural aptitude been fortified, in the neighbourhood of Buckingham Palace (there was scarcely anything they didn't sell in the great shop of which she was an ornament), by daily contact with the freshest products of modern industry? Hyacinth laughed this establishment to scorn, and told her there was nothing in it, from top to bottom, that a real artist would look at. She inquired, with answering derision, if this were a description of his own few inches; but in reality she was fascinated, as much as she was provoked, by his air of being difficult to please, of seeing indescribable differences among things. She had given herself out, originally, as very knowing, but he could make her feel stupid. When once in a while he pointed out a commodity that he condescended to like (this didn't happen

often, because the only shops in which there was a chance
of his making such a discovery were closed at nightfall),
she stared, bruised him more or less with her elbow, and
declared that if any one should give her such a piece of
rubbish she would sell it for fourpence.   Once or twice she
asked him to be so good as to explain to her in what its
superiority consisted—she could not rid herself of a suspicion that there might be something in his opinion, and
she was angry at not finding herself as positive as any one.
But Hyacinth replied that it was no use attempting to tell
her; she wouldn't understand, and she had better continue
to admire the insipid productions of an age which had lost
the sense of quality—a phrase which she remembered,
proposing to herself even to make use of it, on some
future occasion, but was quite unable to interpret.

When her companion demeaned himself in this manner
it was not with a view of strengthening the tie which united
him to his childhood's friend; but the effect followed, on
Millicent's side, and the girl was proud to think that she
was in possession of a young man whose knowledge was of
so high an order that it was inexpressible.   In spite of her
vanity she was not so convinced of her perfection as not
to be full of ungratified aspirations; she had an idea that
it might be to her advantage some day to exhibit a sample
of that learning; and at the same time, when, in consideration, for instance, of a jeweller's gas-lighted display in Great
Portland Street, Hyacinth lingered for five minutes in
perfect silence, while she delivered herself according to
her wont at such junctures, she was a thousand miles from
guessing the feelings which made it impossible for him to
speak.   She could long for things she was not likely to
have; envy other people for possessing them, and say it
was a regular shame (she called it a *shime*); draw brilliant
pictures of what she should do with them if she did have
them; and pass immediately, with a mind unencumbered
by superfluous inductions, to some other topic, equally
intimate and personal.   The sense of privation, with her,
was often extremely acute; but she could always put her
finger on the remedy.   With the imaginative, irresponsible
little bookbinder the case was very different; the remedy,

with him, was terribly vague and impracticable. He was liable to moods in which the sense of exclusion from all that he would have liked most to enjoy in life settled upon him like a pall. They had a bitterness, but they were not invidious—they were not moods of vengeance, of imaginary spoliation : they were simply states of paralysing melancholy, of infinite sad reflection, in which he felt that in this world of effort and suffering life was endurable, the spirit able to expand, only in the best conditions, and that a sordid struggle, in which one should go down to the grave without having tasted them, was not worth the misery it would cost, the dull demoralisation it would entail.

In such hours the great, roaring, indifferent world of London seemed to him a huge organisation for mocking at his poverty, at his inanition; and then its vulgarest ornaments, the windows of third-rate jewellers, the young man in a white tie and a crush-hat who dandled by, on his way to a dinner-party, in a hansom that nearly ran over one—these familiar phenomena became symbolic, insolent, defiant, took upon themselves to make him smart with the sense that *he* was out of it. He felt, moreover, that there was no con- solation or refutation in saying to himself that the immense majority of mankind were out of it with him, and appeared to put up well enough with the annoyance. That was their own affair ; he knew nothing of their reasons or their resignation, and if they chose neither to rebel nor to com- pare, he, at least, among the disinherited, would keep up the standard. When these fits were upon the young man, his brothers of the people fared, collectively, badly at his hands ; their function then was to represent in massive shape precisely the grovelling interests which attracted one's contempt, and the only acknowledgment one owed them was for the completeness of the illustration. Everything which, in a great city, could touch the sentient faculty of a youth on whom nothing was lost ministered to his convic- tion that there was no possible good fortune in life of too ' quiet ' an order for him to appreciate—no privilege, no opportunity, no luxury, to which he should not do justice. It was not so much that he wished to enjoy as that he wished to know; his desire was not to be pampered, but

to be initiated. Sometimes, of a Saturday, in the long
evenings of June and July, he made his way into Hyde
Park at the hour when the throng of carriages, of riders,
of brilliant pedestrians, was thickest; and though lately,
on two or three of these occasions, he had been accompanied by Miss Henning, whose criticism of the scene was
rich and distinct, a tremendous little drama had taken place,
privately, in his soul. He wanted to drive in every carriage,
to mount on every horse, to feel on his arm the hand of
every pretty woman in the place. In the midst of this his
sense was vivid that he belonged to the class whom the
upper ten thousand, as they passed, didn't so much as rest
their eyes upon for a quarter of a second. They looked
at Millicent, who was safe to be looked at anywhere, and
was one of the handsomest girls in any company, but they
only reminded him of the high human walls, the deep
gulfs of tradition, the steep embankments of privilege and
dense layers of stupidity, which fenced him off from social
recognition.

And this was not the fruit of a morbid vanity on his
part, or of a jealousy that could not be intelligent; his
personal discomfort was the result of an exquisite admiration
for what he had missed. There were individuals whom he
followed with his eyes, with his thoughts, sometimes even
with his steps; they seemed to tell him what it was to be
the flower of a high civilisation. At moments he was
aghast when he reflected that the cause he had secretly
espoused, the cause from which M. Poupin and Paul
Muniment (especially the latter) had within the last few
months drawn aside the curtain, proposed to itself to bring
about a state of things in which that particular scene would
be impossible. It made him even rather faint to think that
he must choose; that he couldn't (with any respect for his
own consistency) work, underground, for the enthronement
of the democracy, and continue to enjoy, in however
platonic a manner, a spectacle which rested on a hideous
social inequality. He must either suffer with the people,
as he had suffered before, or he must apologise to others,
as he sometimes came so near doing to himself, for the
rich; inasmuch as the day was certainly near when these

two mighty forces would come to a death-grapple. Hyacinth thought himself obliged, at present, to have reasons
for his feelings; his intimacy with Paul Muniment, which
had now grown very great, laid a good deal of that sort of
responsibility upon him. Muniment laughed at his reasons,
whenever he produced them, but he appeared to expect
him, nevertheless, to have them ready, on demand, and
Hyacinth had an immense desire to do what he expected.
There were times when he said to himself that it might
very well be his fate to be divided, to the point of torture, to be split open by sympathies that pulled him in
different ways; for hadn't he an extraordinarily mingled
current in his blood, and from the time he could remember
was there not one half of him that seemed to be always
playing tricks on the other, or getting snubs and pinches
from it?

That dim, dreadful, confused legend of his mother's
history, as regards which what Pinnie had been able to tell
him when he first began to question her was at once too
much and too little—this stupefying explanation had supplied him, first and last, with a hundred different theories
of his identity. What he knew, what he guessed, sickened
him, and what he didn't know tormented him; but in his
illuminated ignorance he had fashioned forth an article of
faith. This had gradually emerged from the depths of
darkness in which he found himself plunged as a consequence of the challenge he had addressed to Pinnie—while
he was still only a child—on the memorable day which
transformed the whole face of his future. It was one
January afternoon. He had come in from a walk; she
was seated at her lamp, as usual with her work, and she
began to tell him of a letter that one of the lodgers had
got, describing the manner in which his brother-in-law's
shop, at Nottingham, had been rifled by burglars. He
listened to her story, standing in front of her, and then, by
way of response, he said to her, 'Who was that woman you
took me to see ever so long ago?' The expression of her
white face, as she looked up at him, her fear of such an
attack all dormant, after so many years—her strange,
scared, sick glance was a thing he could never forget, any

more than the tone, with her breath failing her, in which she had repeated, 'That woman?'

'That woman, in the prison, years ago—how old was I? —who was dying, and who kissed me so—as I have never been kissed, as I never shall be again! Who *was* she, who WAS she?' Poor Pinnie, to do her justice, had made, after she recovered her breath, a gallant fight: it lasted a week; it was to leave her spent and sore for evermore, and before it was over Anastasius Vetch had been called in. At his instance she retracted the falsehoods with which she had tried to put him off, and she made, at last, a confession, a report, which he had reason to believe was as complete as her knowledge. Hyacinth could never have told you why the crisis occurred on such a day, why his question broke out at that particular moment. The strangeness of the matter to himself was that the germ of his curiosity should have developed so slowly; that the haunting wonder, which now, as he looked back, appeared to fill his whole childhood, should only after so long an interval have crept up to the air. It was only, of course, little by little that he had recovered his bearings in his new and more poignant consciousness; little by little that he reconstructed his antecedents, took the measure, so far as was possible, of his heredity. His having the courage to disinter, in the *Times*, in the reading-room of the British Museum, a report of his mother's trial for the murder of Lord Frederick Purvis, which was very copious, the affair having been quite a *cause célèbre;* his resolution in sitting under that splendid dome, and, with his head bent to hide his hot eyes, going through every syllable of the ghastly record, had been an achievement of comparatively recent years. There were certain things that Pinnie knew which appalled him; and there were others, as to which he would have given his hand to have some light, that it made his heart ache supremely to find she was honestly ignorant of. He scarcely knew what sort of favour Mr. Vetch wished to make with him (as a compensation for the precious part he had played in the business years before), when the fiddler permitted himself to pass judgment on the family of the wretched young nobleman for not having provided in some manner for the infant child of his assassin. Why should they have provided, when it was evident that they refused absolutely to recognise his lordship's responsibility? Pinnie had to admit this, under Hyacinth's terrible cross-questioning; she could not pretend, with any show of evidence, that Lord Whiteroy and the other brothers (there had been no less than seven, most of them still living) had, at the time of the trial, given any symptom of believing Florentine Vivier's asseverations. That was their affair; he had long since made up his mind that his own was very different. One couldn't believe at will, and fortunately, in the case, he had no effort to make; for from the moment he began to consider the established facts (few as they were, and poor and hideous) he regarded himself, irresistibly, as the son of the recreant, sacrificial Lord Frederick.

He had no need to reason about it; all his nerves and pulses pleaded and testified. His mother had been a daughter of the wild French people (all that Pinnie could tell him of her parentage was that Florentine had once mentioned that in her extreme childhood her father had fallen, in the blood-stained streets of Paris, on a barricade, with his gun in his hand); but on the other side it took an English aristocrat—though a poor specimen, apparently, had to suffice—to account for him. This, with its further implications, became Hyacinth's article of faith; the reflection that he was a bastard involved in a remarkable manner the reflection that he was a gentleman. He was conscious that he didn't hate the image of his father, as he might have been expected to do; and he supposed this was because Lord Frederick had paid so tremendous a penalty. It was in the exaction of that penalty that the moral proof, for Hyacinth, resided; his mother would not have armed herself on account of any injury less cruel than the episode of which her miserable baby was the living sign. She had avenged herself because she had been thrown over, and the bitterness of that wrong had been in the fact that he, Hyacinth, lay there in her lap. *He* was the one to have been killed: that remark our young man often made to himself. That his attitude on this whole subject was of a tolerably exalted, transcendent character, and took little account of any refutation that might be based on a vulgar glance at three or four obtrusive items, is proved by the importance that he attached, for instance, to the name by which his mother had told poor Pinnie (when this excellent creature consented to take him) that she wished him to be called. Hyacinth had been the name of her father, a republican clockmaker, the martyr of his opinions, whose memory she professed to worship; and when Lord Frederick insinuated himself into her confidence he had reasons for preferring to be known as plain Mr. Robinson—reasons, however, which, in spite of the light thrown upon them at the trial, it was difficult, after so many years, to enter into.

Hyacinth never knew that Mr. Vetch had said more than once to Pinnie, ' If her contention as regards that dissolute young swell was true, why didn't she make the child bear his real name, instead of his false one ?'—an inquiry which the dressmaker answered with some ingenuity, by remarking that she couldn't call him after a man she had murdered, and that she supposed the unhappy girl didn't wish to publish to every one the boy's connection with a crime that had been so much talked about. If Hyacinth had assisted at this little discussion it is needless to say that he would have sided with Miss Pynsent; though that his judgment was independently formed is proved by the fact that Pinnie's fearfully indiscreet attempts at condolence should not have made him throw up his version in disgust. It was after the complete revelation that he understood the romantic. innuendoes with which his childhood had been surrounded, and of which he had never caught the meaning; they having seemed but part and parcel of the habitual and promiscuous divagations of his too constructive companion. When it came over him that, for years, she had made a fool of him, to himself and to others, he could have beaten her, for grief and shame; and yet, before he administered this rebuke he had to remember that she only chattered (though she professed to have been extraordinarily dumb) about a matter which he spent nine-tenths of his time in brooding over. When she tried to console him for the horror of his mother's history by des-

canting on the glory of the Purvises, and reminding him
that he was related, through them, to half the aristocracy
of England, he felt that she was turning the tragedy of his
life into a monstrous farce ; and yet he none the less continued to cherish the belief that he was a gentleman born.
He allowed her to tell him nothing about the family in
question, and his stoicism on this subject was one of the
reasons of the deep dejection of her later years. If he
had only let her idealise him a little to himself she would
have felt that she was making up, by so much, for her
grand mistake. He sometimes saw the name of his
father's relations in the newspaper, but he always turned
away his eyes from it. He had nothing to ask of them,
and he wished to prove to himself that he could ignore
them (who had been willing to let him die like a rat) as
completely as they ignored him. Decidedly, he cried to
himself at times, he was with the people, and every possible vengeance of the people, as against such shameless
egoism as that ; but all the same he was happy to feel
that he had blood in his veins which would account for the
finest sensibilities.

He had no money to pay for places at a theatre in the
Strand ; Millicent Henning having made it clear to him
that on this occasion she expected something better than
the pit. 'Should you like the royal box, or a couple of
stalls at ten shillings apiece?' he asked of her, with a
frankness of irony which, with this young lady, fortunately,
it was perfectly possible to practise. She had answered
that she would content herself with a seat in the second
balcony, in the very front ; and as such a position involved an expenditure which he was still unable to meet,
he waited one night upon Mr. Vetch, to whom he had
already, more than once, had recourse in moments of
pecuniary embarrassment. His relations with the caustic
fiddler were peculiar ; they were much better in fact than
they were in theory. Mr. Vetch had let him know—long
before this, and with the purpose of covering Pinnie to the
utmost—the part he had played when the question of the
child's being taken to Mrs. Bowerbank's institution was so
distressingly presented ; and Hyacinth, in the face of this

information, had inquired, with some sublimity, what the
devil the fiddler had to do with his private affairs. Anastasius Vetch had replied that it was not as an affair of his,
but as an affair of Pinnie's, that he had considered the
matter; and Hyacinth afterwards had let the question
drop, though he had never been formally reconciled to
his officious neighbour. Of course his feeling about him
had been immensely modified by the trouble Mr. Vetch
had taken to get him a place with old Crookenden; and
at the period of which I write it had long been familiar to
him that the fiddler didn't care a straw what he thought of
his advice at the famous crisis, and entertained himself
with watching the career of a youth put together of such
queer pieces. It was impossible to Hyacinth not to perceive that the old man's interest was kindly; and to-day,
at any rate, our hero would have declared that nothing
could have made up to him for not knowing the truth,
horrible as the truth might be. His miserable mother's
embrace seemed to furnish him with an inexhaustible fund
of motive, and under the circumstances that was a benefit. What he chiefly objected to in Mr. Vetch was a
certain air of still regarding him as extremely juvenile; he
would have got on with him much better if the fiddler had
consented to recognise the degree in which he was already
a man of the world. Vetch knew an immense deal about
society, and he seemed to know the more because he never
swaggered—it was only little by little you discovered it;
but that was no reason for his looking as if his chief
entertainment resided in a private, diverting commentary
on the conversation of his young friend. Hyacinth felt
that he himself gave considerable evidence of liking his
fellow-resident in Lomax Place when he asked him to lend
him half-a-crown. Somehow, circumstances, of old, had
tied them together, and though this partly vexed the little
bookbinder it also touched him; he had more than once
solved the problem of deciding how to behave (when the
fiddler exasperated him) by simply asking him some service. The old man had never refused. It was satisfactory
to Hyacinth to remember this, as he knocked at his door,
very late, after he had allowed him time to come home

from the theatre. He knew his habits : Mr. Vetch never went straight to bed, but sat by his fire an hour, smoking his pipe, mixing a grog, and reading some old book. Hyacinth knew when to go up by the light in his window, which he could see from a court behind.

'Oh, I know I haven't been to see you for a long time,' he said, in response to the remark with which the fiddler greeted him; 'and I may as well tell you immediately what has brought me at present—in addition to the desire to ask after your health. I want to take a young lady to the theatre.'

Mr. Vetch was habited in a tattered dressing-gown ; his apartment smelt strongly of the liquor he was consuming. Divested of his evening-gear he looked to our hero so plucked and blighted that on the spot Hyacinth ceased to hesitate as to his claims in the event of a social liquidation ; he, too, was unmistakably a creditor. 'I'm afraid you find· your young lady rather expensive.'

'I find everything expensive,' said Hyacinth, as if to finish that subject.

'Especially, I suppose, your secret societies.'

'What do you mean by that ?' the young man asked, staring.

'Why, you told me, in the autumn, that you were just about to join a few.'

'A few ? How many do you suppose ?' And Hyacinth checked himself. 'Do you suppose if I had been serious I would tell ?'

'Oh dear, oh dear,' Mr. Vetch murmured, with a sigh. Then he went on : 'You want to take her to my shop, eh ?'

'I'm sorry to say she won't go there. She wants something in the Strand : that's a great point. She wants very much to see the *Pearl of Paraguay*. I don't wish to pay anything, if possible ; I am sorry to say I haven't a penny. But as you know people at the other theatres, and I have heard you say that you do each other little favours, from place to place—*à charge de revanche*, as the French say— it occurred to me that you might be able to get me an order. The piece has been running a long time, and most people (except poor devils like me) must have seen it : therefore there probably isn't a rush.'

Mr. Vetch listened in silence, and presently he said, ' Do you want a box ? '

' Oh no ; something more modest.'

' Why not a box ? ' asked the fiddler, in a tone which Hyacinth knew.

' Because I haven't got the clothes that people wear in that sort of place, if you must have such a definite reason.'

' And your young lady—has she got the clothes ? '

' Oh, I daresay ; she seems to have everything.'

' Where does she get them ? '

' Oh, I don't know. She belongs to a big shop ; she has to be fine.'

' Won't you have a pipe ? ' Mr. Vetch asked, pushing an old tobacco-pouch across the table to his visitor ; and while the young man helped himself he puffed a while in silence. ' What will she do with you ? ' he inquired at last.

' What will who do with me ? '

' Your big beauty—Miss Henning. I know all about her from Pinnie.'

' Then you know what she'll do with me ! ' Hyacinth returned, with rather a scornful laugh.

' Yes, but, after all, it doesn't very much matter.'

' I don't know what you are talking about,' said Hyacinth.

' Well, now the other matter—the International—are you very deep in that ? ' the fiddler went on, as if he had not heard him.

' Did Pinnie tell you also about that ? ' his visitor asked.

' No, our friend Eustace has told me a good deal. He knows you have put your head into something. Besides, I see it,' said Mr. Vetch.

' How do you see it, pray ? '

' You have got such a speaking eye. Any one can tell, to look at you, that you have become a nihilist, that you're a member of a secret society. You seem to say to every one, " Slow torture won't induce me to tell where it meets ! " '

'You won't get me an order, then?' Hyacinth said, in a moment.

'My dear boy, I offer you a box. I take the greatest interest in you.'

They smoked together a while, and at last Hyacinth remarked, 'It has nothing to do with the International.'

'Is it more terrible—more deadly secret?' his companion inquired, looking at him with extreme seriousness.

'I thought you pretended to be a radical,' answered Hyacinth.

'Well, so I am—of the old-fashioned, constitutional, milk-and-water, jog-trot sort. I'm not an exterminator.'

'We don't know what we may be when the time comes,' Hyacinth rejoined, more sententiously than he intended.

'Is the time coming, then, my dear boy?'

'I don't think I have a right to give you any more of a warning than that,' said our hero, smiling.

'It's very kind of you to do so much, I'm sure, and to rush in here at the small hours for the purpose. Meanwhile, in the few weeks, or months, or years, or whatever they are, that are left, you wish to put in as much enjoyment as you can squeeze, with the young ladies : that's a very natural inclination.' Then, irrelevantly, Mr. Vetch inquired, 'Do you see many foreigners?'

'Yes, I see a good many.'

'And what do you think of them?'

'Oh, all sorts of things. I rather like Englishmen better.'

'Mr. Muniment, for example?'

'I say, what do you know about him?' Hyacinth asked.

'I've seen him at Eustace's. I know that you and he are as thick as thieves.'

'He will distinguish himself some day, very much,' said Hyacinth, who was perfectly willing, and indeed very proud, to be thought a close ally of the chemist's assistant.

'Very likely—very likely. And what will *he* do with you?' the fiddler inquired.

Hyacinth got up; the two men looked at each other

for an instant. 'Do get me two good places in the second balcony,' said Hyacinth.

Mr. Vetch replied that he would do what he could, and three days afterwards he gave the coveted order to his young friend. As he placed it in his hands he exclaimed, 'You had better put in all the fun you can, you know!'

BOOK SECOND

Hyacinth and his companion took their seats with extreme
promptitude before the curtain rose upon the *Pearl of
Paraguay.* Thanks to Millicent's eagerness not to be late
they encountered the discomfort which had constituted her
main objection to going into the pit : they waited for twenty
minutes at the door of the theatre, in a tight, stolid crowd,
before the official hour of opening. Millicent, bareheaded
and very tightly laced, presented a most splendid appearance and, on Hyacinth's part, gratified a certain youthful,
ingenuous pride of possession in every respect save a
tendency, while ingress was denied them, to make her
neighbours feel her elbows and to comment, loudly and
sarcastically, on the situation. It was more clear to him
even than it had been before that she was a young lady who
in public places might easily need a champion or an
apologist. Hyacinth knew there was only one way to
apologise for a ' female,' when the female was attached very
closely and heavily to one's arm, and was reminded afresh
how little constitutional aversion Miss Henning had to a
row. He had an idea she might think his own taste ran
even too little in that direction, and had visions of violent,
confused scenes, in which he should in some way distinguish
himself : he scarcely knew in what way, and imagined himself more easily routing some hulking adversary by an
exquisite application of the retort courteous than by flying
at him with a pair of very small fists.

By the time they had reached their places in the balcony
Millicent was rather flushed and a good deal ruffled ; but
she had composed herself in season for the rising of the curtain
upon the farce which preceded the melodrama and which
the pair had had no intention of losing. At this stage a

more genial agitation took possession of her, and she
surrendered her sympathies to the horse-play of the
traditional prelude.   Hyacinth found it less amusing, but
the theatre, in any conditions, was full of sweet deception for
him.   His imagination projected itself lovingly across the
footlights, gilded and coloured the shabby canvas and
battered accessories, and lost itself so effectually in the
fictive world that the end of the piece, however long, or
however short, brought with it a kind of alarm, like a
stoppage of his personal life.   It was impossible to be more
friendly to the dramatic illusion.   Millicent, as the audience
thickened, rejoiced more largely and loudly, held herself as
a lady, surveyed the place as if she knew all about it, leaned
back and leaned forward, fanned herself with majesty, gave
her opinion upon the appearance and coiffure of every
woman within sight, abounded in question and conjecture,
and produced from her pocket, a little paper of peppermint-
drops, of which, under cruel threats, she compelled Hyacinth
to partake.   She followed with attention, though not always
with success, the complicated adventures of the Pearl of
Paraguay, through scenes luxuriantly tropical, in which the
male characters wore sombreros and stilettos, and the ladies
either danced the cachucha or fled from licentious pursuit ;
but her eyes wandered, during considerable periods, to the
occupants of the boxes and stalls, concerning several of
whom she had theories which she imparted to Hyacinth
while the play went on, greatly to his discomfiture, he being
unable to conceive of such levity.   She had the pretension
of knowing who every one was ; not individually and by
name, but as regards their exact social station, the quarter
of London in which they lived, and the amount of money
they were prepared to spend in the neighbourhood of
Buckingham Palace.   She had seen the whole town pass
through her establishment there, and though Hyacinth,
from his infancy, had been watching it from his own point
of view, his companion made him feel that he had missed a
thousand characteristic points, so different were most of her
interpretations from his, and so very bold and irreverent.
Miss Henning's observation of human society had not been
of a nature to impress her with its high moral tone, and she

had a free off-hand cynicism which imposed itself. She thought most ladies were hypocrites, and had, in all ways, a low opinion of her own sex, which, more than once, before this, she had justified to Hyacinth by narrating observations of the most surprising kind, gathered during her career as a shop-girl. There was a pleasing inconsequence, therefore, in her being moved to tears in the third act of the play, when the Pearl of Paraguay, dishevelled and distracted, dragging herself on her knees, implored the stern hidalgo her father, to believe in her innocence in spite of the circumstances which seemed to condemn her—a midnight meeting with the wicked hero in the grove of cocoanuts. It was at this crisis, none the less, that she asked Hyacinth who his friends were in the principal box on the left of the stage, and let him know that a gentleman seated there had been watching him, at intervals, for the past half hour.

'Watching *me!* I like that!' said the young man. 'When I want to be watched I take you with me.'

'Of course he has looked at me,' Millicent answered, as if she had no interest in denying that. 'But you're the one he wants to get hold of.'

'To get hold of!'

'Yes, you ninny : don't hang back. He may make your fortune.'

'Well, if you would like him to come and sit by you I'll go and take a walk in the Strand,' said Hyacinth, entering into the humour of the occasion but not seeing, from where he was placed, any gentleman in the box. Millicent explained that the mysterious observer had just altered his position ; he had gone into the back of the box, which had considerable depth. There were other persons in it, out of sight ; she and Hyacinth were too much on the same side. One of them was a lady, concealed by the curtain ; her arm, bare save for its bracelets, was visible at moments on the cushioned ledge. Hyacinth saw it, in effect, reappear there, and even while the play went on contemplated it with a certain interest ; but until the curtain fell at the end of the act there was no further symptom that a gentleman wished to get hold of him.

'Now do you say it's me he's after?' Millicent asked

abruptly, giving him a sidelong dig, as the fiddlers in the orchestra began to scrape their instruments for the interlude.

'Of course; I am only the pretext,' Hyacinth replied, after he had looked a moment, in a manner which he flattered himself was a proof of quick self-possession. The gentleman designated by his companion was once more at the front, leaning forward, with his arms on the edge. Hyacinth saw that he was looking straight at him, and our young man returned his gaze—an effort not rendered the more easy by the fact that, after an instant, he recognised him.

'Well, if he knows us he might give some sign, and if he doesn't he might leave us alone,' Millicent declared, abandoning the distinction she had made between herself and her companion. She had no sooner spoken than the gentleman complied with the first mentioned of these con- ditions; he smiled at Hyacinth across the house—he nodded to him with unmistakable friendliness. Millicent, perceiving this, glanced at the young man from Lomax Place and saw that the demonstration had brought a deep colour to his cheek. He was blushing, flushing; whether with pleasure or embarrassment was not immediately apparent to her. 'I say, I say—is it one of your grand relations?' she promptly exclaimed. 'Well, I can stare as well as him;' and she told Hyacinth it was a 'shime' to bring a young lady to the play when you hadn't so much as an opera-glass for her to look at the company. 'Is he one of those lords your aunt was always talking about in the Plice? Is he your uncle, or your grandfather, or your first or second cousin? No, he's too young for your grand- father. What a pity I can't see if he looks like you!'

At any other time Hyacinth would have thought these inquiries in the worst possible taste, but now he was too much given up to other reflections. It pleased him that the gentleman in the box should recognise and notice him, because even so small a fact as this was an extension of his social existence; but it also surprised and puzzled him, and it produced, generally, in his easily-excited organism, an agitation of which, in spite of his attempted self-control, the appearance he presented to Millicent was the sign.

They had met three times, he and his fellow-spectator; but they had met under circumstances which, to Hyacinth's mind, would have made a furtive wink, a mere tremor of the eyelid, a more judicious reference to the fact than so public a salutation. Hyacinth would never have permitted himself to greet him first; and this was not because the gentleman in the box belonged—conspicuously as he did so—to a different walk of society. He was apparently a man of forty, tall and lean and loose-jointed; he fell into lounging, dawdling attitudes, and even at a distance he looked lazy. He had a long, smooth, amused, contented face, unadorned with moustache or whisker, and his brown hair parted itself evenly over his forehead, and came forward on either temple in a rich, well-brushed lock which gave his countenance a certain analogy to portraits of English gentlemen about the year 1820. Millicent Henning had a glance of such range and keenness that she was able to make out the details of his evening-dress, of which she appreciated the ' form '; to observe the character of his large hands; and to note that he appeared to be perpetually smiling, that his eyes were extraordinarily light in colour, and that in spite of the dark, well-marked brows arching over them, his fine skin never had produced, and never would produce, a beard. Our young lady pronounced him mentally a ' swell ' of the first magnitude, and wondered more than ever where he had picked up Hyacinth. Her companion seemed to echo her thought when he exclaimed, with a little surprised sigh, almost an exhalation of awe, ' Well, I had no idea he was one of that lot ! '

' You might at least tell me his name, so that I shall know what to call him when he comes round to speak to us,' the girl said, provoked at her companion's incommunicativeness.

' Comes round to speak to us—a chap like that ! ' Hyacinth exclaimed.

' Well, I'm sure if he had been your own brother he couldn't have grinned at you more ! He may want to make my acquaintance after all ; he won't be the first.'

The gentleman had once more retreated from sight, and there was as much evidence as that of the intention

Millicent attributed to him. 'I don't think I'm at all clear that I have a right to tell his name,' he remarked, with sincerity, but with a considerable disposition at the same time to magnify an incident which deepened the brilliancy of the entertainment he had been able to offer Miss Henning. 'I met him in a place where he may not like to have it known that he goes.'

'Do you go to places that people are ashamed of? Is it one of your political clubs, as you call them, where that dirty young man from Camberwell, Mr. Monument (what do you call him?) fills your head with ideas that'll bring you to no good? I'm sure your friend over there doesn't look as if he'd be on *your* side.'

Hyacinth had indulged in this reflection himself; but the only answer he made to Millicent was, 'Well, then, perhaps he'll be on yours!'

'Laws, I hope *she* ain't one of the aristocracy!' Millicent exclaimed, with apparent irrelevance; and following the direction of her eyes Hyacinth saw that the chair his mysterious acquaintance had quitted in the stage-box was now occupied by a lady hitherto invisible—not the one who had given them a glimpse of her shoulder and bare arm. This was an ancient personage, muffled in a voluminous, crumpled white shawl—a stout, odd, foreign-looking woman, whose head apparently was surmounted with a light-coloured wig. She had a placid, patient air and a round, wrinkled face, in which, however, a small, bright eye moved quickly enough. Her rather soiled white gloves were too large for her, and round her head, horizontally arranged, as if to keep her wig in its place, she wore a narrow band of tinsel, decorated, in the middle of the forehead, by a jewel which the rest of her appearance would lead the spectator to suppose false. 'Is the old woman his mother? Where did she dig up her clothes? They look as if she had hired them for the evening. Does *she* come to your wonderful club, too? I daresay she cuts it fine, don't she?' Millicent went on; and when Hyacinth suggested, sportively, that the old lady might be, not the gentleman's mother, but his wife or his 'fancy,' she declared that in that case, if he should come to see them, she wasn't

afraid.   No wonder he wanted to get out of *that* box !   The
woman in the wig was sitting there on purpose to look at
them, but she couldn't say she was particularly honoured
by the notice of such an old guy.   Hyacinth pretended
that he liked her appearance and thought her very handsome ; he offered to bet another paper of peppermints that
if they could find out she would be some tremendous old
dowager, some one with a handle to her name.   To this
Millicent replied, with an air of experience, that she had
never thought the greatest beauty was in the upper class ;
and her companion could see that she was covertly looking
over her shoulder to watch for his political friend and that
she would be disappointed if he did not come.   This idea
did not make Hyacinth jealous, for his mind was occupied
with another side of the business ; and if he offered sportive
suggestions it was because he was really excited, dazzled,
by an incident of which the reader will have failed as yet
to perceive the larger relations.   What moved him was not
the pleasure of being patronised by a rich man ; it was
simply the prospect of new experience—a sensation for
which he was always ready to exchange any present boon ;
and he was convinced that if the gentleman with whom he
had conversed in a small occult back-room in Bloomsbury
as Captain Godfrey Sholto—the Captain had given him his
card—had more positively than in Millicent's imagination
come out of the stage-box to see him, he would bring with
him rare influences.   This nervous presentiment, lighting on
our young man, was so keen that it constituted almost a pre-
paration ; therefore, when at the end of a few minutes he
became aware that Millicent, with her head turned (her
face was in his direction), was taking the measure of some
one who had come in behind them, he felt that fate was
doing for him, by way of a change, as much as could be
expected.   He got up in his place, but not too soon to
see that Captain Sholto had been standing there a moment
in contemplation of Millicent, and that this young lady
had performed with deliberation the ceremony of taking his
measure.   The Captain had his hands in his pockets, and
wore a crush-hat, pushed a good deal backward.   He
laughed at the young couple in the balcony in the friend-

liest way, as if he had known them both for years, and Millicent could see, on a nearer view, that he was a fine distinguished, easy, genial gentleman, at least six feet high, in spite of a habit, or an affectation, of carrying himself in a casual, relaxed, familiar manner. Hyacinth felt a little, after the first moment, as if he were treating them rather too much as a pair of children whom he had stolen upon, to startle ; but this impression was speedily removed by the air with which he said, laying his hand on our hero's shoulder as he stood in the little passage at the end of the bench where the holders of Mr. Vetch's order occupied the first seats, ' My dear fellow, I really thought I must come round and speak to you. My spirits are all gone with this brute of a play. And those boxes are fearfully stuffy, you know,' he added, as if Hyacinth had had at least an equal experience of that part of the theatre.

' It's hot here, too,' Millicent's companion murmured. He had suddenly become much more conscious of the high temperature, of his proximity to the fierce chandelier, and he added that the plot of the play certainly was un-natural, though he thought the piece rather well acted.

' Oh, it's the good old stodgy British tradition. This is the only place where you find it still, and even here it can't last much longer ; it can't survive old Baskerville and Mrs. Ruffler. 'Gad, how old they are ! I remember her, long past her prime, when I used to be taken to the play, as a boy, in the Christmas holidays. Between them, they must be something like a hundred and eighty, eh ? I believe one is supposed to cry a good deal about the middle,' Captain Sholto continued, in the same friendly, familiar, encouraging way, addressing himself to Millicent, upon whom, indeed, his eyes had rested almost uninterruptedly from the first. She sustained his glance with composure, but with just enough of an expression of reserve to intimate (what was perfectly true) that she was not in the habit of conversing with gentlemen with whom she was not ac-quainted. She turned away her face at this (she had already given the visitor the benefit of a good deal of it), and left him, as in the little passage he leaned against the parapet of the balcony with his back to the stage, confronted with Hyacinth, who was now wondering, with rather more vivid a sense of the relations of things, what he had come for. He wanted to do him honour, in return for his civility, but he did not know what one could talk about, at such short notice, to a person whom he immediately perceived to be, in a most extensive, a really transcendent sense of the term, a man of the world. He instantly saw Captain Sholto did not take the play seriously, so that he felt himself warned off that topic, on which, otherwise, he might have had much to say. On the other hand he could not, in the presence of a third person, allude to the matters they had discussed at the 'Sun and Moon'; nor could he suppose his visitor would expect this, though indeed he impressed him as a man of humours and whims, who was amusing himself with everything, including esoteric socialism and a little bookbinder who had so much more of the gentleman about him than one would expect. Captain Sholto may have been a little embarrassed, now that he was completely launched in his attempt at fraternisation, especially after failing to elicit a smile from Millicent's respectability; but he left to Hyacinth the burden of no initiative, and went on to say that it was just this prospect of the dying-out of the old British tradition that had brought him to-night. He was with a friend, a lady who had lived much abroad, who had never seen anything of the kind, and who liked everything that was characteristic. 'You know the foreign school of acting is a very different affair,' he said again to Millicent, who this time replied, 'Oh yes, of course,' and considering afresh the old lady in the box, reflected that she looked as if there were nothing in the world that she, at least, hadn't seen.

'We have never been abroad,' said Hyacinth, candidly, looking into his friend's curious light-coloured eyes, the palest in tint he had ever encountered.

'Oh, well, there's a lot of nonsense talked about that!' Captain Sholto replied; while Hyacinth remained uncertain as to exactly what he referred to, and Millicent decided to volunteer a remark.

'They are making a tremendous row on the stage. I should think it would be very bad in those boxes.' There was a banging and thumping behind the curtain, the sound of heavy scenery pushed about.

'Oh yes; it's much better here, every way. I think you have the best seats in the house,' said Captain Sholto. 'I should like very much to finish my evening beside you. The trouble is I have ladies—a pair of them,' he went on, as if he were seriously considering this possibility. Then, laying his hand again on Hyacinth's shoulder, he smiled at him a moment and indulged in a still greater burst of frankness. 'My dear fellow, that is just what, as a partial reason, has brought me up here to see you. One of my ladies has a great desire to make your acquaintance!'

'To make my acquaintance?' Hyacinth felt himself turning pale; the first impulse he could have, in connection with such an announcement as that—and it lay far down, in the depths of the unspeakable—was a conjecture that it had something to do with his parentage on his father's side. Captain Sholto's smooth, bright face, irradiating such unexpected advances, seemed for an instant to swim before him. The Captain went on to say that he had told the lady of the talks they had had, that she was immensely interested in such matters—'You know what I mean, she really is'—and that as a consequence of what he had said she had begged him to come and ask his —a—his young friend (Hyacinth saw in a moment that the Captain had forgotten his name) to descend into her box for a little while.

'She has a tremendous desire to talk with some one who looks at the whole business from your standpoint, don't you see? And in her position she scarcely ever has a chance, she doesn't come across them—to her great annoyance. So when I spotted you to-night she immediately said that I must introduce you at any cost. I hope you don't mind, for a quarter of an hour. I ought perhaps to tell you that she is a person who is used to having nothing refused her. "Go up and bring him down," you know, as if it were the simplest thing in the world. She is really very much in earnest: I don't mean about wishing to see you— that goes without saying—but about the whole matter that you and I care for. Then I should add—it doesn't spoil

anything—that she is the most charming woman in the
world, simply ! Honestly, my dear boy, she is perhaps the
most remarkable woman in Europe.'

So Captain Sholto delivered himself, with the highest
naturalness and plausibility, and Hyacinth, listening, felt
that he himself ought perhaps to resent the idea of being
served up for the entertainment of imperious triflers, but
that somehow he didn't, and that it was more worthy of the
part he aspired to play in life to meet such occasions calmly
and urbanely than to take the trouble of dodging and going
roundabout. Of course the lady in the box couldn't be
sincere ; she might think she was, though even that was
questionable ; but you couldn't really care for the cause
that was exemplified in the little back room in Bloomsbury
if you came to the theatre in that style. It was Captain
Sholto's style as well, but it had been by no means clear
to Hyacinth hitherto that *he* really cared. All the same,
this was no time for going into the question of the lady's
sincerity, and at the end of sixty seconds our young man
had made up his mind that he could afford to humour her.
None the less, I must add, the whole proposal continued to
make things dance, to appear fictive, delusive ; so that it
sounded, in comparison, like a note of reality when Millicent, who had been looking from one of the men to the
other, exclaimed—

'That's all very well, but who is to look after me ? ' Her
assumption of the majestic had broken down, and this was
the cry of nature.

Nothing could have been pleasanter and more indulgent
of her alarm than the manner in which Captain Sholto reassured her. ' My dear young lady, can you suppose I have
been unmindful of that ? I have been hoping that after I
have taken down our friend and introduced him you
would allow me to come back and, in his absence, occupy his
seat.'

Hyacinth was preoccupied with the idea of meeting the
most remarkable woman in Europe ; but at this juncture he
looked at Millicent Henning with some curiosity. She rose
to the situation, and replied, ' I am much obliged to you,
but I don't know who you are.'

'Oh, I'll tell you all about that!' the Captain exclaimed, benevolently.

'Of course I should introduce you,' said Hyacinth, and he mentioned to Miss Henning the name of his distinguished acquaintance.

'In the army?' the young lady inquired, as if she must have every guarantee of social position.

'Yes—not in the navy! I have left the army, but it always sticks to one.'

'Mr. Robinson, is it your intention to leave me?' Millicent asked, in a tone of the highest propriety.

Hyacinth's imagination had taken such a flight that the idea of what he owed to the beautiful girl who had placed herself under his care for the evening had somehow effaced itself. Her words put it before him in a manner that threw him quickly and consciously back upon his honour; yet there was something in the way she uttered them that made him look at her harder still before he replied, 'Oh dear, no, of course it would never do. I must defer to some other occasion the honour of making the acquaintance of your friend,' he added, to Captain Sholto.

'Ah, my dear fellow, we might manage it so easily now,' this gentleman murmured, with evident disappointment. 'It is not as if Miss—a—Miss—a—were to be alone.'

It flashed upon Hyacinth that the root of the project might be a desire of Captain Sholto to insinuate himself into Millicent's graces; then he asked himself why the most remarkable woman in Europe should lend herself to that design, consenting even to receive a visit from a little bookbinder for the sake of furthering it. Perhaps, after all, she was not the most remarkable; still, even at a lower estimate, of what advantage could such a complication be to her? To Hyacinth's surprise, Millicent's eye made acknowledgment of his implied renunciation; and she said to Captain Sholto, as if she were considering the matter very impartially, 'Might one know the name of the lady who sent you?'

'The Princess Casamassima.'

'Laws!' cried Millicent Henning. And then, quickly, as if to cover up the crudity of this ejaculation, 'And might

one also know what it is, as you say, that she wants to talk
to him about?'

'About the lower orders, the rising democracy, the spread
of nihilism, and all that.'

'The lower orders?   Does she think we belong to
them?' the girl demanded, with a strange, provoking
laugh.

Captain Sholto was certainly the readiest of men.   'If
she could see you, she would think you one of the first
ladies in the land.'

'She'll never see me!' Millicent replied, in a manner
which made it plain that she, at least, was not to be whistled
for.

Being whistled for by a princess presented itself to Hyacinth as an indignity endured gracefully enough by the
heroes of several French novels in which he had found
a thrilling interest; nevertheless, he said, incorruptibly, to
the Captain, who hovered there like a Mephistopheles converted to disinterested charity, 'Having been in the army,
you will know that one can't desert one's post.'

The Captain, for the third time, laid his hand on his
young friend's shoulder, and for a minute his smile rested,
in silence, on Millicent Henning.   'If I tell you simply I
want to talk with this young lady, that certainly won't help
me, particularly, and there is no reason why it should.
Therefore I'll tell you the whole truth : I want to talk with
her about *you !*'   And he patted Hyacinth in a way which
conveyed at once that this idea must surely commend him
to the young man's companion and that he himself liked
him infinitely.

Hyacinth was conscious of the endearment, but he remarked to Millicent that he would do just as she liked ; he
was determined not to let a member of the bloated upper
class suppose that he held any daughter of the people
cheap.

'Oh, I don't care if you go,' said Miss Henning.   'You
had better hurry—the curtain's going to rise.'

'That's charming of you!   I'll rejoin you in three
minutes!' Captain Sholto exclaimed.

He passed his hand into Hyacinth's arm, and as our

hero lingered still, a little uneasy and questioning Millicent always with his eyes, the girl went on, with her bright boldness, 'That kind of princess—I should like to hear all about her.'

'Oh, I'll tell you that, too,' the Captain rejoined, with his imperturbable pleasantness, as he led his young friend away. It must be confessed that Hyacinth also rather wondered what kind of princess she was, and his suspense on this point made his heart beat fast when, after traversing steep staircases and winding corridors, they reached the small door of the stage-box.

HYACINTH'S first consciousness, after his companion had
opened it, was of his nearness to the stage, on which the
curtain had now risen again. The play was in progress,
the actors' voices came straight into the box, and it was
impossible to speak without disturbing them. This at least
was his inference from the noiseless way his conductor drew
him in, and, without announcing or introducing him, simply
pointed to a chair and whispered, 'Just drop into that;
you'll see and hear beautifully.' He heard the door close
behind him, and became aware that Captain Sholto had
already retreated. Millicent, at any rate, would not be left
to languish in solitude very long. Two ladies were seated
in the front of the box, which was so large that there was
a considerable space between them ; and as he stood there,
where Captain Sholto had planted him—they appeared not
to have noticed the opening of the door—they turned their
heads and looked at him. The one on whom his eyes first
rested was the old lady whom he had already contemplated
at a distance ; she looked queerer still on a closer view, and
gave him a little friendly, jolly nod. Her companion was
partly overshadowed by the curtain of the box, which she
had drawn forward with the intention of shielding herself
from the observation of the house ; she had still the air of
youth, and the simplest way to express the instant effect
upon Hyacinth of her fair face of welcome is to say that she
was dazzling. He remained as Sholto had left him, staring
rather confusedly and not moving an inch ; whereupon the
younger lady put out her hand—it was her left, the other
rested on the ledge of the box—with the expectation, as he
perceived, to his extreme mortification, too late, that he
would give her his own. She converted the gesture into a

sign of invitation, and beckoned him, silently but graciously, to move his chair forward. He did so, and seated himself between the two ladies; then, for ten minutes, stared straight before him, at the stage, not turning his eyes sufficiently even to glance up at Millicent in the balcony. He looked at the play, but he was far from seeing it; he had no sense of anything but the woman who sat there, close to him, on his right, with a fragrance in her garments and a light about her which he seemed to see even while his head was averted. The vision had been only of a moment, but it hung before him, threw a vague white mist over the proceedings on the stage. He was embarrassed, overturned, bewildered, and he knew it; he made a great effort to collect himself, to consider the situation lucidly. He wondered whether he ought to speak, to look at her again, to behave differently, in some way; whether she would take him for a clown, for an idiot; whether she were really as beautiful as she had seemed or it were only a superficial glamour, which a renewed inspection would dissipate. While he asked himself these questions the minutes went on, and neither of his hostesses spoke; they watched the play in perfect stillness, so that Hyacinth divined that this was the proper thing and that he himself must remain dumb until a word should be bestowed upon him. Little by little he recovered himself, took possession of his predicament, and at last transferred his eyes to the Princess. She immediately perceived this, and returned his glance, with a soft smile. She might well be a princess—it was impossible to conform more to the finest evocations of that romantic word. She was fair, brilliant, slender, with a kind of effortless majesty. Her beauty had an air of perfection; it astonished and lifted one up, the sight of it seemed a privilege, reward. If the first impression it had given Hyacinth was to make him feel strangely transported, he need not have been too much agitated, for this was the effect the Princess Casamassima produced upon persons of a wider experience and greater pretensions. Her dark eyes, blue or gray, something that was not brown, were as sweet as they were splendid, and there was an extraordinary light nobleness in the way she held her head. That head, where two or three diamond stars glittered in the thick, delicate hair which defined its shape, suggested to Hyacinth something antique and celebrated, which he had admired of old—the memory was vague—in a statue, in a picture, in a museum. Purity of line and form, of cheek and chin and lip and brow, a colour that seemed to live and glow, a radiance of grace and eminence and success—these things were seated in triumph in the face of the Princess, and Hyacinth, as he held himself in his chair, trembling with the revelation, wondered whether she were not altogether of some different substance from the humanity he had hitherto known. She might be divine, but he could see that she understood human needs —that she wished him to be at his ease and happy; there was something familiar in her smile, as if she had seen him many times before. Her dress was dark and rich; she had pearls round her neck, and an old rococo fan in her hand. Hyacinth took in all these things, and finally said to himself that if she wanted nothing more of him than that, he was content, he would like it to go on ; so pleasant was it to sit with fine ladies, in a dusky, spacious receptacle which framed the bright picture of the stage and made one's own situation seem a play within the play. The act was a long one, and the repose in which his companions left him might have been a calculated indulgence, to enable him to get used to them, to see how harmless they were. He looked at Millicent, in the course of time, and saw that Captain Sholto, seated beside her, had not the same standard of propriety, inasmuch as he made a remark to her every few minutes. Like himself, the young lady in the balcony was losing the play, thanks to her eyes being fixed on her friend from Lomax Place, whose position she thus endeavoured to gauge. Hyacinth had quite given up the Paraguayan complications ; by the end of the half hour his attention might have come back to them, had he not then been engaged in wondering what the Princess would say to him after the descent of the curtain—or whether she would say anything. The consideration of this problem, as the moment of the solution drew nearer, made his heart again beat faster. He watched the old lady on his left, and supposed it was natural that a princess should have an attendant—he took

for granted she was an attendant—as different as possible
from herself. This ancient dame was without majesty or
grace; huddled together, with her hands folded on her
stomach and her lips protruding, she solemnly followed the
performance. Several times, however, she turned her head
to Hyacinth, and then her expression changed; she repeated
the jovial, encouraging, almost motherly nod with which she
had greeted him when he had made his bow, and by which
she appeared to wish to intimate that, better than the serene
beauty on the other side, she could enter into the oddity,
the discomfort, of his situation. She seemed to say to him
that he must keep his head, and that if the worst should
come to the worst she was there to look after him. Even
when, at last, the curtain descended, it was some moments
before the Princess spoke, though she rested her smile upon
Hyacinth as if she were considering what he would best like
her to say. He might at that instant have guessed what he
discovered later—that among this lady's faults (he was
destined to learn that they were numerous), not the least
eminent was an exaggerated fear of the commonplace. He
expected she would make some remark about the play, but
what she said was, very gently and kindly, ' I like to know
all sorts of people.'

' I shouldn't think you would find the least difficulty in
that,' Hyacinth replied.

' Oh, if one wants anything very much, it's sure to be
difficult. Every one isn't as obliging as you.'

Hyacinth could think, immediately, of no proper rejoinder to this; but the old lady saved him the trouble by
declaring, with a foreign accent, ' I think you were most
extraordinarily good-natured. I had no idea you would
come—to two strange women.'

' Yes, we are strange women,' said the Princess, musingly.

' It's not true that she finds things difficult; she makes
every one do everything,' her companion went on.

The Princess glanced at her; then remarked to Hyacinth,
' Her name is Madame Grandoni.' Her tone was not
familiar, but there was a friendly softness in it, as if he had
really taken so much trouble for them that it was only
just he should be entertained a little at their expense. It

seemed to imply, also, that Madame Grandoni's fitness for
supplying such entertainment was obvious.

'But I am not Italian—ah no!' the old lady cried.
'In spite of my name, I am an honest, ugly, unfortunate
German. But it doesn't matter. She, also, with such a
name, isn't Italian, either. It's an accident; the world is
full of accidents. But she isn't German, poor lady, any
more.' Madame Grandoni appeared to have entered into
the Princess's view, and Hyacinth thought her exceedingly
amusing. In a moment she added, 'That was a very
charming person you were with.'

'Yes, she is very charming,' Hyacinth replied, not sorry
to have a chance to say it.

The Princess made no remark on this subject, and
Hyacinth perceived not only that from her position in the
box she could have had no glimpse of Millicent, but that
she would never take up such an allusion as that. It was
as if she had not heard it that she asked, 'Do you consider
the play very interesting?'

Hyacinth hesitated a moment, and then told the simple
truth. 'I must confess that I have lost the whole of this
last act.'

'Ah, poor bothered young man!' cried Madame Grandoni. 'You see—you see!'

'What do I see?' the Princess inquired. 'If you are
annoyed at being here now, you will like us later; probably,
at least. We take a great interest in the things you care
for. We take a great interest in the people,' the Princess
went on.

'Oh, allow me, allow me, and speak only for yourself!'
the elder lady interposed. 'I take no interest in the
people; I don't understand them, and I know nothing
about them. An honourable nature, of any class, I
always respect it; but I will not pretend to a passion for
the ignorant masses, because I have it not. Moreover,
that doesn't touch the gentleman.'

The Princess Casamassima had, evidently, a faculty of
completely ignoring things of which she wished to take no
account; it was not in the least the air of contempt, but
a kind of thoughtful, tranquil absence, after which she came

back to the point where she wished to be. She made no
protest against her companion's speech, but said to Hyacinth,
as if she were only vaguely conscious that the old lady
had been committing herself in some absurd way, 'She
lives with me; she is everything to me; she is the best
woman in the world.'

'Yes, fortunately, with many superficial defects, I am
very good,' Madame Grandoni remarked.

Hyacinth, by this time, was less embarrassed than when
he presented himself to the Princess Casamassima, but he
was not less mystified; he wondered afresh whether he
were not being practised upon for some inconceivable end;
so strange did it seem to him that two such fine ladies
should, of their own movement, take the trouble to explain
each other to a miserable little bookbinder. This idea
made him flush; it was as if it had come over him that he
had fallen into a trap. He was conscious that he looked
frightened, and he was conscious the moment afterwards
that the Princess noticed it. This was, apparently, what
made her say, 'If you have lost so much of the play I
ought to tell you what has happened.'

'Do you think he would follow that any more?' Madame
Grandoni exclaimed.

'If you would tell me—if you would tell me——' And
then Hyacinth stopped. He had been going to say, 'If
you would tell me what all this means and what you want
of me, it would be more to the point!' but the words died
on his lips, and he sat staring, for the woman at his right
hand was simply too beautiful. She was too beautiful to
question, to judge by common logic; and how could he
know, moreover, what was natural to a person in that
exaltation of grace and splendour? Perhaps it was her
habit to send out every evening for some *naïf* stranger, to
amuse her; perhaps that was the way the foreign aristocracy lived. There was no sharpness in her face, at the
present moment at least; there was nothing but luminous
sweetness, yet she looked as if she knew what was going on
in his mind. She made no eager attempt to reassure him,
but there was a world of delicate consideration in the tone
in which she said, 'Do you know, I am afraid I have already

forgotten what they have been doing in the play? It's terribly complicated; some one or other was hurled over a precipice.'

'Ah, you're a brilliant pair,' Madame Grandoni remarked, with a laugh of long experience. 'I could describe everything. The person who was hurled over the precipice was the virtuous hero, and you will see, in the next act, that he was only slightly bruised.'

'Don't describe anything; I have so much to ask.' Hyacinth had looked away, in tacit deprecation, at hearing himself 'paired' with the Princess, and he felt that she was watching him. 'What do you think of Captain Sholto?' she went on, suddenly, to his surprise, if anything, in his position, could excite that sentiment more than anything else; and as he hesitated, not knowing what to say, she added, 'Isn't he a very curious type?'

'I know him very little,' Hyacinth replied; and he had no sooner uttered the words than it struck him they were far from brilliant—they were poor and flat, and very little calculated to satisfy the Princess. Indeed, he reflected that he had said nothing at all that could·place him in a favourable light; so he continued, at a venture : 'I mean I have never seen him at home.' That sounded still more silly.

'At home? Oh, he is never at home; he is all over the world. To-night he was as likely to have been in Paraguay, for instance, as here. He is what they call a cosmopolite. I don't know whether you know that species; very modern, more and more frequent, and exceedingly tiresome. I prefer the Chinese! He had told me he had had a great deal of interesting talk with you. That was what made me say to him, "Oh, do ask him to come in and see me. A little interesting talk, that would be a change!"'

'She is very complimentary to me!' said Madame Grandoni.

'Ah, my dear, you and I, you know, we never talk : we understand each other without that!' Then the Princess pursued, addressing herself to Hyacinth, 'Do you never admit women?'

'Admit women ?'

'Into those *séances*—what do you call them?—those little meetings that Captain Sholto described to me. I should like so much to be present. Why not ?'

'I haven't seen any ladies,' Hyacinth said. 'I don't know whether it's a rule, but I have seen nothing but men ;' and he added, smiling, though he thought the dereliction rather serious, and couldn't understand the part Captain Sholto was playing, nor, considering the grand company he kept, how he had originally secured admittance into the subversive little circle in Bloomsbury, 'You know I'm not sure Captain Sholto ought to go about reporting our proceedings.'

'I see. Perhaps you think he's a spy, or something of that sort.'

'No,' said Hyacinth, after a moment. 'I think a spy would be more careful—would disguise himself more. Besides, after all, he has heard very little.' And Hyacinth smiled again.

'You mean he hasn't really been behind the scenes ?' the Princess asked, bending forward a little, and now covering the young man steadily with her deep, soft eyes, as if by this time he must have got used to her and wouldn't flinch from such attention. 'Of course he hasn't, and he never will be ; he knows that, and that it's quite out of his power to tell any real secrets. What he repeated to me was interesting, but of course I could see that there was nothing the authorities, anywhere, could put their hand on. It was mainly the talk he had had with you which struck him so very much, and which struck me, as you see. Perhaps you didn't know how he was drawing you out.'

'I am afraid that's rather easy,' said Hyacinth, with perfect candour, as it came over him that he *had* chattered, with a vengeance, in Bloomsbury, and had thought it natural enough then that his sociable fellow-visitor should offer him cigars and attach importance to the views of a clever and original young artisan.

'I am not sure that I find it so ! However, I ought to tell you that you needn't have the least fear of Captain

Sholto. He's a perfectly honest man, so far as he goes;
and even if you had trusted him much more than you
appear to have done, he would be incapable of betraying
you.   However, don't trust him : not because he's not
safe, but because—— No matter, you will see for yourself.
He has gone into that sort of thing simply to please me.
I should tell you, merely to make you understand, that
he would do anything for that.   That's his own affair.   I
wanted to know something, to learn something, to ascertain
what really is going on; and for a woman everything of
that sort is so difficult, especially for a woman in my position, who is known, and to whom every sort of bad faith is
sure to be imputed.   So Sholto said he would look into
the subject for me ; poor man, he has had to look into so
many subjects !   What I particularly wanted was that he
should make friends with some of the leading spirits,
really characteristic types.'   The Princess's voice was low
and rather deep, and her tone very quick; her manner of
speaking was altogether new to her listener, for whom the
pronunciation of her words and the very punctuation of
her sentences were a kind of revelation of ' society.'

'Surely Captain Sholto doesn't suppose that *I* am a
leading spirit !' Hyacinth exclaimed, with the determination
not to be laughed at any more than he could help.

The Princess hesitated a moment; then she said, ' He
told me you were very original.'

' He doesn't know, and—if you will allow me to say so
—I don't think you know.   How should you ?   I am one
of many thousands of young men of my class—you know,
I suppose, what that is—in whose brains certain ideas are
fermenting.   There is nothing original about me at all.   I
am very young and very ignorant ; it's only a few months
since I began to talk of the possibility of a social revolution
with men who have considered the whole ground much
more than I have done.   I'm a mere particle in the immensity of the people.   All I pretend to is my good faith,
and a great desire that justice shall be done.'

The Princess listened to him intently, and her attitude
made him feel how little *he*, in comparison, expressed himself like a person who had the habit of conversation ; he

seemed to himself to stammer and emit common sounds. For a moment she said nothing, only looking at him with her pure smile. 'I do draw you out!' she exclaimed, at last. 'You are much more interesting to me than if you were an exception.' At these last words Hyacinth flinched a hair's breadth; the movement was shown by his dropping his eyes. We know to what extent he really regarded himself as of the stuff of the common herd. The Princess doubtless guessed it as well, for she quickly added, 'At the same time, I can see that you are remarkable enough.'

'What do you think I am remarkable for?'

'Well, you have general ideas.'

'Every one has them to-day. They have them in Bloomsbury to a terrible degree. I have a friend (who understands the matter much better than I) who has no patience with them: he declares they are our danger and our bane. A few very special ideas—if they are the right ones—are what we want.'

'Who is your friend?' the Princess asked, abruptly.

'Ah, Christina, Christina,' Madame Grandoni murmured from the other side of the box.

Christina took no notice of her, and Hyacinth, not understanding the warning, and only remembering how personal women always are, replied, 'A young man who lives in Camberwell, an assistant at a wholesale chemist's.'

If he had expected that this description of his friend was a bigger dose than his hostess would be able to digest, he was greatly mistaken. She seemed to look tenderly at the picture suggested by his words, and she immediately inquired whether the young man were also clever, and whether she might not hope to know him. Hadn't Captain Sholto seen him; and if so, why hadn't he spoken of him, too? When Hyacinth had replied that Captain Sholto had probably seen him, but that he believed he had had no particular conversation with him, the Princess inquired, with startling frankness, whether her visitor wouldn't bring his friend, some day, to see her.

Hyacinth glanced at Madame Grandoni, but that worthy woman was engaged in a survey of the house, through an old-fashioned eye-glass with a long gilt handle.

He had perceived, long before this, that the Princess Casamassima had no desire for vain phrases, and he had the good taste to feel that, from himself to such a personage, compliments, even if he had wished to pay them, would have had no suitability. 'I don't know whether he would be willing to come. He's the sort of man that, in such a case, you can't answer for.'

'That makes me want to know him all the more. But you'll come yourself, at all events, eh?'

Poor Hyacinth murmured something about the unexpected honour; for, after all, he had a French heredity, and it was not so easy for him to make unadorned speeches. But Madame Grandoni, laying down her eye-glass, almost took the words out of his mouth, with the cheerful exhortation, 'Go and see her—go and see her once or twice. She will treat you like an angel.'

'You must think me very peculiar,' the Princess remarked, sadly.

'I don't know what I think. It will take a good while.'

'I wish I could make you trust me—inspire you with confidence,' she went on. 'I don't mean only you, personally, but others who think as you do. You would find I would go with you—pretty far. I was answering just now for Captain Sholto; but who in the world is to answer for me?' And her sadness merged itself in a smile which appeared to Hyacinth extraordinarily magnanimous and touching.

'Not I, my dear, I promise you!' her ancient companion ejaculated, with a laugh which made the people in the stalls look up at the box.

Her mirth was contagious; it gave Hyacinth the audacity to say to her, 'I would trust *you*, if you did!' though he felt, the next minute, that this was even a more familiar speech than if he had said he wouldn't trust her.

'It comes, then, to the same thing,' the Princess went on. 'She would not show herself with me in public if I were not respectable. If you knew more about me you would understand what has led me to turn my attention to the great social question. It is a long story, and the details wouldn't interest you; but perhaps some day, if we

have more talk, you will put yourself a little in my place.
I am very serious, you know; I am not amusing myself
with peeping and running away. I am convinced that we
are living in a fool's paradise, that the ground is heaving
under our feet.'

'It's not the ground, my dear; it's you that are turning
somersaults,' Madame Grandoni interposed.

'Ah, you, my friend, you have the happy faculty of
believing what you like to believe. I have to believe what
I see.'

'She wishes to throw herself into the revolution, to
guide it, to enlighten it,' Madame Grandoni said to Hyacinth, speaking now with imperturbable gravity.

'I am sure she could direct it in any sense she would
wish!' the young man responded, in a glow. The pure,
high dignity with which the Princess had just spoken,
and which appeared to cover a suppressed tremor of
passion, set Hyacinth's pulses throbbing, and though he
scarcely saw what she meant—her aspirations seeming so
vague—her tone, her voice, her wonderful face, showed
that she had a generous soul.

She answered his eager declaration with a serious smile
and a melancholy head-shake. 'I have no such pretensions, and my good old friend is laughing at me. Of
course that is very easy; for what, in fact, can be more
absurd, on the face of it, than for a woman with a title,
with diamonds, with a carriage, with servants, with a
position, as they call it, to sympathise with the upward
struggles of those who are below? "Give all that up,
and we'll believe you," you have a right to say. I am
ready to give them up the moment it will help the cause;
I assure you that's the least difficulty. I don't want to
teach, I want to learn; and, above all, I want to know
à quoi m'en tenir. Are we on the eve of great changes,
or are we not? Is everything that is gathering force,
underground, in the dark, in the night, in little hidden
rooms, out of sight of governments and policemen and
idiotic "statesmen"—heaven save them!—is all this going
to burst forth some fine morning and set the world on
fire? Or is it to sputter out and spend itself in vain con-

spiracies, be dissipated in sterile heroisms and abortive
isolated movements? I want to know *à quoi m'en tenir,'*
she repeated, fixing her visitor with more brilliant eyes, as
if he could tell her on the spot.   Then, suddenly, she
added in a totally different tone, ' Excuse me, I have an
idea you speak French. Didn't Captain Sholto tell me so?'

' I have some little acquaintance with it,' Hyacinth murmured. ' I have French blood in my veins.'

She considered him as if he had proposed to her some
kind of problem. ' Yes, I can see that you are not
le premier venu.   Now, your friend, of whom you were
speaking, is a chemist; and you, yourself—what is your
occupation?'

' I'm just a bookbinder.'

'That must be delightful. I wonder if you would bind
some books for me.'

' You would have to bring them to our shop, and I can
do there only the work that's given out to me. I might
manage it by myself, at home,' Hyacinth added, smiling.

' I should like that better. And what do you call
home?'

' The place I live in, in the north of London : a little
street you certainly never heard of.'

' What is it called ?'

' Lomax Place, at your service,' said Hyacinth, laughing.

She laughed back at him, and he didn't know whether
her brightness or her gravity were the more charming.
' No, I don't think I have heard of it. I don't know London very well; I haven't lived here long. I have spent
most of my life abroad. My husband is a foreigner, an
Italian. We don't live together much. I haven't the
manners of this country—not of any class ; have I, eh ?
Oh, this country—there is a great deal to be said about it;
and a great deal to be done, as you, of course, understand
better than any one. But I want to know London ; it
interests me more than I can say—the huge, swarming,
smoky, human city. I mean real London, the people and
all their sufferings and passions ; not Park Lane and Bond
Street. Perhaps you can help me—it would be a great
kindness : that's what I want to know men like you for

You see it isn't idle, my having given you so much trouble to-night.'

'I shall be very glad to show you all I know. But it isn't much, and above all it isn't pretty,' said Hyacinth.

'Whom do you live with, in Lomax Place?' the Princess asked, by way of rejoinder to this.

'Captain Sholto is leaving the young lady—he is coming back here,' Madame Grandoni announced, inspecting the balcony with her instrument. The orchestra had been for some time playing the overture to the following act.

Hyacinth hesitated a moment. 'I live with a dress-maker.'

'With a dressmaker? Do you mean—do you mean —— ?' And the Princess paused.

'Do you mean she's your wife?' asked Madame Grandoni, humorously.

'Perhaps she gives you rooms,' remarked the Princess.

'How many do you think I have? She gives me everything, or she has done so in the past. She brought me up; she is the best little woman in the world.'

'You had better command a dress!' exclaimed Madame Grandoni.

'And your family, where are they?' the Princess continued.

'I have no family.'

'None at all?'

'None at all. I never had.'

'But the French blood that you speak of, and which I see perfectly in your face—you haven't the English expression, or want of expression—that must have come to you through some one.'

'Yes, through my mother.'

'And she is dead?'

'Long ago.'

'That's a great loss, because French mothers are usually so much to their sons.' The Princess looked at her painted fan a moment, as she opened and closed it; after which she said, 'Well, then, you'll come some day. We'll arrange it.'

Hyacinth felt that the answer to this could be only

a silent inclination of his little person ; and to make it he rose from his chair. As he stood there, conscious that he had stayed long enough and yet not knowing exactly how to withdraw, the Princess, with her fan closed, resting upright on her knee, and her hands clasped on the end of it, turned up her strange, lovely eyes at him, and said—

'Do you think anything will occur soon ? '

'Will occur ? '

'That there will be a crisis—that you'll make yourselves felt ? '

In this beautiful woman's face there was to Hyacinth's bewildered perception something at once inspiring, tempting and mocking; and the effect of her expression was to make him say, rather clumsily, ' I'll try and ascertain ;' as if she had asked him whether her carriage were at the door.

'I don't quite know what you are talking about; but please don't have it for another hour or two. I want to see what becomes of the Pearl ! ' Madame Grandoni interposed.

'Remember what I told you : I would give up every-thing—everything ! ' the Princess went on, looking up at the young man in the same way. Then she held out her hand, and this time he knew sufficiently what he was about to take it.

When he bade good-night to Madame Grandoni the old lady exclaimed to him, with a comical sigh, ' Well, she *is* respectable ! ' and out in the lobby, when he had closed the door of the box behind him, he found himself echoing these words and repeating mechanically, ' She *is* respectable ! ' They were on his lips as he stood, suddenly, face to face with Captain Sholto, who laid his hand on his shoulder once more and shook him a little, in that free yet insinuating manner for which this officer appeared to be remarkable.

' My dear fellow, you were born under a lucky star.'

' I never supposed it,' said Hyacinth, changing colour.

'Why, what in the world would you have ? You have the faculty, the precious faculty, of inspiring women with an interest—but an interest ! '

'Yes, ask them in the box there ! I behaved like a cretin,' Hyacinth declared, overwhelmed now with a sense of opportunities missed.

'They won't tell me that.   And the lady upstairs?'

'Well,' said Hyacinth gravely, 'what about her?'

The Captain considered him a moment.   'She wouldn't talk to me of anything but you.   You may imagine how I liked it!'

'I don't like it, either.   But I must go up.'

'Oh yes, she counts the minutes.   Such a charming person!' Captain Sholto added, with more propriety of tone.   As Hyacinth left him he called after him, 'Don't be afraid—you'll go far.'

When the young man took his place in the balcony beside Millicent this damsel gave him no greeting, nor asked any question about his adventures in the more aristocratic part of the house. . She only turned her fine complexion upon him for some minutes, and as he himself was not in the mood to begin to chatter, the silence continued—continued till after the curtain had risen on the last act of the play.   Millicent's attention was now, evidently, not at her disposal for the stage, and in the midst of a violent scene, which included pistol-shots and shrieks, she said at last to her companion, 'She's a tidy lot, your Princess, by what I learn.'

'Pray, what do you know about her?'

'I know what that fellow told me.'

'And pray, what was that?'

'Well, she's a bad 'un, as ever was.   Her own husband has had to turn her out of the house.'

Hyacinth remembered the allusion the lady herself had made to her matrimonial situation; nevertheless, what he would have liked to reply to Miss Henning was that he didn't believe a word of it.   He withheld the doubt, and after a moment remarked quietly, 'I don't care.'

'You don't care?   Well, I do, then!' Millicent cried. And as it was impossible, in view of the performance and the jealous attention of their neighbours, to continue the conversation in this pitch, she contented herself with ejaculating, in a somewhat lower key, at the end of five minutes, during which she had been watching the stage, 'Gracious, what dreadful common stuff!'

Hyacinth did not mention to Pinnie or Mr. Vetch that he
had been taken up by a great lady; but he mentioned it to
Paul Muniment, to whom he now confided a great many
things. He had, at first, been in considerable fear of his
straight, loud, north-country friend, who showed signs of
cultivating logic and criticism to a degree that was hostile
to free conversation; but he discovered later that he was
a man to whom one could say anything in the world, if one
didn't think it of more importance to be sympathised with
than to be understood. For a revolutionist, he was
strangely good-natured. The sight of all the things he
wanted to change had seemingly no power to irritate him,
and if he joked about questions that lay very near his
heart his pleasantry was not bitter nor invidious; the fault
that Hyacinth sometimes found with it, rather, was that it
was innocent to puerility. Our hero envied his power of
combining a care for the wide misery of mankind with the
apparent state of mind of the cheerful and virtuous young
workman who, on Sunday morning, has put on a clean
shirt, and, not having taken the gilt off his wages the night
before, weighs against each other, for a happy day, the
respective attractions of Epping Forest and Gravesend.
He was never sarcastic about his personal lot and his daily
life; it had not seemed to occur to him, for instance, that
'society' was really responsible for the condition of his
sister's spinal column, though Eustache Poupin and his
wife (who practically, however, were as patient as he), did
everything they could to make him say so, believing,
evidently, that it would relieve him. Apparently he cared
nothing for women, talked of them rarely, and always
decently, and had never a sign of a sweetheart, unless Lady

Aurora Langrish might pass for one. He never drank a drop of beer nor touched a pipe; he always had a clear tone, a fresh cheek and a smiling eye, and once excited on Hyacinth's part a kind of elder-brotherly indulgence by the open-mouthed glee and credulity with which, when the pair were present, in the sixpenny gallery, at Astley's, at an equestrian pantomime, he followed the tawdry spectacle. He once told the young bookbinder that he was a suggestive little beggar, and Hyacinth's opinion of him, by this time, was so exalted that the remark had almost the value of a patent of nobility. Our hero treated himself to an unlimited belief in him; he had always dreamed of having some grand friendship, and this was the best opening he had ever encountered. No one could entertain a sentiment of that sort better than Hyacinth, or cultivate a greater luxury of confidence. It disappointed him, sometimes, that it was not more richly repaid; that on certain important points of the socialistic programme Muniment would never commit himself; and that he had not yet shown the *fond du sac*, as Eustache Poupin called it, to so ardent an admirer. He answered particular questions freely enough, and answered them occasionally in a manner that made Hyacinth jump, as when, in reply to an inquiry in regard to his view of capital punishment, he said that, so far from wishing it abolished, he should go in for extending it much further—he should impose it on those who habitually lied or got drunk; but his friend had always a feeling that he kept back his best card and that even in the listening circle in Bloomsbury, when only the right men were present, there were unspoken conclusions in his mind which he didn't as yet think any one good enough to be favoured with. So far, therefore, from suspecting him of half-heartedness, Hyacinth was sure that he had extraordinary things in his head; that he was thinking them out to the logical end, wherever it might land him ; and that the night he should produce them, with the door of the club-room guarded and the company bound by a tremendous oath, the others would look at each other and turn pale.

‘ She wants to see you ; she asked me to bring you ; she was very serious,’ Hyacinth said, relating his interview with the ladies in the box at the play; which, however, now that he looked back upon it, seemed as queer as a dream, and not much more likely than that sort of experience to have a continuation in one's waking hours.

'To bring me—to bring me where?' asked Muniment. 'You talk as if I were a sample out of your shop, or a little dog you had for sale. Has she ever seen me? Does she think I'm smaller than you? What does she know about me?'

'Well, principally, that you're a friend of mine—that's enough for her.'

'Do you mean that it ought to be enough for me that she's a friend of yours? I have a notion you'll have some queer ones before you're done; a good many more than I have time to talk to. And how can I go to see a delicate female, with those paws?' Muniment inquired, exhibiting ten work-stained fingers.

'Buy a pair of gloves,' said Hyacinth, who recognised the serious character of this obstacle. But after a moment he added, 'No, you oughtn't to do that; she wants to see dirty hands.'

'That's easy enough; she needn't send for me for the purpose. But isn't she making game of you?'

'It's very possible, but I don't see what good it can do her.'

'You are not obliged to find excuses for the pampered classes. Their bloated luxury begets evil, impudent desires; they are capable of doing harm for the sake of harm. Besides, is she genuine?'

'If she isn't, what becomes of your explanation?' asked Hyacinth.

'Oh, it doesn't matter; at night all cats are gray. Whatever she is, she's an idle, bedizened jade.'

'If you had seen her, you wouldn't talk of her that way.'

'God forbid I should see her, then, if she's going to corrupt me!'

'Do you suppose she'll corrupt *me?*' Hyacinth demanded, with an expression of face and a tone of voice which produced, on his friend's part, an explosion of mirth.

'How can she, after all, when you are already such a little mass of corruption?'

'You don't think that,' said Hyacinth, looking very grave.

'Do you mean that if I did I wouldn't say it? Haven't you noticed that I say what I think?'

'No, you don't, not half of it : you're as close as a fish.'

Paul Muniment looked at his companion a moment, as if he were rather struck with the penetration of that remark ; then he said, 'Well, then, if I should give you the other half of my opinion of you, do you think you'd fancy it?'

'I'll save you the trouble. I'm a very clever, conscientious, promising young chap, and any one would be proud to claim me as a friend.'

'Is that what your Princess told you? She must be a precious piece of goods!' Paul Muniment exclaimed. 'Did she pick your pocket meanwhile?'

'Oh yes; a few minutes later I missed a silver cigarcase, engraved with the arms of the Robinsons. Seriously,' Hyacinth continued, 'don't you consider it possible that a woman of that class should want to know what is going on among the like of us?'

'It depends upon what class you mean.'

'Well, a woman with a lot of jewels and the manners of an angel. It's queer of course, but it's conceivable ; why not? There may be unselfish natures ; there may be disinterested feelings.'

'And there may be fine ladies in an awful funk about their jewels, and even about their manners. Seriously, as you say, it's perfectly conceivable. I am not in the least surprised at the aristocracy being curious to know what we are up to, and wanting very much to look into it ; in their place I should be very uneasy, and if I were a woman with angelic manners very likely I too should be glad to get hold of a soft, susceptible little bookbinder, and pump him dry, bless his heart!'

'Are you afraid I'll tell her secrets?' cried Hyacinth, flushing with virtuous indignation.

'Secrets? What secrets could you tell her, my pretty lad?'

Hyacinth stared a moment. 'You don't trust me—you never have.'

'We will, some day—don't be afraid,' said Muniment,
who, evidently, had no intention of unkindness, a thing that
appeared to be impossible to him. 'And when we do,
you'll cry with disappointment.'

'Well, *you* won't,' Hyacinth declared. And then he
asked whether his friend thought the Princess Casamassima
a spy; and why, if she were in that line, Mr. Sholto was
not—inasmuch as it must be supposed he was not, since
they had seen fit to let him walk in and out, at that rate,
in the place in Bloomsbury. Muniment did not even know
whom he meant, not having had any relations with the
gentleman; but he summoned a sufficient image when his
companion had described the Captain's appearance. He
then remarked, with his usual geniality, that he didn't take
him for a spy—he took him for an ass; but even if he had
edged himself into the place with every intention to betray
them, what handle could he possibly get—what use, against
them, could he make of anything he had seen or heard?
If he had a fancy to dip into working-men's clubs (Muniment
remembered, now, the first night he came; he had been
brought by that German cabinetmaker, who had a stiff neck
and smoked a pipe with a bowl as big as a stove); if it
amused him to put on a bad hat, and inhale foul tobacco,
and call his 'inferiors' 'my dear fellow'; if he thought that
in doing so he was getting an insight into the people and
going half-way to meet them and preparing for what was
coming—all this was his own affair, and he was very welcome,
though a man must be a flat who would spend his evening
in a hole like that when he might enjoy his comfort in one
of those flaming big shops, full of armchairs and flunkies,
in Pall Mall. And what did he see, after all, in Bloomsbury? Nothing but a 'social gathering,' where there were
clay pipes, and a sanded floor, and not half enough gas, and
the principal newspapers; and where the men, as any one
would know, were advanced radicals, and mostly advanced
idiots. He could pat as many of them on the back as he
liked, and say the House of Lords wouldn't last till midsummer; but what discoveries would he make? He was
simply on the same lay as Hyacinth's Princess; he was nervous and scared, and he thought he would see for himself.

'Oh, he isn't the same sort as the Princess. I'm sure he's in a very different line!' Hyacinth exclaimed.

'Different, of course; she's a handsome woman, I suppose, and he's an ugly man; but I don't think that either of them will save us or spoil us. Their curiosity is natural, but I have got other things to do than to show them over; therefore you can tell her serene highness that I'm much obliged.'

Hyacinth reflected a moment, and then he said, 'You show Lady Aurora over; you seem to wish to give her the information she desires; and what's the difference? If it's right for her to take an interest, why isn't it right for my Princess?'

'If she's already yours, what more can she want?' Muniment asked. 'All I know of Lady Aurora, and all I look at, is that she comes and sits with Rosy, and brings her tea, and waits upon her. If the Princess will do as much I'll tell her she's a woman of genius; but apart from that I shall never take a grain of interest in her interest in the masses—or in this particular mass!' And Paul Muniment, with his discoloured thumb, designated his own substantial person. His tone was disappointing to Hyacinth, who was surprised at his not appearing to think the episode at the theatre more remarkable and romantic. Muniment seemed to regard his explanation of such a proceeding as all-sufficient; but when, a moment later, he made use, in referring to the mysterious lady, of the expression that she was 'quaking,' Hyacinth broke out—'Never in the world; she's not afraid of anything!'

'Ah, my lad not afraid of you, evidently!'

Hyacinth paid no attention to this coarse sally, but asked in a moment, with a candour that was proof against further ridicule, 'Do you think she can do me a hurt of any kind, if we follow up our acquaintance?'

'Yes, very likely, but you must hit her back! That's your line, you know: to go in for what's going, to live your life, to gratify the women. I'm an ugly, grimy brute, I've got to watch the fires and mind the shop; but you are one of those taking little beggars who ought to run about and see the world; you ought to be an ornament

to society, like a young man in an illustrated story-book.
Only,' Muniment added in a moment, 'you know, if
she should hurt you very much, *then* I would go and see
her !'

Hyacinth had been intending for some time to take
Pinnie to call on the prostrate damsel in Audley Court, to
whom he had promised that his benefactress (he had told
Rose Muniment that she was 'a kind of aunt') should pay
this civility; but the affair had been delayed by wan hesitations on the part of the dressmaker, for the poor woman
had hard work to imagine, to-day, that there were people
in London so forlorn that her countenance could be of
value to them. Her social curiosities had become very
nearly extinct, and she knew that she no longer made the
same figure in public as when her command of the fashions
enabled her to illustrate them in her own little person, by
the aid of a good deal of whalebone. Moreover she felt
that Hyacinth had strange friends and still stranger opinions;
she suspected that he took an unnatural interest in politics
and was somehow not on the right side, little as she knew
about parties or causes; and she had a vague conviction
that this kind of perversity only multiplied the troubles of
the poor, who, according to theories which Pinnie had never
reasoned out, but which, in her bosom, were as deep as
religion, ought always to be of the same way of thinking as
the rich. They were unlike them enough in their poverty,
without trying to add other differences. When at last
she accompanied Hyacinth to Camberwell, one Saturday
evening at midsummer, it was in a sighing, sceptical, second-
best manner ; but if he had told her he wished it she would
have gone with him to a *soirée* at a scavenger's. There
was no more danger of Rose Muniment's being out than of
one of the bronze couchant lions in Trafalgar Square having
walked down Whitehall; but he had let her know in advance, and he perceived, as he opened her door in obedience to a quick, shrill summons, that she had had the
happy thought of inviting Lady Aurora to help her to
entertain Miss Pynsent. Such, at least, was the inference
he drew from seeing her ladyship's memorable figure rise
before him for the first time since his own visit. He pre-

sented his companion to their reclining hostess, and Rosy immediately repeated her name to the representative of Belgrave Square. Pinnie curtsied down to the ground, as Lady Aurora put out her hand to her, and slipped noiselessly into a chair beside the bed. Lady Aurora laughed and fidgeted, in a friendly, cheerful, yet at the same time rather pointless manner, and Hyacinth gathered that she had no recollection of having met him before. His attention, however, was mainly given to Pinnie : he watched her jealously, to see whether, on this important occasion, she would not put forth a certain stiff, quaint, polished politeness, of which she possessed the secret and which made her resemble a pair of old-fashioned sugar-tongs. Not only for Pinnie's sake, but for his own as well, he wished her to pass for a superior little woman, and he hoped she wouldn't lose her head if Rosy should begin to talk about Inglefield. She was, evidently, much impressed by Rosy, and kept repeating, ' Dear, dear ! ' under her breath, as the small, strange person in the bed rapidly explained to her that there was nothing in the world she would have liked so much as to follow *her* delightful profession, but that she couldn't sit up to it, and had never had a needle in her hand but once, when at the end of three minutes it had dropped into the sheets and got into the mattress, so that she had always been afraid it would work out again and stick into her ; but it hadn't done so yet, and perhaps it never would—she lay so quiet, she didn't push it about much. ' Perhaps you would think it's me that trimmed the little handkerchief I wear round my neck,' Miss Muniment said ; ' perhaps you would think I couldn't do less, lying here all day long, with complete command of my time. Not a stitch of it. I'm the finest lady in London ; I never lift my finger for myself. It's a present from her ladyship—it's her ladyship's own beautiful needlework. What do you think of that ? Have you ever met any one so favoured before ? And the work —just look at the work, and tell me what you think of that ! ' The girl pulled off the bit of muslin from her neck and thrust it at Pinnie, who looked at it confusedly and exclaimed, ' Dear, dear, dear ! ' partly in sympathy, partly as if, in spite of the consideration she owed every one, those were very strange proceedings.

' It's very badly done ; surely you see that,' said Lady Aurora.   ' It was only a joke.'

' Oh yes, everything's a joke ! ' cried the irrepressible invalid—' everything except my state of health ; that's admitted to be serious.   When her ladyship sends me five shillings' worth of coals it's only a joke ; and when she brings me a bottle of the finest port, that's another ; and when she climbs up seventy-seven stairs (there are seventy-seven, I know perfectly, though I never go up or down), at the height of the London season, to spend the evening with me, that's the best of all.   I know all about the London season, though I never go out, and I appreciate what her ladyship gives up.   She is very jocular indeed, but, fortunately, I know how to take it.   You can see that it wouldn't do for me to be touchy, can't you, Miss Pynsent ? '

' Dear, dear, I should be so glad to make you anything myself ; it would be better—it would be better——' Pinnie murmured, hesitating.

' It would be better than my poor work.   I don't know how to do that sort of thing, in the least,' said Lady Aurora.

' I'm sure I didn't mean that, my lady—I only meant it would be more convenient.   Anything in the world she might fancy,' the dressmaker went on, as if it were a question of the invalid's appetite.

' Ah, you see I don't wear things—only a flannel jacket, to be a bit tidy,' Miss Muniment rejoined.   ' I go in only for smart counterpanes, as you can see for yourself ; ' and she spread her white hands complacently over her coverlet of brilliant patch-work.   ' Now doesn't that look to you, Miss Pynsent, as if it might be one of her ladyship's jokes ? '

' Oh, my good friend, how can you ?   I never went so far as that ! ' Lady Aurora interposed, with visible anxiety.

' Well, you've given me almost everything ; I sometimes forget.   This only cost me sixpence ; so it comes to the same thing as if it had been a present.   Yes, only sixpence, in a raffle in a bazaar at Hackney, for the benefit of the Wesleyan Chapel, three years ago.   A young man who works with my brother, and lives in that part, offered him a couple of tickets ; and he took one, and I took one. When I say " I," of course I mean that he took the two ; for how should I find (by which I mean, of course, how should *he* find) a sixpence in that little cup on the chimney-piece unless he had put it there first? Of course my ticket took a prize, and of course, as my bed is my dwelling-place, the prize was a beautiful counterpane, of every colour of the rainbow. Oh, there never was such luck as mine !' Rosy exclaimed, flashing her gay, strange eyes at Hyacinth, as if on purpose to irritate him with her contradictious optimism.

'It's very lovely ; but if you would like another, for a change, I've got a great many pieces,' Pinnie remarked, with a generosity which made the young man feel that she was acquitting herself finely.

Rose Muniment laid her little hand on the dressmaker's arm, and responded, quickly, ' No, not a change, not a change. How can there be a change when there's already everything? There's everything here—every colour that was ever seen, or composed, or dreamed of, since the world began.' And with her other hand she stroked, affectionately, her variegated quilt. ' You have a great many pieces, but you haven't as many as there are here ; and the more you should patch them together the more the whole thing would resemble this dear, dazzling old friend. I have another idea, very, very charming, and perhaps her ladyship can guess what it is.' Rosy kept her fingers on Pinnie's arm, and, smiling, turned her brilliant eyes from one of her female companions to the other, as if she wished to associate them as much as possible in their interest in her. ' In connection with what we were talking about a few minutes ago—couldn't your ladyship just go a little further, in the same line ?' Then, as Lady Aurora looked troubled and embarrassed, blushing at being called upon to answer a conundrum, as it were, so publicly, her infirm friend came to her assistance. ' It will surprise you at first, but it won't when I have explained it : my idea is just simply a pink dressing-gown !'

'A pink dressing-gown!' Lady Aurora repeated.

'With a neat black trimming! Don't you see the connection with what we were talking of before our good visitors came in?'

'That would be very pretty,' said Pinnie. 'I have made them like that, in my time. Or blue, trimmed with white.'

'No, pink and black, pink and black—to suit my complexion. Perhaps you didn't know I have a complexion; but there are very few things I haven't got! Anything at all I should fancy, you were so good as to say. Well now, I fancy that! Your ladyship does see the connection by this time, doesn't she?'

Lady Aurora looked distressed, as if she felt that she certainly ought to see it but was not sure that even yet it didn't escape her, and as if, at the same time, she were struck with the fact that this sudden evocation might result in a strain on the little dressmaker's resources. 'A pink dressing-gown would certainly be very becoming, and Miss Pynsent would be very kind,' she said; while Hyacinth made the mental comment that it was a largeish order, as Pinnie would have, obviously, to furnish the materials as well as the labour. The amiable coolness with which the invalid laid her under contribution was, however, to his sense, quite in character, and he reflected that, after all, when you were stretched on your back like that you had the right to reach out your hands (it wasn't far you could reach at best), and seize what you could get. Pinnie declared that she knew just the article Miss Muniment wanted, and that she would undertake to make a sweet thing of it; and Rosy went on to say that she must explain of what use such an article would be, but for this purpose there must be another guess. She would give it to Miss Pynsent and Hyacinth—as many times as they liked: What *had* she and Lady Aurora been talking about before they came in? She clasped her hands, and her eyes glittered with her eagerness, while she continued to turn them from Lady Aurora to the dressmaker. What would they imagine? What would they think natural, delightful, magnificent—if one could only end, at last, by making out the right place to put it? Hyacinth suggested, successively, a cage of Java sparrows, a music-box and a shower-bath—or perhaps even a full-length portrait of her ladyship; and Pinnie looked at him askance, in a frightened way, as if perchance he were joking too broadly. Rosy at last relieved their suspense and announced, ' A sofa, just a sofa, now! What do you say to that? Do you suppose that's an idea that could have come from any one but her ladyship? She must have all the credit of it; she came out with it in the course of conversation. I believe we were talking of the peculiar feeling that comes just under the shoulder-blades if one never has a change. She mentioned it as she might have mentioned a plaster, or another spoonful of that American stuff. We are thinking it over, and one of these days, if we give plenty of time to the question, we shall find the place, the very nicest and snuggest of all, and no other. I hope *you* see the connection with the pink dressing-gown,' she remarked to Pinnie, ' and I hope you see the importance of the question, Shall anything go? I should like you to look round a bit, and tell me what you would answer if I were to say to you, *Can* anything go?'

'I'm sure there's nothing *I* should like to part with,'
Pinnie returned; and while she surveyed the scene Lady
Aurora, with delicacy, to lighten Amanda's responsibility,
got up and turned to the window, which was open to the
summer-evening and admitted still the last rays of the
long day. Hyacinth, after a moment, placed himself
beside her, looking out with her at the dusky multitude of
chimney-pots and the small black houses, roofed with
grimy tiles. The thick, warm air of a London July
floated beneath them, suffused with the everlasting uproar of the town, which appeared to have sunk into quietness but again became a mighty voice as soon as one
listened for it; here and there, in poor windows, glimmered
a turbid light, and high above, in a clearer, smokeless zone,
a sky still fair and luminous, a faint silver star looked
down. The sky was the same that, far away in the
country, bent over golden fields and purple hills and
gardens where nightingales sang; but from this point of
view everything that covered the earth was ugly and
sordid, and seemed to express, or to represent, the weariness of toil. In an instant, to Hyacinth's surprise, Lady
Aurora said to him, 'You never came, after all, to get the
books.'

'Those you kindly offered to lend me? I didn't know
it was an understanding.'

Lady Aurora gave an uneasy laugh. 'I have picked
them out; they are quite ready.'

'It's very kind of you,' the young man rejoined. 'I
will come and get them some day, with pleasure.' He
was not very sure that he would; but it was the least he
could say.

'She'll tell you where I live, you know,' Lady Aurora
went on, with a movement of her head in the direction of
the bed, as if she were too shy to mention it herself.

'Oh, I have no doubt she knows the way—she could
tell me every street and every turn!' Hyacinth exclaimed.

'She has made me describe to her, very often, how I
come and go.   I think that few people know more about
London than she.   She never forgets anything.'

'She's a wonderful little witch — she terrifies me!'
said Hyacinth.

Lady Aurora turned her modest eyes upon him.   'Oh,
she's so good, she's so patient!'

'Yes, and so wise, and so self-possessed.'

'Oh, she's immensely clever,' said her ladyship.
'Which do you think the cleverest?'

'The cleverest?'

'I mean of the girl and her brother.'

'Oh, I think he, some day, will be prime minister of
England.'

'Do you really?   I'm so glad!' cried Lady Aurora,
with a flush of colour in her face.   'I'm so glad you think
that will be possible.   You know it ought to be, if things
were right.'

Hyacinth had not professed this high faith for the purpose of playing upon her ladyship's feelings, but when he
perceived her eager responsiveness he felt almost as if he
had been making sport of her.   Still, he said no more
than he believed when he remarked, in a moment, that
he had the greatest expectations of Paul Muniment's
future : he was sure that the world would hear of him,
that England would feel him, that the public, some day,
would acclaim him.   It was impossible to associate with
him without feeling that he was very strong, that he must
play an important part.

'Yes, people wouldn't believe—they wouldn't believe,'
Lady Aurora murmured softly, appreciatively.   She was
evidently very much pleased with what Hyacinth was
saying.   It was moreover a pleasure to himself to place
on record his opinion of his friend ; it seemed to make
that opinion more clear, to give it the force of an invoca-

tion, a prophecy. This was especially the case when he asked why on earth nature had endowed Paul Muniment with such extraordinary powers of mind, and powers of body too—because he was as strong as a horse—if it had not been intended that he should do something great for his fellow-men. Hyacinth confided to her ladyship that he thought the people in his own class generally very stupid —what he should call third-rate minds. He wished it were not so, for heaven knew that he felt kindly to them and only asked to cast his lot with theirs; but he was obliged to confess that centuries of poverty, of ill-paid toil, of bad, insufficient food and wretched homes, had not a favourable effect upon the higher faculties. All the more reason that when there was a splendid exception, like Paul Muniment, it should count for a tremendous force—it had so much to make up for, to act for. And then Hyacinth repeated that in his own low walk of life people had really not the faculty of thought; their minds had been simplified —reduced to two or three elements. He saw that this declaration made his interlocutress very uncomfortable; she turned and twisted herself, vaguely, as if she wished to protest, but she was far too considerate to interrupt him. He had no desire to distress her, but there were times in which it was impossible for him to withstand the perverse satisfaction he took in insisting on his lowliness of station, in turning the knife about in the wound inflicted by such explicit reference, and in letting it be seen that if his place in the world was immeasurably small he at least had no illusions about either himself or his fellows. Lady Aurora replied, as quickly as possible, that she knew a great deal about the poor—not the poor like Rose Muniment, but the terribly, hopelessly poor, with whom she was more familiar than Hyacinth would perhaps believe—and that she was often struck with their great talents, with their quick wit, with their conversation being really much more entertaining, to her at least, than what one usually heard in drawing-rooms. She often found them immensely clever.

Hyacinth smiled at her, and said, ' Ah, when you get to the lowest depths of poverty, they may become very brilliant again. But I'm afraid I haven't gone so far down. In spite of my opportunities, I don't know many absolute paupers.'

'I know a great many.' Lady Aurora hesitated, as if she didn't like to boast, and then she added, 'I daresay I know more than any one.' There was something touching, beautiful, to Hyacinth, in this simple, diffident admission; it confirmed his impression that Lady Aurora was in some mysterious, incongruous, and even slightly ludicrous manner a heroine, a creature of a noble ideal. She perhaps guessed that he was indulging in reflections that might be favourable to her, for she said, precipitately, the next minute, as if there were nothing she dreaded so much as the danger of a compliment, 'I think your aunt's so very attractive—and I'm sure Rose Muniment thinks so.' No sooner had she spoken than she blushed again; it appeared to have occurred to her that he might suppose she wished to contradict him by presenting this case of his aunt as a proof that the baser sort, even in a prosaic upper layer, were not without redeeming points. There was no reason why she should not have had this intention; so without sparing her, Hyacinth replied—

'You mean that she's an exception to what I was saying?'

Lady Aurora stammered a little; then, at last, as if, since he wouldn't spare her, she wouldn't spare him, either, 'Yes, and you're an exception, too; you'll not make me believe you're wanting in intelligence. The Muniments don't think so,' she added.

'No more do I myself; but that doesn't prove that exceptions are not frequent. I have blood in my veins that is not the blood of the people.'

'Oh, I see,' said Lady Aurora, sympathetically. And with a smile she went on : 'Then you're all the more of an exception—in the upper class !'

Her smile was the kindest in the world, but it did not blind Hyacinth to the fact that from his own point of view he had been extraordinarily indiscreet. He believed a moment before that he would have been proof against the strongest temptation to refer to the mysteries of his lineage, inasmuch as, if made in a boastful spirit (and he had no desire as yet to make it an exercise in humility) any such

reference would inevitably contain an element of the
grotesque. He had never opened his lips to any one about
his birth (since the dreadful days when the question was
discussed, with Mr. Vetch's assistance, in Lomax Place);
never even to Paul Muniment, never to Millicent Henning
nor to Eustache Poupin. He had an impression that
people had ideas about him, and with some of Miss
Henning's he had been made acquainted : they were
of such a nature that he sometimes wondered whether
the tie which united him to her were not, on her
own side, a secret determination to satisfy her utmost
curiosity before she had done with him. But he flattered
himself that he was impenetrable, and none the less he had
begun to swagger, idiotically, the first time a temptation (to
call a temptation) presented itself. He turned crimson as
soon as he had spoken, partly at the sudden image of what
he had to swagger about, and partly at the absurdity of a
challenge having appeared to proceed from the bashful
gentlewoman before him. He hoped she didn't particularly regard what he had said (and indeed she gave no
sign whatever of being startled by his claim to a pedigree
—she had too much quick delicacy for that ; she appeared
to notice only the symptoms of confusion that followed it),
but as soon as possible he gave himself a lesson in humility
by remarking, ' I gather that you spend most of your time
among the poor, and I am sure you carry blessings with
you. But I frankly confess that I don't understand a lady
giving herself up to people like us when there is no obligation. Wretched company we must be, when there is so
much better to be had.'

' I like it very much—you don't understand.'

' Precisely—that is what I say. Our little friend on
the bed is perpetually talking about your house, your
family, your splendours, your gardens and green-houses ;
they must be magnificent, of course——'

' Oh, I wish she wouldn't ; really, I wish she wouldn't.
It makes one feel dreadfully !' Lady Aurora interposed,
with vehemence.

' Ah, you had better give her her way ; it's such a
pleasure to her.'

'Yes, more than to any of us!' sighed her ladyship, helplessly.

'Well, how can you leave all those beautiful things, to come and breathe this beastly air, surround yourself with hideous images, and associate with people whose smallest fault is that they are ignorant, brutal and dirty? I don't speak of the ladies here present,' Hyacinth added, with the manner which most made Millicent Henning (who at once admired and hated it), wonder where on earth he had got it.

'Oh, I wish I could make you understand!' cried Lady Aurora, looking at him with troubled, appealing eyes, as if he were unexpectedly discouraging.

'After all, I do understand! Charity exists in your nature as a kind of passion.'

'Yes, yes, it's a kind of passion!' her ladyship repeated, eagerly, very thankful for the word. 'I don't know whether it's charity—I don't mean that. But whatever it is, it's a passion—it's my life—it's all I care for.' She hesitated a moment, as if there might be something indecent in the confession, or dangerous in the recipient; and then, evidently, she was mastered by the comfort of being able to justify herself for an eccentricity that had excited notice, as well as by the luxury of discharging her soul of a long accumulation of timid, sacred sentiment. 'Already, when I was fifteen years old, I wanted to sell all I had and give to the poor. And ever since, I have wanted to do something; it has seemed as if my heart would break if I shouldn't be able!'

Hyacinth was struck with a great respect, which, however, did not prevent him (the words sounded patronising, even to himself), from saying in a moment, 'I suppose you are very religious.'

Lady Aurora looked away, into the thickening dusk, at the smutty housetops, the blurred emanation, above the streets, of lamplight. 'I don't know—one has one's ideas—some of them may be strange. I think a great many clergymen do good, but there are others I don't like at all. I daresay we had too many, always, at home; my father likes them so much. I think I have known too many bishops; I have had the church too much on my back. I daresay they wouldn't think at home, you know, that one was quite what one ought to be ; but of course they consider me very odd, in every way, as there's no doubt I am. I should tell you that I don't tell them everything ; for what's the use, when people don't understand ? We are twelve at home, and eight of us are girls ; and if you think it's so very splendid, and *she* thinks so, I should like you both to try it for a little ! My father isn't rich, and there is only one of us married, and we are not at all handsome, and— oh, there are all kinds of things,' the young woman went on, looking round at him an instant, shyly but excitedly.   ' I don't like society ; and neither would you if you were to see the kind there is in London—at least in some parts,' Lady Aurora added, considerately.   ' I daresay you wouldn't believe all the humbuggery and the tiresomeness that one has to go through. But I've got out of it ; I do as I like, though it has been rather a struggle. I have my liberty, and that is the greatest blessing in life, except the reputation of being queer, and even a little mad, which is a greater advantage still. I'm a little mad, you know ; you needn't be surprised if you hear it. That's because I stop in town when they go into the country ; all the autumn, all the winter, when there's no one here (except three or four millions), and the rain drips, drips, drips, from the trees in the big, dull park, where my people live. I daresay I oughtn't to say such things to you, but, as I tell you, I'm a little mad, and I might as well keep up my character. When one is one of eight daughters, and there's very little money (for any of us, at least), and there's nothing to do but to go out with three or four others in a mackintosh, one can easily go off one's head. Of course there's the village, and it's not at all a nice one, and there are the people to look after, and heaven knows they're in want of it ; but one must work with the vicarage, and at the vicarage there are four more daughters, all old maids, and it's dreary, and it's dreadful, and one has too much of it, and they don't under- stand what one thinks or feels, or a single word one says to them ! Besides they *are* stupid, I admit—the country poor ; they are very, very dense.   I like Camberwell better,' said Lady Aurora, smiling and taking breath, at the end of her

nervous, hurried, almost incoherent speech, of which she
had delivered herself pantingly, with strange intonations and
grotesque movements of her neck, as if she were afraid
from one moment to the other that she would repent, not
of her confidence, but of her egotism.

It placed her, for Hyacinth, in an unexpected light, and
made him feel that her awkward, aristocratic spinsterhood
was the cover of tumultuous passions. No one could have
less the appearance of being animated by a vengeful irony;
but he saw that this delicate, shy, generous, and evidently
most tender creature was not a person to spare, wherever
she could prick them, the institutions among which she had
been brought up and against which she had violently reacted.
Hyacinth had always supposed that a reactionary meant a
backslider from the liberal faith, but Rosy's devotee gave a
new value to the term; she appeared to have been driven
to her present excesses by the squire and the parson and
the conservative influences of that upper-class British home
which our young man had always supposed to be the highest
fruit of civilisation. It was clear that her ladyship was an
original, and an original with force; but it gave Hyacinth
a real pang to hear her make light of Inglefield (especially
the park), and of the opportunities that must have abounded
in Belgrave Square. It had been his belief that in a world
of suffering and injustice these things were, if not the most
righteous, at least the most fascinating. If they didn't give
one the finest sensations, where were such sensations to be
had? He looked at Lady Aurora with a face which was a
tribute to her sudden vividness, and said, 'I can easily
understand your wanting to do some good in the world,
because you're a kind of saint.'

'A very curious kind!' laughed her ladyship.

'But I don't understand your not liking what your
position gives you.'

'I don't know anything about my position. I want to
live!'

'And do you call *this* life?'

'I'll tell you what my position is, if you want to know:
it's the deadness of the grave!'

Hyacinth was startled by her tone, but he nevertheless

laughed back at her, ' Ah, as I say, you're a kind of saint ! '
She made no reply, for at that moment the door opened,
and Paul Muniment's tall figure emerged from the blackness
of the staircase into the twilight, now very faint, of the
room.   Lady Aurora's eyes, as they rested upon him, seemed
to declare that such a vision as that, at least, was life.
Another person, as tall as himself, appeared behind him,
and Hyacinth recognised with astonishment their insinuating
friend Captain Sholto.   Muniment had brought him up for
Rosy's entertainment, being ready, and more than ready,
always, to usher in any one in the world, from the prime
minister to the common hangman, who might give that
young lady a sensation.   They must have met at the ' Sun
and Moon,' and if the Captain, some accident smoothing
the way, had made him half as many advances as he had
made some other people Hyacinth could see that it wouldn't
take long for Paul to lay him under contribution.   But what
the mischief was the Captain up to ?   It cannot be said
that our young man arrived, this evening, at an answer to
that question.   The occasion proved highly festal, and the
hostess rose to it without lifting her head from the pillow.
Her brother introduced Captain Sholto as a gentleman who
had a great desire to know extraordinary people, and she
made him take possession of the chair at her bedside, out
of which Miss Pynsent quickly edged herself, and asked him
who he was, and where he came from, and how Paul had
made his acquaintance, and whether he had many friends
in Camberwell.   Sholto had not the same grand air that
hovered about him at the theatre ; he was shabbily dressed,
very much like Hyacinth himself ; but his appearance gave
our young man an opportunity to wonder what made him
so unmistakably a gentleman in spite of his seedy coat and
trousers—in spite too, of his rather overdoing the manner
of being appreciative even to rapture and thinking everything and every one most charming and curious.   He stood
out, in poor Rosy's tawdry little room, among her hideous
attempts at decoration, and looked to Hyacinth a being
from another sphere, playing over the place and company
a smile (one couldn't call it false or unpleasant, yet it was
distinctly not natural), of which he had got the habit in

camps and courts.   It became brilliant when it rested on
Hyacinth, and the Captain greeted him as he might have
done a dear young friend from whom he had been long and
painfully separated.   He was easy, he was familiar, he was
exquisitely benevolent and bland, and altogether incomprehensible.

Rosy was a match for him, however.   He evidently didn't
puzzle her in the least; she thought his visit the most
natural thing in the world.   She expressed all the gratitude
that decency required, but appeared to assume that people
who climbed her stairs would always find themselves repaid.
She remarked that her brother must have met him for the first
time that day, for the way that he sealed a new acquaintance
was usually by bringing the person immediately to call upon
her.   And when the Captain said that if she didn't like
them he supposed the poor wretches were dropped on the
spot, she admitted that this would be true if it ever happened
that she disapproved ; as yet, however, she had not been
obliged to draw the line.   This was perhaps partly because
he had not brought up any of his political friends—people
that he knew only for political reasons.   Of these people,
in general, she had a very small opinion, and she would not
conceal from Captain Sholto that she hoped he was not one
of them.   Rosy spoke as if her brother represented the
Camberwell district in the House of Commons and she had
discovered that a parliamentary career lowered the moral
tone.   The Captain, however, entered quite into her views,
and told her that it was as common friends of Mr. Hyacinth
Robinson that Mr. Muniment and he had come together ;
they were both so fond of him that this had immediately
constituted a kind of tie.   On hearing himself commemorated
in such a brilliant way Mr. Hyacinth Robinson averted
himself ; he saw that Captain Sholto might be trusted to
make as great an effort for Rosy's entertainment as he
gathered that he had made for that of Millicent Henning,
that evening at the theatre.   There were not chairs enough
to go round, and Paul fetched a three-legged stool from his
own apartment, after which he undertook to make tea for
the company, with the aid of a tin kettle and a spirit-lamp ;
these implements having been set out, flanked by half a

dozen cups, in honour, presumably, of the little dressmaker, who was to come such a distance. The little dressmaker, Hyacinth observed with pleasure, fell into earnest conversation with Lady Aurora, who bent over her, flushed, smiling, stammering, and apparently so nervous that Pinnie, in comparison, was majestic and serene. They communicated presently to Hyacinth a plan they had unanimously evolved, to the effect that Miss Pynsent should go home to Belgrave Square with her ladyship, to settle certain preliminaries in regard to the pink dressing-gown, toward which, if Miss Pynsent assented, her ladyship hoped to be able to contribute sundry morsels of stuff which had proved their quality in honourable service and might be dyed to the proper tint. Pinnie, Hyacinth could see, was in a state of religious exaltation ; the visit to Belgrave Square and the idea of co-operating in such a manner with the nobility were privileges she could not take solemnly enough. The latter luxury, indeed, she began to enjoy without delay ; Lady Aurora suggesting that Mr. Muniment might be rather awkward about making tea, and that they should take the business off his hands. Paul gave it up to them, with a pretence of compassion for their conceit, remarking that at any rate it took two women to supplant one man ; and Hyacinth drew him to the window, to ask where he had encountered Sholto and how he liked him.

They had met in Bloomsbury, as Hyacinth supposed, and Sholto had made up to him very much as a country curate might make up to an archbishop. He wanted to know what he thought of this and that : of the state of the labour market at the East End, of the terrible case of the old woman who had starved to death at Walham Green, of the practicability of more systematic out-of-door agitation, and the prospects of their getting one of their own men — one of the Bloomsbury lot —into Parliament. 'He was mighty civil,' Muniment said, 'and I don't find that he has picked my pocket. He looked as if he would like me to suggest that *he* should stand as one of our own men, one of the Bloomsbury lot. He asks too many questions, but he makes up for it by not paying any attention to the answers. He told me he would give the world to see a working-man's "interior." I didn't know what he meant at first: he wanted a favourable specimen, one of the best; he had seen one or two that he didn't believe to be up to the average. I suppose he meant Schinkel, the cabinetmaker, and he wanted to compare. I told him I didn't know what sort of a specimen my place would be, but that he was welcome to look round, and that it contained at any rate one or two original features. I expect he has found that's the case—with Rosy and the noble lady. I wanted to show him off to Rosy; he's good for that, if he isn't good for anything else. I told him we expected a little company this evening, so it might be a good time; and he assured me that to mingle in such an occasion as that was the dream of his existence. He seemed in a rare hurry, as if I were going to show him a hidden treasure, and insisted on driving me over in a hansom. Perhaps his idea is to introduce the use of cabs among the working-classes; certainly, I'll vote for him for Parliament, if that's his line. On our way over he talked to me about you; told you were an intimate friend of his.'

'What did he say about me?' Hyacinth inquired, with promptness.

'Vain little beggar!'

'Did he call me that?' said Hyacinth, ingenuously.

'He said you were simply astonishing.'

'Simply astonishing?' Hyacinth repeated.

'For a person of your low extraction.'

'Well, I may be queer, but he is certainly queerer. Don't you think so, now you know him?'

Paul Muniment looked at his young friend a moment. 'Do you want to know what he is? He's a tout.'

'A tout? What do you mean?'

'Well, a cat's-paw, if you like better.'

Hyacinth stared. 'For whom, pray?'

'Or a fisherman, if you like better still. I give you your choice of comparisons. I made them up as we came along in the hansom. He throws his nets and hauls in the little fishes—the pretty little shining, wriggling fishes. They are all for her; she swallows 'em down.'

' For her ?   Do you mean the Princess ? '

' Who else should I mean ?   Take care, my tadpole ! '

' Why should I take care ?   The other day you told me not to.'

' Yes, I remember.   But now I see more.'

' Did he speak of her ?   What did he say ? ' asked Hyacinth, eagerly.

' I can't tell you now what he said, but I'll tell you what I guessed.'

' And what's that ? '

They had been talking, of course, in a very low tone, and their voices were covered by Rosy's chatter in the corner, by the liberal laughter with which Captain Sholto accompanied it, and by the much more discreet, though earnest, intermingled accents of Lady Aurora and Miss Pynsent.   But Paul Muniment spoke more softly still— Hyacinth felt a kind of suspense—as he replied in a moment, ' Why, she's a monster ! '

' A monster ? ' repeated our young man, from whom, this evening, Paul Muniment seemed destined to elicit ejaculations and echoes.

Muniment glanced toward the Captain, who was apparently more and more fascinated by Rosy.   ' In him I think there's no great harm.   He's only a conscientious fisherman ! '

It must be admitted that Captain Sholto justified to a certain extent this definition by the manner in which he baited his hook for such little facts as might help him to a more intimate knowledge of his host and hostess. When the tea was made, Rose Muniment asked Miss Pynsent to be so good as to hand it about.   They must let her poor ladyship rest a little, must they not ?—and Hyacinth could see that in her innocent but inveterate self-complacency she wished to reward and encourage the dressmaker, draw her out and present her still more, by offering her this graceful exercise.   Sholto sprang up at this, and begged Pinnie to let him relieve her, taking a cup from her hand ; and poor Pinnie, who perceived in a moment that he was some kind of masquerading gentleman, who was bewildered by the strange mixture of

elements that surrounded her and unused to being treated
like a duchess (for the Captain's manner was a triumph
of respectful gallantry), collapsed, on the instant, into a
chair, appealing to Lady Aurora with a frightened smile
and conscious that, deeply versed as she might be in the
theory of decorum, she had no precedent that could meet
such an occasion. 'Now, how many families would there
be in such a house as this, and what should you say about
the sanitary arrangements? Would there be others on
this floor—what is it, the third, the fourth?—beside yourselves, you know, and should you call it a fair specimen of
a tenement of its class?' It was with such inquiries as
this that Captain Sholto beguiled their tea-drinking, while
Hyacinth made the reflection that, though he evidently
meant them very well, they were characterised by a want
of fine tact, by too patronising a curiosity. The Captain
requested information as to the position in life, the avoca-
tions and habits, of the other lodgers, the rent they paid,
their relations with each other, both in and out of the
family. 'Now, would there be a good deal of close packing,
do you suppose, and any perceptible want of—a—sobriety?'

Paul Muniment, who had swallowed his cup of tea at
a single gulp—there was no offer of a second—gazed out
of the window into the dark, which had now come on,
with his hands in his pockets, whistling, impolitely, no
doubt, but with brilliant animation. He had the manner
of having made over their visitor altogether to Rosy and of
thinking that whatever he said or did it was all so much
grist to her indefatigable little mill. Lady Aurora looked
distressed and embarrassed, and it is a proof of the degree
to which our little hero had the instincts of a man of the
world that he guessed exactly how vulgar she thought this
new acquaintance. She was doubtless rather vexed, also
—Hyacinth had learned this evening that Lady Aurora
could be vexed—at the alacrity of Rosy's responses; the
little person in the bed gave the Captain every satisfaction,
considered his questions as a proper tribute to humble respectability, and supplied him, as regards the population
of Audley Court, with statistics and anecdotes which she
had picked up by mysterious processes of her own. At last

Lady Aurora, upon whom Paul Muniment had not been at
pains to bestow much conversation, took leave of her, and
signified to Hyacinth that for the rest of the evening she
would assume the care of Miss Pynsent. Pinnie looked
very tense and solemn, now that she was really about to be
transported to Belgrave Square, but Hyacinth was sure she
would acquit herself only the more honourably ; and when
he offered to call for her there, later, she reminded him,
under her breath, with a little sad smile, of the many years
during which, after nightfall, she had carried her work,
pinned up in cloth, about London.

Paul Muniment, according to his habit, lighted Lady
Aurora downstairs, and Captain Sholto and Hyacinth were
alone for some minutes with Rosy ; which gave the former,
taking up his hat and stick, an opportunity to say to his
young friend, 'Which way are you going ? Not my way,
by chance ?' Hyacinth saw that he hoped for his company, and he became conscious that, strangely as Muniment had indulged him and too promiscuously investigating
as he had just shown himself, this ingratiating personage
was not more easy to resist than he had been the other
night at the theatre. The Captain bent over Rosy's bed as
if she had been a fine lady on a satin sofa, promising
to come back very soon and very often, and the two men
went downstairs. On their way they met Paul Muniment
coming up, and Hyacinth felt rather ashamed, he could
scarcely tell why, that his friend should see him marching
off with the 'tout.' After all, if Muniment had brought
him to see his sister, might not he at least walk with him ?
'I'm coming again, you know, very often. I daresay you'll
find me a great bore !' the Captain announced, as he bade
good-night to his host. 'Your sister is a most interesting
creature, one of the most interesting creatures I have ever
seen, and the whole thing, you know, exactly the sort
of thing I wanted to get at, only much more—really, much
more—original and curious. It has been a great success,
a grand success !'

And the Captain felt his way down the dusky shaft, while
Paul Muniment, above, gave him the benefit of rather a
wavering candlestick, and answered his civil speech with an

'Oh, well, you take us as you find us, you know!' and an outburst of frank but not unfriendly laughter.

Half-an-hour later Hyacinth found himself in Captain Sholto's chambers, seated on a big divan covered with Persian rugs and cushions and smoking the most delectable cigar that had ever touched his lips. As they left Audley Court the Captain had taken his arm, and they had walked along together in a desultory, colloquial manner, till on Westminster Bridge (they had followed the embankment, beneath St. Thomas's Hospital) Sholto said, 'By the way, why shouldn't you come home with me and see my little place? I've got a few things that might amuse you—some pictures, some odds and ends I've picked up, and a few bindings; you might tell me what you think of them.' Hyacinth assented, without hesitation; he had still in his ear the reverberation of the Captain's inquiries in Rose Muniment's room, and he saw no reason why he, on his side, should not embrace an occasion of ascertaining how, as his companion would have said, a man of fashion would live now.

This particular specimen lived in a large, old-fashioned house in Queen Anne Street, of which he occupied the upper floors, and whose high, wainscoted rooms he had filled with the spoils of travel and the ingenuities of modern taste. There was not a country in the world he did not appear to have ransacked, and to Hyacinth his trophies represented a wonderfully long purse. The whole establishment, from the low-voiced, inexpressive valet who, after he had poured brandy into tall tumblers, gave dignity to the popping of soda-water corks, to the quaint little silver receptacle in which he was invited to deposit the ashes of his cigar, was such a revelation for our appreciative hero that he felt himself hushed and made sad, so poignant was the thought that it took thousands of things which he, then, should never possess nor know to make an accomplished man. He had often, in evening-walks, wondered what was behind the walls of certain spacious, bright-windowed houses in the West End, and now he got an idea. The first effect of the idea was to overwhelm him.

'Well, now, tell me what you thought of our friend the

Princess,' the Captain said, thrusting out the loose yellow slippers which his servant had helped to exchange for his shoes. He spoke as if he had been waiting impatiently for the proper moment to ask that question, so much might depend on the answer.

'She's beautiful—beautiful,' Hyacinth answered, almost dreamily, with his eyes wandering all over the room.

'She was so interested in all you said to her; she would like so much to see you again. She means to write to you—I suppose she can address to the "Sun and Moon"?—and I hope you'll go to her house, if she proposes a day.'

'I don't know—I don't know. It seems so strange.'

'What seems strange, my dear fellow?'

'Everything! My sitting here with you; my introduction to that lady; the idea of her wanting, as you say, to see me again, and of her writing to me; and this whole place of yours, with all these dim, rich curiosities hanging on the walls and glinting in the light of that rose-coloured lamp. You yourself, too—you are strangest of all.'

The Captain looked at him, in silence, so fixedly for a while, through the fumes of their tobacco, after he had made this last charge, that Hyacinth thought he was perhaps offended; but this impression was presently dissipated by further manifestations of sociability and hospitality, and Sholto took occasion, later, to let him know how important it was, in the days they were living in, not to have too small a measure of the usual, destined as they certainly were—'in the whole matter of the relations of class with class, and all that sort of thing, you know'—to witness some very startling developments. The Captain spoke as if, for his part, he were a child of his age (so that he only wanted to see all it could show him), down to the point of his yellow slippers. Hyacinth felt that he himself had not been very satisfactory about the Princess; but as his nerves began to tremble a little more into tune with the situation he repeated to his host what Millicent Henning had said about her at the theatre—asked if this young lady had correctly understood him in believing that she had been turned out of the house by her husband.

'Yes, he literally pushed her into the street—or into the garden ; I believe the scene took place in the country. But perhaps Miss Henning didn't mention, or perhaps I didn't mention, that the Prince would at the present hour give everything he owns in the world to get her back. Fancy such a scene !' said the Captain, laughing in a manner that struck Hyacinth as rather profane.

He stared, with dilated eyes, at this picture, which seemed to evoke a comparison with the only incident of the sort that had come within his experience—the forcible ejection of intoxicated females from public houses. 'That magnificent being—what had she done ? '

'Oh, she had made him feel he was an ass !' the Captain answered, promptly. He turned the conversation to Miss Henning ; said he was so glad Hyacinth gave him an opportunity to speak of her. He got on with her famously ; perhaps she had told him. They became immense friends—*en tout bien tout honneur, s'entend.* Now, *there* was another London type, plebeian but brilliant ; and how little justice one usually did it, how magnificent it was ! But she, of course, was a wonderful specimen. 'My dear fellow, I have seen many women, and the women of many countries,' the Captain went on, 'and I have seen them intimately, and I know what I am talking about ; and when I tell you that that one—that one——' Then he suddenly paused, laughing in his democratic way. 'But perhaps I am going too far : you must always pull me up, you know, when I do. At any rate, I congratulate you ; I do, heartily. Have another cigar. Now what sort of— a—salary would she receive at her big shop, you know ? I know where it is ; I mean to go there and buy some pocket-handkerchiefs.'

Hyacinth knew neither how far Captain Sholto had been going, nor exactly on what he congratulated him ; and he pretended, at least, an equal ignorance on the subject of Millicent's salary. He didn't want to talk about her, moreover, nor about his own life ; he wanted to talk about the Captain's, and to elicit information that would be in harmony with his romantic chambers, which reminded our hero somehow of Bulwer's novels. His host gratified this

desire most liberally, and told him twenty stories of things
that had happened to him in Albania, in Madagascar, and
even in Paris.   Hyacinth induced him easily to talk about
Paris (from a different point of view from M. Poupin's), and
sat there drinking in enchantments.   The only thing that
fell below the high level of his entertainment was the
bindings of the Captain's books, which he told him frankly,
with the conscience of an artist, were not very good.   After
he left Queen Anne Street he was quite too excited to go
straight home ; he walked about with his mind full of
images and strange speculations, till the gray London
streets began to grow clear with the summer dawn.

THE aspect of South Street, Mayfair, on a Sunday afternoon in August, is not enlivening, yet the Prince had stood for ten minutes gazing out of the window at the genteel vacancy of the scene; at the closed blinds of the opposite houses, the lonely policeman on the corner, covering a yawn with a white cotton hand, the low-pitched light itself, which seemed conscious of an obligation to observe the decency of the British Sabbath. The Prince, however, had a talent for that kind of attitude; it was one of the things by which he had exasperated his wife; he could remain motionless, with the aid of some casual support for his high, lean person, considering serenely and inexpressively any object that might lie before him and presenting his aristocratic head at a favourable angle, for periods of extraordinary length. On first coming into the room he had given some attention to its furniture and decorations, perceiving at a glance that they were rich and varied; some of the things he recognised as old friends, odds and ends the Princess was fond of, which had accompanied her in her remarkable wanderings, while others were unfamiliar, and suggested vividly that she had not ceased to 'collect.' The Prince made two reflections: one was that she was living as expensively as ever; the other that, however this might be, no one had such a feeling as she for the *mise-en-scène* of life, such a talent for arranging a room. She had still the most charming salon in Europe.

It was his impression that she had taken the house in South Street but for three months; yet, gracious heaven, what had she not put into it? The Prince asked himself this question without violence, for that was not to be his line to-day. He could be angry to a point at which he

himself was often frightened, but he honestly believed that
this was only when he had been baited beyond endurance
and that as a usual thing he was really as mild and accommodating as the extreme urbanity of his manner appeared
to announce.   There was indeed nothing to suggest to the
world in general that he was an impracticable or vindictive
nobleman : his features were not regular, and his complexion
had a bilious tone ; but his dark brown eye, which was at
once salient and dull, expressed benevolence and melancholy ; his head drooped from his long neck in a considerate,
attentive style ; and his close-cropped black hair, combined
with a short, fine, pointed beard, completed his resemblance
to some old portrait of a personage of distinction under
the Spanish dominion at Naples.   To-day, at any rate, he
had come in conciliation, almost in humility, and that is
why he did not permit himself even to murmur at the long
delay to which he was subjected.   He knew very well that
if his wife should consent to take him back it would be
only after a probation to which this little wait in her
drawing-room was a trifle.   It was a quarter of an hour
before the door opened, and even then it was not the
Princess who appeared, but only Madame Grandoni.

Their greeting was a very silent one.   She came to him
with both hands outstretched, and took his own and held
them awhile, looking up at him in a kindly, motherly
manner.   She had elongated her florid, humorous face to a
degree that was almost comical, and the pair might have
passed, in their speechless solemnity, for acquaintances
meeting in a house in which a funeral was about to take
place.   It was indeed a house on which death had descended, as he very soon learned from Madame Grandoni's
expression ; something had perished there for ever, and he
might proceed to bury it as soon as he liked.   His wife's
ancient German friend, however, was not a person to keep
up a manner of that sort very long, and when, after she had
made him sit down on the sofa beside her, she shook her
head, slowly and definitely, several times, it was with a face
in which a more genial appreciation of the circumstances
had already begun to appear.

‘ Never—never—never ? ’ said the Prince, in a deep,

hoarse voice, which was at variance with his aristocratic slimness. He had much of the aspect which, in late-coming members of long-descended races, we qualify to-day as effete; but his speech might have been the speech of some deep-chested fighting ancestor.

'Surely you know your wife as well as I,' she replied, in Italian, which she evidently spoke with facility, though with a strong guttural accent. 'I have been talking with her : that is what has made me keep you. I have urged her to see you. I have told her that this could do no harm and would pledge her to nothing. But you know your wife,' Madame Grandoni repeated, with a smile which was now distinctly facetious.

Prince Casamassima looked down at his boots. 'How can one ever know a person like that? I hoped she would see me for five minutes.'

'For what purpose? Have you anything to propose?'

'For what purpose? To rest my eyes on her beautiful face.'

'Did you come to England for that?'

'For what else should I have come?' the Prince inquired, turning his blighted gaze to the opposite side of South Street.

'In London, such a day as this, *già*,' said the old lady, sympathetically. 'I am very sorry for you; but if I had known you were coming I would have written to you that you might spare yourself the pain.'

The Prince gave a low, interminable sigh. 'You ask me what I wish to propose. What I wish to propose is that my wife does not kill me inch by inch.'

'She would be much more likely to do that if you lived with her!' Madame Grandoni cried.

'*Cara signora*, she doesn't appear to have killed you,' the melancholy nobleman rejoined.

'Oh, me? I am past killing. I am as hard as a stone. I went through my miseries long ago; I suffered what you have not had to suffer; I wished for death many times, and I survived it all. Our troubles don't kill us, Prince; it is we who must try to kill them. I have buried not a

few.   Besides Christina is fond of me, God knows why!'
Madame Grandoni added.

'And you are so good to her,' said the Prince, laying
his hand on her fat, wrinkled fist.

'*Che vuole?* I have known her so long. And she has
some such great qualities.'

'Ah, to whom do you say it?' And Prince Casamassima gazed at his boots again, for some moments, in
silence. Suddenly he inquired, 'How does she look to-
day?'

'She always looks the same : like an angel who came
down from heaven yesterday and has been rather disappointed in her first day on earth!'

The Prince was evidently a man of a simple nature,
and Madame Grandoni's rather violent metaphor took his
fancy. His face lighted up for a moment, and he replied
with eagerness, 'Ah, she is the only woman I have ever
seen whose beauty never for a moment falls below itself.
She has no bad days. She is so handsome when she is
angry!'

'She is very handsome to-day, but she is not angry,'
said the old lady.

'Not when my name was announced?'

'I was not with her then ; but when she sent for me
and asked me to see you, it was quite without passion.
And even when I argued with her, and tried to persuade
her (and she doesn't like that, you know), she was still
perfectly quiet.'

'She hates me, she despises me too much, eh?'

'How can I tell, dear Prince, when she never mentions
you?'

'Never, never?'

'That's much better than if she railed at you and abused
you.'

'You mean it should give me more hope for the future?'
the young man asked, quickly.

Madame Grandoni hesitated a moment. 'I mean it's
better for me,' she answered, with a laugh of which the
friendly ring covered as much as possible her equivoca-
tion.

' Ah, you like me enough to care,' he murmured, turning on her his sad, grateful eyes.

' I am very sorry for you.   *Ma che vuole ?* '

The Prince had, apparently, nothing to suggest, and he only exhaled, in reply, another gloomy groan.   Then he inquired whether his wife pleased herself in that country, and whether she intended to pass the summer in London. Would she remain long in England, and—might he take the liberty to ask?—what were her plans?   Madame Grandoni explained that the Princess had found the British metropolis much more to her taste than one might have expected, and that as for plans, she had as many, or as few, as she had always had.   Had he ever known her to carry out any arrangement, or to do anything, of any kind, she had selected or determined upon?   She always, at the last moment, did the other thing, the one that had been out of the question; and it was for this that Madame Grandoni herself privately made her preparations.   Christina, now that everything was over, would leave London from one day to the other; but they should not know where they were going until they arrived.   The old lady concluded by asking the Prince if he himself liked England. He thrust forward his thick lips.   ' How can I like anything?   Besides, I have been here before ; I have friends,' he said.

His companion perceived that he had more to say to her, to extract from her, but that he was hesitating nervously, because he feared to incur some warning, some rebuff, with which his dignity—which, in spite of his position of discomfiture, was really very great—might find it difficult to square itself.   He looked vaguely round the room, and presently he remarked, ' I wanted to see for myself how she is living.'

' Yes, that is very natural.'

' I have heard—I have heard——'   And Prince Casamassima stopped.

' You have heard great rubbish, I have no doubt.' Madame Grandoni watched him, as if she foresaw what was coming.

'She spends a terrible deal of money,' said the young man.

'Indeed she does.' The old lady knew that, careful as he was of his very considerable property, which at one time had required much nursing, his wife's prodigality was not what lay heaviest on his mind. She also knew that expensive and luxurious as Christina might be she had never yet exceeded the income settled upon her by the Prince at the time of their separation—an income determined wholly by himself and his estimate of what was required to maintain the social consequence of his name, for which he had a boundless reverence. 'She thinks she is a model of thrift—that she counts every shilling,' Madame Grandoni continued. 'If there is a virtue she prides herself upon, it's her economy. Indeed, it's the only thing for which she takes any credit.'

'I wonder if she knows that I'—the Prince hesitated a moment, then he went on—'that I spend really nothing. But I would rather live on dry bread than that, in a country like this, in this English society, she should not make a proper appearance.'

'Her appearance is all you could wish. How can it help being proper, with me to set her off?'

'You are the best thing she has, dear lady. So long as you are with her I feel a certain degree of security; and one of the things I came for was to extract from you a promise that you won't leave her.'

'Ah, let us not tangle ourselves up with promises!' Madame Grandoni exclaimed. 'You know the value of any engagement one may take with regard to the Princess; it's like promising you I will stay in the bath when the hot water is turned on. When I begin to be scalded, I have to jump out! I will stay while I can; but I shouldn't stay if she were to do certain things.' Madame Grandoni uttered these last words very gravely, and for a minute she and her companion looked deep into each other's eyes.

'What things do you mean?'

'I can't say what things. It is utterly impossible to predict, on any occasion, what Christina will do. She is capable of given us great surprises. The things I mean are things I should recognise as soon as I saw them, and they would make me leave the house on the instant.'

'So that if you have not left it yet——?' the Prince asked, in a low tone, with extreme eagerness.

'It is because I have thought I may do some good by staying.'

The young man seemed only half satisfied with this answer; nevertheless he said in a moment—'To me it makes all the difference. And if anything of the kind you speak of should happen, that would be only the greater reason for your staying—that you might interpose, that you might arrest——' He stopped short; Madame Grandoni was laughing, with her Teutonic homeliness, in his face.

'You must have been in Rome, more than once, when the Tiber had overflowed, *è vero?* What would you have thought then if you had heard people telling the poor wretches in the Ghetto, on the Ripetta, up to their knees in liquid mud, that they ought to interpose, to arrest?'

'*Capisco bene*,' said the Prince, dropping his eyes. He appeared to have closed them, for some moments, as if a slow spasm of pain were passing through him. 'I can't tell you what torments me most,' he presently went on, 'the thought that sometimes makes my heart rise into my mouth. It's a haunting fear.' And his pale face and disturbed respiration might indeed have been those of a man before whom some horrible spectre had risen.

'You needn't tell me. I know what you mean, my poor friend.'

'Do you think, then, there *is* a danger—that she will drag my name, do what no one has ever dared to do? That I would never forgive,' said the young man, almost under his breath; and the hoarseness of his whisper lent a great effect to the announcement.

Madame Grandoni wondered for a moment whether she had not better tell him (as it would prepare him for the worst), that his wife cared about as much for his name as for any old label on her luggage; but after an instant's reflection she reserved this information for another hour. Besides, as she said to herself, the Prince ought already to know perfectly to what extent Christina attached the idea of an obligation or an interdict to her ill-starred connection with an ignorant and superstitious Italian race whom she

despised for their provinciality, their parsimony and their
tiresomeness (she thought their talk the climax of puerility),
and whose fatuous conception of their importance in the
great modern world she had on various public occasions
sufficiently covered with her derision.   The old lady finally
contented herself with remarking, 'Dear Prince, your wife
is a very proud woman.'

'Ah, how could my wife be anything else?   But her
pride is not my pride.   And she has such ideas, such
opinions!   Some of them are monstrous.'

Madame Grandoni smiled.   'She doesn't think it so
necessary to have them when you are not there.'

'Why then do you say that you enter into my fears—
that you recognise the stories I have heard?'

I know not whether the good lady lost patience with
his persistence; at all events, she broke out, with a certain
sharpness, 'Understand this—understand this: Christina
will never consider you—your name, your illustrious traditions—in any case in which she doesn't consider, much
more, herself!'

The Prince appeared to study, for a moment, this somewhat ambiguous yet portentous phrase; then he slowly
got up, with his hat in his hand, and walked about the
room, softly, solemnly, as if he were suffering from his long
thin feet.   He stopped before one of the windows, and
took another survey of South Street; then, turning, he
suddenly inquired, in a voice into which he had evidently
endeavoured to infuse a colder curiosity, 'Is she admired
in this place?   Does she see many people?'

'She is thought very strange, of course.   But she sees
whom she likes.   And they mostly bore her to death!'
Madame Grandoni added, with a laugh.

'Why then do you tell me this country pleases her?'

Madame Grandoni left her place.   She had promised
Christina, who detested the sense of being under the same
roof with her husband, that the Prince's visit should be
kept within narrow limits; and this movement was intended
to signify as kindly as possible that it had better terminate.
'It is the common people that please her,' she replied,
with her hands folded on her crumpled satin stomach and

her humorous eyes raised to his face. ' It is the lower
orders, the *basso popolo.*'

' The *basso popolo ?* ' The Prince stared, at this fantastic announcement.

' The *povera gente,*' pursued the old lady, laughing at
his amazement.

' The London mob — the most horrible, the most
brutal—— ?'

' Oh, she wishes to raise them.'

' After all, something like that is no more than I had
heard,' said the Prince gravely.

' *Che vuole ?* Don't trouble yourself ; it won't be for
long ! '

Madame Grandoni saw that this comforting assurance
was lost upon him ; his face was turned to the door of the
room, which had been thrown open, and all his attention
was given to the person who crossed the threshold.   Madame Grandoni transferred her own to the same quarter,
and recognised the little artisan whom Christina had, in a
manner so extraordinary and so profoundly characteristic,
drawn into her box that night at the theatre, and whom she
had since told her old friend she had sent for to come and
see her.

' Mr. Robinson ! ' the butler, who had had a lesson,
announced in a loud, colourless tone.

' It won't be for long,' Madame Grandoni repeated, for
the Prince's benefit ; but it was to Mr. Robinson the words
had the air of being addressed.

He stood there while Madame Grandoni signalled to
the servant to leave the door open and wait, looking from
the queer old lady, who was as queer as before, to the tall
foreign gentleman (he recognised his foreignness at a glance),
whose eyes seemed to challenge him, to devour him ;
wondering whether he had made some mistake, and need-
ing to remind himself that he had the Princess's note in
his pocket, with the day and hour as clear as her magnificent handwriting could make them.

' Good-morning, good-morning. I hope you are well,'
said Madame Grandoni, with quick friendliness, but turning her back upon him at the same time, to ask of the

Prince, in Italian, as she extended her hand, ' And do you
not leave London soon—in a day or two ? '

The Prince made no answer; he still scrutinised the
little bookbinder from head to foot, as if he were wondering who the deuce he could be. His eyes seemed to
Hyacinth to search for the small neat bundle he ought to
have had under his arm, and without which he was incom-
plete. To the reader, however, it may be confided that,
dressed more carefully than he had ever been in his life
before, stamped with that extraordinary transformation
which the British Sunday often operates in the person of
the wage-earning cockney, with his handsome head uncovered and suppressed excitement in his brilliant little
face, the young man from Lomax Place might have passed
for anything rather than a carrier of parcels. ' The Princess wrote to me, madam, to come and see her,' he
remarked, as a precaution, in case he should have incurred
the reproach of bad taste, or at least of precipitation.

' Oh yes, I daresay.' And Madame Grandoni guided
the Prince to the door, with an expression of the hope
that he would have a comfortable journey back to Italy.

A faint flush had come into his face; he appeared to
have satisfied himself on the subject of Mr. Robinson.   ' I
must see you once more—I must—it's impossible ! '

' Ah, well, not in this house, you know.'

' Will you do me the honour to meet me, then ?'   And
as the old lady hesitated, he added, with sudden passion,
' Dearest friend, I entreat you on my knees ! '   After she
had agreed that if he would write to her, proposing a day
and place, she would see him, he raised her ancient
knuckles to his lips and, without further notice of
Hyacinth, turned away.   Madame Grandoni requested
the servant to announce the other visitor to the Princess,
and then approached Mr. Robinson, rubbing her hands
and smiling, with her head on one side.   He smiled back
at her, vaguely; he didn't know what she might be going
to say.   What she said was, to his surprise—

' My poor young man, may I take the liberty of asking
your age ? '

' Certainly, madam; I am twenty-four.'

'And I hope you are industrious, and sober, and—what do you call it in English?—steady.'

'I don't think I am very wild,' said Hyacinth, smiling still. He though the old woman patronising, but he forgave her.

'I don't know how one speaks, in this country, to young men like you. Perhaps one is considered meddling, impertinent.'

'I like the way you speak,' Hyacinth interposed.

She stared, and then with a comical affectation of dignity, replied, 'You are very good. I am glad it amuses you. You are evidently intelligent and clever,' she went on, 'and if you are disappointed it will be a pity.'

'How do you mean, if I am disappointed?' Hyacinth looked more grave.

'Well, I daresay you expect great things, when you come into a house like this. You must tell me if I wound you. I am very old-fashioned, and I am not of this country. I speak as one speaks to young men, like you, in other places.'

'I am not so easily wounded!' Hyacinth exclaimed, with a flight of imagination. 'To expect anything, one must know something, one must understand: isn't it so? And I am here without knowing, without understanding. I have come only because a lady who seems to me very beautiful and very kind has done me the honour to send for me.'

Madame Grandoni examined him a moment, as if she were struck by his good looks, by something delicate that was stamped upon him everywhere. 'I can see you are very clever, very intelligent; no, you are not like the young men I mean. All the more reason'—— And she paused, giving a little sigh. 'I want to warn you a little, and I don't know how. If you were a young Roman, it would be different.'

'A young Roman?'

'That's where I live, properly, in Rome. If I hurt you, you can explain in that way. No, you are not like them.'

'You don't hurt me—please believe that; you interest me very much,' said Hyacinth, to whom it did not occur that he himself might appear patronising. 'Of what do you want to warn me?'

'Well—only to advise you a little. Do not give up anything.'

'What can I give up?'

'Do not give up *yourself*. I say that to you in your interest. I think you have some little trade—I forget what; but whatever it may be, remember that to do it well is the best thing—it is better than paying visits, better even than a Princess!'

'Ah yes, I see what you mean!' Hyacinth exclaimed, exaggerating a little. 'I am very fond of my trade, I assure you.'

'I am delighted to hear it. Hold fast to it, then, and be quiet; be diligent, and honest, and good. I gathered the other night that you are one of the young men who want everything changed—I believe there are a great many in Italy, and also in my own dear old Deutschland—and even think it's useful to throw bombs into innocent crowds, and shoot pistols at their rulers, or at any one. I won't go into that. I might seem to be speaking for myself, and the fact is that for myself I don't care; I am so old that I may hope to spend the few days that are left me without receiving a bullet. But before you go any further please think a little whether you are right.'

'It isn't just that you should impute to me ideas which I may not have,' said Hyacinth, turning very red, but taking more and more of a fancy, all the same, to Madame Grandoni. 'You talk at your ease about our ways and means, but if we were only to make use of those that you would like to see'——— And while he blushed, smiling, the young man shook his head two or three times, with great significance.

'I shouldn't like to see any!' the old lady cried. 'I like people to bear their troubles as one has done one's self. And as for injustice, you see how kind I am to you when I say to you again, don't, don't give anything up. I will tell them to send you some tea,' she added, as she took her way out of the room, presenting to him her round, low, aged back, and dragging over the carpet a scanty and lustreless train.

HYACINTH had been warned by Mr. Vetch as to what
brilliant women might do with him (it was only a word on
the old fiddler's lips, but the word had had a point), he
had been warned by Paul Muniment, and now he was
admonished by a person supremely well placed for knowing—a fact that could not fail to deepen the emotion
which, any time these three days, had made him draw his
breath more quickly. That emotion, however, was now
not of a kind to make him fear remote consequences; as
he looked over the Princess Casamassima's drawing-room
and inhaled an air that seemed to him inexpressibly delicate
and sweet, he hoped that his adventure would throw him
upon his mettle only half as much as the old lady had
wished to intimate. He considered, one after the other,
the different chairs, couches and ottomans the room contained—he wished to treat himself to the most sumptuous
—and then, for reasons he knew best, sank into a seat
covered with rose-coloured brocade, of which the legs and
frame appeared to be of pure gold. Here he sat perfectly
still, with only his heart beating very sensibly and his eyes
coursing again and again from one object to another.
The splendours and suggestions of Captain Sholto's apartment were thrown completely into the shade by the scene
before him, and as the Princess did not scruple to keep
him waiting for twenty minutes (during which the butler
came in and set out, on a small table, a glittering tea-
service), Hyacinth had time to count over the innumerable
bibelots (most of which he had never dreamed of), involved
in the personality of a woman of high fashion, and to feel
that their beauty and oddity revealed not only whole pro-
vinces of art, but refinements of choice, on the part of

their owner, complications of mind, and—almost—terrible
depths of character.

When at last the door opened and the servant, re-
appearing, threw it far back, as if to make a wide passage
for a person of the importance of his mistress, Hyacinth's
suspense became very acute; it was much the same feeling
with which, at the theatre, he had sometimes awaited the
entrance of a celebrated actress. In this case the actress
was to perform for him alone. There was still a moment
before she came on, and when she did so she was so
simply dressed—besides his seeing her now on her feet—
that she looked like a different person. She approached
him rapidly, and a little stiffly and shyly, but in the manner
in which she shook hands with him there was an evident
desire to be frank, and even fraternal. She looked like a
different person, but that person had a beauty even more
radiant; the fairness of her face shone forth at our young
man as if to dissipate any doubts that might have crept
over him as to the reality of the vision bequeathed to him
by his former interview. And in this brightness and richness of her presence he could not have told you whether
she struck him as more proud or more kind.

'I have kept you a long time, but it's supposed not,
usually, to be a bad place, my salon; there are various
things to look at, and perhaps you have noticed them.
Over on that side, for instance, there is rather a curious
collection of miniatures.' She spoke abruptly, quickly, as
if she were conscious that their communion might be
awkward and she were trying to strike, instantly (to con-
jure that element away), the sort of note that would make
them both most comfortable. Quickly, too, she sat down
before her tea-tray and poured him out a cup, which she
handed him without asking whether he would have it. He
accepted it with a trembling hand, though he had no
desire for it; he was too nervous to swallow the tea, but
it would not have occurred to him that it was possible to
decline. When he had murmured that he had indeed
looked at all her things but that it would take hours to
do justice to such treasures, she asked if he were fond of
works of art; adding, however immediately, that she was

afraid he had not many opportunities of seeing them, though of course there were the public collections, open to all.   Hyacinth said, with perfect veracity, that some of the happiest moments of his life had been spent at the British Museum and the National Gallery, and this reply appeared to interest her greatly, so that she immediately begged him to tell her what he thought of certain pictures and antiques.   In this way it was that in an incredibly short space of time, as it appeared to him, he found himself discussing the Bacchus and Ariadne and the Elgin marbles with one of the most remarkable women in Europe. It is true that she herself talked most, passing precipitately from one point to another, asking him questions and not waiting for answers; describing and qualifying things, expressing feelings, by the aid of phrases that he had never heard before but which seemed to him illuminating and happy—as when, for instance, she asked what art was, after all, but a synthesis made in the interest of pleasure, or said that she didn't like England at all, but loved it.   It did not occur to him to think these discriminations pedantic. Suddenly she remarked, ' Madame Grandoni told me you saw my husband.'

' Ah, was the gentleman your husband ?'

' Unfortunately !   What do you think of him ?'

' Oh, I can't think—— ' Hyacinth murmured.

' I wish I couldn't, either !   I haven't seen him for nearly three years.   He wanted to see me to-day, but I refused.'

' Ah !' said Hyacinth, staring and not knowing how he ought to receive so unexpected a confidence.   Then, as the suggestions of inexperience are sometimes the happiest of all, he spoke simply what was in his mind and said, gently, ' It has made you very nervous.'   Afterwards, when he had left the house, he wondered how, at that stage, he could have ventured on such a familiar remark.

The Princess took it with a quick, surprised laugh. ' How do you know that ?'   But before he had time to tell how, she added, ' Your saying that—that way—shows me how right I was to ask you to come to see me.   You know, I hesitated.   It shows me you have perceptions ; I guessed as much the other night at the theatre. If I hadn't, I wouldn't have asked you. I may be wrong, but I like people who understand what one says to them, and also what one doesn't say.'

'Don't think I understand too much. You might easily exaggerate that,' Hyacinth declared, conscientiously.

'You confirm, completely, my first impression,' the Princess returned, smiling in a way that showed him he really amused her. 'We shall discover the limits of your comprehension! I *am* atrociously nervous. But it will pass. How is your friend the dressmaker?' she inquired, abruptly. And when Hyacinth had briefly given some account of poor Pinnie—told her that she was tolerably well for her, but old and tired and sad, and not very successful—she exclaimed, impatiently, 'Ah, well, she's not the only one!' and came back, with irrelevance, to the former question. 'It's not only my husband's visit— absolutely unexpected !—that has made me fidgety, but the idea that now you have been so kind as to come here you may wonder why, after all, I made such a point of it, and even think any explanation I might be able to give you entirely insufficient.'

'I don't want any explanation,' said Hyacinth.

'It's very nice of you to say that, and I shall take you at your word. Explanations usually make things worse. All the same, I don't want you to think (as you might have done so easily the other evening), that I wish only to treat you as a curious animal.'

'I don't care how you treat me!' said Hyacinth, smiling.

There was a considerable silence, after which the Princess remarked, 'All I ask of my husband is to let me alone. But he won't. He won't reciprocate my indifference.'

Hyacinth asked himself what reply he ought to make to such an announcement as that, and it seemed to him that the least civility demanded was that he should say—as he could with such conviction—'It can't be easy to be indifferent to you.'

'Why not, if I am odious? I can be—oh, there is no doubt of that ! However, I can honestly say that with the

Prince I have been exceedingly reasonable, and that most of the wrongs—the big ones, those that settled the question—have been on his side. You may tell me of course that that's the pretension of every woman who has made a mess of her marriage. But ask Madame Grandoni.'

'She will tell me it's none of my business.'

'Very true—she might!' the Princess admitted, laughing. 'And I don't know, either, why I should talk to you about my domestic affairs; except that I have been wondering what I could do to show confidence in you, in return for your showing so much in me. As this matter of my separation from my husband happens to have been turned uppermost by his sudden descent upon me, I just mention it, though the subject is tiresome enough. Moreover I ought to let you know that I have very little respect for distinctions of class—the sort of thing they make so much of in this country. They are doubtless convenient in some ways, but when one has a reason—a reason of feeling—for overstepping them, and one allows one's self to be deterred by some dreary superstition about one's place, or some one else's place, then I think it's ignoble. It always belongs to one's place not to be a poor creature. I take it that if you are a socialist you think about this as I do; but lest, by chance, as the sense of those differences is the English religion, it may have rubbed off even on you, though I am more and more impressed with the fact that you are scarcely more British than I am; lest you should, in spite of your theoretic democracy, be shocked at some of the applications that I, who cherish the creed, am capable of making of it, let me assure you without delay that in that case we shouldn't get on together at all, and had better part company before we go further.' She paused, long enough for Hyacinth to declare, with a great deal of emphasis, that he was not easily shocked; and then, restlessly, eagerly, as if it relieved her to talk, and made their queer interview less abnormal that she should talk most, she arrived at the point that she wanted to know the *people*, and know them intimately—the toilers and strugglers and sufferers—because she was convinced they were the most interesting portion of society, and at the inquiry, 'What could possibly be in worse

taste than for me to carry into such an undertaking a pretension of greater delicacy and finer manners? If I must
do that,' she continued, 'it's simpler to leave them alone.
But I can't leave them alone ; they press upon me, they
haunt me, they fascinate me. There it is (after all, it's
very simple) : I want to know them, and I want you to
help me!'

'I will help you with pleasure, to the best of my humble
ability. But you will be awfully disappointed,' Hyacinth
said. Very strange it seemed to him that within so few
days two ladies of rank should have found occasion to
express to him the same mysterious longing. A breeze
from a thoroughly unexpected quarter was indeed blowing
over the aristocracy. Nevertheless, though there was much
of the same accent of passion in the Princess Casamassima's
communication that there had been in Lady Aurora's, and
though he felt bound to discourage his present interlocutress
as he had done the other, the force that pushed her struck
him as a very different mixture from the shy, conscientious,
anxious heresies of Rose Muniment's friend. The temper
varied in the two women as much as the face and the
manner, and that perhaps made their curiosity the more
significant.

'I haven't the least doubt of it : there is nothing in life
in which I have not been awfully disappointed. But disappointment for disappointment I shall like it better than
some others. You'll not persuade me, either, that among
the people I speak of, characters and passions and motives
are not more natural, more complete, more naïf. The
upper classes are so insipid! My husband traces his
descent from the fifth century, and he's the greatest bore
on earth. That is the kind of people I was condemned to
live with after my marriage. Oh, if you knew what I have
been through, you would allow that intelligent mechanics
(of course I don't want to know idiots), would be a pleasant
change. I must begin with some one—mustn't I?—so I
began, the other night, with you!' As soon as she had
uttered these words the Princess added a correction, with
the consciousness of her mistake in her face. It made that
face, to Hyacinth, more nobly, tenderly pure. 'The only

objection to you, individually, is that you have nothing of the people about you—to-day not even the dress.' Her eyes wandered over him from head to foot, and their friendly beauty made him ashamed. ' I wish you had come in the clothes you wear at your work ! '

' You see you do regard me as a curious animal,' he answered.

It was perhaps to contradict this that, after a moment, she began to tell him more about her domestic affairs. He ought to know who she was, unless Captain Sholto had told him ; and she related her parentage—American on the mother's side, Italian on the father's—and how she had led, in her younger years, a wandering, Bohemian life, in a thousand different places (always in Europe ; she had never been in America and knew very little about it, though she wanted greatly to cross the Atlantic), and largely, at one period, in Rome. She had been married by her people, in a mercenary way, for the sake of a fortune and a title, and ,it had turned out as badly as her worst enemy could wish. Her parents were dead, luckily for them, and she had no one near her of her own except Madame Grandoni, who belonged to her only in the sense that she had known her as a girl ; was an association of her—what should she call them ?—her innocent years. Not that she had ever been very innocent ; she had had a horrible education. However, she had known a few good people— people she respected, then ; but Madame Grandoni was the only one who had stuck to her. She, too, was liable to leave her any day ; the Princess appeared to intimate that her destiny might require her to take some step which would test severely the old lady's adhesive property. It would detain her too long to make him understand the stages by which she had arrived at her present state of mind : her disgust with a thousand social arrangements, her rebellion against the selfishness, the corruption, the iniquity, the cruelty, the imbecility, of the people who, all over Europe, had the upper hand. If he could have seen her life, the *milieu* in which, for several years, she had been condemned to move, the evolution of her opinions (Hyacinth was delighted to hear her use that term), would strike him as perfectly logical. She had been humiliated, out-raged, tortured ; she considered that she too was one of the numerous class who could be put on a tolerable footing only by a revolution. At any rate, she had some self-respect left, and there was still more that she wanted to recover ; the only way to arrive at that was to throw herself into some effort which would make her forget her own affairs and comprehend the troubles and efforts of others. Hyacinth listened to her with a wonderment which, as she went on, was transformed into fascinated submission ; she seemed so natural, so vivid, so exquisitely generous and sincere. By the time he had been with her for half an hour she had made the situation itself appear natural and usual, and a third person who should have joined them at this moment would have observed nothing to make him suppose that friendly social intercourse between little bookbinders and Neapolitan princesses was not, in London, a matter of daily occurrence.

Hyacinth had seen plenty of women who chattered about themselves and their affairs—a vulgar garrulity of confidence was indeed a leading characteristic of the sex as he had hitherto learned to know it—but he was quick to perceive that the great lady who now took the trouble to open herself to him was not of a gossiping habit ; that she must be, on the contrary, as a general thing, proudly, ironically, reserved, even to the point of passing, with many people, for a model of the unsatisfactory. It was very possible she was capricious ; yet the fact that her present sympathies and curiosities might be a caprice wore, in Hyacinth's eyes, no sinister aspect. Why was it not a noble and interesting whim, and why might he not stand, for the hour at any rate, in the silvery moonshine it threw upon his path ? It must be added that he was far from understanding everything she said, and some of her allusions and implications were so difficult to seize that they mainly served to reveal to him the limits of his own acquaintance with life. Her words evoked all sorts of shadowy sugges-tions of things he was condemned not to know, touching him most when he had not the key to them. This was especially the case with her reference to her career in Italy,

on her husband's estates, and her relations with his family ;
who considered that they had done her a great honour in
receiving her into their august circle (putting the best face
on a bad business), after they had moved heaven and earth
to keep her out of it. The position made for her among
these people, and what she had had to suffer from their
family tone, their opinions and customs (though what these
might be remained vague to her listener), had evidently
planted in her soul a lasting resentment and contempt ; and
Hyacinth gathered that the force of reaction and revenge
might carry her far, make her modern and democratic and
heretical *à outrance*—lead her to swear by Darwin and
Spencer as well as by the revolutionary spirit. He
surely need not have been so sensible of the weak spots
in his comprehension of the Princess, when he could
already surmise that personal passion had counted for so
much in the formation of her views. This induction, however, which had no harshness, did not make her appear to
him any the less a creature compounded of the finest
elements ; brilliant, delicate, complicated, but complicated
with something divine. It was not until after he had left
her that he became conscious she had forced him to talk,
as well as talked herself. He drew a long breath as he
reflected that he had not made quite such an ass of himself
as might very well have happened ; he had been saved by
his enjoyment and admiration, which had not gone to his
head and prompted him to show that he too, in his improbable little way, was remarkable, but had kept him in a
state of anxious, delicious tension, as if the occasion had
been a great solemnity. He had said, indeed, much more
than he had warrant for, when she questioned him about
his socialistic affiliations ; he had spoken as if the movement were vast and mature, whereas, in fact, so far, at least,
as he was as yet concerned with it, and could answer for
it from personal knowledge, it was circumscribed by the
hideously papered walls of the little club-room at the ' Sun
and Moon.' He reproached himself with this laxity, but it
had not been engendered by vanity. He was only afraid
of disappointing his hostess too much ; of making her say,
' Why in the world, then, did you come to see me, if you

have nothing more remarkable to relate ? '—an inquiry to
which, of course, he would have had an answer ready, if it
had not been impossible to him to say that he had never
asked to come : his coming was her own affair. He wanted
too much to come a second time to have the courage to
make that speech. Nevertheless, when she exclaimed,
changing the subject abruptly, as she always did, from
something else they had been talking about, 'I wonder
whether I shall ever see you again ! ' he replied, with
perfect sincerity, that it was very difficult for him to believe
anything so delightful could be repeated. There were some
kinds of happiness that to many people never came at all,
and to others could come only once. He added, 'It is
very true I had just that feeling after I left you the other
night at the theatre. And yet here I am ! '

'Yes, there you are,' said the Princess thoughtfully, as if
this might be a still graver and more embarrassing fact than
she had yet supposed it. 'I take it there is nothing
essentially impossible in my seeing you again ; but it may
very well be that you will never again find it so pleasant.
Perhaps that's the happiness that comes but once. At any
rate, you know, I am going away.'

'Oh yes, of course; every one leaves town,' Hyacinth
commented, sagaciously.

'Do you, Mr. Robinson ? ' asked the Princess.

'Well, I don't as a general thing. Nevertheless, it is
possible that, this year, I may get two or three days at the
seaside. I should like to take my old lady. I have done
it before.'

'And except for that you shall be always at work ? '

'Yes ; but you must understand that I like my work.
You must understand that it's a great blessing for a young
fellow like me to have it.'

'And if you didn't have it, what would you do ? Should
you starve ? '

'Oh, I don't think I should starve,' the young man
replied, judicially.

The Princess looked a little chagrined, but after a
moment she remarked, 'I wonder whether you would come
to see me, in the country, somewhere.'

'Oh, dear!' Hyacinth exclaimed, catching his breath. 'You are so kind, I don't know what to do.'

'Don't be *banal*, please.   That's what other people are. What's the use of my looking for something fresh in other walks of life, if you are going to be *banal* too?   I ask you, would you come?'

Hyacinth hesitated a moment.   'Yes, I think I would come.   I don't know, at all, how I should do it—there would be several obstacles; but wherever you should call for me, I would come.'

'You mean you can't leave your work, like that; you might lose it, if you did, and be in want of money and much embarrassed?'

'Yes, there would be little difficulties of that kind.   You see that immediately, in practice, great obstacles come up, when it's a question of a person like you making friends with a person like me.'

'That's the way I like you to talk,' said the Princess, with a pitying gentleness that seemed to her visitor quite sacred.   'After all, I don't know where I shall be.   I have got to pay stupid visits, myself, where the only comfort will be that I shall make the people jump.   Every one here thinks me exceedingly odd—as there is no doubt I am!   I might be ever so much more so if you would only help me a little.   Why shouldn't I have my bookbinder, after all? In attendance, you know, it would be awfully *chic*.   We might have immense fun, don't you think so?   No doubt it will come.   At any rate, I shall return to London when I have got through that *corvée;* I shall be here next year. In the meantime, don't forget me,' she went on, rising to her feet.   'Remember, on the contrary, that I expect you to take me into the slums—into very bad places.'   Why the idea of these scenes of misery should have lighted up her face is more than may be explained; but she smiled down at Hyacinth—who, even as he stood up, was of slightly smaller stature—with all her strange, radiant sweetness.   Then, in a manner almost equally incongruous, she added a reference to what she had said a moment before. 'I recognise perfectly the obstacles, in practice, as you call them; but though I am not, by nature, persevering,

and am really very easily put off, I don't consider that they
will prove insurmountable. They exist on my side as well,
and if you will help me to overcome mine I will do the
same for you, with yours.'

These words, repeating themselves again and again in
Hyacinth's consciousness, appeared to give him wings,
to help him to float and soar, as he turned that afternoon
out of South Street. He had at home a copy of Tennyson's
poems—a single, comprehensive volume, with a double
column on the page, in a tolerably neat condition, though
he had handled it much. He took it to pieces that same
evening, and during the following week, in his hours of
leisure, at home in his little room, with the tools he kept
there for private use, and a morsel of delicate, blue-tinted
Russia leather, of which he obtained possession at the place
in Soho, he devoted himself to the task of binding the book
as perfectly as he knew how. He worked with passion, with
religion, and produced a masterpiece of firmness and finish,
of which his own appreciation was as high as that of M.
Poupin, when, at the end of the week, he exhibited the
fruit of his toil, and much more freely expressed than that
of old Crookenden, who grunted approbation, but was
always too long-headed to create precedents. Hyacinth
carried the volume to South Street, as an offering to the
Princess ; hoping she would not yet have left London, in
which case he would ask the servant to deliver it to her,
along with a little note he had sat up all night to compose.
But the majestic butler, in charge of the house, opening the
door yet looking down at him as if from a second-storey
window, took the life out of his vision and erected himself
as an impenetrable medium. The Princess had been
absent for some days ; the butler was so good as to inform
the young man with the parcel that she was on a visit to a
'juke,' in a distant part of the country. He offered however to receive, and even to forward, anything Hyacinth
might wish to leave ; but our hero felt a sudden indisposition to launch his humble tribute into the vast, the possibly
cold, unknown of a ducal circle. He decided to retain his
little package for the present ; he would give it to her when
he should see her again, and he turned away without part-

ing with it. Later, it seemed to create a sort of material link between the Princess and himself, and at the end of three months it almost appeared to him, not that the exquisite book was an intended present from his own hand, but that it had been placed in that hand by the most remarkable woman in Europe. Rare sensations and impressions, moments of acute happiness, almost always, with Hyacinth, in retrospect, became rather mythic and legendary; and the superior piece of work he had done after seeing her last, in the immediate heat of his emotion, turned into a kind of proof and gage, as if a ghost, in vanishing from sight, had left a palpable relic.

XVIII

THE matter concerned him only indirectly, but it may concern the reader more closely to know that before the visit
to the duke took place Madame Grandoni granted to
Prince Casamassima the private interview she had promised him on that sad Sunday afternoon. She crept out of
South Street after breakfast — a repast which under the
Princess's roof was served at twelve o'clock, in the foreign
fashion—crossed the sultry solitude into which, at such a
season, that precinct resolves itself, and entered the Park,
where the grass was already brown and a warm, smoky
haze prevailed, a sort of summer edition of what was most
characteristic in the London air. The Prince met her, by
appointment, at the gate, and they went and sat down
together under the trees beside the drive, amid a wilderness
of empty chairs and with nothing to distract their attention
from an equestrian or two, left over from the cavalcades of
a fortnight before, and whose vain agitation in the saddle
the desolate scene seemed to throw into high relief. They
remained there for nearly an hour, though Madame Grandoni, in spite of her leaning to friendly interpretations,
could not have told herself what comfort it was to the
depressed, embarrassed young man at her side. She had
nothing to say to him which could better his case, as he
bent his mournful gaze on a prospect which was not, after
all, perceptibly improved by its not being Sunday, and could
only feel that, with her, he must seem to himself to be
nearer his wife—to be touching something she had touched.
The old lady wished he would resign himself more, but she
was willing to minister to that thin illusion, little as she approved of the manner in which he had conducted himself
at the time of the last sharp crisis in the remarkable history

of his relations with Christina. He had behaved like a spoiled child, with a bad little nature, in a rage ; he had been fatally wanting in dignity and wisdom, and had given the Princess an advantage which she took on the spot and would keep for ever. He had acted without manly judgment, had put his uncles upon her (as if she cared for his uncles ! though one of them was a powerful prelate), had been suspicious and jealous on exactly the wrong occasions—occasions on which such ideas were a gratuitous injury. He had not been clever enough or strong enough to make good his valid rights, and had transferred the whole quarrel to a ground where his wife was far too accomplished a woman not to obtain the appearance of victory.

There was another reflection that Madame Grandoni made, as her interview with her dejected friend prolonged itself. She could make it the more freely as, besides being naturally quick and appreciative, she had always, during her Roman career, in the dear old days (mingled with bitterness as they had been for her), lived with artists, archæologists, ingenious strangers, people who abounded in good talk, threw out ideas and played with them. It came over her that, really, even if things had not come to that particular crisis, Christina's active, various, ironical mind, with all its audacities and impatiences, could not have tolerated for long the simple dulness of the Prince's company. The old lady had said to him, on meeting him, ' Of course, what you want to know immediately is whether she has sent you a message. No, my poor friend, I must tell you the truth. I asked her for one, but she told me that she had nothing whatever, of any kind, to say to you. She knew I was coming out to see you. I haven't done so *en cachette*. She doesn't like it, but she accepts the necessity for this once, since you have made the mistake, as she considers it, of approaching her again. We talked about you, last night, after your note came to me — for five minutes ; that is, I talked, and Christina was good enough to listen. At the end she said this (what I shall tell you), with perfect calmness, and the appearance of being the most reasonable woman in the world. She didn't ask me

to repeat it to you, but I do so because it is the only substitute I can offer you for a message.   " I try to occupy
my life, my mind, to create interests, in the odious position
in which I find myself; I endeavour to get out of myself,
my small personal disappointments and troubles, by the aid
of such poor faculties as I possess.   There are things in the
world more interesting, after all, and I hope to succeed in
giving my attention to them.   It appears to me not too
much to ask that the Prince, on his side, should make the
same conscientious effort—and leave me alone ! "   Those
were your wife's remarkable words; they are all I have to
give you.'

   After she had given them Madame Grandoni felt a pang
of regret; the Prince turned upon her a face so white, bewildered and wounded.   It had seemed to her that they
might form a wholesome admonition, but it was now impressed upon her that, as coming from his wife, they were
cruel, and she herself felt almost cruel for having repeated
them.   What they amounted to was an exquisite taunt of
his mediocrity—a mediocrity which was, after all, not a
crime.   How could the Prince occupy himself, what interests could he create, and what faculties, gracious heaven,
did he possess ?   He was as ignorant as a fish, and as
narrow as his hat-band.   His expression became pitiful ; it
was as if he dimly measured the insult, felt it more than saw
it—felt that he could not plead incapacity without putting
the Princess largely in the right.   He gazed at Madame
Grandoni, his face worked, and for a moment she thought
he was going to burst into tears.   But he said nothing—
perhaps because he was afraid of that—so that suffering
silence, during which she gently laid her hand upon his
own, remained his only answer.   He might doubtless do
so much he didn't, that when Christina touched upon this
she was unanswerable.   The old lady changed the subject :
told him what a curious country England was, in so many
ways ; offered information as to their possible movements
during the summer and autumn, which, within a day or two,
had become slightly clearer.   But at last, abruptly, as if he had
not heard her, he inquired, appealingly, who the young man
was who had come in the day he called, just as he was going.

Madame Grandoni hesitated a moment. ' He was the Princess's bookbinder.'

' Her bookbinder ?   Do you mean her lover ? '

' Prince, how can you dream she will ever live with you again ? ' the old lady asked, in reply to this.

' Why, then, does she have him in her drawing-room— announced like an ambassador, carrying a hat in his hand like mine ? Where were his books, his bindings ? I shouldn't say this to her,' the Prince added, as if the declaration justi- fied him.

' I told you the other day that she is making studies of the people—the lower orders.   The young man you saw is a study.'   Madame Grandoni could not help laughing out as she gave her explanation this turn; but her mirth elicited no echo from her interlocutor.

' I have thought that over—over and over; but the more I think the less I understand.   Would it be your idea that she is quite crazy ?   I must tell you I don't care if she is ! '

' We are all quite crazy, I think,' said Madame Gran- doni ; ' but the Princess no more than the rest of us.   No, she must try everything ; at present she is trying democracy and socialism.'

' *Santo Dio !*' murmured the young man.   ' And what do they say here when they see her bookbinder ? '

' They haven't seen him, and perhaps they won't.   But if they do, it won't matter, because here everything is for- given.   That a person should be singular is all they want. A bookbinder will do as well as anything else.'

The Prince mused a while, and then he said, ' How can she bear the dirt, the bad smell ? '

' I don't know what you are talking about.   If you mean the young man you saw at the house (I may tell you, by the way, that it was only the first time he had been there, and that the Princess had only seen him once)—if you mean the little bookbinder, he isn't dirty, especially what we should call.   The people of that kind, here, are not like our dear Romans.   Every one has a sponge, as big as your head ; you can see them in the shops.'

' They are full of gin ; their faces are purple,' said

the Prince; after which he immediately asked, 'If she had only seen him once, how could he have come into her drawing-room that way?'

The old lady looked at him with a certain severity. 'Believe, at least, what *I* say, my poor friend! Never forget that this was how you spoiled your affairs most of all—by treating a person (and such a person!) as if, as a matter of course, she lied. Christina has many faults, but she hasn't that one; that's why I can live with her. She will speak the truth always.'

It was plainly not agreeable to the Prince to be reminded so sharply of his greatest mistake, and he flushed a little as Madame Grandoni spoke. But he did not admit his error, and she doubted whether he even perceived it. At any rate he remarked rather grandly, like a man who has still a good deal to say for himself, 'There are things it is better to conceal.'

'It all depends on whether you are afraid. Christina never is. Oh, I admit that she is very strange, and when the entertainment of watching her, to see how she will carry out some of her inspirations, is not stronger than anything else, I lose all patience with her. When she doesn't fascinate she can only exasperate. But, as regards yourself, since you are here, and as I may not see you again for a long time, or perhaps ever (at my age—I'm a hundred and twenty!) I may as well give you the key of certain parts of your wife's conduct. It may make it seem to you a little less fantastic. At the bottom, then, of much that she does is the fact that she is ashamed of having married you.'

'Less fantastic?' the young man repeated, staring.

'You may say that there can be nothing more eccentric than that. But you know—or, if not, it isn't for want of her having told you—that the Princess considers that in the darkest hour of her life she sold herself for a title and a fortune. She regards her doing so as such a horrible piece of frivolity that she can never, for the rest of her days, be serious enough to make up for it.'

'Yes, I know that she pretends to have been forced. And does she think she's so serious now?'

'The young man you saw the other day thinks so,' said

the old woman, smiling. ' Sometimes she calls it by another
name : she says she has thrown herself with passion into
being "modern." That sums up the greatest number of
things that you and your family are not.'

' Yes, we are not, thank God ! *Dio mio, Dio mio !* '
groaned the Prince. He seemed so exhausted by his
reflections that he remained sitting in his chair after his
companion, lifting her crumpled corpulence out of her own,
had proposed that they should walk about a little. She had
no ill-nature, but she had already noticed that whenever she
was with Christina's husband the current of conversation
made her, as she phrased it, bump against him. After
administering these small shocks she always steered away,
and now, the Prince having at last got up and offered her
his arm, she tried again to talk with him of things he could
consider without bitterness. She asked him about the
health and habits of his uncles, and he replied, for the
moment, with the minuteness which he had been taught
that in such a case courtesy demanded ; but by the time
that, at her request, they had returned to the gate nearest
to South Street (she wished him to come no farther) he had
prepared a question to which she had not opened the way.

' And who and what, then, is this English captain ?
About him there is a great deal said.'

' This English captain ? '

' Godfrey Gerald Cholto—you see I know a good deal
about him,' said the Prince, articulating the English names
with difficulty.

They had stopped near the gate, on the edge of Park
Lane, and a couple of predatory hansoms dashed at them
from opposite quarters. ' I thought that was coming, and
at bottom it is he that has occupied you most ! ' Madame
Grandoni exclaimed, with a sigh. ' But in reality he is the
last one you need trouble about ; he doesn't count.'

' Why doesn't he count ? '

' I can't tell you—except that some people don't, you
know. He doesn't even think he does.'

' Why not, when she receives him always—lets him go
wherever she goes ? '

' Perhaps that is just the reason. When people give her

a chance to get tired of them she takes it rather easily. At any rate, you needn't be any more jealous of him than you are of me. He's a convenience, a *factotum*, but he works without wages.'

'Isn't he, then, in love with her?'

'Naturally. He has, however, no hope.'

'Ah, poor gentleman!' said the Prince, lugubriously.

'He accepts the situation better than you. He occupies himself—as she has strongly recommended him, in my hearing, to do—with other women.'

'Oh, the brute!' the Prince exclaimed. 'At all events, he sees her.'

'Yes, but she doesn't see him!' laughed Madame Grandoni, as she turned away.

XIX

THE pink dressing-gown which Pinnie had engaged to make
for Rose Muniment became, in Lomax Place, a conspicuous
object, supplying poor Amanda with a constant theme for
reference to one of the great occasions of her life—her visit
to Belgrave Square with Lady Aurora, after their meeting
at Rosy's bedside. She described this episode vividly to
her companion, repeating a thousand times that her ladyship's affability was beyond anything she could have expected.
The grandeur of the house in Belgrave Square figured in
her recital as something oppressive and fabulous, tempered
though it had been by shrouds of brown holland and the
nudity of staircases and saloons of which the trappings had
been put away. 'If it's so noble when they're out of town,
what can it be when they are all there together and everything is out?' she inquired suggestively; and she permitted
herself to be restrictive only on two points, one of which
was the state of Lady Aurora's gloves and bonnet-strings.
If she had not been afraid to appear to notice the disrepair
of these objects, she would have been so happy to offer to
do any little mending. 'If she would only come to me
every week or two, I would keep up her rank for her,' said
Pinnie, with visions of a needle that positively flashed in the
disinterested service of the aristocracy. She added that her
ladyship got all dragged out with her long expeditions to
Camberwell; she might be in tatters, for all they could do
to help her at the top of those dreadful stairs, with that
strange sick creature (she was too unnatural), thinking only
of her own finery and talking about her complexion. If
she wanted pink, she should have pink; but to Pinnie there
was something almost unholy in it, like decking out a corpse,
or the next thing to it. This was the other element that

left Miss Pynsent cold; it could not be other than difficult
for her to enter into the importance her ladyship appeared
to attach to those pushing people.   The girl was unfortunate,
certainly, stuck up there like a kitten on a shelf, but in her
ladyship's place she would have found some topic more in
keeping, while they walked about under those tremendous
gilded ceilings.   Lady Aurora, seeing how she was struck,
showed her all over the house, carrying the lamp herself
and telling an old woman who was there—a kind of house-
keeper, with ribbons in her cap, who would have pushed
Pinnie out if you could push with your eyes—that they
would do very well without her.   If the pink dressing-gown,
in its successive stages of development, filled up the little
brown parlour (it was terribly long on the stocks), making
such a pervasive rose-coloured presence as had not been
seen there for many a day, this was evidently because it was
associated with Lady Aurora, not because it was dedicated
to her humble friend.

One day, when Hyacinth came home from his work,
Pinnie announced to him as soon as he entered the room
that her ladyship had been there to look at it—to pass
judgment before the last touches were conferred.   The
dressmaker intimated that in such a case as that her
judgment was rather wild, and she had made an embarrassing suggestion about pockets.   Whatever could
poor Miss Muniment want of pockets, and what had she
to put in them?   But Lady Aurora had evidently found
the garment far beyond anything she expected, and
she had been more affable than ever, and had wanted to
know about every one in the Place; not in a meddling,
prying way, either, like some of those upper-class visitors,
but quite as if the poor people were the high ones and she
was afraid her curiosity might be 'presumptious.'   It was
in the same discreet spirit that she had invited Amanda to
relate her whole history, and had expressed an interest in
the career of her young friend.

'She said you had charming manners,' Miss Pynsent
hastened to remark; 'but, before heaven, Hyacinth Robinson, I never mentioned a scrap that it could give you pain
that any one should talk about.'   There was an heroic

explicitness in this, on Pinnie's part, for she knew in advance just how Hyacinth would look at her—fixedly,
silently, hopelessly, as if she were still capable of tattling
horribly (with the idea that her revelations would increase
her importance), and putting forward this hollow theory of
her supreme discretion to cover it up.   His eyes seemed
to say, ' How can I believe you, and yet how can I prove
you are lying ?   I am very helpless, for I can't prove that
without applying to the person to whom your incorrigible
folly has probably led you to brag, to throw out mysterious
and tantalising hints.   You know, of course, that I would
never condescend to that.'   Pinnie suffered, acutely, from
this imputation ; yet she exposed herself to it often, because
she could never deny herself the pleasure, keener still than
her pain, of letting Hyacinth know that he was appreciated,
admired and, for those ' charming manners ' commended
by Lady Aurora, even wondered at ; and this kind of
interest always appeared to imply a suspicion of his secret
—something which, when he expressed to himself the sense
of it, he called, resenting it at once and yet finding a certain
softness in it, ' a beastly *attendrissement.*'   When Pinnie
went on to say to him that Lady Aurora appeared to feel a
certain surprise at his never yet having come to Belgrave
Square for the famous books, he reflected that he must
really wait upon her without more delay, if he wished to
keep up his reputation for charming manners ; and meanwhile he considered much the extreme oddity of this new
phase of his life (it had opened so suddenly, from one
day to the other) ; a phase in which his society should
have become indispensable to ladies of high rank and the
obscurity of his condition only an attraction the more.
They were taking him up then, one after the other, and
they were even taking up poor Pinnie, as a means of getting
at him ; so that he wondered, with humorous bitterness,
whether it meant that his destiny was really seeking him
out—that the aristocracy, recognising a mysterious affinity
(with that fineness of *flair* for which they were remarkable),
were coming to him to save him the trouble of coming to
them.

It was late in the day (the beginning of an October

evening), and Lady Aurora was at home. Hyacinth had made a mental calculation of the time at which she would have risen from dinner; the operation of 'rising from dinner' having always been, in his imagination, for some reason or other, highly characteristic of the nobility. He was ignorant of the fact that Lady Aurora's principal meal consisted of a scrap of fish and a cup of tea, served on a little stand in the dismantled breakfast-parlour. The door was opened for Hyacinth by the invidious old lady whom Pinnie had described, and who listened to his inquiry, conducted him through the house, and ushered him into her ladyship's presence, without the smallest relaxation of a pair of tightly-closed lips. Hyacinth's hostess was seated in the little breakfast-parlour, by the light of a couple of candles, immersed apparently in a collection of tolerably crumpled papers and account-books. She was ciphering, consulting memoranda, taking notes; she had had her head in her hands, and the silky entanglement of her tresses resisted the rapid effort she made to smooth herself down as she saw the little bookbinder come in. The impression of her fingers remained in little rosy streaks on her pink skin. She exclaimed, instantly, 'Oh, you have come about the books—it's so very kind of you;' and she hurried him off to another room, to which, as she explained, she had had them brought down for him to choose from. The effect of this precipitation was to make him suppose at first that she might wish him to execute his errand as quickly as possible and take himself off; but he presently perceived that her nervousness, her shyness, were of an order that would always give false ideas. She wanted him to stay, she wanted to talk with him, and she had rushed with him at the books in order to gain time and composure for exercising some subtler art. Hyacinth stayed half an hour, and became more and more convinced that her ladyship was, as he had ventured to pronounce her on the occasion of their last meeting, a regular saint. He was privately a little disappointed in the books, though he selected three or four, as many as he could carry, and promised to come back for others: they denoted, on Lady Aurora's part, a limited acquaintance with French literature and even a certain puerility of taste. There were several volumes of Lamartine and a set of the spurious memoirs of the Marquise de Créqui; but for the rest the little library consisted mainly of Marmontel and Madame de Genlis, the Récit d'une Sœur and the tales of M. J. T. de Saint-Germain. There were certain members of an intensely modern school, advanced and scientific realists, of whom Hyacinth had heard and on whom he had long desired to put his hand; but, evidently, none of them had ever stumbled into Lady Aurora's candid collection, though she did possess a couple of Balzac's novels, which, by ill-luck, happened to be just those that Hyacinth had read more than once.

There was, nevertheless, something very agreeable to him in the moments he passed in the big, dim, cool, empty house, where, at intervals, monumental pieces of furniture—not crowded and miscellaneous, as he had seen the appurtenances of the Princess—loomed and gleamed, and Lady Aurora's fantastic intonations awakened echoes which gave him a sense of privilege, of rioting, decently, in the absence of jealous influences. She talked again about the poor people in the south of London, and about the Muniments in particular; evidently, the only fault she had to find with these latter was that they were not poor enough—not sufficiently exposed to dangers and privations against which she could step in. Hyacinth liked her for this, even though he wished she would talk of something else—he hardly knew what, unless it was that, like Rose Muniment, he wanted to hear more about Inglefield. He didn't mind, with the poor, going into questions of poverty —it even gave him at times a strange, savage satisfaction —but he saw that in discussing them with the rich the interest must inevitably be less; they could never treat them *à fond*. Their mistakes and illusions, their thinking they had got hold of the sensations of the destitute when they hadn't at all, would always be more or less irritating. It came over Hyacinth that if he found this want of perspective in Lady Aurora's deep conscientiousness, it would be a queer enough business when he should come to go into the detail of such matters with the Princess Casamassima.

His present hostess said not a word to him about
Pinnie, and he guessed that she had an instinctive desire
to place him on the footing on which people do not express
approbation or surprise at the decency or good-breeding of
each other's relatives.   He saw that she would always treat
him as a gentleman, and that even if he should be basely
ungrateful she would never call his attention to the fact
that she had done so.   He should not have occasion to
say to her, as he had said to the Princess, that she regarded him as a curious animal; and it gave him immediately that sense, always so delightful to him, of learning
more about life, to perceive there were such different ways
(which implied still a good many more), of being a lady of
rank.   The manner in which Lady Aurora appeared to
wish to confer with him on the great problems of pauperism
might have implied that he was a benevolent nobleman (of
the type of Lord Shaftesbury), who had endowed many
charities and was noted, in philanthropic schemes, for his
practical sense.   It was not less present to him that Pinnie
might have tattled, put forward his claims to high con-
sanguinity, than it had been when the dressmaker herself
descanted on her ladyship's condescensions; but he remembered now that he too had only just escaped being
asinine, when, the other day, he flashed out an allusion to
his accursed origin.   At all events, he was much touched
by the delicacy with which the earl's daughter comported
herself, simply assuming that he was ' one of themselves ';
and he reflected that if he did know his history (he was
sure he might pass twenty years in her society without
discovering whether she did or not), this shade of courtesy,
this natural tact, coexisting even with extreme awkwardness,
illustrated that ' best breeding' which he had seen alluded
to in novels portraying the aristocracy.   The only remark
on Lady Aurora's part that savoured in the least of looking
down at him from a height was when she said, cheerfully,
encouragingly, ' I suppose that one of these days you will
be setting up in business for yourself;' and this was not
so cruelly patronising that he could not reply, with a smile
equally free from any sort of impertinence, ' Oh dear, no,
I shall never do that.   I should make a great mess of any

attempt to carry on a business. I haven't a particle of
that kind of aptitude.'

Lady Aurora looked a little surprised; then she said,
'Oh, I see; you don't like—you don't like'—— She
hesitated : he saw she was going to say that he didn't
like the idea of going in, to that extent, for a trade ; but he
stopped her in time from attributing to him a sentiment so
foolish, and declared that what he meant was simply that
the only faculty he possessed was the faculty of doing his
little piece of work, whatever it was, of liking to do it skill-
fully and prettily, and of liking still better to get his money
for it when it was done. His conception of ' business,' or
of rising in the world, didn't go beyond that. ' Oh yes, I
can fancy !' her ladyship exclaimed ; but she looked at him
a moment with eyes which showed that he puzzled her, that
she didn't quite understand his tone. Before he went away
she inquired of him, abruptly (nothing had led up to it), what
he thought of Captain Sholto, whom she had seen that
other evening in Audley Court. Didn't Hyacinth think he
was very odd ? Hyacinth confessed to this impression ;
whereupon Lady Aurora went on anxiously, eagerly : ' Don't
you consider that—that—he is decidedly vulgar ? '

' How can I know ? '

' You can know perfectly—as well as any one ! ' Then
she added, ' I think it's a pity they should—a—form relations
with any one of that kind.'

' They,' of course, meant Paul Muniment and his sister.
' With a person that may be vulgar ? ' Hyacinth asked,
regarding this solicitude as exquisite. ' But think of the
people they know—think of those they are surrounded with
—think of all Audley Court ! '

' The poor, the unhappy, the labouring classes ? Oh, I
don't call *them* vulgar ! ' cried her ladyship, with radiant eyes.
The young man, lying awake a good deal that night, laughed
to himself, on his pillow, not unkindly, at her fear that he
and his friends would be contaminated by the familiar of a
princess. He even wondered whether she would not find
the Princess herself rather vulgar.

XX

It must not be supposed that Hyacinth's relations with
Millicent Henning had remained unaffected by the remarkable incident she had witnessed at the theatre. It had
made a great impression on the young lady from Pimlico ;
he never saw her, for several weeks afterwards, that she had
not an immense deal to say about it ; and though it suited
her to take the line of being shocked at the crudity of such
proceedings, and of denouncing the Princess for a bold-
faced foreigner, of a kind to which any one who knew
anything of what could go on in London would give a wide
berth, it was easy to see that she was pleased at being
brought even into roundabout contact with a person so
splendid and at finding her own discriminating approval of
Hyacinth confirmed in such high quarters. She professed
to derive her warrant for her low opinion of the lady in the
box from information given her by Captain Sholto as he sat
beside her—information of which at different moments she
gave a different version ; her anecdotes having nothing in
common, at least, save that they were alike unflattering to
the Princess. Hyacinth had many doubts of the Captain's
pouring such confidences into Miss Henning's ear ; under
the circumstances it would be such a very unnatural thing
for him to do. He *was* unnatural—that was true—and he
might have told Millicent, who was capable of having plied
him with questions, that his distinguished friend was separated
from her husband ; but, for the rest, it was more probable
that the girl had given the rein to a certain inventive faculty
which she had already showed him she possessed, when it
was a question of exercising her primitive, half-childish,
half-plebeian impulse of destruction, the instinct of pulling
down what was above her, the reckless energy that would,

precisely, make her so effective in revolutionary scenes. Hyacinth (it has been mentioned) did not consider that Millicent was false, and it struck him as a proof of positive candour that she should make up absurd, abusive stories about a person concerning whom she knew nothing at all, save that she disliked her, and could not hope for esteem, or, indeed, for recognition of any kind, in return. When people were really false you didn't know where you stood with them, and on such a point as this Miss Henning could never be accused of leaving you in obscurity. She said little else about the Captain, and did not pretend to repeat the remainder of his conversation; taking it with an air of grand indifference when Hyacinth amused himself with repaying her strictures on his new acquaintance by drawing a sufficiently derisive portrait of hers.

He took the ground that Sholto's admiration for the high-coloured beauty in the second balcony had been at the bottom of the whole episode : he had persuaded the Princess to pretend she was a socialist and should like therefore to confer with Hyacinth, in order that he might slip into the seat of this too easily deluded youth. At the same time, it never occurred to our young man to conceal the fact that the lady in the box had followed him up; he contented himself with saying that this had been no part of the original plot, but a simple result—not unnatural, after all—of his turning out so much more fascinating than one might have supposed. He narrated, with sportive variations, his visit in South Street, and felt that he would never feel the need, with his childhood's friend, of glossing over that sort of experience. She might make him a scene of jealousy and welcome—there were things that would have much more terror for him than that; her jealousy, with its violence, its energy, even a certain inconsequent, dare-devil humour that played through it, entertained him, illustrated the frankness, the passion and pluck, that he admired her for. He should never be on the footing of sparing Miss Henning's susceptibilities; how fond she might really be of him he could not take upon himself to say, but her affection would never take the form of that sort of delicacy, and their intercourse was plainly foredoomed to be an exchange of thumps

and concussions, of sarcastic shouts and mutual *défis*. He
liked her, at bottom, strangely, absurdly ; but after all it
was only well enough to torment her—she could bear so
much—not well enough to spare her. Of there being any
justification of her jealousy of the Princess he never thought ;
it could not occur to him to weigh against each other the
sentiments he might excite in such opposed bosoms or those
that the spectacle of either emotion might have kindled in
his own. He had, no doubt, his share of fatuity, but he
found himself unable to associate, mentally, a great lady and
a shop-girl in a contest for a prize which should present
analogies with his own personality. How could they have
anything in common—even so small a thing as a desire to
possess themselves of Hyacinth Robinson ? A fact that he
did not impart to Millicent, and that he could have no wish
to impart to her, was the matter of his pilgrimage to Belgrave
Square. He might be in love with the Princess (how could
he qualify, as yet, the bewildered emotion she had produced
in him ?), and he certainly never would conceive a passion
for poor Lady Aurora ; yet it would have given him pain
much greater than any he felt in the other case, to hear the
girl make free with the ministering angel of Audley Court.
The difference was, perhaps, somehow in that she appeared
really not to touch or arrive at the Princess at all, whereas
Lady Aurora was within her range and compass.

After paying him that visit at his rooms Hyacinth lost
sight of Captain Sholto, who had not again reappeared at
the 'Sun and Moon,' the little tavern which presented so
common and casual a face to the world and yet, in its
unsuspected rear, offered a security as yet unimpugned to
machinations going down to the very bottom of things.
Nothing was more natural than that the Captain should be
engaged at this season in the recreations of his class ; and
our young man took for granted that if he were not hanging
about the Princess, on that queer footing as to which he
himself had a secret hope that he should some day have
more light, he was probably ploughing through northern
seas on a yacht or creeping after stags in the Highlands ;
our hero's acquaintance with the light literature of his
country being such as to assure him that in one or other

of these occupations people of leisure, during the autumn,
were necessarily immersed. If the Captain were giving his
attention to neither, he must have started for Albania, or at
least for Paris. Happy Captain, Hyacinth reflected, while
his imagination followed him through all kinds of vivid
exotic episodes and his restless young feet continued to
tread, through the stale, flat weeks of September and
October, the familiar pavements of Soho, Islington, and
Pentonville, and the shabby sinuous ways which unite these
laborious districts. He had told the Princess that he sometimes had a holiday at this period and that there was a
chance of his escorting his respectable companion to the
seaside ; but as it turned out, at present, the spare cash for
such an excursion was wanting. Hyacinth had indeed, for
the moment, an exceptionally keen sense of the absence of
this article, and was forcibly reminded that it took a good
deal of money to cultivate the society of agreeable women.
He not only had not a penny, but he was much in debt,
and the explanation of his pinched feeling was in a vague,
half-remorseful, half-resigned reference to the numerous
occasions when he had had to put his hand in his pocket
under penalty of disappointing a young lady whose needs
were positive, and especially to a certain high crisis (as it
might prove to be) in his destiny, when it came over him
that one couldn't call on a princess just as one was. So,
this year, he did not ask old Crookenden for the week
which some of the other men took (Eustache Poupin, who
had never quitted London since his arrival, launched
himself, precisely that summer, supported by his brave wife,
into the British unknown, on the strength of a return
ticket to Worthing) ; simply because he shouldn't know
what to do with it. The best way not to spend money,
though it was no doubt not the best in the world to make
it, was still to take one's daily course to the old familiar,
shabby shop, where, as the days shortened and November
thickened the air to a livid yellow, the uncovered flame of
the gas, burning often from the morning on, lighted up the
ugliness amid which the hand of practice endeavoured to
disengage a little beauty—the ugliness of a dingy, belittered
interior, of battered, dispapered walls, of work-tables stained

and hacked, of windows opening into a foul, drizzling street, of the bared arms, the sordid waistcoat-backs, the smeared aprons, the personal odour, the patient, obstinate, irritating shoulders and vulgar, narrow, inevitable faces, of his fellow-labourers.   Hyacinth's relations with his comrades would form a chapter by itself, but all that may be said of the matter here is that the clever little operator from Lomax Place had a kind of double identity, and that much as he lived in Mr. Crookenden's establishment he lived out of it still more.   In this busy, pasty, sticky, leathery little world, where wages and beer were the main objects of consideration, he played his part in a manner which caused him to be regarded as a queer lot, but capable of queerness in the line of good-nature too.   He had not made good his place there without discovering that the British workman, when animated by the spirit of mirth, has rather a heavy hand, and he tasted of the practical joke in every degree of violence.   During his first year he dreamed, with secret passion and suppressed tears, of a day of bliss when at last they would let him alone— a day which arrived in time, for it is always an advantage to be clever, if only one is clever enough.   Hyacinth was sufficiently so to have invented a *modus vivendi* in respect to which M. Poupin said to him, ' *Enfin vous voilà ferme !* ' (the Frenchman himself, terribly *éprouvé* at the beginning, had always bristled with firmness and opposed to insular grossness a refined dignity), and under the influence of which the scenery of Soho figured as a daily, dusky phantasmagoria, relegated to the mechanical, passive part of experience and giving no hostages to reality, or at least to ambition, save an insufficient number of shillings on Saturday night and spasmodic reminiscences of delicate work that might have been more delicate still, as well as of certain applications of the tool which he flattered himself were unsurpassed, unless by the supreme Eustache.

One evening in November, after discharging himself of a considerable indebtedness to Pinnie, he had still a sovereign in his pocket—a sovereign which seemed to spin there at the opposed solicitation of a dozen exemplary uses. He had come out for a walk, with a vague intention of

pushing as far as Audley Court; and lurking within this
nebulous design, on which the damp breath of the streets,
making objects seem that night particularly dim and places
particularly far, had blown a certain chill, was a sense that
it would be rather nice to take something to Rose Muniment, who delighted in a sixpenny present and to whom,
for some time, he had not rendered any such homage. At
last, after he had wandered a while, hesitating between the
pilgrimage to Lambeth and the possibility of still associating
his evening in some way or other with that of Miss Henning,
he reflected that if a sovereign was to be pulled to pieces
it was a simplification to get it changed. He had been
traversing the region of Mayfair, partly with the preoccupation of a short cut and partly from an instinct of self-defence;
if one was in danger of spending one's money precipitately
it was so much gained to plunge into a quarter in which,
at that hour especially, there were no shops for little bookbinders. Hyacinth's victory, however, was imperfect when
it occurred to him to turn into a public-house in order to
convert his gold into convenient silver. When it was a
question of entering these establishments he selected in
preference the most decent; he never knew what unpleasant
people he might find on the other side of the swinging
door. Those which glitter, at intervals, amid the residential
gloom of Mayfair partake of the general gentility of the
neighbourhood, so that Hyacinth was not surprised (he
had passed into the compartment marked 'private bar') to
see but a single drinker leaning against the counter on
which, with his request very civilly enunciated, he put down
his sovereign. He was surprised, on the other hand, when,
glancing up again, he became aware that this solitary drinker
was Captain Godfrey Sholto.

'Why, my dear boy, what a remarkable coincidence!'
the Captain exclaimed. 'For once in five years that I
come into a place like this!'

'I don't come in often myself. I thought you were in
Madagascar,' said Hyacinth.

'Ah, because I have not been at the "Sun and Moon"?
Well, I have been constantly out of town, you know. And
then—don't you see what I mean?—I want to be tremen-

dously careful. That's the way to get on, isn't it ? But I
daresay you don't believe in my discretion ! ' Sholto
laughed. 'What shall I do to make you understand? I
say, have a brandy and soda,' he continued, as if this might
assist Hyacinth's comprehension. He seemed a trifle
flurried, and, if it were possible to imagine such a thing of
so independent and whimsical a personage, the least bit
abashed or uneasy at having been found in such a low
place. It was not any lower, after all, than the ' Sun and
Moon.' He was dressed on this occasion according to his
station, without the pot-hat and the shabby jacket, and
Hyacinth looked at him with a sense that a good tailor
must really add a charm to life. Our hero was struck more
than ever before with his being the type of man whom, as
he strolled about, observing people, he had so often regarded with wonder and envy—the sort of man of whom
one said to one's self that he was the ' finest white,' feeling
that he had the world in his pocket. Sholto requested the
bar-maid to please not dawdle in preparing the brandy and
soda which Hyacinth had thought to ease off the situation
by accepting : this, indeed, was perhaps what the finest
white would naturally do. And when the young man had
taken the glass from the counter Sholto appeared to
encourage him not to linger as he drank it, and smiled down
at him very kindly and amusedly, as if the combination of
a very small bookbinder and a big tumbler were sufficiently
droll. The Captain took time, however, to ask Hyacinth
how he had spent his autumn and what was the news in
Bloomsbury ; he further inquired about those delightful
people over the river. ' I can't tell you what an impression
they made upon me—that evening, you know.' After this
he remarked to Hyacinth, suddenly, irrelevantly, ' And so
you are just going to stay on for the winter, quietly ?' Our
young man stared : he wondered what other project any
one could attribute to him ; he could not reflect, immediately, that this was the sort of thing the finest whites said to
each other when they met, after their fashionable dispersals,
and that his friend had only been guilty of a momentary in-
advertence. In point of fact the Captain recovered himself. ' Oh, of course you have got your work, and that sort

of thing ;' and, as Hyacinth did not succeed in swallowing
at a gulp the contents of his big tumbler, he asked him
presently whether he had heard anything from the Princess.
Hyacinth replied that he could have no news except what
the Captain might be good enough to give him ; but he
added that he did go to see her just before she left town.

'Ah, you did go to see her ?   That's quite right—quite
right.'

'I went, because she very kindly wrote to me to come.'

'Ah, she wrote to you to come ?'   The Captain fixed
Hyacinth for a moment with his curious colourless eyes.
'Do you know you are a devilish privileged mortal ?'

'Certainly, I know that.'   Hyacinth blushed and felt
foolish ; the bar-maid, who had heard this odd couple talking about a princess, was staring at him too, with her elbows
on the counter.

'Do you know there are people who would give their
heads that she should write to them to come ?'

'I have no doubt of it whatever !' Hyacinth exclaimed,
taking refuge in a laugh which did not sound as natural as
he would have liked, and wondering whether his interlocutor
were not precisely one of these people.   In this case the
bar-maid might well stare ; for deeply convinced as our
young man might be that he was the son of Lord Frederick
Purvis, there was really no end to the oddity of his being
preferred—and by a princess—to Captain Sholto.   If anything could have reinforced, at that moment, his sense of
this anomaly, it would have been the indescribably gentle-
manly way, implying all sorts of common initiations, in
which his companion went on.

'Ah, well, I see you know how to take it !   And if you
are in correspondence with her why do you say that you
can hear from her only through me ?   My dear fellow, I
am not in correspondence with her.   You might think I
would naturally be, but I am not.'   He subjoined, as Hyacinth had laughed again, in a manner that might have
passed for ambiguous, 'So much the worse for me—is that
what you mean ?'   Hyacinth replied that he himself had
had the honour of hearing from the Princess only once,
and he mentioned that she had told him that her letter-

writing came only in fits, when it was sometimes very profuse : there were months together that she didn't touch a
pen. 'Oh, I can imagine what she told you!' the Captain
exclaimed. 'Look out for the next fit! She is visiting
about. It's a great thing to be in the same house with
her—an immense comedy.' He remarked that he had
heard, now he remembered, that she either had taken, or
was thinking of taking, a house in the country for a few
months, and he added that if Hyacinth didn't propose to
finish his brandy and soda they might as well turn out.
Hyacinth's thirst had been very superficial, and as they
turned out the Captain observed, by way of explanation of
his having been found in a public-house (it was the only
attempt of this kind he made), that any friend of his would
always know him by his love of curious out-of-the-way
nooks. 'You must have noticed that,' he said—'my taste
for exploration. If I hadn't explored I never should have
known you, should I? That was rather a nice little girl in
there ; did you twig her figure? It's a pity they always
have such beastly hands.' Hyacinth, instinctively, had
made a motion to go southward, but Sholto, passing a hand
into his arm, led him the other way. The house they had
quitted was near a corner, which they rounded, the Captain
pushing forward as if there were some reason for haste.
His haste was checked, however, by an immediate collision
with a young woman who, coming in the opposite direction,
turned the angle as briskly as themselves. At this moment
the Captain gave Hyacinth a great jerk, but not before he
had caught a glimpse of the young woman's face — it
seemed to flash upon him out of the dusk — and given
quick voice to his surprise.

'Hallo, Millicent!' This was the simple cry that
escaped from his lips, while the Captain, still going on,
inquired, 'What's the matter? Who's your pretty friend?'
Hyacinth declined to go on, and repeated Miss Henning's baptismal name so loudly that the young woman,
who had passed them without looking back, was obliged
to stop. Then Hyacinth saw that he was not mistaken,
though Millicent gave no audible response. She stood
looking at him, with her head very high, and he ap-

proached her, disengaging himself from Sholto, who however hung back only an instant before joining them.
Hyacinth's heart had suddenly begun to beat very fast;
there was a sharp shock in the girl's turning up just in
that place at that moment. Yet when she began to
laugh, abruptly, with violence, and to ask him why he
was looking at her as if she were a kicking horse, he
recognised that there was nothing so very extraordinary,
after all, in a casual meeting between persons who
were such frequenters of the London Streets. Millicent
had never concealed the fact that she 'trotted about,' on
various errands, at night; and once, when he had said to her
that the less a respectable young woman took the evening
air alone the better for her respectability, she had asked
how respectable he thought she pretended to be, and had
remarked that if he would make her a present of a
brougham, or even call for her three or four times a week
in a cab, she would doubtless preserve more of her social
purity. She could turn the tables quickly enough, and
she exclaimed, now, professing, on her own side, great
astonishment—

'What are you prowling about here for? You're after
no good, I'll be bound!'

'Good evening, Miss Henning; what a jolly meeting!'
said the Captain, removing his hat with a humorous
flourish.

'Oh, how d'ye do?' Millicent returned, as if she did
not immediately place him.

'Where were you going so fast? What are you doing?'
asked Hyacinth, who had looked from one to the other.

'Well, I never did see such a manner—from one that
knocks about like *you!*' cried Miss Henning. 'I'm going
to see a friend of mine—a lady's-maid in Curzon Street.
Have you anything to say to that?'

'Don't tell us—don't tell us!' Sholto interposed, after
she had spoken (she had not hesitated an instant). 'I,
at least, disavow the indiscretion. Where may not a
charming woman be going when she trips with a light foot
through the gathering dusk?'

'I say, what are you talking about?' the girl inquired,

with dignity, of Hyacinth's companion. She spoke as if
with a resentful suspicion that her foot had not really
been perceived to be light.

'On what errand of mercy, of secret tenderness?' the
Captain went on, laughing.

'Secret yourself!' cried Millicent. 'Do you two always
hunt in couples?'

'All right, we'll turn round and go with you as far as
your friend's,' Hyacinth said.

'All right,' Millicent replied.

'All right,' the Captain added; and the three took
their way together in the direction of Curzon Street. They
walked for a few moments in silence, though the Captain
whistled, and then Millicent suddenly turned to Hyacinth.

'You haven't told me where *you* were going, yet.'

'We met in that public-house,' the Captain said, 'and
we were each so ashamed of being found in such a place
by the other that we tumbled out together, without much
thinking what we should do with ourselves.'

'When he's out with me he pretends he can't abide
them houses,' Miss Henning declared. 'I wish I had
looked in that one, to see who was there.'

'Well, she's rather nice,' the Captain went on. 'She
told me her name was Georgiana.'

'I went to get a piece of money changed,' Hyacinth
said, with a sense that there was a certain dishonesty in
the air; glad that he, at least, could afford to speak the
truth.

'To get your grandmother's nightcap changed! I
recommend you to keep your money together—you've
none too much of it!' Millicent exclaimed.

'Is that the reason you are playing me false?' Hyacinth
flashed out. He had been thinking, with still intentness,
as they walked; at once nursing and wrestling with a
kindled suspicion. He was pale with the idea that he was
being bamboozled; yet he was able to say to himself that
one must allow, in life, for the element of coincidence, and
that he might easily put himself immensely in the wrong
by making a groundless charge. It was only later that he

pieced his impressions together and saw them—as it
appeared—justify each other; at present, as soon as he
had uttered it, he was almost ashamed of his quick retort
to Millicent's taunt.   He ought at least to have waited to
see what Curzon Street would bring forth.

The girl broke out upon him immediately, repeating
' False, false ? ' with high derision, and wanting to know
whether that was the way to knock a lady about in public.
She had stopped short on the edge of a crossing, and
she went on, with a voice so uplifted that he was glad
they were in a street that was rather empty at such an
hour : ' You're a pretty one to talk about falsity, when a
woman has only to leer at you out of an opera-box ! '

' Don't say anything about *her*,' the young man interposed, trembling.

' And pray why not about " her," I should like to
know ?   You don't pretend she's a decent woman, I suppose ? '   Millicent's laughter rang through the quiet
neighbourhood.

' My dear fellow, you know you *have* been to her,'
Captain Sholto remarked, smiling.

Hyacinth turned upon him, staring, at once challenged
and baffled by his ambiguous part in an incident it was
doubtless possible to magnify but it was not possible to
treat as perfectly simple.   ' Certainly, I have been to the
Princess Casamassima, thanks to you.   When you came
and begged me, when you dragged me, do you make it a
reproach ?   Who the devil are you, any way, and what do
you want of me ? ' our hero cried—his mind flooded in a
moment with everything in the Captain that had puzzled
and eluded him.   This swelling tide obliterated on
the spot everything that had entertained and gratified
him.

' My dear fellow, whatever I am, I am not an ass,' this
gentleman replied, with imperturbable good-humour.   ' I
don't reproach you with anything.   I only wanted to put
in a word as a peacemaker.   My good friends—my good
friends,' and he laid a hand, in his practised way, on
Hyacinth's shoulder, while, with the other pressed to his
heart, he bent on the girl a face of gallantry which had

something paternal in it, ' I am determined this absurd misunderstanding shall end as lovers' quarrels ought always to end.'

Hyacinth withdrew himself from the Captain's touch and said to Millicent, 'You are not really jealous of—of any one. You pretend that, only to throw dust in my eyes.'

To this sally Miss Henning returned him an answer which promised to be lively, but the Captain swept it away in the profusion of his protests. He pronounced them a dear delightful, abominable young couple ; he declared it was most interesting to see how, in people of their sort, the passions lay near the surface ; he almost pushed them into each other's arms ; and he wound up by proposing that they should all terminate their little differences by proceeding together to the Pavilion music-hall, the nearest place of entertainment in that neighbourhood, leaving the lady's-maid in Curzon Street to dress her mistress's wig in peace. He has been presented to the reader as an accomplished man, and it will doubtless be felt that the picture is justified when I relate that he placed this idea in so attractive a light that his companions finally entered a hansom with him and rattled toward the haunt of pleasure, Hyacinth sandwiched, on the edge of the seat, between the others. Two or three times his ears burned ; he felt that if there was an understanding between them they had now, behind him, a rare opportunity for carrying it out. If it was at his expense, the whole evening constituted for them, indeed, an opportunity, and this thought rendered his diversion but scantily absorbing, though at the Pavilion the Captain engaged a private box and ordered ices to be brought in. Hyacinth cared so little for his little pink pyramid that he suffered Millicent to consume it after she had disposed of her own. It was present to him, however, that if he should make a fool of himself the folly would be of a very gross kind, and this is why he withheld a question which rose to his lips repeatedly—a disposition to inquire of his entertainer why the mischief he had hurried him so out of the public-house, if he had not been waiting there, preconcertedly, for Millicent. We know that in Hyacinth's eyes one of this young lady's compensatory merits had been that she was not deceitful, and he asked himself if a girl could change, that way, from one month to the other. This was optimistic, but, all the same, he reflected, before leaving the Pavilion, that he could see quite well what Lady Aurora meant by thinking Captain Sholto vulgar.

XXI

PAUL MUNIMENT had fits of silence, while the others were talking; but on this occasion he had not opened his lips for half an hour. When he talked Hyacinth listened, almost holding his breath; and when he said nothing Hyacinth watched him fixedly, listening to the others only through the medium of his candid countenance. At the 'Sun and Moon' Muniment paid very little attention to his young friend, doing nothing that should cause it to be perceived they were particular pals; and Hyacinth even thought, at moments, that he was bored or irritated by the serious manner in which the bookbinder could not conceal from the world that he regarded him. He wondered whether this were a system, a calculated prudence, on Muniment's part, or only a manifestation of that superior brutality, latent in his composition, which never had an intention of unkindness but was naturally intolerant of palaver. There was plenty of palaver at the 'Sun and Moon'; there were nights when a blast of imbecility seemed to blow over the place, and one felt ashamed to be associated with so much insistent ignorance and flat-faced vanity. Then every one, with two or three exceptions, made an ass of himself, thumping the table and repeating over some inane phrase which appeared for the hour to constitute the whole furniture of his mind. There were men who kept saying, 'Them was my words in the month of February last, and what I say I stick to—what I say I stick to;' and others who perpetually inquired of the company, 'And what the plague am I to do with seventeen shillings—with seventeen shillings? What am I to do with them—will ye tell me that?' an interrogation which, in truth, usually ended by eliciting a ribald reply.

There were still others who remarked, to satiety, that if it
was not done to-day it would have to be done to-morrow,
and several who constantly proclaimed their opinion that
the only way was to pull up the Park rails again—just to
pluck them straight up. A little shoemaker, with red eyes
and a grayish face, whose appearance Hyacinth deplored,
scarcely ever expressed himself but in the same form of
words : ' Well, are we in earnest, or ain't we in earnest ?—
that's the thing *I* want to know.' He was terribly in
earnest himself, but this was almost the only way he had
of showing it ; and he had much in common (though they
were always squabbling) with a large red-faced man, of
uncertain attributes and stertorous breathing, who was
understood to know a good deal about dogs, had fat
hands, and wore on his forefinger a big silver ring, containing some one's hair—Hyacinth believed it to be that
of a terrier, snappish in life. He had always the same
refrain : ' Well, now, are we just starving, or ain't we just
starving ? I should like the v'ice of the company on that
question.'

When the tone fell as low as this Paul Muniment held
his peace, except that he whistled a little, leaning back,
with his hands in his pockets and his eyes on the table.
Hyacinth often supposed him to be on the point of breaking out and letting the company know what he thought of
them—he had a perfectly clear vision of what he must
think : but Muniment never compromised his popularity
to that degree ; he judged it—this he once told Hyacinth
—too valuable an instrument, and cultivated the faculty of
patience, which had the advantage of showing one more
and more that one must do one's thinking for one's self.
His popularity, indeed, struck Hyacinth as rather an
uncertain quantity, and the only mistake he had seen a
symptom of on his friend's part was a tendency to over-
estimate it. Muniment thought many of their colleagues
asinine, but it was Hyacinth's belief that he himself knew
still better how asinine they were ; and this inadequate
conception supported, in some degree, on Paul's part, his
theory of his influence—an influence that would be stronger
than any other on the day he should choose to exert it.

Hyacinth only wished that day would come; it would not be till then, he was sure, that they would all know where they were, and that the good they were striving for, blindly, obstructedly, in a kind of eternal dirty intellectual fog, would pass from the stage of crude discussion and mere sharp, tantalising desirableness into that of irresistible reality.   Muniment was listened to unanimously, when he spoke, and was much talked about, usually with a knowing, implicit allusiveness, when he was absent; it was generally admitted that he could see further than most.   But it was suspected that he wanted to see further than was necessary; as one of the most inveterate frequenters of the club remarked one evening, if a man could see as far as he could chuck a brick, that was far enough.   There was an idea that he had nothing particular to complain of, personally, or that if he had he didn't complain of it—an attitude which perhaps contained the germs of a latent disaffection. Hyacinth could easily see that he himself was exposed to the same imputation, but he couldn't help it; it would have been impossible to him to keep up his character for sincerity by revealing, at the 'Sun and Moon,' the condition of his wardrobe, or announcing that he had not had a pennyworth of bacon for six months.   There were members of the club who were apparently always in the enjoyment of involuntary leisure—narrating the vainest peregrinations in search of a job, the cruelest rebuffs, the most vivid anecdotes of the insolence of office.   They made Hyacinth uncomfortably conscious, at times, that if *he* should be out of work it would be wholly by his own fault; that he had in his hand a bread-winning tool on which he might absolutely count.   He was also aware, however, that his position in this little band of malcontents (it was little only if measured by the numbers that were gathered together on any one occasion; he liked to think it was large in its latent possibilities, its mysterious ramifications and affiliations), was peculiar and distinguished; it would be favourable if he had the kind of energy and assurance that would help him to make use of it.   He had an intimate conviction—the proof of it was in the air, in the sensible facility of his footing at the 'Sun and Moon'—that Eustache Poupin

had taken upon himself to disseminate the anecdote of his
origin, of his mother's disaster ; in consequence of which,
as the victim of social infamy, of heinous laws, it was conceded to him that he had a larger account to settle even
than most.   He was *ab ovo* a revolutionist, and that
balanced against his smart neckties, a certain suspicious
security that was perceived in him as to the *h* (he had had
from his earliest years a natural command of it), and the
fact that he possessed the sort of hand on which there is
always a premium—an accident somehow to be guarded
against in a thorough-going system of equality.   He never
challenged Poupin on the subject, for he owed the Frenchman too much to reproach him with any officious step that
was meant in kindness ; and moreover his fellow-labourer
at old Crookenden's had said to him, as if to anticipate
such an impugnment of his discretion, 'Remember, my
child, that I am incapable of drawing aside any veil that
you may have preferred to drop over your lacerated personality.   Your moral dignity will always be safe with me.
But remember at the same time that among the disinherited
there is a mystic language which dispenses with proofs—a
freemasonry, a reciprocal divination ; they understand each
other with half a word.'   It was with half a word, then, in
Bloomsbury, that Hyacinth had been understood ; but
there was a certain delicacy within him that forbade him
to push his advantage, to treat implications of sympathy,
none the less definite for being roundabout, as steps in the
ladder of success.   He had no wish to be a leader because
his mother had murdered her lover and died in penal
servitude : these circumstances recommended intentness
but they also suggested modesty.   When the gathering at
the 'Sun and Moon' was at its best, and its temper
seemed really an earnest of what was the basis of all its
calculations—that the people was only a sleeping lion,
already breathing shorter and beginning to stretch its limbs
—at these hours, some of them thrilling enough, Hyacinth
waited for the voice that should allot to him the particular
part he was to play.   His ambition was to play it with
brilliancy, to offer an example—an example, even, that
might survive him—of pure youthful, almost juvenile,

consecration.   He was conscious of no commission to
give the promises, to assume the responsibilities, of a
redeemer, and he had no envy of the man on whom this
burden should rest.   Muniment, indeed, might carry it,
and it was the first article of his faith that to help him to
carry it the better he himself was ready for any sacrifice.
Then it was—on these nights of intenser vibration—that
Hyacinth waited for a sign.

They came oftener, this second winter, for the season
was terribly hard; and as in that lower world one walked
with one's ear nearer the ground, the deep perpetual groan
of London misery seemed to swell and swell and form the
whole undertone of life.   The filthy air came into the place
in the damp coats of silent men, and hung there till it was
brewed to a nauseous warmth, and ugly, serious faces
squared themselves through it, and strong-smelling pipes
contributed their element in a fierce, dogged manner which
appeared to say that it now had to stand for everything—
for bread and meat and beer, for shoes and blankets and
the poor things at the pawnbroker's and the smokeless
chimney at home.   Hyacinth's colleagues seemed to him
wiser then, and more permeated with intentions boding ill
to the satisfied classes; and though the note of popularity
was still most effectively struck by the man who could
demand oftenest, unpractically, 'What the plague am I to
do with seventeen shillings?' it was brought home to our
hero on more than one occasion that revolution was ripe at
last.   This was especially the case on the evening I began
by referring to, when Eustache Poupin squeezed in and announced, as if it were a great piece of news, that in the
east of London, that night, there were forty thousand men
out of work.   He looked round the circle with his dilated
foreign eye, as he took his place; he seemed to address
the company individually as well as collectively, and to
make each man responsible for hearing him.   He owed his
position at the 'Sun and Moon' to the brilliancy with
which he represented the political exile, the magnanimous
immaculate citizen wrenched out of bed at dead of night,
torn from his hearthstone, his loved ones and his profession,
and hurried across the frontier with only the coat on his

back. Poupin had performed in this character now for
many years, but he had never lost the bloom of the out-
raged proscript, and the passionate pictures he had often
drawn of the bitterness of exile were moving even to those
who knew with what success he had set up his household
gods in Lisson Grove. He was recognised as suffering
everything for his opinions ; and his hearers in Bloomsbury
—who, after all, even in their most concentrated hours,
were very good-natured—appeared never to have made the
subtle reflection, though they made many others, that there
was a want of tact in his calling upon them to sympathise with him for being one of themselves. He imposed
himself by the eloquence of his assumption that if one were
not in the beautiful France one was nowhere worth speaking
of, and ended by producing an impression that that country
had an almost supernatural charm. Muniment had once
said to Hyacinth that he was sure Poupin would be very
sorry if he should be enabled to go home again (as he
might, from one week to the other, the Republic being
so indulgent and the amnesty to the Communards constantly extended), for over there he couldn't be a refugee ;
and however this might be he certainly flourished a good
deal in London on the basis of this very fact that he
was miserable there.

'Why do you tell us that, as if it was so very striking ?
Don't we know it, and haven't we known it always ? But
you are right ; we behave as if we knew nothing at all,'
said Mr. Schinkel, the German cabinet-maker, who had
originally introduced Captain Sholto to the 'Sun and Moon.'
He had a long, unhealthy, benevolent face and greasy hair,
and constantly wore a kind of untidy bandage round his
neck, as if for a local ailment. 'You remind us—that is
very well ; but we shall forget it in half an hour. We are
not serious.'

'*Pardon, pardon ;* for myself, I do not admit that ! '
Poupin replied, striking the table with his finger-tips several
times, very fast. 'If I am not serious, I am nothing.'

'Oh no, you are something,' said the German, smoking
his monumental pipe with a contemplative air. 'We are
all something ; but I am not sure it is anything very useful.'

'Well, things would be worse without us. I'd rather be in here, in *this* kind of muck, than outside,' remarked the fat man who understood dogs.

'Certainly, it is very pleasant, especially if you have your beer; but not so pleasant in the east, where fifty thousand people starve. It is a very unpleasant night,' the cabinet-maker went on.

'How can it be worse?' Eustache Poupin inquired, looking defiantly at the German, as if to make him responsible for the fat man's reflection. 'It is so bad that the imagination recoils, refuses.'

'Oh, we don't care for the imagination!' the fat man declared. 'We want a compact body, in marching order.'

'What do you call a compact body?' the little gray-faced shoemaker demanded. 'I daresay you don't mean your kind of body.'

'Well, I know what I mean,' said the fat man, severely.

'That's a grand thing. Perhaps one of these days you'll tell us.'

'You'll see it for yourself, perhaps, before that day comes,' the gentleman with the silver ring rejoined. 'Perhaps when you do, you'll remember.'

'Well, you know, Schinkel says we don't,' said the shoemaker, nodding at the cloud-compelling German.

'I don't care what no man says!' the dog-fancier exclaimed, gazing straight before him.

'They say it's a bad year—the blockheads in the newspapers,' Mr. Schinkel went on, addressing himself to the company at large. 'They say that on purpose—to convey the impression that there are such things as good years. I ask the company, has any gentleman present ever happened to notice that article? The good year is yet to come: it might begin to-night, if we like; it all depends on our being able to be serious for a few hours. But that is too much to expect. Mr. Muniment is very serious; he looks as if he was waiting for the signal; but he doesn't speak—he never speaks, if I want particularly to hear him. He only considers, very deeply, I am sure. But it is almost as bad to think without speaking as to speak without thinking.'

Hyacinth always admired the cool, easy way in which Muniment comported himself when the attention of the public was directed towards him.   These manifestations of curiosity, or of hostility, would have put him out immensely, himself.   When a lot of people, especially the kind of people who were collected at the 'Sun and Moon,' looked at him, or listened to him, at once, he always blushed and stammered, feeling that if he couldn't have a million of spectators (which would have been inspiring), he should prefer to have but two or three; there was something very embarrassing in twenty.

Muniment smiled, for an instant, good-humouredly; then, after a moment's hesitation, looking across at the German, and the German only, as if his remark were worth noticing, but it didn't matter if the others didn't understand the reply, he said simply, 'Hoffendahl's in London.'

'Hoffendahl?   *Gott in Himmel!*' the cabinet-maker exclaimed, taking the pipe out of his mouth.   And the two men exchanged a longish glance.   Then Mr. Schinkel remarked, 'That surprises me, *sehr*.   Are you very sure?'

Muniment continued, for a moment, to look at him. 'If I keep quiet for half an hour, with so many valuable suggestions flying all round me, you think I say too little. Then if I open my head to give out three words, you appear to think I say too much.'

'Ah, no; on the contrary, I want you to say three more. If you tell me you have seen him I shall be perfectly satisfied.'

'Upon my word, I should hope so!   Do you think he's the kind of party a fellow says he has seen?'

'Yes, when he hasn't!' said Eustache Poupin, who had been listening.   Every one was listening now.

'It depends on the fellow he says it to.   Not even here?' the German asked.

'Oh, here!' Paul Muniment exclaimed, in a peculiar tone, and resumed his muffled whistle again.

'Take care—take care; you will make me think you haven't!' cried Poupin, with his excited expression.

'That's just what I want,' said Muniment.

'*Nun*, I understand,' the cabinetmaker remarked, restoring his pipe to his lips after an interval almost as momentous as the stoppage of a steamer in mid-ocean.

'*'Ere*, 'ere ?' repeated the small shoemaker, indignantly. 'I daresay it's as good as the place he came from. He might look in and see what he thinks of it.'

'That's a place you might tell us a little about now,' the fat man suggested, as if he had been waiting for his chance.

Before the shoemaker had time to notice this challenge some one inquired, with a hoarse petulance, who the blazes they were talking about; and Mr. Schinkel took upon himself to reply that they were talking about a man who hadn't done what he had done by simply exchanging abstract ideas, however valuable, with his friends in a respectable pot-house.

'What the devil has he done, then?' some one else demanded; and Muniment replied, quietly, that he had spent twelve years in a Prussian prison, and was consequently still an object of a good deal of interest to the police.

'Well, if you call that very useful, I must say I prefer a pot-house !' cried the shoemaker, appealing to all the company and looking, as it appeared to Hyacinth, particularly hideous.

'*Doch, doch*, it is useful,' the German remarked, philosophically, among his yellow clouds.

'Do you mean to say you are not prepared for that, yourself?' Muniment inquired of the shoemaker.

'Prepared for that ? I thought we were going to smash that sort of shop altogether; I thought that was the main part of the job.'

'They will smash best, those who have been inside,' the German declared; 'unless, perhaps, they are broken, enervated. But Hoffendahl is not enervated.'

'Ah, no ; no smashing, no smashing,' Muniment went on. 'We want to keep them standing, and even to build a few more ; but the difference will be that we shall put the correct sort in.'

'I take your idea—that Griffin is one of the correct sort,' the fat man remarked, indicating the shoemaker.

'I thought we was going to 'ave their 'eads—all that bloomin' lot !' Mr. Griffin declared, protesting ; while

Eustache Poupin began to enlighten the company as to the great Hoffendahl, one of the purest martyrs of their cause, a man who had been through everything—who had been scarred and branded, tortured, almost flayed, and had never given them the names they wanted to have. Was it possible they didn't remember that great combined attempt, early in the sixties, which took place in four Continental cities at once and which, in spite of every effort to smother it up—there had been editors and journalists transported even for hinting at it—had done more for the social question than anything before or since? 'Through him being served in the manner you describe?' some one asked, with plainness ; to which Poupin replied that it was one of those failures that are more glorious than any success. Muniment said that the affair had been only a flash in the pan, but that the great value of it was this—that whereas some forty persons (and of both sexes) had been engaged in it, only one had been seized and had suffered. It had been Hoffendahl himself who was collared. Certainly he had suffered much, he had suffered for every one ; but from that point of view—that of the economy of material—the thing had been a rare success.

'Do you know what I call the others? I call 'em bloody sneaks!' the fat man cried ; and Eustache Poupin, turning to Muniment, expressed the hope that he didn't really approve of such a solution—didn't consider that an economy of heroism was an advantage to any cause. He himself esteemed Hoffendahl's attempt because it had shaken, more than anything—except, of course, the Commune—had shaken it since the French Revolution, the rotten fabric of the actual social order, and because that very fact of the impunity, the invisibility, of the persons concerned in it had given the predatory classes, had given all Europe, a shudder that had not yet subsided ; but for his part, he must regret that some of the associates of the devoted victim had not come forward and insisted on sharing with him his tortures and his captivity.

'*C'aurait été d'un bel exemple!*' said the Frenchman, with an impressive moderation of statement which made even those who could not understand him see that he was saying something fine; while the cabinet-maker remarked that in Hoffendahl's place any of them would have stood out just the same. He didn't care if they set it down to self-love (Mr. Schinkel called it 'loaf'), but he might say that he himself would have done so if he had been trusted and had been bagged.

'I want to have it all drawn up clear first; then I'll go in,' said the fat man, who seemed to think it was expected of him to be reassuring.

'Well, who the dickens is to draw it up, eh? That's what we happen to be talking about,' returned his antagonist the shoemaker.

'A fine example, old man? Is that your idea of a fine example?' Muniment, with his amused face, asked of Poupin. 'A fine example of asininity! Are there capable people, in such plenty, about the place?'

'Capable of greatness of soul, I grant you not.'

'Your greatness of soul is usually greatness of blundering. A man's foremost duty is not to get collared. If you want to show you're capable, that's the way.'

At this Hyacinth suddenly felt himself moved to speak. 'But some one must be caught, always, must he not? Hasn't some one always been?'

'Oh, I daresay you'll be, if you like it!' Muniment replied, without looking at him. 'If they succeed in potting you, do as Hoffendahl did, and do it as a matter of course; but if they don't, make it your supreme duty, make it your religion, to lie close and keep yourself for another go. The world is full of unclean beasts whom I shall be glad to see shovelled away by the thousand; but when it's a question of honest men and men of courage, I protest against the idea that two should be sacrificed where one will serve.'

'*Trop d'arithmétique — trop d'arithmétique!* That is fearfully English!' Poupin cried.

'No doubt, no doubt; what else should it be? You shall never share my fate, if I have a fate and I can prevent it!' said Muniment, laughing.

Eustache Poupin stared at him and his·merriment, as if he thought the English frivolous as well as calculating;

then he rejoined, ' If I suffer, I trust it may be for suffering humanity, but I trust it may also be for France.'

' Oh, I hope you ain't going to suffer any more for France,' said Mr Griffin. ' Hasn't it done that insatiable old country of yours some good, by this time, all you've had to put up with ? '

' Well, I want to know what Hoffendahl has come over for ; it's very kind of him, I'm sure. What is he going to do for *us* ?—that's what *I* want to know,' remarked in a loud, argumentative tone a personage at the end of the table most distant from Muniment's place. His name was Delancey, and he gave himself out as holding a position in a manufactory of soda-water ; but Hyacinth had a secret belief that he was really a hairdresser—a belief connected with a high, lustrous curl, or crest, which he wore on the summit of his large head, and the manner in which he thrust over his ear, as if it were a barber's comb, the pencil with which he was careful to take notes of the discussions carried on at the ' Sun and Moon.' His opinions were distinct and frequently expressed ; he had a watery (Muniment had once called it a soda-watery) eye, and a personal aversion to a lord. He desired to change everything except religion, of which he approved.

Muniment answered that he was unable to say, as yet, what the German revolutionist had come to England for, but that he hoped to be able to give some information on the matter the next time they should meet. It was very certain Hoffendahl hadn't come for nothing, and he would undertake to declare that they would all feel, within a short time, that he had given a lift to the cause they were interested in. He had had a great experience, and they might very well find it useful to consult. If there was a way for them, then and there, he was sure to know the way. ' I quite agree with the majority of you—as I take it to be,' Muniment went on, with his fresh, cheerful, reasonable manner—' I quite agree with you that the time has come to settle upon it and to follow it. I quite agree with you that the actual state of things is '—he paused a moment, and then went on in the same pleasant tone—' is hellish.'

These remarks were received with a differing demonstration : some of the company declaring that if the Dutchman cared to come round and smoke a pipe they would be glad to see him—perhaps he'd show where the thumbscrews had been put on ; others being strongly of the opinion that they didn't want any more advice—they had already had advice enough to turn a donkey's stomach. What they wanted was to put forth their might without any more palaver ; to do something, or for some one ; to go out somewhere and smash something, on the spot—why not? —that very night. While they sat there and talked, there were about half a million of people in London that didn't know where the h—— the morrow's meal was to come from ; what they wanted to do, unless they were just a collection of pettifogging old women, was to show them where to get it, to take it to them with heaped-up hands. Hyacinth listened, with a divided attention, to interlaced iterations, while the talk blew hot and cold ; there was a genuine emotion, to-night, in the rear of the ' Sun and Moon,' and he felt the contagion of excited purpose. But he was following a train of his own ; he was wondering what Muniment had in reserve (for he was sure he was only playing with the company), and his imagination, quickened by the sense of impending relations with the heroic Hoffendahl and the discussion as to the alternative duty of escaping or of facing one's fate, had launched itself into possible perils— into the idea of how he might, in a given case, settle for himself that question of paying for the lot. The loud, contradictory, vain, unpractical babble went on about him, but he was definitely conscious only that the project of breaking into the bakers' shops was well before the assembly and was receiving a vigorous treatment, and that there was likewise a good deal of reference to the butchers and grocers, and even to the fishmongers. He was in a state of inward exaltation ; he was seized by an intense desire to stand face to face with the sublime Hoffendahl, to hear his voice, to touch his mutilated hand. He was ready for anything : he knew that he himself was safe to breakfast and dine, poorly but sufficiently, and that his colleagues were perhaps even more crude and clumsy than usual ; but a breath of

popular passion had passed over him, and he seemed to see,
immensely magnified, the monstrosity of the great ulcers
and sores of London—the sick, eternal misery crying, in
the darkness, in vain, confronted with granaries and trea-
sure-houses and places of delight where shameless satiety
kept guard. In such a mood as this Hyacinth felt that
there was no need to consider, to reason : the facts themselves were as imperative as the cry of the drowning ; for
while pedantry gained time didn't starvation gain it too ?
He knew that Muniment disapproved of delay, that he held
the day had come for a forcible rectification of horrible inequalities. In the last conversation they had had together
his chemical friend had given him a more definite warrant
than he had ever done before for numbering him in the
party of immediate action, though indeed he remarked on
this occasion, once more, that that particular formula which
the little bookbinder appeared to have taken such a fancy
to was mere gibberish. He hated that sort of pretentious
label ; it was fit only for politicians and amateurs. None
the less he had been as plain as possible on the point
that their game must be now to frighten society, and
frighten it effectually ; to make it believe that the swindled
classes were at last fairly in league—had really grasped
the idea that, closely combined, they would be irresistible.
They were not in league, and they hadn't in their totality
grasped any idea at all—Muniment was not slow to make
that equally plain. All the same, society was scareable,
and every great scare was a gain for the people. If Hyacinth had needed warrant to-night for a faith that tran-
scended logic, he would have found it in his recollection
of this quiet profession ; but his friend's words came back
to him mainly to make him wonder what that friend had in
his head just now. He took no part in the violence of the
talk ; he had called Schinkel to come round and sit beside
him, and the two appeared to confer together in comfortable absorption, while the brown atmosphere grew denser,
the passing to and fro of fire-brands more lively, and the
flush of faces more portentous. What Hyacinth would have
liked to know most of all was why Muniment had not mentioned to him, first, that Hoffendahl was in London, and

that he had seen him ; for he *had* seen him, though he had
dodged Schinkel's question—of that Hyacinth instantly felt
sure.   He would ask for more information later ; and
meanwhile he wished, without resentment, but with a
certain helpless, patient longing, that Muniment would treat
him with a little more confidence.   If there were a secret
in regard to Hoffendahl (and there evidently was : Muniment, quite rightly, though he had dropped the announcement of his arrival, for a certain effect, had no notion of
sharing the rest of what he knew with that raw roomful),
if there were something to be silent and devoted about,
Hyacinth ardently hoped that to him a chance would be
given to show how he could practise this superiority.   He
felt hot and nervous ; he got up suddenly, and, through the
dark, tortuous, greasy passage which communicated with the
outer world, he went forth into the street.   The air was
foul and sleety, but it refreshed him, and he stood in front
of the public-house and smoked another pipe.   Bedraggled
figures passed in and out, and a damp, tattered, wretched
man, with a spongy, purple face, who had been thrust
suddenly across the threshold, stood and whimpered in the
brutal blaze of the row of lamps.   The puddles glittered
roundabout, and the silent vista of the street, bordered with
low black houses, stretched away, in the wintry drizzle, to
right and left, losing itself in the huge tragic city, where
unmeasured misery lurked beneath the dirty night,
ominously, monstrously, still, only howling, in its pain,
in the heated human cockpit behind him.   Ah, what could
he do ? What opportunity would rise ?   The blundering,
divided counsels he had been listening to only made the
helplessness of every one concerned more abject.   If he
had a definite wish while he stood there it was that that
exalted, deluded company should pour itself forth, with
Muniment at its head, and surge through the sleeping city,
gathering the myriad miserable out of their slums and bur-
rows, and roll into the selfish squares, and lift a tremendous
hungry voice, and awaken the gorged indifferent to a terror
that would bring them down.   Hyacinth lingered a quarter
of an hour, but this grand spectacle gave no sign of coming
off, and he finally returned to the noisy club-room, in

a state of tormented wonder as to what better idea than this very bad one (which seemed to our young man to have at the least the merit that it *was* an idea) Muniment could be revolving in that too-comprehensive brain of his.

As he re-entered the place he saw that the meeting was breaking up in disorder, or at all events in confusion, and that, certainly, no organised attempt at the rescue of the proletariat would take place that night. All the men were on their feet and were turning away, amid a shuffling of benches and chairs, a hunching of shaggy shoulders, a frugal lowering of superflous gas, and a varied vivacity of disgust and resignation. The moment after Hyacinth came in, Mr. Delancey, the supposititious hairdresser, jumped upon a chair at the far end of the room, and shrieked out an accusation which made every one stop and stare at him.

' Well, I want you all to know what strikes me, before we part company. There isn't a man in the blessed lot that isn't afraid of his bloody skin—afraid, afraid, afraid ! I'll go anywhere with any one, but there isn't another, by G——, by what I can make out ! There isn't a mother's son of you that'll risk his precious bones !'

This little oration affected Hyacinth like a quick blow in the face ; it seemed to leap at him personally, as if a three-legged stool, or some hideous hob-nailed boot, had been shied at him. The room surged round, heaving up and down, while he was conscious of a loud explosion of laughter and scorn ; of cries of ' Order, order !' of some clear word of Muniment's, ' I say, Delancey, just step down ;' of Eustache Poupin shouting out, ' *Vous insultez le peuple—vous insultez le peuple !*' of other retorts, not remarkable for refinement. The next moment Hyacinth found that he had sprung up on a chair, opposite to the barber, and that at the sight of so rare a phenomenon the commotion had suddenly checked itself. It was the first time he had asked the ear of the company, and it was given on the spot. He was sure he looked very white, and it was even possible they could see him tremble. He could only hope that this didn't make him ridiculous when he said, ' I don't think it's right of him to say that. There are others, besides him. At all events, I want to speak for myself : it

may do some good; I can't help it. I'm not afraid; I'm
very sure I'm not. I'm ready to do anything that will do
any good; anything, anything—I don't care a rap. In
such a cause I should like the idea of danger. I don't
consider my bones precious in the least, compared with
some other things. If one is sure one isn't afraid, and
one is accused, why shouldn't one say so?'

It appeared to Hyacinth that he was talking a long
time, and when it was over he scarcely knew what happened.
He felt himself, in a moment, down almost under the feet
of the other men; stamped upon with intentions of ap-
plause, of familiarity; laughed over and jeered over,
hustled and poked in the ribs. He felt himself also
pressed to the bosom of Eustache Poupin, who apparently
was sobbing, while he heard some one say, 'Did ye hear
the little beggar, as bold as a lion?' A trial of personal
prowess between him and Mr. Delancey was proposed,
but somehow it didn't take place, and at the end of five
minutes the club-room emptied itself, not, evidently, to be
reconstituted, outside, in a revolutionary procession. Paul
Muniment had taken hold of Hyacinth, and said, ' I'll
trouble you to stay, you little desperado. I'll be blowed if
I ever expected to see *you* on the stump!' Muniment
remained, and M. Poupin and Mr. Schinkel lingered in
their overcoats, beneath a dim, surviving gasburner, in
the unventilated medium in which, at each renewed
gathering, the Bloomsbury club seemed to recognise itself.

'Upon my word, I believe you're game,' said Muniment,
looking down at him with a serious face.

'Of course you think it's swagger, "self-loaf," as
Schinkel says. But it isn't.' Then Hyacinth asked, ' In
God's name, why don't we do something?'

'Ah, my child, to whom do you say it?' Eustache
Poupin exclaimed, folding his arms, despairingly.

'Whom do you mean by "we"?' said Muniment.

'All the lot of us. There are plenty of them ready.'

'Ready for what? There is nothing to be done here.'

Hyacinth stared. 'Then why the deuce do you come?'

'I daresay I shan't come much more. This is a place
you have always overestimated.'

'I wonder if I have overestimated you,' Hyacinth murmured, gazing at his friend.

'Don't say that — he's going to introduce us to Hoffendahl!' Schinkel exclaimed, putting away his pipe in a receptacle almost as large as a fiddlecase.

'Should you like to see the genuine article, Robinson?' Muniment asked, with the same unusual absence of jocosity in his tone.

'The genuine article?' Hyacinth looked from one of his companions to the other.

'You have never seen it yet—though you think you have.'

'And why haven't you shown it to me before?'

'Because I had never seen you on the stump.' This time Muniment smiled.

'Bother the stump! I was trusting you.'

'Exactly so. That gave me time.'

'Don't come unless your mind is made up, *mon petit*,' said Poupin.

'Are you going now—to see Hoffendahl?' Hyacinth cried.

'Don't shout it all over the place. He wants a genteel little customer like you,' Muniment went on.

'Is it true? Are we all going?' Hyacinth demanded, eagerly.

'Yes, these two are in it; they are not very artful, but they are safe,' said Muniment, looking at Poupin and Schinkel.

'Are *you* the genuine article, Muniment?' asked Hyacinth, catching this look.

Muniment dropped his eyes on him; then he said, 'Yes, you're the boy he wants. It's at the other end of London; we must have a growler.'

'Be calm, my child; *me voici !*' And Eustache Poupin led Hyacinth out.

They all walked away from the 'Sun and Moon,' and it was not for some five minutes that they encountered the four-wheeled cab which deepened so the solemnity of their expedition. After they were seated in it, Hyacinth learned that Hoffendahl was in London but for three days, was

liable to hurry away on the morrow, and was accustomed
to receive visits at all kinds of queer hours. It was
getting to be midnight; the drive seemed interminable,
to Hyacinth's impatience and curiosity. He sat next to
Muniment, who passed his arm round him, as if by way
of a tacit expression of indebtedness. They all ended by
sitting silent, as the cab jogged along murky miles, and
by the time it stopped Hyacinth had wholly lost, in the
drizzling gloom, a sense of their whereabouts.

BOOK THIRD

XXII

HYACINTH got up early—an operation attended with very little effort, as he had scarcely closed his eyes all night. What he saw from his window made him dress as rapidly as a young man could do who desired more than ever that his appearance should not give strange ideas about him : an old garden, with parterres in curious figures, and little intervals of lawn which appeared to our hero's cockney vision fantastically green. At one end of the garden was a parapet of mossy brick, which looked down on the other side into a canal, or moat, or quaint old pond ; and from the same standpoint there was also a view of a considerable part of the main body of the house (Hyacinth's room appeared to be in a wing commanding the extensive, irregular back), which was richly gray wherever it was not green with ivy and other dense creepers, and everywhere infinitely like a picture, with a high-piled, ancient, russet roof, broken by huge chimneys and queer peep-holes and all manner of odd gables and windows on different lines and antique patches and protrusions, and a particularly fascinating architectural excrescence in which a wonderful clock-face was lodged—a clock-face covered with gilding and blazonry but showing many traces of the years and the weather. Hyacinth had never in his life been in the country—the real country, as he called it, the country which was not the mere raveled fringe of London—and there entered through his open casement the breath of a world enchantingly new and, after his recent feverish hours, inexpressibly refreshing to him ; a sense of sweet, sunny air and mingled odours, all strangely pure and agreeable, and a kind of musical silence, the greater part of which seemed to consist of the voices of birds. There were tall, quiet trees near by, and

afar off, and everywhere ; and the group of objects which
greeted Hyacinth's eyes evidently formed only a corner of
larger spaces and a more complicated scene. There was a
world to be revealed to him : it lay waiting, with the dew
upon it, under his windows, and he must go down and take
his first steps in it.

The night before, at ten o'clock, when he arrived, he had
only got the impression of a mile-long stretch of park, after
turning in at a gate ; of the cracking of gravel under the
wheels of the fly ; and of the glow of several windows,
suggesting in-door cheer, in a façade that lifted a variety of
vague pinnacles into the starlight. It was much of a relief
to him then to be informed that · the Princess, in consideration of the lateness of the hour, begged to be excused
till the morrow ; the delay would give him time to recover
his balance and look about him. This latter opportunity
was offered him first as he sat at supper in a vast dining-room,
with the butler, whose acquaintance he had made in South
Street, behind his chair. He had not exactly wondered
how he should be treated : there was too much vagueness in
his conception of the way in which, at a country-house,
invidious distinctions might be made and shades of importance
illustrated ; but it was plain that the best had been ordered
for him. He was, at all events, abundantly content with
his reception and more and more excited by it. The repast
was delicate (though his other senses were so awake that
hunger dropped out and he ate, as it were, without eating),
and the grave mechanical servant filled his glass with a liquor
that reminded him of some lines in Keats—in the ' Ode to
a Nightingale.' He wondered whether he should hear a
nightingale at Medley (he knew nothing about the seasons
of this vocalist), and also whether the butler would attempt
to talk to him, had ideas about him, knew or suspected who
he was and what ; which, after all, there was no reason for
his doing, unless it might be the poverty of the luggage that
had been transported from Lomax Place. Mr. Withers,
however (it was in this manner that Hyacinth heard him
addressed by the cabman who conveyed the visitor from the
station), gave no further symptom of sociability than to ask
him at what time he would be called in the morning ; to

which our young man replied that he preferred not to be
called at all—he would get up by himself. The butler
rejoined, ' Very good, sir,' while Hyacinth thought it probable
that he puzzled him a good deal, and even considered the
question of giving him a glimpse of his identity, lest it should
be revealed, later, in a manner less graceful. The object
of this anticipatory step, in Hyacinth's mind, was that he
should not be oppressed and embarrassed with attentions
to which he was unused ; but the idea came to nothing, for
the simple reason that before he spoke he found that he
already *was* inured to being waited upon. His impulse to
deprecate attentions departed, and he became conscious that
there were none he should care to miss, or was not quite
prepared for. He knew he probably thanked Mr. Withers
too much, but he couldn't help this—it was an irrepressible
tendency and an error he should doubtless always commit.

He lay in a bed constituted in a manner so perfect to
insure rest that it was probably responsible in some degree
for his restlessness, and in a large, high room, where long
dressing-glasses emitted ghostly glances even after the light
was extinguished. Suspended on the walls were many
prints, mezzotints and old engravings, which Hyacinth
supposed, possibly without reason, to be fine and rare. He
got up several times in the night, lighted his candle and
walked about looking at them. He looked at himself in
one of the long glasses, and in a place where everything was
on such a scale it seemed to him more than ever that
Mademoiselle Vivier's son was a tiny particle. As he came
downstairs he encountered housemaids, with dusters and
brooms, or perceived them, through open doors, on their
knees before fireplaces ; and it was his belief that they
regarded him more boldly than if he had been a guest of
the usual kind. Such a reflection as that, however, ceased
to trouble him after he had passed out of doors and begun
to roam through the park, into which he let himself loose
at first, and then, in narrowing circles, through the nearer
grounds. He rambled for an hour, in a state of breathless
ecstasy ; brushing the dew from the deep fern and bracken
and the rich borders of the garden, tasting the fragrant air,
and stopping everywhere, in murmuring rapture, at the touch

of some exquisite impression.   His whole walk was peopled
with recognitions; he had been dreaming all his life of
just such a place and such objects, such a morning and such
a chance.   It was the last of April, and everything was
fresh and vivid ; the great trees, in the early air, were a blur
of tender shoots.   Round the admirable house he revolved
repeatedly; catching every point and tone, feasting on its
expression, and wondering whether the Princess would
observe his proceedings from the window, and whether, if
she did, they would be offensive to her.   The house was
not hers, but only hired for three months, and it could flatter
no princely pride that he should be struck with it.   There
was something in the way the gray walls rose from the green
lawn that brought tears to his eyes ; the spectacle of long
duration unassociated with some sordid infirmity or poverty
was new to him ; he had lived with people among whom
old age meant, for the most part, a grudged and degraded
survival.   In the majestic preservation of Medley there was
a kind of serenity of success, an accumulation of dignity and
honour.

A footman sought him out, in the garden, to tell him
that breakfast was ready.   He had never thought of breakfast, and as he walked back to the house, attended by the
inscrutable flunkey, this offer appeared a free, extravagant
gift, unexpected and romantic.   He found he was to breakfast alone, and he asked no questions ; but when he had
finished the butler came in and informed him that the
Princess would see him after luncheon, but that in the
meanwhile she wished him to understand that the library was
entirely at his service.   'After luncheon'—that threw the
hour he had come for very far into the future, and it caused
him some confusion of mind that the Princess should think
it worth while to invite him to stay at her house from
Saturday evening to Monday morning if it had been her
purpose that so much of his visit should elapse without their
meeting.   But he felt neither slighted nor impatient; the
impressions that had already crowded upon him were in
themselves a sufficient reward, and what could one do better,
precisely, in such a house as that, than wait for a princess?
The butler showed him the way to the library, and left him

planted in the middle of it, staring at the treasures that he instantly perceived it contained. It was an old brown room, of great extent—even the ceiling was brown, though there were figures in it dimly gilt—where row upon row of finely-lettered backs returned his discriminating professional gaze. A fire of logs crackled in a great chimney, and there were alcoves with deep window-seats, and arm-chairs such as he had never seen, luxurious, leather-covered, with an adjustment for holding one's volume ; and a vast writing-table, before one of the windows, furnished with a perfect magazine of paper and pens, inkstands and blotters, seals, stamps, candlesticks, reels of twine, paper-weights, book-knives. Hyacinth had never imagined so many aids to correspondence, and before he turned away he had written a note to Millicent, in a hand even more beautiful than usual—his penmanship was very minute, but at the same time wonderfully free and fair—largely for the pleasure of seeing ' Medley Hall ' stamped in crimson, heraldic-looking characters at the top of his paper. In the course of an hour he had ravaged the collection, taken down almost every book, wishing he could keep it a week, and put it back quickly, as his eye caught the next, which appeared even more desirable. He discovered many rare bindings, and gathered several ideas from an inspection of them—ideas which he felt himself perfectly capable of reproducing. Altogether, his vision of true happiness, at that moment, was that, for a month or two, he should be locked into the library at Medley. He forgot the outer world, and the morning waned—the beautiful vernal Sunday—while he lingered there.

He was on the top of a ladder when he heard a voice remark, ' I am afraid they are very dusty ; in this house, you know, it is the dust of centuries ;' and, looking down, he saw Madame Grandoni stationed in the middle of the room. He instantly prepared to descend, to make her his salutation, when she exclaimed, ' Stay, stay, if you are not giddy ; we can talk from here ! I only came in to show you we *are* in the house, and to tell you to keep up your patience. The Princess will probably see you in a few hours.'

' I really hope so,' said Hyacinth, from his perch, rather dismayed at the ' probably.'

'*Natürlich*,' the old lady rejoined; 'but people have come, sometimes, and gone away without seeing her. It all depends upon her mood.'

'Do you mean even when she has sent for them?'

'Oh, who can tell whether she has sent for them or not?'

'But she sent for me, you know,' Hyacinth declared, staring down—struck with the odd effect of Madame Grandoni's wig in that bird's-eye view.

'Oh yes, she sent for you, poor young man!' The old lady looked up at him with a smile, and they remained a moment exchanging a silent scrutiny. Then she added, 'Captain Sholto has come, like that, more than once; and he has gone away no better off.'

'Captain Sholto?' Hyacinth repeated.

'Very true, if we talk at this distance I must shut the door.' She took her way back to it (she had left it open), and pushed it to; then advanced into the room again, with her superannuated, shuffling step, walking as if her shoes were too big for her. Hyacinth meanwhile descended the ladder. '*Ecco!* She's a *capricciosa*,' said the old lady.

'I don't understand how you speak of her,' Hyacinth remarked, gravely. 'You seem to be her friend, yet you say things that are not favourable to her.'

'Dear young man, I say much worse to her about herself than I should ever say to you. I am rude, oh yes—even to you, to whom, no doubt, I ought to be particularly kind. But I am not false. It is not our German nature. You will hear me some day. I *am* the friend of the Princess; it would be well enough if she never had a worse one! But I should like to be yours, too—what will you have? Perhaps it is of no use. At any rate, here you are.'

'Yes, here I am, decidedly!' Hyacinth laughed, uneasily.

'And how long shall you stay? Excuse me if I ask that; it is part of my rudeness.'

'I shall stay till to-morrow morning. I must be at my work by noon.'

'That will do very well. Don't you remember, the other time, how I told you to remain faithful?'

'That was very good advice. But I think you exaggerate my danger.'

'So much the better,' said Madame Grandoni; 'though now that I look at you well I doubt it a little. I see you you are one of those types that ladies like. I can be sure of that, because I like you myself. At my age—a hundred and twenty—can I not say that? If the Princess were to do so, it would be different; remember that—that any flattery she may ever offer you will be on her lips much less discreet. But perhaps she will never have the chance ; you may never come again. There are people who have come only once. *Vedremo bene.* I must tell you that I am not in the least against a young man taking a holiday, a little quiet recreation, once in a while,' Madame Grandoni continued, in her disconnected, discursive, confidential way. 'In Rome they take it every five days ; that is, no doubt, too often. In Germany, less often. In this country, I cannot understand whether it is an increase of effort : the English Sunday is so difficult ! This one will, however, in any case, have been beautiful for you. Be happy, make yourself comfortable ; but go home to-morrow !' And with this injunction Madame Grandoni took her way again to the door, while Hyacinth went to open it for her. 'I can say that, because it is not my house. I am only here like you. And sometimes I think I also shall go to-morrow !'

'I imagine you have not, like me, your living to get, every day. That is reason enough for me,' said Hyacinth.

She paused in the doorway, with her expressive, ugly, kindly little eyes on his face. 'I believe I am nearly as poor as you. And I have not, like you, the appearance of nobility. Yet I am noble,' said the old lady, shaking her wig.

'And I am not !' Hyacinth rejoined, smiling.

'It is better not to be lifted up high, like our friend. It does not give happiness.'

'Not to one's self, possibly ; but to others !' From where they stood, Hyacinth looked out into the great panelled and decorated hall, lighted from above and roofed with a far-away dim fresco, and the reflection of this grandeur came into his appreciative eyes.

'Do you admire everything here very much—do you receive great pleasure ?' asked Madame Grandoni.

' Oh, so much—so much ! '

She considered him a moment longer. ' *Poverino !* ' she murmured, as she turned away.

A couple of hours later the Princess sent for Hyacinth, and he was conducted upstairs, through corridors carpeted with crimson and hung with pictures, and ushered into a kind of bright drawing-room, which he afterwards learned that his hostess regarded as her boudoir. The sound of music had come to him outside the door, so that he was prepared to find her seated at the piano, if not to see her continue to play after he appeared. Her face was turned in the direction from which he entered, and she smiled at him while the servant, as if he had just arrived, formally pronounced his name, without lifting her hands from the keys. The room, placed in an angle of the house and lighted from two sides, was large and sunny, upholstered in fresh, gay chintz, furnished with all sorts of sofas and low, familiar seats and convenient little tables, most of them holding great bowls of early flowers, littered over with books, newspapers, magazines, photographs of celebrities, with their signatures, and full of the marks of luxurious and rather indolent habitation. Hyacinth stood there, not advancing very far, and the Princess, still playing and smiling, nodded toward a seat near the piano. ' Put yourself there and listen to me.' Hyacinth obeyed, and she played a long time without glancing at him. This left him the more free to rest his eyes on her own face and person, while she looked about the room, vaguely, absently, but with an expression of quiet happiness, as if she were lost in her music, soothed and pacified by it. A window near her was half open, and the soft clearness of the day and all the odour of the spring diffused themselves, and made the place cheerful and pure. The Princess struck him as extraordinarily young and fair, and she seemed so slim and simple, and friendly too, in spite of having neither abandoned her occupation nor offered him her hand, that he sank back in his seat at last, with the sense that all his uneasiness, his nervous tension, was leaving him, and that he was safe in her kindness, in the free, original way with which she evidently would always treat him. This peculiar

manner—half consideration, half fellowship—seemed to
him already to have the sweetness of familiarity.   She
played ever so movingly, with different pieces succeeding
each other ; he had never listened to music, nor to a talent,
of that order.   Two or three times she turned her eyes
upon him, and then they shone with the wonderful expression which was the essence of her beauty ; that profuse,
mingled light which seemed to belong to some everlasting
summer, and yet to suggest seasons that were past and gone,
some experience that was only an exquisite memory.   She
asked him if he cared for music, and then added, laughing,
that she ought to have made sure of this before ; while he
answered—he had already told her so in South Street ;
she appeared to have forgotten—that he was awfully fond
of it.

The sense of the beauty of women had been given to
our young man in a high degree ; it was a faculty that
made him conscious, to adoration, of every element of loveliness, every delicacy of feature, every shade and tone, that
contributed to charm.   Even, therefore, if he had appreciated less the deep harmonies the Princess drew from the
piano, there would have been no lack of interest in his
situation, in such an opportunity to watch her admirable
outline and movement, the noble form of her head and
face, the gathered-up glories of her hair, the living flower-
like freshness which had no need to turn from the light.
She was dressed in fair colours, as simply as a young girl.
Before she ceased playing she asked Hyacinth what he
would like to do in the afternoon : would he have any
objection to taking a drive with her ?   It was very possible
he might enjoy the country.   She seemed not to attend to
his answer, which was covered by the sound of the piano ;
but if she had done so it would have left her very little
doubt as to the reality of his inclination.   She remained
gazing at the cornice of the room, while her hands wandered
to and fro ; then suddenly she stopped, got up and came
toward her companion.   ' It is probable that is the most I
shall ever bore you ; you know the worst.   Would you
very kindly close the piano ? '   He complied with her
request, and she went to another part of the room and sank

into an arm-chair. When he approached her again she
said, ' Is it really true that you have never seen a park, nor
a garden, nor any of the beauties of nature, and that sort
of thing?' She was alluding to something he had said
in his letter, when he answered the note by which she proposed to him to run down to Medley; and after he assured
her that it was perfectly true she exclaimed, ' I'm so glad
—I'm so glad! I have never been able to show any one
anything new, and I have always thought I should like it
so—especially to a sensitive nature. Then you *will* come
and drive with me?' She asked this as if it would be a
great favour.

That was the beginning of the communion—so singular,
considering their respective positions—which he had come
to Medley to enjoy ; and it passed into some very remarkable phases. The Princess had the most extraordinary
way of taking things for granted, of ignoring difficulties, of
assuming that her preferences might be translated into fact.
After Hyacinth had remained with her ten minutes longer
—a period mainly occupied with her exclamations of delight
at his having seen so little of the sort of thing of which
Medley consisted (Where should he have seen it, gracious
heaven? he asked himself); after she had rested, thus
briefly, from her exertions at the piano, she proposed that
they should go out-of-doors together. She was an immense
walker—she wanted her walk. She left him for a short
time, giving him the last number of the *Revue des Deux
Mondes* to entertain himself withal, and calling his attention, in particular, to a story of M. Octave Feuillet (she
should be so curious to know what he thought of it) ; and
reappeared with her hat and parasol, drawing on her long
gloves and presenting herself to our young man, at that
moment, as a sudden incarnation of the heroine of M.
Feuillet's novel, in which he had instantly become immersed. On their way downstairs it occurred to her that
he had not yet seen the house and that it would be amusing for her to show it to him ; so she turned aside and took
him through it, up and down and everywhere, even into the
vast, old-fashioned kitchen, where there was a small, red-
faced man in a white jacket and apron and a white cap (he

removed the latter ornament to salute the little bookbinder),
with whom his companion spoke Italian, which Hyacinth
understood sufficiently to perceive that she addressed her
cook in the second person singular, as if he had been a
feudal retainer. He remembered that was the way the
three Musketeers spoke to their lackeys. The Princess
explained that the gentleman in the white cap was a delightful creature (she couldn't endure English servants,
though she was obliged to have two or three), who would
make her plenty of risottos and polentas—she had quite
the palate of a contadina. She showed Hyacinth everything : the queer transmogrified corner that had once been
a chapel ; the secret stairway which had served in the per-
secutions of the Catholics (the owners of Medley were,
like the Princess herself, of the old persuasion) ; the
musicians' gallery, over the hall ; the tapestried room,
which people came from a distance to see ; and the haunted
chamber (the two were sometimes confounded, but they
were quite distinct), where a dreadful individual at certain
times made his appearance—a dwarfish ghost, with an
enormous head, a dispossessed brother, of long ago (the
eldest), who had passed for an idiot, which he wasn't, and
had somehow been made away with. The Princess offered
her visitor the privilege of sleeping in this apartment, declaring, however, that nothing would induce *her* even to enter
it alone, she being a benighted creature, consumed with
abject superstitions. ' I don't know whether I am religious,
and whether, if I were, my religion would be superstitious,
But my superstitions are certainly religious.' She made
her young friend pass through the drawing-room very
cursorily, remarking that they should see it again : it was
rather stupid—drawing-rooms in English country-houses
were always stupid ; indeed, if it would amuse him, they
would sit there after dinner. Madame Grandoni and she
usually sat upstairs, but they would do anything that he
should find more comfortable.

At last they went out of the house together, and as they
did so she explained, as if she wished to justify herself
against the imputation of extravagance, that, though the
place doubtless struck him as absurdly large for a couple of

quiet women, and the whole thing was not in the least what she would have preferred, yet it was all far cheaper than he probably imagined; she would never have looked at it if it hadn't been cheap. It must appear to him so preposterous for a woman to associate herself with the great uprising of the poor and yet live in palatial halls—a place with forty or fifty rooms. This was one of only two allusions she made that day to her democratic sympathies; but it fell very happily, for Hyacinth had been reflecting precisely upon the anomaly she mentioned. It had been present to him all day; it added much to the way life practised on his sense of the tragic-comical to think of the Princess's having retired to that magnificent residence in order to concentrate her mind upon the London slums. He listened, therefore, with great attention while she related that she had taken the house only for three months, in any case, because she wanted to rest, after a winter of visiting and living in public (as the English spent their lives, with all their celebrated worship of the 'home'), and yet didn't wish as yet to return to town—though she was obliged to confess that she had still the place in South Street on her hands, thanks to her deciding unexpectedly to go on with it rather than move out her things. But one had to keep one's things somewhere, and why wasn't that as good a receptacle as another? Medley was not what she would have chosen if she had been left to herself; but she had not been left to herself—she never was; she had been bullied into taking it by the owners, whom she had met somewhere and who had made up to her immensely, persuading her that she might really have it for nothing—for no more than she would give for the little honeysuckle cottage, the old parsonage embowered in clematis, which were really what she had been looking for. Besides it was one of those old musty mansions, ever so far from town, which it was always difficult to let, or to get a price for; and then it was a wretched house for living in. Hyacinth, for whom his three hours in the train had been a series of happy throbs, had not been struck with its geographical remoteness, and he asked the Princess what she meant, in such a connection, by using the word 'wretched.' To this she replied

that the place was tumbling to pieces, inconvenient in every
respect, full of ghosts and bad smells. ' That is the only
reason I come to have it. I don't want you to think me
more luxurious than I am, or that I throw away money.
Never, never !' Hyacinth had no standard by which he
could measure the importance his opinion would have for
her, and he perceived that though she judged him as a
creature still open to every initiation, whose *naïveté* would
entertain her, it was also her fancy to treat him as an old
friend, a person to whom she might have had the habit of
referring her difficulties. Her performance of the part she
had undertaken to play was certainly complete, and everything lay before him but the reason she had for playing it.

One of the gardens at Medley took the young man's
heart beyond the others ; it had high brick walls, on the
sunny sides of which was a great training of apricots and
plums, and straight walks, bordered with old-fashioned
homely flowers, inclosing immense squares where other
fruit-trees stood upright and mint and lavender floated in
the air. In the southern quarter it overhung a small, dis-
used canal, and here a high embankment had been raised,
which was also long and broad and covered with fine turf ;
so that the top of it, looking down at the canal, made a
magnificent grassy terrace, than which, on a summer's day,
there could be no more delightful place for strolling up and
down with a companion—all the more that, at either end,
was a curious pavilion, in the manner of a tea-house, which
completed the scene in an old-world sense and offered rest
and privacy, a refuge from sun or shower. One of these
pavilions was an asylum for gardeners' tools and superfluous
flower-pots ; the other was covered, inside, with a queer
Chinese paper, representing ever so many times over a
group of people with faces like blind kittens, having tea
while they sat on the floor. It also contained a big, clumsy
inlaid cabinet, in which cups and saucers showed themselves through doors of greenish glass, together with a
carved cocoanut and a pair of outlandish idols. On a
shelf, over a sofa, not very comfortable though it had
cushions of faded tapestry, which looked like samplers,
was a row of novels, out of date and out of print—novels

that one couldn't have found any more and that were only
there.   On the chimney-piece was a bowl of dried rose-
leaves, mixed with some aromatic spice, and the whole place
suggested a certain dampness.

On the terrace Hyacinth paced to and fro with the
Princess until she suddenly remembered that he had not
had his luncheon.   He protested that this was the last
thing he wished to think of, but she declared that she had
not asked him down to Medley to starve him and that he
must go back and be fed.   They went back, but by a very
roundabout way, through the park, so that they really had
half an hour's more talk.   She explained to him that she
herself breakfasted at twelve o'clock, in the foreign fashion,
and had tea in the afternoon; as he too was so foreign he
might like that better, and in this case, on the morrow,
they would breakfast together.   He could have coffee, and
anything else he wanted, brought to his room when he woke
up.   When Hyacinth had sufficiently composed himself, in
the presence of this latter image—he thought he saw a
footman arranging a silver service at his bedside—he mentioned that really, as regarded the morrow, he should have
to be back in London.   There was a train at nine o'clock;
he hoped she didn't mind his taking it.   She looked at him
a moment, gravely and kindly, as if she were considering
an abstract idea, and then she said, 'Oh yes, I mind it
very much.   Not to-morrow—some other day.'   He made
no rejoinder, and the Princess spoke of something else;
that is, his rejoinder was private, and consisted of the
reflection that he *would* leave Medley in the morning,
whatever she might say.   He simply couldn't afford to stay;
he couldn't be out of work.   And then Madame Grandoni
thought it so important; for though the old lady was obscure
she was decidedly impressive.   The Princess's protest, however, was to be reckoned with; he felt that it might take
a form less cursory than the words she had just uttered,
which would make it embarrassing.   She was less solemn,
less explicit, than Madame Grandoni had been, but there
was something in her slight seriousness and the delicate
way in which she signified a sort of command that seemed
to tell him his liberty was going—the liberty he had

managed to keep (till the other day, when he gave Hoffendahl a mortgage on it), and the possession of which had in
some degree consoled him for other forms of penury. This
made him uneasy ; what would become of him if he should
add another servitude to the one he had undertaken, at the
end of that long, anxious cab-drive in the rain, in that dim
back-bedroom of a house as to whose whereabouts he was
even now not clear, while Muniment and Poupin and
Schinkel, all visibly pale, listened and accepted the vow ?
Muniment and Poupin and Schinkel—how disconnected,
all the same, he felt from them at the present hour ; how
little he was the young man who had made the pilgrimage in
the cab ; and how the two latter, at least, if they could have
a glimpse of him now, would wonder what he was up to !

As to this, Hyacinth wondered sufficiently himself, while
the Princess touched upon the people and places she had
seen, the impressions and conclusions she had gathered,
since their former meeting. It was to such matters as these
that she directed the conversation ; she appeared to wish
to keep it off his own concerns, and he was surprised at her
continued avoidance of the slums and the question of her
intended sacrifices. She mentioned none of her friends by
name, but she talked of their character, their houses, their
manners, taking for granted, as before, that Hyacinth would
always follow. So far as he followed he was edified, but
he had to admit to himself that half the time he didn't
know what she was talking about. At all events, if *he* had
been with the dukes (she didn't call her associates dukes,
but Hyacinth was sure they were of that order), he would
have got more satisfaction from them. She appeared, on
the whole, to judge the English world severely ; to think
poorly of its wit, and even worse of its morals. 'You
know people oughtn't to be both corrupt and dull,' she
said ; and Hyacinth turned this over, feeling that he
certainly had not yet caught the point of view of a person
for whom the aristocracy was a collection of bores. He
had sometimes taken great pleasure in hearing that it was
fabulously profligate, but he was rather disappointed in the
bad account the Princess gave of it. She remarked that
she herself was very corrupt—she ought to have mentioned

that before—but she had never been accused of being stupid. Perhaps he would discover it, but most of the people she had had to do with thought her only too lively. The second allusion that she made to their ulterior designs (Hyacinth's and hers) was when she said, ' I determined to see it '—she was speaking still of English society—'to learn for myself what it really is, before we blow it up. I have been here now a year and a half, and, as I tell you, I feel that I have seen. It is the old régime again, the rottenness and extravagance, bristling with every iniquity and every abuse, over which the French Revolution passed like a whirlwind; or perhaps even more a reproduction of Roman society in its decadence, gouty, apoplectic, depraved, gorged and clogged with wealth and spoils, selfishness and scepticism, and waiting for the onset of the barbarians. You and I are the barbarians, you know.' The Princess was pretty general, after all, in her animadversions, and regaled him with no anecdotes (he rather missed them) that would have betrayed the hospitality she had enjoyed. She couldn't treat him absolutely as if he had been an ambassador. By way of defending the aristocracy he said to her that it couldn't be true they were all a bad lot (he used that expression because she had let him know that she liked him to speak in the manner of the people), inasmuch as he had an acquaintance among them—a noble lady—who was one of the purest, kindest, most conscientious human beings it was possible to imagine. At this she stopped short and looked at him; then she asked, ' Whom do you mean—a noble lady ? '

' I suppose there is no harm saying. Lady Aurora Langrish.'

' I don't know her. Is she nice ? '

' I like her ever so much.'

' Is she pretty, clever ? '

' She isn't pretty, but she is very uncommon,' said Hyacinth.

' How did you make her acquaintance ? ' As he hesitated, she went on, ' Did you bind some books for her ? '

' No. I met her in a place called Audley Court.'

' Where is that ? '

' In Camberwell.'

' And who lives there ? '

' A young woman I was calling on, who is bedridden.'

' And the lady you speak of—what do you call her, Lydia Languish?—goes to see her ? '

' Yes, very often.'

The Princess was silent a moment, looking at him. ' Will you take me there ? '

' With great pleasure. The young woman I speak of is the sister of the chemist's assistant you will perhaps remember that I mentioned to you.'

' Yes, I remember. It must be one of the first places we go to. I am sorry,' the Princess added, walking on. Hyacinth inquired what she might be sorry for, but she took no notice of his question, and presently remarked, ' Perhaps she goes to see him.'

' Goes to see whom ? '

' The chemist's assistant—the brother.' She said this very seriously.

' Perhaps she does,' Hyacinth rejoined, laughing. ' But she is a fine sort of woman.'

The Princess repeated that she was sorry, and he again asked her for what—for Lady Aurora's being of that sort ? To which she replied, ' No ; I mean for my not being the first—what is it you call them ?—noble lady that you have encountered.'

' I don't see what difference that makes. You needn't be afraid you don't make an impression on me.'

' I was not thinking of that. I was thinking that you might be less fresh than I thought.'

' Of course I don't know what you thought,' said Hyacinth, smiling.

' No ; how should you ? '

He was in the library, after luncheon, when word was
brought to him that the carriage was at the door, for
their drive; and when he went into the hall he found
Madame Grandoni, bonneted and cloaked, awaiting the
descent of the Princess. 'You see I go with you. I am
always there,' she remarked, jovially. 'The Princess has
me with her to take care of her, and this is how I do it.
Besides, I never miss my drive.'

'You are different from me; this will be the first I have
ever had in my life.' He could establish that distinction
without bitterness, because he was too pleased with his
prospect to believe the old lady's presence could spoil it.
He had nothing to say to the Princess that she might not
hear. He didn't dislike her for coming, even after she had
said to him, in answer to his own announcement, speaking
rather more sententiously than was her wont, 'It doesn't
surprise me that you have not spent your life in carriages.
They have nothing to do with your trade.'

'Fortunately not,' he answered. 'I should have made
a ridiculous coachman.'

The Princess appeared, and they mounted into a great
square barouche, an old-fashioned, high-hung vehicle, with
a green body, a faded hammer-cloth and a rumble where
the footman sat (the Princess mentioned that it had been
let with the house), which rolled ponderously and smoothly
along the winding avenue and through the gilded gates
(they were surmounted with an immense escutcheon) of the
park. The progress of this oddly composed trio had a
high respectability, and that is one of the reasons why
Hyacinth felt the occasion to be tremendously memorable.
There might still be greater joys in store for him—he was

by this time quite at sea, and could recognise no shores—
but he would never again in his life be so respectable.
The drive was long and comprehensive, but very little was
said while it lasted.   ' I shall show you the whole country :
it is exquisitely beautiful; it speaks to the heart.'   Of so
much as this his hostess had informed him at the start ; and
she added, in French, with a light, allusive nod at the rich,
humanised landscape, ' *Voilà ce que j'aime en Angleterre.*'
For the rest, she sat there opposite to him, in quiet fairness,
under her softly-swaying, lace-fringed parasol : moving her
eyes to where she noticed that his eyes rested; allowing
them, when the carriage passed anything particularly
charming, to meet his own ; smiling as if she enjoyed the
whole affair very nearly as much as he ; and now and then
calling his attention to some prospect, some picturesque
detail, by three words of which the cadence was sociable.
Madame Grandoni dozed most of the time, with her chin
resting on rather a mangy ermine tippet, in which she had
enveloped herself; expanding into consciousness at moments,
however, to greet the scenery with comfortable polyglot
ejaculations.   If Hyacinth was exalted, during these
delightful hours, he at least measured his exaltation, and it
kept him almost solemnly still, as if with the fear that a
wrong movement of any sort would break the charm, cause
the curtain to fall upon the play   This was especially the
case when his senses oscillated back from the objects that
sprang up by the way, every one of which was a rich image
of something he had longed for, to the most beautiful
woman in England, who sat there, close to him, as completely for his benefit as if he had been a painter engaged
to make her portrait.   More than once he saw everything
through a mist; his eyes were full of tears.

That evening they sat in the drawing-room after dinner,
as the Princess had promised, or, as he was inclined to
consider it, threatened him.   The force of the threat was in
his prevision that the ladies would make themselves fine,
and that in contrast with the setting and company he should
feel dingier than ever ; having already on his back the only
tolerably decent coat he possessed, and being unable to
exchange it for a garment of the pattern that civilised

people (so much he knew, if he couldn't emulate them),
put on about eight o'clock.   The ladies, when they came
to dinner, looked festal indeed; but Hyacinth was able to
make the reflection that he was more pleased to be dressed
as he was dressed, meanly and unsuitably as it was, than he
should have been to present such a figure as Madame
Grandoni, in whose toggery there was something comical.
He was coming more and more round to the sense that if
the Princess didn't mind his poorness, in every way, he had
no call to mind it himself.   His present circumstances were
not of his seeking—they had been forced upon him; they
were not the fruit of a disposition to push.   How little the
Princess minded—how much, indeed, she enjoyed the consciousness that in having him about her in that manner she
was playing a trick upon society, the false and conventional
society she had measured and despised—was manifest from
the way she had introduced him to the people they found
awaiting them in the hall on the return from their drive:
four ladies, a mother and three daughters, who had come
over to call, from Broome, a place some five miles off.
Broome was also a great house, as he gathered, and Lady
Marchant, the mother, was the wife of a county magnate.
She explained that they had come in on the persuasion of
the butler, who had represented the return of the Princess
as imminent, and who then had administered tea without
waiting for this event.   The evening had drawn in chill;
there was a fire in the hall, and they all sat near it, round
the tea-table, under the great roof which rose to the top of
the house.   Hyacinth conversed mainly with one of the
daughters, a very fine girl with a straight back and long
arms, whose neck was encircled so tightly with a fur boa
that, to look a little to one side, she was obliged to move
her whole body.   She had a handsome, inanimate face,
over which the firelight played without making it more
lively, a beautiful voice, and the occasional command of a
few short words.   She asked Hyacinth with what pack he
hunted, and whether he went in much for tennis, and she
ate three muffins.

Our young man perceived that Lady Marchant and her
daughters had already been at Medley, and even guessed

that their reception by the Princess, who probably thought them of a tiresome type, had not been enthusiastic ; and his imagination projected itself, further still, into the motives which, in spite of this tepidity, must have led them, in consideration of the rarity of princesses in that country, to come a second time. The talk, in the firelight, while Hyacinth laboured, rather recklessly (for the spirit of the occasion, on his hostess's part, was passing into his own blood), with his muffin-eating beauty—the conversation, accompanied with the light click of delicate tea-cups, was as well-bred as could be consistent with an odd, evident *parti-pris* of the Princess's to make poor Lady Marchant explain everything. With great urbanity of manner, she professed complete inability to understand the sense in which her visitor meant her thin remarks ; and Hyacinth was scarcely able to follow her here, he wondered so what interest she could have in trying to appear dense. It was only afterwards he learned that the Marchant family produced a very peculiar, and at moments almost maddening, effect upon her nerves. He asked himself what would happen to that member of it with whom he was engaged if it should be revealed to her that she was conversing (how little soever) with a beggarly London artisan ; and though he was rather pleased at her not having discovered his station (for he didn't attribute her brevity to this idea), he entertained a little the question of its being perhaps his duty not to keep it hidden from her, not to flourish in a cowardly disguise. What did she take him for—or, rather, what didn't she take him for—when she asked him if he hunted ? Perhaps that was because it was rather dark ;. if there had been more light in the great vague hall she would have seen he was not one of themselves. Hyacinth felt that by this time he had associated a good deal with swells, but they had always known what he was and had been able to elect how to treat him. This was the first occasion on which a young gentlewoman had not been warned, and, as a consequence, he appeared to pass muster. He determined not to unmask himself, on the simple ground that he should by the same stroke betray the Princess. It was quite open to her to lean over and say to Miss

Marchant, 'You know he's a wretched little bookbinder, earning a few shillings a week in a horrid street in Soho. There are all kinds of low things—and I suspect even something very horrible—connected with his birth. It seems to me I ought to mention it.' He almost wished she would mention it, for the sake of the strange, violent sensation of the thing, a curiosity quivering within him to know what Miss Marchant would do at such a pinch, and what chorus of ejaculations—or, what appalled, irremediable silence—would rise to the painted roof. The responsibility, however, was not his; he had entered a phase of his destiny where responsibilities were suspended. Madame Grandoni's tea had waked her up; she came, at every crisis, to the rescue of the conversation, and talked to the visitors about Rome, where they had once spent a winter, describing with much drollery the manner in which the English families she had seen there for nearly half a century (and had met, of an evening, in the Roman world) inspected the ruins and monuments and squeezed into the great ceremonies of the church. Clearly, the four ladies didn't know what to make of the Princess; but, though they perhaps wondered if she were a paid companion, they were on firm ground in the fact that the queer, familiar, fat person had been acquainted with the Millingtons, the Bunburys and the Tripps.

After dinner (during which the Princess allowed herself a considerable license of pleasantry on the subject of her recent visitors, declaring that Hyacinth must positively go with her to return their call, and must see their interior, their manner at home), Madame Grandoni sat down to the piano, at Christina's request, and played to her companions for an hour. The spaces were large in the big drawing-room, and our friends had placed themselves at a distance from each other. The old lady's music trickled forth discreetly into the pleasant dimness of the candlelight; she knew dozens of Italian local airs, which sounded like the forgotten tunes of a people, and she followed them by a series of tender, plaintive German *Lieder*, awaking, without violence, the echoes of the high, pompous apartment. It was the music of an old woman, and seemed to quaver a little, as her singing might have done. The Princess, buried in a deep chair, listened, behind her fan. Hyacinth at least supposed she listened; at any rate, she never moved. At last Madame Grandoni left the piano and came toward the young man. She had taken up, on the way, a French book, in a pink cover, which she nursed in the hollow of her arm, and she stood looking at Hyacinth.

'My poor little friend, I must bid you good-night. I shall not see you again for the present, as, to take your early train, you will have left the house before I put on my wig—and I never show myself to gentlemen without it. I have looked after the Princess pretty well, all day, to keep her from harm, and now I give her up to you, for a little. Take the same care, I beg you. I must put myself into my dressing-gown; at my age, at this hour, it is the only thing. What will you have? I hate to be tight,' pursued Madame Grandoni, who appeared even in her ceremonial garment to have evaded this discomfort successfully enough. 'Do not sit up late,' she added; 'and do not keep him, Christina. Remember that for an active young man like Mr. Robinson, going every day to his work, there is nothing more exhausting than such an unoccupied life as ours. For what do we do, after all? His eyes are very heavy. *Basta !'*

During this little address the Princess, who made no rejoinder to that part of it which concerned herself, remained hidden behind her fan; but after Madame Grandoni had wandered away she lowered this emblazoned shield and rested her eyes for a while on Hyacinth. At last she said, 'Don't sit half a mile off. Come nearer to me. I want to say something to you that I can't shout across the room.' Hyacinth instantly got up, but at the same moment she also rose; so that, approaching each other, they met half-way, before the great marble chimney-piece. She stood a little, opening and closing her fan; then she remarked, 'You must be surprised at my not having yet spoken to you about our great interest.'

'No, indeed, I am not surprised at anything.'

'When you take that tone I feel as if we should never, after all, become friends,' said the Princess.

'I hoped we were, already. Certainly, after the kindness you have shown me, there is no service of friendship that you might ask of me——'

'That you wouldn't gladly perform? I know what you are going to say, and have no doubt you speak truly. But what good would your service do me if, all the while, you think of me as a hollow-headed, hollow-hearted trifler, behaving in the worst possible taste and oppressing you with her attentions? Perhaps you can think of me as—what shall I call it?—as a kind of coquette.'

Hyacinth demurred. 'That would be very conceited.'

'Surely, you have the right to be as conceited as you please, after the advances I have made you! Pray, who has a better one? But you persist in remaining humble, and that is very provoking.'

'It is not I that am provoking; it is life, and society, and all the difficulties that surround us.'

'I am precisely of that opinion—that they are exasperating; that when I appeal to you, frankly, candidly, disinterestedly—simply because I like you, for no other reason in the world—to help me to disregard and surmount these obstructions, to treat them with the contempt they deserve, you drop your eyes, you even blush a little, and make yourself small, and try to edge out of the situation by pleading general devotion and insignificance. Please remember this : you cease to be insignificant from the moment I have anything to do with you. My dear fellow,' the Princess went on, in her free, audacious, fraternising way, to which her beauty and simplicity gave nobleness, 'there are people who would be very glad to enjoy, in your place, that form of obscurity.'

'What do you wish me to do?' Hyacinth asked, as quietly as he could.

If he had had an idea that this question, to which, as coming from his lips, and even as being uttered with perceptible impatience, a certain unexpectedness might attach, would cause her a momentary embarrassment, he was completely out in his calculation. She answered on the instant : 'I want you to give me time! That's all I ask of my friends, in general—all I ever asked of the best I have had. But none of them ever did it; none of them, that is, save the excellent creature who has just left us. She understood me long ago.'

'That's all I, on my side, ask of you,' said Hyacinth, smiling. 'Give me time, give me time,' he murmured, looking up at her splendour.

'Dear Mr. Hyacinth, I have given you months!—months since our first meeting. And at present, haven't I given you the whole day? It has been intentional, my not speaking to you of our plans. Yes, our plans; I know what I am saying. Don't try to look stupid; you will never succeed. I wished to leave you free to amuse yourself.'

'Oh, I have amused myself,' said Hyacinth.

'You would have been very fastidious if you hadn't! However, that is precisely, in the first place, what I wished you to come here for. To observe the impression made by such a place as this on such a nature as yours, introduced to it for the first time, has been, I assure you, quite worth my while. I have already given you a hint of how extraordinary I think it that you should be what you are without having seen—what shall I call them?—beautiful, delightful old things. I have been watching you; I am frank enough to tell you that. I want you to see more—more—more!' the Princess exclaimed, with a sudden flicker of passion. 'And I want to talk with you about this matter, as well as others. That will be for to-morrow.'

'To-morrow?'

'I noticed Madame Grandoni took for granted just now that you are going. But that has nothing to do with the business. She has so little imagination!'

Hyacinth shook his head, smiling. 'I can't stay!' He had an idea his mind was made up.

She returned his smile, but there was something strangely touching—it was so sad, yet, as a rebuke, so gentle—in the tone in which she replied, 'You oughtn't to force me to beg. It isn't nice.'

He had reckoned without that tone; all his reasons suddenly seemed to fall from under him, to liquefy. He remained a moment, looking on the ground; then he said,

'Princess, you have no idea—how should you have?—into the midst of what abject, pitiful preoccupations you thrust yourself. I have no money—I have no clothes.'

'What do you want of money? This isn't an hotel.'

'Every day I stay here I lose a day's wages; and I live on my wages from day to day.'

'Let me, then, give you wages. You will work for me.'

'What do you mean—work for you?'

'You will bind all my books. I have ever so many foreign ones, in paper.'

'You speak as if I had brought my tools!'

'No, I don't imagine that. I will give you the wages now, and you can do the work, at your leisure and convenience, afterwards. Then, if you want anything, you can go over to Bonchester and buy it. There are very good shops; I have used them.' Hyacinth thought of a great many things at this juncture; the Princess had that quickening effect upon him. Among others, he thought of these two: first, that it was indelicate (though such an opinion was not very strongly held either in Pentonville or in Soho) to accept money from a woman; and second, that it was still more indelicate to make such a woman as that go down on her knees to him. But it took more than a minute for one of these convictions to prevail over the other, and before that he had heard the Princess continue, in the tone of mild, disinterested argument: 'If we believe in the coming democracy, if it seems to us right and just, and we hold that in sweeping over the world the great wave will wash away a myriad iniquities and cruelties, why not make some attempt, with our own poor means—for one must begin somewhere—to carry out the spirit of it in our lives and our manners? I want to do that. I try to do it —in my relations with you, for instance. But you hang back; you are not democratic!'

The Princess accusing him of a patrician offishness was a very fine stroke; nevertheless it left him lucidity enough (though he still hesitated an instant, wondering whether the words would not offend her) to say, with a smile, 'I have been strongly warned against you.'

The offence seemed not to touch her. 'I can easily

understand that. Of course my proceedings—though, after all, I have done little enough as yet—must appear most unnatural. *Che vuole?* as Madame Grandoni says.'

A certain knot of light blue ribbon, which formed part of the trimming of her dress, hung down, at her side, in the folds of it. On these glossy loops Hyacinth's eyes happened for a moment to have rested, and he now took one of them up and carried it to his lips. ' I will do all the work for you that you will give me. If you give it on purpose, by way of munificence, that is your own affair. I myself will estimate the price. What decides me is that I shall do it so well; at least it shall be better than any one else can do—so that if you employ me there will have been that reason. I have brought you a book—so you can see. I did it for you last year, and went to South Street to give it to you, but you had already gone.'

' Give it to me to-morrow.' These words appeared to express so exclusively the calmness of relief at finding that he could be reasonable, as well as that of a friendly desire to see the proof of his talent, that he was surprised when she said, in the next breath, irrelevantly, ' Who was it warned you against me?'

He feared she might suppose he meant Madame Grandoni, so he made the plainest answer, having no desire to betray the old lady, and reflecting that, as the likelihood was small that his friend in Camberwell would ever consent to meet the Princess (in spite of her plan of going there), no one would be hurt by it. ' A friend of mine in London—Paul Muniment.'

' Paul Muniment?'

' I think I mentioned him to you the first time we met.'

' The person who said something good? I forget what it was.'

' It was sure to be something good if he said it; he is very wise.'

' That makes his warning very flattering to me ! What does he know about me?'

'Oh, nothing, of course, except the little that I could tell him. He only spoke on general grounds.'

'I like his name—Paul Muniment,' the Princess said.
'If he resembles it, I think I should like him.'

'You would like him much better than me.'

'How do you know how much—or how little—I like
you? I am determined to keep hold of you, simply for
what you can show me.' She paused a moment, with
her beautiful, intelligent eyes smiling into his own, and
then she continued, 'On general grounds, *bien entendu*,
your friend was quite right to warn you. Now those
general grounds are just what I have undertaken to make
as small as possible. It is to reduce them to nothing
that I talk to you, that I conduct myself with regard to
you as I have done. What in the world is it I am
trying to do but, by every device that my ingenuity
suggests, fill up the inconvenient gulf that yawns between
my position and yours? You know what I think of
"positions"; I told you in London. For Heaven's sake
let me feel that I have—a little—succeeded!' Hyacinth
satisfied her sufficiently to enable her, five minutes later,
apparently to entertain no further doubt on the question
of his staying over. On the contrary, she burst into a
sudden ebullition of laughter, exchanging her bright, lucid
insistence for one of her singular sallies. 'You must
absolutely go with me to call on the Marchants; it will be
too delightful to see you there!'

As he walked up and down the empty drawing-room
it occurred to him to ask himself whether that was mainly
what she was keeping him for—so that he might help her
to play one of her tricks on the good people at Broome.
He paced there, in the still candlelight, for a longer time
than he measured; until the butler came and stood
in the doorway, looking at him silently and fixedly, as if to
let him know that he interfered with the custom of the
house. He had told the Princess that what determined
him was the thought of the manner in which he might
exercise his craft in her service; but this was only half the
influence that pressed him into forgetfulness of what he had
most said to himself when, in Lomax Place, in an hour of
unprecedented introspection, he wrote the letter by which
he accepted the invitation to Medley. He would go there

(so he said), because a man must be gallant, especially if he be a little bookbinder; but after he should be there he would insist at every step upon knowing what he was in for. The change that had taken place in him now, from one moment to another, was that he had simply ceased to care what he was in for. All warnings, reflections, considerations of verisimilitude, of the delicate, the natural and the possible, of the value of his independence, had become as nothing to him. The cup of an exquisite experience—a week in that enchanted palace, a week of such immunity from Lomax Place and old Crookenden as he had never dreamed of—was at his lips; it was purple with the wine of novelty, of civilisation, and he couldn't push it aside without drinking. He might go home ashamed, but he would have for evermore in his mouth the taste of nectar. He went upstairs, under the eye of the butler, and on his way to his room, at the turning of a corridor, found himself face to face with Madame Grandoni. She had apparently just issued from her own apartment, the door of which stood open, near her; she might have been hovering there in expectation of his footstep. She had donned her dressing-gown, which appeared to give her every facility for respiration, but she had not yet parted with her wig. She still had her pink French book under her arm; and her fat little hands, tightly locked together in front of her, formed the clasp of her generous girdle.

'Do tell me it is positive, Mr. Robinson!' she said, stopping short.

'What is positive, Madame Grandoni?'

'That you take the train in the morning.'

'I can't tell you that, because it wouldn't be true. On the contrary, it has been settled that I shall stay over. I am very sorry if it distresses you—but *che vuole?*' Hyacinth added, smiling.

Madame Grandoni was a humorous woman, but she gave him no smile in return; she only looked at him a moment, and then, shrugging her shoulders silently but expressively, shuffled back to her room.

' I CAN give you your friend's name—in a single guess. He
is Diedrich Hoffendahl!' They had been strolling more
and more slowly, the next morning, and as she made
this announcement the Princess stopped altogether, standing
there under a great beech with her eyes upon Hyacinth's
and her hands full of primroses. He had breakfasted at
noon, with his hostess and Madame Grandoni, but the old
lady had fortunately not joined them when the Princess
afterwards proposed that he should accompany her on her
walk in the park. She told him that her venerable friend
had let her know, while the day was still very young, that
she thought it in the worst possible taste of the Princess not
to have allowed Mr. Robinson to depart; to which Christina
had replied that concerning tastes there was no disputing
and that they had disagreed on such matters before without
any one being the worse. Hyacinth expressed the hope
that they wouldn't dispute about *him*—of all thankless
subjects in the world; and the Princess assured him that
she never disputed about anything. She held that there
were other ways than that of arranging one's relations with
people; and Hyacinth guessed that she meant that when
a difference became sharp she broke off altogether. On her
side, then, there was as little possibility as on his that they
should ever quarrel; their acquaintance would be a solid
friendship or it would be nothing at all. The Princess
gave it from hour to hour more of this quality, and it may
be imagined how safe Hyacinth felt by the time he began
to tell her that something had happened to him, in London,
three months before, one night (or rather in the small
hours of the morning), that had altered his life altogether—
had, indeed, as he might say, changed the terms on which

he held it.   He was aware that he didn't know exactly
what he meant by this last phrase; but it expressed
sufficiently well the new feeling that had come over him
since that interminable, tantalising cab-drive in the rain.

The Princess had led to this, almost as soon as they left
the house; making up for her avoidance of such topics the
day before by saying, suddenly, ' Now tell me what is going
on among your friends.   I don't mean your worldly acquaintances, but your colleagues, your brothers.   *Où en êtes-vous*,
at the present time?   Is there anything new, is anything
going to be done ; I am afraid you are always simply dawdling
and muddling.'   Hyacinth felt as if, of late, he had by no
means either dawdled or muddled ; but before he had committed himself so far as to refute the imputation the Princess
exclaimed, in another tone, ' How annoying it is that I can't
ask you anything without giving you the right to say to
yourself, " After all, what do I know?   May she not be in
the pay of the police ? " '

' Oh, that doesn't occur to me,' said Hyacinth, with a
smile.

' It might, at all events; by which I mean it may, at any
moment.   Indeed, I think it ought.'

' If you were in the pay of the police you wouldn't trouble
your head about me.'

' I should make you think that, certainly !   That would
be my first care.   However, if you have no tiresome suspicions so much the better,' said the Princess; and she
pressed him again for some news from behind the scenes.

In spite of his absence of doubt on the subject of her
honesty—he felt that he should never again entertain any
such trumpery idea as that she might be an agent on the
wrong side—he did not open himself immediately ; but at
the end of half an hour he let her know that the most
important event of his life had taken place, scarcely more
than the other day, in the most unexpected manner.   And
to explain in what it had consisted, he said, ' I pledged
myself, by everything that is sacred.'

' To what did you pledge yourself ? '

' I took a vow—a tremendous, terrible vow—in the
presence of four witnesses,' Hyacinth went on.

'And what was it about, your vow ? '

'I gave my life away,' said Hyacinth, smiling.

She looked at him askance, as if to see how he would make such an announcement as that ; but she wore no smile—her face was politely grave. They moved together a moment, exchanging a glance, in silence, and then she said, 'Ah, well, then, I'm all the more glad you stayed ! '

'That was one of the reasons.'

'I wish you had waited—till after you had been here,' the Princess remarked.

'Why till after I had been here ? '

'Perhaps then you wouldn't have given away your life. You might have seen reasons for keeping it.' And now, at last, she treated the matter gaily, as Hyacinth had done. He replied that he had not the least doubt that, on the whole, her influence was relaxing ; but without heeding this remark she went on : 'Be so good as to tell me what you are talking about.'

'I'm not afraid of you, but I'll give you no names,' said Hyacinth ; and he related what had happened in the back-room in Bloomsbury, in the course of that evening of which I have given some account. The Princess listened, intently, while they strolled under the budding trees with a more interrupted step. Never had the old oaks and beeches, renewing themselves in the sunshine as they did to-day, or naked in some gray November, witness such an extraordinary series of confidences, since the first pair that sought isolation wandered over the grassy slopes and ferny dells beneath them. Among other things Hyacinth mentioned to his companion that he didn't go to the 'Sun and Moon' any more ; he now perceived, what he ought to have perceived long before, that this particular temple of their faith, and everything that pretended to get hatched there, was a hopeless sham. He had been a rare muff, from the first, to take it seriously. He had done so mainly because a friend of his, in whom he had confidence, appeared to set him the example ; but now it turned out that this friend (it was Paul Muniment again, by the way) had always thought the men who went there a pack of duffers and was only trying them because he tried everything. There was nobody

you could begin to call a first-rate man there, putting aside
another friend of his, a Frenchman named Poupin—and
Poupin was magnificent, but he wasn't first-rate.   Hyacinth
had a standard, now that he had seen a man who was the
very incarnation of a programme.   You felt that *he* was a
big chap the very moment you came into his presence.

'Into whose presence, Mr. Robinson?' the Princess
inquired.

'I don't know that I ought to tell you, much as I believe in you!   I am speaking of the very remarkable individual with whom I entered into that engagement.'

'To give away your life?'

'To do something which in a certain contingency he
will require of me.   He will require my poor little carcass.'

'Those plans have a way of failing—unfortunately,' the
Princess murmured, adding the last word more quickly.

'Is that a consolation, or a lament?' Hyacinth asked.
'This one shall not fail, so far as it depends on me.   They
wanted an obliging young man—the place was vacant—I
stepped in.'

'I have no doubt you are right.   We must pay for what
we do.'   The Princess made that remark calmly and coldly;
then she said, 'I think I know the person in whose power
you have placed yourself.'

'Possibly, but I doubt it.'

'You can't believe I have already gone so far?   Why
not?   I have given you a certain amount of proof that I
don't hang back.'

'Well, if you know my friend, you have gone very far
indeed.'

The Princess appeared to be on the point of pronouncing a name; but she checked herself, and asked suddenly,
smiling, 'Don't they also want, by chance, an obliging
young woman?'

'I happen to know he doesn't think much of women,
my first-rate man.   He doesn't trust them.'

'Is that why you call him first-rate?   You have very
nearly betrayed him to me.'

'Do you imagine there is only one of that opinion?'
Hyacinth inquired.

'Only one who, having it, still remains a superior man. That's a very difficult opinion to reconcile with others which it is important to have.'

'Schopenhauer did so, successfully,' said Hyacinth.

'How delightful that you should know Schopenhauer!' the Princess exclaimed. 'The gentleman I have in my eye is also German.' Hyacinth let this pass, not challenging her, because he wished not to be challenged in return, and the Princess went on, 'Of course such an engagement as you speak of must make a tremendous difference, in everything.'

'It has made this difference, that I have now a far other sense from any I had before of the reality, the solidity, of what is being prepared. I was hanging about outside, on the steps of the temple, among the loafers and the gossips, but now I have been in the innermost sanctuary—I have seen the holy of holies.'

'And it's very dazzling?'

'Ah, Princess!' sighed the young man.

'Then it *is* real, it *is* solid?' she pursued. 'That's exactly what I have been trying to make up my mind about, for so long.'

'It is more strange than I can say. Nothing of it appears above the surface; but there is an immense underworld, peopled with a thousand forms of revolutionary passion and devotion. The manner in which it is organised is what astonished me; I knew that, or thought I knew it, in a general way, but the reality was a revelation. And on top of it all, society lives! People go and come, and buy and sell, and drink and dance, and make money and make love, and seem to know nothing and suspect nothing and think of nothing; and iniquities flourish, and the misery of half the world is prated about as a 'necessary evil,' and generations rot away and starve, in the midst of it, and day follows day, and everything is for the best in the best of possible worlds. All that is one-half of it; the other half is that everything is doomed! In silence, in darkness, but under the feet of each one of us, the revolution lives and works. It is a wonderful, immeasurable trap, on the lid of which society performs its antics. When once the machin-

ery is complete, there will be a great rehearsal. That
rehearsal is what they want me for. The invisible, impalpable wires are everywhere, passing through everything,
attaching themselves to objects in which one would never
think of looking for them. What could be more strange
and incredible, for instance, than that they should exist just
here ? '

'You make me believe it,' said the Princess, thoughtfully.

' It matters little whether one believes it or not ! '

' You have had a vision,' the Princess continued.

' *Parbleu*, I have had a vision ! So would you, if you
had been there.'

' I wish I had ! ' she declared, in a tone charged with
such ambiguous implications that Hyacinth, catching them
a moment after she had spoken, rejoined, with a quick,
incongruous laugh—

' No, you would have spoiled everything. He made
me see, he made me feel, he made me do, everything he
wanted.'

' And why should he have wanted you, in particular ? '

' Simply because I struck him as the right person.
That's his affair : I can't tell you. When he meets the right
person he chalks him. I sat on the bed. (There were only
two chairs in the dirty little room, and by way of a curtain
his overcoat was hung up before the window.) He didn't sit,
himself ; he leaned against the wall, straight in front of me,
with his hands behind him. He told me certain things,
and his manner was extraordinarily quiet. So was mine, I
think I may say ; and indeed it was only poor Poupin who
made a row. It was for my sake, somehow : he didn't
think we were all conscious enough ; he wanted to call
attention to my sublimity. There was no sublimity about
it—I simply couldn't help myself. He and the other
German had the two chairs, and Muniment sat on a queer
old battered, hair-covered trunk, a most foreign-looking
article.' Hyacinth had taken no notice of the little ejaculation with which his companion greeted, in this last sentence,
the word ' other.'

' And what did Mr. Muniment say ? ' she presently
inquired.

'Oh, he said it was all right. Of course he thought that, from the moment he determined to bring me. He knew what the other fellow was looking for.'

'I see.' Then the Princess remarked, 'We have a curious way of being fond of you.'

'Whom do you mean by "we"?'

'Your friends. Mr. Muniment and I, for instance.'

'I like it as well as any other. But you don't feel alike. I have an idea you are sorry.'

'Sorry for what?'

'That I have put my head in a noose.'

'Ah, you're severe—I thought I concealed it so well!' the Princess exclaimed. He admitted that he had been severe, and begged her pardon, for he was by no means sure that there was not a hint of tears in her voice. She looked away from him for a minute, and it was after this that, stopping short, she remarked, as I have related, 'He is Diedrich Hoffendahl.'

Hyacinth stared for a moment, with parted lips. 'Well, you *are* in it, more than I supposed!'

'You know he doesn't trust women,' his companion smiled.

'Why in the world should you have cared for any light *I* can throw, if you have ever been in relation with him?'

She hesitated a little. 'Oh, you are very different. I like you better,' she added.

'Ah, if it's for that!' murmured Hyacinth.

The Princess coloured, as he had seen her colour before, and in this accident, on her part, there was an unexpectedness, something touching. 'Don't try to fix my inconsistencies on me,' she said, with a humility which matched her blush. 'Of course there are plenty of them, but it will always be kinder of you to let them pass. Besides, in this case they are not so serious as they seem. As a product of the 'people,' and of that strange, fermenting underworld (what you say of it is so true!) you interest me more, and have more to say to me, even than Hoffendahl—wonderful creature as he assuredly is.'

'Would you object to telling me how and where you came to know him?'

'Through a couple of friends of mine in Vienna, two of
the affiliated, both passionate revolutionists and clever men.
They are Neapolitans, originally *poveretti*, like yourself,
who emigrated, years ago, to seek their fortune. One of
them is a teacher of singing, the wisest, most accomplished
person in his line I have ever known. The other, if you
please, is a confectioner! He makes the most delicious
pâtisserie fine. It would take long to tell you how I made
their acquaintance, and how they put me into relation
with the Maestro, as they called him, of whom they spoke
with bated breath. It is not from yesterday—though you
don't seem able to believe it—that I have had a care for
all this business. I wrote to Hoffendahl, and had several
letters from him; the singing-master and the pastry-cook
went bail for my sincerity. The next year I had an interview with him at Wiesbaden; but I can't tell you the
circumstances of our meeting, in that place, without im-
plicating another person, to whom, at present at least, I
have no right to give you a clue. Of course Hoffendahl
made an immense impression on me; he seemed to me
the Master indeed, the very genius of a new social order,
and I fully understand the manner in which you were
affected by him. When he was in London, three months
ago, I knew it, and I knew where to write to him. I did
so, and asked him if he wouldn't see me somewhere. I
said I would meet him in any hole he should designate.
He answered by a charming letter, which I will show you
—there is nothing in the least compromising in it—but he
declined my offer, pleading his short stay and a press of
engagements. He will write to me, but he won't trust
me. However, he shall some day!'

Hyacinth was thrown quite off his balance by this
representation of the ground the Princess had already
traversed, and the explanation was still but half restorative
when, on his asking her why she hadn't exhibited her titles
before, she replied, 'Well, I thought my being quiet was
the better way to draw you out.' There was but little
difficulty in drawing him out now, and before their walk
was over he had told her more definitely what Hoffendahl
demanded. This was simply that he should hold himself

ready, for the next five years, to do, at a given moment, an act which would in all probability cost him his life. The act was as yet indefinite, but one might get an idea of it from the penalty involved, which would certainly be capital. The only thing settled was that it was to be done instantly and absolutely, without a question, a hesitation or a scruple, in the manner that should be prescribed, at the moment, from headquarters. Very likely it would be to kill some one—some humbug in a high place; but whether the individual should deserve it or should not deserve it was not Hyacinth's affair. If he recognised generally Hoffendahl's wisdom—and the other night it had seemed to shine like a northern aurora—it was not in order that he might challenge it in the particular case. He had taken a vow of blind obedience, as the Jesuit fathers did to the head of their order. It was because they had carried out their vows (having, in the first place, great administrators) that their organisation had been mighty, and that sort of mightiness was what people who felt as Hyacinth and the Princess felt should go in for. It was not certain that he should be collared, any more than it was certain that he should bring down his man; but it was much to be looked for, and it was what he counted on and indeed preferred. He should probably take little trouble to escape, and he should never enjoy the idea of hiding (after the fact), or running away. If it were a question of putting a bullet into some one, he himself should naturally deserve what would come to him. If one did that sort of thing there was an indelicacy in not being ready to pay for it; and he, at least, was perfectly willing. He shouldn't judge; he should simply execute. He didn't pretend to say what good his little job might do, or what *portée* it might have; he hadn't the data for appreciating it, and simply took upon himself to believe that at headquarters they knew what they were about. The thing was to be a feature in a very large plan, of which he couldn't measure the scope—something that was to be done simultaneously in a dozen different countries. The effect was to be very much in this immense coincidence. It was to be hoped it wouldn't be spoiled. At any rate, *he* wouldn't hang fire, whatever the other fellows might do. He didn't say it because Hoffendahl had done him the honour of giving him the business to do, but he believed the Master knew how to pick out his men. To be sure, Hoffendahl had known nothing about him in advance; he had only been suggested by those who were looking out, from one day to the other. The fact remained however that when Hyacinth stood before him he recognised him as the sort of little chap that he had in his eye (one who could pass through a small orifice). Humanity, in his scheme, was classified and sub-divided with a truly German thoroughness, and altogether of course from the point of view of the revolution, as it might forward or obstruct it. Hyacinth's little job was a very small part of what Hoffendahl had come to England for; he had in his hand innumerable other threads. Hyacinth knew nothing of these, and didn't much want to know, except that it was marvellous, the way Hoffendahl kept them apart. He had exactly the same mastery of them that a great musician—that the Princess herself—had of the keyboard of the piano; he treated all things, persons, institutions, ideas, as so many notes in his great symphonic revolt. The day would come when Hyacinth, far down in the treble, would feel himself touched by the little finger of the composer, would become audible (with a small, sharp crack) for a second.

It was impossible that our young man should not feel, at the end of ten minutes, that he had charmed the Princess into the deepest, most genuine attention; she was listening to him as she had never listened before. He enjoyed having that effect upon her, and his sense of the tenuity of the thread by which his future hung, renewed by his hearing himself talk about it, made him reflect that at present anything in the line of enjoyment was so much gained. The reader may judge whether he had passed through a phase of excitement after finding himself on his new footing of utility in the world; but that had finally spent itself, through a hundred forms of restlessness, of vain conjecture —through an exaltation which alternated with despair and which, equally with the despair, he concealed more suc-cessfully than he supposed. He would have detested the idea that his companion might have heard his voice tremble while he told his story; but though to-day he had really grown used to his danger and resigned, as it were, to his consecration, and though it could not fail to be agreeable to him to perceive that he was thrilling, he could still not guess how very remarkable, in such a connection, the Princess thought his composure, his lucidity and good-humour. It is true she tried to hide her wonder, for she owed it to her self-respect to let it still appear that even she was prepared for a personal sacrifice as complete. She had the air—or she endeavoured to have it—of accepting for him everything that he accepted for himself; nevertheless, there was something rather forced in the smile (lovely as it was) with which she covered him, while she said, after a little, 'It's very serious—it's very serious indeed, isn't it?' He replied that the serious part was to come—there was no particular grimness for him (comparatively) in strolling in that sweet park and gossiping with her about the matter; and it occurred to her presently to suggest to him that perhaps Hoffendahl would never give him any sign at all, and he would wait all the while, *sur les dents*, in a false suspense. He admitted that this would be a sell, but declared that either way he would be sold, though differently; and that at any rate he would have conformed to the great religious rule—to live each hour as if it were to be one's last.

'In holiness, you mean—in great *recueillement?*' the Princess asked.

'Oh dear, no; simply in extreme thankfulness for every minute that's added.'

'Ah, well, there will probably be a great many,' she rejoined.

'The more the better—if they are like this.'

'That won't be the case with many of them, in Lomax Place.'

'I assure you that since that night Lomax Place has improved.' Hyacinth stood there, smiling, with his hands in his pockets and his hat pushed back a little.

The Princess appeared to consider this fact with an extreme intellectual curiosity. 'If, after all, then, you are not called, you will have been positively happy.'

' I shall have had some fine moments.   Perhaps Hoffen-dahl's plot is simply for that ; Muniment may have put him up to it ! '

' Who knows ?   However, with me you must go on as if nothing were changed.'

' Changed from what ? '

' From the time of our first meeting at the theatre.'

' I'll go on in any way you like,' said Hyacinth ; ' only the real difference will be there.'

' The real difference ? '

' That I shall have ceased to care for what you care about.'

' I don't understand,' said the Princess.

' Isn't it enough, now, to give my life to the beastly cause,' the young man broke out, ' without giving my sympathy ? '

' The beastly cause ? ' the Princess murmured, opening her deep eyes.

' Of course it is really just as holy as ever ; only the people I find myself pitying now are the rich, the happy.'

' I see.   You are very curious.   Perhaps you pity my husband,' the Princess added in a moment.

' Do you call him one of the happy ? ' Hyacinth in-quired, as they walked on again.

In answer to this she only repeated, ' You are very curious ! '

I have related the whole of this conversation, because it supplies a highly important chapter of Hyacinth's history, but it will not be possible to trace all the stages through which the friendship of the Princess Casamassima with the young man she had constituted her bookbinder was con-firmed.   By the end of a week the standard of fitness she had set up in the place of exploded proprieties appeared the model of justice and convenience ; and during this period many other things happened.   One of them was that Hyacinth drove over to Broome with his hostess, and called on Lady Marchant and her daughters ; an episode from which the Princess appeared to derive an exquisite gratification.   When they came away he asked her why

she hadn't told the ladies who he was.   Otherwise, where
was the point?   And she replied, 'Simply because they
wouldn't have believed me.   That's your fault!'   This
was the same note she had struck when, the third day of
his stay (the weather had changed for the worse, and a
rainy afternoon kept them in-doors), she remarked to him,
irrelevantly and abruptly, 'It *is* most extraordinary, your
knowing about Schopenhauer!'   He answered that she
really seemed quite unable to accustom herself to his
little talents; and this led to a long talk, longer than
the one I have already narrated, in which he took her
still further into his confidence.   Never had the pleasure
of conversation (the greatest he knew), been so largely
opened to him.   The Princess admitted, frankly, that he
would, to her sense, take a great deal of accounting for;
she observed that he was, no doubt, pretty well used to
himself, but he must give other people time.   'I have
watched you, constantly, since you have been here, in
every detail of your behaviour, and I am more and more
intriguée.   You haven't a vulgar intonation, you haven't
a common gesture, you never make a mistake, you do
and say everything exactly in the right way.   You come
out of the hole you have described to me, and yet you
might have stayed in country-houses all your life.   You
are much better than if you had!   *Jugez donc,* from the
way I talk to you!   I have to make no allowances.   I have
seen Italians with that sort of natural tact and taste, but
I didn't know one ever found it in any Anglo-Saxon in
whom it hadn't been cultivated at a vast expense; unless,
indeed, in certain little American women.'

    'Do you mean I'm a gentleman?' asked Hyacinth, in
a peculiar tone, looking out into the wet garden.

    She hesitated, and then she said, 'It's I who make the
mistakes!'   Five minutes later she broke into an exclamation which touched him almost more than anything she
had ever done, giving him the highest opinion of her
delicacy and sympathy and putting him before himself as
vividly as if the words were a little portrait.   'Fancy the
strange, the bitter fate: to be constituted as you are constituted, to feel the capacity that you must feel, and yet to

look at the good things of life only through the glass of
the pastry-cook's window ! '

'Every class has its pleasures,' Hyacinth rejoined, with
perverse sententiousness, in spite of his emotion ; but the
remark didn't darken their mutual intelligence, and before
they separated that evening he told her the things that
had never yet passed his lips—the things to which he had
awaked when he made Pinnie explain to him the visit to
the prison.   He told her, in a word, what he was.

HYACINTH took several long walks by himself, beyond the gates of the park and through the neighbouring country—walks during which, committed as he was to reflection on the general 'rumness' of his destiny, he had still a delighted attention to spare for the green dimness of leafy lanes, the attraction of meadow-paths that led from stile to stile and seemed a clue to some pastoral happiness, some secret of the fields; the hedges thick with flowers, bewilderingly common, for which he knew no names, the picture-making quality of thatched cottages, the mystery and sweetness of blue distances, the bloom of rural complexions, the quaintness of little girls bobbing curtsies by waysides (a sort of homage he had never prefigured); the soft sense of the turf under feet that had never ached but from paving-stones. One morning, as he had his face turned homeward, after a long stroll, he heard behind him the sound of a horse's hoofs, and, looking back, perceived a gentleman, who would presently pass him, advancing up the road which led to the lodge-gates of Medley. He went his way and, as the horse overtook him, noticed that the rider slackened pace. Then he turned again, and recognised in this personage his brilliant occasional friend Captain Sholto. The Captain pulled up alongside of him, saluting him with a smile and a movement of the whip-handle. Hyacinth stared with surprise, not having heard from the Princess that she was expecting him. He gathered, however, in a moment, that she was not; and meanwhile he received an impression, on Sholto's part, of riding-gear that was 'knowing'—of gaiters and spurs and a curious waistcoat; perceiving that this was a phase of the Captain's varied nature which he had not yet had an opportunity to observe. He struck him as very high in the air, perched on his big, lean chestnut, and Hyacinth noticed that if the horse was heated the rider was cool.

'Good-morning, my dear fellow. I thought I should find you here!' the Captain exclaimed. 'It's a good job I've met you this way, without having to go to the house.'

'Who gave you reason to think I was here?' Hyacinth asked; partly occupied with the appositeness of this inquiry and partly thinking, as his eyes wandered over his handsome friend, bestriding so handsome a beast, what a jolly thing it would be to know how to ride. He had already, during the few days he had been at Medley, had time to observe that the knowledge of luxury and the extension of one's sensations beget a taste for still newer pleasures.

'Why, I knew the Princess was capable of asking you,' Sholto said; 'and I learned at the "Sun and Moon" that you had not been there for a long time. I knew furthermore that as a general thing you go there a good deal, don't you? So I put this and that together, and judged you were out of town.'

This was very luminous and straightforward, and might have satisfied Hyacinth were it not for that irritating reference to the Princess's being 'capable of asking him.' He knew as well as the Captain that it had been tremendously eccentric in her to do so, but somehow a transformation had lately taken place in him which made it disagreeable for him to receive that view from another, and particularly from a gentleman of whom, on a certain occasion, several months before, he had had strong grounds for thinking unfavourably. He had not seen Sholto since the evening when a queer combination of circumstances caused him, more queerly still, to sit and listen to comic songs in the company of Millicent Henning and this admirer. The Captain did not conceal his admiration; Hyacinth had his own ideas about his taking that line in order to look more innocent. That evening, when he accompanied Millicent to her lodgings (they parted with Sholto on coming out of the Pavilion), the situation was tense between the young lady and her childhood's friend. She let him have it, as she said; she gave him a dressing which she evidently intended should be memorable, for having suspected her, for having insulted her before a military gentleman. The tone she took, and the magnificent audacity with which she took it, reduced him to a kind of gratified helplessness; he watched her at last with something of the excitement with which he would have watched a clever but uncultivated actress, while she worked herself into a passion which he believed to be fictitious. He gave more credence to his jealousy and to the whole air of the case than to her vehement repudiations, enlivened though these were by tremendous head-tossings and skirt-shakings. But he felt baffled and outfaced, and took refuge in sarcasms which after all proved as little as her high gibes; seeking a final solution in one of those beastly little French shrugs, as Millicent called them, with which she had already reproached him with interlarding his conversation.

The air was never cleared, though the subject of their dispute was afterwards dropped, Hyacinth promising himself to watch his playmate as he had never done before. She let him know, as may well be supposed, that she had her eye on *him*, and it must be confessed that as regards the exercise of a right of supervision he had felt himself at a disadvantage ever since the night at the theatre. It mattered little that she had pushed him into the Princess's box (for she herself had not been jealous beforehand; she had wanted too much to know what such a person could be 'up to,' desiring, perhaps, to borrow a hint), and it mattered little, also, that his relations with the great lady were all for the sake of suffering humanity; the atmosphere, none the less, was full of thunder for many weeks, and it scarcely signified from which quarter the flash and the explosion proceeded. Hyacinth was a good deal surprised to find that he should care whether Millicent deceived him or not, and even tried to persuade himself that he didn't; but there was a grain of conviction in his heart that some kind of personal affinity existed between them and that it would torment him more never to see her at all than to see her go into tantrums in order to cover her tracks. An inner sense told him that her mingled beauty and grossness,

her vulgar vitality, the spirit of contradiction yet at the
same time of attachment that was in her, had ended by
making her indispensable to him. She bored him as much
as she irritated him; but if she was full of execrable taste
she was also full of life, and her rustlings and chatterings,
her wonderful stories, her bad grammar and good health,
her insatiable thirst, her shrewd perceptions and grotesque
opinions, her mistakes and her felicities, were now all part
of the familiar human sound of his little world. He could
say to himself that she came after him much more than he
went after her, and this helped him, a little, to believe,
though the logic was but lame, that she was not making a
fool of him. If she were really taking up with a swell he
didn't see why she wished to retain a bookbinder. Of late,
it must be added, he had ceased to devote much consideration to Millicent's ambiguities; for although he was lingering on at Medley for the sake of suffering humanity he was
quite aware that to say so (if she should ask him for a
reason) would have almost as absurd a sound as some of
the girl's own speeches. As regards Sholto, he was in the
awkward position of having let him off, as it were, by
accepting his hospitality, his bounty; so that he couldn't
quarrel with him except on a fresh pretext. This pretext
the Captain had apparently been careful not to give, and
Millicent had told him, after the triple encounter in the
street, that he had driven him out of England, the poor
gentleman whom he insulted by his low insinuations even
more (why 'even more' Hyacinth hardly could think) than
he outraged herself. When he asked her what she knew
about the Captain's movements she made no scruple to
announce to him that the latter had come to her great shop
to make a little purchase (it was a pair of silk braces, if she
remembered rightly, and she admitted, perfectly, the transparency of the pretext), and had asked her with much concern whether his gifted young friend (that's what he called
him—Hyacinth could see he meant well) was still in a huff.
Millicent had answered that she was afraid he was—the
more shame to him; and then the Captain had said that
it didn't matter, for he himself was on the point of leaving
England for several weeks (Hyacinth—he called him

Hyacinth this time—couldn't have ideas about a man in a foreign country, could he ?), and he hoped that by the time he returned the little cloud would have blown over. Sholto had added that she had better tell him frankly— recommending her at the same time to be gentle with their morbid friend—about his visit to the shop.   Their candour, their humane precautions, were all very well ; but after this, two or three evenings, Hyacinth passed and repassed the Captain's chambers in Queen Anne Street, to see if, at the window, there were signs of his being in London. Darkness, however, prevailed, and he was forced to comfort himself a little when, at last making up his mind to ring at the door and inquire, by way of a test, for the occupant, he was informed, by the superior valet whose acquaintance he had already made, and whose air of wearing a jacket left behind by his master confirmed the statement, that the gentleman in question was at Monte Carlo.

'Have you still got your back up a little ?' the Captain demanded, without rancour ; and in a moment he had swung a long leg over the saddle and dismounted, walking beside his young friend and leading his horse by the bridle. Hyacinth pretended not to know what he meant, for it came over him that after all, even if he had not condoned, at the time, the Captain's suspected treachery, he was in no position, sitting at the feet of the Princess, to sound the note of jealousy in relation to another woman.   He reflected that the Princess had originally been, in a manner, Sholto's property, and if he did *en fin de compte* wish to quarrel with him about Millicent he would have to cease to appear to poach on the Captain's preserves.   It now occurred to him, for the first time, that the latter had intended a kind of exchange ; though it must be added that the Princess, who on a couple of occasions had alluded slightingly to her military friend, had given him no sign of recognising this gentleman's claim.   Sholto let him know, at present, that he was staying at Bonchester, seven miles off ; he had come down from London and put up at the inn.   That morning he had ridden over on a hired horse (Hyacinth had supposed this steed was a very fine animal, but Sholto spoke of it as an infernal screw); he had been taken by the sudden fancy of seeing how his young friend was coming on.

'I'm coming on very well, thank you,' said Hyacinth, with some shortness, not knowing exactly what business it was of the Captain's.

'Of course you understand my interest in you, don't you? I'm responsible for you—I put you forward.'

'There are a great many things in the world that I don't understand, but I think the thing I understand least is your interest in me. Why the devil——' And Hyacinth paused, breathless with the force of his inquiry. Then he went on, 'If I were you, I shouldn't care a filbert for the sort of person that I happen to be.'

'That proves how different my nature is to yours! But I don't believe it, my boy; you are too generous for that.' Sholto's imperturbability always appeared to grow with the irritation it produced, and it was proof even against the just resentment excited by his want of tact. That want of tact was sufficiently marked when he went on to say, 'I wanted to see you here, with my own eyes. I wanted to see how it looked; it *is* a rum sight! Of course you know what I mean, though you are always trying to make a fellow explain. I don't explain well, in any sense, and that's why I go in only for clever people, who can do without it. It's very grand, her having brought you down.'

'Grand, no doubt, but hardly surprising, considering that, as you say, I was put forward by you.'

'Oh, that's a great thing for me, but it doesn't make any difference to her!' Sholto exclaimed. 'She may care for certain things for themselves, but it will never signify a jot to her what I may have thought about them. One good turn deserves another. I wish you would put *me* forward!'

'I don't understand you, and I don't think I want to,' said Hyacinth, as his companion strolled beside him.

The latter put a hand on his arm, stopping him, and they stood face to face a moment. 'I say, my dear Robinson, you're not spoiled already, at the end of a week —how long is it? It isn't possible you're jealous!'

'Jealous of whom?' asked Hyacinth, whose failure to comprehend was perfectly genuine.

Sholto looked at him a moment; then, with a laugh, 'I don't mean Miss Henning.' Hyacinth turned away, and the Captain resumed his walk, now taking the young man's arm and passing his own through the bridle of the horse. 'The courage of it, the insolence, the *crânerie!* There isn't another woman in Europe who could carry it off.'

Hyacinth was silent a little; after which he remarked, 'This is nothing, here. You should have seen me the other day over at Broome, at Lady Marchant's.'

'Gad, did she take you there? I'd have given ten pounds to see it. There's no one like her!' cried the Captain, gaily, enthusiastically.

'There's no one like me, I think—for going.'

'Why, didn't you enjoy it?'

'Too much—too much. Such excesses are dangerous.'

'Oh, I'll back you,' said the Captain; then, checking their pace, he inquired, 'Is there any chance of our meeting her? I won't go into the park.'

'You won't go to the house?' Hyacinth demanded, staring.

'Oh dear, no, not while you're there.'

'Well, I shall ask the Princess about you, and have done with it, once for all.'

'Lucky little beggar, with your fireside talks!' the Captain exclaimed. 'Where does she sit now, in the evening? She won't tell you anything except that I'm a nuisance; but even if she were willing to take the trouble to throw some light upon me it wouldn't be of much use, because she doesn't understand me herself.'

'You are the only thing in the world then of which that can be said,' Hyacinth returned.

'I dare say I am, and I am rather proud of it. So far as the head is concerned, the Princess is all there. I told you, when I presented you, that she was the cleverest woman in Europe, and that is still my opinion. But there are some mysteries you can't see into unless you happen to have a little heart. The Princess hasn't, though doubt-

less just now you think that's her strong point.   One of
these days you'll see.   I don't care a straw, myself, whether
she has or not.   She has hurt me already so much she
can't hurt me any more, and my interest in her is quite
independent of that.   To watch her, to adore her, to see
her lead her life and act out her extraordinary nature, all
the while she treats me like a brute, is the only thing I care
for to-day.   It doesn't do me a scrap of good, but, all the
same, it's my principal occupation.   You may believe me
or not—it doesn't in the least matter; but I'm the most
disinterested human being alive.   She'll tell you I'm a
tremendous ass, and so one is.   But that isn't all.'

It was Hyacinth who stopped this time, arrested by
something new and natural in the tone of his companion,
a simplicity of emotion which he had not hitherto associated
with him.   He stood there a moment looking up at him,
and thinking again what improbable confidences it decidedly
appeared to be his lot to receive from gentlefolks.   To
what quality in himself were they a tribute?   The honour
was one he could easily dispense with; though as he
scrutinised Sholto he found something in his curious light
eyes—an expression of cheerfulness not disconnected from
veracity—which put him into a less fantastic relation with
this jaunty, factitious personage.   'Please go on,' he said,
in a moment.

'Well, what I mentioned just now is my real and only
motive, in anything.   The rest is mere gammon and rubbish,
to cover it up—or to give myself the change, as the French
say.'

'What do you mean by the rest?' asked Hyacinth,
thinking of Millicent Henning.

'Oh, all the straw one chews, to cheat one's appetite;
all the rot one dabbles in, because it may lead to something which it never does lead to; all the beastly buncombe
(you know) that you and I have heard together in Bloomsbury and that I myself have poured out, damme, with an
eloquence worthy of a better cause.   Don't you remember
what I have said to you—all as my own opinion—about
the impending change of the relations of class with class?
Impending fiddlesticks!   I believe those that are on top

the heap are better than those that are under it, that they mean to stay there, and that if they are not a pack of poltroons they will.'

'You don't care for the social question, then?' Hyacinth inquired, with an aspect of which he was conscious of the blankness.

'I only took it up because she did. It hasn't helped me,' Sholto remarked, smiling. 'My dear Robinson,' he went on, 'there is only one thing I care for in life : to have a look at that woman when I can, and when I can't, to approach her in the sort of way I'm doing now.'

'It's a very curious sort of way.'

'Indeed it is ; but if it is good enough for me it ought to be good enough for you. What I want you to do is this —to induce her to ask me over to dine.'

'To induce her——?' Hyacinth murmured.

'Tell her I'm staying at Bonchester and it would be an act of common humanity.'

They proceeded till they reached the gates, and in a moment Hyacinth said, 'You took up the social question, then, because she did ; but do you happen to know why she took it up ?'

'Ah, my dear fellow, you must find that out for yourself. I found you the place, but I can't do your work for you !'

'I see—I see. But perhaps you'll tell me this : if you had free access to the Princess a year ago, taking her to the theatre and that sort of thing, why shouldn't you have it now ?'

This time Sholto's white pupils looked strange again. '*You* have it now, my dear fellow, but I'm afraid it doesn't follow that you'll have it a year hence. She was tired of me then, and of course she's still more tired of me now, for the simple reason that I'm more tiresome. She has sent me to Coventry, and I want to come out for a few hours. See how conscientious I am—I won't pass the gates.'

'I'll tell her I met you,' said Hyacinth. Then, irrelevantly, he added, 'Is that what you mean by her having no heart ?'

'Her treating me as she treats me ? Oh, dear, no ; her treating you !'

This had a portentous sound, but it did not prevent Hyacinth from turning round with his visitor (for it was the greatest part of the oddity of the present meeting that the hope of a little conversation with him, if accident were favourable, had been the motive not only of Sholto's riding over to Medley but of his coming down to stay, in the neighbourhood, at a musty inn in a dull market-town), it did not prevent him, I say, from bearing the Captain company for a mile on his backward way. Our young man did not pursue this particular topic much further, but he discovered still another reason or two for admiring the light, free action with which his companion had unmasked himself, and the nature of his interest in the revolutionary idea, after he had asked him, abruptly, what he had had in his head when he travelled over that evening, the summer before (he didn't appear to have come back as often as he promised), to Paul Muniment's place in Camberwell. What was he looking for, whom was he looking for, there?

'I was looking for anything that would turn up, that might take her fancy. Don't you understand that I'm always looking? There was a time when I went in immensely for illuminated missals, and another when I collected horrible ghost-stories (she wanted to cultivate a belief in ghosts), all for her. The day I saw she was turning her attention to the rising democracy I began to collect little democrats. That's how I collected you.'

'Muniment read you exactly, then. And what did you find to your purpose in Audley Court?'

'Well, I think the little woman with the popping eyes— she reminded me of a bedridden grasshopper—will do. And I made a note of the other one, the old virgin with the high nose, the aristocratic sister of mercy. I'm keeping them in reserve for my next propitiatory offering.'

Hyacinth was silent a moment. 'And Muniment himself—can't you do anything with him?'

'Oh, my dear fellow, after you he's poor!'

'That's the first stupid thing you have said. But it doesn't matter, for he dislikes the Princess—what he knows of her—too much ever to consent to see her.'

'That's his line, is it? Then he'll do!' Sholto cried.

'Of course he may come, and stay as long as he likes!'
the Princess exclaimed, when Hyacinth, that afternoon, told
her of his encounter, with the sweet, bright surprise her face
always wore when people went through the form (supererogatory she apparently meant to declare it) of asking her
leave. From the manner in which she granted Sholto's
petition—with a geniality that made light of it, as if the
question were not worth talking of, one way or the other—
it might have been supposed that the account he had given
Hyacinth of their relations was an elaborate but none the
less foolish hoax. She sent a messenger with a note over
to Bonchester, and the Captain arrived just in time to dress
for dinner. The Princess was always late, and Hyacinth's
toilet, on these occasions, occupied him considerably (he
was acutely conscious of its deficiencies, and yet tried to
persuade himself that they were positively honourable and
that the only garb of dignity, for him, was the costume, as
it were, of his profession); therefore when the fourth
member of the little party descended to the drawing-room
Madame Grandoni was the only person he found there.

'*Santissima Vergine!* I'm glad to see you! What good
wind has sent you?' she exclaimed, as soon as Sholto came
into the room.

'Didn't you know I was coming?' he asked. 'Has the
idea of my arrival produced so little agitation?'

'I know nothing of the affairs of this house. I have
given them up at last, and it was time. I remain in my
room.' There was nothing at present in the old lady's
countenance of her usual spirit of cheer; it expressed
anxiety, and even a certain sternness, and the excellent
woman had perhaps at this moment more than she had

ever had in her life of the air of a duenna who took her duties seriously. She looked almost august. 'From the moment you come it's a little better. But it is very bad.'

'Very bad, dear madam?'

'Perhaps you will be able to tell me where Christina *veut en venir.* I have always been faithful to her—I have always been loyal. But to-day I have lost patience. It has no sense.'

'I am not sure I know what you are talking about,' Sholto said; 'but if I understand you I must tell you I think it's magnificent.'

'Yes, I know your tone; you are worse than she, because you are cynical. It passes all bounds. It is very serious. I have been thinking what I should do.'

'Precisely; I know what you would do.'

'Oh, this time I shouldn't come back!' the old lady declared. 'The scandal is too great; it is intolerable. My only fear is to make it worse.'

'Dear Madame Grandoni, you can't make it worse, and you can't make it better,' Sholto rejoined, seating himself on the sofa beside her. 'In point of fact, no idea of scandal can possibly attach itself to our friend. She is above and outside of all such considerations, such dangers. She carries everything off; she heeds so little, she cares so little. Besides, she has one great strength—she does no wrong.'

'Pray, what do you call it when a lady sends for a book-binder to come and live with her?'

'Why not for a bookbinder as well as for a bishop? It all depends upon who the lady is, and what she is.'

'She had better take care of one thing first,' cried Madame Grandoni—'that she shall not have been separated from her husband!'

'The Princess can carry off even that. It's unusual, it's eccentric, it's fantastic, if you will, but it isn't necessarily wicked. From her own point of view our friend goes straight. Besides, she has her opinions.'

'Her opinions are perversity itself.'

'What does it matter,' asked Sholto, 'if they keep her quiet?'

' Quiet !   Do you call this quiet ? '

' Surely, if you'll only be so yourself.   Putting the case at the worst, moreover, who is to know he's her bookbinder ? It's the last thing you'd take him for.'

'Yes, for that she chose him carefully,' the old lady murmured, still with a discontented eyebrow.

' *She* chose him ?   It was I who chose him, dear lady ! ' the Captain exclaimed, with a laugh which showed how little he shared her solicitude.

' Yes, I had forgotten ; at the theatre,' said Madame Grandoni, gazing at him as if her ideas were confused but a certain repulsion from her interlocutor nevertheless disengaged itself.   ' It was a fine turn you did him there, poor young man ! '

' Certainly, he will have to be sacrificed.   But why was I bound to consider him so much ?   Haven't I been sacrificed myself ? '

' Oh, if he bears it like you ! ' cried the old lady, with a short laugh.

' How do you know how I bear it ?   One does what one can,' said the Captain, settling his shirt-front.   ' At any rate, remember this : she won't tell people who he is, for his own sake ; and he won't tell them, for hers.   So, as he looks much more like a poet, or a pianist, or a painter, there won't be that sensation you fear.'

' Even so it's bad enough,' said Madame Grandoni. ' And he's capable of bringing it out, suddenly, himself.'

' Ah, if he doesn't mind it, she won't !   But that's his affair.'

' It's too terrible, to spoil him for his station,' the old lady went on.   ' How can he ever go back ? '

' If you want him kept, then, indefinitely, you are inconsistent.   Besides, if he pays for it, he deserves to pay.   He's an abominable little conspirator against society.'

Madame Grandoni was silent a moment ;   then she looked at the Captain with a gravity which might have been impressive to him, had not his accomplished jauntiness suggested an insensibility to that sort of influence. ' What, then, does Christina deserve ? ' she asked, 'with solemnity.

'Whatever she may get; whatever, in the future, may make her suffer. But it won't be the loss of her reputation. She is too distinguished.'

'You English are strange. Is it because she's a princess?' Madame Grandoni reflected, audibly.

'Oh, dear, no, her princedom is nothing here. We can easily beat that. But we can't beat——' And Sholto paused a moment.

'What then?' his companion asked.

'Well, the perfection of her indifference to public opinion and the unaffectedness of her originality; the sort of thing by which she has bedeviled me.'

'Oh, *you!*' murmured Madame Grandoni.

'If you think so poorly of me why did you say just now that you were glad to see me?' Sholto demanded, in a moment.

'Because you make another person in the house, and that is more regular; the situation is by so much less— what did you call it?—eccentric. *Nun,*' the old lady went on, in a moment, 'so long as you are here I won't go off.'

'Depend upon it that I shall be here until I'm turned out.'

She rested her small, troubled eyes upon him, but they betrayed no particular enthusiasm at this announcement. 'I don't understand how, for yourself, on such an occasion, you should like it.'

'Dear Madame Grandoni, the heart of man, without being such a hopeless labyrinth as the heart of woman, is still sufficiently complicated. Don't I know what will become of the little beggar?'

'You are very horrible,' said the ancient woman. Then she added, in a different tone, 'He is much too good for his fate.'

'And pray wasn't I, for mine?' the Captain asked.

'By no manner of means!' Madame Grandoni answered, rising and moving away from him.

The Princess had come into the room, accompanied by Hyacinth. As it was now considerably past the dinner-hour the old lady judged that this couple, on their side, had met in the hall and had prolonged their conversation

there. Hyacinth watched with extreme interest the way
the Princess greeted the Captain—observed that it was
very simple, easy and friendly. At dinner she made no
stranger of him, including him in everything, as if he had
been a useful familiar, like Madame Grandoni, only a little
less venerable, yet not giving him any attention that might
cause their eyes to meet. She had told Hyacinth that she
didn't like his eyes, nor indeed, very much, any part of him.
Of course any admiration, from almost any source, could
not fail to be in some degree agreeable to a woman, but of
any little impression that one might ever have produced the
mark she had made on Godfrey Sholto was the one that
ministered least to her vanity. He had been useful, un-
doubtedly, at times, but at others he had been an intolerable bore. He was so uninteresting in himself, so shallow,
so unoccupied and superfluous, and really so frivolous, in
spite of his pretension (of which she was unspeakably
weary) of being all wrapped up in a single idea. It had
never, by itself, been sufficient to interest her in any man,
the fact that he was in love with her ; but indeed she could
honestly say that most of the people who had liked her had
had, on their own side, something—something in their
character or circumstances—that one could care a little
about. Not so far as would do any harm, save perhaps in
one or two cases ; but still, something.

Sholto was a curious and not particularly edifying English
type (as the Princess further described him) ; one of those
strange beings produced by old societies that have run to seed,
corrupt, exhausted civilisations. He was a cumberer of the
earth, and purely selfish, in spite of his devoted, disinterested
airs. He was nothing whatever in himself, and had no
character or merit save by tradition, reflection, imitation,
superstition. He had a longish pedigree—he came of some
musty, mouldy 'county family,' people with a local reputation and an immense lack of general importance ; he had
taken the greatest care of his little fortune. He had
travelled all over the globe several times, 'for the shooting,'
in that brutal way of the English. That was a pursuit which
was compatible with the greatest stupidity. He had a little
taste, a little cleverness, a little reading, a little good furni-

ture, a little French and Italian (he exaggerated these latter quantities), an immense deal of assurance, and complete leisure. That, at bottom, was all he represented—idle, trifling, luxurious, yet at the same time pretentious leisure, the sort of thing that led people to invent false, humbugging duties, because they had no real ones. Sholto's great idea of himself (after his profession of being her slave), was that he was a cosmopolite—exempt from every prejudice. About the prejudices the Princess couldn't say and didn't care; but she had seen him in foreign countries, she had seen him in Italy, and she was bound to say he understood nothing about those people. It was several years before, shortly after her marriage, that she had first encountered him. He had not begun immediately to take the adoring line, but it had come little by little. It was only after she had separated from her husband that he had begun really to hang about her; since when she had suffered much from him. She would do him one justice, however: he had never, so far as she knew, had the impudence to represent himself as anything but hopeless and helpless. It was on this that he took his stand; he wished to pass for the great model of unrewarded constancy. She couldn't imagine what he was waiting for; perhaps it was for the death of the Prince. But the Prince would never die, nor had she the least desire that he should. She had no wish to be harsh, for of course that sort of thing, from any one, was very flattering; but really, whatever feeling poor Sholto might have, four-fifths of it were purely theatrical. He was not in the least a natural human being, but had a hundred affectations and attitudes, the result of never having been obliged to put his hand to anything; having no serious tastes and yet being born to a little 'position.' The Princess remarked that she was so glad Hyacinth had no position, had been forced to do something else in life but amuse himself; that was the way she liked her friends now. She had said to Sholto again and again, 'There are plenty of others who will be much more pleased; why not go to *them*? It's such a waste of time:' and she was sure he had taken her advice, and was by no means, as regards herself, the absorbed, annihilated creature he endeavoured

to appear.   He had told her once that he tried to take an
interest in other women—though indeed he had added that
it was of no use.   Of what use did he expect anything he
could possibly do to be?   Hyacinth did not tell the Princess that he had reason to believe the Captain's effort in
this direction had not been absolutely vain ; but he made
that reflection, privately, with increased confidence.   He
recognised a further truth even when his companion said,
at the end, that, with all she had touched upon, he was a
queer combination.   Trifler as he was, there was something
sinister in him too ; and she confessed she had had a vague
feeling, at times, that some day he might do her a hurt.
Hyacinth, at this, stopped short, on the threshold of the
drawing-room, and asked in a low voice, ' Are you afraid of
him ? '

The Princess looked at him a moment; then smiling,
' *Dio mio*, how you say that !   Should you like to kill him
for me ? '

' I shall have to kill some one, you know.   Why not
him, while I'm about it, if he troubles you ? '

' Ah, my friend, if you should begin to kill every one
who had troubled me ! ' the Princess murmured, as they
went into the room.

HYACINTH knew there was something out of the way as
soon as he saw Lady Aurora's face look forth at him, in
answer to his tap, while she held the door ajar. What was
she doing in Pinnie's bedroom?—a very poor place, into
which the dressmaker, with her reverence, would never have
admitted a person of that quality unless things were pretty
bad. She was solemn, too; she didn't laugh, as usual;
she had removed her large hat, with its limp, old-fashioned
veil, and she raised her finger to her lips. Hyacinth's first
alarm had been immediately after he let himself into the
house, with his latch-key, as he always did, and found the
little room on the right of the passage, in which Pinnie had
lived ever since he remembered, fireless and untenanted.
As soon as he had paid the cabman, who put down his
portmanteau for him in the hall (he was not used to paying
cabmen, and was conscious he gave him too much, but was
too impatient, in his sudden anxiety, to care), he hurried
up the vile staircase, which seemed viler, even through his
preoccupation, than ever, and gave the knock, accompanied
by a call the least bit tremulous, immediately answered by
Lady Aurora. She drew back into the room a moment,
while he stared, in his dismay; then she emerged again,
closing the door behind her—all with the air of enjoining
him to be terribly quiet. He felt, suddenly, so sick at the
idea of having lingered at Medley while there was distress
in the wretched little house to which he owed so much, that
he scarcely found strength for an articulate question, and
obeyed, mechanically, the mute, urgent gesture by which
Lady Aurora appealed to him to go downstairs with her.
It was only when they stood together in the deserted
parlour (it was as if he perceived for the first time what an

inelegant odour prevailed there), that he asked, 'Is she
dying—is she dead?' That was the least the strained
sadness looking out from the face of the noble visitor
appeared to announce.

'Dear Mr. Robinson, I'm so sorry for you. I wanted
to write, but I promised her I wouldn't. She is very ill
—we are very anxious. It began ten days ago, and I suppose I *must* tell you how much she has gone down.'
Lady Aurora spoke with more than all her usual embarrassments and precautions, eagerly, yet as if it cost her
much pain: pausing a little after everything she said,
to see how he would take it; then going on, with a
propitiatory rush. He learned presently what was the
matter, what doctor she had sent for, and that if he
would wait a little before going into the room it would
be so much better; the invalid having sunk, within half
an hour, into a doze of a less agitated kind than she
had had for some time, from which it would be an immense pity to run the risk of waking her. The doctor
gave her the right things, as it seemed to her ladyship,
but he admitted that she had very little power of resistance.
He was of course not a very large practitioner, Mr. Buffery, from round the corner, but he seemed really clever;
and she herself had taken the liberty (as she confessed
to this she threw off one of her odd laughs, and her colour
rose), of sending an elderly, respectable person—a kind of
nurse. She was out just then; she had to go, for an
hour, for the air—'only when I come, of course,' said
Lady Aurora. Dear Miss Pynsent had had a cold hanging about her, and had not taken care of it. Hyacinth
would know how plucky she was about that sort of
thing; she took so little interest in herself. 'Of course
a cold is a cold, whoever has it; isn't it?' said Lady
Aurora. Ten days before, she had taken an additional
chill through falling asleep in her chair, in the evening,
down there, and letting the fire go out. 'It would have
been nothing if she had been like you or me, you know,'
her ladyship went on; 'but just as she was then,
it made the difference. The day was horribly damp,
and it had struck into the lungs, and inflammation

had set in. Mr. Buffery says she was impoverished, just rather low and languid, you know.' The next morning she had bad pains and a good deal of fever, yet she had got up. Poor Pinnie's gracious ministrant did not make clear to Hyacinth what time had elapsed before she came to her relief, nor by what means she had been notified, and he saw that she slurred this over from the admirable motive of wishing him not to feel that the little dressmaker had suffered by his absence or called for him in vain. This, apparently, had indeed not been the case, if Pinnie had opposed, successfully, his being written to. Lady Aurora only said, ' I came in very soon, it was such a delightful chance. Since then she has had everything; only it's sad to see a person *need* so little. She did want you to stay; she has clung to that idea. I speak the simple truth, Mr. Robinson.'

'I don't know what to say to you—you are so extraordinarily good, so angelic,' Hyacinth replied, bewildered and made weak by a strange, unexpected shame. The episode he had just traversed, the splendour he had been living in and drinking so deep of, the unnatural alliance to which he had given himself up while his wretched little foster-mother struggled alone with her death-stroke—he could see it was that; the presentiment of it, the last stiff horror, was in all the place—the contrast seemed to cut him like a knife, and to make the horrible accident of his absence a perversity of his own. 'I can never blame you, when you are so kind, but I wish to God I had known!' he broke out.

Lady Aurora clasped her hands, begging him to judge her fairly. 'Of course it was a great responsibility for us, but we thought it right to consider what she urged upon us. She went back to it constantly, that your visit should *not* be cut short. When you should come of yourself, it would be time enough. I don't know exactly where you have been, but she said it was such a pleasant house. She kept repeating that it would do you so much good.'

Hyacinth felt his eyes filling with tears. 'She's dying—she's dying! How can she live when she's like that?'

He sank upon the old yellow sofa, the sofa of his

lifetime and of so many years before, and buried his head on the shabby, tattered arm. A succession of sobs broke from his lips—sobs in which the accumulated emotion of months and the strange, acute conflict of feeling that had possessed him for the three weeks just past found relief and a kind of solution. Lady Aurora sat down beside him and laid her finger-tips gently on his hand. So, for a minute, while his tears flowed and she said nothing, he felt her timid, consoling touch. At the end of the minute he raised his head; it came back to him that she had said ' we ' just before, and he asked her whom she meant.

'Oh, Mr. Vetch, don't you know? I have made his acquaintance ; it's impossible to be more kind.' Then, while, for an instant, Hyacinth was silent, wincing, pricked with the thought that Pinnie had been beholden to the fiddler while *he* was masquerading in high life, Lady Aurora added, ' He's a charming musician. She asked him once, at first, to bring his violin ; she thought it would soothe her.'

' I'm much obliged to him, but now that I'm here we needn't trouble him,' said Hyacinth.

Apparently there was a certain dryness in his tone, which was the cause of her ladyship's venturing to reply, after an hesitation, ' Do let him come, Mr. Robinson ; let him be near you ! I wonder whether you know that— that he has a great affection for you.'

' The more fool he ; I have always treated him like a brute !' Hyacinth exclaimed, colouring.

The way Lady Aurora spoke proved to him, later, that she now definitely did know his secret, or one of them, rather ; for at the rate things had been going for the last few months he was making a regular collection. She knew the smaller—not, of course, the greater ; she had, decidedly, been illuminated by Pinnie's divagations. At the moment he made that reflection, however, he was almost startled to perceive how completely he had ceased to resent such betrayals and how little it suddenly seemed to signify that the innocent source of them was about to be quenched. The sense of his larger secret swallowed up that particular anxiety, making him ask himself what it mattered, for the

time that was left to him, that people should whisper to
each other his little mystery. The day came quickly when
he believed, and yet didn't care, that it had been univer-
sally imparted.

After Lady Aurora left him, promising she would call
him the first moment it should seem prudent, he walked up
and down the cold, stale parlour, immersed in his meditations. The shock of the danger of losing Pinnie had
already passed away; he had achieved so much, of late, in
the line of accepting the idea of death that the little dressmaker, in taking her departure, seemed already to benefit
by this curious discipline. What was most vivid to him, in
the deserted scene of Pinnie's unsuccessful industry, was the
changed vision with which he had come back to objects
familiar for twenty years. The picture was the same, and
all its horrid elements, wearing a kind of greasy gloss in the
impure air of Lomax Place, made, through the mean win-
dow-panes, a dismal *chiaroscuro*—showed, in their polished
misery, the friction of his own little life; but the eyes with
which he looked at it had new terms of comparison. He
had known the place was hideous and sordid, but its aspect
to-day was pitiful to the verge of the sickening; he couldn't
believe that for years together he had accepted and even, a
little, revered it. He was frightened at the sort of service
that his experience of grandeur had rendered him. It was
all very well to have assimilated that element with a rapidity
which had surprises even for himself; but with sensibilities
now so improved what fresh arrangement could one come
to with the very humble, which was in its nature uncompro-
mising? Though the spring was far advanced the day was
a dark drizzle, and the room had the clamminess of a
finished use, an ooze of dampness from the muddy street,
where the areas were a narrow slit. No wonder Pinnie had
felt it at last, and her small under-fed organism had grown
numb and ceased to act. At the thought of her limited,
stinted life, the patient, humdrum effort of her needle and
scissors, which had ended only in a show-room where
there was nothing to show and a pensive reference to the
cut of sleeves no longer worn, the tears again rose to
his eyes; but he brushed them aside when he heard a

cautious tinkle at the house-door, which was presently
opened by the little besmirched slavey retained for the
service of the solitary lodger — a domestic easily bewildered, who had a squint and distressed Hyacinth by
wearing shoes that didn't match, though they were of an
equal antiquity and resembled each other in the facility
with which they dropped off. Hyacinth had not heard Mr.
Vetch's voice in the hall, apparently because he spoke in
a whisper ; but the young man was not surprised when,
taking every precaution not to make the door creak, he
came into the parlour. The fiddler said nothing to him
at first ; the two men only looked at each other for a
long minute. Hyacinth saw what he most wanted to
know—whether *he* knew the worst about Pinnie ; but what
was further in his eyes (they had an expression considerably
different from any he had hitherto seen in them), defined
itself to our hero only little by little.

'Don't you think you might have written me a word ? '
said Hyacinth, at last. His anger at having been left in
ignorance had quitted him, but he thought the question
fair. None the less, he expected a sarcastic answer, and
was surprised at the mild reasonableness with which Mr.
Vetch replied—

'I assure you, no responsibility, in the course of my
life, ever did more to distress me. There were obvious
reasons for calling you back, and yet I couldn't help wishing you might finish your visit. I balanced one thing
against the other ; it was very difficult.'

'I can imagine nothing more simple. When people's
nearest and dearest are dying, they are usually sent
for.'

The fiddler gave a strange, argumentative smile. If
Lomax Place and Miss Pynsent's select lodging-house wore
a new face of vulgarity to Hyacinth, it may be imagined
whether the renunciation of the niceties of the toilet, the
resigned seediness, which marked Mr. Vetch's old age was
unlikely to lend itself to comparison. The glossy butler at
Medley had had a hundred more of the signs of success
in life. 'My dear boy, this case was exceptional,' said
the old man. 'Your visit had a character of importance.'

' I don't know what you know about it. I don't remember that I told you anything.'

' No, certainly, you have never told me much. But if, as is probable, you have seen that kind lady who is now upstairs, you will have learned that Pinnie made a tremendous point of your not being disturbed. She threatened us with her displeasure if we should hurry you back. You know what Pinnie's displeasure is ! ' As, at this, Hyacinth turned away with a gesture of irritation, Mr. Vetch went on, ' No doubt she is absurdly fanciful, poor dear thing ; but don't, now, cast any disrespect upon it. I assure you, if she had been here alone, suffering, sinking, without a creature to tend her, and nothing before her but to die in a corner, like a starved cat, she would still have faced that fate rather than cut short by a single hour your experience of novel scenes.'

Hyacinth was silent for a moment. ' Of course I know what you mean. But she spun her delusion—she always did, all of them—out of nothing. I can't imagine what she knows about my "experience" of any kind of scenes. I told her, when I went out of town, very little more than I told you.'

' What she guessed, what she gathered, has been, at any rate, enough. She has made up her mind that you have formed a connection by means of which you will come, somehow or other, into your own. She has done nothing but talk about your grand kindred. To her mind, you know, it's all one, the aristocracy, and nothing is simpler than that the person—very exalted, as she believes—with whom you have been to stay should undertake your business with her friends.'

' Oh, well,' said Hyacinth, ' I'm very glad not to have deprived you of that entertainment.'

' I assure you the spectacle was exquisite.' Then the fiddler added, ' My dear fellow, please leave her the idea.'

' Leave it ? I'll do much more ! ' Hyacinth exclaimed. ' I'll tell her my great relations have adopted me and that I have come back in the character of Lord Robinson.'

' She will need nothing more to die happy,' Mr. Vetch observed.

Five minutes later, after Hyacinth had obtained from his old friend a confirmation of Lady Aurora's account of Miss Pynsent's condition, Mr. Vetch explaining that he came over, like that, to see how she was, half a dozen times a day—five minutes later a silence had descended upon the pair, while Hyacinth waited for some sign from Lady Aurora that he might come upstairs. The fiddler, who had lighted a pipe, looked out of the window, studying intently the physiognomy of Lomax Place ; and Hyacinth, making his tread discreet, walked about the room with his hands in his pockets. At last Mr. Vetch observed, without taking his pipe out of his lips or looking round, ' I think you might be a little more frank with me at this time of day and at such a crisis.'

Hyacinth stopped in his walk, wondering for a moment, sincerely, what his companion meant, for he had no consciousness at present of an effort to conceal anything he could possibly tell (there were some things, of course, he couldn't) ; on the contrary, his life seemed to him particularly open to the public view and exposed to invidious comment. It was at this moment he first observed a certain difference ; there was a tone in Mr. Vetch's voice that he had never perceived before—an absence of that note which had made him say, in other days, that the impenetrable old man was diverting himself at his expense. It was as if his attitude had changed, become more explicitly considerate, in consequence of some alteration or promotion on Hyacinth's part, his having grown older, or more important, or even simply more surpassingly curious. If the first impression made upon him by Pinnie's old neighbour, as to whose place in the list of the sacrificial (his being a gentleman or one of the sovereign people) he formerly was so perplexed ; if the sentiment excited by Mr. Vetch in a mind familiar now for nearly a month with forms of indubitable gentility was not favourable to the idea of fraternisation, this secret impatience on Hyacinth's part was speedily corrected by one of the sudden reactions or quick conversions of which the young man was so often the victim. In the light of the fiddler's appeal, which evidently meant more than it said, his musty antiquity, his

typical look of having had, for years, a small, definite use
and taken all the creases and contractions of it, his visible
expression, even, of ultimate parsimony and of having
ceased to care for the shape of his trousers because he
cared more for something else—these things became so
many reasons for turning round, going over to him, touching signs of an invincible fidelity, the humble, continuous,
single-minded practice of daily duties and an art after all
very charming; pursued, moreover, while persons of the
species our restored prodigal had lately been consorting
with fidgeted from one selfish sensation to another and
couldn't even live in the same place for three months
together.

'What should you like me to do, to say, to tell you?
Do you want to know what I have been doing in the
country?   I should have first to know, myself,' Hyacinth
said.

'Have you enjoyed it very much?'

'Yes, certainly, very much—not knowing anything
about Pinnie.   I have been in a beautiful house, with a
beautiful woman.'

Mr. Vetch had turned round; he looked very impartial,
through the smoke of his pipe.

'Is she really a princess?'

'I don't know what you mean by "really."   I suppose
all titles are great rot.   But every one seems agreed to call
her so.'

'You know I have always liked to enter into your life;
and to-day the wish is stronger than ever,' the old man observed, presently, fixing his eyes very steadily on Hyacinth's.

The latter returned his gaze for a moment; then he
asked, 'What makes you say that just now?'

The fiddler appeared to deliberate, and at last he replied,
'Because you are in danger of losing the best friend you
have ever had.'

'Be sure I feel it.   But if I have got you——' Hyacinth added.

'Oh, me!   I'm very old, and very tired of life.'

'I suppose that that's what one arrives at.   Well, if I

can help you in any way you must lean on me, you must
make use of me.'

'That's precisely what I was going to say to you,' said
Mr. Vetch.   'Should you like any money?'

'Of course I should!   But why should you offer it to
me?'

'Because in saving it up, little by little, I have had you
in mind.'

'Dear Mr. Vetch,' said Hyacinth, 'you have me too
much in mind.   I'm not worth it, please believe that; for
all sorts of reasons.   I should make money enough for any
uses I have for it, or have any right to have, if I stayed
quietly in London and attended to my work.   As you
know, I can earn a decent living.'

'Yes, I can see that.   But if you stayed quietly in
London what would become of your princess?'

'Oh, they can always manage, ladies in that position.'

'Hanged if I understand her position!' cried Mr.
Vetch, but without laughing.   'You have been for three
weeks without work, and yet you look uncommonly smart.'

'You see, my living has cost me nothing.   When you
stay with great people you don't pay your score,' Hyacinth
explained, with great gentleness.   'Moreover, the lady
whose hospitality I have been enjoying has made me a very
handsome offer of work.'

What kind of work?'

'The only kind I know.   She is going to send me a
lot of books, to do up for her.'

'And to pay you fancy prices?'

'Oh, no ; I am to fix the prices myself.'

'Are not transactions of that kind rather disagreeable,
with a lady whose hospitality one has been enjoying?'
Mr. Vetch inquired.

'Exceedingly!   That is exactly why I shall do the
books and then take no money.'

'Your princess is rather clever!' the fiddler exclaimed,
in a moment, smiling.

'Well, she can't force me to take it if I won't,' said
Hyacinth.

'No ; you must only let *me* do that.'

'You have curious ideas about me,' the young man declared.

Mr. Vetch turned about to the window again, remarking that he had curious ideas about everything. Then he added, after an interval—

'And have you been making love to your great lady?'

He had expected a flash of impatience in reply to this inquiry, and was rather surprised at the manner in which Hyacinth answered: 'How shall I explain? It is not a question of that sort.'

'Has she been making love to you, then?'

'If you should ever see her you would understand how absurd that supposition is.'

'How shall I ever see her?' returned Mr. Vetch. 'In the absence of that privilege I think there is something in my idea.'

'She looks quite over my head,' said Hyacinth, simply. 'It's by no means impossible you may see her. She wants to know my friends, to know the people who live in the Place. And she would take a particular interest in you, on account of your opinions.'

'Ah, I have no opinions now, none any more!' the old man broke out, sadly. 'I only had them to frighten Pinnie.'

'She was easily frightened,' said Hyacinth.

'Yes, and easily reassured. Well, I like to know about your life,' his neighbour sighed, irrelevantly. 'But take care the great lady doesn't lead you too far.'

'How do you mean, too far?'

'Isn't she an anarchist—a nihilist? Doesn't she go in for a general rectification, as Eustace calls it?'

Hyacinth was silent a moment. 'You should see the place—you should see what she wears, what she eats and drinks.'

'Ah, you mean that she is inconsistent with her theories? My dear boy, she would be a droll woman if she were not. At any rate, I'm glad of it.'

'Glad of it?' Hyacinth repeated.

'For you, I mean, when you stay with her; it's more luxurious!' Mr. Vetch exclaimed, turning round and smil-

ing.   At this moment a little rap on the floor above, given
by Lady Aurora, announced that Hyacinth might at last
come up and see Pinnie.   Mr. Vetch listened and recognised it, and it led him to say, with considerable force,
' *There's* a woman whose theories and conduct do square !'

Hyacinth, on the threshold, leaving the room, stopped
long enough to reply, ' Well, when the day comes for my
friend to give up—you'll see.'

' Yes, I have no doubt there are things she will bring
herself to sacrifice,' the old man remarked ; but Hyacinth
was already out of hearing.

MR. VETCH waited below till Lady Aurora should come down and give him the news he was in suspense for. His mind was pretty well made up about Pinnie. It had seemed to him, the night before, that death was written in her face, and he judged it on the whole a very good moment for her to lay down her earthly burden. He had reasons for believing that the future could not be sweet to her. As regards Hyacinth, his mind was far from being at ease; for though he was aware in a general way that he had taken up with strange company, and though he had flattered himself of old that he should be pleased to see the boy act out his life and solve the problem of his queer inheritance, he was worried by the absence of full knowledge. He put out his pipe, in anticipation of Lady Aurora's reappearance, and without this consoler he was more accessible still to certain fears that had come to him in consequence of a recent talk, or rather an attempt at a talk, with Eustache Poupin. It was through the Frenchman that he had gathered the little he knew about the occasion of Hyacinth's unprecedented excursion. His ideas on the subject had been very infer-ential; for Hyacinth had made a mystery of his absence to Pinnie, merely letting her know that there was a lady in the case and that the best luggage he could muster and the best way his shirts could be done up would still not be good enough. Poupin had seen Godfrey Sholto at the 'Sun and Moon,' and it had come to him, through Hyacinth, that there was a remarkable feminine influence in the Captain's life, mixed up in some way with his presence in Bloomsbury —an influence, moreover, by which Hyacinth himself, for good or for evil, was in peril of being touched. Sholto was the young man's visible link with a society for which Lisson

Grove could have no importance in the scheme of the
universe but as a short cut (too disagreeable to be frequently
used) out of Bayswater; therefore if Hyacinth left town
with a new hat and a pair of kid gloves it must have been
to move in the direction of that superior circle and in some
degree, at least, at the solicitation of the before-mentioned
feminine influence. So much as this the Frenchman suggested, explicitly enough, as his manner was, to the old
fiddler; but his talk had a flavour of other references which
excited Mr. Vetch's curiosity much more than they satisfied
it. They were obscure; they evidently were painful to the
speaker; they were confused and embarrassed and totally
wanting in the luminosity which usually characterised the
lightest allusions of M. Poupin. It was the fiddler's fancy
that his friend had something on his mind which he was not
at liberty to impart, and that it related to Hyacinth and
might, for those who took an interest in the singular lad,
constitute a considerable anxiety. Mr. Vetch, on his own
part, nursed this anxiety into a tolerably definite shape: he
persuaded himself that the Frenchman had been leading
the boy too far in the line of social criticism, had given him
a push on some crooked path where a slip would be a likely
accident. When on a subsequent occasion, with Poupin,
he indulged in a hint of this suspicion, the bookbinder
flushed a good deal and declared that his conscience was
pure. It was one of his peculiarities that when his colour
rose he looked angry, and Mr. Vetch held that his displeasure was a proof that in spite of his repudiations he
had been unwise; though before they parted Eustache gave
this sign of softness, that he shed tears of emotion, of which
the reason was not clear to the fiddler and which appeared
in a general way to be dedicated to Hyacinth. The interview had taken place in Lisson Grove, where Madame
Poupin, however, had not shown herself.

Altogether the old man was a prey to suppositions which
led him to feel how much he himself had outlived the
democratic glow of his prime. He had ended by accepting
everything (though, indeed, he couldn't swallow the idea
that a trick should be played upon Hyacinth), and even by
taking an interest in current politics, as to which, of old, he

had held the opinion (the same that the Poupins held to-day),
that they had been invented on purpose to throw dust in
the eyes of disinterested reformers and to circumvent the
social solution. He had given up that problem some time
ago ; there was no way to clear it up that didn't seem to
make a bigger mess than the actual muddle of human
affairs, which, by the time one had reached sixty-five, had
mostly ceased to exasperate. Mr. Vetch could still feel a
certain sharpness on the subject of the prayer-book and the
bishops ; and if at moments he was a little ashamed of
having accepted this world he could reflect that at all events
he continued to repudiate every other. The idea of great
changes, however, took its place among the dreams of his
youth ; for what was any possible change in the relations of
men and women but a new combination of the same
elements ? If the elements could be made different the
thing would be worth thinking of; but it was not only
impossible to introduce any new ones—no means had yet
been discovered for getting rid of the old. The figures on
the chessboard were still the passions and jealousies and
superstitions and stupidities of man, and their position with
regard to each other, at any given moment, could be of
interest only to the grim, invisible fates who played the
game—who sat, through the ages, bow-backed over the
table. This laxity had come upon the old man with the
increase of his measurement round the waist, of the little
heap of half-crowns and half-sovereigns that had accumulated
in a tin box with a very stiff padlock, which he kept under
his bed, and of the interwoven threads of sentiment and
custom that united him to the dressmaker and her foster-
son. If he was no longer pressing about the demands he
felt he should have a right to make of society, as he had
been in the days when his conversation scandalised Pinnie,
so he was now not pressing for Hyacinth, either ; reflecting
that though, indeed, the constituted powers might have to
' count ' with him, it would be in better taste for him not to
be importunate about a settlement. What he had come to
fear for him was that he should be precipitated by crude
agencies, with results in which the deplorable might not
exclude the ridiculous. It may even be said that Mr.

Vetch had a secret project of settling a little on his behalf.

Lady Aurora peeped into the room, very noiselessly, nearly half an hour after Hyacinth had left it, and let the fiddler know that she was called to other duties but that the nurse had come back and the doctor had promised to look in at five o'clock. She herself would return in the evening, and meanwhile Hyacinth was with his aunt, who had recognised him, without a protest; indeed seemed intensely happy that he should be near her again, and lay there with closed eyes, very weak and speechless, with his hand in hers. Her restlessness had passed and her fever abated, but she had no pulse to speak of and Lady Aurora did not disguise the fact that, in her opinion, she was rapidly sinking. Mr. Vetch had already accepted it, and after her ladyship had quitted him he lighted another philosophic pipe upon it, lingering on, till the doctor came, in the dressmaker's dismal, forsaken bower, where, in past years, he had indulged in so many sociable droppings-in and hot tumblers. The echo of all her little simple surprises and pointless contradictions, her gasping reception of contemplative paradox, seemed still to float in the air; but the place felt as relinquished and bereaved as if she were already beneath the sod. Pinnie had always been a wonderful hand at 'putting away'; the litter that testified to her most elaborate efforts was often immense, but the reaction in favour of an unspeckled carpet was greater still; and on the present occasion, before taking to her bed, she had found strength to sweep and set in order as daintily as if she had been sure that the room would never again know her care. Even to the old fiddler, who had not Hyacinth's sensibility to the scenery of life, it had the cold propriety of a place arranged for an interment. After the doctor had seen Pinnie, that afternoon, there was no doubt left as to its soon being the stage of dismal preliminaries.

Miss Pynsent, however, resisted her malady for nearly a fortnight more, during which Hyacinth was constantly in her room. He never went back to Mr. Crookenden's, with whose establishment, through violent causes, his relations seemed indefinitely suspended; and in fact, for the rest of

the time that Pinnie demanded his care he absented himself
but twice from Lomax Place for more than a few minutes.
On one of these occasions he travelled over to Audley Court
and spent an hour there ; on the other he met Millicent
Henning, by appointment, and took a walk with her on the
Embankment.   He tried to find a moment to go and thank
Madame Poupin for a sympathetic offering, many times
repeated, of *tisane*, concocted after a receipt thought supreme
by the couple in Lisson Grove (though little appreciated in
the neighbourhood generally) ; but he was obliged to acknowledge her kindness only by a respectful letter, which he
composed with some trouble, though much elation, in the
French tongue, peculiarly favourable, as he believed, to
little courtesies of this kind.   Lady Aurora came again and
again to the darkened house, where she diffused her beneficent
influence in nightly watches, in the most modern sanative suggestions, in conversations with Hyacinth, directed with more
ingenuity than her fluttered embarrassments might have led
one to attribute to her, to the purpose of diverting his mind,
and in tea-makings (there was a great deal of this liquid consumed on the premises during Pinnie's illness), after a
system more enlightened than the usual fashion of Pentonville.   She was the bearer of several messages and of a good
deal of medical advice from Rose Muniment, whose interest
in the dressmaker's case irritated Hyacinth by its fine
courage, which even at second-hand was still obtrusive ;
she appeared very nearly as resigned to the troubles of
others as she was to her own.

Hyacinth had been seized, the day after his return from
Medley, with a sharp desire to do something enterprising
and superior on Pinnie's behalf.   He felt the pressure of a
sort of angry sense that she was dying of her poor career,
of her uneffaced remorse for the trick she had played him
in his boyhood (as if he hadn't long ago, and indeed at the
time, forgiven it, judging it to have been the highest
wisdom !) of something basely helpless in the attitude of
her little circle.   He wanted to do something which should
prove to himself that he had got the best opinion about
the invalid that it was possible to have : so he insisted that
Mr. Buffery should consult with a West End doctor, if the

West End doctor would consent to meet Mr. Buffery. A physician capable of this condescension was discovered through Lady Aurora's agency (she had not brought him of her own movement, because on the one hand she hesitated to impose on the little household in Lomax Place the expense of such a visit, and on the other, with all her narrow personal economies for the sake of her charities, had not the means to meet it herself); and in prevision of the great man's fee Hyacinth applied to Mr. Vetch, as he had applied before, for a loan. The great man came, and was wonderfully civil to Mr. Buffery, whose conduct of the case he pronounced judicious; he remained several minutes in the house, while he gazed at Hyacinth over his spectacles (he seemed rather more occupied with him than with the patient), and almost the whole of the Place turned out to stare at his chariot. After all, he consented to accept no fee. He put the question aside with a gesture full of urbanity—a course disappointing and displeasing to Hyacinth, who felt in a manner cheated of the full effect of the fine thing he had wished to do for Pinnie; though when he said as much (or something like it) to Mr. Vetch, the caustic fiddler greeted the observation with a face of amusement which, considering the situation, verged upon the unseemly

Hyacinth, at any rate, had done the best he could, and the fashionable doctor had left directions which foreshadowed relations with an expensive chemist in Bond Street—a prospect by which our young man was to some extent consoled. Poor Pinnie's decline, however, was not arrested, and one evening, more than a week after his return from Medley, as he sat with her alone, it seemed to Hyacinth that her spirit must already have passed away. The nurse had gone down to her supper, and from the staircase a perceptible odour of fizzling bacon indicated that a more cheerful state of things prevailed in the lower regions. Hyacinth could not make out whether Miss Pynsent were asleep or awake; he believed she had not lost consciousness, yet for more than an hour she had given no sign of life. At last she put out her hand, as if she knew he was near her and wished to feel for his, and murmured, 'Why did she come? I didn't want to see her.' In a moment, as she went on, he perceived to whom she was alluding: her mind had travelled back, through all the years, to the dreadful day (she had described every incident of it to him), when Mrs. Bowerbank had invaded her quiet life and startled her sensitive conscience with a message from the prison. 'She sat there so long—so long. She was very large, and I was frightened. She moaned, and moaned, and cried—too dreadful. I couldn't help it—I couldn't help it!' Her thought wandered from Mrs. Bowerbank in the discomposed show-room, enthroned on the yellow sofa, to the tragic creature at Milbank, whose accents again, for the hour, lived in her ears; and mixed with this mingled vision was still the haunting sense that she herself might have acted differently. That had been cleared up in the past, so far as Hyacinth's intention was concerned; but what was most alive in Pinnie at the present moment was the passion of repentance, of still further expiation. It sickened Hyacinth that she should believe these things were still necessary, and he leaned over her and talked tenderly, with words of comfort and reassurance. He told her not to think of that dismal, far-off time, which had ceased long ago to have any consequences for either of them; to consider only the future, when she should be quite strong again and he would look after her and keep her all to himself and take care of her better, far better, than he had ever done before. He had thought of many things while he sat with Pinnie, watching the shadows made by the night-lamp—high, imposing shadows of objects low and mean—and among them he had followed, with an imagination that went further in that direction than ever before, the probable consequences of his not having been adopted in his babyhood by the dressmaker. The work-house and the gutter, ignorance and cold, filth and tatters, nights of huddling under bridges and in doorways, vermin, starvation and blows, possibly even the vigorous efflorescence of an inherited disposition to crime—these things, which he saw with unprecedented vividness, suggested themselves as his natural portion. Intimacies with a princess, visits to fine old country-houses, intelligent consideration, even, of the best means of inflicting a scare on the classes of privilege, would in that case not have been within his compass; and that Pinnie should have rescued him from such a destiny and put these luxuries within his reach was an amelioration which really amounted to success, if he could only have the magnanimity to regard it so.

Her eyes were open and fixed on him, but the sharp ray the little dressmaker used to direct into Lomax Place as she plied her needle at the window had completely left them. 'Not there—what should I do there?' she inquired, very softly. 'Not with the great—the great——' and her voice failed.

'The great what? What do you mean?'

'You know—you know,' she went on, making another effort. 'Haven't you been with them? Haven't they received you?'

'Ah, they won't separate us, Pinnie; they won't come between us as much as that,' said Hyacinth, kneeling by her bed.

'*You* must be separate—that makes me happier. I knew they would find you at last.'

'Poor Pinnie, poor Pinnie,' murmured the young man.

'It was only for that—now I'm going,' she went on.

'If you'll stay with me you needn't fear,' said Hyacinth, smiling at her.

'Oh, what would *they* think?' asked the dressmaker.

'I like you best,' said Hyacinth.

'You have had me always. Now it's their turn; they have waited.'

'Yes, indeed, they have waited!' Hyacinth exclaimed.

'But they will make it up; they will make up everything!' the invalid panted. Then she added, 'I couldn't —couldn't help it!'—which was the last flicker of her strength. She gave no further sign of consciousness, and four days later she ceased to breathe. Hyacinth was with her, and Lady Aurora, but neither of them could recognise the moment.

Hyacinth and Mr. Vetch carried her bier, with the help of Eustache Poupin and Paul Muniment. Lady Aurora was at the funeral, and Madame Poupin as well, and twenty neighbours from Lomax Place ; but the most distinguished person (in appearance at least) in the group of mourners was Millicent Henning, the grave yet brilliant beauty of whose countenance, the high propriety of whose demeanour, and the fine taste and general style of whose black 'costume' excited no little attention. Mr. Vetch had his idea ; he had been nursing it ever since Hyacinth's return from Medley, and three days after Pinnie had been consigned to the earth he broached it to his young friend. The funeral had been on a Friday, and Hyacinth had mentioned to him that he should return to Mr. Crookenden's on the Monday morning. This was Sunday night, and Hyacinth had been out for a walk, neither with Millicent Henning nor with Paul Muniment, but alone, after the manner of old days. When he came in he found the fiddler waiting for him, and burning a tallow candle, in the blighted show-room. He had three or four little papers in his hand, which exhibited some jottings of his pencil, and Hyacinth guessed, what was the truth but not all the truth, that he had come to speak to him about business. Pinnie had left a little will, of which she had appointed her old friend executor ; this fact had already become known to our hero, who thought such an arrangement highly natural. Mr. Vetch informed him of the purport of this simple and judicious document, and mentioned that he had been looking into the dress-maker's 'affairs.' They consisted, poor Pinnie's affairs, of the furniture of the house in Lomax Place, of the obliga-tion to pay the remainder of a quarter's rent, and of a sum of money in the savings-bank. Hyacinth was surprised to learn that Pinnie's economies had produced fruit at this late day (things had gone so ill with her in recent years, and there had been often such a want of money in the house), until Mr. Vetch explained to him, with eager clearness, that he himself had watched over the little hoard, accumulated during the period of her comparative prosperity, with the stiff determination that it should be sacrificed only in case of desperate necessity. Work had become scarce with Pinnie, but she could still do it when it came, and the money was to be kept for the very possible period when she should be helpless. Mercifully enough, she had not lived to see that day, and the sum in the bank had survived her, though diminished by more than half. She had left no debts but the matter of the house and those incurred during her illness. Of course the fiddler had known—he hastened to give his young friend this assurance—that Pinnie, had she become infirm, would have been able to count absolutely upon *him* for the equivalent, in her old age, of the protection she had given him in his youth. But what if an accident had overtaken Hyacinth ? What if he had incurred some nasty penalty for his revolutionary dabblings, which, little dangerous as they might be to society, were quite capable, in a country where authority, though good-natured, liked occasionally to make an example, to put him on the wrong side of a prison-wall ? At any rate, for better or worse, by pinching and scraping, she had saved a little, and of that little, after everything was paid off, a fraction would still be left. Everything was bequeathed to Hyacinth—everything but a couple of plated candlesticks and the old 'cheffonier,' which had been so handsome in its day; these Pinnie begged Mr. Vetch to accept in recognition of services beyond all price. The furniture, everything he didn't want for his own use, Hyacinth could sell in a lump, and with the proceeds he could wipe out old scores. The sum of money would remain to him ; it amounted, in its reduced condition, to about thirty-seven pounds. In mentioning this figure Mr. Vetch appeared to imply that Hyacinth would be master of a very pretty little fortune. Even to the young man himself, in spite of his recent initiations, it seemed far from contemptible ; it represented sudden possibilities of still not returning to old Crookenden's. It represented them, that is, till, presently, he remembered the various advances made him by the fiddler, and reflected that by the time these had been repaid there would hardly be twenty pounds left. That, however, was a far larger sum than he had ever had in his pocket at once. He thanked the old man for his information, and remarked—and there was no hypocrisy in the speech—that he was very sorry Pinnie had not given herself the benefit of the whole of the little fund in her lifetime. To this her executor replied that it had yielded

her an interest far beyond any other investment; for he
was persuaded she believed she should never live to enjoy
it, and this faith was rich in pictures, visions of the effect
such a windfall would produce in Hyacinth's career.

'What effect did she mean—do you mean?' Hyacinth
inquired. As soon as he had spoken he felt that he knew
what the old man would say (it would be a reference to
Pinnie's belief in his reunion with his ' relations,' and the
facilities that thirty-seven pounds would afford him for
cutting a figure among them); and for a moment Mr. Vetch
looked at him as if exactly that response were on his lips.
At the end of the moment, however, he replied, quite
differently—

'She hoped you would go abroad and see the world.'
The fiddler watched his young friend; then he added,
' She had a particular wish that you should go to Paris.'

Hyacinth had turned pale at this suggestion, and for a
moment he said nothing. ' Ah, Paris!' he murmured, at
last.

'She would have liked you even to take a little run
down to Italy.'

' Doubtless that would be pleasant. But there is a limit
to what one can do with twenty pounds.'

' How do you mean, with twenty pounds?' the old man
asked, lifting his eyebrows, while the wrinkles in his forehead made deep shadows in the candle-light.

'That's about what will remain, after I have settled my
account with you.'

' How do you mean, your account with me? I shall
not take any of your money.'

Hyacinth's eyes wandered over his interlocutor's suggestive rustiness. ' I don't want to be ungracious, but
suppose *you* should lose your powers.'

' My dear boy, I shall have one of the resources that
was open to Pinnie. I shall look to you to be the support
of my old age.'

'You may do so with perfect safety, except for that
danger you just mentioned, of my being imprisoned or
hanged.'

' It's precisely because I think it will be less if you go

abroad that I urge you to take this chance. You will see
the world, and you will like it better. You will think
society, even as it is, has some good points,' said Mr.
Vetch.

'I have never liked it better than the last few months.'

'Ah well, wait till you see Paris !'

'Oh, Paris—Paris,' Hyacinth repeated, vaguely, staring
into the turbid flame of the candle as if he made out the
most brilliant scenes there ; an attitude, accent and expression which the fiddler interpreted both as the vibration of
a latent hereditary chord and a symptom of the acute sense
of opportunity.

BOOK FOURTH

THE boulevard was all alive, brilliant with illuminations, with the variety and gaiety of the crowd, the dazzle of shops and cafés seen through uncovered fronts or immense lucid plates, the flamboyant porches of theatres and the flashing lamps of carriages, the far-spreading murmur of talkers and strollers, the uproar of pleasure and prosperity, the general magnificence of Paris on a perfect evening in June. Hyacinth had been walking about all day—he had walked from rising till bed-time every day of the week that had elapsed since his arrival—and now an extraordinary fatigue, which, however, was not without its delight (there was a kind of richness, a sweet satiety, in it), a tremendous lassitude had fallen upon him, and he settled himself in a chair beside a little table in front of Tortoni's, not so much to rest from it as to enjoy it. He had seen so much, felt so much, learned so much, thrilled and throbbed and laughed and sighed so much, during the past several days, that he was conscious at last of the danger of becoming incoherent to himself, of the need of balancing his accounts.

To-night he came to a full stop; he simply sat at the door of the most dandified café in Paris and felt his pulse and took stock of his impressions. He had been intending to visit the Variétés theatre, which blazed through intermediate lights and through the thin foliage of trees not favoured by the asphalt, on the other side of the great avenue. But the impression of Chaumont—he relinquished that, for the present; it added to the luxury of his situation to reflect that he should still have plenty of time to see the *succès du jour*. The same effect proceeded from his determination to order a *marquise*, when the waiter, whose

superior shirt-front and whisker emerged from the long
white cylinder of an apron, came to take his commands.
He knew the decoction was expensive—he had learnt as
much at the moment he happened to overhear, for the first
time, a mention of it; which had been the night before, in
his place in a stall, during an *entr'acte*, at the Comédie
Française. A gentleman beside him, a young man in
evening-dress, conversing with an acquaintance in the row
behind, recommended the latter to refresh himself with the
article in question after the play: there was nothing like it,
the speaker remarked, of a hot evening, in the open air,
when one was thirsty. The waiter brought Hyacinth a tall
glass of champagne, in which a pine-apple ice was in solution, and our hero felt that he had hoped for a sensation
no less delicate when he looked for an empty table on
Tortoni's terrace. Very few tables were empty, and it was
his belief that the others were occupied by high celebrities;
at any rate they were just the types he had had a prevision
of and had wanted most to meet, when the extraordinary
opportunity to come abroad with his pocket full of money
(it was more extraordinary, even, than his original meeting
with the Princess), became real to him in Lomax Place.
He knew about Tortoni's from his study of the French
novel, and as he sat there he had a vague sense of fraternising with Balzac and Alfred de Musset; there were
echoes and reminiscences of their works in the air, con-
founding themselves with the indefinable exhalations, the
strange composite odour, half agreeable, half impure, of
the boulevard. 'Splendid Paris, charming Paris'—that
refrain, the fragment of an invocation, a beginning without
an end, hummed itself perpetually in Hyacinth's ears; the
only articulate words that got themselves uttered in the
hymn of praise which his imagination had been offering
to the French capital from the first hour of his stay. He
recognised, he greeted, with a thousand palpitations, the
seat of his maternal ancestors—was proud to be associated with so much of the superb, so many proofs of a
civilisation that had no visible rough spots. He had his
perplexities, and he had even now and then a revulsion
for which he had made no allowance, as when it came

over him that the most brilliant city in the world was also the most blood-stained ; but the great sense that he understood and sympathised was preponderant, and his comprehension gave him wings—appeared to transport him to still wider fields of knowledge, still higher sensations.

In other days, in London, he had thought again and again of his mother's father, the revolutionary watch-maker who had known the ecstasy of the barricade and had paid for it with his life, and his reveries had not been sensibly chilled by the fact that he knew next to nothing about him. He figured him in his mind, had a conviction that he was very short, like himself, and had curly hair, an immense talent for his work and an extraordinary natural eloquence, together with many of the most attractive qualities of the French character. But he was reckless, and a little cracked, and probably immoral ; he had difficulties and debts and irrepressible passions ; his life had been an incurable fever and its tragic termination was a matter of course. None the less it would have been a charm to hear him talk, to feel the influence of a gaiety which even political madness could never quench ; for his grandson had a theory that he spoke the French tongue of an earlier time, delightful and sociable in accent and phrase, exempt from the commonness of modern slang. This vague yet vivid personage became Hyacinth's constant companion, from the day of his arrival ; he roamed about with Florentine's boy, hand in hand, sat opposite to him at dinner, at the small table in the restaurant, finished the bottle with him, made the bill a little longer, and treated him to innumerable revelations and counsels. He knew the lad's secret without being told, and looked at him across the diminutive tablecloth, where the great tube of bread, pushed aside a little, left room for his elbows (it puzzled Hyacinth that the people of Paris should ever have had the fierceness of hunger when the loaves were so big), gazed at him with eyes of deep, kind, glowing comprehension and with lips which seemed to murmur that when one was to die to-morrow one was wise to eat and drink to-day. There was nothing venerable, no constraint of importance or disapproval, in this edifying and impalpable presence ; the young man

considered that Hyacinthe Vivier was of his own time of
life and could enter into his pleasures as well as his pains.
Wondering, repeatedly, where the barricade on which his
grandfather fell had been erected, he at last satisfied himself (but I am unable to trace the process of the induction)
that it had bristled across the Rue Saint-Honoré, very near
to the church of Saint-Roch. The pair had now roamed
together through all the museums and gardens, through the
principal churches (the republican martyr was very good-
natured about this), through the passages and arcades, up
and down the great avenues, across all the bridges, and
above all, again and again, along the river, where the
quays were an endless entertainment to Hyacinth, who
lingered by the half-hour beside the boxes of old books on
the parapets, stuffing his pockets with five-penny volumes,
while the bright industries of the Seine flashed and glittered
beneath him, and on the other bank the glorious Louvre
stretched either way for a league. Our young man took
almost the same sort of satisfaction in the Louvre as if he
had erected it ; he haunted the muséum during all the first
days, couldn't look enough at certain pictures, nor sufficiently
admire the high polish of the great floors in which the
golden, frescoed ceilings repeated themselves. All Paris
struck him as tremendously artistic and decorative ; he felt
as if hitherto he had lived in a dusky, frowsy, Philistine
world, in which the taste was the taste of Little Peddlington
and the idea of beautiful arrangement had never had an
influence. In his ancestral city it had been active from the
first, and that was why his quick sensibility responded ; and
he murmured again his constant refrain, when the fairness
of the great monuments arrested him, in the pearly, silvery
light, or he saw them take gray-blue, delicate tones at the
end of stately vistas. It seemed to him that Paris expressed
herself, and did it in the grand style, while London remained
vague and blurred, inarticulate, blunt and dim.

Eustache Poupin had given him letters to three or four
democratic friends, ardent votaries of the social question,
who had by a miracle either escaped the cruelty of exile or
suffered the outrage of pardon, and, in spite of republican
mouchards, no less infamous than the imperial, and the

periodical swoops of a despotism which had only changed
its buttons and postage-stamps, kept alive the sacred spark
which would some day become a consuming flame.
Hyacinth, however, had not had the thought of delivering
these introductions ; he had accepted them because Poupin
had had such a solemn glee in writing them, and also
because he had not the courage to let the couple in Lisson
Grove know that since that terrible night at Hoffendahl's a
change had come over the spirit of his dream. He had
not grown more concentrated, he had grown more relaxed,
and it was inconsistent with relaxation that he should
rummage out Poupin's friends—one of whom lived in the
Batignolles and the others in the Faubourg Saint-Antoine—
and pretend that he cared for what they cared for in the
same way as they cared for it. What was supreme in his
mind to-day was not the idea of how the society that surrounded him should be destroyed ; it was, much more, the
sense of the wonderful, precious things it had produced, of
the brilliant, impressive fabric it had raised. That destruction was waiting for it there was forcible evidence, known
to himself and others, to show; but since this truth had
risen before him, in its magnitude he had become conscious
of a transfer, partial if not complete, of his sympathies ; the
same revulsion of which he had given a sign to the Princess
in saying that now he pitied the rich, those who were
regarded as happy. While the evening passed, therefore,
as he kept his place at Tortoni's, the emotion that was last
to visit him was a compunction for not having put himself
in relation to poor Poupin's friends, for having neglected
to make the acquaintance of earnest people.

Who in the world, if one should come to that, was as
earnest as he himself, or had given such signal even though
secret proofs of it ? He could lay that unction to his soul
in spite of his having amused himself cynically, spent all his
time in theatres, galleries, walks of pleasure. The feeling
had not failed him with which he accepted Mr. Vetch's
furtherance—the sense that since he was destined to perish
in his flower he was right to make a dash at the beautiful,
horrible world. That reflection had been natural enough,
but what was strange was the fiddler's own impulse, his

desire to do something pleasant for him, to beguile him and ship him off. What had been most odd in that was the way Mr. Vetch appeared to overlook the fact that his young friend had already had, that year, such an episode of dissipation as was surely rare in the experience of London artisans. This was one of the many things Hyacinth thought of; he thought of the others in turn and out of turn; it was almost the first time he had sat still long enough (except at the theatre), to collect himself. A hundred confused reverberations of the recent past crowded upon him, and he saw that he had lived more intensely in the previous six months than in all the rest of his existence. The succession of events finally straightened itself, and he tasted some of the rarest, strangest moments over again. His last week at Medley, in especial, had already become a kind of fable, the echo of a song; he could read it over like a story, gaze at it as he would have gazed at some exquisite picture. His visit there had been perfect to the end, and even the three days that Captain Sholto's sojourn lasted had not broken the spell, for the three more that had elapsed before his own departure (the Princess herself had given him the signal), were the most important of all. It was then the Princess had made it clear to him that she was in earnest, was prepared for the last sacrifice. She was now his standard of comparison, his authority, his measure, his perpetual reference; and in taking possession of his mind to this extent she had completely renewed it. She was altogether a new term, and now that he was in a foreign country he observed how much her conversation, itself so foreign, had prepared him to understand it. In Paris he saw, of course, a great many women, and he noticed almost all of them, especially the actresses; confronting, mentally, their movement, their speech, their manner of dressing, with that of his extraordinary friend. He judged that she was beyond them in every respect, though there were one or two actresses who had the air of trying to copy her.

The recollection of the last days he had spent with her affected him now like the touch of a tear-washed cheek. She had shed tears for him, and it was his suspicion that her secret idea was to frustrate the redemption of his vow to Hoffendahl, to the immeasurable body that Hoffendahl represented.   She pretended to have accepted it, and what she said was simply that when he should have played his part she would engage to save him—to fling a cloud about him, as the goddess-mother of the Trojan hero used, in Virgil's poem, to *escamoter* Æneas.   What she meant was, in his view, to prevent him from playing his part at all. She was in earnest for herself, not for him.   The main result of his concentrated intimacy with her had been to make him feel that he was good enough for anything. When he had asked her, the last day, if he might write to her she had said, Yes, but not for two or three weeks.   He had written after Pinnie's death, and again just before coming abroad, and in doing so had taken account of something else she had said in regard to their correspondence— that she didn't wish vague phrases, protestations or compliments ; she wanted the realities of his life, the smallest, most personal details.   Therefore he had treated her to the whole business of the break-up in Lomax Place, including the sale of the rickety furniture.   He had told her what that transaction brought—a beggarly sum, but sufficient to help a little to pay debts ; and he had informed her furthermore that one of the ways Mr. Vetch had taken to hurry him off to Paris was to offer him a present of thirty pounds out of his curious little hoard, to add to the sum already inherited from Pinnie—which, in a manner that none of Hyacinth's friends, of course, could possibly regard as frugal, or even as respectable, was now consecrated to a mere excursion.   He even mentioned that he had ended by accepting the thirty pounds, adding that he feared there was something demoralising in his peculiar situation (she would know what he meant by that) : it disposed one to take what one could get, made one at least very tolerant of whims that happened to be munificent.

What he did not mention to the Princess was the manner in which he had been received by Paul Muniment and by Millicent Henning on his return from Medley.   Millicent's reception had been the queerest ; it had been quite unexpectedly mild.   She made him no scene of violence, and appeared to have given up the line of throwing a blur

of recrimination over her own nefarious doings. She treated
him as if she liked him for having got in with the swells ;
she had an appreciation of success which would lead her to
handle him more tenderly now that he was really successful. She tried to make him describe the style of life that
was led in a house where people were invited to stay like
that without having to pay, and she surprised him almost
as much as she gratified him by not indulging in any of
her former digs at the Princess. She was lavish of ejaculations when he answered certain of her questions—
ejaculations that savoured of Pimlico, ' Oh, I say ! ' and
' Oh, my stars ! '—and he was more than ever struck with
her detestable habit of saying, ' Aye, that's where it is,'
when he had made some remark to which she wished
to give an intelligent and sympathetic assent. But she
didn't jeer at the Princess's private character ; she stayed
her satire, in a case where there was such an opening for
it. Hyacinth reflected that this was lucky for her : he
couldn't have stood it (nervous and anxious as he was
about Pinnie), if she had had the bad taste, at such a time
as that, to be profane and insulting. In that case he
would have broken with her completely—he would have
been too disgusted. She displeased him enough, as it was,
by her vulgar tricks of speech. There were two or three
little recurrent irregularities that aggravated him to a degree
quite out of proportion to their importance, as when she
said ' full up ' for full, ' sold out ' for sold, or remarked to
him that she supposed he was now going to chuck up his
work at old Crookenden's. These phrases had fallen upon
his ear many a time before, but now they seemed almost
unpardonable enough to quarrel about. Not that he had
any wish to quarrel, for if the question had been pushed he
would have admitted that to-day his intimacy with the
Princess had caused any rights he might have had upon
Millicent to lapse. Millicent did not push it, however ;
she only, it was evident, wished to convey to him that
it was better for both parties they should respect each
other's liberty. A genial understanding on this subject was
what Miss Henning desired, and Hyacinth forbade himself
to inquire what use she proposed to make of her freedom.

During the month that elapsed between Pinnie's death and his visit to Paris he had seen her several times, for the respect for each other's freedom had somehow not implied cessation of intercourse, and it was only natural she should have been soft to him in his bereaved condition. Hyacinth's sentiment about Pinnie was deep, and Millicent was clever enough to guess it; the consequence of which was that on these occasions she was very soft indeed. She talked to him almost as if she had been his mother and he a convalescent child; called him her dear, and a young rascal, and her old boy; moralised a good deal, abstained from beer (till she learned he had inherited a fortune), and when he remarked once (moralising a little, too), that after the death of a person we have loved we are haunted by the memory of our failures of kindness, of generosity, rejoined, with a dignity that made the words almost a contribution to philosophy, 'Yes, that's where it is!'

Something in her behaviour at this period had even made Hyacinth wonder whether there were not some mystical sign in his appearance, some subtle betrayal in the very expression of his face, of the predicament in which he had been placed by Diedrich Hoffendahl; he began to suspect afresh the operation of that 'beastly *attendrissement*' he had detected of old in people who had the benefit of Miss Pynsent's innuendoes. The compassion Millicent felt for him had never been one of the reasons why he liked her; it had fortunately been corrected, moreover, by his power to make her furious. This evening, on the boulevard, as he watched the interminable successions, one of the ideas that came to him was that it was odd he should like her even yet; for heaven knew he liked the Princess better, and he had hitherto supposed that when a sentiment of this kind had the energy of a possession it made a clean sweep of all minor predilections. But it was clear to him that Millicent still existed for him; that he couldn't feel he had quite done with her, or she with him; and that in spite of his having now so many other things to admire there was still a comfort in the recollection of her robust beauty and her primitive passions. Hyacinth thought of her as some clever young barbarian

who in ancient days should have made a pilgrimage to
Rome might have thought of a Dacian or Iberian mistress
awaiting his return on the rough provincial shore.   If
Millicent considered his visit at a 'hall' a proof of the
sort of success that was to attend him (how he reconciled this with the supposition that she perceived, as a
ghostly irradiation, intermingled with his curly hair, the
aureola of martyrdom, he would have had some difficulty in
explaining), if Miss Henning considered, on his return from
Medley, that he had taken his place on the winning side,
it was only consistent of her to borrow a grandeur from
his further travels; and, indeed, by the time he was
ready to start she spoke of the plan as if she had invented
it herself and had even contributed materially to the funds
required.   It had been her theory, from the first, that she
only liked people of spirit; and Hyacinth certainly had
never had so much spirit as when he launched himself into
Continental adventures.   He could say to himself, quite
without bitterness, that of course she would profit by his
absence to put her relations with Sholto on a comfortable
footing; yet, somehow, at this moment, as her face came
back to him amid the crowd of faces about him, it had not
that gentleman's romantic shadow across it.   It was the
brilliancy of Paris, perhaps, that made him see things rosy;
at any rate, he remembered with kindness something that
she had said to him the last time he saw her and that had
touched him exceedingly at the moment.   He had happened to observe to her, in a friendly way, that now Miss
Pynsent had gone she was, with the exception of Mr.
Vetch, the person in his whole circle who had known him
longest.   To this Millicent had replied that Mr. Vetch
wouldn't live for ever, and then she should have the satisfaction of being his very oldest friend.   'Oh, well, I
shan't live for ever, either,' said Hyacinth; which led her
to inquire whether by chance he had a weakness of the
chest.   'Not that I know of, but I might get killed in a
row;' and when she broke out into scorn of his silly notion
of turning everything up (as if any one wanted to know
what a costermonger would like, or any of that low sort
at the East End!) he amused himself with asking her if she

were satisfied with the condition of society and thought
nothing ought to be done for people who, at the end of a
lifetime of starvation-wages, had only the reward of the
hideous workhouse and a pauper's grave.

'I shouldn't be satisfied with anything, if ever you was
to slip up,' Millicent answered, simply, looking at him with
her beautiful boldness. Then she added, 'There's one
thing I can tell *you*, Mr. Robinson : that if ever any one
was to do you a turn——' And she paused again, tossing
back the head she carried as if it were surmounted by a
tiara, while Hyacinth inquired what would occur in that
contingency. 'Well, there'd be *one* left behind who would
take it up!' she announced; and in the tone of the declaration there was something brave and genuine. It
struck Hyacinth as a strange fate—though not stranger,
after all, than his native circumstances—that one's memory
should come to be represented by a shop-girl overladen
with bracelets of imitation silver; but he was reminded
that Millicent was a fine specimen of a woman of a type
opposed to the whining, and that in her free temperament
many disparities were reconciled.

XXX

On the other hand the brilliancy of Paris had not much
power to transfigure the impression made upon him by
such intercourse with Paul Muniment as he had enjoyed
during the weeks that followed Pinnie's death—an impression considerably more severe than any idea of renunciation
or oblivion that could connect itself with Millicent. Why
it should have had the taste of sadness was not altogether
clear, for Muniment's voice was as distinct as any in the
chorus of approbation excited by the news that Hyacinth
was about to cultivate the most characteristic of the
pleasures of gentility—a sympathetic unanimity, of which
the effect was to place his journey to Paris in a light
almost ridiculous. What had got into them all, and did
they think he was good for nothing but to amuse himself?
Mr. Vetch had been the most zealous, but the others
clapped him on the back in almost exactly the same
manner as he had seen his mates in Soho bring their
palms down on one of their number when it was disclosed
to them that his 'missus' had made him yet once again
a father. That had been Poupin's tone, and his wife's as
well; and even poor Schinkel, with his everlasting bandage,
whom he had met in Lisson Grove, appeared to think it
necessary to remark that a little run across the Rhine,
while he was about it, would open his eyes to a great many
wonders. The Poupins shed tears of joy, and the letters
which have already been mentioned, and which lay day
after day on the mantel-shelf of the little room our hero
occupied in a *hôtel garni*, tremendously tall and somewhat
lopsided, in the Rue Jacob (that recommendation proceeded also from Lisson Grove, the garni being kept by
a second cousin of Madame Eustache), these valuable

documents had been prepared by the obliging exile many
days before his young friend was ready to start.   It was
almost refreshing to Hyacinth when old Crookenden, the
sole outspoken dissentient, told him he was a blockhead
to waste his money on the bloody French.   This worthy
employer of labour was evidently disgusted at such an
innovation; if he wanted a little recreation why couldn't
he take it as it had been taken in Soho from the beginning
of time, in the shape of a trip to Hampton Court or two
or three days of alcoholic torpor?   Old Crookenden was
right.   Hyacinth conceded freely that he was a blockhead,
and was only a little uncomfortable that he couldn't explain why he didn't pretend not to be and had a kind of
right to that compensatory luxury.

Paul guessed why, of course, and smiled approval with
a candour which gave Hyacinth a strange, inexpressible
heartache.   He already knew that his friend's view of him
was that he was ornamental and adapted to the lighter
kinds of socialistic utility—constituted to show that the
revolution was not necessarily brutal and illiterate; but in
the light of the cheerful stoicism with which Muniment
regarded the sacrifice our hero was committed to, the latter
had found it necessary to remodel a good deal his original
conception of the young chemist's nature.   The result of
this process was not that he admired it less but that he
felt almost awe-stricken in the presence of it.   There had
been an element of that sort in his appreciation of Muniment from the first, but it had been infinitely deepened by
the spectacle of his sublime consistency.   Hyacinth felt
that he himself could never have risen to that point.   He
was competent to make the promise to Hoffendahl, and
he was equally competent to keep it; but he could not
have had the same fortitude for another, could not have
detached himself from personal prejudice so effectually as
to put forward, in that way, for the terrible 'job,' a little
chap he liked.   That Muniment liked him it never
occurred to Hyacinth to doubt, and certainly he had all
the manner of it to-day: he had never been more good-
humoured, more placidly talkative; he was like an elder
brother who knew that the 'youngster' was clever, and

was rather proud of it even when there was no one there to see. That air of suspending their partnership for the moment, which had usually marked him at the 'Sun and Moon,' was never visible in other places; in Audley Court he only chaffed Hyacinth occasionally for taking him too seriously. To-day his young friend hardly knew just how to take him; the episode of which Hoffendahl was the central figure had, as far as one could see, made so little change in his life. As a conspirator he was so extraordinarily candid, and bitterness and denunciation so rarely sat on his lips. It was as if he had been ashamed to complain; and indeed, for himself, as the months went on, he had nothing particular to complain of. He had had a rise, at the chemical works, and a plan of getting a larger room for Rosy was under serious consideration. On behalf of others he never sounded the pathetic note— he thought that sort of thing unbusiness-like; and the most that he did in the way of expatiation on the wrongs of humanity was occasionally to mention certain statistics, certain 'returns,' in regard to the remuneration of industries, applications for employment and the discharge of hands. In such matters as these he was deeply versed, and he moved in a dry statistical and scientific air in which it cost Hyacinth an effort of respiration to accompany him. Simple and kindly as he was, and thoughtful of the woes of beasts, attentive and merciful to small insects, and addicted even to kissing dirty babies in Audley Court, he sometimes emitted a short satiric gleam which showed that his esteem for the poor was small and that if he had no illusions about the people who had got everything into their hands he had as few about those who had egregiously failed to do so. He was tremendously reasonable, which was largely why Hyacinth admired him, having a desire to be so himself but finding it terribly difficult.

Muniment's absence of passion, his fresh-coloured coolness, his easy, exact knowledge, the way he kept himself clean (except for the chemical stains on his hands), in circumstances of foul contact, constituted a group of qualities that had always appeared to Hyacinth singularly enviable. Most enviable of all was the force that enabled

him to sink personal sentiment where a great public good
was to be attempted and yet keep up the form of caring
for that minor interest.   It seemed to Hyacinth that if *he*
had introduced a young fellow to Hoffendahl for his purposes, and Hoffendahl had accepted him on such a recommendation, and everything had been settled, he would
have preferred never to look at the young fellow again.
That was his weakness, and Muniment carried it off far
otherwise.   It must be added that he had never made an
allusion to their visit to Hoffendahl; so that Hyacinth
also, out of pride, held his tongue on the subject.   If his
friend didn't wish to express any sympathy for him he was
not going to beg for it (especially as he didn't want it), by
restless references.   It had originally been a surprise to
him that Muniment should be willing to countenance a
possible assassination; but after all none of his ideas were
narrow (Hyacinth had a sense that they ripened all the
while), and if a pistol-shot would do any good he was not
the man to raise pedantic objections.   It is true that, as
regards his quiet acceptance of the predicament in which
Hyacinth might be placed by it, our young man had given
him the benefit of a certain amount of doubt; it had
occurred to him that perhaps Muniment had his own
reasons for believing that the summons from Hoffendahl
would never really arrive, so that he might only be treating
himself to the entertainment of judging of a little bookbinder's nerve.   But in this case, why did he take an
interest in the little bookbinder's going to Paris?   That
was a thing he would not have cared for had he held that
in fact there was nothing to fear.   He despised the sight
of idleness, and in spite of the indulgence he had more
than once been good enough to express on the subject of
Hyacinth's epicurean tendencies what he would have been
most likely to say at present was, 'Go to Paris?   Go to
the dickens!   Haven't you been out at grass long enough
for one while, didn't you lark enough in the country there
with the noble lady, and hadn't you better take up your
tools again before you forget how to handle them?'   Rosy
had said something of that sort, in her free, familiar way
(whatever her intention, she had been, in effect, only a little

less sarcastic than old Crookenden) : that Mr. Robinson
was going in for a life of leisure, a life of luxury, like herself; she must congratulate him on having the means and
the time. Oh, the time—that was the great thing! She
could speak with knowledge, having always enjoyed these
advantages herself. And she intimated—or was she mistaken?—that his good fortune emulated hers also in the
matter of his having a high-born and beneficent friend
(such a blessing, now he had lost dear Miss Pynsent), who
covered him with little attentions. Rose Muniment, in
short, had been more exasperating than ever.

The boulevard became even more brilliant as the evening went on, and Hyacinth wondered whether he had a
right to occupy the same table for so many hours. The
theatre on the other side discharged its multitude; the
crowd thickened on the wide asphalt, on the terrace of the
café ; gentlemen, accompanied by ladies of whom he knew
already how to characterise the type—*des femmes très-chic*
—passed into the portals of Tortoni. The nightly emanation of Paris seemed to rise more richly, to float and
hang in the air, to mingle with the universal light and the
many-voiced sound, to resolve itself into a thousand soli-
citations and opportunities, addressed however mainly to
those in whose pockets the chink of a little loose gold
might respond. Hyacinth's retrospections had not made
him drowsy, but quite the reverse; he grew restless and
excited, and a kind of pleasant terror of the place and hour
entered into his blood. But it was nearly midnight, and
he got up to walk home, taking the line of the boulevard
toward the Madeleine. He passed down the Rue Royale,
where comparative stillness reigned ; and when he reached
the Place de la Concorde, to cross the bridge which faces the
Corps Législatif, he found himself almost isolated. He
had left the human swarm and the obstructed pavements
behind, and the wide spaces of the splendid square lay
quiet under the summer stars. The plash of the great
fountains was audible, and he could almost hear the wind-
stirred murmur of the little wood of the Tuileries on one
side, and of the vague expanse of the Champs Elysées on
the other. The place itself—the Place Louis Quinze, the

Place de la Révolution—had given him a sensible emotion, from the day of his arrival; he had recognised so quickly its tremendously historic character. He had seen, in a rapid vision, the guillotine in the middle, on the site of the inscrutable obelisk, and the tumbrils, with waiting victims, were stationed round the circle now made majestic by the monuments of the cities of France. The great legend of the French Revolution, sanguinary and heroic, was more real to him here than anywhere else; and, strangely, what was most present was not its turpitude and horror, but its magnificent energy, the spirit of life that had been in it, not the spirit of death. That shadow was effaced by the modern fairness of fountain and statue, the stately perspective and composition; and as he lingered, before crossing the Seine, a sudden sense overtook him, making his heart sink with a kind of desolation—a sense of everything that might hold one to the world, of the sweetness of not dying, the fascination of great cities, the charm of travel and discovery, the generosity of admiration. The tears rose to his eyes, as they had done more than once in the past six months, and a question, low but poignant, broke from his lips, ending in nothing. 'How could he—how *could* he——?' It may be explained that 'he' was a reference to Paul Muniment; for Hyacinth had dreamed of the religion of friendship.

Three weeks after this he found himself in Venice, whence he addressed to the Princess Casamassima a letter of which I reproduce the principal passages.

'This is probably the last time I shall write to you before I return to London. Of course you have been in this place, and you will easily understand why here, especially here, the spirit should move me. Dear Princess, what an enchanted city, what ineffable impressions, what a revelation of the exquisite! I have a room in a little *campo* opposite to a small old church, which has cracked marble slabs let into the front; and in the cracks grow little wild delicate flowers, of which I don't know the name. Over the door of the church hangs an old battered leather curtain, polished and tawny, as thick as a mattress, and with buttons in it, like a sofa; and it flops to and fro, laboriously, as

women and girls, with shawls on their heads and their feet
in little wooden shoes which have nothing but toes, pass in
and out.   In the middle of the campo is a fountain, which
looks still older than the church ; it has a primitive, bar-
baric air, and I have an idea it was put there by the first
settlers—those who came to Venice from the mainland,
from Aquileia.   Observe how much historical information
I have already absorbed ; it won't surprise you, however, for
you never wondered at anything after you discovered I
knew something of Schopenhauer.   I assure you, I don't
think of that musty misogynist in the least to-day, for I
bend a genial eye on the women and girls I just spoke of,
as they glide, with a small clatter and with their old copper
water-jars, to the fountain.   The Venetian girl-face is wonderfully sweet and the effect is charming when its pale, sad
oval (they all look underfed), is framed in the old faded
shawl.   They also have very fascinating hair, which never
has done curling, and they slip along together, in couples or
threes, interlinked by the arms and never meeting one's
eye (so that its geniality doesn't matter), dressed in thin,
cheap cotton gowns, whose limp folds make the same delightful line that everything else in Italy makes.   The
weather is splendid and I roast—but I like it ; apparently,
I was made to be spitted and "done," and I discover that
I have been cold all my life, even when I thought I was
warm.   I have seen none of the beautiful patricians who
sat for the great painters—the gorgeous beings whose golden
hair was intertwined with pearls ; but I am studying Italian
in order to talk with the shuffling, clicking maidens who
work in the bead-factories—I am determined to make one
or two of them look at me.   When they have filled their old
water-pots at the fountain it is jolly to see them perch them
on their heads and patter away over the polished Venetian
stones.   It's a charm to be in a country where the women
don't wear the hideous British bonnet.   Even in my own
class (excuse the expression—I remember it used to offend
you), I have never known a young female, in London, to
put her nose out of the door without it ; and if you had
frequented such young females as much as I have you
would have learned of what degradation that dreary neces-

sity is the source. The floor of my room is composed of
little brick tiles, and to freshen the air, in this temperature,
one sprinkles it, as you no doubt know, with water. Before
long, if I keep on sprinkling, I shall be able to swim about ;
the green shutters are closed, and the place makes a very
good tank. Through the chinks the hot light of the campo
comes in. I smoke cigarettes, and in the pauses of this
composition recline on a faded magenta divan in the corner.
Convenient to my hand, in that attitude, are the works of
Leopardi and a second-hand dictionary. I am very happy
—happier than I have ever been in my life save at Medley
—and I don't care for anything but the present hour. It
won't last long, for I am spending all my money. When I
have finished this I shall go forth and wander about in
the splendid Venetian afternoon ; and I shall spend the
evening in that enchanted square of St. Mark's, which resembles an immense open-air drawing-room, listening to
music and feeling the sea-breeze blow in between those
two strange old columns, in the piazzetta, which seem to
make a portal for it. I can scarcely believe that it's of
myself that I am telling these fine things ; I say to myself
a dozen times a day that Hyacinth Robinson is not in it
—I pinch my leg to see if I'm not dreaming. But a
short time hence, when I have resumed the exercise of my
profession, in sweet Soho, I shall have proof enough that
it has been my very self : I shall know that by the terrible
grind I shall feel my work to be.

'That will mean, no doubt, that I'm deeply demoralised.
It won't be for you, however, in this case, to cast the stone
at me ; for my demoralisation began from the moment I
first approached you. Dear Princess, I may have done you
good, but you haven't done me much. I trust you will
understand what I mean by that speech, and not think it
flippant or impertinent. I may have helped you to understand and enter into the misery of the people (though I
protest I don't know much about it), but you have led my
imagination into quite another train. However, I don't
mean to pretend that it's all your fault if I have lost sight
of the sacred cause almost altogether in my recent adventures.
It is not that it has not been there to see, for that perhaps

is the clearest result of extending one's horizon—the sense, increasing as we go, that want and toil and suffering are the constant lot of the immense majority of the human race.   I have found them everywhere, but I haven't minded them. Excuse the cynical confession.   What has struck me is the great achievements of which man has been capable in spite of them—the splendid accumulations of the happier few, to which, doubtless, the miserable many have also in their degree contributed.   The face of Europe appears to be covered with them, and they have had much the greater part of my attention.   They seem to me inestimably precious and beautiful, and I have become conscious, more than ever before, of how little I understand what, in the great rectification, you and Poupin propose to do with them.   Dear Princess, there are things which I shall be sorry to see you touch, even you with your hands divine; and—shall I tell you *le fond de ma pensée*, as you used to say?—I feel myself capable of fighting for them.   You can't call me a traitor, for you know the obligation that I recognise.   The monuments and treasures of art, the great palaces and properties, the conquests of learning and taste, the general fabric of civilisation as we know it, based, if you will, upon all the despotisms, the cruelties, the exclusions, the monopolies and the rapacities of the past, but thanks to which, all the same, the world is less impracticable and life more tolerable—our friend Hoffendahl seems to me to hold them too cheap and to wish to substitute for them something in which I can't somehow believe as I do in things with which the aspirations and the tears of generations have been mixed. You know how extraordinary I think our Hoffendahl (to speak only of him); but if there is one thing that is more clear about him than another it is that he wouldn't have the least feeling for this incomparable, abominable old Venice.   He would cut up the ceilings of the Veronese into strips, so that every one might have a little piece.   I don't want every one to have a little piece of anything, and I have a great horror of that kind of invidious jealousy which is at the bottom of the idea of a redistribution.   You will say that I talk of it at my ease, while, in a delicious capital, I smoke cigarettes on a magenta divan; and I give you leave

to scoff at me if it turns out that, when I come back to
London without a penny in my pocket, I don't hold the
same language.   I don't know what it comes from, but
during the last three months there has crept over me a deep
mistrust of that same grudging attitude—the intolerance of
positions and fortunes that are higher and brighter than
one's own ; a fear, moreover, that I may, in the past, have
been actuated by such motives, and a devout hope that if I
am to pass away while I am yet young it may not be with
that odious stain upon my soul.'

HYACINTH spent three days, after his return to London, in a process which he supposed to be the quest of a lodging; but in reality he was pulling himself together for the business of his livelihood—an effort he found by no means easy or agreeable. As he had told the Princess, he was demoralised, and the perspective of Mr. Crookenden's dirty staircase had never seemed so steep. He lingered on the brink, before he plunged again into Soho; he wished not to go back to the shop till he should be settled, and he delayed to get settled in order not to go back to the shop. He saw no one during this interval, not even Mr. Vetch; he waited to call upon the fiddler till he should have the appearance of not coming as a beggar or a borrower—have recovered his employment and be able to give an address, as he had heard Captain Sholto say. He went to South Street—not meaning to go in at once but wishing to look at the house—and there he had the surprise of perceiving a bill of sale in the window of the Princess's late residence. He had not expected to find her in town (he had heard from her the last time three weeks before, and then she said nothing about her prospects), but he was puzzled by this indication that she had moved away altogether. There was something in this, however, which he felt that at bottom he had looked for; it appeared a proof of the justice of a certain suspicious, uneasy sentiment from which one could never be quite free, in one's intercourse with the Princess—a vague apprehension that one might suddenly stretch out one's hand and miss her altogether from one's side. Hyacinth decided to ring at the door and ask for news of her; but there was no response to his summons: the stillness of an August afternoon (the year had come round again from his first visit) hung over

the place, the blinds were down and the caretaker appeared
to be absent. Under these circumstances Hyacinth was
much at a loss; unless, indeed, he should address a letter
to his wonderful friend at Medley. It would doubtless be
forwarded, though her short lease of the country-house had
terminated, as he knew, several weeks before. Captain
Sholto was of course a possible medium of communication;
but nothing would have induced Hyacinth to ask such a
service of him.

He turned away from South Street with a curious sinking
of the heart; his state of ignorance struck inward, as it were
—had the force of a vague, disquieting portent. He went
to old Crookenden's only when he had arrived at his last
penny. This, however, was very promptly the case. He
had disembarked at London Bridge with only seventeen
pence in his pocket, and he had lived on that sum for three
days. The old fiddler in Lomax Place was having a chop
before he went to the theatre, and he invited Hyacinth to
share his repast, sending out at the same time for another
pot of beer. He took the youth with him to the play,
where, as at that season there were very few spectators, he
had no difficulty in finding him a place. He seemed to
wish to keep hold of him, and looked at him strangely,
over his spectacles (Mr. Vetch wore the homely double
glass in these latter years), when he learned that Hyacinth
had taken a lodging not in their old familiar quarter but in
the unexplored purlieus of Westminster. What had determined our young man was the fact that from this part of
the town the journey was comparatively a short one to
Camberwell; he had suffered so much, before Pinnie's
death, from being separated by such a distance from his
best friends. There was a pang in his heart connected
with the image of Paul Muniment, but none the less the
prospect of an evening hour in Audley Court, from time to
time, appeared one of his most definite sources of satisfaction
in the future. He could have gone straight to Camberwell
to live, but that would carry him too far from the scene of
his profession; and in Westminster he was much nearer
to old Crookenden's than he had been in Lomax Place.
He said to Mr. Vetch that if it would give him pleasure he

would abandon his lodging and take another in Pentonville.
But the old man replied, after a moment, that he should be
sorry to put that constraint upon him ; if he were to make
such an exaction Hyacinth would think he wanted to watch
him.

'How do you mean, to watch me ? '

Mr. Vetch had begun to tune his fiddle, and he scraped
it a little before answering. 'I mean it as I have always
meant it. Surely you know that in Lomax Place I had my
eyes on you. I watched you as a child on the edge of a
pond watches the little boat he has constructed and set
afloat.'

'You couldn't discover much. You saw, after all, very
little of me,' Hyacinth said.

'I made what I could of that little ; it was better than
nothing.'

Hyacinth laid his hand gently on the old man's arm ; he
had never felt so kindly to him, not even when he accepted
the thirty pounds, before going abroad, as at this moment.
'Certainly I will come and see you.'

'I was much obliged to you for your letters,' Mr. Vetch
remarked, without heeding these words, and continuing to
scrape. He had always, even into the shabbiness of his
old age, kept that mark of English good-breeding (which
is composed of some such odd elements), that there was a
shyness, an aversion to possible phrase-making, in his
manner of expressing gratitude for favours, and that in spite
of this cursory tone his acknowledgment had ever the
accent of sincerity.

Hyacinth took but little interest in the play, which was
an inanimate revival ; he had been at the Théâtre Français
and the tradition of that house was still sufficiently present
to him to make any other style of interpretation appear of
the clumsiest. He sat in one of the front stalls, close to
the orchestra ; and while the piece went forward—or backward, ever backward, as it seemed to him—his thoughts
wandered far from the shabby scene and the dusty boards,
revolving round a question which had come up immensely
during the last few hours. The Princess was a *capricciosa*
—that, at least, was Madame Grandoni's account of her ;

and was that blank, expressionless house in South Street
a sign that an end had come to the particular caprice in
which he had happened to be involved? He had returned
to London with an ache of eagerness to be with her again
on the same terms as at Medley, a throbbing sense that
unless she had been abominably dishonest he might count
upon her. This state of mind was by no means complete
security, but it was so sweet that it mattered little whether
it were sound. Circumstances had favoured in an extraordinary degree his visit to her, and it was by no means
clear that they would again be so accommodating or that
what had been possible for a few days should be possible
with continuity, in the midst of the ceremonies and complications of London. Hyacinth felt poorer than he had
ever felt before, inasmuch as he had had money and spent
it, whereas in previous times he had never had it to spend.
He never for an instant regretted his squandered fortune,
for he said to himself that he had made a good bargain
and become master of a precious equivalent. The equivalent was a rich experience—an experience which would
become richer still as he should talk it over, in a low chair,
close to hers, with the all-comprehending, all-suggesting lady
of his life. His poverty would be no obstacle to their
intercourse so long as he should have a pair of legs to
carry him to her door; for she liked him better shabby
than when he was furbished up, and she had given him too
many pledges, they had taken together too many appoint-
ments, worked out too many programmes, to be disconcerted
(on either side) by obstacles that were merely a part of the
general conventionality. He was to go with her into the
slums, to introduce her to the worst that London contained
(he should have, precisely, to make acquaintance with it
first), to show her the reality of the horrors of which she
dreamed that the world might be purged. He had ceased,
himself, to care for the slums, and had reasons for not
wishing to spend his remnant in the contemplation of foul
things; but he would go through with his part of the
engagement. He might be perfunctory, but any dreariness
would have a gilding that should involve an association
with her. What if she should have changed, have ceased

to care ? What if, from a kind of royal insolence which
he suspected to lurk somewhere in the side-scenes of her
nature, though he had really not once seen it peep out, she
should toss back her perfect head with a movement signi-
fying that he was too basely literal and that she knew him
no more ? Hyacinth's imagination represented her this
evening in places where a barrier of dazzling light shut her
out from access, or even from any appeal. He saw her
with other people, in splendid rooms, where 'the dukes'
had possession of her, smiling, satisfied, surrounded, covered
with jewels. When this vision grew intense he found a
reassurance in reflecting that after all she would be unlikely
to throw him personally over so long as she should remain
mixed up with what was being planned in the dark,
and that it would not be easy for her to liberate herself
from that entanglement. She had of course told him
more, at Medley, of the manner in which she had
already committed herself, and he remembered, with a
strange perverse elation, that she had gone very far
indeed.

In the intervals of the foolish play Mr. Vetch, who
lingered in his place in the orchestra while his mates
descended into the little hole under the stage, leaned
over the rail and asked his young friend occasional questions,
carrying his eyes at the same time up about the dingy house,
at whose smoky ceiling and tarnished galleries he had been
staring for so many a year. He came back to Hyacinth's
letters, and said, ' Of course you know they were clever ;
they entertained me immensely. But as I read them I
thought of poor Pinnie : I wished she could have listened
to them ; they would have made her so happy.'

'Yes, poor Pinnie,' Hyacinth murmured, while Mr.
Vetch went on :

' I was in Paris in 1840 ; I stayed at a small hotel in
the Rue Mogador. I judge everything is changed, from
your letters. Does the Rue Mogador still exist ? Yes,
everything is changed. I daresay it's all much finer, but
I liked it very much as it was then. At all events, I am
right in supposing—am I not ?—that it cheered you up
considerably, made you really happy.'

'Why should I have wanted any cheering? I was happy enough,' Hyacinth replied.

The fiddler turned his old white face upon him; it had the unhealthy smoothness which denotes a sedentary occupation, thirty years spent in a close crowd, amid the smoke of lamps and the odour of stage-paint. 'I thought you were sad about Pinnie,' he remarked.

'When I jumped, with that avidity, at your proposal that I should take a tour? Poor old Pinnie!' Hyacinth added.

'Well, I hope you think a little better of the world. We mustn't make up our mind too early in life.'

'Oh, I have made up mine: it's an awfully jolly place.'

'Awfully jolly, no; but I like it as I like an old pair of shoes—I like so much less the idea of putting on the new ones.'

'Why should I complain?' Hyacinth asked. 'What have I known but kindness? People have done such a lot for me.'

'Oh, well, of course, they have liked you. But that's all right,' murmured Mr. Vetch, beginning to scrape again. What remained in Hyacinth's mind from this conversation was the fact that the old man, whom he regarded distinctly as cultivated, had thought his letters clever. He only wished that he had made them cleverer still; he had no doubt of his ability to have done so.

It may be imagined whether the first hours he spent at old Crookenden's, after he took up work again, were altogether to his taste, and what was the nature of the reception given him by his former comrades, whom he found exactly in the same attitudes and the same clothes (he knew and hated every article they wore), and with the same primitive pleasantries on their lips. Our young man's feelings were mingled; the place and the people appeared to him loathsome, but there was something delightful in handling his tools. He gave a little private groan of relief when he discovered that he still liked his work and that the pleasant swarm of his ideas (in the matter of sides and backs), returned to him. They came in still brighter, more suggestive form, and he had the satisfaction of feeling that his taste had improved, that it had been purified by experience, and that the covers of a book might be made to express an astonishing number of high conceptions. Strange enough it was, and a proof, surely, of our little hero's being a genuine artist, that the impressions he had accumulated during the last few months appeared to mingle and confound themselves with the very sources of his craft and to be susceptible of technical representation. He had quite determined, by this time, to carry on his life as if nothing were hanging over him, and he had no intention of remaining a little bookbinder to the end of his days ; for that medium, after all, would translate only some of his conceptions. Yet his trade was a resource, an undiminished resource, for the present, and he had a particular as well as a general motive in attempting new flights — the prevision of the exquisite work which he was to do during the coming year for the Princess and which it was very definite to him he owed her. When that debt should have been paid and his other arrears made up he proposed to himself to write something. He was far from having decided as yet what it should be ; the only point settled was that it should be very remarkable and should not, at least on the face of it, have anything to do with a fresh deal of the social pack. That was to be his transition —into literature ; to bind the book, charming as the process might be, was after all much less fundamental than to write it. It had occurred to Hyacinth more than once that it would be a fine thing to produce a brilliant death-song.

It is not surprising that among such reveries as this he should have been conscious of a narrow range in the tone of his old workfellows. They had only one idea : that he had come into a thousand pounds and had gone to spend them in France with a regular high one. He was aware, in advance, of the diffusion of this legend, and did his best to allow for it, taking the simplest course, which was not to contradict it but to catch the ball as it came and toss it still further, enlarging and embroidering humorously until Grugan and Roker and Hotchkin and all the rest, who struck him as not having washed since he left them, seemed really to begin to understand how it was he could have spent such a rare sum in so short a time. The impressiveness of this achievement helped him greatly to slip into his place; he could see that, though the treatment it received was superficially irreverent, the sense that he was very sharp and that the springs of his sharpness were somehow secret gained a good deal of strength from it. Hyacinth was not incapable of being rather pleased that it *should* be supposed, even by Grugan, Roker and Hotchkin, that he could get rid of a thousand pounds in less than five months, especially as to his own conscience the fact had altogether yet to be proved. He got off, on the whole, easily enough to feel a little ashamed, and he reflected that the men at Crookenden's, at any rate, showed no symptoms of the social jealousy lying at the bottom of the desire for a fresh deal. This was doubtless an accident, and not inherent in the fact that they were highly skilled workmen (old Crookenden had no others), and therefore sure of constant employment; for it was impossible to be more skilled, in one's own line, than Paul Muniment was, and yet he (though not out of jealousy, of course), went in for the great restitution. What struck him most, after he had got used again to the sense of his apron and bent his back a while over his battered table, was the simple, synthetic patience of the others, who had bent *their* backs and felt the rub of that dirty drapery all the while he was lounging in the halls of Medley, dawdling through boulevards and museums, and admiring the purity of the Venetian girl-face. With Poupin, to be sure, his relations were special; but the explanations that he owed the sensitive Frenchman were not such as could make him very unhappy, once he had determined to resist as much as possible the friction of his remaining days. There was moreover more sorrow than anger in Poupin's face when he learned that his young friend and pupil had failed to cultivate, in Paris, the rich opportunities he had offered him. 'You are cooling off, my child; there is something about you! Have you the weakness to flatter yourself that anything has been done, or that humanity suffers a particle less? *Enfin*, it's between you and your conscience.'

'Do you think I want to get out of it?' Hyacinth asked, smiling; Eustache Poupin's phrases about humanity, which used to thrill him so, having grown of late strangely hollow and *rococo*.

'You owe me no explanations; the conscience of the individual is absolute, except, of course, in those classes in which, from the very nature of the infamies on which they are founded, no conscience can exist. Speak to me, however, of my Paris; *she* is always divine,' Poupin went on; but he showed signs of irritation when Hyacinth began to praise to him the magnificent creations of the arch-fiend of December. In the presence of this picture he was in a terrible dilemma: he was gratified as a Parisian and a patriot but he was disconcerted as a lover of liberty; it cost him a pang to admit that anything in the sacred city was defective, yet he saw still less his way to concede that it could owe any charm to the perjured monster of the second Empire, or even to the hypocritical, mendacious republicanism of the régime before which the sacred Commune had gone down in blood and fire. 'Ah, yes, it's very fine, no doubt,' he remarked at last, 'but it will be finer still when it's ours!'—a speech which caused Hyacinth to turn back to his work with a slight feeling of sickness. Everywhere, everywhere, he saw the ulcer of envy—the passion of a party which hung together for the purpose of despoiling another to its advantage. In old Eustace, one of the 'pure,' this was particularly sad.

XXXII

THE landing at the top of the stairs in Audley Court was always dark ; but it seemed darker than ever to Hyacinth while he fumbled for the door-latch, after he had heard Rose Muniment's penetrating voice bid him come in. During that instant his ear caught the sound—if it could trust itself—of another voice, which prepared him, a little, for the spectacle that offered itself as soon as the door (his attempt to reach the handle, in his sudden agitation, proving fruitless), was opened to him by Paul. His friend stood there, tall and hospitable, saying something loud and jovial, which he didn't distinguish. His eyes had crossed the threshold in a flash, but his step faltered a moment, only to obey, however, the vigour of Muniment's outstretched hand. Hyacinth's glance had gone straight, and though with four persons in it Rosy's little apartment looked crowded, he saw no one but the object of his quick preconception— no one but the Princess Casamassima, seated beside the low sofa (the grand feature introduced during his absence from London), on which, arrayed in the famous pink dressing-gown, Miss Muniment now received her visitors. He wondered afterwards why he should have been so startled ; for he had said, often enough, both to himself and to the Princess, that so far as she was concerned he was proof against astonishment ; it was so evident that, in her behaviour, the unexpected was the only thing to be looked for. In fact, now that he perceived she had made her way to Camberwell without his assistance, the feeling that took possession of him was a kind of embarrassment ; he blushed a little as he entered the circle, the fourth member of which was inevitably Lady Aurora Langrish. Was it that his intimacy with the Princess gave him a certain sense

of responsibility for her conduct in respect to people who
knew her as yet but a little, and that there was something
that required explanation in the confidence with which she
had practised a descent upon them ? It is true that it
came over our young man that by this time, perhaps, they
knew her a good deal ; and moreover a woman's conduct
spoke for itself when she could sit looking, in that fashion,
like a radiant angel dressed in a simple bonnet and mantle
and immensely interested in an appealing corner of the
earth. It took Hyacinth but an instant to perceive that
her character was in a different phase from any that had
yet been exhibited to him. There had been a brilliant
mildness about her the night he made her acquaintance,
and she had never ceased, at any moment since, to strike
him as an exquisitely human, sentient, pitying organisation ;
unless it might be, indeed, in relation to her husband,
against whom—for reasons, after all, doubtless, very sufficient
—her heart appeared absolutely steeled. But now her face
turned to him through a sort of glorious charity. She had
put off her splendour, but her beauty was unquenchably
bright ; she had made herself humble for her pious excursion ; she had, beside Rosy (who, in the pink dressing-
gown, looked much the more luxurious of the two), almost
the attitude of an hospital nurse; and it was easy to see,
from the meagre line of her garments, that she was tremendously in earnest. If Hyacinth was flurried her own countenance expressed no confusion ; for her, evidently, this
queer little chamber of poverty and pain was a place in
which it was perfectly natural that *he* should turn up. The
sweet, still greeting her eyes offered him might almost have
conveyed to him that she had been waiting for him, that
she knew he would come and that there had been a tacit
appointment for that very moment. They said other things
beside, in their beautiful friendliness ; they said, ' Don't
notice me too much, or make any kind of scene. I have
an immense deal to say to you, but remember that I have
the rest of our life before me to say it in. Consider only
what will be easiest and kindest to these people, these delightful people, whom I find enchanting (why didn't you
ever tell me more—I mean really more—about them ?) It

won't be particularly complimentary to them if you have
the air of seeing a miracle in my presence here. I am
very glad of your return. The quavering, fidgety "ladyship" is as fascinating as the others.'

Hyacinth's reception at the hands of his old friends was
cordial enough quite to obliterate the element of irony that
had lurked, three months before, in their godspeed; their
welcome was not boisterous, but it seemed to express the
idea that the occasion was already so rare and agreeable
that his arrival was all that was needed to make it perfect.
By the time he had been three minutes in the room he was
able to measure the impression produced by the Princess,
who, it was clear, had thrown a spell of adoration over the
little company. This was in the air, in the face of each,
in their excited, smiling eyes and heightened colour; even
Rosy's wan grimace, which was at all times screwed up to
ecstasy, emitted a supererogatory ray. Lady Aurora looked
more than ever dishevelled with interest and wonder; the
long strands of her silky hair floated like gossamer, as, in
her extraordinary, religious attention (her hands were raised
and clasped to her bosom, as if she were praying), her
respiration rose and fell. She had never seen any one like
the Princess; but Hyacinth's apprehension, of some months
before, had been groundless—she evidently didn't think her
vulgar. She thought her divine, and a revelation of beauty
and benignity; and the illuminated, amplified room could
contain no dissentient opinion. It was her beauty, primarily,
that 'fetched' them, Hyacinth could easily see, and it was
not hidden from him that the sensation was as active in
Paul Muniment as in his companions. It was not in Paul's
nature to be jerkily demonstrative, and he had not lost his
head on the present occasion; but he had already appreciated the difference between one's preconception of a
meretricious, factitious fine lady and the actual influence of
such a personage. She was gentler, fairer, wiser, than a
chemist's assistant could have guessed in advance. In
short, she held the trio in her hand (she had reduced Lady
Aurora to exactly the same simplicity as the others), and
she performed, admirably, artistically, for their benefit.
Almost before Hyacinth had had time to wonder how she

had found the Muniments out (he had no recollection of
giving her specific directions), she mentioned that Captain
Sholto had been so good as to introduce her; doing so as
if she owed him that explanation and were a woman who
would be scrupulous in such a case.   It was rather a blow
to him to hear that she had been accepting the Captain's
mediation, and this was not softened by her saying that
she was too impatient to wait for his own return ; he was
apparently so happy on the Continent that one couldn't be
sure it would ever take place.   The Princess might at least
have been sure that to see her again very soon was still
more necessary to his happiness than anything the Continent
could offer.

It came out in the conversation he had with her, to
which the others listened with respectful curiosity, that
Captain Sholto had brought her a week before, but then
she had seen only Miss Muniment.   'I took the liberty of
coming again, by myself, to-day, because I wanted to see
the whole family,' the Princess remarked, looking from
Paul to Lady Aurora, with a friendly gaiety in her face
which purified the observation (as regarded her ladyship), of
impertinence.   The Princess added, frankly, that she had
now been careful to arrive at an hour when she thought
Mr. Muniment might be at home.   'When I come to see
gentlemen, I like at least to find them,' she continued,
and she was so great a lady that there was no small
diffidence in her attitude ; it was a simple matter for her
to call on a chemist's assistant, if she had a reason.
Hyacinth could see that the reason had already been
brought forward—her immense interest in problems that
Mr. Muniment had completely mastered, and in particular
their common acquaintance with the extraordinary man
whose mission it was to solve them.   Hyacinth learned
later that she had pronounced the name of Hoffendahl.
A part of the lustre in Rosy's eye came no doubt from
the explanation she had inevitably been moved to make
in respect to any sympathy with wicked theories that
might be imputed to *her ;* and of course the effect of
this intensely individual little protest (such was always
its effect), emanating from the sofa and the pink dressing-

gown, was to render the Muniment interior still more
quaint and original. In that spot Paul always gave the
go-by, humorously, to any attempt to draw out his views,
and you would have thought, to hear him, that he allowed
himself the reputation of having them only in order to get
a 'rise' out of his sister and let their visitors see with what
wit and spirit she could repudiate them. This, however,
would only be a reason the more for the Princess's following
up her scent. She would doubtless not expect to get at
the bottom of his ideas in Audley Court; the opportunity
would occur, rather, in case of his having the civility (on
which surely she might count), to come and talk them over
with her in her own house.

Hyacinth mentioned to her the disappointment he had
had in South Street, and she replied, 'Oh, I have given up
that house, and taken quite a different one.'   But she didn't
say where it was, and in spite of her having given him so
much the right to expect she would communicate to him a
matter so nearly touching them both as a change of address,
he felt a great shyness about asking.

Their companions watched them as if they considered
that something rather brilliant, now, would be likely to come
off between them; but Hyacinth was too full of regard to
the Princess's tacit notification to him that they must not
appear too thick, which was after all more flattering than
the most pressing inquiries or the most liberal announcements about herself could have been. She never asked
him when he had come back; and indeed it was not long
before Rose Muniment took that business upon herself.
Hyacinth, however, ventured to assure himself whether
Madame Grandoni were still with the Princess, and even to
remark (when she had replied, 'Oh yes, still, still. The
great refusal, as Dante calls it, has not yet come off'),
'You ought to bring her to see Miss Rosy. She is a person
Miss Rosy would particularly appreciate.'

'I am sure I should be most happy to receive any friend
of the Princess Casamassima,' said this young lady, from
the sofa; and when the Princess answered that she certainly
would not fail to produce Madame Grandoni some day,
Hyacinth (though he doubted whether the presentation

would really take place), guessed how much she wished her
old friend might have heard the strange bedizened little
invalid make that speech.

There were only three other seats, for the introduction
of the sofa (a question so profoundly studied in advance),
had rendered necessary the elimination of certain articles;
so that Muniment, on his feet, hovered round the little
circle, with his hands in his pockets, laughing freely and
sociably but not looking at the Princess; though, as Hyacinth
was sure, he was none the less agitated by her presence.

'You ought to tell us about foreign parts and the grand
things you have seen; except that, doubtless, our distinguished visitor knows all about them,' Muniment said to
Hyacinth.   Then he added, 'Surely, at any rate, you have
seen nothing more worthy of your respect than Camberwell.'

'Is this the worst part?' the Princess asked, looking up
with her noble, interested face.

'The worst, madam?   What grand ideas you must have!
We admire Camberwell immensely.'

'It's my brother's ideas that are grand!' cried Rose
Muniment, betraying him conscientiously.   'He does want
everything changed, no less than you, Princess; though he
is more cunning than you, and won't give one a handle
where one can take him up.   He thinks all this part most
objectionable—as if dirty people won't always make everything dirty where they live!   I dare say he thinks there
ought to be no dirty people, and it may be so; only if every
one was clean, where would be the merit?   You would get
no credit for keeping yourself tidy.   At any rate, if it's a
question of soap and water, every one can begin by himself.
My brother thinks the whole place ought to be as handsome
as Brompton.'

'Ah, yes, that's where the artists and literary people live,
isn't it?' asked the Princess, attentively.

'I have never seen it, but it's very well laid out,' Rosy
rejoined, with her competent air.

'Oh, I like Camberwell better than that,' said Muniment,
hilariously.

The Princess turned to Lady Aurora, and with the air of

appealing to her for her opinion gave her a glance which
travelled in a flash from the topmost bow of her large, misfitting hat to the crumpled points of her substantial shoes.
'I must get *you* to tell me the truth,' she murmured.   'I
want so much to know London—the real London.   It seems
so difficult!'

Lady Aurora looked a little frightened, but at the same
time gratified, and after a moment she responded, 'I
believe a great many artists live in St. John's Wood.'

'I don't care about the artists!' the Princess exclaimed,
shaking her head, slowly, with the sad smile which sometimes made her beauty so inexpressibly touching.

'Not when they have painted you such beautiful pictures?'
Rosy demanded.   'We know about your pictures—we have
admired them so much.   Mr. Hyacinth has described to us
your precious possessions.'

The Princess transferred her smile to Rosy, and rested
it on that young lady's shrunken countenance with the same
ineffable head-shake.   'You do me too much honour.   I
have no possessions.'

'Gracious, was it all a make-believe?' Rosy cried, flashing at Hyacinth an eye that was never so eloquent as when
it demanded an explanation.

'I have nothing in the world—nothing but the clothes
on my back!' the Princess repeated, very gravely, without
looking at the young man.

The words struck him as an admonition, so that, though
he was much puzzled, he made no attempt, for the moment,
to reconcile the contradiction.   He only replied, 'I meant
the things in the house.   Of course I didn't know whom
they belonged to.'

'There are no things in my house now,' the Princess
went on; and there was a touch of pure, high resignation
in the words.

'Laws, I shouldn't like that!' Rose Muniment declared,
glancing, with complacency, over her own decorated walls.
'Everything here belongs to me.'

'I shall bring Madame Grandoni to see you,' said the
Princess, irrelevantly but kindly.

'Do you think it's not right to have a lot of things

about?' Lady Aurora, with sudden courage, queried of her distinguished companion, pointing her chin at her but looking into the upper angle of the room.

'I suppose one must always settle that for one's self. I don't like to be surrounded with objects I don't care for ; and I can care only for one thing—that is, for one class of things —at a time. Dear lady,' the Princess went on, 'I fear I must confess to you that my heart is not in *bibelots*. When thousands and tens of thousands haven't bread to put in their mouths, I can dispense with tapestry and old china.' And her fair face, bent charmingly, conciliatingly, on Lady Aurora, appeared to argue that if she was narrow at least she was candid.

Hyacinth wondered, rather vulgarly, what strange turn she had taken, and whether this singular picture of her denuded personality were not one of her famous caprices, a whimsical joke, a nervous perversity. Meanwhile, he heard Lady Aurora urge, anxiously, 'But don't you think we ought to make the world more beautiful?'

'Doesn't the Princess make it so by the mere fact of her existence?' Hyacinth demanded; his perplexity escaping, in a harmless manner, through this graceful hyperbole. He had observed that, though the lady in question could dispense with old china and tapestry, she could not dispense with a pair of immaculate gloves, which fitted her like a charm.

'My people have a mass of things, you know, but I have really nothing myself,' said Lady Aurora, as if she owed this assurance to such a representative of suffering humanity.

'The world will be beautiful enough when it becomes good enough,' the Princess resumed. 'Is there anything so ugly as unjust distinctions, as the privileges of the few contrasted with the degradation of the many? When we want to beautify, we must begin at the right end.'

'Surely there are none of us but what have our privileges!' Rose Muniment exclaimed, with eagerness. 'What do you say to mine, lying here between two members of the aristocracy, and with Mr. Hyacinth thrown in?'

'You are certainly lucky—with Lady Aurora Langrish.

I wish she would come and see *me*,' the Princess murmured, getting up.

'Do go, my lady, and tell me if it's so poor!' Rosy went on, gaily.

'I think there can't be too many pictures and statues and works of art,' Hyacinth broke out. 'The more the better, whether people are hungry or not. In the way of ameliorating influences, are not those the most definite?'

'A piece of bread and butter is more to the purpose, if your stomach's empty,' the Princess declared.

'Robinson has been corrupted by foreign influences,' Paul Muniment suggested. 'He doesn't care for bread and butter now; he likes French cookery.'

'Yes, but I don't get it. And have you sent away the little man, the Italian, with the white cap and apron?' Hyacinth asked of the Princess.

She hesitated a moment, and then she replied, laughing, and not in the least offended at his question, though it was an attempt to put her in the wrong from which Hyacinth had not been able to refrain, in his astonishment at these ascetic pretensions, 'I have sent him away many times!'

Lady Aurora had also got up ; she stood there gazing at her beautiful fellow-visitor with a timidity which made her wonder only more apparent. 'Your servants must be awfully fond of you,' she said.

'Oh, my servants!' murmured the Princess, as if it were only by a stretch of the meaning of the word that she could be said to enjoy the ministrations of menials. Her manner seemed to imply that she had a charwoman for an hour a day. Hyacinth caught the tone, and determined that since she was going, as it appeared, he would break off his own visit and accompany her. He had flattered himself, at the end of three weeks of Medley, that he knew her in every phase, but here was a field of freshness. She turned to Paul Muniment and put out her hand to him, and while he took it in his own his face was visited by the most beautiful eyes that had ever rested there. 'Will you come and see me, one of these days?' she asked, with a voice as sweet and clear as her glance.

Hyacinth waited for Paul's answer with an emotion

that could only be accounted for by his affectionate
sympathy, the manner in which he had spoken of him to
the Princess and which he wished him to justify, the
interest he had in his appearing, completely, the fine
fellow he believed him. Muniment neither stammered
nor blushed; he held himself straight, and looked back
at his interlocutress with an eye almost as crystalline as
her own. Then, by way of answer, he inquired, 'Well,
madam, pray what good will it do me?' And the tone of
the words was so humorous and kindly, and so instinct
with a plain manly sense, that though they were not
gallant Hyacinth was not ashamed for him. At the same
moment he observed that Lady Aurora was watching their
friend as if she had at least an equal stake in what he
might say.

'Ah, none; only me, perhaps, a little.' With this
rejoinder, and with a wonderful sweet, indulgent dignity,
in which there was none of the stiffness of pride or resentment, the Princess quitted him and approached Lady
Aurora. She asked her if *she* wouldn't do her the kindness
to come. She should like so much to know her, and she
had an idea there was a great deal they might talk about.
Lady Aurora said she should be delighted, and the Princess took one of her cards out of her pocket and gave it to
the noble spinster. After she had done so she stood a
moment holding her hand, and remarked, 'It has really
been such a happiness to me to meet you. Please don't
think it's very clumsy if I say I *do* like you so!' Lady
Aurora was evidently exceedingly moved and impressed;
but Rosy, when the Princess took farewell of her, and the
irrepressible invalid had assured her of the pleasure with
which she should receive her again, admonished her that
in spite of this she could never conscientiously enter into
such theories.

'If every one was equal,' she asked, 'where would be
the gratification I feel in getting a visit from a grandee?
That's what I have often said to her ladyship, and I consider that I've kept her in her place a little. No, no; no
equality while *I*'m about the place!'

The company appeared to comprehend that there was

a natural fitness in Hyacinth's seeing the great lady on her
way, and accordingly no effort was made to detain him.
He guided her, with the help of an attendant illumination
from Muniment, down the dusky staircase, and at the
door of the house there was a renewed brief leave-taking
with the young chemist, who, however, showed no signs of
relenting or recanting in respect to the Princess's invitation.
The warm evening had by this time grown thick, and the
population of Audley Court appeared to be passing it, for
the most part, in the open air.   As Hyacinth assisted his
companion to thread her way through groups of sprawling,
chattering children, gossiping women with bare heads and
babies at the breast,. and heavily-planted men smoking
very bad pipes, it seemed to him that their project of
exploring the slums was already in the way of execution.
He said nothing till they had gained the outer street, and
then, pausing a moment, he inquired how she would be
conveyed.   Had she a carriage somewhere, or should he
try and get a cab?

'A carriage, my dear fellow?   For what do you take
me?   I won't trouble you about a cab : I walk everywhere
now.'

'But if I had not been here?'

'I should have gone alone,' said the Princess, smiling
at him through the turbid twilight of Camberwell.

'And where, please, gracious heaven?   I may at least
have the honour of accompanying you.'

'Certainly, if you can walk so far.'

'So far as what, dear Princess?'

'As Madeira Crescent, Paddington.'

'Madeira Crescent, Paddington?'   Hyacinth stared.

'That's what I call it when I'm with people with whom
I wish to be fine, like you.   I have taken a small house
there.'

'Then it's really true that you have given up your
beautiful things?'

'I have sold them all, to give to the poor.'

'Ah, Princess!' the young man almost moaned; for the
memory of some of her treasures was vivid within him.

She became very grave, even stern, and with an accent

of reproach that seemed to show she had been wounded where she was most sensitive, she demanded, ' When I said I was willing to make the last sacrifice, did you then believe I was lying?'

' Haven't you kept *anything?*' Hyacinth went on, without heeding this challenge.

She looked at him a moment. ' I have kept *you!*' Then she took his arm, and they moved forward. He saw what she had done; she was living in a little ugly, bare, middle-class house and wearing simple gowns; and the energy and good faith of her behaviour, with the abruptness of the transformation, took away his breath. ' I thought I should please you so much,' she added, after they had gone a few steps. And before he had time to reply, as they came to a part of the street where there were small shops, those of butchers, greengrocers and pork-pie men, with open fronts, flaring lamps and humble purchasers, she broke out, joyously, ' Ah, this is the way I like to see London!'

The house in Madeira Crescent was a low, stucco-fronted
edifice, in a shabby, shallow semicircle, and Hyacinth
could see, as they approached it, that the window-place in
the parlour (which was on a level with the street-door), was
ornamented by a glass case containing stuffed birds and
surmounted by an alabaster Cupid. He was sufficiently
versed in his London to know that the descent in the scale
of the gentility was almost immeasurable for a person who
should have moved into that quarter from the neighbourhood of Park Lane. The street was not squalid, and it
was strictly residential; but it was mean and meagre and
fourth-rate, and had in the highest degree that paltry, paro-
chial air, that absence of style and elevation, which is the
stamp of whole districts of London and which Hyacinth
had already more than once mentally compared with the
high-piled, important look of the Parisian perspective. It
possessed in combination every quality which should have
made it detestable to the Princess; it was almost as bad as
Lomax Place. As they stopped before the narrow, ill-
painted door, on which the number of the house was
marked with a piece of common porcelain, cut in a fanciful
shape, it appeared to Hyacinth that he had felt, in their
long walk, the touch of the passion which led his companion to divest herself of her superfluities, but that it
would take the romantic out of one's heroism to settle one's
self in such a *mesquin*, Philistine row. However, if the
Princess had wished to mortify the flesh she had chosen an
effective means of doing so, and of mortifying the spirit as
well. The long light of the gray summer evening was still
in the air, and Madeira Crescent wore a soiled, dusty expression. A hand-organ droned in front of a neighbouring

house, and the cart of the local washerwoman, to which a donkey was harnessed, was drawn up opposite. The local children, as well, were dancing on the pavement, to the music of the organ, and the scene was surveyed, from one of the windows, by a gentleman in a dirty dressing-gown, smoking a pipe, who made Hyacinth think of Mr. Micawber. The young man gave the Princess a deep look, before they went into the house, and she smiled, as if she understood everything that was passing in his mind.

The long, circuitous walk with her, from the far-away south of London, had been strange and delightful ; it reminded Hyacinth, more queerly than he could have expressed, of some of the rambles he had taken on summer evenings with Millicent Henning. It was impossible to resemble this young lady less than the Princess resembled her, but in her enjoyment of her unwonted situation (she had never before, on a summer's evening—to the best of Hyacinth's belief, at least—lost herself in the unfashionable districts on the arm of a seedy artisan), the distinguished personage exhibited certain coincidences with the shop-girl. She stopped, as Millicent had done, to look into the windows of vulgar establishments, and amused herself with picking out abominable objects that she should like to possess ; selecting them from a new point of view, that of a reduced fortune and the domestic arrangements of the 'lower middle class,' deriving extreme diversion from the idea that she now belonged to that aggrieved body. She was in a state of light, fresh, sociable exhilaration which Hyacinth had hitherto, in the same degree, not seen in her, and before they reached Madeira Crescent it had become clear to him that her present phase was little more than a brilliant *tour de force*, which he could not imagine her keeping up long, for the simple reason that after the novelty and strangeness of the affair had passed away she would not be able to endure the contact of so much that was common and ugly. For the moment her discoveries in this line diverted her, as all discoveries did, and she pretended to be sounding, in a scientific spirit —that of the social philosopher, the student and critic of manners—the depths of the British Philistia. Hyacinth

was struck, more than ever, with the fund of life that was
in her, the energy of feeling, the high, free, reckless spirit.
These things expressed themselves, as the couple proceeded,
in a hundred sallies and droll proposals, kindling the young
man's pulses and making him conscious of the joy with
which, in any extravagance, he would bear her company to
the death. She appeared to him, at this moment, to be
playing with life so audaciously and defiantly that the end
of it all would inevitably be some violent catastrophe.

She desired exceedingly that Hyacinth should take her
to a music-hall or a coffee-tavern; she even professed a
curiosity to see the inside of a public-house. As she still
had self-possession enough to remember that if she stayed
out beyond a certain hour Madame Grandoni would begin
to worry about her, they were obliged to content themselves
with the minor ' lark,' as the Princess was careful to designate their peep into an establishment, glittering with polished
pewter and brass, which bore the name of the ' Happy
Land.' Hyacinth had feared that she would be nervous
after the narrow, befingered door had swung behind her, or
that, at all events, she would be disgusted at what she
might see and hear in such a place and would immediately
wish to retreat. By good luck, however, there were only
two or three convivial spirits in occupancy, and the presence
of the softer sex was apparently not so rare as to excite
surprise. The softer sex, furthermore, was embodied in a
big, hard, red woman, the publican's wife, who looked as
if she were in the habit of dealing with all sorts and mainly
interested in seeing whether even the finest put down their
money before they were served. The Princess pretended
to ' have something,' and to admire the ornamentation of
the bar; and when Hyacinth asked her in a low tone what
disposal they should make, when the great changes came,
of such an embarrassing type as that, replied, off-hand,
' Oh, drown her in a barrel of beer ! ' She professed, when
they came out, to have been immensely interested in the
' Happy Land,' and was not content until Hyacinth had
fixed an evening on which they might visit a music-hall
together. She talked with him largely, by fits and starts,
about his adventures abroad and his impressions of France

and Italy; breaking off, suddenly, with some irrelevant but almost extravagantly appreciative allusion to Rose Muniment and Lady Aurora ; then returning with a question as to what he had seen and done, the answer to which, however, in many cases, she was not at pains to wait for.   Yet it implied that she had paid considerable attention to what he told her that she should be able to say, towards the end, with that fraternising frankness which was always touching because it appeared to place her at one's mercy, to show that she counted on one's having an equal loyalty, ' Well, my dear friend, you have not wasted your time ; you know everything, you have missed nothing ; there are lots of things you can tell me, and we shall have some famous talks in the winter evenings.'   This last reference was apparently to the coming season, and there was something in the tone of quiet friendship with which it was uttered, and which seemed to involve so many delightful things, something that, for Hyacinth, bound them still closer together.   To live out of the world with her that way, lost among the London millions, in a queer little cock-neyfied retreat, was a refinement of intimacy, and better even than the splendid chance he had enjoyed at Medley.

They found Madame Grandoni sitting alone in the twilight, very patient and peaceful, and having, after all, it was clear, accepted the situation too completely to fidget at such a trifle as her companion's not coming home at a ladylike hour.   She had placed herself in the back part of the tawdry little drawing-room, which looked into a small, smutty garden, and from the front window, which was open, the sound of the hurdy-gurdy and the voices of the children, who were romping to its music, came in to her through the summer dusk.   The influence of London was there, in a kind of mitigated, far-away hum, and for some reason or other, at that moment, the place, to Hyacinth, took on the semblance of the home of an exile —a spot and an hour to be remembered with a throb of fondness in some danger or sorrow of after years.   The old lady never moved from her chair as she saw the Princess come in with the little bookbinder, and her eyes rested on Hyacinth as familiarly as if she had seen him go out with her in the afternoon. The Princess stood before Madame Grandoni a moment, smiling. 'I have done a great thing. What do you think I have done?' she asked, as she drew off her gloves.

'God knows! I have ceased to think!' said the old woman, staring up, with her fat, empty hands on the arms of her chair.

'I have come on foot from the far south of London— how many miles? four or five—and I'm not a particle tired.'

'*Che forza, che forza!*' murmured Madame Grandoni. 'She will knock you up, completely,' she added, turning to Hyacinth with a kind of customary compassion.

'Poor darling, *she* misses the carriage,' Christina remarked, passing out of the room.

Madame Grandoni followed her with her eyes, and Hyacinth thought he perceived a considerable lassitude, a plaintive bewilderment and *hébétement,* in the old woman's face. 'Don't you like to use cabs—I mean hansoms?' he asked, wishing to say something comforting to her.

'It is not true that I miss anything; my life is only too full,' she replied. 'I lived worse than this—in my bad days.' In a moment she went on: 'It's because you are here—she doesn't like Assunta to come.'

'Assunta—because I am here?' Hyacinth did not immediately catch her meaning.

'You must have seen her Italian maid at Medley. She has kept her, and she's ashamed of it. When we are alone Assunta comes for her bonnet. But she likes you to think she waits on herself.'

'That's a weakness—when she's so strong! And what does Assunta think of it?' Hyacinth asked, looking at the stuffed birds in the window, the alabaster Cupid, the wax flowers on the chimney-piece, the florid antimacassars on the chairs, the sentimental engravings on the walls—in frames of *papier-mâché* and 'composition,' some of them enveloped in pink tissue-paper—and the prismatic glass pendants which seemed attached to everything.

'She says, "What on earth will it matter to-morrow?"'

'Does she mean that to-morrow the Princess will have her luxury back again? Hasn't she sold all her beautiful things?'

Madame Grandoni was silent a moment.   'She has kept a few.   They are put away.'

'*A la bonne heure !*' cried Hyacinth, laughing.   He sat down with the ironical old woman ; he spent nearly half an hour in desultory conversation with her, before candles were brought in, and while Christina was in Assunta's hands.   He noticed how resolutely the Princess had withheld herself from any attempt to sweeten the dose she had taken it into her head to swallow, to mitigate the ugliness of her vulgar little house.   She had respected its horrible idiosyncrasies, and left, rigidly, in their places the gimcracks which found favour in Madeira Crescent.   She had flung no draperies over the pretentious furniture and disposed no rugs upon the staring carpet ; and it was plainly her theory that the right way to acquaint one's self with the sensations of the wretched was to suffer the anguish of exasperated taste.   Presently a female servant came in —not the sceptical Assunta, but a stunted young woman of the maid-of-all-work type, the same who had opened the door to the pair a short time before—and informed Hyacinth that the Princess wished him to understand that he was expected to remain to tea.   He learned from Madame Grandoni that the custom of an early dinner, followed in the evening by the frugal repast of the lower orders, was another of Christina's mortifications ; and when, shortly afterwards, he saw the table laid in the back parlour, which was also the dining-room, and observed the nature of the crockery with which it was decorated, he perceived that whether or no her earnestness were durable, it was at any rate, for the time, intense.   Madame Grandoni narrated to him, definitely, as the Princess had done only in scraps, the history of the two ladies since his departure from Medley, their relinquishment of that fine house and the sudden arrangements Christina had made to change her mode of life, after they had been only ten days in South Street.   At the climax of the London season, in a society which only desired to treat her as one of its brightest orna- ments, she had retired to Madeira Crescent, concealing her address (with only partial success, of course), from every one, and inviting a celebrated curiosity-monger to come

and look at her *bibelots* and tell her what he would give
her for the lot.   In this manner she had parted with them
at a fearful sacrifice.   She had wished to avoid the nine
days' wonder of a public sale ; for, to do her justice,
though she liked to be original she didn't like to be
notorious, an occasion of vulgar chatter.   What had precipitated her determination was a remonstrance received
from her husband, just after she left Medley, on the subject
of her excessive expenditure ; he had written to her that
it was past a joke (as she had appeared to consider it), and
that she must really pull up.   Nothing could gall her more
than an interference on that head (she maintained that she
knew the exact figure of the Prince's income, and that her
allowance was an insignificant part of it), and she had
pulled up with a vengeance, as Hyacinth perceived.   The
young man divined on this occasion one of the Princess's
sharpest anxieties (he had never thought of it before), the
danger of Casamassima's really putting the screw on—
attempting to make her come back and live with him by
withholding supplies altogether.   In this case she would
find herself in a very tight place, though she had a theory
that if she should go to law about the matter the courts
would allow her a separate maintenance.   This course,
however, it would scarcely be in her character to adopt ;
she would be more likely to waive her right and support
herself by lessons in music and the foreign tongues, supple-
mented by the remnant of property that had come to her
from her mother.   That she was capable of returning to
the Prince some day, through not daring to face the loss
of luxury, was an idea that could not occur to Hyacinth,
in the midst of her assurances, uttered at various times,
that she positively yearned for a sacrifice ; and such an
apprehension was less present to him than ever as he
listened to Madame Grandoni's account of the manner in
which her rupture with the fashionable world had been
effected.   It must be added that the old lady remarked,
with a sigh, that she didn't know how it would all end, as
some of Christina's economies were very costly ; and when
Hyacinth pressed her a little she went on to say that it was
not at present the question of complications arising from the

Prince that troubled her most, but the fear that Christina
was seriously compromised by her reckless, senseless cor-
respondences—letters arriving from foreign countries, from
God knew whom (Christina never told her, nor did she
desire it), all about uprisings and liberations (of so much
one could be sure), and other matters that were no concern
of honest folk. Hyacinth scarcely knew what Madame
Grandoni meant by this allusion, which seemed to show
that, during the last few months, the Princess had considerably extended her revolutionary connection : he only
thought of Hoffendahl, whose name, however, he was
careful not to pronounce, and wondered whether his
hostess had been writing to the Master to intercede for
him, to beg that he might be let off. His cheeks burned
at the thought, but he contented himself with remarking
to Madame Grandoni that their extraordinary friend enjoyed
the sense of danger. The old lady wished to know how
she would enjoy the hangman's rope (with which, *du train
dont elle allait*, she might easily make acquaintance) ; and
when he expressed the hope that she didn't regard him as
a counsellor of imprudence, replied, ' You, my poor child ?
Oh, I saw into you at Medley. You are a simple *codino !* '

The Princess came in to tea in a very dull gown, with
a bunch of keys at her girdle ; and nothing could have
suggested the thrifty housewife better than the manner in
which she superintended the laying of the cloth and the
placing on it of a little austere refreshment—a pile of bread
and butter, flanked by a pot of marmalade and a morsel of
bacon. She filled the teapot out of a little tin canister
locked up in a cupboard, of which the key worked with
difficulty, and made the tea with her own superb hands ;
taking pains, however, to explain to Hyacinth that she was
far from imposing that régime on Madame Grandoni, who
understood that the grocer had a standing order to supply
her, for her private consumption, with any delicacy she
might desire. For herself, she had never been so well as
since she followed a homely diet. On Sundays they had
muffins, and sometimes, for a change, a smoked haddock,
or even a fried sole. Hyacinth was lost in adoration of
the Princess's housewifely ways and of the exquisite figure

that she made as a little *bourgeoise;* judging that if her
attempt to combine plain living with high thinking were all
a comedy, at least it was the most finished entertainment
she had yet offered him. She talked to Madame Grandoni
about Lady Aurora; described her with much drollery,
even to the details of her dress; declared that she was a
delightful creature and one of the most interesting persons
she had seen for an age; expressed to Hyacinth the conviction that she should like her exceedingly, if Lady Aurora
would only believe a little in *her.* 'But I shall like her,
whether she does or not,' said the Princess. 'I always
know when that's going to happen; it isn't so common.
She will begin very well with me, and be "fascinated"—
isn't that the way people begin with me?—but she won't
understand me at all, or make out in the least what kind of
a queer fish I am, though I shall try to show her. When
she thinks she does, at last, she will give me up in disgust,
and will never know that she has understood me quite
wrong. That has been the way with most of the people I
have liked; they have run away from me *à toutes jambes.*
Oh, I have inspired aversions!' laughed the Princess, hand-
ing Hyacinth his cup of tea. He recognised it by the
aroma as a mixture not inferior to that of which he had
partaken at Medley. 'I have never succeeded in knowing
any one who would do me good; for by the time I began
to improve, under their influence, they could put up with
me no longer.'

'You told me you were going to visit the poor. I don't
understand what your Gräfin was doing there,' said Madame
Grandoni.

'She had come out of charity—in the same way as I.
She evidently goes about immensely over there; I shall
entreat her to take me with her.'

'I thought you had promised to let me be your guide,
in those explorations,' Hyacinth remarked.

The Princess looked at him a moment. 'Dear Mr.
Robinson, Lady Aurora knows more than you.'

'There have been times, surely, when you have com-
plimented me on my knowledge.'

'Oh, I mean more about the lower classes!' the Princess

exclaimed; and, oddly enough, there was a sense in which Hyacinth was unable to deny the allegation.   He presently returned to something she had said a moment before, declaring that it had not been the way with Madame Grandoni and him to take to their heels, and to this she replied, 'Oh, you'll run away yet; don't be afraid!'

'I think that if I had been capable of quitting you I should have done it by this time; I have neglected such opportunities,' the old lady sighed.   Hyacinth now perceived that her eye had quite lost its ancient twinkle; she was troubled about many things.

'It is true that if you didn't leave me when I was rich, it wouldn't look well for you to leave me at present,' the Princess suggested; and before Madame Grandoni could reply to this speech she said to Hyacinth, 'I liked the man, your friend Muniment, so much for saying he wouldn't come to see me. "What good would it do him," poor fellow?   What good would it do him, indeed?   You were not so difficult: you held off a little and pleaded obstacles, but one could see you would come down,' she continued, covering her guest with her mystifying smile.   'Besides, I was smarter then, more splendid; I had on gewgaws and suggested worldly lures.   I must have been more attractive. But I liked him for refusing,' she repeated; and of the many words she uttered that evening it was these that made most impression on Hyacinth.   He remained for an hour after tea, for on rising from the table she had gone to the piano (she had not deprived herself of this resource, and had a humble instrument, of the so-called 'cottage' kind), and begun to play in a manner that reminded him of her playing the day of his arrival at Medley.   The night had grown close, and as the piano was in the front room he opened, at her request, the window that looked into Madeira Crescent. Beneath it assembled the youth of both sexes, the dingy loiterers who had clustered an hour before around the hurdy-gurdy.   But on this occasion they did not caper about; they remained still, leaning against the area-rails and listening to the wondrous music.   When Hyacinth told the Princess of the spell she had thrown upon them she declared that it made her singularly happy; she added that she was really glad, almost proud, of her day ; she felt as if she had begun to do something for the people. Just before he took leave she encountered some occasion for saying to him that she was certain the man in Audley Court wouldn't come ; and Hyacinth forebore to contradict her, because he believed that in fact he wouldn't.

How right she had been to say that Lady Aurora would
probably be fascinated at first was proved the first time
Hyacinth went to Belgrave Square, a visit he was led to
pay very promptly, by a deep sense of the obligations under
which her ladyship had placed him at the time of Pinnie's
death. The circumstances in which he found her were
quite the same as those of his visit the year before ; she was
spending the unfashionable season in her father's empty
house, amid a desert of brown holland and the dormant
echoes of heavy conversation. He had seen so much of
her during Pinnie's illness that he felt (or had felt then)
that he knew her almost intimately—that they had become
real friends, almost comrades, and might meet henceforth
without reserves or ceremonies ; yet she was as fluttered
and awkward as she had been on the other occasion : not
distant, but entangled in new coils of shyness and apparently
unmindful of what had happened to draw them closer.
Hyacinth, however, always liked extremely to be with her,
for she was the person in the world who quietly, delicately,
and as a matter of course treated him most like a gentleman. She had never said the handsome, flattering things
to him that had fallen from the lips of the Princess, and
never explained to him her view of him ; but her timid,
cursory, receptive manner, which took all sorts of equalities
for granted, was a homage to the idea of his refinement. It
was in this manner that she now conversed with him on the
subject of his foreign travels ; he found himself discussing
the political indications of Paris and the Ruskinian theories
of Venice, in Belgrave Square, quite like one of the cos-
mopolites bred in that region. It took him, however, but
a few minutes to perceive that Lady Aurora's heart was not

in these considerations ; the deferential smile she bent upon
him, while she sat with her head thrust forward and her
long hands clasped in her lap, was slightly mechanical, her
attitude perfunctory.   When he gave her his views of some
of the *arrière-pensées* of M. Gambetta (for he had views not
altogether, as he thought, deficient in originality), she did
not interrupt, for she never interrupted ; but she took
advantage of his first pause to say, quickly, irrelevantly,
'Will the Princess Casamassima come again to Audley
Court ? '

'I have no doubt she will come again, if they would
like her to.'

'I do hope she will.   She is very wonderful,' Lady Aurora
continued.

'Oh, yes, she is very wonderful.   I think she gave Rosy
pleasure,' said Hyacinth.

'Rosy can talk of nothing else.   It would really do her
great good to see the Princess again.   Don't you think she
is different from anybody that one has ever seen ?'   But
her ladyship added, before waiting for an answer to this,
'I liked her quite extraordinarily.'

'She liked you just as much.   I know it would give
her great pleasure if you should go to see her.'

'Fancy !' exclaimed Lady Aurora ; but she instantly
obtained the Princess's address from Hyacinth, and made
a note of it in a small, shabby book.   She mentioned that
the card the Princess had given her in Camberwell proved
to contain no address, and Hyacinth recognised that
vagary—the Princess was so off-hand.   Then she said,
hesitating a little, ' Does she really care for the poor ? '

'If she doesn't,' the young man replied, 'I can't imagine
what interest she has in pretending to.'

'If she does, she's very remarkable—she deserves great
honour.'

'You really care ; why is she more remarkable than you ?'
Hyacinth demanded.

'Oh, it's very different—she's so wonderfully attractive !'
Lady Aurora replied, making, recklessly, the only allusion
to the oddity of her own appearance in which Hyacinth
was destined to hear her indulge.   She became conscious

of it the moment she had spoken, and said, quickly, to turn it off, 'I should like to talk with her, but I'm rather afraid. She's tremendously clever.'

'Ah, what she is you'll find out when you know her!' Hyacinth sighed, expressively.

His hostess looked at him a little, and then, vaguely, exclaimed, 'How very interesting!' The next moment she continued, 'She might do so many other things; she might charm the world.'

'She does that, whatever she does,' said Hyacinth, smiling. 'It's all by the way; it needn't interfere.'

'That's what I mean, that most other people would be content—beautiful as she is. There's great merit, when you give up something.'

'She has known a great many bad people, and she wants to know some good,' Hyacinth rejoined. 'Therefore be sure to go to her soon.'

'She looks as if she had known nothing bad since she was born,' said Lady Aurora, rapturously. 'I can't imagine her going into all the dreadful places that she would have to.'

'You have gone into them, and it hasn't hurt you,' Hyacinth suggested.

'How do you know that? My family think it has.'

'You make me glad that I haven't a family,' said the young man.

'And the Princess—has she no one?'

'Ah, yes, she has a husband. But she doesn't live with him.'

'Is he one of the bad persons?' asked Lady Aurora, as earnestly as a child listening to a tale.

'Well, I don't like to abuse him, because he is down.'

'If I were a man, I should be in love with her,' said Lady Aurora. Then she pursued, 'I wonder whether we might work together.'

'That's exactly what she hopes.'

'I won't show her the worst places,' said her ladyship, smiling.

To which Hyacinth replied, 'I suspect you will do what every one else has done, namely, exactly what she wants!'

Before he took leave he said to her, 'Do you know whether Paul Muniment liked the Princess?'

Lady Aurora meditated a moment, apparently with some intensity. 'I think he considered her extraordinarily beautiful—the most beautiful person he had ever seen.'

'Does he still believe her to be a humbug?'

'Still?' asked Lady Aurora, as if she didn't understand.

'I mean that that was the impression apparently made upon him last winter by my description of her.'

'Oh, I'm sure he thinks her tremendously plucky!' That was all the satisfaction Hyacinth got just then as to Muniment's estimate of the Princess.

A few days afterward he returned to Madeira Crescent, in the evening, the only time he was free, the Princess having given him a general invitation to take tea with her. He felt that he ought to be discreet in acting upon it, though he was not without reasons that would have warranted him in going early and often. He had a peculiar dread of her growing tired of him—boring herself in his society; yet at the same time he had rather a sharp vision of her boring herself without him, in the dull summer evenings, when even Paddington was out of town. He wondered what she did, what visitors dropped in, what pastimes she cultivated, what saved her from the sudden vagary of throwing up the whole of her present game. He remembered that there was a complete side of her life with which he was almost unacquainted (Lady Marchant and her daughters, at Medley, and three or four other persons who had called while he was there, being, in his experience, the only illustrations of it), and knew not to what extent she had, in spite of her transformation, preserved relations with her old friends; but he could easily imagine a day when she should discover that what she found in Madeira Crescent was less striking than what she missed. Going thither a second time Hyacinth perceived that he had done her great injustice; she was full of resources, she had never been so happy, she found time to read, to write, to commune with her piano, and above all to think—a delightful detachment from the invasive, vulgar, gossiping, distracting world she had known hitherto. The only interruption to her felicity was that she received quantities of notes from her former acquaintance, challenging her to give some account of herself, to say what had become of her, to come and stay with them in the country; but with these importunate missives she took a very short way—she simply burned them, without answering. She told Hyacinth immediately that Lady Aurora had called on her, two days before, at an hour when she was not in, and she had straightway addressed her, in return, an invitation to come to tea, any evening, at eight o'clock. That was the way the people in Madeira Crescent entertained each other (the Princess knew everything about them now, and was eager to impart her knowledge); and the evening, she was sure, would be much more convenient to Lady Aurora, whose days were filled with good works, peregrinations of charity. Her ladyship arrived ten minutes after Hyacinth; she told the Princess that her invitation had been expressed in a manner so irresistible that she was unwilling to wait more than a day to respond. She was introduced to Madame Grandoni, and tea was immediately served; Hyacinth being gratefully conscious the while of the supersubtle way in which Lady Aurora forebore to appear bewildered at meeting him in such society. She knew he frequented it, and she had been witness of his encounter with the Princess in Audley Court; but it might have startled her to have ocular evidence of the footing on which he stood. Everything the Princess did or said, at this time, had for effect, whatever its purpose, to make her seem more rare and fine; and she had seldom given him greater pleasure than by the exquisite art she put forward to win Lady Aurora's confidence, to place herself under the pure and elevating influence of the noble spinster. She made herself small and simple; she spoke of her own little aspirations and efforts; she appealed and persuaded; she laid her white hand on Lady Aurora's, gazing at her with an interest which was evidently deeply sincere, but which, all the same, derived half its effect from the contrast between the quality of her beauty, the whole air of her person, and

the hard, dreary problems of misery and crime. It was
touching, and Lady Aurora was touched; that was very
evident as they sat together on the sofa, after tea, and the
Princess protested that she only wanted to know what her
new friend was doing—what she had done for years—in
order that she might go and do likewise. She asked personal questions with a directness that was sometimes embarrassing to the subject—Hyacinth had seen that habit in
her from the first—and Lady Aurora, though she was
charmed and excited, was not quite comfortable at being
so publicly probed and sounded. The public was formed
of Madame Grandoni and Hyacinth; but the old lady
(whose intercourse with the visitor had consisted almost
wholly of watching her with a quiet, speculative anxiety),
presently shuffled away, and was heard, through the thin
partitions that prevailed in Madeira Crescent, to ascend to
her own apartment. It seemed to Hyacinth that he ought
also, in delicacy, to retire, and this was his intention, from
one moment to the other; to him, certainly (and the second
time she met him), Lady Aurora had made as much of her
confession as he had a right to look for. After that one
little flash of egotism he had never again heard her allude
to her own feelings or circumstances.

'Do you stay in town, like this, at such a season, on
purpose to attend to your work?' the Princess asked; and
there was something archly rueful in the tone in which she
made this inquiry, as if it cost her just a pang to find that
in taking such a line she herself had not been so original
as she hoped. 'Mr. Robinson has told me about your big
house in Belgrave Square—you must let me come and see
you there. Nothing would make me so happy as that you
should allow me to help you a little—how little soever.
Do you like to be helped, or do you like to go alone?
Are you very independent, or do you need to look up, to
cling, to lean upon some one? Excuse me if I ask impertinent questions; we speak that way—rather, you know
—in Rome, where I have spent a large part of my life.
That idea of your being there alone in your great dull
house, with all your charities and devotions, makes a kind
of picture in my mind; it's quaint and touching, like some-

thing in some English novel. Englishwomen are so accomplished, are they not? I am really a foreigner, you know,
and though I have lived here a while it takes one some
time to find those things out *au juste*. Therefore, is your
work for the people only one of your occupations, or is it
everything, does it absorb your whole life? That's what I
should like it to be for me! Do your family like you to
throw yourself into all this, or have you had to brave a
certain amount of ridicule? I dare say you have; that's
where you English are strong, in braving ridicule. They
have to do it so often, haven't they? I don't know whether
I could do it. I never tried; but with you I would brave
anything. Are your family clever and sympathetic? No?
the kind of thing that one's family generally is? Ah, well,
dear lady, we must make a little family together. Are you
encouraged or disgusted? Do you go on doggedly, or
have you any faith, any great idea, that lifts you up? Are
you religious, now, *par exemple?* Do you do your work
in connection with any ecclesiasticism, any missions, or
priests or sisters? I'm a Catholic, you know—but so
little! I shouldn't mind in the least joining hands with
any one who is really doing anything. I express myself
awkwardly, but perhaps you know what I mean. Possibly
you don't know that I am one of those who believe that a
great social cataclyism is destined to take place, and that it
can't make things worse than they are already. I believe,
in a word, in the people doing something for themselves
(the others will never do anything for them), and I am
quite willing to help them. If that shocks you I shall be
immensely disappointed, because there is something in the
impression you make on me that seems to say that you
haven't the usual prejudices, and that if certain things were
to happen you wouldn't be afraid. You are shy, are you
not?—but you are not timorous. I suppose that if you
thought the inequalities and oppressions and miseries which
now exist were a necessary part of life, and were going on
for ever, you wouldn't be interested in those people over the
river (the bedridden girl and her brother, I mean); because
Mr. Robinson tells me that they are advanced socialists—
or at least the brother is. Perhaps you'll say that you don't

care for him ; the sister, to your mind, being the remarkable one. She is, indeed, a perfect little *femme du monde*
—she talks so much better than most of the people in
society. I hope you don't mind my saying that, because
I have an idea that you are not in society. You can
imagine whether I am ! Haven't you judged it, like me,
condemned it, and given it up ? Are you not sick of the
egotism, the snobbery, the meanness, the frivolity, the
immorality, the hypocrisy ? Isn't there a great resemblance in our situation ? I don't mean in our nature,
for you are far better than I shall ever be. Aren't you
quite divinely good ? When I see a woman of your sort
(not that I often do !) I try to be a little less bad. You
have helped hundreds, thousands, of people ; you must
help me !'

These remarks, which I have strung together, did not,
of course, fall from the Princess's lips in an uninterrupted
stream ; they were arrested and interspersed by frequent
inarticulate responses and embarrassed protests. Lady
Aurora shrank from them even while they gratified her,
blinking and fidgeting in the brilliant, direct light of her
hostess's attentions. I need not repeat her answers, the
more so as they none of them arrived at completion, but
passed away into nervous laughter and averted looks, the
latter directed at the ceiling, the floor, the windows, and
appearing to constitute a kind of entreaty to some occult
or supernatural power that the conversation should become
more impersonal. In reply to the Princess's allusion to
the convictions prevailing in the Muniment family, she
said that the brother and sister thought differently about
public questions, but were of the same mind with regard
to persons of the upper class taking an interest in the
working people, attempting to enter into their life : they
held it was a great mistake. At this information the
Princess looked much disappointed ; she wished to know
if the Muniments thought it was impossible to do them any
good. ' Oh, I mean a mistake from *our* point of view,'
said Lady Aurora. ' They wouldn't do it in our place ;
they think we had much better occupy ourselves with our
own pleasures.' And as the Princess stared, not compre-

hending, she went on : ' Rosy thinks we have a right to
our own pleasures under all circumstances, no matter how
badly off the poor may be ; and her brother takes the
ground that we will not have them long, and that in view
of what may happen we are great fools not to make the
most of them.'

' I see, I see.   That is very strong,' the Princess murmured, in a tone of high appreciation.

' I dare say.   But all the same, whatever is going to
come, one *must* do something.'

' You do think, then, that something is going to come ?'
said the Princess.

' Oh, immense changes, I dare say.   But I don't belong
to anything, you know.'

The Princess hesitated a moment.   ' No more do I.
But many people do.   Mr. Robinson, for instance.'   And
she gave Hyacinth a familiar smile.

' Oh, if the changes depend on me !' the young man
exclaimed, blushing.

' They won't set the Thames on fire—I quite agree to
that !'

Lady Aurora had the manner of not considering that
she had a warrant for going into the question of Hyacinth's affiliations ; so she stared abstractedly at the
piano and in a moment remarked to the Princess, ' I
am sure you play awfully well ; I should like so much to
hear you.'

Hyacinth felt that their hostess thought this *banal.*
She had not asked Lady Aurora to spend the evening
with her simply that they should fall back on the resources
of the vulgar.   Nevertheless, she replied with perfect good-
nature that she should be delighted to play ; only there was
a thing she should like much better, namely, that Lady
Aurora should narrate her life.

' Oh, don't talk about mine ; yours, yours !' her ladyship cried, colouring with eagerness and, for the first time
since her arrival, indulging in the free gesture of laying her
hand upon that of the Princess.

' With so many narratives in the air, I certainly had
better take myself off,' said Hyacinth, and the Princess

offered no opposition to his departure. She and Lady Aurora were evidently on the point of striking up a tremendous intimacy, and as he turned this idea over, walking away, it made him sad, for strange, vague reasons, which he could not have expressed.

THE Sunday following this occasion Hyacinth spent almost
entirely with the Muniments, with whom, since his return
to his work, he had been able to have no long, fraternising
talk, of the kind that had marked their earlier relations.
The present, however, was a happy day; it refreshed
exceedingly the sentiments with which he now regarded
the inscrutable Paul. The warm, bright September
weather gilded even the dinginess of Audley Court, and
while, in the morning, Rosy's brother and their visitor sat
beside her sofa, the trio amused themselves with discussing
a dozen different plans for giving a festive turn to the day.
There had been moments, in the last six months, when
Hyacinth had the sense that he should never again be able
to enter into such ideas as that, and these moments had
been connected with the strange perversion taking place in
his mental image of the man whose hardness (of course he
was obliged to be hard), he had never expected to see
turned upon a passionate admirer. But now, for the hour
at least, the darkness had cleared away, and Paul's company was in itself a comfortable, inspiring influence. He
had never been kinder, jollier, safer, as it were; it had
never appeared more desirable to hold fast to him and
trust him. Less than ever would an observer have guessed
there was a reason why the two young men might have
winced as they looked at each other. Rosy naturally took
part in the question debated between her companions—
the question whether they should limit their excursion to a
walk in Hyde Park; should embark at Lambeth pier on
the penny steamer, which would convey them to Greenwich; or should start presently for Waterloo station and
go thence by train to Hampton Court. Miss Muniment

had visited none of these places, but she contributed largely
to the discussion, for which she seemed perfectly qualified ;
talked about the crowd on the steamer, and the inconveni-
ence arising from drunken persons on the return, quite as
if she had suffered from these drawbacks ; said that the
view from the hill at Greenwich was terribly smoky, and
at that season the fashionable world—half the attraction, of
course—was wholly absent from Hyde Park ; and expressed
strong views in favour of Wolsey's old palace, with whose
history she appeared intimately acquainted. She threw
herself into her brother's holiday with eagerness and glee,
and Hyacinth marvelled again at the stoicism of the hard,
bright creature, polished, as it were, by pain, whose imagination appeared never to concern itself with her own
privations, so that she could lie in her close little room the
whole golden afternoon, without bursting into sobs as she
saw the western sunbeams slant upon the shabby, ugly,
familiar paper of her wall and thought of the far-off fields
and gardens which she should never see. She talked immensely of the Princess, for whose beauty, grace and benevolence she could find no sufficient praise ; declaring that
of all the fair faces that had ever hung over her couch (and
Rosy spoke as from immense opportunities for comparison),
she had far the noblest and most refreshing. She seemed
to make a kind of light in the room and to leave it behind
her after she had gone. Rosy could call up her image as
she could hum a tune she had heard, and she expressed in
her quaint, particular way how, as she lay there in the quiet
hours, she repeated over to herself the beautiful air. The
Princess might be anything, she might be royal or imperial,
and Rosy was well aware how little *she* should complain of
the dullness of her life when such apparitions as that could
pop in any day. She made a difference in the place—it
gave it a kind of finish for her to have come there ; if it
was good enough for a princess, it was good enough for
her, and she hoped she shouldn't hear again of Paul's
wishing her to move out of a room with which she should
have henceforth such delightful associations. The Princess
had found her way to Audley Court, and perhaps she
wouldn't find it to another lodging—they couldn't expect

her to follow them about London at their pleasure; and at any rate she had evidently been very much struck with the little room, so that if they were quiet and patient who could say but the fancy would take her to send them a bit of carpet, or a picture, or even a mirror with a gilt frame, to make it a bit more tasteful? Rosy's transitions from pure enthusiasm to the imaginative calculation of benefit were performed with a serenity peculiar to herself. Her chatter had so much spirit and point that it always commanded attention, but to-day Hyacinth was less tolerant of it than usual, because so long as it lasted Muniment held his tongue, and what he had been anxious about was much more Paul's impression of the Princess. Rosy made no remark to him on the monopoly he had so long enjoyed of this wonderful lady; she had always had the manner of a kind of indulgent incredulity about Hyacinth's social adventures, and he saw the day might easily come when she would begin to talk of the Princess as if she herself had been the first to discover her. She had much to say, however, about the nature of the acquaintance Lady Aurora had formed with her, and she was mainly occupied with the glory she had drawn upon herself by bringing two such exalted persons together. She fancied them alluding, in the great world, to the occasion on which 'we first met, at Miss Muniment's, you know;' and she related how Lady Aurora, who had been in Audley Court the day before, had declared that she owed her a debt she could never repay. The two ladies had liked each other more, almost, than they liked any one; and wasn't it a rare picture to think of them moving hand in hand, like twin roses, through the bright upper air? Muniment inquired, in rather a coarse, unsympathetic way, what the mischief she ever wanted of *her*; which led Hyacinth to demand in return, 'What do you mean? What does who want of whom?'

'What does the beauty want of *our* poor lady? She has a totally different stamp. I don't know much about women, but I can see that.'

'How do you mean—a different stamp? They both have the stamp of their rank!' cried Rosy.

'Who can ever tell what women want, at any time?'

Hyacinth said, with the off-handedness of a man of the world.

'Well, my boy, if you don't know any more than I, you disappoint me! Perhaps if we wait long enough she will tell us some day herself.'

'Tell you what she wants of Lady Aurora?'

'I don't mind about Lady Aurora so much; but what in the name of long journeys does she want with *us*?'

'Don't you think you're worth a long journey?' Rosy asked, gaily. 'If you were not my brother, which is handy for seeing you, and I were not confined to my sofa, I would go from one end of England to the other to make your acquaintance! He's in love with the Princess,' she went on, to Hyacinth, 'and he asks those senseless questions to cover it up. What does any one want of anything?'

It was decided, at last, that the two young men should go down to Greenwich, and after they had partaken of bread and cheese with Rosy they embarked on a penny-steamer. The boat was densely crowded, and they leaned, rather squeezed together, in the fore part of it, against the rail of the deck, and watched the big black fringe of the yellow stream. The river was always fascinating to Hyacinth. The mystified entertainment which, as a child, he had found in all the aspects of London came back to him from the murky scenery of its banks and the sordid agitation of its bosom: the great arches and pillars of the bridges, where the water rushed, and the funnels tipped, and sounds made an echo, and there seemed an overhanging of interminable processions; the miles of ugly wharves and warehouses; the lean protrusions of chimney, mast, and crane; the painted signs of grimy industries, staring from shore to shore; the strange, flat, obstructive barges, straining and bumping on some business as to which everything was vague but that it was remarkably dirty; the clumsy coasters and colliers, which thickened as one went down; the small, loafing boats, whose occupants, somehow, looking up from their oars at the steamer, as they rocked in the oily undulations of its wake, appeared profane and sarcastic; in short, all the grinding, puffing, smoking, splashing activity of the turbid flood. In the good-natured crowd, amid the fumes of vile tobacco, beneath the shower of sooty particles, and to the accompaniment of a bagpipe of a dingy Highlander, who sketched occasionally a smothered reel, Hyacinth forbore to speak to his companion of what he had most at heart; but later, as they lay on the brown, crushed grass, on one of the slopes of Greenwich Park, and saw the river stretch away and shine beyond the pompous colonnades of the hospital, he asked him whether there was any truth in what Rosy had said about his being sweet on their friend the Princess. He said 'their friend' on purpose, speaking as if, now that she had been twice to Audley Court, Muniment might be regarded as knowing her almost as well as he himself did. He wished to con- jure away the idea that he was jealous of Paul, and if he desired information on the point I have mentioned this was because it still made him almost as uncomfortable as it had done at first that his comrade should take the scoffing view. He didn't easily see such a fellow as Muniment wheel about from one day to the other, but he had been present at the most exquisite exhibition he had ever observed the Princess make of that divine power of conciliation which was not perhaps in social intercourse the art she chiefly exercised but was certainly the most wonderful of her secrets, and it would be remarkable indeed that a sane young man should not have been affected by it. It was familiar to Hyacinth that Muniment was not easily touched by women, but this might perfectly have been the case without detriment to the Princess's ability to work a miracle. The companions had wandered through the great halls and courts of the hospital; had gazed up at the glories of the famous painted chamber and admired the long and lurid series of the naval victories of England—Muniment remarking to his friend that he supposed he had seen the match to all that in foreign parts, offensive little travelled beggar that he was. They had not ordered a fish-dinner either at the 'Tra- falgar' or the 'Ship' (having a frugal vision of tea and shrimps with Rosy, on their return), but they had laboured up and down the steep undulations of the shabby, charming park; made advances to the tame deer and seen them amble foolishly away; watched the young of both sexes, hilarious

and red in the face, roll in promiscuous entanglement over
the slopes; gazed at the little brick observatory, perched
on one of the knolls, which sets the time of English history
and in which Hyacinth could see that his companion took
a kind of technical interest; wandered out of one of the
upper gates and admired the trimness of the little villas at
Blackheath, where Muniment declared that it was his idea
of supreme social success to be able to live. He pointed
out two or three small, semi-detached houses, faced with
stucco, and with 'Mortimer Lodge' or 'The Sycamores'
inscribed upon the gate-posts, and Hyacinth guessed that
these were the sort of place where he would like to end his
days—in high, pure air, with a genteel window for Rosy's
couch and a cheerful view of suburban excursions. It was
when they came back into the park that, being rather hot
and a little satiated, they stretched themselves under a tree
and Hyacinth yielded to his curiosity.

'Sweet on her—sweet on her, my boy!' said Muniment.
'I might as well be sweet on the dome of St. Paul's, which
I just make out off there.'

'The dome of St. Paul's doesn't come to see you, and
doesn't ask you to return the visit.'

'Oh, I don't return visits—I've got a lot of jobs of my
own to do. If I don't put myself out for the Princess,
isn't that a sufficient answer to your question?'

'I'm by no means sure,' said Hyacinth. 'If you went
to see her, simply and civilly, because she asked you, I
shouldn't regard it as a proof that you had taken a fancy
to her. Your hanging off is more suspicious; it may
mean that you don't trust yourself—that you are in
danger of falling in love if you go in for a more intimate
acquaintance.'

'It's a rum job, your wanting me to make up to her.
I shouldn't think it would suit your book,' Muniment
rejoined, staring at the sky, with his hands clasped under
his head.

'Do you suppose I'm afraid of you?' his companion
asked. 'Besides,' Hyacinth added in a moment, 'why the
devil should I care, now?'

Muniment, for a little, made no rejoinder; he turned

over on his side, and with his arm resting on the ground leaned his head on his hand. Hyacinth felt his eyes on his face, but he also felt himself colouring, and didn't meet them. He had taken a private vow never to indulge, to Muniment, in certain inauspicious references, and the words he had just spoken had slipped out of his mouth too easily. 'What do you mean by that?' Paul demanded, at last; and when Hyacinth looked at him he saw nothing but his companion's strong, fresh, irresponsible face. Muniment, before speaking, had had time to guess what he meant by it.

Suddenly, an impulse that he had never known before, or rather that he had always resisted, took possession of him. There was a mystery which it concerned his happiness to clear up, and he became unconscious of his scruples, of his pride, of the strength that he had believed to be in him —the strength for going through his work and passing away without a look behind. He sat forward on the grass, with his arms round his knees, and bent upon Muniment a face lighted up by his difficulties. For a minute the two men's eyes met with extreme clearness, and then Hyacinth exclaimed, 'What an extraordinary fellow you are!'

'You've hit it there!' said Muniment, smiling.

'I don't want to make a scene, or work on your feelings, but how will you like it when I'm strung up on the gallows?'

'You mean for Hoffendahl's job? That's what you were alluding to just now?' Muniment lay there, in the same attitude, chewing a long blade of dry grass, which he held to his lips with his free hand.

'I didn't mean to speak of it; but after all, why shouldn't it come up? Naturally, I have thought of it a good deal.'

'What good does that do?' Muniment returned. 'I hoped you didn't, and I noticed you never spoke of it. You don't like it; you would rather throw it up,' he added.

There was not in his voice the faintest note of irony or contempt, no sign whatever that he passed judgment on such a tendency. He spoke in a quiet, human, memorising manner, as if it had originally quite entered into his thought to allow for weak regrets. Nevertheless the complete reasonableness of his tone itself cast a chill on his companion's spirit; it was like the touch of a hand at once very firm and very soft, but strangely cold.

' I don't want in the least to throw the business up, but did you suppose I liked it?' Hyacinth asked, with rather a forced laugh.

' My dear fellow, how could I tell? You like a lot of things I don't. You like excitement and emotion and change, you like remarkable sensations, whereas I go in for a holy calm, for sweet repose.'

' If you object, for yourself, to change, and are so fond of still waters, why have you associated yourself with a revolutionary movement?' Hyacinth demanded, with a little air of making rather a good point.

' Just for that reason !' Muniment answered, with a smile. ' Isn't our revolutionary movement as quiet as the grave? Who knows, who suspects, anything like the full extent of it?'

' I see—you take only the quiet parts !'

In speaking these words Hyacinth had had no derisive intention, but a moment later he flushed with the sense that they had a sufficiently petty sound. Muniment, however, appeared to see no offence in them, and it was in the gentlest, most suggestive way, as if he had been thinking over what might comfort his comrade, that he replied, ' There's one thing you ought to remember—that it's quite on the cards it may never come off.'

' I don't desire that reminder,' Hyacinth said ; ' and, moreover, you must let me say that, somehow, I don't easily fancy *you* mixed up with things that don't come off. Anything you have to do with will come off, I think.'

Muniment reflected a moment, as if his little companion were charmingly ingenious. ' Surely, I have nothing to do with this idea of Hoffendahl's.'

' With the execution, perhaps not; but how about the conception? You seemed to me to have a great deal to do with it the night you took me to see him.'

Muniment changed his position, raising himself, and in a moment he was seated, Turk-fashion, beside his mate. He put his arm over his shoulder and held him, studying his face ; and then, in the kindest manner in the world, he remarked, ' There are three or four definite chances in your favour.'

' I don't want comfort, you know,' said Hyacinth, with his eyes on the distant atmospheric mixture that represented London.

' What the devil *do* you want ? ' Muniment asked, still holding him, and with perfect good-humour.

' Well, to get inside of *you* a little ; to know how a chap feels when he's going to part with his best friend.'

' To part with him ? ' Muniment repeated.

' I mean, putting it at the worst.'

' I should think you would know by yourself, if you're going to part with me ! '

At this Hyacinth prostrated himself, tumbled over on the grass, on his face, which he buried in his arms.   He remained in this attitude, saying nothing, for a long time ; and while he lay there he thought, with a sudden, quick flood of association, of many strange things.   Most of all, he had the sense of the brilliant, charming day ; the warm stillness, touched with cries of amusement ; the sweetness of loafing there, in an interval of work, with a friend who was a tremendously fine fellow, even if he didn't understand the inexpressible.   Muniment also kept silent, and Hyacinth perceived that he was unaffectedly puzzled.   He wanted now to relieve him, so that he pulled himself together again and turned round, saying the first thing he could think of, in relation to the general subject of their conversation, that would carry them away from the personal question.   ' I have asked you before, and you have told me, but somehow I have never quite grasped it (so I just touch on the matter again), exactly what good you think it will do.'

' This idea of Hoffendahl's ?   You must remember that as yet we know only very vaguely what it is.   It is difficult, therefore, to measure closely the importance it may have, and I don't think I have ever, in talking with you, pretended to fix that importance.   I don't suppose it will matter immensely whether your own engagement is carried out or not ; but if it is it will have been a detail in a scheme of which the general effect will be decidedly useful.   I believe, and you pretend to believe, though I am not sure you do,

in the advent of the democracy.   It will help the democracy
to get possession ·that the classes that keep them down shall
be admonished from time to time that they have a very
definite and very determined intention of doing so.   An
immense deal will depend upon that.   Hoffendahl is a
capital admonisher.'

Hyacinth listened to this explanation with an expression
of interest that was not feigned ; and after a moment he
rejoined, 'When you say you believe in the democracy,
I take for granted you mean you positively wish for their
coming into power, as I have always supposed.   Now what
I really have never understood is this—why you should
desire to put forward a lot of people whom you regard,
almost without exception, as donkeys.'

' Ah, my dear lad,' laughed Muniment, ' when one under-
takes to meddle in human affairs one must deal with
human material.   The upper classes have the longest
ears.'

' I have heard you say that you were working for an
equality in human conditions, to abolish the immemorial
inequality.   What you want, then, for all mankind is a
similar *nuance* of asininity.'

' That's very clever ; did you pick it up in France ?   The
low tone of our fellow-mortals is a result of bad conditions ;
it is the conditions I want to alter.   When those that have
no start to speak of have a good one, it is but fair to infer
that they will go further.   I want to try them, you know.'

' But why equality ? ' Hyacinth asked.   ' Somehow, that
word doesn't say so much to me as it used to.   Inequality
—inequality !   I don't know whether it's by dint of repeating
it over to myself, but *that* doesn't shock me as it used.'

' They didn't put you up to that in France, I'm sure ! '
Muniment exclaimed.   ' Your point of view has changed ;
you have risen in the world.'

' Risen ?   Good God, what have I risen to ? '

' True enough ; you were always a bloated little swell ! '
And Muniment gave his young friend a sociable slap on
the back.   There was a momentary bitterness in its being
imputed to such a one as Hyacinth, even in joke, that he
had taken sides with the fortunate ones of the earth, and

he had it on his tongue's end to ask his friend if he had
never guessed what his proud titles were—the bastard of a
murderess, spawned in a gutter, out of which he had been
picked by a sewing-girl. But his life-long reserve on this
point was a habit not easily broken, and before such an
inquiry could flash through it Muniment had gone on : ' If
you've ceased to believe we can do anything, it will be
rather awkward, you know.'

' I don't know what I believe, God help me !' Hyacinth
remarked, in a tone of an effect so lugubrious that Paul
gave one of his longest, most boyish-sounding laughs. And
he added, ' I don't want you to think I have ceased to care
for the people. What am I but one of the poorest and
meanest of them ? '

'You, my boy? You're a duke in disguise, and so I
thought the first time I ever saw you. That night I took
you to Hoffendahl you had a little way with you that made
me forget it ; I mean that your disguise happened to be
better than usual. As regards caring for the people, there's
surely no obligation at all,' Muniment continued. ' I
wouldn't if I could help it—I promise you that. It all
depends on what you see. The way *I*'ve used my eyes in
this abominable metropolis has led to my seeing that present
arrangements won't do. They won't do,' he repeated,
placidly.

'Yes, I see that, too,' said Hyacinth, with the same
dolefulness that had marked his tone a moment·before—a
dolefulness begotten of the rather helpless sense that, whatever he saw, he saw (and this was always the case), so
many other things beside. He saw the immeasurable
misery of the people, and yet he saw all that had been, as
it were, rescued and redeemed from it : the treasures, the
felicities, the splendours, the successes, of the world. All
this took the form, sometimes, to his imagination, of a vast,
vague, dazzling presence, an irradiation of light from objects
undefined, mixed with the atmosphere of Paris and of
Venice. He presently added that a hundred things Muniment had told him about the foul horrors of the worst
districts of London, pictures of incredible shame and suffering that he had put before him, came back to him now,

with the memory of the passion they had kindled at the
time.

'Oh, I don't want you to go by what I have told you;
I want you to go by what you have seen yourself. I remember there were things you told me that weren't bad in
their way.' And at this Paul Muniment sprang to his feet,
as if their conversation had drawn to an end, or they must
at all events be thinking of their homeward way. Hyacinth
got up, too, while his companion stood there. Muniment
was looking off toward London, with a face that expressed
all the healthy singleness of his vision. Suddenly Paul
remarked, as if it occurred to him to complete, or at any
rate confirm, the declaration he had made a short time
before, 'Yes, I don't believe in the millennium, but I do
believe in the democracy.'

The young man, as he spoke these words, struck his
comrade as such a fine embodiment of the spirit of the
people; he stood there, in his powerful, sturdy newness,
with such an air of having learnt what he had learnt
and of good-nature that had purposes in it, that our hero
felt the simple inrush of his old, frequent pride at having
a person of that promise, a nature of that capacity, for a
friend. He passed his hand into Muniment's arm and
said, with an imperceptible tremor in his voice, 'It's no
use your saying I'm not to go by what you tell me. I
would go by what you tell me, anywhere. There's no
awkwardness to speak of. I don't know that I believe
exactly what you believe, but I believe in you, and doesn't
that come to the same thing?'

Muniment evidently appreciated the cordiality and
candour of this little tribute, and the way he showed it was
by a movement of his arm, to check his companion, before
they started to leave the spot, and by looking down at him
with a certain anxiety of friendliness. 'I should never have
taken you to Hoffendahl if I hadn't thought you would
jump at the job. It was that flaring little oration of yours,
at the club, when you floored Delancey for saying you were
afraid, that put me up to it.'

'I did jump at it—upon my word I did; and it was
just what I was looking for. That's all correct!' said Hya-

cinth, cheerfully, as they went forward.   There was a strain
of heroism in these words—of heroism of which the sense
was not conveyed to Muniment by a vibration in their
interlocked arms.   Hyacinth did not make the reflection
that he was infernally literal ; he dismissed the sentimental
problem that had bothered him ; he condoned, excused,
admired—he merged himself, resting happy for the time in
the consciousness that Paul was a grand fellow, that friendship was a purer feeling than love, and that there was an
immense deal of affection between them.   He did not even
observe at that moment that it was preponderantly on his
own side.

A CERTAIN Sunday in November, more than three months
after she had gone to live in Madeira Crescent, was so important an occasion for the Princess Casamassima that I
must give as complete an account of it as the limits of my
space will allow.   Early in the afternoon a loud peal from
her door-knocker came to her ear ; it had a sound of resolution, almost of defiance, which made her look up from
her book and listen.   She was sitting by the fire, alone,
with a volume of a heavy work on Labour and Capital in
her hand.   It was not yet four o'clock, but she had had
candles for an hour ; a dense brown fog made the daylight
impure, without suggesting an answer to the question
whether the scheme of nature had been to veil or to deepen
the sabbatical dreariness.   She was not tired of Madeira
Crescent—such an idea she would indignantly have repu-
diated ; but the prospect of a visitor was rather pleasant to
her—the possibility even of his being an ambassador, or a
cabinet minister, or another of the eminent personages with
whom she had associated before embracing the ascetic life.
They had not knocked at her present door hitherto in any
great numbers, for more reasons than one ; they were out
of town, and she had taken pains to diffuse the belief that
she had left England.   If the impression prevailed, it was
exactly the impression she had desired ; she forgot this fact
whenever she felt a certain surprise, even, it may be, a certain irritation, in perceiving that people were not taking the
way to Madeira Crescent.   She was making the discovery,
in which she had had many predecessors, that in London
it is only too possible to hide one's self.   It was very much
in that fashion that Godfrey Sholto was in the habit of
announcing himself, when he reappeared after the intervals

she explictly imposed upon him; there was a kind of art-
lessness, for so world-worn a personage, in the point he
made of showing that he knocked with confidence, that he
had as good a right as any other.   This afternoon she was
ready to accept a visit from him: she was perfectly detached
from the shallow, frivolous world in which he lived, but
there was still a freshness in her renunciation which coveted
reminders and enjoyed comparisons ; he would prove to her
how right she had been to do exactly what she was doing.
It did not occur to her that Hyacinth Robinson might be
at her door, for it was understood between them that,
except by special appointment, he was to come to see
her only in the evening.   She heard in the hall, when the
servant arrived, a voice that she failed to recognise ; but in
a moment the door of the room was thrown open and
the name of Mr. Muniment was pronounced.   It may be
said at once that she felt great pleasure in hearing it, for
she had both wished to see more of Hyacinth's extraordinary friend and had given him up, so little likely had it
begun to appear that he would put himself out for her.
She had been glad he wouldn't come, as she had told Hyacinth three months before ; but now that he had come she
was still more glad.

Presently he was sitting opposite to her, on the other
side of the fire, with his big foot crossed over his big knee,
his large, gloved hands fumbling with each other, drawing
and smoothing the gloves (of very red, new-looking dog-
skin) in places, as if they hurt him.   So far as the size of
his extremities, and even his attitude and movement, went,
he might have belonged to her former circle.   With the
details of his dress remaining vague in the lamp-light,
which threw into relief mainly his powerful, important
head, he might have been one of the most considerable men she had ever known.   The first thing she
said to him was that she wondered extremely what had
brought him at last to come to see her : the idea,
when she proposed it, evidently had so little attraction
for him.   She had only seen him once since then—the
day she met him coming into Audley Court as she
was leaving it, after a visit to his sister—and, as he

probably remembered, she had not on that occasion
repeated her invitation.

'It wouldn't have done any good, at the time, if you
had,' Muniment rejoined, with his natural laugh.

'Oh, I felt that; my silence wasn't accidental!' the
Princess exclaimed, joining in his merriment.

'I have only come now—since you have asked me the
reason—because my sister hammered at 'me, week after
week, dinning it into me that I ought to. Oh, I've been
under the lash! If she had left me alone I wouldn't have
come.'

The Princess blushed on hearing these words, but not
with shame or with pain; rather with the happy excitement
of being spoken to in a manner so fresh and original. She
had never before had a visitor who practised so racy a
frankness, or who, indeed, had so curious a story to tell.
She had never before so completely failed, and her failure
greatly interested her, especially as it seemed now to be
turning a little to success. She had succeeded promptly
with every one, and the sign of it was that every one had
rendered her a monotony of homage. Even poor little
Hyacinth had tried, in the beginning, to say sweet things
to her. This very different type of man appeared to have
his thoughts fixed on anything but sweetness; she felt the
liveliest hope that he would move further and further away
from it. 'I remember what you asked me—what good it
would do you. I couldn't tell you then; and though I now
have had a long time to turn it over, I haven't thought of
it yet.'

'Oh, but I hope it will do me some,' said Paul. 'A
fellow wants a reward, when he has made a great effort.'

'It does me some,' the Princess remarked, gaily.

'Naturally, the awkward things I say amuse you. But
I don't say them for that, but just to give you an
idea.'

'You give me a great many ideas. Besides, I know you
already a good deal.'

'From little Robinson, I suppose,' said Muniment.

The Princess hesitated. 'More particularly from Lady
Aurora.'

'Oh, she doesn't know much about me !' the young man exclaimed.

'It's a pity you say that, because she likes you.'

'Yes, she likes me,' Muniment replied, serenely.

Again the Princess hesitated. 'And I hope you like her.'

'Ay, she's a dear old girl !'

The Princess reflected that her visitor was not a gentleman, like Hyacinth ; but this made no difference in her present attitude. The expectation that he would be a gentleman had had nothing to do with her interest in him ; that, in fact, had rested largely on the supposition that he had a rich plebeian strain. 'I don't know that there is any one in the world I envy so much,' she remarked ; an observation which her visitor received in silence. 'Better than any one I have ever met she has solved the problem — which, if we are wise, we all try to solve, don't we ?—of getting out of herself. She has got out of herself more perfectly than any one I have ever known. She has merged herself in the passion of doing something for others. That's why I envy her,' said the Princess, with an explanatory smile, as if perhaps he didn't understand her.

'It's an amusement, like any other,' said Paul Muniment.

'Ah, not like any other ! It carries light into dark places ; it makes a great many wretched people considerably less wretched.'

'How many, eh ?' asked the young man, not exactly as if he wished to dispute, but as if it were always in him to enjoy an argument.

The Princess wondered why he should desire to argue at Lady Aurora's expense. 'Well, one who is very near to you, to begin with.'

'Oh, she's kind, most kind ; it's altogether wonderful. But Rosy makes *her* considerably less wretched,' Paul Muniment rejoined.

'Very likely, of course ; and so she does me.'

'May I inquire what you are wretched about ?' Muniment went on.

'About nothing at all. That's the worst of it. But I am much happier now than I have ever been.'

'Is that also about nothing?'

'No, about a sort of change that has taken place in my life. I have been able to do some little things.'

'For the poor, I suppose you mean. Do you refer to the presents you have made to Rosy?' the young man inquired.

'The presents?' The Princess appeared not to remember. 'Oh, those are trifles. It isn't anything one has been able to give; it's some talks one has had, some convictions one has arrived at.'

'Convictions are a source of very innocent pleasure,' said the young man, smiling at his interlocutress with his bold, pleasant eyes, which seemed to project their glance further than any she had seen.

'Having them is nothing. It's the acting on them,' the Princess replied.

'Yes; that doubtless, too, is good.' He continued to look at her peacefully, as if he liked to consider that this might be what she had asked him to come for. He said nothing more, and she went on :

'It's far better, of course, when one is a man.'

'I don't know. Women do pretty well what they like. My sister and you have managed, between you, to bring me to this.'

'It's more your sister, I suspect, than I. But why, after all, should you have disliked so much to come?'

'Well, since you ask me,' said Paul Muniment, 'I will tell you frankly, though I don't mean it uncivilly, that I don't know what to make of you.'

'Most people don't,' returned the Princess. 'But they usually take the risk.'

'Ah, well, I'm the most prudent of men.'

'I was sure of it; that is one of the reasons why I wanted to know you. I know what some of your ideas are —Hyacinth Robinson has told me; and the source of my interest in them is partly the fact that you consider very carefully what you attempt.'

'That I do—I do,' said Muniment, simply.

The tone in which he said this would have been almost ignoble, as regards a kind of northern canniness which it expressed, had it not been corrected by the character of his face, his youth and strength, and his military eye. The Princess recognised both the shrewdness and the latent audacity as she rejoined, 'To do anything with you would be very safe. It would be sure to succeed.'

'That's what poor Hyacinth thinks,' said Paul Muniment.

The Princess wondered a little that he could allude in that light tone to the faith their young friend had placed in him, considering the consequences such a trustfulness might yet have ; but this curious mixture of qualities could only make her visitor, as a tribune of the people, more interesting to her. She abstained for the moment from touching on the subject of Hyacinth's peculiar position, and only said, 'Hasn't he told you about me? Hasn't he explained me a little?'

'Oh, his explanations are grand!' Muniment exclaimed, hilariously. 'He's fine sport when he talks about you.'

'Don't betray him,' said the Princess, gently.

'There's nothing to betray. You would be the first to admire it if you were there. Besides, I don't betray,' the young man added.

'I love him very much,' said the Princess ; and it would have been impossible for the most impudent cynic to smile at the manner in which she made the declaration.

Paul accepted it respectfully. 'He's a sweet little lad, and, putting her ladyship aside, quite the light of our home.'

There was a short pause after this exchange of amenities, which the Princess terminated by inquiring, 'Wouldn't some one else do his work quite as well?'

'His work? Why, I'm told he's a master-hand.'

'Oh, I don't mean his bookbinding.' Then the Princess added, 'I don't know whether you know it, but I am in correspondence with Hoffendahl. I am acquainted with many of our most important men.'

'Yes, I know it. Hyacinth has told me. Do you

mention it as a guarantee, so that I may know you are
genuine?'

'Not exactly; that would be weak, wouldn't it?' the
Princess asked.   'My genuineness must be in myself—a
matter for you to appreciate as you know me better; not in
my references and vouchers.'

'I shall never know you better.   What business is it of
mine?'

'I want to help you,' said the Princess, and as she made
this earnest appeal her face became transfigured; it wore
an expression of the most passionate yet the purest longing.
'I want to do something for the cause you represent; for
the millions that are rotting under our feet—the millions
whose whole life is passed on the brink of starvation, so
that the smallest accident pushes them over.   Try me, test
me; ask me to put my hand to something, to prove that I
am as deeply in earnest as those who have already given
proof.   I know what I am talking about—what one must
meet and face and count with, the nature and the immensity
of your organisation.   I am not playing.   No, I am not
playing.'

Paul Muniment watched her with his steady smile until
this sudden outbreak had spent itself.   'I was afraid you
would be like this—that you would turn on the fountains
and let off the fireworks.'

'Permit me to believe you thought nothing about it.
There is no reason my fireworks should disturb you.'

'I have always had a fear of women.'

'I see—that's a part of your prudence,' said the Princess, reflectively.   'But you are the sort of man who ought
to know how to use them.'

Muniment said nothing, immediately, in answer to this;
the way he appeared to consider the Princess suggested that
he was not following closely what she said, so much as
losing himself in certain matters which were beside that
question—her beauty, for instance, her grace, her fragrance,
the spectacle of a manner and quality so new to him.   After
a little, however, he remarked, irrelevantly, 'I'm afraid I'm
very rude.'

'Of course you are, but it doesn't signify.   What I

mainly object to is that you don't answer my questions.
Would not some one else do Hyacinth Robinson's work
quite as well? Is it necessary to take a nature so delicate,
so intellectual? Oughtn't we to keep him for something
finer?'

'Finer than what?'

'Than what Hoffendahl will call upon him to do.'

'And pray what is that?' the young man demanded.
'You know nothing about it; no more do I,' he added in
a moment. 'It will require whatever it will. Besides, if
some one else might have done it, no one else volunteered.
It happened that Robinson did.'

'Yes, and you nipped him up!' the Princess exclaimed.

At this expression Muniment burst out laughing. 'I
have no doubt you can easily keep him, if you want
him.'

'I should like to do it in his place—that's what I should
like,' said the Princess.

'As I say, you don't even know what it is.'

'It may be nothing,' she went on, with her grave eyes
fixed on her visitor. 'I dare say you think that what I
wanted to see you for was to beg you to let him off. But
it wasn't. Of course it's his own affair, and you can do
nothing. But oughtn't it to make some difference, when
his opinions have changed?'

'His opinions? He never had any opinions,' Muniment replied. 'He is not like you and me.'

'Well, then, his feelings, his attachments. He hasn't
the passion for democracy he had when I first knew him.
He's much more tepid.'

'Ah, well, he's quite right.'

The Princess stared. 'Do you mean that *you* are giving
up—— ?'

'A fine stiff conservative is a thing I perfectly understand,' said Paul Muniment. 'If I were on the top, I'd
stick there.'

'I see, you are not narrow,' the Princess murmured,
appreciatively.

'I beg your pardon, I am. I don't call that wide. One
must be narrow to penetrate.'

'Whatever you are, you'll succeed,' said the Princess.
'Hyacinth won't, but you will.'

'It depends upon what you call success!' the young
man exclaimed.   And in a moment, before she replied, he
added, looking about the room, 'You've got a very lovely
dwelling.'

'Lovely?   My dear sir, it's hideous.   That's what I
like it for,' the Princess added.

'Well, I like it; but perhaps I don't know the reason.
I thought you had given up everything—pitched your
goods out of window, for a grand scramble.

'Well, so I have.   You should have seen me before.'

'I should have liked that,' said Muniment, smiling.   'I
like to see solid wealth.'

'Ah, you're as bad as Hyacinth.   I am the only consistent one!' the Princess sighed.

'You have a great deal left, for a person who has given
everything away.'

'These are not mine—these abominations—or I would
give them, too!' Paul's hostess rejoined, artlessly.

Muniment got up from his chair, still looking about the
room.   'I would give my nose for such a place as this.
At any rate, you are not yet reduced to poverty.'

'I have a little left—to help you.'

'I dare say you've a great deal,' said Paul, with his north-
country accent.

'I could get money—I could get money,' the Princess
continued, gravely.   She had also risen, and was standing
before him.

These two remarkable persons faced each other, their
eyes met again, and they exchanged a long, deep glance of
mutual scrutiny.   Each seemed to drop a plummet into
the other's mind.   Then a strange and, to the Princess,
unexpected expression passed over the countenance of the
young man; his lips compressed themselves, as if he were
making a strong effort, his colour rose, and in a moment he
stood there blushing like a boy.   He dropped his eyes and
stared at the carpet, while he observed, 'I don't trust
women—I don't trust women!'

'I am sorry, but, after all, I can understand it,' said the

Princess; 'therefore I won't insist on the question of your
allowing me to work with you.   But this appeal I will make
to you : help me a little yourself—help me ! '

'How do you mean, help you?' Muniment demanded,
raising his eyes, which had a new, conscious look.

'Advise me ; you will know how.   I am in trouble—I
have gone very far.'

'I have no doubt of that !' said Paul, laughing.

'I mean with some of those people abroad.   I'm not
frightened, but I'm perplexed ; I want to know what to
do.'

'No, you are not frightened,' Muniment rejoined, after
a moment.

'I am, however, in a sad entanglement.   I think you
can straighten it out.   I will give you the facts, but not
now, for we shall be interrupted ; I hear my old lady on
the stairs.   For this, you must come to see me again.'

At this point the door opened, and Madame Grandoni
appeared, cautiously, creepingly, as if she didn't know what
might be going on in the parlour.   'Yes, I will come again,'
said Paul Muniment, in a low but distinct tone ; and he
walked away, passing Madame Grandoni on the threshold,
without having exchanged the hand-shake of farewell with
his hostess.   In the hall he paused an instant, feeling she
was behind him ; and he learned that she had not come to
exact from him this omitted observance, but to say once
more, dropping her voice, so that her companion, through
the open door, might not hear—

'I *could* get money—I could ! '

Muniment passed his hand through his hair, and, as if
he had not heard her, remarked, 'I have not given you,
after all, half Rosy's messages.'

'Oh, that doesn't matter !' the Princess answered, turning
back into the parlour.

Madame Grandoni was in the middle of the room,
wrapped in her old shawl, looking vaguely around her, and
the two ladies heard the house-door close.   'And pray,
who may that be?   Isn't it a new face?' the elder one
inquired.

'He's the brother of the little person I took you to see

over the river—the chattering cripple with the wonderful manners.'

'Ah, she had a brother! That, then, was why you went?'

It was striking, the good-humour with which the Princess received this rather coarse thrust, which could have been drawn from Madame Grandoni only by the petulance and weariness of increasing age, and the antipathy she now felt to Madeira Crescent and everything it produced. Christina bent a calm, charitable smile upon her ancient companion, and replied—

'There could have been no question of our seeing him. He was, of course, at his work.'

'Ah, how do I know, my dear? And is he a successor?'

'A successor?'

'To the little bookbinder.'

'My darling,' said the Princess, 'you will see how absurd that question is when I tell you he's his greatest friend!'

HALF an hour after Paul Muniment's departure the Princess
heard another rat-tat-tat at her door; but this was a briefer,
discreeter peal, and was accompanied by a faint tintinnabu-
lation. The person who had produced it was presently
ushered in, without, however, causing Madame Grandoni to
look round, or rather to look up, from an arm-chair as low
as a sitz-bath, and of very much the shape of such a
receptacle, in which, near the fire, she had been immersed.
She left this care to the Princess, who rose on hearing the
name of the visitor pronounced, inadequately, by her maid.
' Mr. Fetch,' Assunta called it; but the Princess recognised
without difficulty the little fat, ' reduced ' fiddler of whom
Hyacinth had talked to her, who, as Pinnie's most intimate
friend, had been so mixed up with his existence, and whom
she herself had always had a curiosity to see. Hyacinth
had not told her he was coming, and the unexpectedness
of the apparition added to its interest. Much as she
liked seeing queer types and exploring out-of-the-way social
corners, she never engaged in a fresh encounter, nor formed
a new relation of this kind, without a fit of nervousness, a
fear that she might be awkward and fail to hit the right
tone. She perceived in a moment, however, that Mr. Vetch
would take her as she was and require no special adjust-
ments; he was a gentleman and a man of experience, and
she would only have to leave the tone to him. He stood
there with his large, polished hat in his two hands, a hat of
the fashion of ten years before, with a rusty sheen and an
undulating brim——stood there without a salutation or a
speech, but with a little fixed, acute, tentative smile, which
seemed half to inquire and half to explain. What he
explained was that he was clever enough to be trusted, and

that if he had come to see her that way, abruptly, without
an invitation, he had a reason which she would be sure to
think good enough when she should hear it.   There was
even a certain jauntiness in this confidence—an insinuation
that he knew how to present himself to a lady ; and though
it quickly appeared that he really did, that was the only
thing about him that was inferior—it suggested a long
experience of actresses at rehearsal, with whom he had
formed habits of advice and compliment.

'I know who you are—I know who you are,' said the
Princess, though she could easily see that he knew she did.

'I wonder whether you also know why I have come to
see you,' Mr. Vetch replied, presenting the top of his hat to
her as if it were a looking-glass.

'No, but it doesn't matter.   I am very glad ; you might
even have come before.'   Then the Princess added, with
her characteristic honesty, 'Don't you know of the great
interest I have taken in your nephew?'

'In my nephew?   Yes, my young friend Robinson.   It
is in regard to him that I have ventured to intrude upon
you.'

The Princess had been on the point of pushing a chair
toward him, but she stopped in the act, staring, with a
smile.   'Ah, I hope you haven't come to ask me to give
him up !'

'On the contrary—on the contrary!' the old man
rejoined, lifting his hand expressively, and with his head on
one side, as if he were holding his violin.

'How do you mean, on the contrary?' the Princess
demanded, after he had seated himself and she had sunk
into her former place.   As if that might sound contradictious,
she went on : 'Surely he hasn't any fear that I shall cease
to be a good friend to him?'

'I don't know what he fears ; I don't know what he
hopes,' said Mr. Vetch, looking at her now with a face in
which she could see there was something more tonic than
old-fashioned politeness.   'It will be difficult to tell you,
but at least I must try.   Properly speaking, I suppose, it's
no business of mine, as I am not a blood-relation to the
boy ; but I have known him since he was an urchin, and I

can't help saying that I thank you for your great kindness
to him.'

'All the same, I don't think you like it,' the Princess
remarked. 'To me it oughtn't to be difficult to say anything.'

'He has told me very little about you ; he doesn't know
I have taken this step,' the fiddler said, turning his eyes
about the room, and letting them rest on Madame Grandoni.

'Why do you call it a "step"?' the Princess asked.
'That's what people say when they have to do something
disagreeable.'

'I call very seldom on ladies.   It's a long time since I
have been in the house of a person like the Princess
Casamassima.   I remember the last time,' said the old man.
'It was to get some money from a lady at whose party I
had been playing—for a dance.'

'You must bring your fiddle, sometime, and play to us.
Of course I don't mean for money,' the Princess rejoined.

'I will do it with pleasure, or anything else that will
gratify you.   But my ability is very small.   I only know
vulgar music—things that are played at theatres.'

'I don't believe that; there must be things you play for
yourself, in your room, alone.'

For a moment the old man made no reply; then he
said, 'Now that I see you, that I hear you, it helps me to
understand.'

'I don't think you do see me !' cried the Princess,
kindly, laughing ; while the fiddler went on to ask whether
there were any danger of Hyacinth's coming in while he was
there.   The Princess replied that he only came, unless by
prearrangement, in the evening, and Mr. Vetch made a
request that she would not let their young friend know that
he himself had been with her.   'It doesn't matter; he will
guess it, he will know it by instinct, as soon as he comes in.
He is terribly subtle,' said the Princess ; and she added
that she had never been able to hide anything from him.
Perhaps it served her right, for attempting to make a mystery
of things that were not worth it.

'How well you know him !' Mr. Vetch murmured, with

his eyes wandering again to Madame Grandoni, who paid
no attention to him as she sat staring at the fire.   He
delayed, visibly, to say what he had come for, and his
hesitation could only be connected with the presence of the
old lady.   He said to himself that the Princess might have
divined this from his manner ; he had an idea that he could
trust himself to convey such an intimation with clearness and
yet with delicacy.   But the most she appeared to apprehend
was that he desired to be presented to her companion.

'You must know the most delightful of women.   She
also takes a particular interest in Mr. Robinson : of a
different kind from mine—much more sentimental !'   And
then she explained to the old lady, who seemed absorbed
in other ideas, that Mr. Vetch was a distinguished musician,
a person whom she, who had known so many in her day,
and was so fond of that kind of thing, would like to talk
with.   The Princess spoke of 'that kind of thing' quite as
if she herself had given it up, though Madame Grandoni
heard her by the hour together improvising on the piano
revolutionary battle-songs and pæans.

'I think you are laughing at me,' Mr. Vetch said to the
Princess, while Madame Grandoni twisted herself slowly
round in her chair and considered him.   She looked at
him leisurely, up and down, and then she observed, with a
sigh—

'Strange people—strange people !'

'It is indeed a strange world, madam,' the fiddler
replied ; after which he inquired of the Princess whether he
might have a little conversation with her in private.

She looked about her, embarrassed and smiling.   'My
dear sir, I have only this one room to receive in.   We live
in a very small way.'

'Yes, your excellency *is* laughing at me.   Your ideas
are very large, too.   However, I would gladly come at any
other time that might suit you.'

'You impute to me higher spirits than I possess.   Why
should I be so gay?' the Princess asked.   'I should be
delighted to see you again.   I am extremely curious as to
what you may have to say to me.   I would even meet you
anywhere—in Kensington Gardens or the British Museum.'

The fiddler looked at her a moment before replying; then, with his white old face flushing a little, he exclaimed, ' Poor dear little Hyacinth ! '

Madame Grandoni made an effort to rise from her chair, but she had sunk so low that at first it was not successful. Mr. Vetch gave her his hand, to help her, and she slowly erected herself, keeping hold of him for a moment after she stood there. ' What did she tell me ? That you are a great musician ? Isn't that enough for any man ? You ought to be content, my dear gentleman. It has sufficed for people whom I don't believe you surpass.'

' I don't surpass any one,' said poor Mr. Vetch. ' I don't know what you take me for.'

' You are not a conspirator, then ? You are not an assassin ? It surprises me, but so much the better. In this house one can never know. It is not a good house, and if you are a respectable person it is a pity you should come here. Yes, she is very gay, and I am very sad. I don't know how it will end. After me, I hope. The world is not good, certainly ; but God alone can make it better.' And as the fiddler expressed the hope that he was not the cause of her leaving the room, she went on, '*Doch, doch*, you are the cause; but why not you as well as another? I am always leaving it for some one or for some thing, and I would sooner do so for an honest man, if you *are* one— but, as I say, who can tell ?—than for a .destroyer. I wander about. I have no rest. I have, however, a very nice room, the best in the house. Me, at least, she does not treat ill. It looks to-day like the end of all things. If you would turn your climate the other side up, the rest would do well enough. Good-night to you, whoever you are.'

The old lady shuffled away, in spite of Mr. Vetch's renewed apologies, and the Princess stood before the fire, watching her companions, while he opened the door. ' She goes away, she comes back ; it doesn't matter. She thinks it's a bad house, but she knows it would be worse without her. I remember now,' the Princess added. ' Mr. Robinson told me that you had been a great democrat in old days, but that now you had ceased to care for the people.'

'The people—the people? That is a vague term. Whom do you mean?'

The Princess hesitated. Those you used to care for, to plead for; those who are underneath every one, every thing, and have the whole social mass crushing them.'

'I see you think I'm a renegade. The way certain classes arrogate to themselves the title of the people has never pleased me. Why are some human beings the people, and the people only, and others not? I am of the people myself, I have worked all my days like a knife-grinder, and I have really never changed.'

'You must not let me make you angry,' said the Princess, laughing and sitting down again. 'I am sometimes very provoking, but you must stop me off. You wouldn't think it, perhaps, but no one takes a snub better than I.'

Mr. Vetch dropped his eyes a minute; he appeared to wish to show that he regarded such a speech as that as one of the Princess's characteristic humours, and knew that he should be wanting in respect to her if he took it seriously or made a personal application of it. 'What I want is this,' he began, after a moment: 'that you will—that you will——' But he stopped before he had got further. She was watching him, listening to him, and she waited while he paused. It was a long pause, and she said nothing. 'Princess,' the old man broke out at last, 'I would give my own life many times for that boy's!'

'I always told him you must have been fond of him!' she cried, with bright exultation.

'Fond of him? Pray, who can doubt it? I made him, I invented him!'

'He knows it, moreover,' said the Princess, smiling. 'It is an exquisite organisation.' And as the old man gazed at her, not knowing, apparently, what to make of her tone, she continued: 'It is a very interesting opportunity for me to learn certain things. Speak to me of his early years. How was he as a child? When I like people I want to know everything about them.'

'I shouldn't have supposed there was much left for you to learn about our young friend. You have taken possession of his life,' the fiddler added, gravely.

'Yes, but as I understand you, you don't complain of it? Sometimes one does so much more than one has intended. One must use one's influence for good,' said the Princess, with the noble, gentle air of accessibility to reason that sometimes lighted up her face. And then she went on, irrelevantly: 'I know the terrible story of his mother. He told it me himself, when he was staying with me; and in the course of my life I think I have never been more affected.'

'That was my fault, that he ever learned it. I suppose he also told you that.'

'Yes, but I think he understood your idea. If you had the question to determine again, would you judge differently?'

'I thought it would do him good,' said the old man, simply and rather wearily.

'Well, I dare say it has,' the Princess rejoined, with the manner of wishing to encourage him.

'I don't know what was in my head. I wanted him to quarrel with society. Now I want him to be reconciled to it,' Mr. Vetch remarked, earnestly. He appeared to wish the Princess to understand that he made a great point of this.

'Ah, but he is!' she immediately returned. 'We often talk about that; he is not like me, who see all kinds of abominations. He's a tremendous aristocrat. What more would you have?'

'Those are not the opinions that he expresses to me,' said Mr. Vetch, shaking his head sadly. 'I am greatly distressed, and I don't understand. I have not come here with the presumptuous wish to cross-examine you, but I should like very much to know if I *am* wrong in believing that he has gone about with you in the bad quarters—in St. Giles's and Whitechapel.'

'We have certainly inquired and explored together,' the Princess admitted, 'and in the depths of this huge, luxurious, wanton, wasteful city we have seen sights of unspeakable misery and horror. But we have been not only in the slums; we have been to a music hall and a penny-reading.'

The fiddler received this information at first in silence,

so that his hostess went on to mention some of the phases
of life they had observed; describing with great vividness,
but at the same time with a kind of argumentative moderation, several scenes which did little honour to 'our boasted
civilisation.' 'What wonder is it, then, that he should tell
me that things cannot go on any longer as they are?' he
asked, when she had finished. 'He said only the other
day that he should regard himself as one of the most contemptible of human beings if he should do nothing to alter
them, to better them.'

'What wonder, indeed? But if he said that, he was in
one of his bad days. He changes constantly, and his impressions change. The misery of the people is by no
means always weighing on his heart. You tell me what he
has told you; well, he has told me that the people may
perish over and over, rather than the conquests of civilisation shall be sacrificed to them. He declares, at such
moments, that they will be sacrificed—sacrificed utterly—
if the ignorant masses get the upper hand.'

'He needn't be afraid! That will never happen.'

'I don't know. We can at least try!'

'Try what you like, madam, but, for God's sake, get the
boy out of his mess!'

The Princess had suddenly grown excited, in speaking
of the cause she believed in, and she gave, for the moment,
no heed to this appeal, which broke from Mr. Vetch's lips
with a sudden passion of anxiety. Her beautiful head raised
itself higher, and the deep expression that was always in her
eyes became an extraordinary radiance. 'Do you know
what I say to Mr. Robinson when he makes such remarks
as that to me? I ask him what he means by civilisation.
Let civilisation come a little, first, and then we will talk
about it. For the present, face to face with those horrors,
I scorn it, I deny it!' And the Princess laughed ineffable
things, like some splendid syren of the Revolution.

'The world is very sad and very hideous, and I am
happy to say that I soon shall have done with it. But
before I go I want to save Hyacinth. If he's a little
aristocrat, as you say, there is so much the less fitness in his
being ground in your mill. If he doesn't even believe in what

he pretends to do, that's a pretty situation ! What is he in for, madam ? What devilish folly has he undertaken ?'

'He is a strange mixture of contradictory impulses,' said the Princess, musingly. Then, as if calling herself back to the old man's question, she continued : ' How can I enter into his affairs with you ? How can I tell you his secrets ? In the first place, I don't know them, and if I did—fancy me !'

The fiddler gave a long, low sigh, almost a moan, of discouragement and perplexity. He had told the Princess that now he saw her he understood how Hyacinth should have become her slave, but he would not have been able to tell her that he understood her own motives and mysteries, that he embraced the immense anomaly of her behaviour. It came over him that she was incongruous and perverse, a more complicated form of the feminine character than any he had hitherto dealt with, and he felt helpless and baffled, foredoomed to failure. He had come prepared to flatter her without scruple, thinking that would be the clever, the efficacious, method of dealing with her ; but he now had a sense that this primitive device had, though it was strange, no application to such a nature, while his embarrassment was increased rather than diminished by the fact that the lady at least made the effort to be accommodating. He had put down his hat on the floor beside him, and his two hands were clasped on the knob of an umbrella which had long since renounced pretensions to compactness ; he collapsed a little, and his chin rested on his folded hands. 'Why do you take such a line ? Why do you believe such things ?' he asked ; and he was conscious that his tone was weak and his inquiry beside the question.

'My dear sir, how do you know what I believe ? However, I have my reasons, which it would take too long to tell you, and which, after all, would not particularly interest you. One must see life as one can ; it comes, no doubt, to each of us in different ways. You think me affected, of course, and my behaviour a fearful *pose ;* but I am only trying to be natural. Are you not yourself a little inconsequent ?' the Princess went on, with the bright mildness which had the effect of making Mr. Vetch feel that he should not extract any pledge of assistance from her. 'You don't want our young friend to pry into the wretchedness of London, because it excites his sense of justice. It is a strange thing to wish, for a person of whom one is fond and whom one esteems, that his sense of justice shall not be excited.'

'I don't care a fig for his sense of justice—I don't care a fig for the wretchedness of London; and if I were young, and beautiful, and clever, and brilliant, and of a noble position, like you, I should care still less. In that case I should have very little to say to a poor mechanic—a youngster who earns his living with a glue-pot and scraps of old leather.'

'Don't misrepresent him; don't make him out what you know he's not!' the Princess retorted, with her baffling smile. 'You know he's one of the most civilised people possible.'

The fiddler sat breathing unhappily. 'I only want to keep him—to get him free.' Then he added, 'I don't understand you very well. If you like him because he's one of the lower orders, how can you like him because he's a swell?'

The Princess turned her eyes on the fire a moment, as if this little problem might be worth considering, and presently she answered, 'Dear Mr. Vetch, I am very sure you don't mean to be impertinent, but some things you say have that effect. Nothing is more annoying than when one's sincerity is doubted. I am not bound to explain myself to you. I ask of my friends to trust me, and of the others to leave me alone. Moreover, anything not very nice you may have said to me, out of awkwardness, is nothing to the insults I am perfectly prepared to see showered upon me before long. I shall do things which will produce a fine crop of them—oh, I shall do things, my dear sir! But I am determined not to mind them. Come, therefore, pull yourself together. We both take such an interest in young Robinson that I can't see why in the world we should quarrel about him.'

'My dear lady,' the old man pleaded, 'I have indeed not the least intention of failing in respect or courtesy, and

you must excuse me if I don't look after my manners.
How can I when I am so worried, so haunted? God
knows I don't want to quarrel. As I tell you, I only want
to get Hyacinth free.'

'Free from what?' the Princess asked.

'From some abominable brotherhood or international
league that he belongs to, the thought of which keeps me
awake at night. He's just the sort of youngster to be
made a catspaw.'

'Your fears seem very vague.'

'I hoped you would give me chapter and verse.'

'On what do your suspicions rest? What grounds have
you?' the Princess inquired.

'Well, a great many; none of them very definite, but
all contributing something—his appearance, his manner, the
way he strikes me. Dear madam, one feels those things,
one guesses. Do you know that poor, infatuated phrase-
monger, Eustache Poupin, who works at the same place as
Hyacinth? He's a very old friend of mine, and he's an
honest man, considering everything. But he is always
conspiring, and corresponding, and pulling strings that
make a tinkle which he takes for the death-knell of
society. He has nothing in life to complain of, and he
drives a roaring trade. But he wants folks to be equal,
heaven help him; and when he has made them so I suppose he's going to start a society for making the stars in
the sky all of the same size. He isn't serious, though he
thinks that he's the only human being who never trifles;
and his machinations, which I believe are for the most
part very innocent, are a matter of habit and tradition with
him, like his theory that Christopher Columbus, who discovered America, was a Frenchman, and his hot foot-
bath on Saturday nights. He has *not* confessed to me that
Hyacinth has taken some secret engagement to do something for the cause which may have nasty consequences,
but the way he turns off the idea makes me almost as
uncomfortable as if he had. He and his wife are very
sweet on Hyacinth, but they can't make up their minds to
interfere; perhaps for them, indeed, as for me, there is no
way in which interference can be effective. Only *I* didn't

put him up to those devil's tricks—or, rather, I did originally! The finer the work, I suppose, the higher the privilege of doing it; yet the Poupins heave socialistic sighs over the boy, and their peace of mind evidently isn't all that it ought to be, if they have given him a noble opportunity. I have appealed to them, in good round terms, and they have assured me that every hair of his head is as precious to them as if he were their own child. That doesn't comfort me much, however, for the simple reason that I believe the old woman (whose grandmother, in Paris, in the Revolution, must certainly have carried bloody heads on a pike), would be quite capable of chopping up her own child, if it would do any harm to proprietors. Besides, they say, what influence have they on Hyacinth any more? He is a deplorable little backslider; he worships false gods. In short, they will give me no information, and I dare say they themselves are tied up by some unholy vow. They may be afraid of a vengeance if they tell tales. It's all sad rubbish, but rubbish may be a strong motive.'

The Princess listened attentively, following her visitor with patience. 'Don't speak to me of the French; I have never liked them.'

'That's awkward, if you're a socialist. You are likely to meet them.'

'Why do you call me a socialist? I hate labels and tickets,' she declared. Then she added, 'What is it you suppose on Mr. Robinson's part?—for you must suppose something.'

'Well, that he may have drawn some accursed lot, to do some idiotic thing—something in which even he himself doesn't believe.'

'I haven't an idea of what sort of thing you mean. But, if he doesn't believe in it he can easily let it alone.'

'Do you think he's a customer who will back out of an engagement?' the fiddler asked.

The Princess hesitated a moment. 'One can never judge of people, in that way, until they are tested.' The next thing, she inquired, 'Haven't you even taken the trouble to question him?'

'What would be the use? He would tell me nothing. It would be like a man giving notice when he is going to fight a duel.'

The Princess sat for some moments in thought; she looked up at Mr. Vetch with a pitying, indulgent smile. 'I am sure you are worrying about a mere shadow; but that never prevents, does it? I still don't see exactly how I can help you.'

'Do you want him to commit some atrocity, some infamy?' the old man murmured.

'My dear sir, I don't want him to do anything in all the wide world. I have not had the smallest connection with any arrangement of any kind, that he may have entered into. Do me the honour to trust me,' the Princess went on, with a certain dryness of tone. 'I don't know what I have done to deprive myself of your confidence. Trust the young man a little, too. He is a gentleman, and he will behave like a gentleman.'

The fiddler rose from his chair, smoothing his hat, silently, with the cuff of his coat. He stood there, whimsical and piteous, as if the sense that he had still something to urge mingled with that of his having received his dismissal, and both of them were tinged with the oddity of another idea. 'That's exactly what I am afraid of!' he exclaimed. Then he added, continuing to look at her, 'But he *must* be very fond of life.'

The Princess took no notice of the insinuation contained in these words, and indeed it was of a sufficiently impalpable character. 'Leave him to me—leave him to me. I am sorry for your anxiety, but it was very good of you to come to see me. That has been interesting, because you have been one of our friend's influences.'

'Unfortunately, yes! If it had not been for me, he would not have known Poupin, and if he hadn't known Poupin he wouldn't have known his chemical friend—what's his name? Muniment.'

'And has that done him harm, do you think?' the Princess asked. She had got up.

'Surely: that fellow has been the main source of his infection.'

'I lose patience with you,' said the Princess, turning away.

And indeed her visitor's persistence was irritating. He went on, lingering, with his head thrust forward and his short arms out at his sides, terminating in his hat and umbrella, which he held grotesquely, as if they were intended for emphasis or illustration : 'I have supposed for a long time that it was either Muniment or you that had got him into his scrape. It was you I suspected most— much the most; but if it isn't you, it must be he.'

'You had better go to him, then !'

'Of course I will go to him. I scarcely know him—I have seen him but once—but I will speak my mind.'

The Princess rang for her maid to usher the fiddler out, but at the moment he laid his hand on the door of the room she checked him with a quick gesture. 'Now that I think of it, don't go to Mr. Muniment. It will be better to leave him quiet. Leave him to me,' she added, smiling.

'Why not, why not?' he pleaded. And as she could not tell him on the instant why not, he asked, 'Doesn't he know?'

'No, he doesn't know; he has nothing to do with it.' She suddenly found herself desiring to protect Paul Muniment from the imputation that was in Mr. Vetch's mind— the imputation of an ugly responsibility; and though she was not a person who took the trouble to tell fibs, this repudiation, on his behalf, issued from her lips before she could check it. It was a result of the same desire, though it was also an inconsequence, that she added, 'Don't do that—you'll spoil everything !' She went to him, suddenly eager, and herself opened the door for him. 'Leave him to me—leave him to me,' she continued, persuasively, while the fiddler, gazing at her, dazzled and submissive, allowed himself to be wafted away. A thought that excited her had come to her with a bound, and after she had heard the house door close behind Mr. Vetch she walked up and down the room half an hour, restlessly, under the possession of it.

BOOK FIFTH

HYACINTH found, this winter, considerable occupation for
his odd hours, his evenings and holidays and scraps of
leisure, in putting in hand the books which he had promised himself, at Medley, to inclose in covers worthy of
the high station and splendour of the lady of his life
(these brilliant attributes had not then been shuffled out of
sight), and of the confidence and generosity she showed
him. He had determined she should receive from him
something of value, and took pleasure in thinking that
after he was gone they would be passed from hand to
hand as specimens of rare work, while connoisseurs bent
their heads over them, smiling and murmuring, handling
them delicately. His invention stirred itself, and he had
a hundred admirable ideas, many of which he sat up late
at night to execute. He used all his skill, and by this
time his skill was of a very high order. Old Crookenden
recognised it by raising the rates at which he was paid;
and though it was not among the traditions of the pro-
prietor of the establishment in Soho, who to the end wore
the apron with his workmen, to scatter sweet speeches,
Hyacinth learned accidentally that several books that he
had given him to do had been carried off and placed on a
shelf of treasures at the villa, where they were exhibited to
the members of the Crookenden circle who came to tea on
Sundays. Hyacinth himself, indeed, was included in this
company on a great occasion—invited to a musical party
where he made the acquaintance of half a dozen Miss
Crookendens, an acquaintance which consisted in his
standing in a corner, behind several broad-backed old
ladies, and watching the rotation, at the piano and the
harp, of three or four of his master's thick-fingered daughters.

'You know it's a tremendously musical house,' said one of the old ladies to another (she called it ''ouse'); but the principal impression made upon him by the performance of the Miss Crookendens was that it was wonderfully different from the Princess's playing.

He knew that he was the only young man from the shop who had been invited, not counting the foreman, who was sixty years old and wore a wig which constituted in itself a kind of social position, besides being accompanied by a little frightened, furtive wife, who closed her eyes, as if in the presence of a blinding splendour, when Mrs. Crookenden spoke to her. The Poupins were not there—which, however, was not a surprise to Hyacinth, who knew that (even if they had been asked, which they were not), they had objections of principle to putting their feet *chez les bourgeois*. They were not asked because, in spite of the place Eustache had made for himself in the prosperity of the business, it had come to be known that his wife was somehow not his wife (though she was certainly no one's else); and the evidence of this irregularity was conceived to reside, vaguely, in the fact that she had never been seen save in a camisole. There had doubtless been an apprehension that if she had come to the villa she would not have come with the proper number of hooks and eyes, though Hyacinth, on two or three occasions, notably the night he took the pair to Mr. Vetch's theatre, had been witness of the proportions to which she could reduce her figure when she wished to give the impression of a lawful tie.

It was not clear to him how the distinction conferred upon him became known in Soho, where, however, it excited no sharpness of jealousy — Grugan, Roker and Hotchkin being hardly more likely to envy a person condemned to spend a genteel evening than they were to envy a monkey performing antics on a barrel-organ : both forms of effort indicated an urbanity painfully acquired. But Roker took his young comrade's breath half away with his elbow and remarked that he supposed he saw the old man had spotted him for one of the darlings at home ; inquiring, furthermore, what would become in that case of the little thing he took to France, the one to whom he had stood

champagne and lobster.   This was the first allusion Hyacinth had heard made to the idea that he might some day
marry his master's daughter, like the virtuous apprentice of
tradition; but the suggestion, somehow, was not inspiring,
even when he had thought of an incident or two which
gave colour to it.   None of the Miss Crookendens spoke
to him—they all had large faces and short legs and a comical resemblance to that elderly male with wide nostrils,
their father, and, unlike the Miss Marchants, at Medley,
they knew who he was—but their mother, who had on
her head the plumage of a cockatoo, mingled with a structure of glass beads, looked at him with an almost awful
fixedness and asked him three distinct times if he would
have a glass of negus.

He had much difficulty in getting his books·from the
Princess; for when he reminded her of the promise she
had given him at Medley to make over to him as many
volumes as he should require, she answered that everything was changed since then, that she was completely
dépouillée, that she had now no pretension to have a
library, and that, in fine, he had much better leave the
matter alone.   He was welcome to any books that were
in the house, but, as he could see for himself, these were
cheap editions, on which it would be foolish to expend
such work as his.   He asked Madame Grandoni to help
him—to tell him, at least, whether there were not some
good volumes among the things the Princess had
sent to be warehoused; it being known to him, through
casual admissions of her own, that she had allowed her
maid to save certain articles from the wreck and·pack
them away at the Pantechnicon.   This had all been
Assunta's work, the woman had begged so hard for a few
reservations—a loaf of bread for their old days; but the
Princess herself had washed her hands of the business.
'*Chè, chè*, there are boxes, I am sure, in that place, with
a little of everything,' said the old lady, in answer to
his inquiry; and Hyacinth conferred with Assunta, who
took a sympathetic, talkative, Italian interest in his undertaking and promised to fish out for him whatever worthy
volumes should remain.   She came to his lodging, one

evening, in a cab, with an armful of pretty books, and
when he asked her where they had come from waved
her forefinger in front of her nose, in a manner both
mysterious and expressive. He brought each volume to
the Princess, as it was finished ; but her manner of receiving it was to shake her head over it with a kind,
sad smile. ' It's beautiful, I am sure, but I have lost
my sense for such things. Besides, you must always
remember what you once told me, that a woman, even
the most cultivated, is incapable of feeling the difference
between a bad binding and a good. I remember your
once saying that fine ladies had brought shoemaker's
bindings to your shop, and wished them imitated. Certainly those are not the differences I most feel. My dear
fellow, such things have ceased to speak to me ; they
are doubtless charming, but they leave me cold. What
will you have ? One can't serve God and mammon.' Her
thoughts were fixed on far other matters than the delight
of dainty covers, and she evidently considered that in
caring so much for them Hyacinth resembled the mad
emperor who fiddled in the flames of Rome. European
society, to her mind, was in flames, and no frivolous occupation could give the measure of the emotion with which
she watched them. It produced occasionally demonstra-
tions of hilarity, of joy and hope, but these always took
some form connected with the life of the people. It was
the people she had gone to see, when she accompanied
Hyacinth to a music-hall in the Edgeware Road ; and all
her excursions and pastimes, this winter, were prompted
by her interest in the classes on whose behalf the revolution was to be wrought.

To ask himself whether she were in earnest was now
an old story to him, and, indeed, the conviction he
might arrive at on this head had ceased to have any
practical relevancy. It was just as she was, superficial
or profound, that she held him, and she was, at any
rate, sufficiently animated by a purpose for her doings
to have consequences, actual and possible. Some of
these might be serious, even if she herself were not, and
there were times when Hyacinth was much visited by

the apprehension of them.   On the Sundays that she
had gone with him into the darkest places, the most
fetid holes, in London, she had always taken money
with her, in considerable quantities, and always left it
behind.   She said, very naturally, that one couldn't go
and stare at people, for an impression, without paying
them, and she gave alms right and left, indiscriminately,
without inquiry or judgment, as simply as the abbess of
some beggar-haunted convent, or a lady-bountiful of the
superstitious, unscientific ages who should have hoped to
be assisted to heaven by her doles.   Hyacinth never
said to her, though he sometimes thought it, that since
she was so full of the modern spirit her charity should
be administered according to the modern lights, the prin-
ciples of economical science ; partly because she was not
a woman to be directed and regulated—she could take
other people's ideas, but she could never take their way.
Besides, what did it matter?   To himself, what did it
matter to-day whether he were drawn into right methods
or into wrong ones, his time being too short for regret
or for cheer?   The Princess was an embodied passion—
she was not a system ; and her behaviour, after all, was
more addressed to relieving herself than to relieving
others.   And then misery was sown so thick in her path
that wherever her money was dropped it fell into some
trembling palm.   He wondered that she should still have
so much cash to dispose of, until she explained to him
that she came by it through putting her personal expenditure on a rigid footing.   What she gave away was her
savings, the margin she had succeeded in creating ; and
now that she had tasted of the satisfaction of making
little hoards for such a purpose she regarded her other
years, with their idleness and waste, their merely personal
motives, as a long, stupid sleep of the conscience.   To
do something for others was not only so much more
human, but so much more amusing !

She made strange acquaintances, under Hyacinth's conduct ; she listened to extraordinary stories, and formed
theories about them, and about the persons who narrated
them to her, which were often still more extraordinary.

She took romantic fancies to vagabonds of either sex, attempted to establish social relations with them, and was the cause of infinite agitation to the gentleman who lived near her in the Crescent, who was always smoking at the window, and who reminded Hyacinth of Mr. Micawber. She received visits that were a scandal to the Crescent, and Hyacinth neglected his affairs, whatever they were, to see what tatterdemalion would next turn up at her door. This intercourse, it is true, took a more fruitful form as her intimacy with Lady Aurora deepened; her ladyship practised discriminations which she brought the Princess to recognise, and before the winter was over Hyacinth's services in the slums were found unnecessary. He gave way with relief, with delight, to Lady Aurora, for he had not in the least understood his behaviour for the previous four months, nor taken himself seriously as a *cicerone*. He had plunged into a sea of barbarism without having any civilising energy to put forth. He was conscious that the people were miserable—more conscious, it often seemed to him, than they themselves were; so frequently was he struck with their brutal insensibility, a grossness impervious to the taste of better things or to any desire for them. He knew it so well that the repetition of contact could add no vividness to the conviction; it rather smothered and befogged his impression, peopled it with contradictions and difficulties, a violence of reaction, a sense of the inevitable and insurmountable. In these hours the poverty and ignorance of the multitude seemed so vast and preponderant, and so much the law of life, that those who had managed to escape from the black gulf were only the happy few, people of resource as well as children of luck; they inspired in some degree the interest and sympathy that one should feel for survivors and victors, those who have come safely out of a shipwreck or a battle. What was most in Hyacinth's mind was the idea, of which every pulsation of the general life of his time was a syllable, that the flood of democracy was rising over the world; that it would sweep all the traditions of the past before it; that, whatever it might fail to bring, it would at least carry in its bosom a magnificent energy; and that it might be trusted to look after its own. When

democracy should have its way everywhere, it would be its
fault (whose else ?) if want and suffering and crime should
continue to be ingredients of the human lot. With his
mixed, divided nature, his conflicting sympathies, his eternal
habit of swinging from one view to another, Hyacinth
regarded this prospect, in different moods, with different
kinds of emotion. In spite of the example Eustache
Poupin gave him of the reconcilement of disparities, he
was afraid the democracy wouldn't care for perfect bindings
or for the finest sort of conversation. The Princess gave
up these things in proportion as she advanced in the
direction she had so audaciously chosen ; and if the Princess could give them up it would take very transcendent
natures to stick to them. At the same time there was joy,
exultation, in the thought of surrendering one's self to the
wave of revolt, of floating in the tremendous tide, of
feeling one's self lifted and tossed, carried higher on the
sun-touched crests of billows than one could ever be by a
dry, lonely effort of one's own. That vision could deepen
to a kind of ecstasy ; make it indifferent whether one's
ultimate fate, in such a heaving sea, were not almost
certainly to be submerged in bottomless depths or dashed
to pieces on resisting cliffs. Hyacinth felt that, whether
his personal sympathy should rest finally with the victors
or the vanquished, the victorious force was colossal and
would require no testimony from the irresolute.

The reader will doubtless smile at his mental debates
and oscillations, and not understand why a little bastard
bookbinder should attach importance to his conclusions.
They were not important for either cause, but they were
important for himself, if only because they would rescue
him from the torment of his present life, the perpetual
laceration of the rebound. There was no peace for him
between the two currents that flowed in his nature, the
blood of his passionate, plebeian mother and that of his
long-descended, supercivilised sire. They continued to
toss him from one side to the other ; they arrayed him in
intolerable defiances and revenges against himself. He had
a high ambition : he wanted neither more nor less than to
get hold of the truth and wear it in his heart. He believed,

with the candour of youth, that it is brilliant and clear-
cut, like a royal diamond ; but in whatever direction he
turned in the effort to find it, he seemed to know that
behind him, bent on him in reproach, was a tragic,
wounded face. The thought of his mother had filled him,
originally, with the vague, clumsy fermentation of his first
impulses toward social criticism ; but since the problem
had become more complex by the fact that many things in
the world as it was constituted grew intensely dear to him,
he had tried more and more to construct some conceivable
and human countenance for his father—some expression of
honour, of tenderness and recognition, of unmerited suffering,
or at least of adequate expiation. To desert one of these
presences for the other—that idea had a kind of shame in
it, as an act of treachery would have had ; for he could
almost hear the voice of his father ask him if it were the
conduct of a gentleman to take up the opinions and emulate
the crudities of fanatics and cads. He had got over
thinking that it would not have become his father to talk
of what was proper to gentlemen, and making the mental
reflection that from him, at least, the biggest cad in London
could not have deserved less consideration. He had worked
himself round to allowances, to interpretations, to such
hypotheses as the evidence in the *Times*, read in the British
Museum on that never-to-be-forgotten afternoon, did not
exclude ; though they had been frequent enough, and too
frequent, his hours of hot resentment against the man who
had attached to him the stigma he was to carry for ever, he
threw himself, in other conditions, and with a certain
success, into the effort to find condonations, excuses, for
him. It was comparatively easy for him to accept himself
as the son of a terribly light Frenchwoman ; there seemed
a deeper obloquy even than that in his having for his other
parent a nobleman altogether wanting in nobleness. He
was too poor to afford it. Sometimes, in his imagination,
he sacrificed one to the other, throwing over Lord Frederick
much the oftener ; sometimes, when the theory failed that
his father would have done great things for him if he had
lived, or the assumption broke down that he had been
Florentine Vivier's only lover, he cursed and disowned

them alike; sometimes he arrived at conceptions which presented them side by side, looking at him with eyes infinitely sad but quite unashamed—eyes which seemed to tell him that they had been hideously unfortunate but had not been base. Of course his worst moments now, as they had always been the worst, were those in which his grounds for thinking that Lord Frederick had really been his father perversely fell away from him. It must be added that they always passed, for the mixture that he felt himself so tormentingly, so insolubly, to be could be accounted for in no other manner.

I mention these dim broodings not because they belong in an especial degree to the history of our young man during the winter of the Princess's residence in Madeira Crescent, but because they were a constant element in his moral life and need to be remembered in any view of him at a given time. There were nights of November and December, as he trod the greasy pavements that lay between Westminster and Paddington, groping his way through the baffled lamp-light and tasting the smoke-seasoned fog, when there was more happiness in his heart than he had ever known. The influence of his permeating London had closed over him again; Paris and Milan and Venice had shimmered away into reminiscence and picture; and as the great city which was most his own lay round him under her pall, like an immeasurable breathing monster, he felt, with a vague excitement, as he had felt before, only now with more knowledge, that it was the richest expression of the life of man. His horizon had been immensely widened, but it was filled, again, by the expanse that sent dim night-gleams and strange blurred reflections and emanations into a sky without stars. He suspended, as it were, his small sensibility in the midst of it, and it quivered there with joy and hope and ambition, as well as with the effort of renunciation. The Princess's quiet fireside glowed with deeper assurances, with associations of intimacy, through the dusk and the immensity; the thought of it was with him always, and his relations with the mistress of it were more organised than they had been in his first vision of her. Whether or no it was better for the cause she cherished that she should have been reduced to her present simplicity, it was better, at least, for Hyacinth. It made her more near and him more free ; and if there had been a danger of her nature seeming really to take the tone of the vulgar things about her, he would only have had to remember her as she was at Medley to restore the perspective. In truth, her beauty always appeared to have the setting that best became it ; her fairness made the element in which she lived and, among the meanest accessories, constituted a kind of splendour. Nature had multiplied the difficulties in the way of her successfully representing herself as having properties in common with the horrible populace of London. Hyacinth used to smile at this pretension in his night-walks to Paddington, or homeward ; the populace of London were scattered upon his path, and he asked himself by what wizardry they could ever be raised to high participations. There were nights when every one he met appeared to reek with gin and filth, and he found himself elbowed by figures as foul as lepers. Some of the women and girls, in particular, were appalling—saturated with alcohol and vice, brutal, bedraggled, obscene. ' What remedy but another deluge, what alchemy but annihilation ? ' he asked himself, as he went his way ; and he wondered what fate there could be, in the great scheme of things, for a planet overgrown with such vermin, what redemption but to be hurled against a ball of consuming fire. If it was the fault of the rich, as Paul Muniment held, the selfish, congested rich, who allowed such abominations to flourish, that made no differ-ence, and only shifted the shame ; for the terrestrial globe, a visible failure, produced the cause as well as the effect.

It did not occur to Hyacinth that the Princess had with-drawn her confidence from him because, for the work of investigating still further the condition of the poor, she placed herself in the hands of Lady Aurora. He could have no jealousy of the noble spinster ; he had too much respect for her philanthropy, the thoroughness of her know-ledge, and her capacity to answer any question it could come into the Princess's extemporising head to ask, and too acute a consciousness of his own desultory and superficial attitude toward the great question. It was enough for him

that the little parlour in Madeira Crescent was a spot round
which his thoughts could revolve, and toward which his
steps could direct themselves, with an unalloyed sense of
security and privilege.   The picture of it hung before him
half the time, in colours to which the feeling of the place
gave a rarity that doubtless did not literally characterise the
scene.   His relations with the Princess had long since
ceased to appear to him to belong to the world of fable ;
they were as natural as anything else (everything in life was
queer enough) ; he had by this time assimilated them, as it
were, and they were an indispensable part of the happiness
of each.   ' Of each '—Hyacinth risked that, for there was no
particular vanity now involved in his perceiving that the most
remarkable woman in Europe was, simply, very fond of him.
The quiet, familiar, fraternal welcome he found on the nasty
winter nights was proof enough of that.   They sat together
like very old friends, whom long pauses, during which they
simply looked at each other with kind, acquainted eyes,
could not make uncomfortable.   Not that the element of
silence was the principal part of their conversation, for it
interposed only when they had talked a great deal.   Hyacinth,
on the opposite side of the fire, felt at times almost as if he
were married to his hostess, so many things were taken for
granted between them.   For intercourse of that sort, intimate,
easy, humorous, circumscribed by drawn curtains and shaded
lamp-light, and interfused with domestic embarrassments and
confidences, all turning to the jocular, the Princess was
incomparable.   It was her theory of her present existence
that she was picnicking ; but all the accidents of the business were happy accidents.   There was a household quietude
in her steps and gestures, in the way she sat, in the way she
listened, in the way she played with the cat, or looked after
the fire, or folded Madame Grandoni's ubiquitous shawl ;
above all, in the inveteracy with which she spent her evenings at home, never dining out nor going to parties, ignorant
of the dissipations of the town.   There was something in
the isolation of the room, when the kettle was on the hob
and he had given his wet umbrella to the maid and the
Princess made him sit in a certain place near the fire, the
better to dry his shoes—there was something that evoked

the idea of the *vie de province*, as he had read about it in
French works. The French term came to him because it
represented more the especial note of the Princess's company, the cultivation, the facility, of talk. She expressed
herself often in the French tongue itself; she could borrow
that convenience, for certain shades of meaning, though she
had told Hyacinth that she didn't like the people to whom
it was native. Certainly, the quality of her conversation
was not provincial; it was singularly free and unrestricted;
there was nothing one mightn't say to her or that she was
not liable to say herself. She had cast off prejudices and
gave no heed to conventional danger-posts. Hyacinth
admired the movement—his eyes seemed to see it—with
which, in any direction, intellectually, she could fling open
her windows. There was an extraordinary charm in this
mixture of liberty and humility—in seeing a creature capable,
socially, of immeasurable flights sit dove-like, with folded
wings.

The young man met Lady Aurora several times in
Madeira Crescent (her days, like his own, were filled with
work, and she came in the evening), and he knew that her
friendship with the Princess had arrived at a rich maturity.
The two ladies were a source of almost rapturous interest
to each other, and each rejoiced that the other was not
a bit different. The Princess prophesied freely that her
visitor would give her up—all nice people did, very soon;
but to Hyacinth the end of her ladyship's almost breathless enthusiasm was not yet in view. She was bewildered,
but she was fascinated; and she thought the Princess not
only the most distinguished, the most startling, the most
edifying and the most original person in the world, but the
most amusing and the most delightful to have tea with. As
for the Princess, her sentiment about Lady Aurora was the
same that Hyacinth's had been : she thought her a saint,
the first she had ever seen, and the purest specimen conceivable; as good in her way as St. Francis of Assisi, as
tender and naïve and transparent, of a spirit of charity as
sublime. She held that when one met a human flower as
fresh as that in the dusty ways of the world one should
pluck it and wear it; and she was always inhaling Lady

Aurora's fragrance, always kissing her and holding her hand. The spinster was frightened at her generosity, at the way her imagination embroidered; she wanted to convince her (as the Princess did on her own side), that such exaggerations destroyed their unfortunate subject. The Princess delighted in her clothes, in the way she put them on and wore them, in the economies she practised in order to have money for charity and the ingenuity with which these slender resources were made to go far, in the very manner in which she spoke, a kind of startled simplicity. She wished to emulate her in all these particulars; to learn how to economise still more cunningly, to get her bonnets at the same shop, to care as little for the fit of her gloves, to ask, in the same tone, 'Isn't it a bore Susan Crotty's husband has got a ticket-of-leave?' She said Lady Aurora made her feel like a French milliner, and that if there was anything in the world she loathed it was a French milliner. Each of these persons was powerfully affected by the other's idiosyncrasies, and each wanted the other to remain as she was while she herself should be transformed into the image of her friend.

One evening, going to Madeira Crescent a little later than usual, Hyacinth met Lady Aurora on the doorstep, leaving the house. She had a different air from any he had seen in her before; appeared flushed and even a little agitated, as if she had been learning a piece of bad news. She said, 'Oh, how do you do?' with her customary quick, vague laugh; but she went her way, without stopping to talk.

Hyacinth, on going in, mentioned to the Princess that he had encountered her, and this lady replied, 'It's a pity you didn't come a little sooner. You would have assisted at a scene.'

'At a scene?' Hyacinth repeated, not understanding what violence could have taken place between mutual adorers.

'She made me a scene of tears, of earnest remonstrance —perfectly well meant, I needn't tell you. She thinks I am going too far.'

'I imagine you tell her things that you don't tell me,' said Hyacinth.

'Oh, you, my dear fellow!' the Princess murmured. She spoke absent-mindedly, as if she were thinking of what had passed with Lady Aurora, and as if the futility of telling things to Hyacinth had become a commonplace.

There was no annoyance for him in this, his pretension to keep pace with her 'views' being quite extinct. The tone they now, for the most part, took with each other was one of mutual derision, of shrugging commiseration for insanity on the one hand and benightedness on the other. In discussing with her he exaggerated deliberately, went to fantastic lengths in the way of reaction; and it was their habit and their entertainment to hurl all manner of denunciation at each other's head. They had given up serious discussion altogether, and when they were not engaged in bandying, in the spirit of burlesque, the amenities I have mentioned, they talked of matters as to which it could not occur to them to differ. There were evenings when the Princess did nothing but relate her life and all that she had seen of humanity, from her earliest years, in a variety of countries. If the evil side of it appeared mainly to have been presented to her view, this did not diminish the interest and vividness of her reminiscences, nor her power, the greatest Hyacinth had ever encountered, of light pictorial, dramatic evocation. She was irreverent and invidious, but she made him hang on her lips; and when she regaled him with anecdotes of foreign courts (he delighted to know how sovereigns lived and conversed), there was often, for hours together, nothing to indicate that she would have liked to get into a conspiracy and he would have liked to get out of one. Nevertheless, his mind was by no means exempt from wonder as to what she was really doing in the dark and in what queer consequences she might find herself landed. When he questioned her she wished to know by what title, with his sentiments, he pretended to inquire. He did so but little, not being himself altogether convinced of the validity of his warrant; but on one occasion, when she challenged him, he replied, smiling and hesitating, 'Well, I must say, it seems to me that, from what I have told you, it ought to strike you that I have a title.'

'You mean your famous engagement, your vow? Oh, that will never come to anything.'

'Why won't it come to anything?'

'It's too absurd, it's too vague. It's like some silly humbug in a novel.'

'*Vous me rendez la vie!*' said Hyacinth, theatrically.

'You won't have to do it,' the Princess went on.

'I think you mean I won't do it. I have offered, at least; isn't that a title?'

'Well, then, you won't do it,' said the Princess; and they looked at each other a couple of minutes in silence.

'You will, I think, at the pace you are going,' the young man resumed.

'What do you know about the pace? You are not worthy to know!'

He did know, however; that is, he knew that she was in communication with foreign socialists and had, or believed she had, irons on the fire—that she held in her hand some of the strings that are pulled in great movements. She received letters that made Madame Grandoni watch her askance, of which, though she knew nothing of their contents and had only her general suspicions and her scent for disaster, now become constant, the old woman had spoken more than once to Hyacinth. Madame Grandoni had begun to have sombre visions of the interference of the police: she was haunted with the idea of a search for compromising papers; of being dragged, herself, as an accomplice in direful plots, into a court of justice—possibly into a prison. 'If she would only burn—if she would only burn! But she keeps—I know she keeps!' she groaned to Hyacinth, in her helpless gloom. Hyacinth could only guess what it might be that she kept; asking himself whether she were seriously entangled, were being exploited by revolutionary Bohemians, predatory adventurers who counted on her getting frightened at a given moment and offering hush-money to be allowed to slip out (out of a complicity which they, of course, would never have taken seriously); or were merely coquetting with paper schemes, giving herself cheap sensations, discussing preliminaries

which, for her, could have no second stage.   It would have
been easy for Hyacinth to smile at the Princess's impression
that she was 'in it,' and to conclude that even the cleverest
women do not know when they are superficial, had not the
vibration remained which had been imparted to his nerves
two years before, of which he had spoken to his hostess at
Medley—the sense, vividly kindled and never quenched,
that the forces secretly arrayed against the present social
order were pervasive and universal, in the air one breathed,
in the ground one trod, in the hand of an acquaintance
that one might touch, or the eye of a stranger that might
rest a moment on one's own.   They were above, below,
within, without, in every contact and combination of life ;
and it was no disproof of them to say it was too odd that
they should lurk in a particular improbable form.   To lurk
in improbable forms was precisely their strength, and they
would doubtless exhibit much stranger incidents than this
of the Princess's being a genuine participant even when she
flattered herself that she was.

'You do go too far,' Hyacinth said to her, the evening
Lady Aurora had passed him at the door.

To which she answered, 'Of course I do—that's exactly
what I mean.   How else does one know one has gone far
enough ?   That poor, dear woman !   She's an angel, but
she isn't in the least in it,' she added, in a moment.   She
would give him no further satisfaction on the subject ; when
he pressed her she inquired whether he had brought the
copy of Browning that he had promised the last time.   If
he had, he was to sit down and read it to her.   In such a
case as this Hyacinth had no disposition to insist ; he was
glad enough not to talk about the everlasting nightmare.
He took *Men and Women* from his pocket, and read aloud
for half an hour ; but on his making some remark on one
of the poems, at the end of this time he perceived the
Princess had been paying no attention.   When he charged
her with this levity she only replied, looking at him musingly,
'How *can* one, after all, go too far ?   That's a word of
cowards.'

'Do you mean her ladyship is a coward ? '

'Yes, in not having the courage of her opinions, of her

conclusions. The way the English can go half-way to a thing, and then stick in the middle !' the Princess exclaimed, impatiently.

'That's not your fault, certainly !' said Hyacinth. 'But it seems to me that Lady Aurora, for herself, goes pretty far.'

'We are all afraid of some things, and brave about others,' the Princess went on.

'The thing Lady Aurora is most afraid of is the Princess Casamassima,' Hyacinth remarked.

His companion looked at him, but she did not take this up. 'There is one particular in which she would be very brave. She would marry her friend—your friend—Mr. Muniment.'

'Marry him, do you think ? '

'What else, pray ? ' the Princess asked. 'She adores the ground he walks on.'

'And what would Belgrave Square, and Inglefield, and all the rest of it, say ? '

'What do they say already, and how much does it make her swerve ? She would do it in a moment, and it would be fine to see it, it would be magnificent,' said the Princess, kindling, as she was apt to kindle, at the idea of any great freedom of action.

'That certainly wouldn't be a case of what you call sticking in the middle,' Hyacinth rejoined.

'Ah, it wouldn't be a matter of logic ; it would be a matter of passion. When it's a question of that, the English, to do them justice, don't stick !'

This speculation of the Princess's was by no means new to Hyacinth, and he had not thought it heroic, after all, that their high-strung friend should feel herself capable of sacrificing her family, her name, and the few habits of gentility that survived in her life, of making herself a scandal, a fable, and a nine days' wonder, for Muniment's sake ; the young chemist's assistant being, to his mind, as we know, exactly the type of man who produced convulsions, made ruptures and renunciations easy. But it was less clear to him what ideas Muniment might have on the subject of a union with a young woman who should have come out of her class for him.   He would marry some day, evidently, because he would do all the natural, human, productive things ; but for the present he had business on hand which would be likely to pass first.   Besides—Hyacinth had seen him give evidence of this—he didn't think people could really come out of their class ; he held that the stamp of one's origin is ineffaceable and that the best thing one can do is to wear it and fight for it.   Hyacinth could easily imagine how it would put him out to be mixed up, closely, with a person who, like Lady Aurora, was fighting on the wrong side.   'She can't marry him unless he asks her, I suppose—and perhaps he won't,' he reflected.

'Yes, perhaps he won't,' said the Princess, thoughtfully.

XXXIX

On Saturday afternoons Paul Muniment was able to leave his work at four o'clock and on one of these occasions, some time after his visit to Madeira Crescent, he came into Rosy's room at about five, carefully dressed and brushed, and ruddy with the freshness of an abundant washing. He stood at the foot of her sofa, with a conscious smile, knowing how she chaffed him when his necktie was new; and after a moment, during which she ceased singing to herself as she twisted the strands of her long black hair together and let her eyes travel over his whole person, inspecting every detail, she said to him, 'My dear Mr. Muniment, you are going to see the Princess.'

'Well, have you anything to say against it?' Mr. Muniment asked.

'Not a word; you know I like princesses. But you have.'

'Well, my girl, I'll not speak it to you,' the young man rejoined. 'There's something to be said against everything, if you'll give yourself trouble enough.'

'I should be very sorry if ever anything was said against you.'

'The man's a sneak who is only and always praised,' Muniment remarked. 'If you didn't hope to be finely abused, where would be the encouragement?'

'Ay, but not with reason,' said Rosy, who always brightened to an argument.

'The better the reason, the greater the incentive to expose one's self. However, you won't hear it, if people do heave bricks at me.'

'I won't hear it? Pray, don't I hear everything? I should like any one to keep anything from *me!*' And Miss Muniment gave a toss of her recumbent head.

'There's a good deal I keep from you, my dear,' said Paul, rather dryly.

'You mean there are things I don't want, I don't take any trouble, to know.   Indeed and indeed there are : things that I wouldn't know for the world—that no amount of persuasion would induce me, not if you was to go down on your knees.   But if I did—if I did, I promise you that just as I lie here I should have them all in my pocket. Now there are others,' the young woman went on—'there are others that you will just be so good as to tell me. When the Princess asked you to come and see her you refused, and you wanted to know what good it would do. I hoped you would go, then; I should have liked you to go, because I wanted to know how she lived, and whether she had things handsome, or only in the poor way she said. But I didn't push you, because I couldn't have told you what good it *would* do you : that was only the good it would have done me.   At present I have heard everything from Lady Aurora, and I know that it's all quite decent and tidy (though not really like a princess a bit), and that she knows how to turn everything about and put it best end foremost, just as I do, like, though *I* oughtn't to say it, no doubt. Well, you have been, and more than once, and I have had nothing to do with it; of which I am very glad now, for reasons that you perfectly know—you're too honest a man to pretend you don't.   Therefore, when I see you going again, I just inquire of you, as you inquired of her, what good *does* it do you?'

'I like it—I like it, my dear,' said Paul, with his fresh, unembarrassed smile.

'I dare say you do.   So should I, in your place.   But it's the first time I have heard you express the idea that we ought to do everything we like.'

'Why not, when it doesn't hurt any one else?'

'Oh, Mr. Muniment, Mr. Muniment!' Rosy exclaimed, with exaggerated solemnity, holding up a straight, attenuated forefinger at him.   Then she added, 'No, she doesn't do you good, that beautiful, brilliant woman.'

'Give her time, my dear—give her time,' said Paul, looking at his watch.

'Of course you are impatient, but you *must* hear me. I have no doubt she'll wait for you; you won't lose your turn. Please, what would you do if any one was to break down altogether?'

'My bonny lassie,' the young man rejoined, 'if *you* only keep going, I don't care who fails.'

'Oh, I shall keep going, if it's only to look after my friends and get justice for them,' said Miss Muniment—'the delicate, sensitive creatures who require support and protection. Have you really forgotten that we have such a one as that?'

The young man walked to the window, with his hands in his pockets, and looked out at the fading light. 'Why does she go herself, then, if she doesn't like her?'

Rose Muniment hesitated a moment. 'Well, I'm glad I'm not a man!' she broke out. 'I think a woman on her back is cleverer than a man on his two legs. And you such a wonderful one, too!'

'You are all too clever for me, my dear. If she goes—and twenty times a week, too—why shouldn't I go, once in ever so long? Especially as I like her, and Lady Aurora doesn't.'

'Lady Aurora doesn't? Do you think she'd be guilty of hypocrisy? Lady Aurora delights in her; she won't let me say that she herself is fit to dust the Princess's shoes. I needn't tell *you* how she goes down before them she likes. And I don't believe you care a button; you have got something in your head, some wicked game or other, that you think she can hatch for you.'

At this Paul Muniment turned round and looked at his sister a moment, smiling still and whistling just audibly. 'Why shouldn't I care? Ain't I soft, ain't I susceptible?'

'I never thought I should hear you ask that, after what I have seen these four years. For four years she has come, and it's all for you, as well it might be, and you never showing any more sense of what she'd be willing to do for you than if you had been that woollen cat on the hearth-rug!'

'What would you like me to do? Would you like me

to hang round her neck and hold her hand, the same as
you do?' Muniment asked.

'Yes, it would do me good, I can tell you. It's better
than what I see—the poor lady getting spotted and dim, like
a mirror that wants rubbing.'

'You know a good deal, Rosy, but you don't know
everything,' Muniment remarked in a moment, with a face
that gave no sign of seeing a reason in what she said.
'Your mind is too poetical. There's nothing that I should
care for that her ladyship would be willing to do for me.'

'She would marry you at a day's notice—she'd do
that.'

'I shouldn't care for that. Besides, if I was to ask
her she would never come into the place again. And I
shouldn't care for that, for you.'

'Never mind me; I'll take the risk!' cried Rosy,
gaily.

'But what's to be gained, if I can have her, for you,
without any risk?'

'You won't have her for me, or for any one, when she's
dead of a broken heart.'

'Dead of a broken tea-cup!' said the young man.
'And, pray, what should we live on, when you had got us
set up?—the three of us, without counting the kids.'

He evidently was arguing from pure good-nature, and
not in the least from curiosity; but his sister replied as
eagerly as if he would be floored by her answer: 'Hasn't
she got two hundred a year of her own? Don't I know
every penny of her affairs?'

Paul Muniment gave no sign of any mental criticism he
may have made on Rosy's conception of the delicate course,
or of a superior policy; perhaps, indeed, for it is perfectly
possible, her inquiry did not strike him as having a mixture
of motives. He only rejoined, with a little pleasant, patient
sigh, 'I don't want the dear old girl's money.'

His sister, in spite of her eagerness, waited twenty
seconds; then she flashed at him, 'Pray, do you like the
Princess's better?'

'If I did, there would be more of it,' he answered,
quietly.

'How can she marry you?   Hasn't she got a husband?'
Rosy cried.

'Lord, how you give me away!' laughed her brother.
'Daughters of earls, wives of princes—I have only to pick.'

'I don't speak of the Princess, so long as there's a
prince.   But if you haven't seen that Lady Aurora is a
beautiful, wonderful exception, and quite unlike any one
else in all the wide world—well, all I can say is that *I*
have.'

'I thought it was your opinion,' Paul objected, 'that
the swells should remain swells, and the high ones keep
their place.'

'And, pray, would she lose hers if she were to marry
you?'

'Her place at Inglefield, certainly,' said Paul, as
patiently as if his sister could never tire him with any
insistence or any minuteness.

'Hasn't she lost that already?   Does she ever go
there?'

'Surely you appear to think so, from the way you
always question her about it,' replied Paul.

'Well, they think her so mad already that they can't
think her any madder,' his sister continued.   'They have
given her up, and if she were to marry you——'

'If she were to marry me, they wouldn't touch her with
a ten-foot pole,' Paul broke in.

Rosy flinched a moment; then she said, serenely, 'Oh,
I don't care for that!'

'You ought to, to be consistent, though, possibly, she
shouldn't, admitting that she wouldn't.   You have more
imagination than logic—which of course, for a woman, is
quite right.   That's what makes you say that her ladyship
is in affliction because I go to a place that she herself goes
to without the least compulsion.'

'She goes to keep you off,' said Rosy, with decision.

'To keep me off?'

'To interpose, with the Princess; to be nice to her and
conciliate her, so that she may not take you.'

'Did she tell you any such rigmarole as that?' Paul
inquired, this time staring a little.

'Do I need to be told things, to know them? I am not a fine, strong, superior male; therefore I can discover them for myself,' answered Rosy, with a dauntless little laugh and a light in her eyes which might indeed have made it appear that she was capable of wizardry.

'You make her out at once too passionate and too calculating,' the young man rejoined. 'She has no personal feelings, she wants nothing for herself. She only wants one thing in the world—to make the poor a little less poor.'

'Precisely; and she regards you, a helpless, blundering bachelor, as one of them.'

'She knows I am not helpless so long as you are about the place, and that my blunders don't matter so long as you correct them.'

'She wants to assist me to assist you, then!' the girl exclaimed, with the levity with which her earnestness was always interfused; it was a spirit that seemed, at moments, in argument, to mock at her own contention. 'Besides, isn't that the very thing you want to bring about?' she went on. 'Isn't that what you are plotting and working and waiting for? She wants to throw herself into it—to work with you.'

'My dear girl, she doesn't understand a pennyworth of what I think. She couldn't if she would.'

'And no more do I, I suppose you mean.'

'No more do you; but with you it's different. If you would, you could. However, it matters little who understands and who doesn't, for there's mighty little of it. I'm not doing much, you know.'

Rosy lay there looking up at him. 'It must be pretty thick, when you talk that way. However, I don't care what happens, for I know I shall be looked after.'

'Nothing will happen—nothing will happen,' Paul remarked, simply.

The girl's rejoinder to this was to say in a moment, 'You have a different tone since you have taken up the Princess.'

She spoke with a certain severity, but he broke out, as if he had not heard her, 'I like your idea of the female aristocracy quarrelling over a dirty brute like me.'

'I don't know how dirty you are, but I know you smell of soap,' said Rosy, with serenity. 'They won't quarrel; that's not the way they do it. Yes, you are taking a different tone, for some purpose that I can't discover just yet.'

'What do you mean by that? When did I ever take a tone?' her brother asked.

'Why then do you speak as if you were not remarkable, immensely remarkable—more remarkable than anything any one, male or female, good or bad, of the aristocracy or of the vulgar sort, can ever do for you?'

'What on earth have I ever done to show it?' Paul demanded.

'Oh, I don't know your secrets, and that's one of them. But we're out of the common beyond any one, you and I, and, between ourselves, with the door fastened, we might as well admit it.'

'I admit it for you, with all my heart,' said the young man, laughing.

'Well, then, if I admit it for you, that's all that's required.'

The brother and sister considered each other a while in silence, as if each were tasting, agreeably, the distinction the other conferred; then Muniment said, 'If I'm such an awfully superior chap, why shouldn't I behave in keeping?'

'Oh, you do, you do!'

'All the same, you don't like it.'

'It isn't so much what you do; it's what *she* does.'

'How do you mean, what she does?'

'She makes Lady Aurora suffer.'

'Oh, I can't go into that,' said Paul. 'A man feels like a muff, talking about the women that "suffer" for him.'

'Well, if they do it, I think *you* might bear it!' Rosy exclaimed. 'That's what a man is. When it comes to being sorry, oh, that's too ridiculous!'

'There are plenty of things in the world I'm sorry for,' Paul rejoined, smiling. 'One of them is that you should keep me gossiping here when I want to go out.'

'Oh, I don't care if I worry her a little. Does she do it on purpose?' Rosy continued.

'You ladies must settle all that together,' Muniment answered, rubbing his hat with the cuff of his coat. It was a new one, the bravest he had ever possessed, and in a moment he put it on his head, as if to reinforce his reminder to his sister that it was time she should release him.

'Well, you do look genteel,' she remarked, complacently, gazing up at him. 'No wonder she has lost her head! I mean the Princess,' she explained. 'You never went to any such expense for her ladyship.'

'My dear, the Princess is worth it—she's worth it,' said the young man, speaking seriously now, and reflectively.

'Will she help you very much?' Rosy demanded, with a strange, sudden transition to eagerness.

'Well,' said Paul, 'that's rather what I look for.'

She threw herself forward on her sofa, with a movement that was rare with her, and shaking her clasped hands she exclaimed, 'Then go off, go off quickly!'

He came round and kissed her, as if he were not more struck than usual with her freakish inconsistency. 'It's not bad to have a little person at home who wants a fellow to succeed.'

'Oh, I know they will look after me,' she said, sinking back upon her pillow with an air of agreeable security.

He was aware that whenever she said 'they,' without further elucidation, she meant the populace surging up in his rear, and he rejoined, always hilarious, 'I don't think we'll leave it much to "them."'

'No, it's not much you'll leave to them, I'll be bound.'

He gave a louder laugh at this, and said, 'You're the deepest of the lot, Miss Muniment.'

Her eyes kindled at his praise, and as she rested them on her brother's she murmured, 'Well, I pity the poor Princess, too, you know.'

'Well, now, I'm not conceited, but I don't,' Paul returned, passing in front of the little mirror on the mantel-shelf.

'Yes, you'll succeed, and so shall I—but *she* won't,' Rosy went on.

Muniment stopped a moment, with his hand on the latch of the door, and said, gravely, almost sententiously,

'She is not only beautiful, as beautiful as a picture, but she is uncommon sharp, and she has taking ways, beyond anything that ever was known.'

'I know her ways,' his sister replied. Then, as he left the room, she called after him, 'But I don't care for anything, so long as you become prime minister of England!'

Three quarters of an hour after this Muniment knocked at the door in Madeira Crescent, and was immediately ushered into the parlour, where the Princess, in her bonnet and mantle, sat alone. She made no movement as he came in ; she only looked up at him with a smile.

'You are braver than I gave you credit for,' she said, in her rich voice.

'I shall learn to be brave, if I associate a while longer with you. But I shall never cease to be shy,' Muniment added, standing there and looking tall in the middle of the small room. He cast his eyes about him for a place to sit down, but the Princess gave him no help to choose ; she only watched him, in silence, from her own place, with her hands quietly folded in her lap. At last, when, without remonstrance from her, he had selected the most uncomfortable chair in the room, she replied—

'That's only another name for desperate courage. I put on my bonnet, on the chance, but I didn't expect you.'

'Well, here I am—that's the great thing,' Muniment said, good-humouredly.

'Yes, no doubt it's a very great thing. But it will be a still greater thing when you are there.'

'I am afraid you hope too much,' the young man observed. 'Where is it ? I don't think you told me.'

The Princess drew a small folded letter from her pocket, and, without saying anything, held it out to him. He got up to take it from her, opened it, and, as he read it, remained standing in front of her. Then he went straight to the fire and thrust the paper into it. At this movement she rose quickly, as if to save the document, but the expression of his face, as he turned round to her, made her stop. The smile that came into her own was a little forced. 'What are you afraid of ?' she asked. 'I take it the house is known. If we go, I suppose we may admit that we go.'

Muniment's face showed that he had been annoyed, but he answered, quietly enough, ' No writing—no writing.'

' You are terribly careful,' said the Princess.

' Careful of you—yes.'

She sank down upon her sofa again, asking her companion to ring for tea ; they would do much better to have some before going out. When the order had been given, she remarked, ' I see I shall have much less keen emotion than when I acted by myself.'

' Is that what you go in for—keen emotion ?'

' Surely, Mr. Muniment. Don't you ?'

' God forbid ! I hope to have as little of it as possible.'

' Of course one doesn't want any vague rodomontade , one wants to do something. But it would be hard if one couldn't have a little pleasure by the way.'

' My pleasure is in quietness,' said Paul Muniment, smiling.

' So is mine. But it depends on how you understand it. Quietness, I mean, in the midst of a tumult.'

' You have rare ideas about tumults. They are not good in themselves.'

The Princess considered this a moment ; then she remarked, ' I wonder if you are too prudent. I shouldn't like that. If it is made an accusation against you that you have been—where we are going—shall you deny it ?'

' With that prospect it would be simpler not to go at all, wouldn't it ?' Muniment inquired.

' Which prospect do you mean ? That of being found out, or that of having to lie ?'

' I suppose that if you lie you are not found out,' Muniment replied, humorously.

' You won't take me seriously,' said the Princess. She spoke without irritation, without resentment, with a kind of resigned sadness. But there was a certain fineness of reproach in the tone in which she added, ' I don't believe you want to go at all.'

' Why else should I have come, especially if I don't take you seriously ?'

' That has never been a reason for a man's not going to

see a woman,' said the Princess. 'It's usually a reason in favour of it.'

Muniment turned his smiling eyes over the room, looking from one article of furniture to another : this was a way he had when he was engaged in a discussion, and it suggested not so much that he was reflecting on what his interlocutor said as that his thoughts were pursuing a cheerfully independent course. Presently he observed, 'I don't know that I quite understand what you mean by that question of taking a woman seriously.'

'Ah, you are very perfect,' murmured the Princess. 'Don't you consider that the changes you look for will be also for our benefit ?'

'I don't think they will alter your position.'

'If I didn't hope for that, I wouldn't do anything,' said the Princess.

'Oh, I have no doubt you'll do a great deal.'

The young man's companion was silent for some minutes, during which he also was content to say nothing. 'I wonder you can find it in your conscience to work with me,' she observed at last.

'It isn't in my conscience I find it,' said Muniment, laughing.

The maid-servant brought in the tea, and while the Princess was making a place for it on a little table beside her she exclaimed, 'Well, I don't care, for I think I have you in my power !'

'You have every one in your power, returned Muniment.

'Every one is no one,' the Princess replied, rather dryly ; and a moment later she said to him, 'That extraordinary little sister of yours — surely you take *her* seriously ?'

'I'm wonderful fond of her, if that's what you mean. But I don't think her position will ever be altered.

'Are you alluding to her position in bed ? If you consider that she will never recover her health,' the Princess said, 'I am very sorry to hear it.'

'Oh, her health will do. I mean that she will continue to be, like all the most amiable women, just a kind of ornament to life.'

The Princess had already perceived that he pronounced
amiable 'emiable;' but she had accepted this peculiarity
of her visitor in the spirit of imaginative transfiguration in
which she had accepted several others. 'To your life, of
course. She can hardly be said to be an ornament to her
own.'

'Her life and mine are all one.'

'She is certainly magnificent,' said the Princess. While
he was drinking his tea she remarked to him that for a
revolutionist he was certainly most extraordinary ; and he
inquired, in answer, whether it were not rather in keeping
for revolutionists to be extraordinary. He drank three
cups, declaring that his hostess's decoction was fine ; it
was better, even, than Lady Aurora's. This led him to
observe, as he put down his third cup, looking round the
room again, lovingly, almost covetously, 'You've got everything so handy, I don't see what interest you can have.'

'How do you mean, what interest ?'

'In getting in so uncommon deep.'

On the instant the Princess's expression flashed into
pure passion. 'Do you consider that I am in—really
far ?'

'Up to your neck, ma'am.'

'And do you think that *il y va* of my neck—I mean
that it's in danger ?' she translated, eagerly.

'Oh, I understand your French. Well, I'll look after
you,' Muniment said.

'Remember, then, definitely, that I expect not to lie.'

'Not even for me ?' Then Muniment added, in the
same familiar tone, which was not rough nor wanting in
respect, but only homely and direct, suggestive of growing
acquaintance, 'If I was your husband I would come and
take you away.'

'Please don't speak of my husband,' said the Princess,
gravely. 'You have no qualification for doing so ; you
know nothing whatever about him.'

'I know what Hyacinth has told me.'

'Oh, Hyacinth !' the Princess murmured, impatiently.
There was another silence of some minutes, not disconnected, apparently, from this reference to the little book-

binder; but when Muniment spoke, after the interval, it
was not to carry on the allusion.

'Of course you think me very plain, very rude.'

'Certainly, you have not such a nice address as Hyacinth,' the Princess rejoined, not desiring, on her side, to
evade the topic. 'But that is given to very few,' she
added; 'and I don't know that pretty manners are exactly
what we are working for.'

'Ay, it won't be very endearing when we cut down a
few allowances,' said Muniment. 'But I want to please
you; I want to be as much as possible like Hyacinth,' he
went on.

'That is not the way to please me. I don't forgive
him; he's very silly.'

'Ah, don't say that; he's a little brick!' Muniment
exclaimed.

'He's a dear fellow, with extraordinary qualities, but so
deplorably conventional.'

'Yes, talking about taking things seriously—*he* takes
them seriously,' remarked Muniment.

'Has he ever told you his life?' asked the Princess.

'He hasn't required to tell me. I've seen a good bit
of it.'

'Yes, but I mean before you knew him.'

Muniment reflected a moment. 'His birth, and his
poor mother? I think it was Rosy told me about that.'

'And, pray, how did *she* know?'

'Ah, when you come to the way Rosy knows!' said
Muniment, laughing. 'She doesn't like people in that
predicament. She thinks we ought all to be finely born.'

'Then they agree, for so does poor Hyacinth.' The
Princess hesitated an instant; then she said, as if with a
quick effort, 'I want to ask you something. Have you had
a visit from Mr. Vetch?'

'The old gentleman who fiddles? No, he has never
done me that honour.'

'It was because I prevented him, then. I told him to
leave it to me.'

'To leave what, now?' Muniment looked at her in
placid perplexity.

'He is in great distress about Hyacinth—about the danger he runs. You know what I mean.'

'Yes, I know what you mean,' Muniment replied, slowly. 'But what does *he* know about it? I thought it was supposed to be a deadly secret.'

'So it is. He doesn't know anything; he only suspects.'

'How do you know, then?'

The Princess hesitated again. 'Oh, I'm like Rosy—I find out. Mr. Vetch, as I suppose you are aware, has known Hyacinth all his life; he takes a most affectionate interest in him. He believes there is something hanging over him, and he wants it to be turned off, to be stopped.' The Princess paused at this, but her visitor made no response, and she continued: 'He was going to see you, to beg you to do something, to interfere; he seemed to think that your power, in such a matter, would be very great; but, as I tell you, I requested him, as a particular favour to me, to let you alone.'

'What favour would it be to you?' Muniment asked.

'It would give me the satisfaction of feeling that you were not worried.'

Muniment appeared struck with the curious inadequacy of this explanation, considering what was at stake; he broke into a laugh and remarked, 'That was considerate of you, beyond everything.'

'It was not meant as consideration for you; it was a piece of calculation.' The Princess, having made this announcement, gathered up her gloves and turned away, walking to the chimney-piece, where she stood a moment arranging her bonnet-ribbons in the mirror with which it was decorated. Muniment watched her with evident curiosity; in spite both of his inaccessibility to nervous agitation and of the sceptical theories he entertained about her, he was not proof against her general faculty of creating a feeling of suspense, a tension of interest, on the part of those who associated with her. He followed her movements, but plainly he didn't follow her calculations, so that he could only listen more attentively when she inquired suddenly, 'Do you know why I asked you to come and see me? Do you know why I went to see your sister? It was all a plan,' said the Princess.

'We hoped it was just an ordinary humane, social impulse,' the young man returned.

'It was humane, it was even social, but it was not ordinary. I wanted to save Hyacinth.'

'To save him?'

'I wanted to be able to talk with you just as I am talking now.'

'That was a fine idea!' Muniment exclaimed, ingenuously.

'I have an exceeding, a quite inexpressible, regard for him. I have no patience with some of his opinions, and that is why I permitted myself to say just now that he is silly. But, after all, the opinions of our friends are not what we love them for, and therefore I don't see why they should be what we hate them for. Hyacinth Robinson's nature is singularly generous and his intelligence very fine, though there *are* some things that he muddles up. You just now expressed strongly your own regard for him ; therefore we ought to be perfectly agreed. Agreed, I mean, about getting him out of his scrape.'

Muniment had the air of a man who felt that he must consider a little before he assented to these successive propositions; it being a limitation of his intellect that he could not respond without understanding. After a moment he answered, referring to the Princess's last remark, in which the others appeared to culminate, and at the same time shaking his head a little and smiling, ' His scrape isn't important.'

'You thought it was when you got him into it.'

'I thought it would give him pleasure,' said Muniment.

'That's not a reason for letting people do what isn't good for them.'

'I wasn't thinking so much about what would be good for him as about what would be bad for some others. He can do as he likes.'

'That's easy to say. They must be persuaded not to call upon him.'

'Persuade them, then, dear madam.'

'How can I persuade them? If I could, I wouldn't have approached you. I have no influence, and even if I had my motives would be suspected. You are the one to interpose.'

'Shall I tell them he funks it?' Muniment asked.

'He doesn't—he doesn't!' exclaimed the Princess.

'On what ground, then, shall I put it?'

'Tell them he has changed his opinions.'

'Wouldn't that be rather like denouncing him as a traitor, and doing it hypocritically?'

'Tell them then it's simply my wish.'

'That won't do *you* much good,' Muniment said, with his natural laugh.

'Will it put me in danger? That's exactly what I want.'

'Yes; but as I understand you, you want to suffer *for* the people, not by them. You are very fond of Robinson; it couldn't be otherwise,' the young man went on. 'But you ought to remember that, in the line you have chosen, our affections, our natural ties, our timidities, our shrink-ings——' His voice had become low and grave, and he paused a little, while the Princess's deep and lovely eyes, attaching themselves to his face, showed that in an instant she was affected by this unwonted adjuration. He spoke now as if he were taking her seriously. 'All those things are as nothing, and must never weigh a feather beside our service.'

The Princess began to draw on her gloves. 'You're a most extraordinary man.'

'That's what Rosy tells me.'

'Why don't you do it yourself?'

'Do Hyacinth's job? Because it's better to do my own.'

'And, pray, what is your own?'

'I don't know,' said Paul Muniment, with perfect serenity and good-nature. 'I expect to be instructed.'

'Have you taken an oath, like Hyacinth?'

'Ah, madam, the oaths *I* take I don't tell,' said the young man, gravely.

'Oh, you . . . !' the Princess murmured, with an

ambiguous cadence. She appeared to dismiss the question, but to suggest at the same time that he was very
abnormal. This imputation was further conveyed by the
next words she uttered : ' And can you see a dear friend
whirled away like that ? '

At this, for the first time, Paul Muniment exhibited a
certain irritation. ' You had better leave my dear friend
to me.'

The Princess, with her eyes still fixed upon him, gave a
long, soft sigh. ' Well, then, shall we go ? '

Muniment took up his hat again, but he made no movement toward the door. ' If you did me the honour to seek
my acquaintance, to ask me to come and see you, only in
order to say what you have just said about Hyacinth, perhaps we needn't carry out the form of going to the place
you proposed. Wasn't this only your pretext ? '

' I believe you *are* afraid ! ' the Princess exclaimed ; but
in spite of her exclamation the pair presently went out of
the house. They quitted the door together, after having
stood on the step for a moment, looking up and down,
apparently for a cab. So far as the darkness, which was
now complete, permitted the prospect to be scanned, there
was no such vehicle within hail. They turned to the left,
and after a walk of several minutes, during which they
were engaged in small, dull by-streets, emerged upon a
more populous way, where there were lighted shops and
omnibuses and the evident chance of a hansom. Here
they paused again, and very soon an empty hansom passed,
and, at a sign, pulled up near them. Meanwhile, it should
be recorded, they had been followed, at an interval, by a
cautious figure, a person who, in Madeira Crescent, when
they came out of the house, was stationed on the other side
of the street, at a considerable distance. When they
appeared he retreated a little, still however keeping them
in sight. When they moved away he moved in the same
direction, watching them but maintaining his distance.
He drew nearer, seemingly because he could not control
his eagerness, as they turned into Westbourne Grove, and
during the minute they stood there he was exposed to
recognition by the Princess if she had happened to turn

her head.   In the event of her having felt such an impulse
she would have discovered, in the lamplight, that her noble
husband was hovering in her rear.   But the Princess was
otherwise occupied ; she failed to see that at one moment
he came so close as to suggest that he had an intention of
addressing himself to the couple.   The reader scarcely
needs to be informed that his real intention was to satisfy
himself as to the kind of person his wife was walking with.
The time allowed him for this research was brief, especially
as he had perceived, more rapidly than he sometimes perceived things, that they were looking for a vehicle and that
with its assistance they would pass out of his range—a reflection which caused him to give half his attention to the
business of hailing any second cab which should come that
way.   There are parts of London in which you may never
see a cab at all, but there are none in which you may see
only one ; in accordance with which fortunate truth Prince
Casamassima was able to wave his stick to good purpose as
soon as the two objects of his pursuit had rattled away.
Behind them now, in the gloom, he had no fear of being
seen.   In little more than an instant he had jumped into
another hansom, the driver of which accompanied the usual
exclamation of ' All right, sir ! ' with a small, amused grunt,
which the Prince thought eminently British, after he had
hissed at him, over the hood, expressively, and in a manner
by no means indicative of that nationality, the injunction,
' Follow, follow, follow ! '

AN hour after the Princess had left the house with Paul Muniment, Madame Grandoni came down to supper, a meal of which she partook, in gloomy solitude, in the little back parlour. She had pushed away her plate, and sat motionless, staring at the crumpled cloth, with her hands folded on the edge of the table, when she became aware that a gentleman had been ushered into the drawing-room and was standing before the fire in an attitude of discreet expectancy. At the same moment the maid-servant approached the old lady, remarking with bated breath, 'The Prince, the Prince, mum! It's you he 'ave asked for, mum!' Upon this, Madame Grandoni called out to the visitor from her place, addressed him as her poor illustrious friend and bade him come and give her his arm. He obeyed with solemn alacrity, and conducted her into the front room, near the fire. He helped her to arrange herself in her arm-chair and to gather her shawl about her; then he seated himself near her and remained with his dismal eyes bent upon her. After a moment she said, 'Tell me something about Rome. The grass in Villa Borghese must already be thick with flowers.'

'I would have brought you some, if I had thought,' he answered. Then he turned his gaze about the room. 'Yes, you may well ask, in such a black little hole as this. My wife should not live here,' he added.

'Ah, my dear friend, for all that she's your wife!' the old woman exclaimed.

The Prince sprang up in sudden, passionate agitation, and then she saw that the rigid quietness with which he had come into the room and greeted her was only an effort of his good manners. He was really trembling with excitement. 'It is true—it is true! She *has* lovers—she *has* lovers!' he broke out. 'I have seen it with my eyes, and I have come here to know!'

'I don't know what you have seen, but your coming here to know will not have helped you much. Besides, if you have seen, you know for yourself. At any rate, I have ceased to be able to tell you.'

'You are afraid—you are afraid!' cried the visitor, with a wild accusatory gesture.

Madame Grandoni looked up at him with slow speculation. 'Sit down and be tranquil, very tranquil. I have ceased to pay attention—I take no heed.'

'Well, I do, then,' said the Prince, subsiding a little. 'Don't you know she has gone out to a house, in a horrible quarter, with a man?'

'I think it highly probable, dear Prince.'

'And who is he? That's what I want to discover.'

'How can I tell you? I haven't seen him.'

He looked at her a moment, with his distended eyes. 'Dear lady, is that kind to me, when I have counted on you?'

'Oh, I am not kind any more; it's not a question of that. I am angry—as angry, almost, as you.'

'Then why don't you watch her, eh?'

'It's not with her I am angry. It's with myself,' said Madame Grandoni, meditatively.

'For becoming so indifferent, do you mean?'

'On the contrary, for staying in the house.'

'Thank God, you are still here, or I couldn't have come. But what a lodging for the Princess!' the visitor exclaimed. 'She might at least live in a manner befitting.'

'Eh, the last time you were in London you thought it was too costly!' she cried.

He hesitated a moment. 'Whatever she does is wrong. Is it because it's so bad that you must go?' he went on.

'It is foolish—foolish—foolish,' said Madame Grandoni, slowly, impressively.

'Foolish, *chè, chè!* He was in the house nearly an hour, this one.'

'In the house? In what house?'

'Here, where you sit. I saw him go in, and when he came out it was after a long time, with her.'

'And where were you, meanwhile?'

Again Prince Casamassima hesitated. 'I was on the other side of the street. When they came out I followed them. It was more than an hour ago.'

'Was it for that you came to London?'

'Ah, what I came for! To put myself in hell!'

'You had better go back to Rome,' said Madame Grandoni.

'Of course I will go back, but if you will tell me who this one is! How can you be ignorant, dear friend, when he comes freely in and out of the house where I have to watch, at the door, for a moment that I can snatch? He was not the same as the other.'

'As the other?'

'Doubtless there are fifty! I mean the little one whom I met in the other house, that Sunday afternoon.'

'I sit in my room almost always now,' said the old woman. 'I only come down to eat.'

'Dear lady, it would be better if you would sit here,' the Prince remarked.

'Better for whom?'

'I mean that if you did not withdraw yourself you could at least answer my questions.'

'Ah, but I have not the slightest desire to answer them,' Madame Grandoni replied. 'You must remember that I am not here as your spy.'

'No,' said the Prince, in a tone of extreme and simple melancholy. 'If you had given me more information I should not have been obliged to come here myself. I arrived in London only this morning, and this evening I spent two hours walking up and down opposite the house, like a groom waiting for his master to come back from a ride. I wanted a personal impression. It was so that I saw him come in. He is not a gentleman—not even like some of the strange ones here.'

'I think he is Scotch,' remarked Madame Grandoni.

'Ah, then, you *have* seen him?'

'No, but I have heard him. He speaks very loud—the floors of this house are not built as we build in Italy—and his voice is the same that I have heard in the people of that country. Besides, she has told me—some things. He is a chemist's assistant.'

'A chemist's assistant? *Santo Dio!* And the other one, a year ago—more than a year ago—was a bookbinder.'

'Oh, the bookbinder!' murmured Madame Grandoni.

'And does she associate with no people of good? Has she no other society?'

'For me to tell you more, Prince, you must wait till I am free,' said the old lady.

'How do you mean, free?'

'I must choose. I must either go away—and then I can tell you what I have seen—or if I stay here I must hold my tongue.'

'But if you go away you will have seen nothing,' the Prince objected.

'Ah, plenty as it is—more than I ever expected to!'

The Prince clasped his hands together in tremulous suppliance; but at the same time he smiled, as if to conciliate, to corrupt. 'Dearest friend, you torment my curiosity. If you will tell me this, I will never ask you anything more. Where did they go? For the love of God, what is that house?'

'I know nothing of their houses,' she returned, with an impatient shrug.

'Then there are others—there are many?' She made no answer, but sat brooding, with her chin in her protrusive kerchief. Her visitor presently continued, in a soft, earnest tone, with his beautiful Italian distinctness, as if his lips cut and carved the sound, while his fine fingers quivered into quick, emphasising gestures, 'The street is small and black, but it is like all the streets. It has no importance; it is at the end of an endless imbroglio. They drove for twenty minutes; then they stopped their cab and got out. They went together on foot some minutes more. There were many turns; they seemed to know them well. For me it was very difficult—of course I also got out; I had to stay so far behind—close against the houses. Chiffinch

Street, N.E.—that was the name,' the Prince continued, pronouncing the word with difficulty; 'and the house is number 3 2—I looked at that after they went in. It's a very bad house—worse than this; but it has no sign of a chemist, and there are no shops in the street. They rang the bell—only once, though they waited a long time; it seemed to me, at least, that they did not touch it again. It was several minutes before the door was opened ; and that was a bad time for me, because as they stood there they looked up and down. Fortunately you know the air of this place ! I saw no light in the house—not even after they went in. Who let them enter I couldn't tell. I waited nearly half an hour, to see how long they would stay and what they would do on coming out; then, at last, my impatience brought me here, for to know she was absent made me hope I might see you. While I was there two persons went in—two men, together, smoking, who looked like *artisti* (I didn't see them near), but no one came out. I could see they took their cigars—and you can fancy what tobacco !—into the presence of the Princess. Formerly,' pursued Madame Grandoni's visitor, with a touching attempt at a jocular treatment of this point, ' she never tolerated smoking—never mine, at least. The street is very quiet—very few people pass. Now what is the house ? Is it where that man lives ? ' he asked, almost in a whisper.

He had been encouraged by her consenting, in spite of her first protests, to listen to him—he could see she *was* listening ; and he was still more encouraged when, after a moment, she answered his question by a question of her own. ' Did you cross the river to go there ? I know that he lives over the water.'

' Ah, no, it was not in that part. I tried to ask the cabman who brought me back to explain to me what it is called ; but I couldn't make him understand. They have heavy minds,' the Prince declared. Then he pursued, drawing a little closer to his hostess, ' But what were they doing there ? Why did she go with him ? '

' They are plotting. There ! ' said Madame Grandoni.

' You mean a secret society, a band of revolutionists and

murderers? *Capisco bene*—that is not new to me. But perhaps they only pretend it's for that,' added the Prince.

'Only pretend? Why should they pretend? That is not Christina's way.'

'There are other possibilities,' the Prince observed.

'Oh, of course, when your wife goes away with strange men, in the dark, to far-away houses, you can think any-thing you like, and I have nothing to say to your thoughts. I have my own, but they are my own affair, and I shall not undertake to defend Christina, for she is indefensible. When she does the things she does, she provokes, she invites, the worst construction; there let it rest, save for this one remark, which I will content myself with making: if she were a licentious woman she would not behave as she does now, she would not expose herself to irresistible interpretations; the appearance of everything would be good and proper. I simply tell you what I believe. If I believed that what she is doing concerned you alone, I should say nothing about it—at least sitting here. But it concerns others, it concerns every one, so I will open my mouth at last. She has gone to that house to break up society.'

'To break it up, yes, as she has wanted before?'

'Oh, more than before! She is very much entangled. She has relations with people who are watched by the police. She has not told me, but I have perceived it by simply living with her.'

Prince Casamassima stared. 'And is *she* watched by the police?'

'I can't tell you; it is very possible—except that the police here is not like that of other countries.'

'It is more stupid,' said the Prince. He gazed at Madame Grandoni with a flush of shame on his face. 'Will she bring us to *that* scandal? It would be the worst of all.'

'There is one chance—the chance that she will get tired of it,' the old lady remarked. 'Only the scandal may come before that.'

'Dear friend, she is the devil,' said the Prince, solemnly.

'No, she is not the devil, because she wishes to do good.'

'What good did she ever wish to do to me?' the Italian demanded, with glowing eyes.

Madame Grandoni shook her head very sadly. 'You can do no good, of any kind, to each other. Each on your own side, you must be quiet.

'How can I be quiet when I hear of such infamies?' Prince Casamassima got up, in his violence, and, in a tone which caused his companion to burst into a short, incongruous laugh as soon as she heard the words, exclaimed, 'She shall *not* break up society!'

'No, she will bore herself before the trick is played. Make up your mind to that.'

'That is what I expected to find—that the caprice was over. She has passed through so many follies.'

'Give her time—give her time,' replied Madame Grandoni.

'Time to drag my name into an assize-court? Those people are robbers, incendiaries, murderers!'

'You can say nothing to me about them that I haven't said to her.'

'And how does she defend herself?'

'Defend herself? Did you ever hear Christina do that?' Madame Grandoni asked. 'The only thing she says to me is, " Don't be afraid ; I promise you by all that's sacred that you shan't suffer." She speaks as if she had it all in her hands. That is very well. No doubt I'm a selfish old woman, but, after all, one has a heart for others.'

'And so have I, I think I may pretend,' said the Prince. 'You tell me to give her time, and it is certain that she will take it, whether I give it or not. But I can at least stop giving her money. By heaven, it's my duty, as an honest man.'

'She tells me that as it is you don't give her much.'

'Much, dear lady? It depends on what you call so. It's enough to make all these scoundrels flock around her.'

'They are not all scoundrels, any more than she is. That is the strange part of it,' said the old woman, with a weary sigh.

'But this fellow, the chemist—to-night—what do you call him?'

'She has spoken to me of him as a most estimable young man.'

'But she thinks it's estimable to blow us all up,' the Prince returned. 'Doesn't *he* take her money?'

'I don't know what he takes. But there are some things—heaven forbid one should forget them! The misery of London is something fearful.'

'*Che vuole?* There is misery everywhere,' returned the Prince. 'It is the will of God. *Ci vuol' pazienza!* And in this country does no one give alms?'

'Every one, I believe. But it appears that it is not enough.'

The Prince said nothing for a moment; this statement of Madame Grandoni's seemed to present difficulties. The solution, however, soon suggested itself; it was expressed in the inquiry, 'What will you have in a country which has not the true faith?'

'Ah, the true faith is a great thing; but there is suffering even in countries that have it.'

'*Evidentemente.* But it helps suffering to be borne, and, later, it makes it up; whereas here! . . .' said the old lady's visitor, with a melancholy smile. 'If I may speak of myself, it is to me, in my circumstances, a support.'

'That is good,' said Madame Grandoni.

He stood before her, resting his eyes for a moment on the floor. 'And the famous Cholto—Godfrey Gerald—does he come no more?'

'I haven't seen him for months, and know nothing about him.'

'He doesn't like the chemists and the bookbinders, eh?' asked the Prince.

'Ah, it was he who first brought them—to gratify your wife.'

'If they have turned him out, then, that is very well. Now, if only some one could turn *them* out!'

'*Aspetta, aspetta!*' said the old woman.

'That is very good advice, but to follow it isn't amusing.' Then the Prince added, 'You alluded, just now, as to something particular, to *quel giovane*, the young artisan whom I met in the other house. Is he also estimable, or has he paid the penalty of his crimes?'

'He has paid the penalty, but I don't know of what.   I
have nothing bad to tell you of him, except that I think
his star is on the wane.'

'*Poverino !*' the Prince exclaimed.

'That is exactly the manner in which I addressed him
the first time I saw him.   I didn't know how it would
happen, but I felt that it would happen somehow.   It has
happened through his changing his opinions.   He has now
the same idea as you—*ci vuol' pazienza.*'

'The Prince listened with the same expression of
wounded eagerness, the same parted lips and excited eyes,
to every added fact that dropped from Madame Grandoni's
lips.   'That, at least, is more honest.   Then *he* doesn't go
to Chiffinch Street ? '

'I don't know about Chiffinch Street; but it would be
my impression that he doesn't go anywhere that Christina
and the other one—the Scotchman—go together.   But
these are delicate matters,' the old woman pursued.

They seemed much to interest her interlocutor.   'Do
you mean that the Scotchman is—what shall I call it ?—his
successor ? '

For a moment Madame Grandoni made no reply.   'I
think that this case is different.   But I don't understand ;
it was the other, the little one, who helped her to know the
Scotchman.'

'And now they have quarrelled—about my wife ?   It is
all tremendously edifying ! ' the Prince exclaimed.

'I can't tell you, and shouldn't have attempted it, only
that Assunta talks to me.'

'I wish she would talk to me,' said the Prince, wistfully.

'Ah, my friend, if Christina were to find you getting at
her servants ! '

'How could it be worse for me than it is now ?   However, I don't know why I speak as if I cared, for I don't
care any more.   I have given her up.   It is finished.'

'I am glad to hear it,' said Madame Grandoni, gravely.

'You yourself made the distinction, perfectly.   So long
as she endeavoured only to injure *me*, and in my private
capacity, I could condone, I could wait, I could hope.
But since she has so recklessly thrown herself into the most

criminal undertakings, since she lifts her hand with a determined purpose, as you tell me, against the most sacred
institutions—it is too much; ah, yes, it is too much! She
may go her way; she is no wife of mine. Not another
penny of mine shall go into her pocket, and into that of
the wretches who prey upon her, who have corrupted her.'

'Dear Prince, I think you are right. And yet I am
sorry!' sighed the old woman, extending her hand for
assistance to rise from her chair. 'If she becomes really
poor, it will be much more difficult for me to leave her.
This is not poverty, and not even a good imitation of it, as
she would like it to be. But what will be said of me if
having remained with her through so much of her splendour,
I turn away from her the moment she begins to want?'

'Dear lady, do you ask that to make me relent?' the
Prince inquired, after an hesitation.

'Not in the least; for whatever is said and whatever
you do, there is nothing for me in decency, at present, but
to pack my trunk. Judge, by the way I have tattled.'

'If you will stay on, she shall have everything.' The
Prince spoke in a very low tone, with a manner that betrayed
the shame he felt at his attempt at bribery.

Madame Grandoni gave him an astonished glance and
moved away from him. 'What does that mean? I
thought you didn't care.'

I know not what explanation of his inconsequence her
companion would have given her if at that moment the
door of the room had not been pushed open to permit the
entrance of Hyacinth Robinson. He stopped short on
perceiving that Madame Grandoni had a visitor, but before
he had time to say anything the old lady addressed him
with a certain curtness. 'Ah, you don't fall well; the
Princess isn't at home.'

'That was mentioned to me, but I ventured to come in
to see you, as I have done before,' Hyacinth replied. Then
he added, as if he were retreating, 'I beg many pardons.
I was not told that you were not alone.'

'My visitor is going, but I am going too,' said Madame
Grandoni. 'I must take myself to my room—I am all
falling to pieces. Therefore kindly excuse me.'

Hyacinth had had time to recognise the Prince, and this nobleman paid him the same compliment, as was proved by his asking of Madame Grandoni, in a rapid aside, in Italian, 'Isn't it the bookbinder?'

'*Sicuro*,' said the old lady; while Hyacinth, murmuring a regret that he should find her indisposed, turned back to the door.

'One moment—one moment, I pray!' the Prince interposed, raising his hand persuasively and looking at him with an unexpected, exaggerated smile. 'Please introduce me to the gentleman,' he added, in English, to Madame Grandoni.

She manifested no surprise at the request—she had none left, apparently, for anything—but pronounced the name of Prince Casamassima, and then added, for Hyacinth's benefit, 'He knows who you are.'

'Will you permit me to keep you a very little minute?' the Prince continued, addressing the other visitor; after which he remarked to Madame Grandoni, 'I will speak with him a little. It is perhaps not necessary that we should incommode you, if you do not wish to stay.'

She had for a moment, as she tossed off a satirical little laugh, a return of her ancient drollery. 'Remember that if you talk long she may come back! Yes, yes, I will go upstairs. *Felicissima notte, signori!*' She took her way to the door, which Hyacinth, considerably bewildered, held open for her.

The reasons for which Prince Casamassima wished to converse with him were mysterious; nevertheless, he was about to close the door behind Madame Grandoni, as a sign that he was at the service of her companion. At this moment the latter extended again a courteous, remonstrant hand. 'After all, as my visit is finished and as yours comes to nothing, might we not go out?'

'Certainly, I will go with you,' said Hyacinth. He spoke with an instinctive stiffness, in spite of the Prince's queer affability, and in spite also of the fact that he felt sorry for the nobleman, to whose countenance Madame Grandoni's last injunction, uttered in English, had brought a deep and painful blush. It is needless to go into the

question of what Hyacinth, face to face with an aggrieved
husband, may have had on his conscience, but he assumed,
naturally enough, that the situation might be grave, though
indeed the Prince's manner was, for the moment, incongruously conciliatory.   Hyacinth invited his new acquaintance
to pass, and in a minute they were in the street together.

'Do you go here—do you go there?' the Prince inquired, as they stood a moment before the house.   'If you
will permit, I will take the same direction.'   On Hyacinth's
answering that it was indifferent to him the Prince said,
turning to the right, 'Well, then, here, but slowly, if that
pleases you, and only a little way.'   His English was far
from perfect, but his errors were mainly errors of pronunciation, and Hyacinth was struck with his effort to express
himself very distinctly, so that in intercourse with a little
representative of the British populace his foreignness should
not put him at a disadvantage.   Quick as he was to perceive and appreciate, Hyacinth noted how a certain quality
of breeding that was in his companion enabled him to compass that coolness, and he mentally applauded his success
in a difficult feat.   Difficult he judged it because it seemed
to him that the purpose for which the Prince wished to
speak to him was one which must require a deal of explanation, and it was a sign of training to explain adequately, in
a foreign tongue, especially if one were agitated, to a person
in a social position very different from one's own.   Hyacinth knew what the Prince's estimate of *his* importance
must be (he could have no illusions as to the character of
the people his wife received); but while he heard him carefully put one word after the other he was able to smile to
himself at his needless precautions.   Hyacinth reflected
that at a pinch he could have encountered him in his own
tongue; during his stay at Venice he had picked up an
Italian vocabulary.   'With Madame Grandoni I spoke of
you,' the Prince announced, dispassionately, as they walked
along.   'She told me a thing that interested me,' he added;
'that is why I walk with you.'   Hyacinth said nothing,
deeming that better by silence than in any other fashion he
held himself at the disposal of his interlocutor.   'She told
me you have changed—you have no more the same opinions.'

' The same opinions ? '

'About the arrangement of society. You desire no more the assassination of the rich.'

' I never desired any such thing ! ' said Hyacinth, indignantly.

' Oh, if you have changed, you can confess,' the Prince rejoined, in an encouraging tone. ' It is very good for some people to be rich. It would not be right for all to be poor.'

' It would be pleasant if all could be rich,' Hyacinth suggested.

' Yes, but not by stealing and shooting.'

' No, not by stealing and shooting. I never desired that.'

' Ah, no doubt she was mistaken. But to-day you think we must have patience,' the Prince went on, as if he hoped very much that Hyacinth would allow this valuable conviction to be attributed to him. ' That is also my view.'

' Oh, yes, we must have patience,' said Hyacinth, who was now smiling to himself in the dark.

They had by this time reached the end of the little Crescent, where the Prince paused under the street-lamp. He considered Hyacinth's countenance for a moment by its help, and then he pronounced, ' If I am not mistaken, you know very well the Princess.'

Hyacinth hesitated a moment. ' She has been very kind to me.'

' She is my wife—perhaps you know.'

Again Hyacinth hesitated, but after a moment he replied, ' She has told me that she is married.' As soon as he had spoken these words he thought them idiotic.

' You mean you would not know if she had not told you, I suppose. Evidently, there is nothing to show it. You can think if that is agreeable to me.'

' Oh, I can't think, I can't judge,' said Hyacinth.

' You are right—that is impossible.' The Prince stood before his companion, and in the pale gaslight the latter saw more of his face. It had an unnatural expression, a look of wasted anxiety ; the eyes seemed to glitter, and Hyacinth conceived the unfortunate nobleman to be

feverish and ill.   He continued in a moment : 'Of course
you think it strange—my conversation.   I want you to tell
me something.'

'I am afraid you are very unwell,' said Hyacinth.

'Yes, I am unwell ; but I shall be better if you will tell
me.   It is because you have come back to good ideas—
that is why I ask you.'

A sense that the situation of the Princess's husband was
really pitiful, that at any rate he suffered and was helpless,
that he was a gentleman and even a person who would
never have done any great harm—a perception of these
appealing truths came into Hyacinth's heart, and stirred
there a desire to be kind to him, to render him any service
that, in reason, he might ask.   It appeared to Hyacinth
that he must be pretty sick to ask any service at all, but
that was his own affair.   'If you would like me to see you
safely home, I will do that,' our young man remarked ; and
even while he spoke he was struck with the oddity of his
being already on such friendly terms with a person whom
he had hitherto supposed to be the worst enemy of the
rarest of women.   He found himself unable to consider the
Prince with resentment.

This personage acknowledged the civility of his offer
with a slight inclination of his high slimness.   'I am
very much obliged to you, but I will not go home.
I will not go home till I know this—to what house she
has gone.   Will you tell me that?'

'To what house?' Hyacinth repeated.

'She has gone with a person whom you know.   Madame
Grandoni told me that.   He is a Scotch chemist.'

'A Scotch chemist?' Hyacinth stared.

'I saw them myself— two hours, three hours, ago.
Listen, listen ; I will be very clear,' said the Prince, laying
his forefinger on the other hand with an explanatory
gesture.   'He came to that house—this one, where we
have been, I mean—and stayed there a long time.   I was
here in the street—I have passed my day in the street !
They came out together, and I watched them, I followed
them.'

Hyacinth had listened with wonder, and even with

suspense; the Prince's manner gave an air of such importance, such mystery, to what he had to relate. But at this
he broke out: 'This is not my business—I can't hear it!
I don't watch, *I* don't follow.'

The Prince stared a moment, in surprise; then he
rejoined, more quickly than he had spoken yet, 'But they
went to a house where they conspire, where they prepare
horrible acts. How can you like that?'

'How do you know it, sir?' Hyacinth inquired, gravely.

'It is Madame Grandoni who has told me.'

'Why, then, do you ask me?'

'Because I am not sure, I don't think she knows.
I want to know more, to be sure of what is done in that
house. Does she go there only for the revolution,' the
Prince demanded, 'or does she go there to be alone with
him?'

'With *him?*' The Prince's tone and his excited eyes
infused a kind of vividness into the suggestion.

'With the tall man—the chemist. They got into a
hansom together; the house is far away, in the lost
quarters.'

Hyacinth drew himself together. 'I know nothing
about the matter, and I don't care. If that is all you wish
to ask me, we had better separate.'

The Prince's face elongated; it seemed to grow paler.
'Then it is not true that you hate those abominations!'

Hyacinth hesitated a moment. 'How can you know
about my opinions? How can they interest you?'

The Prince looked at him with sick eyes; he raised
his arms a moment, a certain distance, and then let them
drop at his sides. 'I hoped you would help me.'

'When we are in trouble we can't help each other
much!' our young man exclaimed. But this austere
reflection was lost upon the Prince, who at the moment
Hyacinth spoke had already turned to look in the direction
from which they had proceeded, the other end of the
Crescent, his attention apparently being called thither by
the sound of a rapid hansom. The place was still and
empty, and the wheels of this vehicle reverberated. The
Prince peered at it through the darkness, and in an instant

he cried, under his breath, excitedly, 'They have come
back—they have come back ! Now you can see—yes, the
two !' The hansom had slackened pace and pulled up ;
the house before which it stopped was clearly the house
the two men had lately quitted. Hyacinth felt his arm
seized by the Prince, who, hastily, by a strong effort, drew
him forward several yards. At this moment a part of the
agitation that possessed the unhappy Italian seemed to
pass into his own blood ; a wave of anxiety rushed through
him—anxiety as to the relations of the two persons who
had descended from the cab ; he had, in short, for several
instants, a very exact revelation of the state of feeling of a
jealous husband. If he had been told, half an hour before,
that he was capable of surreptitious peepings, in the interest
of such jealousy, he would have resented the insult ; yet he
allowed himself to be checked by his companion just at
the nearest point at which they might safely consider the
proceedings of the couple who alighted. It was in fact
the Princess, accompanied by Paul Muniment. Hyacinth
noticed that the latter paid the cabman, who immediately
drove away, from his own pocket. He stood with the
Princess for some minutes at the door of the house—
minutes during which Hyacinth felt his heart beat insanely,
ignobly, he couldn't tell why.

'What does he say ? what does *she* say ?' hissed the
Prince ; and when he demanded, the next moment, 'Will
he go in again, or will he go away ?' our sensitive youth
felt that a voice was given to his own most eager thought.
The pair were talking together, with rapid sequences, and
as the door had not yet been opened it was clear that, to
prolong the conversation on the steps, the Princess delayed
to ring. 'It will make three, four, hours he has been with
her,' moaned the Prince.

'He may be with her fifty hours !' Hyacinth answered,
with a laugh, turning away, ashamed of himself.

'He has gone in—*sangue di Dio!*' cried the Prince,
catching his companion again by the arm and making him
look. All that Hyacinth saw was the door just closing ;
the Princess and Muniment were on the other side of it.
'Is *that* for the revolution ?' the trembling nobleman

panted. But Hyacinth made no answer; he only gazed at the closed door an instant, and then, disengaging himself, walked straight away, leaving the Italian, in the darkness, to direct a great helpless, futile shake of his stick at the indifferent house.

HYACINTH waited a long time, but when at last Millicent
came to the door the splendour of her appearance did
much to justify her delay. He heard an immense rustling
on the staircase, accompanied by a creaking of that
inexpensive structure, and then she brushed forward into
the narrow, dusky passage where he had been standing for
a quarter of an hour. She looked flushed; she exhaled a
strong, cheap perfume; and she instantly thrust her muff,
a tight, fat, beribboned receptacle, at him, to be held while
she adjusted her gloves to her large vulgar hands.
Hyacinth opened the door—it was so natural an assumption that they would not be able to talk properly in the
passage—and they came out to the low steps, lingering
there in the yellow Sunday sunshine. A loud ejaculation
on the beauty of the day broke from Millicent, though, as
we know, she was not addicted to facile admirations. The
winter was not over, but the spring had begun, and the
smoky London air allowed the baffled citizens, by way of a
change, to see through it. The town could refresh its
recollections of the sky, and the sky could ascertain the
geographical position of the town. The essential dimness
of the low perspectives had by no means disappeared, but
it had loosened its folds; it lingered as a blur of mist,
interwoven with pretty sun-tints and faint transparencies.
There was warmth and there was light, and a view of the
shutters of shops, and the church bells were ringing. Miss
Henning remarked that it was a 'shime' she couldn't have
a place to ask a gentleman to sit down; but what were
you to do when you had such a grind for your living, and
a room, to keep yourself tidy, no bigger than a pill-box?
She couldn't, herself, abide waiting outside; she knew

something about it when she took things home to ladies to choose (the time they spent was long enough to choose a husband !) and it always made her feel quite miserable. It was something cruel. If she could have what she liked she knew what she would have ; and she hinted at a mystic bower where a visitor could sit and enjoy himself—with the morning paper, or a nice view out of the window, or even a glass of sherry—so that, in an adjacent apartment, she could dress without getting in a fidget, which always made her red in the face.

'I don't know how I 'ave pitched on my things,' she remarked, presenting her magnificence to Hyacinth, who became aware that she had put a small plump book into her muff. He explained that, the day being so fine, he had come to propose to her to take a walk with him, in the manner of ancient times. They might spend an hour or two in the Park and stroll beside the Serpentine, or even paddle about on it, if she liked, and watch the lambkins, or feed the ducks, if she would put a crust in her pocket. The prospect of paddling Miss Henning entirely declined ; she had no idea of wetting her flounces, and she left those rough pleasures, especially of a Sunday, to a lower class of young woman. But she didn't mind if she did go for a turn, though he didn't deserve any such favour, after the way he hadn't been near her, if she had died in her garret. She was not one that was to be dropped and taken up at any man's convenience—she didn't keep one of those offices for servants out of place. Millicent expressed the belief that if the day had not been so lovely she would have sent Hyacinth about his business ; it was lucky for him that she was always forgiving (such was her sensitive, generous nature), when the sun was out. Only there was one thing—she couldn't abide making no difference for Sunday ; it was her personal habit to go to church, and she should have it on her conscience if she gave that up for a lark. Hyacinth had already been impressed, more than once, by the manner in which his blooming friend stickled for the religious observance : of all the queer disparities of her nature, her devotional turn struck him as perhaps the queerest. She held her head erect through

the longest and dullest sermon, and came out of the place
of worship with her fine face embellished by the publicity
of her virtue. She was exasperated by the general
secularity of Hyacinth's behaviour, especially taken in
conjunction with his general straightness, and was only
consoled a little by the fact that if he didn't drink, or fight,
or steal, at least he indulged in unlimited wickedness of
opinion—theories as bad as anything that people got ten
years for. Hyacinth had not yet revealed to her that his
theories had somehow lately come to be held with less
tension; an instinct of kindness had forbidden him to
deprive her of a grievance which ministered so much to
sociability. He had not reflected that she would have
been more aggrieved, and consequently more delightful, if
her condemnation of his godlessness had been deprived of
confirmatory indications.

On the present occasion she let him know that she
would go for a walk with him if he would first accompany
her to church; and it was in vain he represented to her
that this proceeding would deprive them of their morning,
inasmuch as after church she would have to dine, and in
the interval there would be no time left. She replied, with
a toss of her head, that she dined when she liked; besides
on Sundays she had cold fare—it was left out for her; an
argument to which Hyacinth had to assent, his ignorance
of her domestic economy being complete, thanks to the
maidenly mystery, the vagueness of reference and explanation, in which, in spite of great freedom of complaint,
perpetual announcements of intended change, impending
promotion and high bids for her services in other quarters,
she had always enshrouded her private affairs. Hyacinth
walked by her side to the place of worship she preferred—
her choice was made apparently from a large experience;
and as they went he remarked that it was a good job he
wasn't married to her. Lord, how she would bully him,
how she would 'squeeze' him, in such a case! The worst
of it would be that—such was his amiable, peace-loving
nature—he would obey like a showman's poodle. And
pray, whom was a man to obey, asked Millicent, if he was
not to obey his wife? She sat up in her pew with a

majesty that carried out this idea ; she seemed to answer, in her proper person, for creeds and communions and sacraments; she was more than devotional, she was almost pontifical. Hyacinth had never felt himself under such distinguished protection ; the Princess Casamassima came back to him, in comparison, as a Bohemian, a shabby adventuress. He had come to see her to-day not for the sake of her austerity (he had had too gloomy a week for that), but for that of her genial side ; yet now that she treated him to the severer spectacle it struck him for the moment as really grand sport—a kind of magnification of her rich vitality. She had her phases and caprices, like the Princess herself; and if they were not the same as those of the lady of Madeira Crescent they proved at least that she was as brave a woman. No one but a capital girl could give herself such airs ; she would have a consciousness of the large reserve of pliancy required for making up for them. The Princess wished to destroy society and Millicent wished to uphold it ; and as Hyacinth, by the side of his childhood's friend, listened to practised intonings, he was obliged to recognise the liberality of a fate which had sometimes appeared invidious. He had been provided with the best opportunities for choosing between the beauty of the original and the beauty of the conventional.

Fortunately, on this particular Sunday, there was no sermon (fortunately, I mean, from the point of view of Hyacinth's heretical impatience), so that after the congregation dispersed there was still plenty of time for a walk in the Park. Our friends traversed that barely-interrupted expanse of irrepressible herbage which stretches from the Birdcage Walk to Hyde Park Corner, and took their way to Kensington Gardens, beside the Serpentine. Once Millicent's religious exercises were over for the day (she as rigidly forbore to repeat them in the afternoon as she made a point of the first service), once she had lifted her voice in prayer and praise, she changed her *allure ;* moving to a different measure, uttering her sentiments in a high, free manner, and not minding that it should be perceived that she had on her very best gown and was out, if need be, for the day. She was mainly engaged, for some time, in overhauling Hyacinth for his long absence, demanding, as usual, some account of what he had been 'up to.' He listened to her philosophically, liking and enjoying her chaff, which seemed to him, oddly enough, wholesome and refreshing, and absolutely declining to satisfy her. He remarked, as he had had occasion to do before, that if he asked no explanations of her the least he had a right to expect in return was that she should let him off as easily; and even the indignation with which she received this plea did not make him feel that an *éclaircissement* between them could be a serious thing. There was nothing to explain and nothing to forgive; they were a pair of very fallible individuals, united much more by their weaknesses than by any consistency or fidelity that they might pretend to practise toward each other. It was an old acquaintance— the oldest thing, to-day, except Mr. Vetch's friendship, in Hyacinth's life; and strange as this may appear, it inspired our young man with a kind of indulgent piety. The probability that Millicent 'kept company' with other men had quite ceased to torment his imagination; it was no longer necessary to his happiness to be certain about it in order that he might dismiss her from his mind. He could be as happy without it as with it, and he felt a new modesty in regard to prying into her affairs. He was so little in a position to be stern with her that her assumption that he recognised a right on her own part to chide him seemed to him only a part of her perpetual clumsiness—a clumsiness that was not soothing but was nevertheless, in its rich spontaneity, one of the things he liked her for.

'If you have come to see me only to make jokes at my expense, you had better have stayed away altogether,' she said, with dignity, as they came out of the Green Park. 'In the first place it's rude, in the second place it's silly, and in the third place I see through you.'

'My dear Millicent, the motions you go through, the resentment you profess, are purely perfunctory,' her companion replied. 'But it doesn't matter; go on—say anything you like. I came to see you for recreation, for a little entertainment without effort of my own. I scarcely ventured to hope, however, that you would make me laugh

—I have been so dismal for a long time.   In fact, I am
dismal still.   I wish I had your disposition !   My mirth is
feverish.'

'The first thing I require of any friend is that he should
respect me,' Miss Henning announced.   'You lead a bad
life.   I know what to think about that,' she continued,
irrelevantly.

'And is it out of respect for you that you wish me to
lead a better one ?   To-day, then, is so much saved out
of my wickedness.   Let us get on the grass,' Hyacinth
continued ; 'it is innocent and pastoral to feel it under one's
feet.   It's jolly to be with you; you understand everything.'

'I don't understand everything you say, but I understand everything you hide,' the young woman returned, as
the great central expanse of Hyde Park, looking intensely
green and browsable, stretched away before them.

'Then I shall soon become a mystery to you, for I
mean from this time forth to cease to seek safety in con-
cealment.   You'll know nothing about me then, for it will
be all under your nose.'

'Well, there's nothing so pretty as nature,' Millicent
observed, surveying the smutty sheep who find pasturage
in the fields that extend from Knightsbridge to the Bayswater Road.   'What will you do when you're so bad you
can't go to the shop ?' she added, with a sudden transition.
And when he asked why he should ever be so bad as that,
she said she could see he *was* in a fever; she hadn't noticed
it at first, because he never had had any more complexion
than a cheese.   Was it something he had caught in some
of those back slums, where he went prying about with his
wicked ideas ?   It served him right for taking as little good
into such places as ever came out of them.   Would his
fine friends—a precious lot *they* were, that put it off on
him to do all the nasty part !—would they find the doctor,
and the port wine, and the money, and all the rest, when
he was laid up—perhaps for months—through their putting
such rot into his head and his putting it into others
that could carry it even less ?   Millicent stopped on the
grass, in the watery sunshine, and bent on her companion
an eye in which he perceived, freshly, an awakened curiosity,

a friendly, reckless ray, a pledge of substantial comradeship. Suddenly she exclaimed, quitting the tone of exaggerated derision which she had used a moment before, 'You little rascal, you've got something on your heart! Has your Princess given you the sack?'

'My poor girl, your talk is a queer mixture,' Hyacinth murmured. 'But it may well be. It is not queerer than my life.'

'Well, I'm glad you admit that!' the young woman cried, walking on with a flutter of her ribbons.

'Your ideas about my ideas!' Hyacinth continued. 'Yes, you should see me in the back slums. I'm a bigger Philistine than you, Miss Henning.'

'You've got more ridiculous names, if that's what you mean. I don't believe that half the time you know what you do mean, yourself. I don't believe you even know, with all your thinking, what you do think. That's your disease.'

'It's astonishing how you sometimes put your finger on the place,' Hyacinth rejoined. 'I mean to think no more —I mean to give it up. Avoid it yourself, my dear Millicent—avoid it as you would a baleful vice. It confers no true happiness. Let us live in the world of irreflective contemplation—let us live in the present hour.'

'I don't care how I live, nor where I live,' said Millicent, 'so long as I can do as I like. It's them that are over you—it's them that cut it fine! But you never were really satisfactory to me—not as one friend should be to another,' she pursued, reverting irresistibly to the concrete and turning still upon her companion that fine fairness which had no cause to shrink from a daylight exhibition. 'Do you remember that day I came back to Lomax Place ever so long ago, and called on poor dear Miss Pynsent (she couldn't abide me; she didn't like my form), and waited till you came in, and went out for a walk with you, and had tea at a coffee-shop? Well, I don't mind telling you that you weren't satisfactory to me then, and that I consider myself remarkably good-natured, ever since, to have kept you so little up to the mark. You always tried to carry it off as if you were telling one everything, and you never told one nothing at all.'

'What is it you want me to tell, my dear child?'
Hyacinth inquired, putting his hand into her arm. 'I'll
tell you anything you like.'

'I dare say you'll tell me a lot of trash! Certainly, I
tried kindness,' Miss Henning declared.

'Try it again; don't give it up,' said her companion,
strolling along with her in close association.

She stopped short, detaching herself, though not with
intention. 'Well, then, has she—*has* she chucked you
over?'

Hyacinth turned his eyes away; he looked at the green
expanse, misty and sunny, dotted with Sunday-keeping
figures which made it seem larger; at the wooded boundary
of the Park, beyond the grassy moat of Kensington Gardens;
at a shining reach of the Serpentine on the one side and
the far façades of Bayswater, brightened by the fine weather
and the privilege of their view, on the other. 'Well, you
know I rather think so,' he replied, in a moment.

'Ah, the nasty brute!' cried Millicent, as they resumed
their walk.

Upwards of an hour later they were sitting under the
great trees of Kensington Gardens, those scattered over the
slope which rises gently from the side of the water most
distant from the old red palace. They had taken possession of a couple of the chairs placed there for the convenience of that part of the public for which a penny is not,
as the French say, an affair, and Millicent, of whom such
speculations were highly characteristic, had devoted considerable conjecture to the question whether the functionary
charged with collecting the said penny would omit to come
and ask for his fee. Miss Henning liked to enjoy her
pleasures *gratis*, as well as to see others do so, and even
that of sitting in a penny chair could touch her more deeply
in proportion as she might feel that nothing would be paid
for it. The man came round, however, and after that her
pleasure could only take the form of sitting as long as
possible, to recover her money. This question had been
settled, and two or three others, of a much weightier kind,
had come up. At the moment we again participate in the
conversation of the pair Millicent was leaning forward,

earnest and attentive, with her hands clasped in her lap
and her multitudinous silver bracelets tumbled forward
upon her wrists. Her face, with its parted lips and eyes
clouded to gentleness, wore an expression which Hyacinth
had never seen there before and which caused him to say
to her, 'After all, dear Milly, you're a good old fellow!'

'Why did you never tell me before—years ago?' she
asked.

'It's always soon enough to commit an imbecility! I
don't know why I tell you to-day, sitting here in a charming
place, in balmy air, amid pleasing suggestions, without any
reason or practical end. The story is hideous, and I have
held my tongue for so long! It would have been an effort,
an impossible effort, at any time, to do otherwise. Somehow, to-day it hasn't been an effort; and indeed I have
spoken just *because* the air is sweet, and the place ornamental, and the day a holiday, and your company exhila-
rating. All this has had the effect that an object has if you
plunge it into a cup of water—the water overflows. Only
in my case it's not water, but a very foul liquid indeed.
Excuse the bad odour!'

There had been a flush of excitement in Millicent's face
while she listened to what had gone before; it lingered
there, and as a colour heightened by emotion is never
unbecoming to a handsome woman, it enriched her exceptional expression. 'I wouldn't have been so rough with
you,' she presently remarked.

'My dear lass, *this* isn't rough!' her companion exclaimed.

'You're all of a tremble.' She put out her hand and
laid it on his own, as if she had been a nurse feeling his
pulse.

'Very likely. I'm a nervous little beast,' said Hyacinth.

'Any one would be nervous, to think of anything so
awful. And when it's yourself!' And the girl's manner
represented the dreadfulness of such a contingency. 'You
require sympathy,' she added, in a tone that made Hyacinth
smile; the words sounded like a medical prescription.

'A tablespoonful every half-hour,' he rejoined, keeping
her hand, which she was about to draw away.

'You would have been nicer, too,' Millicent went on.

'How do you mean, I would have been nicer?'

'Well, I like you now,' said Miss Henning. And this time she drew away her hand, as if, after such a speech, to recover her dignity.

'It's a pity I have always been so terribly under the influence of women,' Hyacinth murmured, folding his arms.

He was surprised at the delicacy with which Millicent replied : 'You must remember that they have a great deal to make up to you.'

'Do you mean for my mother? Ah, *she* would have made it up, if they had let her! But the sex in general have been very nice to me,' he continued. 'It's wonderful the kindness they have shown me, and the amount of pleasure I have derived from their society.'

It would perhaps be inquiring too closely to consider whether this reference to sources of consolation other than those that sprang from her own bosom had an irritating effect on Millicent; at all events after a moment's silence she answered it by asking, 'Does *she* know—your trumpery Princess?'

'Yes, but she doesn't mind it.'

'That's most uncommonly kind of her!' cried the girl, with a scornful laugh.

'It annoys me very much to hear you apply invidious epithets to her. You know nothing about her.'

'How do you know what I know, please?' Millicent asked this question with the habit of her natural pugnacity, but the next instant she dropped her voice, as if she remembered that she was in the presence of a great misfortune. 'Hasn't she treated you most shamefully, and you such a regular dear?'

'Not in the least. It is I that, as you may say, have rounded on her. She made my acquaintance because I was interested in the same things as she was. Her interest has continued, has increased, but mine, for some reason or other, has declined. She has been consistent, and I have been fickle.'

'Your interest has declined, in the Princess?' Millicent

questioned, following imperfectly this somewhat complicated statement.

'Oh dear, no. I mean only in some views that I used to have.'

'Ay, when you thought everything should go to the lowest! That's a good job!' Miss Henning exclaimed, with an indulgent laugh, as if, after all, Hyacinth's views and the changes in his views were not what was most important. 'And your grand lady still holds for the costermongers?'

'She wants to take hold of the great question of material misery; she wants to do something to make that misery less. I don't care for her means, I don't like her processes. But when I think of what there is to be done, and of the courage and devotion of those that set themselves to do it, it seems to me sometimes that with my reserves and scruples I'm a very poor creature.'

'You *are* a poor creature—to sit there and put such accusations on yourself!' the girl flashed out. 'If you haven't a spirit for yourself, I promise you I've got one for you! If she hasn't chucked you over why in the name of common sense did you say just now that she has? And why is your dear old face as white as my stocking?'

Hyacinth looked at her awhile without answering, as if he took a placid pleasure in her violence. 'I don't know —I don't understand.'

She put out her hand and took possession of his own ; for a minute she held it, as if she wished to check herself, finding some influence in his touch that would help her. They sat in silence, looking at the ornamental water and the landscape-gardening beyond, which was reflected in it ; until Millicent turned her eyes again upon her companion and remarked, 'Well, that's the way I'd have served him too !'

It took him a moment to perceive that she was alluding to the vengeance wrought upon Lord Frederick. 'Don't speak of that; you'll never again hear a word about it on my lips. It's all darkness.'

'I always knew you were a gentleman,' the girl went on. A queer variety, *cara mia*,' her companion rejoined, not

very candidly, as we know the theories he himself had
cultivated on this point. 'Of course you had heard poor
Pinnie's incurable indiscretions. They used to exasperate
me when she was alive, but I forgive her now. It's time I
should, when I begin to talk myself. I think I'm breaking
up.'

'Oh, it wasn't Miss Pynsent; it was just yourself.'

'Pray, what did I ever say, in those days?'

'It wasn't what you said,' Millicent answered, with refinement. 'I guessed the whole business—except, of
course, what she got her time for, and you being taken to
that death-bed—that day I came back to the Place.
Couldn't you see I was turning it over? And did I ever
throw it up at you, whatever high words we might have
had? Therefore what I say now is no more than I thought
then; it only makes you nicer.'

She was crude, she was common, she even had the vice
of unskilful exaggeration, for he himself honestly could not
understand how the situation he had described could make
him nicer. But when the faculty of affection that was in
her rose, as it were, to the surface, it diffused a sense of
rest, almost of protection, deepening, at any rate, the luxury
of the balmy holiday, the interlude in the grind of the
week's work; so that, though neither of them had dined,
Hyacinth would have been delighted to sit with her there
the whole afternoon. It seemed a pause in something
bitter that was happening to him, making it stop awhile or
pushing it off to a distance. His thoughts hovered about
that with a pertinacity of which they themselves were weary;
but they regarded it now with a kind of wounded indifference. It would be too much, no doubt, to say that Millicent's society appeared a compensation, but it seemed at
least a resource. She too, evidently, was highly content;
she made no proposal to retrace their steps. She interro-
gated him about his father's family, and whether they were
going to let him go on like that always, without ever holding out so much as a little finger to him; and she declared,
in a manner that was meant to gratify him by the indignation it conveyed, though the awkwardness of the turn made
him smile, that if she were one of them she couldn't

' abear ' the thought of a relation of hers being in such a
poor way. Hyacinth already knew what Miss Henning
thought of his business at old Crookenden's and of the
feebleness of a young man of his parts contenting himself
with a career which was after all a mere getting of one's
living by one's 'ands. He had to do with books ; but so
had any shop-boy who should carry such articles to the
residence of purchasers ; and plainly Millicent had never
discovered wherein the art he practised differed from that of
a plumber, a glazier. He had not forgotten the shock he
once administered to her by letting her know that he wore
an apron ; she looked down on such conditions from the
summit of her own intellectual profession, for *she* wore
mantles and jackets and shawls, and the long trains of robes
exhibited in the window on dummies of wire and taken
down to be transferred to her own undulating person, and
had never a scrap to do with making them up, but just with
talking about them and showing them off, and persuading
people of their beauty and cheapness. It had been a source
of endless comfort to her, in her arduous evolution, that she
herself never worked with her 'ands. Hyacinth answered
her inquiries, as she had answered his own of old, by asking
her what those people owed to the son of a person who had
brought murder and mourning into their bright sublimities,
and whether she thought he was very highly recommended
to them. His question made her reflect for a moment ;
after which she returned, with the finest spirit, ' Well, if
your position was so miserable, ain't that all the more
reason they should give you a lift ? Oh, it's something
cruel ! ' she cried ; and she added that in his place she
would have found a way to bring herself under their notice.
She wouldn't have drudged out her life in Soho if she had
had gentlefolks' blood in her veins ! ' If they had noticed
you they would have liked you,' she was so good as to observe ; but she immediately remembered, also, that in that
case he would have been carried away quite over her head.
She was not prepared to say that she would have given him
up, little good as she had ever got of him. In that case he
would have been thick with real swells, and she emphasised
the ' real ' by way of a thrust at the fine lady of Madeira

Crescent—an artifice which was wasted, however, inasmuch
as Hyacinth was sure she had extracted from Sholto a
tolerably detailed history of the personage in question.
Millicent was tender and tenderly sportive, and he was
struck with the fact that his base birth really made little
impression upon her; she accounted it an accident much
less grave than he had been in the habit of doing.   She
was touched and moved; but what moved her was his story
of his mother's dreadful revenge, her long imprisonment
and his childish visit to the jail, with the later discovery of
his peculiar footing in the world.   These things produced a
generous agitation—something the same in kind as the impressions she had occasionally derived from the perusal of
the *Family Herald.*   What affected her most, and what she
came back to, was the whole element of Lord Frederick
and the mystery of Hyacinth's having got so little good out
of his affiliation to that nobleman.   She couldn't get over
his friends not having done something, though her imagination was still vague as to what they might have done.   It
was the queerest thing in the world, to Hyacinth, to find
her apparently assuming that if he had not been so in-
efficient he might have ' worked ' the whole dark episode
as a source of distinction, of glory.   *She* wouldn't have
been a nobleman's daughter for nothing!   Oh, the left
hand was as good as the right; her respectability, for the
moment, didn't care for that!   His long silence was what
most astonished her; it put her out of patience, and there
was a strange candour in her wonderment at his not having
bragged about his grand relations.   They had become vivid
and concrete to her now, in comparison with the timid
shadows that Pinnie had set into spasmodic circulation.
Millicent bumped about in the hushed past of her companion with the oddest mixture of sympathy and criticism,
and with good intentions which had the effect of profane
voices halloaing for echoes.

'Me only—me and her?   Certainly, I ought to be
obliged, even though it is late in the day.   The first time
you saw her I suppose you told her—that night you went
into her box at the theatre, eh?   She'd have worse to tell
you, I'm sure, if she could ever bring herself to speak the

truth.   And do you mean to say you never broke it to your
big friend in the chemical line?'

'No, we have never talked about it.'

'Men are rare creatures!' Millicent cried.   'You never
so much as mentioned it?'

'It wasn't necessary.   He knew it otherwise—he knew it
through his sister.'

'How do you know that, if he never spoke?'

'Oh, because he was jolly good to me,' said Hyacinth.

'Well, I don't suppose that ruined him,' Miss Henning
rejoined.   'And how did his sister know it?'

'Oh, I don't know; she guessed it.'

'Millicent stared.   'It was none of her business.'   Then
she added, 'He *was* jolly good to you?   Ain't he good to
you now?'   She asked this question in her loud, free voice,
which rang through the bright stillness of the place.

Hyacinth delayed for a minute to answer her, and when
at last he did so it was without looking at her.   'I don't
know; I can't make it out.'

'Well, I can, then!'   And Millicent jerked him round
toward her and inspected him with her big bright eyes.
'You silly baby, has *he* been serving you?'   She pressed
her question upon him; she asked if that was what disagreed with him.   His lips gave her no answer, but apparently, after an instant, she found one in his face.   'Has
he been making up to her ladyship—is that his game?' she
broke out.   'Do you mean to say she'd look at the likes of
him?'

'The likes of him?   He's as fine a man as stands!' said
Hyacinth.   'They have the same views, they are doing the
same work.'

'Oh, he hasn't changed *his* opinions, then—not like you?'

'No, he knows what he wants; he knows what he
thinks.'

'Very much the same work, I'll be bound!' cried
Millicent, in large derision.   'He knows what he wants,
and I dare say he'll get it.'

Hyacinth got up, turning away from her; but she also
rose, and passed her hand into his arm.   'It's their own
business; they can do as they please.'

'Oh, don't try to be a saint; you put me out of patience!' the girl responded, with characteristic energy. 'They're a precious pair, and it would do me good to hear you say so.'

'A man shouldn't turn against his friends,' Hyacinth went on, with desperate sententiousness.

'That's for them to remember; there's no danger of *your* forgetting it.' They had begun to walk, but she stopped him; she was suddenly smiling at him, and her face was radiant. She went on, with caressing inconsequence: 'All that you have told me—it *has* made you nicer.'

'I don't see that, but it has certainly made you so. My dear girl, you're a comfort,' Hyacinth added, as they strolled on again.

XLII

He had no intention of going in the evening to Madeira
Crescent, and that is why he asked his companion, before
they separated, if he might not see her again, after tea.
The evenings were bitter to him now, and he feared them
in advance. The darkness had become a haunted element;
it had visions for him that passed even before his closed
eyes—sharp doubts and fears and suspicions, suggestions of
evil, revelations of suffering. He wanted company, to light
up his gloom, and this had driven him back to Millicent, in
a manner not altogether consistent with the respect which it
was still his theory that he owed to his nobler part. He
felt no longer free to drop in at the Crescent, and tried to
persuade himself, in case his mistrust should be overdone,
that his reasons were reasons of magnanimity. If Paul
Muniment were seriously occupied with the Princess, if they
had work in hand for which their most earnest attention was
required (and Sunday was very likely to be the day they
would take: they had spent so much of the previous
Sunday together), it would be delicate on his part to stay
away, to leave his friend a clear field. There was something
inexpressibly representative to him in the way that friend
had abruptly decided to re-enter the house, after pausing
outside with its mistress, at the moment he himself stood
peering through the fog with the Prince. The movement
repeated itself innumerable times, to his moral perception, suggesting to him things that he couldn't bear to
learn. Hyacinth was afraid of being jealous, even after he
had become so, and to prove to himself that he was not he
had gone to see the Princess one evening in the middle of
the week. Hadn't he wanted Paul to know her, months
and months before, and now was he to entertain a vile feel-

ing at the first manifestation of an intimacy which rested, in
each party to it, upon aspirations that he respected? The
Princess had not been at home, and he had turned away
from the door without asking for Madame Grandoni; he
had not forgotten that on the occasion of his previous visit
she had excused herself from remaining in the drawing-
room. After the little maid in the Crescent had told him
the Princess was out he walked away with a quick curiosity
—a curiosity which, if he had listened to it, would have
led him to mount upon the first omnibus that travelled in the
direction of Camberwell. Was Paul Muniment, who was
such a rare one, in general, for stopping at home of an
evening—was he also out, and would Rosy, in this case, be
in the humour to mention (for of course she would know),
where he had gone? Hyacinth let the omnibus pass, for
he suddenly became aware, with a throb of horror, that he
was in danger of playing the spy. He had not been near
Muniment since, on purpose to leave his curiosity unsatis-
fied. He allowed himself however to notice that the
Princess had now not written him a word of consolation,
as she had been so kind as to do once or twice before when
he had knocked at her door without finding her. At
present he had missed her twice in succession, and yet she
had given no sign of regret—regret even on his own behalf.
This determined him to stay away awhile longer; it was
such a proof that she was absorbingly occupied. Hyacinth's
glimpse of the Princess in earnest conversation with Muniment as they returned from the excursion described by the
Prince, his memory of Paul's relenting figure crossing the
threshold once more, could leave him no doubt as to the
degree of that absorption.

Millicent hesitated when Hyacinth proposed to her that
they should finish the day together. She smiled, and her
splendid eyes rested on his with an air of indulgent interrogation; they seemed to ask whether it were worth her
while, in face of his probable incredulity, to mention the
real reason why she could not have the pleasure of acceding
to his delightful suggestion. Since he would be sure to
deride her explanation, would not some trumped-up excuse
do as well, since he could knock that about without hurting

her? I know not exactly in what sense Miss Henning decided ; but she confessed at last that there *was* an odious obstacle to their meeting again later—a promise she had made to go and see a young lady, the forewoman of her department, who was kept indoors with a bad face, and nothing in life to help her pass the time. She was under a pledge to spend the evening with her, and it was not her way to disappoint an expectation. Hyacinth made no comment on this speech ; he received it in silence, looking at the girl gloomily.

'I know what's passing in your mind !' Millicent suddenly broke out. 'Why don't you say it at once, and give me a chance to contradict it ? I oughtn't to care, but I do care !'

'Stop, stop—don't let us fight !' Hyacinth spoke in a tone of pleading weariness ; she had never heard just that accent before.

Millicent considered a moment. 'I've a mind to play her false. She's a real lady, highly connected, and the best friend I have—I don't count men,' the girl interpolated, smiling—'and there isn't one in the world I'd do such a thing for but you.'

'No, keep your promise ; don't play any one false,' said Hyacinth.

'Well, you *are* a gentleman !' Miss Henning murmured, with a sweetness that her voice occasionally took.

'Especially'—Hyacinth began ; but he suddenly stopped.

'Especially what? Something impudent, I'll engage ! Especially as you don't believe me ?'

'Oh, no ! Don't let's fight !' he repeated.

'Fight, my darling ? I'd fight *for* you !' Miss Henning declared.

Hyacinth offered himself, after tea, the choice between a visit to Lady Aurora and a pilgrimage to Lisson Grove. He was in a little doubt about the former experiment, having an idea that her ladyship's family might have returned to Belgrave Square. He reflected, however, that he could not recognise that as a reason for not going to see her ; his relations with her were not clandestine, and she had given him the kindest general invitation. If her august progeni-

tors were at home she was probably at dinner with them ;
he would take that risk.   He had taken it before, without
disastrous results.   He was determined not to spend the
evening alone, and he would keep the Poupins as a more
substantial alternative, in case her ladyship should not be
able to receive him.

As soon as the great portal in Belgrave Square was
drawn open before him, he perceived that the house was
occupied and animated—if the latter term might properly
be applied to a place which had hitherto given Hyacinth
the impression of a magnificent mausoleum.   It was pervaded by subdued light and tall domestics ; Hyacinth
found himself looking down a kind of colonnade of colossal
footmen, an array more imposing even than the retinue of
the Princess at Medley.   His inquiry died away on his
lips, and he stood there struggling with dumbness.   It was
manifest to him that some high festival was taking place,
at which his presence could only be deeply irrelevant ; and
when a large official, out of livery, bending over him for a
voice that faltered, suggested, not unencouragingly, that it
might be Lady Aurora he wished to see, he replied in a
low, melancholy accent, 'Yes, yes, but it can't be possible !'
The butler took no pains to controvert this proposition
verbally ; he merely turned round, with a majestic air of
leading the way, and as at the same moment two of the
footmen closed the wings of the door behind the visitor,
Hyacinth judged that it was his cue to follow him.   In
this manner, after traversing a passage where, in the perfect
silence of the servants, he heard the shorter click of his
plebeian shoes upon a marble floor, he found himself
ushered into a small apartment, lighted by a veiled lamp,
which, when he had been left there alone, without further
remark on the part of his conductor, he recognised as the
scene—only now more amply decorated—of one of his
former interviews.   Lady Aurora kept him waiting a few
moments, and then fluttered in with an anxious, incoherent
apology.   The same transformation had taken place in her
own appearance as in the aspect of her parental halls : she
had on a light-coloured, crumpled-looking, faintly-rustling
dress ; her head was adorned with a kind of languid plume,

terminating in little pink tips ; and in her hand she carried
a pair of white gloves. All her repressed eagerness was in
her face, and she smiled as if she wished to anticipate any
scruples or embarrassments on the part of her visitor ;
frankly recognising the brilliancy of her attire and the
startling implications it might convey. Hyacinth said to
her that, no. doubt, on perceiving her family had returned
to town, he ought to have backed out ; he knew that must
make a difference in her life. But he had been marched
in, in spite of himself, and now it was clear that he had
interrupted her at dinner. She answered that no one
who asked for her at any hour was ever turned away ; she
had managed to arrange that, and she was very happy in
her success. She didn't usually dine—there were so many
of them, and it took so long. Most of her friends couldn't
come at visiting-hours, and it wouldn't be right that she
shouldn't ever receive them. On that occasion she *had*
been dining, but it was all over ; she was only sitting there
because she was going to a party. Her parents were dining
out, and she was just in the drawing-room with some of her
sisters. When they were alone it wasn't so long, though it
was rather long afterwards, when they went up again. It
wasn't time yet : the carriage wouldn't come for nearly half
an hour. She hadn't been to an evening thing for months
and months, but—didn't he know ?—one sometimes had to
do it. Lady Aurora expressed the idea that one ought to
be fair all round and that one's duties were not all of the
same species ; some of them would come up from time to
time that were quite different from the others. Of course
it wasn't just, unless one did all, and that was why she was
in for something to-night. It was nothing of consequence ;
only the family meeting the family, as they might do of a
Sunday, at one of their houses. It was there that papa
and mamma were dining. Since they had given her that
room for any hour she wanted (it was really tremendously
convenient), she had determined to do a party now and
then, like a respectable young woman, because it pleased
them—though why it should, to see *her* at a place, was
more than she could imagine. She supposed it was because it would perhaps keep some people, a little, from

thinking she was mad and not safe to be at large—which
was of course a sort of thing that people didn't like to have
thought of their belongings.   Lady Aurora explained and
expatiated with a kind of nervous superabundance; she
talked more continuously than Hyacinth had ever heard
her do before, and the young man saw that she was not in
her natural equilibrium.   He thought it scarcely probable
that she was excited by the simple prospect of again dip-
ping into the great world she had forsworn, and he presently perceived that he himself had an agitating effect
upon her.   His senses were fine enough to make him feel
that he revived certain associations and quickened certain
wounds.   She suddenly stopped talking, and the two sat
there looking at each other, in a kind of occult community
of suffering.   Hyacinth made several mechanical remarks,
explaining, insufficiently, why he had come, and in the
course of a very few moments, quite independently of these
observations, it seemed to him that there was a deeper, a
measurelessly deep, confidence between them.   A tacit
confession passed and repassed, and each understood the
situation of the other.   They wouldn't speak of it—it was
very definite that they would never do that; for there was
something in their common consciousness that was inconsistent with the grossness of accusation.   Besides, the
grievance of each was an apprehension, an instinct of the
soul—not a sharp, definite wrong, supported by proof.   It
was in the air and in their restless pulses, and not in anything that they could exhibit or complain of.   Strange
enough it seemed to Hyacinth that the history of each
should be the counterpart of that of the other.   What had
each done but lose that which he or she had never had?
Things had gone ill with them; but even if they had gone
well, if the Princess had not combined with his friend in
that manner which made his heart sink and produced an
effect exactly corresponding upon that of Lady Aurora—
even in this case what would prosperity, what would success, have amounted to?   They would have been very
barren.   He was sure the singular creature before him
would never have had a chance to take the unprecedented
social step for the sake of which she was ready to go forth

from Belgrave Square for ever; Hyacinth had judged the smallness of Paul Muniment's appetite for that complication sufficiently to have begun really to pity her ladyship long ago. And now, even when he most felt the sweetness of her sympathy, he might wonder what she could have imagined for him in the event of his not having been supplanted—what security, what completer promotion, what honourable, satisfying sequel. They were unhappy because they were unhappy, and they were right not to rail about that.

'Oh, I like to see you—I like to talk with you,' said Lady Aurora, simply. They talked for a quarter of an hour, and he made her such a visit as any gentleman might have made to any lady. They exchanged remarks about the lateness of the spring, about the loan-exhibition at Burlington House—which Hyacinth had paid his shilling to see—about the question of opening the museums on Sunday, about the danger of too much coddling legislation on behalf of the working classes. He declared that it gave him great pleasure to see any sign of her amusing herself; it was unnatural never to do that, and he hoped that now she had taken a turn she would keep it up. At this she looked down, smiling, at her frugal finery, and then she replied, 'I dare say I shall begin to go to balls—who knows?'

'That's what our friends in Audley Court think, you know—that it's the worst mistake you can make, not to drink deep of the cup while you have it.'

'Oh, I'll do it, then—I'll do it for them!' Lady Aurora exclaimed. 'I dare say that, as regards all that, I haven't listened to them enough.' This was the only allusion that passed on the subject of the Muniments.

Hyacinth got up—he had stayed long enough, as she was going out; and as he held out his hand to her she seemed to him a heroine. She would try to cultivate the pleasures of her class if the brother and sister in Camberwell thought it right—try even to be a woman of fashion in order to console herself. Paul Muniment didn't care for her, but she was capable of considering that it might be her duty to regulate her life by the very advice that made an

abyss between them. Hyacinth didn't believe in the success of this attempt; there passed before his imagination a
picture of the poor lady coming home and pulling off her
feathers for ever, after an evening spent in watching the
agitation of a ball-room from the outer edge of the circle,
with a white, irresponsive face. 'Let us eat and drink, for
to-morrow we die,' he said, laughing.

'Oh, I don't mind dying.'

'I think I do,' Hyacinth declared, as he turned away.
There had been no mention whatever of the Princess.

It was early enough in the evening for him to risk a
visit to Lisson Grove; he calculated that the Poupins would
still be sitting up. When he reached their house he found
this calculation justified; the brilliancy of the light in the
window appeared to announce that Madame was holding a
salon. He ascended to this apartment without delay (it
was free to a visitor to open the house-door himself), and,
having knocked, obeyed the hostess's invitation to enter.
Poupin and his wife were seated, with a third person, at a
table in the middle of the room, round a staring kerosene
lamp adorned with a globe of clear glass, of which the
transparency was mitigated only by a circular pattern of
bunches of grapes. The third person was his friend
Schinkel, who had been a member of the little party that
waited upon Hoffendahl. No one said anything as Hyacinth came in; but in their silence the three others got
up, looking at him, as he thought, rather strangely.

BOOK SIXTH

'My child, you are always welcome,' said Eustache Poupin, taking Hyacinth's hand in both his own and holding it for some moments. An impression had come to our young man, immediately, that they were talking about him before he appeared and that they would rather have been left to talk at their ease. He even thought he saw in Poupin's face the kind of consciousness that comes from detection, or at least interruption, in a nefarious act. With Poupin, however, it was difficult to tell; he always looked so heated and exalted, so like a conspirator defying the approach of justice. Hyacinth contemplated the others : they were standing as if they had shuffled something on the table out of sight, as if they had been engaged in the manufacture of counterfeit coin. Poupin kept hold of his hand ; the Frenchman's ardent eyes, fixed, unwinking, always expressive of the greatness of the occasion, whatever the occasion was, had never seemed to him to protrude so far from his head. 'Ah, my dear friend, *nous causions justement de vous*,' Eustache remarked, as if this were a very extraordinary fact.

'Oh, *nous causions—nous causions !*' his wife exclaimed, as if to deprecate an indiscreet exaggeration. 'One may mention a friend, I suppose, in the way of conversation, without taking such a liberty.'

'A cat may look at a king, as your English proverb says,' added Schinkel, jocosely. He smiled so hard at his own pleasantry that his eyes closed up and vanished—an effect which Hyacinth, who had observed it before, thought particularly unbecoming to him, appearing as it did to administer the last perfection to his ugliness. He would have consulted his interests by cultivating immobility of feature.

'Oh, a king, a king!' murmured Poupin, shaking his head up and down. 'That's what it's not good to be, *au point où nous en sommes.*'

'I just came in to wish you good-night,' said Hyacinth. 'I'm afraid it's rather late for a call, though Schinkel is here.'

'It's always too late, my very dear, when you come,' the Frenchman rejoined. 'You know if you have a place at our fireside.'

'I esteem it too much to disturb it,' said Hyacinth, smiling and looking round at the three.

'We can easily sit down again ; we are a comfortable party. Put yourself beside me.' And the Frenchman drew a chair close to the one, at the table, that he had just quitted.

'He has had a long walk, he is tired—he will certainly accept a little glass,' Madame Poupin announced with decision, moving toward the tray containing the small gilded *liqueur* service.

'We will each accept one, *ma bonne;* it is a very good occasion for a drop of *fine*,' her husband interposed, while Hyacinth seated himself in the chair his host had designated. Schinkel resumed his place, which was opposite ; he looked across at Hyacinth without speaking, but his long face continued to flatten itself into a representation of mirth. He had on a green coat, which Hyacinth had seen before ; it was a garment of ceremony, such as our young man judged it would have been impossible to procure in London or in any modern time. It was eminently German and of high antiquity, and had a tall, stiff, clumsy collar, which came up to the wearer's ears and almost concealed his perpetual bandage. When Hyacinth had sat down Eustache Poupin did not take possession of his own chair, but stood beside him, resting his hand on his head. At that touch something came over Hyacinth, and his heart sprang into his throat. The idea that occurred to him, conveyed in Poupin's whole manner as well as in the reassuring intention of that caress and in his wife's uneasy, instant offer of refreshment, explained the embarrassment of the circle and reminded our young man of the engagement he had taken with himself to

exhibit an extraordinary quietness when a certain crisis in
his life should have arrived.   It seemed to him that this
crisis was in the air, very near—that he should touch it if
he made another movement; the pressure of the Frenchman's hand, which was meant as a solvent, only operated as
a warning.   As he looked across at Schinkel he felt dizzy
and a little sick; for a moment, to his senses, the room
whirled round.   His resolution to be quiet appeared only
too easy to keep; he couldn't break it even to the extent of
speaking.   He knew that his voice would tremble, and that
is why he made no answer to Schinkel's rather honeyed
words, uttered after an hesitation.   ' *Also*, my dear Robinson, have you passed your Sunday well—have you had an
'appy day?'   Why was every one so endearing?   His eyes
questioned the table, but encountered nothing but its well-
wiped surface, polished for so many years by the gustatory
elbows of the Frenchman and his wife, and the lady's dirty
pack of cards for 'patience' (she had apparently been
engaged in this exercise when Schinkel came in), which indeed gave a little the impression of gamblers surprised, who
might have shuffled away the stakes.   Madame Poupin,
who had dived into a cupboard, came back with a bottle of
green chartreuse, an apparition which led the German to exclaim, ' *Lieber Gott*, you Vrench, you Vrench, how well you
manage!   What would you have more?'
    The hostess distributed the liquor, but Hyacinth was
scarcely able to swallow it, though it was highly appreciated by his companions.   His indifference to this luxury
excited much discussion and conjecture, the others bandying theories and contradictions, and even ineffectual jokes,
about him, over his head, with a volubility which seemed to
him unnatural.   Poupin and Schinkel professed the belief
that there must be something very curious the matter with a
man who couldn't smack his lips over a drop of that tap; he
must either be in love or have some still more insidious
complaint.   It was true that Hyacinth was always in love—
that was no secret to his friends—and it had never been
observed to stop his thirst.   The Frenchwoman poured
scorn on this view of the case, declaring that the effect
of the tender passion was to make one enjoy one's victual

(when everything went straight, *bien entendu;* and how could an ear be deaf to the whisperings of such a dear little *bon-homme* as Hyacinth?) in proof of which she deposed that she had never eaten and drunk with such relish as at the time—oh, it was far away now—when she had a soft spot in her heart for her rascal of a husband. For Madame Poupin to allude to her husband as a rascal indicated a high degree of conviviality. Hyacinth sat staring at the empty table with the feeling that he was, somehow, a detached, irresponsible witness of the evolution of his fate. Finally he looked up and said to his friends, collectively, ' What on earth's the matter with you all?' And he followed this inquiry by an invitation that they should tell him what it was they had been saying about him, since they admitted that he had been the subject of their conversation. Madame Poupin answered for them that they had simply been saying how much they loved him, but that they wouldn't love him any more if he became suspicious and *grincheux.* She had been telling Mr Schinkel's fortune on the cards, and she would tell Hyacinth's if he liked. There was nothing much for Mr Schinkel, only that he would find something, some day, that he had lost, but would probably lose it again, and serve him right if he did! He objected that he had never had anything to lose, and never expected to have ; but that was a vain remark, inasmuch as the time was fast coming when every one would have something—though indeed it was to be hoped that he would keep it when he had got it. Eustache rebuked his wife for her levity, reminded her that their young friend cared nothing for old women's tricks, and said he was sure Hyacinth had come to talk over a very different matter—the question (he was so good as to take an interest in it, as he had done in everything that related to them), of the terms which M. Poupin might owe it to himself, to his dignity, to a just though not exaggerated senti-ment of his value, to make in accepting Mr Crookenden's offer of the foremanship of the establishment in Soho ; an offer not yet formally enunciated but visibly in the air and destined—it would seem, at least—to arrive within a day or two. The old foreman was going to set up for himself. The Frenchman intimated that before accepting any such

proposal he must have the most substantial guarantees.
'*Il me faudrait des conditions très-particulières.*'   It was
singular to Hyacinth to hear M. Poupin talk so comfortably
about these high contingencies, the chasm by which he
himself was divided from the future having suddenly
doubled its width. His host and hostess sat down on either
side of him, and Poupin gave a sketch, in somewhat sombre
tints, of the situation in Soho, enumerating certain elements
of decomposition which he perceived to be at work there
and which he would not undertake to deal with unless he
should be given a completely free hand. Did Schinkel
understand, and was that what Schinkel was grinning at?
Did Schinkel understand that poor Eustache was the
victim of an absurd hallucination and that there was not
the smallest chance of his being invited to assume a
lieutenancy? He had less capacity for tackling the British
workman to-day than when he began to rub shoulders with
him, and Mr. Crookenden had never in his life made a
mistake, at least in the use of his tools. Hyacinth's
responses were few and mechanical, and he presently
ceased to try to look as if he were entering into the
Frenchman's ideas.

'You have some news—you have some news about me,'
he remarked, abruptly, to Schinkel. 'You don't like it,
you don't like to have to give it to me, and you came
to ask our friends here whether they wouldn't help you out
with it. But I don't think they will assist you particularly,
poor dears! Why do you mind? You oughtn't to mind
more than I do. That isn't the way.'

'*Qu'est-ce qu'il dit—qu'est-ce qu'il dit, le pauvre chéri?*'
Madame Poupin demanded, eagerly; while Schinkel looked
very hard at her husband, as if to ask for direction.

'My dear child, *vous vous faites des idées!*' the latter exclaimed, laying his hand on him remonstrantly.

But Hyacinth pushed away his chair and got up. 'If
you have anything to tell me, it is cruel of you to let me see
it, as you have done, and yet not satisfy me.'

'Why should I have anything to tell you?' Schinkel
asked.

'I don't know that, but I believe you have. I perceive

things, I guess things, quickly. That's my nature at all times, and I do it much more now.'

'You do it indeed; it is very wonderful,' said Schinkel.

'Mr. Schinkel, will you do me the pleasure to go away —I don't care where—out of this house?' Madame Poupin broke out, in French.

'Yes, that will be the best thing, and I will go with you,' said Hyacinth.

'If you would retire, my child, I think it would be a service that you would render us,' Poupin returned, appealing to his young friend. 'Won't you do us the justice to believe that you may leave your interests in our hands?'

Hyacinth hesitated a moment; it was now perfectly clear to him that Schinkel had some sort of message for him, and his curiosity as to what it might be had become nearly intolerable. 'I am surprised at your weakness,' he observed, as sternly as he could manage it, to Poupin.

The Frenchman stared at him an instant, and then fell on his neck. 'You are sublime, my young friend—you are sublime!'

'Will you be so good as to tell me what you are going to do with that young man?' demanded Madame Poupin, glaring at Schinkel.

'It's none of your business, my poor lady,' Hyacinth replied, disengaging himself from her husband. 'Schinkel, I wish you would walk away with me.'

'*Calmons-nous, entendons-nous, expliquons-nous!* The situation is very simple,' Poupin went on.

'I will go with you, if it will give you pleasure,' said Schinkel, very obligingly, to Hyacinth.

'Then you will give me that letter first!' Madame Poupin, erecting herself, declared to the German.

'My wife, you are an imbecile!' Poupin groaned, lifting his hands and shoulders and turning away.

'I may be an imbecile, but I won't be a party—no, God help me, not to that!' protested the Frenchwoman, planted before Schinkel as if to prevent his moving.

'If you have a letter for me, you ought to give it to me,' said Hyacinth to Schinkel. 'You have no right to give it to any one else.'

'I will bring it to you in your house, my good friend,'
Schinkel replied, with a little wink that seemed to say that
Madame Poupin would have to be considered.

'Oh, in his house—I'll go to his house!' cried the lady.
'I regard you, I have always regarded you, as my child,'
she declared to Hyacinth, 'and if this isn't an occasion
for a mother!'

'It's you that are making it an occasion. I don't know
what you are talking about,' said Hyacinth. He had been
questioning Schinkel's eye, and he thought he saw there
a little twinkle of assurance that he might really depend
upon him. 'I have disturbed you, and I think I had
better go away.'

Poupin had turned round again; he seized the young
man's arm eagerly, as if to prevent his retiring before he
had given a certain satisfaction. 'How can you care,
when you know everything is changed?'

'What do you mean—everything is changed?'

'Your opinions, your sympathies, your whole attitude.
I don't approve of it—*je le constate*. You have withdrawn
your confidence from the people; you have said things in
this spot, where you stand now, that have given pain to my
wife and me.'

'If we didn't love you, we should say that you had
betrayed us!' cried Madame Poupin, quickly, taking her
husband's idea.

'Oh, I shall never betray you,' said Hyacinth,
smiling.

'You will never betray us — of course you think so.
But you have no right to act for the people when you have
ceased to believe in the people. *Il faut être conséquent,
nom de Dieu !*' Poupin went on.

'You will give up all thoughts of acting for me—*je ne
permets pas ça !*' exclaimed his wife.

'It is probably not of importance—only a little fraternal
greeting,' Schinkel suggested, soothingly.

'We repudiate you, we deny you, we denounce you!'
shouted Poupin, more and more excited.

'My poor friends, it is you who have broken down, not
I,' said Hyacinth. 'I am much obliged to you for your

solicitude, but the inconsequence is yours.   At all events, good-night.'

He turned away from them, and was leaving the room, when Madame Poupin threw herself upon him, as her husband had done a moment before, but in silence and with an extraordinary force of passion and distress.   Being stout and powerful she quickly got the better of him, and pressed him to her ample bosom in a long, dumb embrace.

'I don't know what you want me to do,' said Hyacinth, as soon as he could speak.   'It's for me to judge of my convictions.'

'We want you to do nothing, because we *know* you have changed,' Poupin replied.   'Doesn't it stick out of you, in every glance of your eye and every breath of your lips?   It's only for that, because that alters everything.'

'Does it alter my engagement?   There are some things in which one can't change.   I didn't promise to believe; I promised to obey.'

'We want you to be sincere—that is the great thing,' said Poupin, edifyingly.   'I will go to see them—I will make them understand.'

'Ah, you should have done that before!'   Madame Poupin groaned.

'I don't know whom you are talking about, but I will allow no one to meddle in my affairs.'   Hyacinth spoke with sudden vehemence; the scene was cruel to his nerves, which were not in a condition to bear it.

'When it is Hoffendahl, it is no good to meddle,' Schinkel remarked, smiling.

'And pray, who is Hoffendahl, and what authority has he got?' demanded Madame Poupin, who had caught his meaning.   'Who has put him over us all, and is there nothing to do but to lie down in the dust before him?   Let him attend to his little affairs himself, and not put them off on innocent children, no matter whether they are with us or against us.'

This protest went so far that, evidently, Poupin felt a little ashamed of his wife.   'He has no authority but what we give him; but you know that we respect him, that he is one of the pure, *ma bonne*.   Hyacinth can do exactly as

he likes; he knows that as well as we do. He knows
there is not a feather's weight of compulsion; he knows
that, for my part, I long since ceased to expect anything
from him.'

'Certainly, there is no compulsion,' said Schinkel.
'It's to take or to leave. Only *they* keep the books.'

Hyacinth stood there before the three, with his eyes on
the floor. 'Of course I can do as I like, and what I like
is what I *shall* do. Besides, what are we talking about,
with such sudden passion?' he asked, looking up. 'I
have no summons, I have no sign. When the call reaches
me, it will be time to discuss it. Let it come or not come :
it's not my affair.'

'Certainly, it is not your affair,' said Schinkel.

'I can't think why M. Paul has never done anything,
all this time, knowing that everything is different now !'
Madame Poupin exclaimed.

'Yes, my dear boy, I don't understand our friend,' her
husband remarked, watching Hyacinth with suspicious,
contentious eyes.

'It's none of his business, any more than ours; it's
none of any one's business !' Schinkel declared.

'Muniment walks straight; the best thing you can do is
to imitate him,' said Hyacinth, trying to pass Poupin, who
had placed himself before the door.

'Promise me only this—not to do anything till I have
seen you first,' the Frenchman begged, almost piteously.

'My poor old friend, you are very weak.' And Hyacinth opened the door, in spite of him, and passed out.

'Ah, well, if you *are* with us, that's all I want to know !'
the young man heard him say, behind him, at the top of
the stairs, in a different voice, a tone of sudden, exaggerated
fortitude.

HYACINTH hurried down and got out of the house, but he
had not the least intention of losing sight of Schinkel. The
odd behaviour of the Poupins was a surprise and annoyance, and he had wished to shake himself free from it. He
was candidly astonished at the alarm they were so good as
to feel for him, for he had never perceived that they had
gone round to the hope that the note he had signed (as it
were) to Hoffendahl would not be presented. What had
he said, what had he done, after all, to give them the right
to fasten on him the charge of apostasy? He had always
been a free critic of everything, and it was natural that, on
certain occasions, in the little parlour in Lisson Grove, he
should have spoken in accordance with that freedom; but
it was only with the Princess that he had permitted himself
really to rail at the democracy and given the full measure
of his scepticism. He would have thought it indelicate to
express contempt for the opinions of his old foreign friends,
to whom associations that made them venerable were
attached; and, moreover, for Hyacinth, a change of heart
was, in the nature of things, much more an occasion for a
hush of publicity and a kind of retrospective reserve; it
couldn't prompt one to aggression or jubilation. When
one had but lately discovered what could be said on the
opposite side one didn't want to boast of one's sharpness—
not even when one's new convictions cast shadows that
looked like the ghosts of the old.

Hyacinth lingered in the street, a certain distance from
the house, watching for Schinkel's exit and prepared to
remain there if necessary till the dawn of another day. He
had said to his friends, just before, that the manner in
which the communication they looked so askance at should

reach him was none of his business—it might reach him as it could.   This was true enough in theory, but in fact his desire was overwhelming to know what Madame Poupin had meant by her allusion to a letter, destined for him, in Schinkel's possession—an allusion confirmed by Schinkel's own virtual acknowledgment.   It was indeed this eagerness that had driven him out of the house, for he had reason to believe that the German would not fail him, and it galled his suspense to see the foolish Poupins try to interpose, to divert the missive from its course.   He waited and waited, in the faith that Schinkel was dealing with them in his slow, categorical Teutonic way, and only objurgated the cabinet-maker for having in the first place paltered with his sacred trust.   Why hadn't he come straight to him—whatever the mysterious document was—instead of talking it over with French featherheads ?   Passers were rare, at this hour, in Lisson Grove, and lights were mainly extinguished ; there was nothing to look at but the vista of the low black houses, the dim, interspaced street-lamps, the prowling cats who darted occasionally across the road, and the terrible, mysterious, far-off stars, which appeared to him more than ever to see everything and tell nothing.   A policeman creaked along on the opposite side of the way, looking across at him as he passed, and stood for some minutes on the corner, as if to keep an eye on him.   Hyacinth had leisure to reflect that the day was perhaps not far off when a policeman might have his eye on him for a very good reason—might walk up and down, pass and repass, as he mounted guard over him.

It seemed horribly long before Schinkel came out of the house, but it was probably only half an hour.   In the still-ness of the street he heard Poupin let his visitor out, and at the sound he stepped back into the recess of a doorway on the same side, so that, in looking out, the Frenchman should not see him waiting.   There was another delay, for the two stood talking together interminably and in a low tone on the doorstep.   At last, however, Poupin went in again, and then Schinkel came down the street towards Hyacinth, who had calculated that he would proceed in that direction, it being, as Hyacinth happened to know,

that of his own lodging.   After he had heard Poupin go in
he stopped and looked up and down ; it was evidently his
idea that Hyacinth would be waiting for him.   Our hero
stepped out of the shallow recess in which he had been
flattening himself, and came straight to him, and the two
men stood there face to face, in the dusky, empty, sordid
street.

'You didn't let them have the letter ? '

'Oh no, I retained it,' said Schinkel, with his eyes more
than ever like invisible points.

'Then hadn't you better give it to me ? '

'We will talk of that—we will talk.'   Schinkel made no
motion to satisfy his friend ; he had his hands in the
pockets of his trousers, and his appearance was characterised by an exasperating assumption that they had
the whole night before them.   He was intolerably
methodical.

'Why should we talk ?   Haven't you talked enough with
those people, all the evening ?   What have they to say
about it ?   What right have you to detain a letter that
belongs to me ? '

'*Erlauben Sie :* I will light my pipe,' the German
remarked.   And he proceeded to this business, method-
ically, while Hyacinth's pale, excited face showed in the
glow of the match that he ignited on the rusty railing beside
them.   'It is not yours unless I have given it to you,'
Schinkel went on, as they walked along.   'Be patient, and
I will tell you,' he added, passing his hand into his companion's arm.   'Your way, not so ?   We will go down
toward the Park.'   Hyacinth tried to be patient, and he
listened with interest when Schinkel said, 'She tried to take
it ; she attacked me with her hands.   But that was not
what I went for, to give it up.'

'Is she mad ?   I don't recognise them,' Hyacinth
murmured.

'No, but they lofe you.'

'Why, then, do they try to disgrace me ? '

'They think it is no disgrace, if you have changed.'

'That's very well for her ; but it's pitiful for him, and I
declare it surprises me.'

'Oh, he came round, and he helped me to resist. He pulled his wife off. It was the first shock,' said Schinkel.

'You oughtn't to have shocked them, my dear fellow,' Hyacinth replied.

'I was shocked myself—I couldn't help it.'

'Lord, how shaky you all are!'

'You take it well. I am very sorry. But it is a fine chance,' Schinkel went on, smoking away. His pipe, for the moment, seemed to absorb him, so that after a silence Hyacinth resumed—

'Be so good as to reflect that all this while I don't in the least understand what you are talking about.'

'Well, it was this morning, early,' said the German. 'You know in my country we don't lie in bed late, and what they do in my country I try to do everywhere. I think it is good enough. In winter I get up, of course, long before the sun, and in summer I get up almost at the same time. I should see the fine spectacle of the sunrise, if in London you could see. The first thing I do of a Sunday is to smoke a pipe at my window, which is at the front, you remember, and looks into a little dirty street. At that hour there is nothing to see there—you English are so slow to leave the bed. Not much, however, at any time; it is not important, my little street. But my first pipe is the one I enjoy most. I want nothing else when I have that pleasure. I look out at the new, fresh light—though in London it is not very fresh—and I think it is the beginning of another day. I wonder what such a day will bring; whether it will bring anything good to us poor devils. But I have seen a great many pass, and nothing has come. This morning, however, brought something—something, at least, to you. On the other side of the way I saw a young man, who stood just opposite to my house, looking up at my window. He looked at me straight, without any ceremony, and I smoked my pipe and looked at him. I wondered what he wanted, but he made no sign and spoke no word. He was a very nice young man; he had an umbrella, and he wore spectacles. We remained that way, face to face, perhaps for a quarter of an hour, and at last he took out his watch—he had a watch, too—and held it in his hand, just glancing at

it every few minutes, as if to let me know that he would
rather not give me the whole day. Then it came over me
that he wanted to speak to me! You would have guessed
that before, but we good Germans are slow. When we
understand, however, we act; so I nodded to him, to let
him know I would come down. I put on my coat and my
shoes, for I was only in my shirt and stockings (though of
course I had on my trousers), and · I went down into the
street. When he saw me come he walked slowly away, but
at the end of a little distance he waited for me. When I
came near him I saw that he was a very nice young man
indeed—very young, with a very pleasant, friendly face. He
was also very neat, and he had gloves, and his umbrella
was of silk. I liked him very much. He said I should
come round the corner, so we went round the corner
together. I thought there would be some one there waiting
for us ; but there was nothing—only the closed shops and
the early light and a little spring mist which told that the
day would be fine. I didn't know what he wanted ; perhaps it was some of our business—that's what I first thought
—and perhaps it was only a little game. So I was very
careful ; I didn't ask him to come into the house. Yet I
told him that he must excuse me for not understanding
more quickly that he wished to speak with me ; and when
I said this he said it was not of consequence—he would
have waited there, for the chance to see me all day. I
told him I was glad I had spared him that, at least, and we
had some very polite conversation. He *was* a very nice
young man. But what he wanted was simply to put a
letter in my hand ; as he said himself, he was only a kind
of private postman. He gave me the letter—it was not
addressed ; and when I had taken it I asked him how he
knew, and if he wouldn't be sorry if it should turn out that
I was not the man for whom the letter was meant. But I
didn't give him a start ; he told me he knew all it was
necessary for him to know—he knew exactly what to do
and how to do it. I think he is a valuable member. I
asked him if the letter required an answer, and he told me
he had nothing to do with that ; he was only to put it in
my hand. He recommended me to wait till I had gone

into the house again to read it. We had a little more talk
—always very polite ; and he mentioned that he had come
so early because he thought I might go out, if he delayed,
and because, also, he had a great deal to do and had to
take his time when he could. It is true that he looked as
if he had plenty to do—as if he was in some very good
occupation. I should tell you that he spoke to me always
in English, but he is not English ; he sounded his words
like some kind of foreigner. I suppose he is not German,
or he would have spoken to me in German. But there
are so many, of all countries ! I said if he had so much
to do I wouldn't keep him ; I would go to my room and
open my letter. He said it wasn't important; and then I
asked him if he wouldn't come into my room, also, and
rest. I told him it wasn't very handsome, my room—
because he looked like a young man who would have, for
himself, a very neat lodging. Then I found he meant it
wasn't important that we should talk any more, and he went
away without even offering to shake hands. I don't know
if he had other letters to give, but he went away, as I have
said, like a postman on his rounds, without giving me any
more information.'

It took Schinkel a long time to tell this story—
his calm and conscientious thoroughness made no
allowance for any painful acuteness of curiosity that
Hyacinth might feel. He went from step to step, and
treated his different points with friendly explicitness, as if
each would have exactly the same interest for his companion. The latter made no attempt to hurry him, and
indeed he listened, now, with a kind of intense patience ;
for he *was* interested, and, moreover, it was clear to him
that he was safe with Schinkel ; the German would satisfy
him in time—wouldn't worry him with attaching conditions
to their transaction, in spite of the mistake he had made in
going for guidance to Lisson Grove. Hyacinth learned in
due course that on returning to his apartment and opening
the little packet of which he had been put into possession,
Mr Schinkel had found himself confronted with two separate articles : one a sealed letter superscribed with our
young man's name, the other a sheet of paper containing in

three lines a request that within two days of receiving it he would hand the letter to the 'young Robinson.' The three lines in question were signed D. H., and the letter was addressed in the same hand. Schinkel professed that he already knew the writing; it was that of Diedrich Hoffendahl. 'Good, good,' he said, exerting a soothing pressure upon Hyacinth's arm. 'I will walk with you to your door, and I will give it to you there; unless you like better that I should keep it till to-morrow morning, so that you may have a quiet sleep—I mean in case it might contain anything that will be disagreeable to you. But it is probably nothing; it is probably only a word to say that you need think no more about your engagement.'

'Why should it be that?' Hyacinth asked.

'Probably he has heard that you repent.'

'That I repent?' Hyacinth stopped him short; they had just reached the top of Park Lane. 'To whom have I given a right to say that?'

'Ah well, if you haven't, so much the better. It may be, then, for some other reason.'

'Don't be an idiot, Schinkel,' Hyacinth returned, as they walked along. And in a moment he went on, 'What the devil did you go and tattle to the Poupins for?'

'Because I thought they would like to know. Besides, I felt my responsibility; I thought I should carry it better if they knew it. And then, I'm like them—I lofe you.'

Hyacinth made no answer to this profession; he asked the next instant, 'Why didn't your young man bring the letter directly to me?'

'Ah, I didn't ask him that! The reason was probably not complicated, but simple—that those who wrote it knew my address and didn't know yours. And wasn't I one of your guarantors?'

'Yes, but not the principal one. The principal one was Muniment. Why was the letter not sent to me through him?'

'My dear Robinson, you want to know too many things. Depend upon it, there are always good reasons. I should have liked it better if it had been Muniment. But if they didn't send to him'—Schinkel interrupted himself;

the remainder of his sentence was lost in a cloud of
smoke.

'Well, if they didn't send to him,'—Hyacinth persisted.

'You're a great friend of his—how can I tell you?'

'At this Hyacinth looked up at his companion askance,
and caught an odd glance, accompanied with a smile, which
the mild, circumspect German directed toward him. 'If
it's anything against him, my being his friend makes me
just the man to hear it. I can defend him.'

'Well, it's a possibility that they are not satisfied.'

'How do you mean it—not satisfied?'

'How shall I say it?—that they don't trust him.'

'Don't trust him? And yet they trust me!'

'Ah, my boy, depend upon it, there are reasons,'
Schinkel replied ; and in a moment he added, 'They know
everything—everything. Oh, they go straight!'

The pair pursued the rest of their course for the most
part in silence, Hyacinth being considerably struck with
something that dropped from his companion in answer to
a question he asked as to what Eustache Poupin had said
when Schinkel, that evening, first told him what he had come
to see him about. '*Il vaut du galme—il vaut du galme:*'
that was the German's version of the Frenchman's words ;
and Hyacinth repeated them over to himself several times,
almost with the same accent. They had a certain soothing
effect. In fact the good Schinkel was soothing altogether,
as our hero felt when they stopped at last at the door of
his lodging in Westminster and stood there face to face, while
Hyacinth waited—waited. The sharpness of his impatience
had passed away, and he watched without irritation the
loving manner in which the German shook the ashes out of
his big pipe and laid it to rest in its coffin. It was only
after he had gone through this business with his usual
attention to every detail of it that he said, '*Also*, now for the
letter,' and, putting his hand inside of his waistcoat, drew
forth the important document. It passed instantly into
Hyacinth's grasp, and our young man transferred it to
his own pocket without looking at it. He thought he saw
a shade of disappointment in Schinkel's ugly, kindly face,
at this indication that he should have no present knowledge

of its contents ; but he liked that better than his pretending to say again that it was nothing—that it was only a
release. Schinkel had now the good sense, or the good
taste, not to repeat that remark, and as the letter pressed
against his heart Hyacinth felt still more distinctly that it
was something—that it was a command. What Schinkel
did say, in a moment, was ' Now that you have got it, I am
very glad. It is more comfortable for me.'

' I should think so !' Hyacinth exclaimed. ' If you
hadn't done your job you would have paid for it.'

Schinkel hesitated a moment while he lingered ; then,
as Hyacinth turned away, putting in his door-key, he replied, ' And if you don't do yours, so will you.'

' Yes, as you say, *they* go straight ! Good-night.' And
our young man let himself in.

The passage and staircase were never lighted, and the
lodgers either groped their way bedward with the infallibility
of practice or scraped the wall with a casual match which,
in the milder gloom of day, was visible in a hundred rich
streaks. Hyacinth's room was on the second floor, behind,
and as he approached it he was startled by seeing a light
proceed from the crevice under the door, the imperfect
fitting of which was in this manner vividly illustrated. He
stopped and considered this mysterious brightness, and his
first impulse was to connect it with the incident just ushered
in by Schinkel ; for what could anything that touched him
now be but a part of the same business ? It was natural
that some punctual emissary should be awaiting him. Then
it occurred to him that when he went out to call on Lady
Aurora, after tea, he had simply left a tallow candle burning, and that it showed a cynical spirit on the part of his
landlady, who could be so close-fisted for herself, not to
have gone in and put it out. Lastly, it came over him that
he had had a visitor, in his absence, and that the visitor
had taken possession of his apartment till his return, seeking
sources of comfort, as was perfectly just. When he opened
the door he found that this last prevision was the right one,
though his visitor was not one of the figures that had risen
before him. Mr. Vetch sat there, beside the little table
at which Hyacinth did his writing, with his head resting on

his hand and his eyes bent on the floor.   He looked
up when Hyacinth appeared, and said, 'Oh, I didn't hear
you; you are very quiet.'

'I come in softly, when I'm late, for the sake of the
house—though I am bound to say I am the only lodger
who has that refinement.   Besides, you have been asleep,'
Hyacinth said.

'No, I have not been asleep,' returned the old man.   'I
don't sleep much nowadays.'

'Then you have been plunged in meditation.'

'Yes, I have been thinking.'   Then Mr. Vetch explained
that the woman of the house wouldn't let him come in, at
first, till he had given proper assurances that his intentions
were pure and that he was moreover the oldest friend Mr.
Robinson had in the world.   He had been there for an
hour; he thought he might find him, coming so late.

Hyacinth answered that he was very glad he had waited
and that he was delighted to see him, and expressed regret
that he hadn't known in advance of his visit, so that he
might have something to offer him.   He sat down on his
bed, vaguely expectant; he wondered what special purpose
had brought the fiddler so far at that unnatural hour.   But
he only spoke the truth in saying that he was glad to see
him.   Hyacinth had come up-stairs in a tremor of desire to
be alone with the revelation that he carried in his pocket,
yet the sight of Anastasius Vetch gave him a sudden relief
by postponing solitude.   The place where he had put his
letter seemed to throb against his side, yet he was thankful to his old friend for forcing him still to leave it so.   'I
have been looking at your books,' the fiddler said; 'you
have two or three exquisite specimens of your own.   Oh
yes, I recognise your work when I see it; there are always
certain little finer touches.   You have a manner, like a
master.   With such a talent, such a taste, your future leaves
nothing to be desired.   You will make a fortune and become
a great celebrity.'

Mr. Vetch sat forward, to sketch this vision; he rested
his hands on his knees and looked very hard at his young
friend, as if to challenge him to dispute his flattering views.
The effect of what Hyacinth saw in his face was to give him

immediately the idea that the fiddler knew something, though it was impossible to guess how he could know it. The Poupins, for instance, had had no time to communicate with him, even granting that they were capable of that baseness; an unwarrantable supposition, in spite of Hyacinth's having seen them, less than an hour before, fall so much below their own standard. With this suspicion there rushed into Hyacinth's mind an intense determination to dissemble before his visitor to the last : he might imagine what he liked, but he should not have a grain of satisfaction—or rather he should have that of being led to believe, if possible, that his suspicions were positively vain and idle. Hyacinth rested his eyes on the books that Mr. Vetch had taken down from the shelf, and admitted that they were very pretty work and that so long as one didn't become blind or maimed the ability to produce that sort of thing was a legitimate source of confidence. Then suddenly, as they continued simply to look at each other, the pressure of the old man's curiosity, the expression of his probing, beseeching eyes, which had become strange and tragic in these latter times and completely changed their character, grew so intolerable that to defend himself Hyacinth took the aggressive and asked him boldly whether it were simply to look at his work, of which he had half a dozen specimens in Lomax Place, that he had made a nocturnal pilgrimage. ' My dear old friend, you have something on your mind— some fantastic fear, some extremely erroneous *idée fixe*. Why has it taken you to-night, in particular ? Whatever it is, it has brought you here, at an unnatural hour, you don't know why. I ought of course to be thankful to anything that brings you here ; and so I am, in so far as that it makes me happy. But I can't like it if makes *you* miserable. You're like a nervous mother whose baby's in bed upstairs; she goes up every five minutes to see if he's all right—if he isn't uncovered or hasn't tumbled out of bed. Dear Mr. Vetch, don't, don't worry ; the blanket's up to my chin, and I haven't tumbled yet.'

Hyacinth heard himself say these things as if he were listening to another person ; the impudence of them, under the circumstances, seemed to him, somehow, so rare. But

he believed himself to be on the edge of an episode in
which impudence, evidently, must play a considerable part,
and he might as well try his hand at it without delay.   The
way the old man gazed at him might have indicated that
he too was able to take the measure of his perversity—
that he knew he was false as he sat there declaring that
there was nothing the matter, while a brand-new revolutionary commission burned in his pocket.   But in a moment
Mr. Vetch said, very mildly, as if he had really been reassured, 'It's wonderful how you read my thoughts.   I
don't trust you; I think there are beastly possibilities.   It's
not true, at any rate, that I come to look at you every five
minutes.   You don't know how often I have resisted my
fears—how I have forced myself to let you alone.'

'You had better let me come and live with you, as I
proposed after Pinnie's death.   Then you will have me
always under your eyes,' said Hyacinth, smiling.

The old man got up eagerly, and, as Hyacinth did the
same, laid his hands upon his shoulders, holding him close.
'Will you now, really, my boy?   Will you come to-night?'

'To-night, Mr. Vetch?'

'To-night has worried me more than any other, I don't
know why.   After my tea I had my pipe and a glass, but
I couldn't keep quiet; I was very, very bad.   I got to
thinking of Pinnie—she seemed to be in the room.   I felt
as if I could put out my hand and touch her.   If I believed
in ghosts I should believe I had seen her.   She wasn't
there for nothing; she was there to add her fears to mine
—to talk to me about you.   I tried to hush her up, but it
was no use—she drove me out of the house.   About ten
o'clock I took my hat and stick and came down here.
You may judge whether I thought it important, as I took
a cab.'

'Ah, why do you spend your money so foolishly?' asked
Hyacinth, in a tone of the most affectionate remonstrance.

'Will you come to-night?' said the old man, for all
rejoinder, holding him still.

'Surely, it would be simpler for you to stay here.   I see
perfectly that you are ill and nervous.   You can take the
bed, and I'll spend the night in the chair.'

The fiddler thought a moment. 'No, you'll hate me if I subject you to such discomfort as that; and that's just what I don't want.'

'It won't be a bit different in your room; there, as here, I shall have to sleep in a chair.'

'I'll get another room; we shall be close together,' the fiddler went on.

'Do you mean you'll get another room at this hour of the night, with your little house stuffed full and your people all in bed? My poor Anastasius, you are very bad; your reason totters on its throne,' said Hyacinth, humorously and indulgently.

'Very good, we'll get a room to-morrow. I'll move into another house, where there are two, side by side.' Hyacinth's tone was evidently soothing to him.

'*Comme vous y allez!*' the young man continued. 'Excuse me if I remind you that in case of my leaving this place I have to give a fortnight's notice.'

'Ah, you're backing out!' the old man exclaimed, dropping his hands.

'Pinnie wouldn't have said that,' Hyacinth returned. 'If you are acting, if you are speaking, at the prompting of her pure spirit, you had better act and speak exactly as she would have done. She would have believed me.'

'Believed you? Believed what? What is there to believe? If you'll make me a promise, I will believe that.'

'I'll make you any promise you like,' said Hyacinth.

'Oh, any promise I like—that isn't what I want! I want just one very particular little pledge; and that is really what I came here for to-night. It came over me that I've been an ass, all this time, never to have demanded it of you before. Give it to me now, and I will go home quietly and leave you in peace.' Hyacinth, assenting in advance, requested again that he would formulate his demand, and then the old man said, 'Well, promise me that you will never, under any circumstances whatever, do anything.'

'Do anything?'

'Anything that those people expect of you.'

'Those people?' Hyacinth repeated.

'Ah, don't torment me with pretending not to understand !' the old man begged. 'You know the people I mean. I can't call them by their names, because I don't know them. But you do, and they know you.'

Hyacinth had no desire to torment Mr. Vetch, but he was capable of reflecting that to enter into his thought too easily would be tantamount to betraying himself. 'I suppose I know the people you have in mind,' he said, in a moment; 'but I'm afraid I don't grasp the idea of the promise.'

'Don't they want to make use of you?'

'I see what you mean,' said Hyacinth. 'You think they want me to touch off some train for them. Well, if that's what troubles you, you may sleep sound. I shall never do any of their work.'

A radiant light came into the fiddler's face, and he stared, as if this assurance were too fair for nature. 'Do you take your oath to that? Never anything, anything, anything?'

'Never anything at all.'

'Will you swear it to me by the memory of that good woman of whom we have been speaking and whom we both loved?'

'My dear old Pinnie's memory? Willingly.'

The old man sank down in his chair and buried his face in his hands; the next moment his companion heard him sobbing. Ten minutes later he was content to take his departure, and Hyacinth went out with him to look for another cab. They found an ancient four-wheeler stationed languidly at a crossing of the ways, and before Mr. Vetch got into it he asked his young friend to kiss him. That young friend watched the vehicle get itself into motion and rattle away; he saw it turn a neighbouring corner. Then he approached the nearest gas-lamp and drew from his breast-pocket the letter that Schinkel had given him.

'AND Madame Grandoni, then?' asked Hyacinth, reluctant to turn away. He felt pretty sure that he should never knock at that door again, and the desire was strong in him to see once more, for the last time, the ancient, troubled *suivante* of the Princess, whom he had always liked. She had seemed to him ever to be in the slightly ridiculous position of a confidant of tragedy in whom the heroine should have ceased to confide.

'*E andata via, caro signorino,*' said Assunta, smiling at him as she stood there holding the door open.

'She has gone away? Bless me, when did she go?'

'It is now five days, dear young sir. She has returned to our country.'

'Is it possible?' exclaimed Hyacinth, disappointedly.

'*E possibilissimo!*' said Assunta. Then she added, 'There were many times when she almost went; but this time—*capisce*——' And without finishing her sentence the Princess's Roman tirewoman indulged in a subtle, suggestive, indefinable play of expression, to which her hands and shoulders contributed, as well as her lips and eyebrows.

Hyacinth looked at her long enough to catch any meaning that she might have wished to convey, but gave no sign of apprehending it. He only remarked, gravely, 'In short she is here no more.'

'And the worst is that she will probably never come back. She didn't go for a long time, but when she decided herself it was finished,' Assunta declared. '*Peccato!*' she added, with a sigh.

'I should have liked to see her again—I should have liked to bid her good-bye.' Hyacinth lingered there in strange, melancholy vagueness; since he had been told the

Princess was not at home he had no reason for remaining, save the possibility that she might return before he turned away. This possibility, however, was small, for it was only nine o'clock, the middle of the evening—too early an hour for her to reappear, if, as Assunta said, she had gone out after tea. He looked up and down the Crescent, gently swinging his stick, and became conscious in a moment that Assunta was regarding him with tender interest.

'You should have come back sooner ; then perhaps she wouldn't have gone, *povera vecchia*,' she rejoined in a moment. 'It is too many days since you have been here. She liked you—I know that.'

'She liked me, but she didn't like me to come,' said Hyacinth. 'Wasn't that why she went, because we came ? '

'Ah, that other one—with the long legs—yes. But you are better.'

'The Princess doesn't think so, and she is the right judge,' Hyacinth replied, smiling.

'Eh, who knows what she thinks ? It is not for me to say. But you had better come in and wait. I dare say she won't be long, and it would gratify her to find you.'

Hyacinth hesitated. 'I am not sure of that.' Then he asked, 'Did she go out alone ? '

'*Sola, sola*,' said Assunta, smiling. 'Oh, don't be afraid ; you were the first ! ' And she flung open the door of the little drawing-room, with an air of irresistible solicitation and sympathy.

He sat there nearly an hour, in the chair the Princess habitually used, under her shaded lamp, with a dozen objects around him which seemed as much a part of herself as if they had been folds of her dress or even tones of her voice. His thoughts were tremendously active, but his body was too tired for restlessness ; he had not been to work, and had been walking about all day, to fill the time ; so that he simply reclined there, with his head on one of the Princess's cushions, his feet on one of her little stools —one of the ugly ones, that belonged to the house—and his respiration coming quickly, like that of a man in a state of acute agitation. Hyacinth was agitated now, but it was not because he was waiting for the Princess ; a deeper

source of emotion had been opened to him, and he had
not on the present occasion more sharpness of impatience
than had already visited him at certain moments of the
past twenty hours. He had not closed his eyes the night
before, and the day had not made up for that torment. A
fever of reflection had descended upon him, and the range
of his imagination had been wide. It whirled him through
circles of immeasurable compass ; and this is the reason
that, thinking of many things while he sat in the Princess's
chair, he wondered why, after all, he had come to Madeira
Crescent, and what interest he could have in seeing the
lady of the house. He had a very complete sense that
everything was over between them ; that the link had
snapped which bound them so closely together for a while.
And this was not simply because for a long time now he
had received no sign nor communication from her, no invitation to come back, no inquiry as to why his visits had
stopped. It was not because he had seen her go in and
out with Paul Muniment, nor because it had suited Prince
Casamassima to point the moral of her doing so, nor even
because, quite independently of the Prince, he believed her
to be more deeply absorbed in her acquaintance with that
superior young man than she had ever been in her relations
with himself. The reason, so far as he became conscious
of it in his fitful meditations, could only be a strange,
detached curiosity—strange and detached because everything else of his past had been engulfed in the abyss that
opened before him as, after Mr. Vetch had left him, he
stood under the lamp in a paltry Westminster street. That
had swallowed up all familiar feelings, and yet out of the
ruin had sprung the impulse which brought him to where
he sat.

The solution of his difficulty—he flattered himself he
had arrived at it—involved a winding-up of his affairs ; and
though, even if no solution had been required, he would
have felt clearly that he had been dropped, yet as even in
that case it would have been sweet to him to bid her good-
bye, so, at present, the desire for some last vision of her
own hurrying fate could still appeal to him. If things had
not gone well for him he was still capable of wondering

whether they looked better for her. It is a singular fact, that there rose in his mind a sort of incongruous desire to pity her. All these were odd feelings enough, and by the time half an hour had elapsed they had throbbed themselves into weariness and into slumber. While he remembered that he was waiting now in a very different frame from that in which he waited for her in South Street the first time he went to see her, he closed his eyes and lost himself. His unconsciousness lasted, he afterwards perceived, nearly half an hour; it terminated in his becoming aware that the lady of the house was standing before him. Assunta was behind her, and as he opened his eyes she took from her mistress the bonnet and mantle of which the Princess divested herself. ' It's charming of you to have waited,' the latter said, smiling down at him with all her old kindness. ' You are very tired—don't get up; that's the best chair, and you must keep it.' She made him remain where he was; she placed herself near him on a smaller seat; she declared that she was not tired herself, that she didn't know what was the matter with her—nothing tired her now; she exclaimed on the time that had elapsed since he had last called, as if she were reminded of it simply by seeing him again; and she insisted that he should have some tea—he looked so much as if he needed it. She considered him with deeper attention, and wished to know what was the matter with him—what he had done to use himself up; adding that she must begin and look after him again, for while she had the care of him that kind of thing didn't happen. In response to this Hyacinth made a great confession: he admitted that he had stayed away from work and simply amused himself—amused himself by loafing about London all day. This didn't pay—he was beginning to discover it as he grew older; it was doubtless a sign of increasing years when one began to perceive that wanton pleasures were hollow and that to stick to one's tools was not only more profitable but more refreshing. However, he did stick to them, as a general thing; that was no doubt partly why, from the absence of the habit of it, a day off turned out to be rather a grind. When Hyacinth had not seen the Princess for some time he always,

on meeting her again, had a renewed, tremendous sense of
her beauty, and he had it to-night in an extraordinary
degree. Splendid as that beauty had ever been, it seemed
clothed at present in transcendant glory, and (if that which
was already supremely fine could be capable of greater refinement), to have worked itself free of all earthly grossness
and been purified and consecrated by her new life. Her
gentleness, when she was in the mood for it, was quite divine
(it had always the irresistible charm that it was the humility
of a high spirit), and on this occasion she gave herself up
to it. Whether it was because he had the consciousness of
resting his eyes upon her for the last time, or because she
wished to be particularly pleasant to him in order to make
up for having, amid other preoccupations, rather dropped
him of late (it was probable the effect was a product of both
causes), at all events the sight of her loveliness seemed
none the less a privilege than it had done the night he went
into her box, at the play, and her presence lifted the weight
from his soul. He suffered himself to be coddled and absently, even if radiantly, smiled at, and his state of mind
was such that it could produce no alteration of his pain to
see that on the Princess's part these were inexpensive gifts.
She had sent Assunta to bring them tea, and when the tray
arrived she gave him cup after cup, with every restorative
demonstration ; but he had not sat with her a quarter of
an hour before he perceived that she scarcely measured
a word he said to her or a word that she herself uttered.
If she had the best intention of being nice to him, by
way of compensation, this compensation was for a wrong
that was far from vividly present to her mind. Two
points became perfectly clear : one was that she was
thinking of something very different from her present,
her past, or her future relations with Hyacinth Robinson ; the other was that he was superseded indeed. This
was so completely the case that it did not even occur
to her, it was evident, that the sense of supersession
might be cruel to the young man. If she was charming
to him it was because she was good-natured and he had
been hanging off, and not because she had done him an
injury. Perhaps, after all, she hadn't, for he got the im-

pression that it might be no great loss of comfort not to
constitute part of her life to-day. It was manifest from her
eye, from her smile, from every movement and tone,
and indeed from all the irradiation of her beauty, that
that life to-day was tremendously wound up. If he had
come to Madeira Crescent because he was curious to see
how she was getting on, it was sufficiently intimated to
him that she was getting on well ; that is that she was
living more than ever on high hopes and bold plans and
far-reaching combinations. These things, from his own
point of view, ministered less to happiness, and to be
mixed up with them was perhaps not so much greater a sign
that one had not lived for nothing, than the grim arrangement which, in the interest of peace, he had just arrived
at with himself. She asked him why he had not been
to see her for so long, quite as if this failure were only
a vulgar form of social neglect ; and she scarcely seemed
to notice whether it were a good or a poor excuse when
he said he had stayed away because he knew her to be
extremely busy. But she did not deny the impeach-
ment ; she admitted that she had been busier than ever
in her life before. She looked at him as if he would
know what that meant, and he remarked that he was
very sorry for her.

'Because you think it's all a mistake? Yes, I know
that. Perhaps it is ; but if it is, it's a magnificent one. If
you were scared about me three or four months ago,
I don't know what you would think to-day—if you knew!
I have risked everything.'

'Fortunately I don't know,' said Hyacinth.

'No, indeed, how should you ? '

'And to tell the truth,' he went on, 'that is really
the reason I haven't been back here till to-night. I
haven't wanted to know—I have feared and hated to
know.'

'Then why did you come at last ? '

Hyacinth hesitated a moment. 'Out of a kind of
inconsistent curiosity.'

I suppose then you would like me to tell you where
I have been to-night, eh ? '

' No, my curiosity is satisfied. I have learned something—what I mainly wanted to know—without your telling me.'

'She stared an instant. 'Ah, you mean whether Madame Grandoni was gone? I suppose Assunta told you.'

' Yes, Assunta told me, and I was sorry to hear it.'

The Princess looked grave, as if her old friend's departure had been indeed a very serious incident. ' You may imagine how I feel it! It leaves me completely alone; it makes, in the eyes of the world, an immense difference in my position. However, I don't consider the eyes of the world. At any rate, she couldn't put up with me any more—it appears that I am more and more shocking; and it was written!' On Hyacinth's asking what the old lady would do, she replied, ' I suppose she will go and live with my husband.' Five minutes later she inquired of him whether the same reason that he had mentioned just before was the explanation of his absence from Audley Court. Mr. Muniment had told her that he had not been near him and his sister for more than a month.

' No, it isn't the fear of learning something that would make me uneasy : because, somehow, in the first place it isn't natural to feel uneasy about Paul, and in the second, if it were, he never lets one see anything. It is simply the general sense of real divergence of view. When that divergence becomes sharp, it is better not to pester each other.'

' I see what you mean. But you might go and see his sister.'

' I don't like her,' said Hyacinth, simply.

' Ah, neither do I !' the Princess exclaimed ; while her visitor remained conscious of the perfect composure, the absence of false shame, with which she had referred to their common friend. But she was silent after this, and he judged that he had stayed long enough and sufficiently taxed a preoccupied attention. He got up, and was bidding her good-night, when she checked him by saying, suddenly, ' By the way, your not going to see so good a friend as Mr. Muniment, because you disapprove to-day of his work, suggests to me that you will be in an awkward fix, with your disapprovals, the day you are called upon to serve the cause according to your vow.'

' Oh, of course I have thought of that,' said Hyacinth, smiling.

'And would it be indiscreet to ask what you have thought ?'

'Ah, so many things, Princess ! It would take me a long time to say.'

' I have never talked to yóu about this, because it seemed to me indelicate, and the whole thing too much a secret of your own breast for even so intimate a friend as I have been to have a right to meddle with it. But I have wondered much—seeing that you cared less and less for the people—how you would reconcile your change of heart with the performance of your engagement. I pity you, my poor friend,' the Princess went on, with a heavenly sweetness, 'for I can imagine nothing more terrible than to find yourself face to face with such an engagement, and to feel at the same time that the spirit which prompted it is dead within you.'

' Terrible, terrible, most terrible,' said Hyacinth, gravely, looking at her.

' But I pray God it may never be your fate !' The Princess hesitated a moment ; then she added, ' I see you feel it. Heaven help us all !' She paused, then went on : ' Why shouldn't I tell you, after all ? A short time ago I had a visit from Mr. Vetch.'

' It was kind of you to see him,' said Hyacinth.

' He was delightful, I assure you. But do you know what he came for ? To beg me, on his knees, to snatch you away.'

' To snatch me away ?'

' From the danger that hangs over you. Poor man, he was very pathetic.'

' Oh yes, he has talked to me about it,' Hyacinth said. ' He has picked up.the idea, but he knows nothing whatever about it. And how did he expect that you would be able to snatch me ? '

' He left that to me ; he had only a general conviction of my influence with you.'

'And he thought you would exercise it to make me back out? He does you injustice; you wouldn't!' Hyacinth exclaimed, with a laugh. 'In that case, taking one false position with another, yours would be no better than mine.'

'Oh, speaking seriously, I am perfectly quiet about you and about myself. I know you won't be called,' the Princess returned.

'May I inquire how you know it?'

After a slight hesitation she replied, 'Mr. Muniment tells me so.'

'And how does he know it?'

'We have information. My dear fellow,' the Princess went on, 'you are so much out of it now that if I were to tell you, you wouldn't understand.'

'Yes, no doubt I am out of it; but I still have a right to say, all the same, in contradiction to your imputation of a moment ago, that I care for the people exactly as much as I ever did.'

'My poor Hyacinth, my dear infatuated little aristocrat, was that ever very much?' the Princess asked.

'It was enough, and it is still enough, to make me willing to lay down my life for anything that will really help them.'

'Yes, and of course you must decide for yourself what that is; or, rather, what it's not.'

'I didn't decide when I gave my promise. I agreed to take the decision of others,' Hyacinth said.

'Well, you said just now that in relation to this business of yours you had thought of many things,' the Princess rejoined. 'Have you ever, by chance, thought of anything that *will* help the people?'

'You call me fantastic names, but I'm one of them myself.'

'I know what you are going to say!' the Princess broke in. 'You are going to say that it will help them to do what you do—to do their work and earn their wages. That's beautiful so far as it goes. But what do you propose for the thousands and thousands for whom no work —on the overcrowded earth, under the pitiless heaven— is to be found? There is less and less work in the world,

and there are more and more people to do the little that
there is. The old ferocious selfishnesses *must* come down.
They won't come down gracefully, so they must be
smashed !'

The tone in which the Princess uttered these words
made Hyacinth's heart beat fast, and there was something
so inspiring in her devoted fairness that the vision of a
great heroism flashed up again before him, in all the
splendour it had lost—the idea of a tremendous risk and
an unregarded sacrifice. Such a woman as that, at such
a moment, made every scruple seem a prudence and every
compunction a cowardice. ' I wish to God I could see it
as you see it !' he exclaimed, after he had looked at her a
minute in silent admiration.

' I see simply this : that what we are doing is at least
worth trying, and that as none of those who have the
power, the place, the means, will try anything else, on *their*
head be the responsibility, on *their* head be the blood !'

' Princess,' said Hyacinth, clasping his hands and feeling
that he trembled, ' dearest Princess, if anything should
happen to *you*'—and his voice fell ; the horror of it, a
dozen hideous images of her possible perversity and her
possible punishment were again before him, as he had
already seen them in sinister musings ; they seemed to
him worse than anything he had imagined for himself.

She threw back her head, looking at him almost in
anger. 'To me ! And pray why not to me ? What title
have I to exemption, to security, more than any one else ?
Why am I so sacrosanct and so precious ?'

' Simply because there is no one in the world, and there
has never been any one in the world, like you.'

' Oh, thank you !' said the Princess, with a kind of dry
impatience, turning away.

The manner in which she spoke put an end to their
conversation. It expressed an indifference to what it
might interest him to think about her to-day, and even a
contempt for it, which brought tears to his eyes. His
tears, however, were concealed by the fact that he bent his
head over her hand, which he had taken to kiss ; after
which he left the room without looking at her.

'I HAVE received a letter from your husband,' Paul Muniment said to the Princess, the next evening, as soon as he came into the room. He announced this fact with a kind of bald promptitude and with a familiarity of manner which showed that his visit was one of a closely-connected series. The Princess was evidently not a little surprised by it, and immediately asked how in the world the Prince could know his address. ' Couldn't it have been by your old lady ?' Muniment inquired. ' He must have met her in Paris. It is from Paris that he writes.'

' What an incorrigible cad !' the Princess exclaimed.

' I don't see that—for writing to me. I have his letter in my pocket, and I will show it to you if you like.'

' Thank you, nothing would induce me to touch anything he has touched,' the Princess replied.

' You touch his money, my dear lady,' Muniment remarked, with the quiet smile of a man who sees things as they are.

The Princess hesitated a little. ' Yes, I make an exception for that, because it hurts him, it makes him suffer.'

' I should think, on the contrary, it would gratify him by showing you in a condition of weakness and dependence.'

' Not when he knows I don't use it for myself. What exasperates him is that it is devoted to ends which he hates almost as much as he hates me and yet which he can't call selfish.'

' He doesn't hate you,' said Muniment, with the tone of pleasant reasonableness that he used when he was most imperturbable. ' His letter satisfies me of that.' The Princess stared, at this, and asked him what he was coming

to—whether he were leading up to advising her to go back
and live with her husband.   ' I don't know that I would go
so far as to advise,' he replied; ' when I have so much
benefit from seeing you here, on your present footing, that
wouldn't sound well.   But I'll just make bold to prophesy
that you will go before very long.'

' And on what does that extraordinary prediction rest ? '

' On this plain fact—that you will have nothing to live
upon.   You decline to read the Prince's letter, but if you
were to look at it it would give you evidence of what I
mean.   He informs me that I need count upon no more
supplies from your hands, as you yourself will receive no
more.'

' He addresses you that way, in plain terms ? '

' I can't call them very plain, because the letter is
written in French, and I naturally have had a certain difficulty in making it out, in spite of my persevering study of
the tongue and the fine example set me by poor Robinson.
But that appears to be the gist of the matter.'

' And you can repeat such an insult to me without the
smallest apparent discomposure ?   You're the most remarkable man !' the Princess broke out.

' Why is it an insult ?   It is the simple truth.   I do
take your money,' said Paul Muniment.

' You take it for a sacred cause ; you don't take it for
yourself.'

' The Prince isn't obliged to look at that,' Muniment
rejoined, laughing.

His companion was silent for a moment ; then, ' I didn't
know you were on his side,' she replied, gently.

' Oh, you know on what side I am !'

' What does he know ?   What business has he to address
you so ? '

' I suppose he knows from Madame Grandoni.   She has
told him that I have great influence with you.'

' She was welcome to tell him that !' the Princess exclaimed.

' His reasoning, therefore, has been that when I find you
have nothing more to give to the cause I will let you go.'

' Nothing more ?   And does he count *me*, myself, and

every pulse of my being, every capacity of my nature, as nothing?' the Princess cried, with shining eyes.

'Apparently he thinks that I do.'

'Oh, as for that, after all, I have known that you care far more for my money than for me. But it has made no difference to me,' said the Princess.

'Then you see that by your own calculation the Prince is right.'

'My dear sir,' Muniment's hostess replied, 'my interest in you never depended on your interest in me. It depended wholly on a sense of your great destinies. I suppose that what you began to tell me is that he stops my allowance.'

'From the first of next month. He has taken legal advice. It is now clear—so he tells me—that you forfeit your settlements.'

'Can I not take legal advice, too?' the Princess asked. Surely I can contest that. I can forfeit my settlements only by an act of my own. The act that led to our separation was *his* act; he turned me out of his house by physical violence.'

'Certainly,' said Muniment, displaying even in this simple discussion his easy aptitude for argument; 'but since then there have been acts of your own——' He stopped a moment, smiling; then he went on : ' Your whole connection with a secret society constitutes an act, and so does your exercise of the pleasure, which you appreciate so highly, of feeding it with money extorted from an old Catholic and princely family. You know how little it is to be desired that these matters should come to light.'

'Why in the world need they come to light? Allegations in plenty, of course, he would have, but not a particle of proof. Even if Madame Grandoni were to testify against me, which is inconceivable, she would not be able to produce a definite fact.'

'She would be able to produce the fact that you had a little bookbinder staying for a month in your house.'

'What has that to do with it?' the Princess demanded. ' If you mean that that is a circumstance which would put me in the wrong as against the Prince, is there not, on the other

side, this circumstance, that while our young friend was
staying with me Madame Grandoni herself, a person of the
highest and most conspicuous respectability, never saw fit
to withdraw from me her countenance and protection?
Besides, why shouldn't I have my bookbinder, just as I
might have (and the Prince should surely appreciate
my consideration in not having) my physician and my
chaplain?'

'Am I not your chaplain?' said Muniment, with a
laugh. 'And does the bookbinder usually dine at the
Princess's table?'

'Why not, if he's an artist? In the old times, I know,
artists dined with the servants; but not to-day.'

'That would be for the court to appreciate,' Muniment
remarked. And in a moment he added, 'Allow me to call
your attention to the fact that Madame Grandoni *has* left
you—*has* withdrawn her countenance and protection.'

'Ah, but not for Hyacinth!' the Princess returned, in a
tone which would have made the fortune of an actress
if an actress could have caught it.

'For the bookbinder or for the chaplain, it doesn't
matter. But that's only a detail,' said Muniment. 'In any
case, I shouldn't in the least care for your going to law.'

The Princess rested her eyes upon him for a while
in silence, and at last she replied, 'I was speaking just now
of your great destinies, but every now and then you do
something, you say something, that makes me doubt of
them. It's when you seem afraid. That's terribly against
your being a first-rate man.'

'Oh, I know you have thought me a coward from the
first of your knowing me. But what does it matter? I
haven't the smallest pretension to being a first-rate man.'

'Oh, you are deep, and you are provoking!' murmured
the Princess, with a sombre eye.

'Don't you remember,' Muniment continued, without
heeding this somewhat passionate ejaculation—'don't you
remember how, the other day, you accused me of being not
only a coward but a traitor; of playing false; of wanting,
as you said, to back out?'

'Most distinctly. How can I help its coming over me,

at times, that you have incalculable ulterior views and are
only using me—only using us all? But I don't care!'

'No, no; I'm genuine,' said Paul Muniment, simply, yet
in a tone which might have implied that the discussion was
idle. And he immediately went on, with a transition too
abrupt for perfect civility: 'The best reason in the world
for your not having a lawsuit with your husband is this:
that when you haven't a penny left you will be obliged to
go back and live with him.'

'How do you mean, when I haven't a penny left?
Haven't I my own property?' the Princess demanded.

'The Prince tells me that you have drawn upon your
own property at such a rate that the income to be derived
from it amounts, to his positive knowledge, to no more than
a thousand francs—forty pounds—a year. Surely, with
your habits and tastes, you can't live on forty pounds. I
should add that your husband implies that your property,
originally, was but a small affair.'

'You have the most extraordinary tone,' observed the
Princess, gravely. 'What you appear to wish to express is
simply this: that from the moment I have no more money
to give you I am of no more value than the skin of an
orange.'

Muniment looked down at his shoe awhile. His companion's words had brought a flush into his cheek; he
appeared to admit to himself and to her that, at the point
at which their conversation had arrived, there was a natural
difficulty in his delivering himself. But presently he raised
his head, showing a face still slightly embarrassed but none
the less bright and frank. 'I have no intention whatever of
saying anything harsh or offensive to you, but since you
challenge me, perhaps it is well that I should let you know
that I *do* consider that in giving your money—or, rather,
your husband's—to our business you gave the most valuable
thing you had to contribute.'

'This is the day of plain truths!' the Princess exclaimed,
with a laugh that was not expressive of pleasure. 'You
don't count then any devotion, any intelligence, that I may
have placed at your service, even rating my faculties
modestly?'

'I count your intelligence, but I don't count your devotion, and one is nothing without the other.   You are not trusted at headquarters.'

'Not trusted!' the Princess repeated, with her splendid stare.   'Why, I thought I could be hanged to-morrow!'

'They may let you hang, perfectly, without letting you act.   You are liable to be weary of us,' Paul Muniment went on; 'and, indeed, I think you are weary of us already.'

'Ah, you *must* be a first-rate man—you are such a brute!' replied the Princess, who noticed, as she had noticed before, that he pronounced 'weary' *weery*.

'I didn't say you were weary of *me*,' said Muniment, blushing again.   'You can never live poor—you don't begin to know the meaning of it.'

'Oh, no, I am not tired of you,' the Princess returned, in a strange tone.   'In a moment you will make me cry with passion, and no man has done that for years.   I was very poor when I was a girl,' she added, in a different manner.   'You yourself recognised it just now, in speaking of the insignificant character of my fortune.'

'It had to be a fortune, to be insignificant,' said Muniment, smiling.   'You will go back to your husband!'

To this declaration she made no answer whatever; she only sat looking at him in a sort of desperate calmness. 'I don't see, after all, why they trust you more than they trust me,' she remarked.

'I am not sure that they do,' said Muniment.   'I have heard something this evening which suggests that.'

'And may one know what it is?'

'A communication which I should have expected to be made through me has been made through another person.'

'A communication?'

'To Hyacinth Robinson.'

'To Hyacinth——' The Princess sprang up; she had turned pale in a moment.

'He has got his ticket; but they didn't send it through me.'

'Do you mean his orders?   He was here last night,' the Princess said.

'A fellow named Schinkel, a German—whom you don't

know, I think, but who was a sort of witness, with me and another, of his undertaking—came to see me this evening. It was through him the summons came, and he put Hyacinth up to it on Sunday night.'

'On Sunday night?' The Princess stared. 'Why, he was here yesterday, and he talked of it, and he told me nothing.'

'That was quite right of him, bless him!' Muniment exclaimed.

The Princess closed her eyes a moment, and when she opened them again Muniment had risen and was standing before her. 'What do they want him to do?' she asked.

'I am like Hyacinth; I think I had better not tell you —at least till it's over.'

'And when will it be over?'

'They give him several days and, I believe, minute instructions,' said Muniment; 'with, however, considerable discretion in respect to seizing his chance. The thing is made remarkably easy for him. All this I know from Schinkel, who himself knew nothing on Sunday, being a a mere medium of transmission, but who saw Hyacinth yesterday morning.'

'Schinkel trusts you, then?' the Princess remarked.

Muniment looked at her steadily a moment. 'Yes, but he won't trust you. Hyacinth is to receive a card of invitation to a certain big house,' he went on, 'a card with the name left in blank, so that he may fill it out himself. It is to be good for each of two grand parties which are to be given at a few days' interval. That's why they give him the job—because at a grand party he'll look in his place.'

'He will like that,' said the Princess, musingly—'repaying hospitality with a pistol-shot.'

'If he doesn't like it he needn't do it.'

The Princess made no rejoinder to this, but in a moment she said, 'I can easily find out the place you mean—the big house where two parties are to be given at a few days' interval and where the master is worth your powder.'

'Easily, no doubt. And do you want to warn him?'

'No, I want to do the business first, so that it won't be left for another. If Hyacinth will look in his place at a

grand party, should not I look still more in mine? And as
I know the individual I should be able to approach him
without exciting the smallest suspicion.'

Muniment appeared to consider her suggestion a moment,
as if it were practical and interesting; but presently he
answered, placidly, ' To fall by your hand would be too
good for him.'

' However he falls, will it be useful, valuable?' the Princess asked.

' It's worth trying. He's a very bad institution.'

' And don't you mean to go near Hyacinth?'

' No, I wish to leave him free,' Muniment answered.

' Ah, Paul Muniment,' murmured the Princess, ' you *are*
a first-rate man!' She sank down upon the sofa and sat
looking up at him. ' In God's name, why have you told
me this?' she broke out.

' So that you should not be able to throw it up at me,
later, that I had not.'

She threw herself over, burying her face in the cushions,
and remained so for some minutes, in silence. Muniment
watched her awhile, without speaking; but at last he
remarked, ' I don't want to aggravate you, but you *will* go
back!' The words failed to cause her even to raise her
head, and after a moment he quietly went out.

THAT the Princess had done with him, done with him for
ever, remained the most vivid impression that Hyacinth
had carried away from Madeira Crescent the night before.
He went home, and he flung himself on his narrow bed,
where the consolation of sleep again descended upon him.
But he woke up with the earliest dawn, and the beginning
of a new day was a quick revival of pain. He was over-
past, he had become vague, he was extinct. The things
that Sholto had said to him came back to him, and the
compassion of foreknowledge that Madame Grandoni had
shown him from the first. Of Paul Muniment he only
thought to wonder whether he knew. An insurmountable
desire to do justice to him, for the very reason that there
might be a temptation to oblique thoughts, forbade him to
challenge his friend even in imagination. He vaguely
wondered whether *he* would ever be superseded; but this
possibility faded away in a stronger light—a kind of dazzling
vision of some great tribuneship, which swept before him
now and again and in which the figure of the Princess
herself seemed merged and extinguished. When full
morning came at last, and he got up, it brought with it,
in the restlessness which made it impossible to him to
remain in his room, a return of that beginning of an
answerless question, 'After all—after all——?' which the
Princess had planted there the night before when she
spoke so bravely in the name of the Revolution. 'After
all—after all, since nothing else was tried, or would, apparently, ever be tried——' He had a sense of his mind,
which had been made up, falling to pieces again; but that
sense in turn lost itself in a shudder which was already
familiar—the horror of the public reappearance, on his part,

of the imbrued hands of his mother. This loathing of the
idea of a *repetition* had not been sharp, strangely enough,
till his summons came; in all his previous meditations the
growth of his reluctance to act for the 'party of action'
had not been the fear of a personal stain, but the simple
extension of his observation. Yet now the idea of the
personal stain made him horribly sick; it seemed by itself
to make service impossible. It rose before him like a
kind of backward accusation of his mother; to suffer it
to start out in the life of her son was in a manner to place
her own forgotten, redeemed pollution again in the eye of
the world. The thought that was most of all with him
was that he had time—he had time; he was grateful for
that, and saw a kind of delicacy in their having given him
a margin—not condemned him to be pressed by the hours.
He had another day, he had two days, he might take three,
he might take several. He knew he should be terribly
weary of them before they were over; but for that matter
they would be over whenever he liked. Anyhow, he went
forth again into the streets, into the squares, into the parks,
solicited by an aimless desire to steep himself yet once
again in the great indifferent city which he knew and loved
and which had had so many of his smiles and tears and
confidences. The day was gray and damp, though no rain
fell, and London had never appeared to him to wear more
proudly and publicly the stamp of her imperial history.
He passed slowly to and fro over Westminster bridge and
watched the black barges drift on the great brown river,
and looked up at the huge fretted palace that rose there as
a fortress of the social order which he, like the young
David, had been commissioned to attack with a sling and
pebble. At last he made his way to St. James's Park, and
he strolled about a long time. He revolved around it, and
he went a considerable distance up the thoroughfare that
communicates with Pimlico. He stopped at a certain
point and came back again, and then he retraced his steps
in the former direction. He looked in the windows of
shops, and he looked in particular into the long, glazed
expanse of that establishment in which, at that hour of the
day, Millicent Henning discharged superior functions.

Millicent's image had descended upon him after he came out, and now it moved before him as he went, it clung to him, it refused to quit him. He made, in truth, no effort to drive it away; he held fast to it in return, and it murmured strange things in his ear. She had been so jolly to him on Sunday; she was such a strong, obvious, simple nature, with such a generous breast and such a freedom from the sophistries of civilisation. All that he had ever liked in her came back to him now with a finer air, and there was a moment, during which he hung over the rail of the bridge that spans the lake in St. James's Park and mechanically followed the movement of the swans, when he asked himself whether, at bottom, he hadn't liked her better, almost, than any one. He tried to think he had, he wanted to think he had, and he seemed to see the look her eyes would have if he should tell her that he had. Something of that sort had really passed between them on Sunday; only the business that had come up since had superseded it. Now the taste of the vague, primitive comfort that his Sunday had given him came back to him, and he asked himself whether he mightn't know it a second time. After he had thought he couldn't again wish for anything, he found himself wishing that he might believe there was something Millicent could do for him. Mightn't she help him—mightn't she even extricate him? He was looking into a window—not that of her own shop—when a vision rose before him of a quick flight with her, for an undefined purpose, to an undefined spot; and he was glad, at that moment, to have his back turned to the people in the street, because his face suddenly grew red to the tips of his ears. Again and again, all the same, he indulged in the reflection that spontaneous, uncultivated minds often have inventions, inspirations. Moreover, whether Millicent should have any or not, he might at least feel her arms around him. He didn't exactly know what good it would do him or what door it would open; but he should like it. The sensation was not one he could afford to defer, but the nearest moment at which he should be able to enjoy it would be that evening. *He* had thrown over everything, but she would be busy all day; nevertheless, it would be a gain, it would be a kind of foretaste, to see her earlier, to have three words with her. He wrestled with the temptation to go into her haberdasher's, because he knew she didn't like it (he had tried it once, of old) ; as the visits of gentlemen, even when ostensible purchasers (there were people watching about who could tell who was who), compromised her in the eyes of her employers. This was not an ordinary case, however ; and though he hovered about the place a long time, undecided, embarrassed, half ashamed, at last he went in, as by an irresistible necessity. He would just make an appointment with her, and a glance of the eye and a single word would suffice. He remembered his way through the labyrinth of the shop ; he knew that her department was on the second floor. He walked through the place, which was crowded, as if he had as good a right as any one else ; and as he had entertained himself, on rising, with putting on his holiday garments, in which he made such a distinguished little figure, he was not suspected of any purpose more nefarious than that of looking for some nice thing to give a lady. He ascended the stairs, and found himself in a large room where made-up articles were exhibited and where, though there were twenty people in it, a glance told him he shouldn't find Millicent. She was perhaps in the next one, into which he passed by a wide opening. Here also were numerous purchasers, most of them ladies ; the men were but three or four, and the disposal of the wares was in the hands of neat young women attired in black dresses with long trains. At first it appeared to Hyacinth that the young woman he sought was even here not within sight, and he was turning away, to look elsewhere, when suddenly he perceived that a tall gentleman, standing in the middle of the room, was none other than Captain Sholto. It next became plain to him that the person standing upright before the Captain, as still as a lay-figure and with her back turned to Hyacinth, was the object of his own quest. In spite of her averted face he instantly recognised Millicent ; he knew her shop-attitude, the dressing of her hair behind, and the long, grand lines of her figure, draped in the last new thing. She was exhibiting this article to the Captain, and he was lost

in contemplation. He had been beforehand with Hyacinth as a false purchaser, but he imitated a real one
better than our young man, as, with his eyes travelling
up and down the front of Millicent's person, he frowned,
consideringly, and rubbed his lower lip slowly with his
walking-stick. Millicent stood admirably still, and the back-
view of the garment she displayed was magnificent. Hyacinth,
for a minute, stood as still as she. At the end of that
minute he perceived that Sholto saw him, and for an instant
he thought he was going to direct Millicent's attention to
him. But Sholto only looked at him very hard, for a few
seconds, without telling her he was there; to enjoy that
satisfaction he would wait till the interloper was gone.
Hyacinth gazed back at him for the same length of time
—what these two pairs of eyes said to each other re-
quires perhaps no definite mention—and then turned
away.

That evening, about nine o'clock, the Princess Casamassima drove in a hansom to Hyacinth's lodgings in Westminster. The door of the house was a little open, and a
man stood on the step, smoking his big pipe and looking up
and down. The Princess, seeing him while she was still at
some distance, had hoped he was Hyacinth, but he proved
to be a very different figure indeed from her devoted young
friend. He had not a forbidding countenance, but he
looked very hard at her as she descended from her hansom
and approached the door. She was used to being looked
at hard, and she didn't mind this; she supposed he was one
of the lodgers in the house. He edged away to let her
pass, and watched her while she endeavoured to impart an
elasticity of movement to the limp bell-pull beside the door.
It gave no audible response, so that she said to him,
' I wish to ask for Mr Hyacinth Robinson. Perhaps you
can tell me——"

'Yes, I too,' the man replied, smiling. ' I have come
also for that.'

The Princess hesitated a moment. ' I think you must
be Mr Schinkel. I have heard of you.'

'You know me by my bad English,' her interlocutor
remarked, with a sort of benevolent coquetry.

'Your English is remarkably good—I wish I spoke German as well. Only just a hint of an accent, and evidently an excellent vocabulary.'

'I think I have heard, also, of you,' said Schinkel, appreciatively.

'Yes, we know each other, in our circle, don't we? We are all brothers and sisters.' The Princess was anxious, she was in a fever; but she could still relish the romance of standing in a species of back-slum and fraternising with a personage looking like a very tame horse whose collar galled him. 'Then he's at home, I hope; he is coming down to you?' she went on.

'That's what I don't know. I am waiting.'

'Have they gone to call him?'

Schinkel looked at her, while he puffed his pipe. 'I have called him myself, but he will not say.'

'How do you mean—he will not say?'

'His door is locked. I have knocked many times.'

'I suppose he is out,' said the Princess.

'Yes, he may be out,' Schinkel remarked, judicially.

He and the Princess stood a moment looking at each other, and then she asked, 'Have you any doubt of it?'

'Oh, *es kann sein.* Only the woman of the house told me five minutes ago that he came in.'

'Well, then, he probably went out again,' the Princess remarked.

'Yes, but she didn't hear him.'

The Princess reflected, and was conscious that she was flushing. She knew what Schinkel knew about their young friend's actual situation, and she wished to be very clear with him and to induce him to be the same with her. She was rather baffled, however, by the sense that he was cautious, and justly cautious. He was polite and inscrutable, quite like some of the high personages—ambassadors and cabinet-ministers—whom she used to meet in the great world. 'Has the woman been here, in the house, ever since?' she asked in a moment.

'No, she went out for ten minutes, half an hour ago.'

'Surely, then, he may have gone out again in that time!'
the Princess exclaimed.

'That is what I have thought. It is also why I have
waited here,' said Schinkel. 'I have nothing to do,' he
added, serenely.

'Neither have I,' the Princess rejoined. 'We can wait
together.'

'It's a pity you haven't got some room,' the German
suggested.

'No, indeed; this will do very well. We shall see him
the sooner when he comes back.'

'Yes, but perhaps it won't be for long.'

'I don't care for that; I will wait. I hope you don't
object to my company,' she went on, smiling.

'It is good, it is good,' Schinkel responded, through his
smoke.

'Then I will send away my cab.' She returned to the
vehicle and paid the driver, who said, 'Thank you, my
lady,' with expression, and drove off.

'You gave him too much,' observed Schinkel, when she
came back.

'Oh, he looked like a nice man. I am sure he deserved it.'

'It is very expensive,' Schinkel went on, sociably.

'Yes, and I have no money, but it's done. Was there
no one else in the house while the woman was away?' the
Princess asked.

'No, the people are out; she only has single men. I
asked her that. She has a daughter, but the daughter
has gone to see her cousin. The mother went only a
hundred yards, round the corner there, to buy a pennyworth of milk. She locked this door, and put the key in
her pocket; she stayed at the grocer's, where she got
the milk, to have a little conversation with a friend she
met there. You know ladies always stop like that—
nicht wahr? It was half an hour later that I came.
She told me that he was at home, and I went up to
his room. I got no sound, as I have told you. I
came down and spoke to her again, and she told me
what I say.'

'Then you determined to wait, as I have done,' said the Princess.

'Oh, yes, I want to see him.'

'So do I, very much.'   The Princess said nothing more, for a minute ; then she added, 'I think we want to see him for the same reason.'

'Das kann sein—das kann sein.'

The two continued to stand there in the brown evening, and they had some further conversation, of a desultory and irrelevant kind.   At the end of ten minutes the Princess broke out, in a low tone, laying her hand on her companion's arm, 'Mr. Schinkel, this won't do.   I'm intolerably nervous.'

'Yes, that is the nature of ladies,' the German replied, imperturbably.

'I wish to go up to his room,' the Princess pursued. 'You will be so good as to show me where it is.'

'It will do you no good, if he is not there.'

The Princess hesitated.   'I am not sure he is not there.'

'Well, if he won't speak, it shows he likes better not to have visitors.'

'Oh, he may like to have me better than he does you !' the Princess exclaimed.

'Das kann sein—das kann sein.'   But Schinkel made no movement to introduce her into the house.

'There is nothing to-night—you know what I mean,' the Princess remarked, after looking at him for a moment.

'Nothing to-night?'

'At the Duke's.   The first party is on Thursday, the other is next Tuesday.'

'*Schön.*   I never go to parties,' said Schinkel.

'Neither do I.'

'Except that *this* is a kind of party—you and me,' suggested Schinkel.

'Yes, and the woman of the house doesn't approve of it.'   The footstep of the personage in question had been audible in the passage, through the open door, which was presently closed, from within, with a little reprehensive bang. Something in this incident appeared to quicken exceedingly the Princess's impatience and emotion; the menace of exclusion from the house made her wish more even than before to enter it. 'For God's sake, Mr. Schinkel, take me up there. If you won't, I will go alone,' she pleaded.

Her face was white now, and it need hardly be added that it was beautiful. The German considered it a moment in silence; then turned and reopened the door and went in, followed closely by his companion.

There was a light in the lower region, which tempered the gloom of the staircase—as high, that is, as the first floor; the ascent the rest of the way was so dusky that the pair went slowly and Schinkel led the Princess by the hand. She gave a suppressed exclamation as she rounded a sharp turn in the second flight. 'Good God, is that his door, with the light?'

'Yes, you can see under it. There was a light before,' said Schinkel, without confusion.

'And why, in heaven's name, didn't you tell me?'

'Because I thought it would worry you.'

'And doesn't it worry *you?*'

'A little, but I don't mind,' said Schinkel. 'Very likely he may have left it.'

'He doesn't leave candles!' the Princess returned, with vehemence. She hurried up the few remaining steps to the door, and paused there with her ear against it. Her hand grasped the handle, and she turned it, but the door resisted. Then she murmured, pantingly, to her companion, 'We must go in—we must go in!'

'What will you do, when it's locked?' he inquired.

'You must break it down.'

'It is very expensive,' said Schinkel.

'Don't be abject!' cried the Princess. 'In a house like this the fastenings are certainly flimsy; they will easily yield.'

'And if he is not there—if he comes back and finds what we have done?'

She looked at him a moment through the darkness, which was mitigated only by the small glow proceeding

from the chink. 'He *is* there! Before God, he is
there!'

'Schön, schön,' said her companion, as if he felt the
contagion of her own dread but was deliberating and meant
to remain calm. The Princess assured him that one or
two vigorous thrusts with his shoulder would burst the bolt
—it was sure to be some wretched morsel of tin—and she
made way for him to come close. He did so, he even
leaned against the door, but he gave no violent push, and
the Princess waited, with her hand against her heart
Schinkel apparently was still deliberating. At last he gave
a low sigh. 'I know they found him the pistol; it is only
for that,' he murmured; and the next moment Christina
saw him sway sharply to and fro in the gloom. She heard
a crack and saw that the lock had yielded. The door
collapsed: they were in the light; they were in a small
room, which looked full of things. The light was that of a
single candle on the mantel; it was so poor that for a
moment she made out nothing definite. Before that
moment was over, however, her eyes had attached themselves to the small bed. There was something on it—
something black, something ambiguous, something outstretched. Schinkel held her back, but only for an instant;
she saw everything, and with the very act she flung herself
beside the bed, upon her knees. Hyacinth lay there as if he
were asleep, but there was a horrible thing, a mess of blood,
on the bed, in his side, in his heart. His arm hung limp
beside him, downwards, off the narrow couch; his face was
white and his eyes were closed. So much Schinkel saw,
but only for an instant; a convulsive movement of the
Princess, bending over the body while a strange low cry
came from her lips, covered it up. He looked about him
for the weapon, for the pistol, but the Princess, in her rush
at the bed, had pushed it out of sight with her knees. 'It's
a pity they found it—if he hadn't had it here!' he exclaimed
to her. He had determined to remain calm, so that, on
turning round at the quick advent of the little woman of
the house, who had hurried up, white, scared, staring, at
the sound of the crashing door, he was able to say, very
quietly and gravely, 'Mr. Robinson has shot himself through

the heart.   He must have done it while you were fetching
the milk.'   The Princess got up, hearing another person in
the room, and then Schinkel perceived the small revolver
lying just under the bed.   He picked it up and carefully
placed it on the mantel-shelf, keeping, equally carefully, to
himself the reflection that it would certainly have served
much better for the Duke.

THE END.